It was hard to see it when she was down there, part of the thousands of milling human beings penned in by streets and walls and harbor guards. But from up here it all looked familiar to Simonis, every single stone and cobble and mule's bray and mosaic tessera of it. It lay as though in the palm of her hand, this place they called the City of Gold, and somehow she knew it. She *knew* it. She was too young to understand the feeling or to shape it into something coherent or profound. But standing high above Visant and looking down upon it, Simonis summarized it to herself with simple, forthright logic, a single thought that was formed in the clarity of a child's mind as yet unburdened with too many layers of adult complexity and complication. A single word.

Home.

She had been born in a small town far from this place, but that was barely a memory now, and she let it go without grief, without grief, without sadness, without regret. It might never have existed at all.

This did. This place. This great city at her feet.

She was home.

Also by Alma Alexander

The Secrets of Jin Shei
Embers of Heaven

The Hidden Queen
Changer of Days

Midnight at Spanish Gardens

Worldweavers
Gift of the Unmage
Spellspam
Cybermage
Dawn of Magic

The Were Chronicles
Random
Wolf
Shifter

Short story collections (ebook only)
The Weight of Worlds
Haunted
Sense of Love
Plaisir d'Amour

River (anthology, ed.)

EMPRESS

Alma Alexander

Empress
Alma Alexander
Copyright © 2015 Alma Alexander
All rights reserved
Published by Book View Café Publishing Cooperative
www.BookViewCafe.com

ISBN:978-1-61138-580-9

Cover artist and design: Elizabeth Leggett
Interior design copyright © Knotted Road Press

EMPRESS

Alma Alexander

Book View Café
www.BookViewCafe.com

ONE

The Bear-keeper's Daughter
and the Peasant's Son

CHAPTER ONE

They called it the City of Gold, and under the heavy dark-gold light of a westering sun it was easy to see why. The light gilded the weathered limestone walls of the great Hippodrome into glowing golden ramparts, and played with the colours on the four enormous banners snapping above the track in the brisk breeze blowing into the harbour from the sea.

Beyond, behind high palace walls, a cascade of domed and tiled roofs and open terraces gleamed through the thick foliage of lush gardens and spilled down toward the shore. Smaller palaces clung to the side of the hillside further in along the Narrows that guided ships inwards towards the Great Harbour and the Inner Sea; on the far side of the Narrows, rows upon rows of houses crowded together on steep streets leading down to small wharfs teeming with fishing boats and ferries, and then yet more houses, built out over the water on stilts.

In this light Simonis first saw the place—Visant, the queen city, the jewel of the Empire. She did not recognise the shape of the Sacred Palace. Hippodrome-bred, though, she saw the flags on top of the curved golden wall and, although it was far bigger than she could ever have imagined one could be, knew it for another Hippodrome, the one for which she and her family were bound. But she wasn't given a lot of time to look—by the time that the small cargo ship on which Simonis and her family had taken passage swept into the Narrows, the shadows were already long, rapidly swallowing the city; the small lamp that had been lit and hung from the curved prow of the ship, where Simonis had taken up her perch when the ship came close to the city, was no match for the encroaching night. Full dark had fallen when the ship finally turned in towards a waiting wharf lit by pitch torches and a few oil-burning lamps. In the red half-light and dancing shadows, men waited on the wharf, ready to help haul the ship in and tie her up.

Behind Simonis, on a ship's deck piled high with packages and baskets and bales, a commotion of movement and raised voices told of a flurry of activity as the ship sidled in to the side of the quay.

"It'll be too late to unload her tonight, we'd better look to a guard on the quayside until first light."

"Hoy! Hoy there! Watch that oar!"

"Throw us the stern rope! Get a move on there!"

And, almost lost in the deeper men's voices, a woman's call, her mother's.

"Simonis? Simonis! Where are you? Come here this instant! *Simonis*!"

Simonis scrambled down from her perch on the prow, where she had been conveniently out of sight behind several mammoth bales, and came sliding down to a thumping halt at her mother's feet. She was too heavy, at five, to be quite lifted off her feet by the scruff of her neck like an errant kitten, but it came close enough to that as her mother's hand closed around the back of Simonis's shift. And then the hand fell flat on the child's back, between her shoulder blades, and propelled her forward.

"How many times do I have to tell you not to stray?" said Apphia, Simonis's mother, sounding tired and exasperated. "I have Danelis to watch, she's only three, and there's the baby—but you ought to know better than to get lost like this. Now come on, we don't have much time. We have to gather up our things, as soon as they're tied up we have to be off the boat…."

"But they said they would wait until morning," Simonis said.

"Wait for what?"

"To unload the ship," Simonis said, trying to get her feet under her as her mother, practically dragged her back to the family's bivouac on the deck.

"Unload the *cargo*," Apphia said, with a trace of impatience. "We aren't cargo. We're getting off tonight."

In a fold of cloth against Apphia's breast, her month-old infant stirred and whimpered and Apphia instinctively let go of her older daughter to cradle the baby with both hands.

"Now he's awake. We'll be lucky if he doesn't scream all the way to the Hippodrome," Apphia said, trying to rock the child back into sleep. "Your bag is ready, Simonis, your father has it, go run ahead. Watch out for Danelis, and don't stray from us when we get off the ship. This isn't Cyrenais, where everyone knows you. You don't want to get lost in the city."

There were only a handful of passengers on the small vessel—there was no room for many people on a ship whose business was ferrying cargo to the ever-hungry wharves of the City of Gold. Aside from Simonis's family, there were only two more passengers who stepped ashore once the unsteady gangplank was laid across the narrow ribbon of water between the ship and the wharf's edge. One of them had been silent and taciturn throughout the voyage, and had been on the ship already when the family had joined it in the small town of Cyrenais on Kypra, one of the islands of the Middle Sea; they had never even learned his name, and he slipped off without a word.

The other passenger had been more gregarious, and he lingered with the small family as they hesitated on the wharf, unsure of what to do next.

"There will be someone to inspect your papers," he told Batzas, Simonis's father. "They let in those who have family in the city, or some legitimate business to pursue; you have to have a reason to come here. But you're fine, you have the letters from the City's White Jewel people…although, really, they *ought* to have sent someone to meet you. It's criminal, letting a provincial loose on the city on their own, especially one with small children in tow. No offence."

"None taken," Batzas said. "There may be someone beyond the barricade on the city side. I can't see from here. Thank you, friend. If there is nobody, then I shall make my way to the Hippodrome…."

"If I were you, I would wait until morning before I'd present myself at the Hippodrome," said the other man. "The people you need to see do not reside at the Hippodrome itself, and their offices would be closed by now, and you have no idea where to seek them at their lodgings—and even if you were lucky enough to find them there, if indeed they have sent nobody to greet you at the wharf they may be none too pleased to be accosted by you at their home after their working hours. I would find a hostelry somewhere for the night, you and your babies, get yourselves a good night's rest and then go to the Hippodrome fresh in the morning."

"Where would I look for a hostelry?" Batzas asked.

"There are signs. You will know. Just avoid the really loud ones with women lingering by the doorways." An eloquent glance at Apphia more than explained the reasoning behind that piece of advice, and Batzas took its meaning immediately.

"I thank you," he said politely, and the other man gave him a wide smile.

"Eh, you can pay me back," he said. "Let me know who I can bet on when the races start again in the spring. It's always good to have a friend inside the Hippodrome. Good luck to you."

He shouldered his bag and strode off into the shadows towards the back of the wharf. Batzas, staring after him, could not help a small sigh.

"At least he's coming home," Batzas said. "I wish I had his confidence. He's right, we'd better have the papers ready for inspection."

He led the way forward, fumbling in his satchel for the letters of appointment he carried from the city's White Jewel faction, one of the two major players in the Hippodrome games, always bickering for top billing with their sworn rival, the Golden Crown. Both factions had secondary groups, the Scarlet Banner for the Jewel faction and the Obsidian Knife for the Crown—but only the two main groupings maintained their own menageries within the Visant Hippodrome, and could employ keepers and trainers for their animals. It was for this purpose that Batzas had been brought from Cyrenais.

Simonis followed her father, keeping close behind and almost treading on his heels, clutching her own bag with one hand and clinging to three-year-old Danelis' hand with the other, dragging her forward at a pace that had the younger girl whimpering quietly to herself. Apphia, cradling the baby against her breast with one hand and steadying a large bundle of belongings on her shoulder with the other, brought up the rear, crooning to the infant quietly to keep him quiet.

"Hold. You seek to enter the city?"

"I have a letter of introduction," Batzas said, thrusting forward the rolled-up scroll which bore his appointment. "I am expected, I am an animal trainer—I have been sent to the city Hippodrome from my own—there, see the seal of the White Jewel...."

The challenge had been peremptory, brusque; Batzas had come to a sudden halt, with Simonis blundering into him from behind. Now she looked up diffidently, biting her lip, to inspect the man who had halted them. He wore the kilt and sculpted breastplate of a soldier, with a round metal helmet, gleaming in torchlight. His features were angular, and his mouth a thin arrogant line as he pored over the letters. But the soldier finally rolled the scroll back up untidily and handed it back with a small sharp motion.

"New assistant bear keeper, eh," he said. "Well, welcome to Visant, bear keeper. It'll be a while before the Hippodrome opens its doors again, though."

"Gives me a few months…to settle in," Batzas said carefully, unsure of whether it was better to make small talk or simply to mutter thanks and press on.

"Indeed," the guard said. He peered down to where the two small girls crowded behind Batzas's knees, and reached out to tilt up the chin of Simonis, who was closest. She flinched, just a little, but then she lifted her eyes and met his, squarely. He chuckled, letting go of her and straightening up. "Your girl has spirit," he said, and there was a tinge of approval in his voice. "Pass. All is well."

Batzas hesitated, and then decided to try and trade on the man's apparent goodwill.

"Please," he said, "we were advised to seek a hostelry for tonight…would you know where…?"

But the soldier's face had settled back to its harsh lines; his moment of warmth done, he was a guard once again, on duty at the city's borders.

"Ask as you pass into the street," he said. "I know nothing of hostelries."

"Thank you," Batzas said, with a small sigh, and motioned his family forward. Simonis needed no urging, scurrying forward with her head down and her eyes on the paving stones at her feet.

"We don't have much coin," Apphia murmured from the rear of the column.

"I know," Batzas replied in a low voice. "I will see what I can find for us. Tomorrow…will be better. Tonight will be hard."

"I wish they had sent someone to meet us," Apphia said in a small voice.

"I am not a charioteer," Batzas said, "or a prize horse. They probably barely know I am coming. There, ahead—that's a light. It might be a place to sleep. Stay close. Watch the children."

He didn't like the look of the first place they approached, nor the next—the first was too close to the wharfs and apparently serving a potent brew, with large brawny off-shift cargo handlers staggering unsteadily against doorways and walls and each other and picking fights in broad dockside patois and half a dozen foreign tongues; the second had two women who appeared to be waiting patiently in the half-shadows under the single lit torch above the hostelry's door, and Batzas remembered the warning of his fellow passenger, veering away. But by this time the baby had set up a thin, persistent wail and the older girls were weaving as they walked. Batzas finally admitted defeat and at the next hostelry in their path he threw caution to the winds and begged for any available corner where his family could rest for the night.

They might have avoided the place had Batzas had a chance to look—it seemed rather classier than they could hope to afford. But the city smiled on them and gave them the first and perhaps the only real free luck that they would find in its walls—they crossed the path of the proprietor of this particular inn on the rebound from a consultation with a wharfside astrologer who had given him dire warnings that some previously committed sin would catch up with him and exact its own price if he did not forestall matters by doing a random good deed to a stranger. Seeing the tired little family adrift in the night he saw his chance and seized it, and although his businessman's soul, astrologer or no astrologer, could not quite allow him to offer them accommodation for nothing, at least he gave them a room in the back at only half his usual price. Danelis and Simonis were asleep on their pallets almost before they were fully horizontal; the baby took a little longer to settle but finally, warm and fed and swaddled comfortably at the foot of his parents' bed, he slept too. There were a few whispers exchanged between the man and the woman, but they were quiet and tired and doled out sparingly. Soon they, too, slept. There would be much that was new to be faced in the morning, and they were grateful for the chance to defer it until then.

The innkeeper's generosity—or the scope of his repentance—did not stretch to a free breakfast. Batzas and his family, gathering their belongings together in the morning, found that they could afford to ask for nothing more than directions to the Hippodrome.

They had still been in the narrower, poorer streets, the ones leading down to the wharf and the main trade harbour—but now they abruptly found themselves in a mixed area. Houses of well-to-do gentry—with closed gates set into blank walls facing into the streets, hiding private gardens and courtyards—stood cheek by jowl with homes of lesser folk, with balconies or open windows thrust out over the street, complete with curious faces peering out at the strangers passing by. Once or twice they turned into narrower, unpaved alley-like streets where Batzas could have touched the walls of the houses on either side if he stretched out his arms; there were no windows here, just bare gratings in the blank walls, and doors that opened straight out into the streets. But despite the odd mix of social and architectural levels, on the whole, the streets became wider and better kept and busier with what was obviously a higher social caste of people, as they steadily climbed the slope of the hill towards the top of the ridge and the centre of the city.

Itinerant food sellers began to appear on the streets wide enough to accommodate them, shouting out their wares. Having ushered his family back on the road without breakfast, Batzas halted a couple of the vendors and handed fresh figs and a small earthenware pot of honey to his enthusiastic daughters. They paused to allow the children to rinse their sticky hands and take a drink from a standing pipe of running water on the corner of a street, having first carefully observed several locals do the same, and then to take stock of the increasing rush and bustle around them.

The street was filling with hurrying people. Several patrician-looking gentlemen thundered past on horseback, and a number of others, obviously less well-off, made do with mules or donkeys laden with mysterious packages. Once a sedan chair rocked past, carried by four strapping young slaves with skins so black that Danelis, who had never seen human beings that shade before, squealed and buried her face in her mother's skirts; the sedan chair's curtains twitched a little, but did not part.

"A lady of the palace, perhaps," Batzas said. He reached out to ruffle Danelis's dark curls. "Nothing to be afraid of, little one. Gone now."

"I'm not sure that travelling like that would not be worse than the boat," Apphia said. She had been miserably seasick on the voyage over to the city, and the swaying of the sedan chair had forcefully brought back that feeling of queasiness. "I don't know why they can't just walk...."

Simonis pointed, with a five-year-old's complete and utter lack of self-consciousness. "Yes, they can. Look, there comes one."

A woman wearing a plain head-dress which covered her hair had turned into the street, followed by three attendants carrying various packages and parcels. The attendants, one of whom was as black as the sedan chair bearers had been, glanced over at Batzas and his family; one of them even gave them a thin ghost of a smile. Their mistress ignored the pointing child with an arrogant tilt of her head, apparently absorbed in studying the houses she was passing. She halted at one door, not too far down the street, and motioned one of the attendants to knock. The door opened, and she and her entourage were admitted, vanishing into the house.

"Come on," Batzas said, "the morning is wasting away. We need a proper place to sleep tonight, and the man to whom I must present myself still needs finding."

Before long they were out of the warren of narrower streets and had stepped into one of the spacious paved forums, which opened up every so often along the wide straight road that cut across the city from the Bronze Gate into the Palace to the great gates on the outermost walls, scented with a heady mix of herbs and spices, piled in boxes and barrels and hempen sacks and displayed on low wooden tables. There were more people there than Batzas's girls had ever seen together in one place before. Traffic threatened to sweep them aside and apart from one another—people pushed past on foot or drove carts along the main road simply assuming that everyone else would get out of the way. Batzas had to snatch one of his daughters out of the path of the plunging horse of an oblivious soldier in the dusty attire of someone from the field; he was closely followed by a long-legged boy riding a mule. The boy, his flaxen-haired head bare and gleaming golden in the sun, half turned as if to apologise for the horseman's actions—but he didn't have much more time than to catch Batzas's gaze with his own and give a small abrupt nod before the mule claimed his attention again and he had to kick its dun sides hard, digging in the scuffed heels of his unfashionable country boots, boots that told even Batzas that here was another bewildered soul newly come to the city and still coming to terms with it.

Their friend from the ship had told them about this road. He had mentioned the spice market; he had also spoken of an entire city block on the broad avenue where the silk sellers hawked their wares, or another of the open forums, the one closest to the Palace gate, where the sweet scents of the perfume-makers paved the path to the bronze Palace gates and the Emperor's own front door. Danelis was entranced by all this; Simonis was fascinated; the baby, its ears assailed by the racket and its tender nose offended by the strange new smells. Before the city distracted them any further, Batzas, pausing only long enough to ask for the shortest way to the Hippodrome, steered his little family down a side street where a number of weavers and spinners and dressmakers plied their trade. It wound down a slight slope and then climbed back up again to spit them out facing an expanse of wall made of glowing golden stone.

Batzas reached out and leaned his hand, open-palmed, on the wall, like a blind man who had been lost but had now finally found his way back to something familiar, something safe, something he understood.

"This is it," he said. "We are here."

"Where's the gate?" Apphia asked, glancing around, shifting the baby to a more comfortable position.

"We follow the wall," Batzas said. "There will be a gate in it somewhere."

There was one, but it was the wrong gate—they first stumbled onto the smaller, narrower back gate of the Hippodrome, known as the Gate of the Dead because this was the door through which the dead bodies were carried out back in the days when the Hippodrome's entertainment still included fights to the death between slave-born gladiators. It was locked—but Batzas knocked anyway, without great hope. It was hard to say who was the more astonished when the gate actually squeaked open at this summons—Batzas himself, or the wizened old man who stood in the opened doorway.

"I have come from Cyrenais," Batzas said helplessly. "I am to take up a position as animal trainer. I need to see Amantius. The…the head of the White Jewel faction."

"Here?" the old man said, glancing around at the gate he tended. "Do you habitually come knocking at the back door? No matter. Come in, now that you're here. You may as well cut across on the inside." He moved aside as Batzas handed Apphia and the girls through the door, where they paused, waiting for further instructions. The old man closed and barred the back gate behind them "This way," he said, and then managed a crooked, toothless grin which sent Danelis backing away cautiously, grabbing for her mother's skirts with both hands. "Welcome to the Hippodrome," the old man said.

"Where…?' Batzas began, but the old man was already pointing.

"Out of the portico, there's a small stair on your left just before you enter the arena—that will take you into the tiers, you can walk along the first row, go all the way across—they just raked the season's sand over the race track, I wouldn't go walking across that if I were you—ask again when you get to the Crown Portico, over at the far end. There should be someone there to direct you to the offices."

Batzas nodded his thanks and swept his family before him in search of the stair the old man had described.

They struggled up the few shallow stairs and emerged into the first row of marble-faced seating, separated from the racing track only by a low stone wall. Behind them, rows upon rows of similar seats sloped sharply up towards a tall colonnade of marching columns linked by curving arches, impossibly far away and high enough to scrape the sky. The place was empty now, except for a couple of silent workers who were busy on esoteric tasks down in the arena itself, on the Spina that rose down the middle of the track, full of ancient obelisks of crumbling stone brought back in triumph from forgotten foreign conquests and pillars upon which statues of ancient emperors and a particularly beloved or renowned charioteer or two gazed down upon the race track with sightless eyes. But the ghost of its races clung to the Hippodrome. Even empty, with its horses safely in their winter stables and its chariots put away into oiled wraps for the winter hiatus, with the voices of its crowds stilled until the new season opened, there was an echo of a many-throated roar that hung above the marble seats and the statues and the sand on the tracks.

Win! Win! Win!

Batzas drew in his breath sharply.

"Come on," he said. "Let's go find this Amantius."

A track sweeper on the far side of the Hippodrome, working right next to where they came down another shallow stair down into what the old man at the Gate of the Dead had called the Crown Portico, pointed them on, and it was mostly by trial and error that they finally found and presented themselves at the office of Amantius, the chief of the White Jewel faction's administrative wing. Batzas gave his name to a minion in an antechamber, and was announced and ushered in after he and his family were left waiting in the antechamber for some ten or fifteen minutes.

He had handed his letter of appointment to the minion when he had first arrived, and Amantius had this flattened out between two meaty palms on the table before him, glancing up appraisingly as Batzas entered into his presence.

"Well," he said. "Assistant bear keeper. Well, I'm afraid that the circumstances have changed a little since this letter was written. The situation is no longer the same."

Behind Batzas, Apphia could not help a small gasp. Sensing her sudden distress, the baby in the crook of her arm whimpered pitifully.

Amantius allowed his mouth to curve into a slight smile.

"Ah, now," he said. "There is no need for that. It is true that we have no particular need for an assistant in the animal pens right now. But we *do* need a bear keeper, as it happens, seeing as we lost our old one at the close of the season."

"*Lost* your bear keeper? What happened?" Batzas said warily.

"Congratulations, Batzas of Cyrenais," Amantius said, as though Batzas had not said anything at all. "You've just been promoted." He raised his voice a little, throwing it behind the little family and through the half-open door behind them. "Cantaxas! In here! Our new bear keeper has arrived. Conduct him to his new quarters, and find one of the other animal handlers to show him down below. Well, good luck, Batzas. And don't worry, we got rid of *that* bear, the one who dispatched your predecessor. He put up a fine fight in the arena at the end of the last season. And it was all an accident, anyway, with the keeper. How *you* deal with the rest of your charges will be up to you. I'll see you in the arena."

Cantaxas rounded them all up again and ushered them out of Amantius's presence, back out of the antechamber and into the portico area, and then through a narrow door that opened into the area beneath the great tiers of stone seats.

"Through here," Cantaxas said. "Out of season, like now, this door is left open—once the races start there will a bar on the inside, and someone on duty to open it when you knock—you will be given the passwords in time. Don't worry about these first few chambers, they're just storage—that one's got the sand for the tracks, and then there's the wardrobe, back there, for the mimes and the actors. One of these rooms will have your tack, bear-keeper—hunt around, you'll find it. But go on, go on now.…" He ushered them down a low corridor, lit by the occasional grating that let in a little bit of daylight but didn't give much of a view and by guttering torches set into sconces in between doors on the inner side of the corridor. Cantaxas finally paused before one of the doors. "These will be your quarters," he said. "You're responsible for your own torch, out here. You'll be shown where to pick up fresh ones."

He pushed open the door as he spoke, and Apphia, the first one inside, stepped into the room and then stood staring around her. It was large enough, but that might have been because there was not all that much inside to take up any room. Pallet beds were piled up against one wall, behind a half-drawn and worn arras curtain hung about a third of the way into the room. High above them, above the doorway, a narrow window let in some light, but was too high to look out of; the roof sloped on the far side, giving an indication of where they were—buried deep beneath the tiers of seating above, where the crowds would stamp their feet and roar their exhilaration or dismay when the races started. There was a charcoal burning stove and heater in one corner with an exhaust built in and letting out next to the high window. One or two other necessities were there, but that was all—just the necessities, not an ounce of comfort, or softness, or gentleness, or sunshine.

"Well," Cantaxas said, with a hint of impatience. "We have to go find one of your peers. I think Cletius the lion keeper might be down in the dens right now, if we hurry we can still catch him. You can leave your family and your baggage here, they will be quite safe."

"Would you…give us a moment?" Batzas said quietly.

Cantaxas gave him a sharp look, and then an unpleasant half-smile. "I will be outside," he said, stepping out of the room and closing the door behind him.

Batzas and Apphia exchanged a long look over the heads of their daughters.

"It could have been worse," Batzas said. "Just think where they would have quartered us if I had been a mere *assistant* bear keeper."

Apphia began to laugh, but somehow ended on a queer hiccup that was something between a giggle and a sob. "It wasn't supposed to be like this," she said.

"We will make it work. We're in the city now, there will be chances I could never have dreamed.…" Batzas broke off, glanced back at the door, squeezed

Apphia's hand and then dropped it. "I'd better not keep him waiting. I'll be back as soon as I can. Settle the baby, and when I get back we will see what we can do about a proper lunch for the rest of us. Hold on, Apphia—all will be well."

"Yes," she said reflexively, her eyes straying to the high window and its narrow rectangle of light. "Yes, I am sure it will."

Danelis was tired and in any event too cowed by her surroundings to do more than simply curl up to where her mother directed her to sit, on one of the pallet beds she had pulled out and laid into a corner of the sleeping area. The baby was fretful and uncooperative, refusing to feed or settle, keeping up a thin and constant unhappy wail.

Simonis didn't wait in the stone chamber. When her mother's back was turned, she slipped out of the door and back along the corridor the way they had come in, out of the door, into the portico, up the side stair and back into the tiers of seats. She climbed along the side of them slowly, where stairs had been cut all the way up to the very top of the amphitheatre wall, up where the colonnade was—and at length she emerged onto the flat uppermost terrace, wider than she had thought it might be, stretching out to where only a stone parapet separated her from the emptiness that yawned below.

But Simonis wasn't interested in looking straight down.

What drew her eye was the view that now opened up before her—the warren of streets through some of which she may well have wended her way as they had walked towards the Hippodrome that morning, the straight slash of the main avenue which they had crossed, the glimpse of imperial gardens behind their walls and the tumbling tiered domed roofs of the palace itself, and beyond all of that the promontory which was the gateway to the Narrows and then, glinting in the golden autumn sunshine, in the distance, the open sea.

It was hard to see it down below, when she was part of the thousands of milling human beings and penned in by streets and walls and harbour guards and the great unknown—but from up here, it all suddenly looked familiar to Simonis, every single stone and cobble and mule's bray and mosaic tessera of it. It lay as though in the palm of her hand, this place they called the City of Gold, and somehow she knew it. She *knew* it. She was too young to understand the feeling or to shape it into something coherent or profound—but standing up there high above Visant and looking down upon it Simonis summarised it to herself with simple, forthright logic, a single thought that was formed in the clarity of a child's mind, as yet unburdened with too many layers of adult complexity and complication. A single word.

Home.

She had been born far from this place, in a small town with a tiny Hippodrome of its own—but she had been a baby then, and it hadn't mattered. The Cyrenais of her earliest childhood was barely a memory now, and she let it go without grief, without sadness, without regret. It might never have existed at all.

This did. This place. This great city at her feet.

Home.

I am home.

CHAPTER TWO

reetings to Marcus, the son of my sister.

G Marcus had known, of course, about his uncle Leontes, his mother Dunia's older brother. He was a family legend—the young man who had left their farm and their village nearly thirty years before, to seek his fortune, and had never returned home. Marcus had never actually set eyes on his uncle, had known him only through his mother's stories and the occasional letters that came and told of his advancement in the Palace guard in the golden city of Visant. The last letter from the city had come some time ago, the letter that had brought news of his appointment to the position of Count of the Palace Guard, the highest honour the old Emperor could bestow in reward for unswerving loyalty and obvious talent for commanding such loyalty in the men of whom he had charge. There had been a long silence, after that, as though Leontes had reached the pinnacle of his life and suddenly had nothing more to write home about.

But now there was another letter. A letter addressed not to his sister or to her husband, but to Marcus, the oldest of Dunia's four sons.

Leontes, who had seen his share of field campaigns, had taken up many years ago with a slave girl named Arethusa, a camp follower whom he had first promoted to cook and then eventually formally freed and then married. Their union seemed happy enough; Arethusa had been mentioned several times in Leontes's dispatches back home, and always with affection. But in the many years that they had shared together there had been no children, no sons, no-one to carry on Leontes's name and his legacy

He had now written directly to his oldest nephew, proposing that the boy travel to Visant and take up residence with his childless uncle and aunt, and eventually be adopted as their own son.

The letter had come as a complete shock to Marcus. At fifteen he already had a burning desire to learn, to study and to understand anything that was thrown at him. Taught by the monks in a monastery close by his home, he was already literate in the High Imperial language with a smattering of one or two of the Eastern tongues, and his teachers, taken by the boy's enthusiasm, had given him a glimpse—a glittering, tempting hoard—of more knowledge which waited to be conquered. He had been given hints of matters of learning that were weightier than just his letters—he had begun to formulate ideas about the law, about philosophy, about a vast storehouse of history which he knew he had barely scratched there in the small monastery in the even smaller settlement out in the Empire's outer provinces. Marcus had grown up with the understanding that he would one day inherit the farm, and continue the life of his father, and his father's father before him, tilling the land, spending his days in this quiet backwater being a dutiful subject to the Emperor far away. But now...now there was a promise of more. Leontes's letter laid it all out:

> I will make sure that you get the best education that money can buy—the finest minds of the Empire work and study in the city's halls of learning, and I have means to ensure that you learn from the best. There are archives here dating from the dawn of our history, there is perhaps knowledge buried deep in the catacombs waiting for an eager young mind to unearth them. The Empire, and the city in particular, value native talent and ability above empty lineage, and if you prove yourself here you will never find yourself passed over for advancement in favour of some Senatorial scion—here, in Visant, you are measured by what and not who you are.

Until his uncle's letter came, Marcus had not known how much he had coveted a chance like this.

His mother had known what he would choose, long before he himself was able to become completely aware of his own decision. She had handed him the letter without having broken its seal, fully aware of the things that it might contain, willing to let her son make up his own mind—but she had been with him when he had broken that seal, and long before he had finished reading and looked up with newly kindled hunger in his eyes, Dunia had sighed, folded her hands in her lap, and accepted the loss of her son and the new possibilities that now lay open before him.

"When do you wish to leave?" she asked, even as he looked up and fought to control his reaction to the news.

"You knew?"

"That he would ask you to Visant? He has no children, Marcus. I have four sons. This day was bound to come."

"You don't want me to go," he said, a flat statement, his hand clenching on the parchment he held in his lap.

"Of course not," Dunia said gently. "You are my son, you are still so young…."

"I am fifteen," Marcus said, with an edge of stubbornness. "You said my uncle was only a couple of years older than this when he…."

"Yes," Dunia said, with a wry smile that acknowledged defeat, "I have said that. And it is true. You are almost grown, Marcus—you are certainly old enough to make this decision on your own. If you choose this life, your father and I will not stand in your way."

Marcus gazed at her in silence for a moment, his grey eyes speculative. "You knew," he said again, and this time it was not a question.

"I knew you would become a man one day, and that you would grow away from your mother," Dunia said. "I just didn't know…it would come so soon. And that you would do it so far from me."

"And if I don't go?"

"You'll go," Dunia said, reaching out to touch her son's cheek with a gentle hand. "We both know that. I may not have wished it, I may have hoped for a different life, but Leontes can give you a broader horizon than your father and I ever could. I cannot say that I am happy at the prospect of having you call Leontes's camp cook your mother, but I…."

"He may adopt me," Marcus said fiercely, "but you will always be my mother."

She smiled again. "That would be kind," she said, acknowledging the emotion behind the words.

Marcus dropped his eyes to the parchment, crumpled in his hand. "How am I to…where do I need to go…."

"As to that, the messenger who brought the letter will probably have been charged with the details of your journey," Dunia said. "At least, that's probably why he is still hanging around. The letter was addressed to you; I expect you will wish to speak to him yourself and give reply to your uncle's words. We have offered him lodging for the night—but I think he is still out by the stable, tending to his horse."

The letter from Visant was still in Marcus's hand as he went to seek his uncle's messenger, but it was not until he saw the stranger in the familiar yard that the idea that he would be *leaving* this place actually took root in his mind. He would be following in his uncle's footsteps, going to the big city to seek his fortune—and his uncle, although he had kept in touch with letters and gifts, had never returned home. Marcus, seized by a sudden desire to cling to everything he would be leaving—his house, the farm, the fields of grain, the woods by the roadside and the hidden places of his boyhood in the hills beyond, the quiet sonorous halls of the little monastery where he had learned his letters—was suddenly and miserably certain that he was not ready for this. He had not said goodbye to the people and places he would be leaving behind, the home and hearth where he had done his growing up, his family, his friends. But the past had to be left behind for the sake of a future that beckoned, and the longer he took about it, the harder it was going to be until it finally became impossible.

They left in the early morning, Marcus and his escort, a stocky, taciturn soldier whose stubbled jaw was raked by a livid white scar from some long-past encounter. Marcus's brothers were still asleep and his mother merely a shape silhouetted in the window in the pearly light of an autumn dawn. She might have waved. Marcus had not dared to turn and look, for fear that he would disgrace himself in his soldier-companion's eyes if he should be so weak as to burst into tears. It wasn't as if either of them were *dying*, Marcus had berated himself. His uncle had written letters to his family about his life in the city. Marcus could do the same.

That buoyed him on the ride to the city; he had stored every new impression and sensation and scent and sound, and wrote about them to his parents and his siblings back home. He had carefully archived the memories of his first sight of the sea and a whiff of its foreign, exotic scent; the nights spent on the road, bivouacking out in the open when the nights were fine or seeking shelter in wayside hostelries and inns against driving rains with the first cold hints of late autumn and early winter in the wind; the massive herds of cattle and pigs for whom they had had to make way on the road more than once as they approached Visant, being driven to the city slaughterhouses to feed the hungry thousands who waited for nourishment; his slack-jawed astonishment at the massive buttresses of the outer walls of Visant, and the way the mention of his uncle's name, like a magic password, cleared their way into the city; the teeming avenue with its shops and bath-houses and milling crowds who got in the way of the peasant boy and the soldier. Marcus registered one man snatching his small daughter from their path, just before the apparently oblivious soldier nearly trampled her under the hooves of his impassive warhorse.

But then his mind had overflowed, and the sights and sounds and smells of the new place began to muddle and mix and tangle in his head, which was beginning to spin with the sensory and emotional overload. He was feeling sick by the time they passed under the Bronze Gate and into the first of the outer courtyards of the Imperial Palace, and his escort gestured for him to dismount. He did so, the muscles in his legs quivering after being on horseback for so long, and had to make a concerted effort to stay on his feet.

"Someone else will take you in from here," the soldier said. "Your uncle, the Count, will be expecting you. Good luck, boy."

Another soldier, much younger and apparently lower in rank than Marcus's escort into the city, conducted him in silence across the inner courtyard which opened from the Palace Guard quarters just inside the Bronze Gate. Another, smaller gate led from that into another paved yard edged with shrubs and small ornamental trees. Marcus followed his guide down a shallow stone stair, through another small gate, across a narrow balcony overlooking a steeper, treed slope below, where Marcus glimpsed a small stone bridge arching over a trickle of clear running water. Then they moved through a solid wooden door which stood open, but had a fully armoured guard in an alcove just inside the inner portico. Marcus already despaired of ever finding his way out of the place again; it was a warren of gardens and colonnades and walkways and stairwells, designed to trap the unwary in its webs. He tried to maintain a sense of direction, something that he had been rather good at back home, but here the walls and the domes of the roofs and glimpses of windows or balconies higher up or lower down from the place played havoc with his perspective and his ability to orient himself. His head was spinning by the time he was deposited by his guide, with a silent salute of fist on heart, in what seemed to be an empty room which opened onto yet another balcony. The year was already wrapped in an air of autumn and there was a hint of chill in the air even with the deceptive sunshine that still spilled from the sky—but the doors to the balcony were ajar, and Marcus diffidently stepped closer, reaching out with one hesitant hand to push the door a little wider, peering outside to see if the view would give him some more information on his location.

"That bag looks heavy. You can lay it down now."

A woman's voice at his back made Marcus snatch his hand back as though the door had burned him.

"I'm sorry," he began, "I didn't mean to presume...."

He might have taken the woman who faced him as some sort of servant, perhaps, had he not been paying attention—she was short, with a broad face and a body which could never have been graceful. Her feet and ankles were hidden by the hem of a gown which made a certain attempt at reflecting a costly elegance—or at the very least at something a dazzled country boy assumed to be such, although it might well have been no more than quite ordinary everyday wear for the city. Her sleeves, immodestly not quite reaching the heel of her hands, revealed thick, bracelet-clasped wrists flowing into square capable hands with thick peasant fingers that could not be disguised even with several rings.

"A-aunt Arethusa...?" Marcus asked, hesitating, testing the name in his mouth.

"She no longer goes by that name," said another voice. A man's. "But she is your aunt, yes. She has been written into the Patrician Register as Euphaedra, and the other name...has been erased. Let me look at you, boy."

Marcus, flushed at having managed to make some sort of social blunder as soon as he had opened his ill-educated country bumpkin mouth, stood without moving as his uncle Leontes crossed the room and closed his hands on Marcus's shoulders, forcing him to straighten up and look Leontes in the eye.

Marcus might have been braced for an expression of mild rebuke, but Leontes was smiling, and there was something about him, some evanescent resemblance to his mother that suddenly stabbed Marcus to the heart.

"You have Dunia's eyes," Leontes said, in an uncanny echo of his nephew's thoughts. "I didn't know what to expect, frankly, but you might do very well. You aren't going to be a big man, you run more to stamina than to power, I would say—but you've got a length of leg to you and you're still growing, after all. You'll do, lad, you'll do. Welcome to Visant."

"Thank you, sir," Marcus said, wary but reflexively polite.

"We will talk of your future at great length," Leontes said. "But before we do that, you must be tired and hungry from your journey. I will make sure that you are shown to the baths later, but in the meantime there's a basin set up in your quarters, and after you've washed up a little and set aside your luggage, there's fruit and cheese set out in the other room—dinner is a long time away and you're probably hungry. You must tell me of your mother, and your family, and I am sure you will have plenty of questions about Visant." A young boy in a simple servant tunic was hovering at the inner doorway, and Leontes slapped

Marcus on the back lightly, sending him staggering forward towards the servant. "He will show you where you need to go. Go on, we will be waiting."

Marcus blinked owlishly, thinking he should respond in some way, but when no response seemed to be required or even expected decided that the best course of action for now would be to simply obey instructions until he could find his feet. His "quarters" turned out to be plain, almost stark—the furniture consisted of a pallet bed, a simple table with a single chair, and, tucked underneath the window, a second low table on which a basin full of warm water and a clean washcloth had been set out. Left to himself for the first time since he had left his home, Marcus dropped the bag he had carried all the way from his chilhood village—and which now seemed to contain not a single item that he would want or need in this strange new world—at the foot of the pallet, and crossed over to the window, peering outside. There wasn't much of a view, he could see mostly trees and more walls, but he committed what he could see to memory, his first real attempt to locate himself in the city and the palace, to claim some part of it for his own. Then he turned away, scrubbed at his grimy hands and face as best he could with the wetted washcloth, leaving the water in the basin faintly grey, and, not knowing what to do with the detritus, left the washcloth draped on the side of the basin and made his way back to where his new family waited for him.

In the few quiet moments that he had had to himself, while scrubbing the dust of the world outside Visant from his face and hands, he'd had a chance to think. His ideas about this venture had always been vast and nebulous—the letter from his uncle had offered education, broader horizons, a chance for the kind of life which would never have been within his grasp had he stayed home on the farm—but the details had been sketchy, and now there was that rather ominous-sounding *You'll do* from his uncle's lips. For the first time since he had leapt at the opportunity to come to the City of Gold, Marcus took a moment to wonder at the road that would take him to destinations which had yet to be formalised and firmed up.

He steeled himself to offer some sort of apology to his aunt, feeling perfectly certain that he had somehow unforgivably insulted or slighted her in that first encounter, but it was only Leontes who waited for him by the side table where fruit and butter-yellow cheese and coarse brown bread had been laid out. A pewter goblet stood beside the trenchers, filled with a pale wine.

"I took the liberty of watering yours," Leontes said, nodding at the goblet as Marcus entered and paused by the door, "I have no idea yet what your head for drink is. But you're near grown, you'll make your own decisions on that score after this. Although I have to warn you, drink yourself senseless in this city and your peers will be quick to take advantage."

Marcus took up the goblet. "I'll keep that in mind," he said.

He had not meant it as a joke, but Leontes appeared to find it funny because he threw his head back and guffawed. "Oh, you'll do indeed," he said.

"What…am I supposed to be doing here, Uncle?" Marcus asked carefully, turning the goblet between his fingers.

Leontes narrowed his eyes just a little. "I wrote you a letter," he said, and then, watching Marcus eyeing the food, "Go on then, we can talk while you eat."

"You said…I could learn.…" Marcus wrapped a piece of bread around a large piece of cheese, bit into it with gusto, and then paused, distracted. "This tastes…just like the cheese from home," he said, his mouth full, sounding vaguely astonished.

"It probably comes from some such village," Leontes said. "That's your first lesson, boy. You can find almost anything you want in this city, so long as you have coin to pay for it. So, why don't you tell me, what did you come here to seek?"

Marcus swallowed his bread and cheese quickly, and had to wash it down with a gulp of the wine before it lodged in the back of his throat and gave him the hiccups. "I went to the monks, back home," he said eagerly. "They taught me what they could, the basics, but they said that there was so much more out there to learn. And your letter said that here at the University.…"

Leontes nodded. "Yes. There is a vast knowledge in this city."

Marcus took a deep breath, and met his uncle's eyes squarely.

"What are your plans for me, uncle?"

"What if they don't match up with your own?"

Marcus felt his heart sink, a little, but his gaze was grey and steady. "You brought me here," he said, "and I owe you for that. I will pay any debt that I owe, in any way that I can."

Leontes sighed. "There can be no debt between us," he said, "we are family. For now, you are my foster-son. In time, as I wrote to you and to your mother, I plan to adopt you as my own son and heir—you notice that Euphaedra and I have no children and are unlikely to, now. You will be enrolled in the Palace Guard—at the lowest level, where I started—and you will get training in the ways of arms and battle; you already, I suspect, ride a horse better than any of the peacocks out in that courtyard."

"And school…?" Marcus said.

"That too. I know some of the scholars who pore over the dusty tomes in the University and I dare say they would welcome a quick young mind. I myself have had little chance at book learning, so whatever you take from them you learn for the both of us, and it will come in useful in some fashion some day. You will live here, for now, in my quarters—once you know the city better, and become of age, I do not have a problem with your taking up lodgings of your own if you wish. Young men do need their privacy, I understand that."

Marcus actually blushed at the blunt soldierly assumption, but did not interrupt.

"I have a Senator's rank," Leontes said, after a pause. "You are my family—my sister-son, my own foster son, in time my own son. You are entitled to be written into the Patrician Register, and indeed you will have to be—it is only a Patrician's rank that will gain you free admittance beyond the first courtyard of the Bronze Gate. It is by the name that I write into the register that you will become known in this city. When your aunt was raised into the Patrician ranks, she chose her own name."

"But Euphaedra is not...." Marcus began, and then stopped, aware of a chasm opening at his feet again. The name was obviously a fake, a clumsy attempt to marry an aristocratic root with an unrelated nomen taken from myth and fable, chosen out of a combination of fancy and ignorance. Even Marcus, whose own knowledge was born from children's hearth tales and the things which simple country monks might have been expected to know, was aware of that much. He was not sure where he stood, exactly, with his aunt—only that he should not laugh at that name, and that nobody else in the Palace who might have wanted to snicker did so in the Count's hearing or to Euphaedra's face.

Leontes might have stopped to explain all that, but in the end he did not need to—Marcus had already taken enough of a measure of his uncle to realise that much. "Yes, she chose it, because she thought it sounded like a Patrician's name ought to sound," was all he said. And then added, slyly, "She was all set to pick the name by which *you* will be known...."

Marcus actually winced.

"Ah, have no fear," Leontes said, not failing to notice that reaction. "I explained that a man's name, particularly a name by which a nephew of the Count of the Palace Guard goes by, has to be something that will command respect—and that she, a woman, could not possibly understand what needs to go into this." He was deprecating, but amused, and Marcus was left in no doubt of how much genuine comfortable affection there was between these two people and in this unlikely marriage. Leontes had indulged his wife's ignorance of the classics and the somewhat unfortunate whimsy of the name she had chosen, and stood perfectly willing to defend it by both word and deed if necessary.

"So did *you* pick...?" Marcus said, feeling a little bit lost, as though the strange city was already stripping his old identity from him little by little, suddenly afraid of how much of his true self, his core, the Marcus Neissus who had first set foot in Visant, would be left by the time the city was done with him.

"It doesn't have to be done tonight," Leontes said. "I'm happy to make a few suggestions, but if you come up with something of your own there's no reason why it can't be done. Did you have an idea?"

"I had not thought about it," Marcus said, attacking another piece of cheese and snaking a couple of figs off another platter with his free hand.

"Well," Leontes said indulgently, "there's time enough for that. In the meantime...." He slipped a signet ring off the little finger of his left hand and offered it to Marcus. "This is your passport, until such time as we can make things more regular," he said. "Do not lose it. It is the ring of the Count of the Palace Guard, and its seal is known—it will admit you to the Palace grounds, and into this house. If it's too large for your hand, I will procure a chain you can use to wear it around your neck for the time being."

"No," Marcus said, slipping the ring on the ring finger of his own left hand, "it will do."

"Good hands," Leontes said approvingly. "Well, as soon as we have settled the small matter of what you are to be addressed by, I will have letters of reference prepared, and you can take them to the University. I'm letting you have a few days off, after your journey, and do use them to find your way around the city. Ask for company if you need to, there are idle lads aplenty in the Bronze Gate courtyard at any hour of the day who would be more than happy to show your around or draw you a map of where you need to go. You start your training with the Guard next week...have you *ever* held a proper sword in your hands, lad?...and we can take it from there."

"Maxentius," Marcus said, squaring his shoulders and straightening his back.

"Eh?" Leontes said, frowning a little.

"The name. The name you want to write into the Register."

"Maxentius."

"Yes, sir."

"And where did that come from? Ready-baked and sudden like this?"

Marcus squirmed a little. "One of the monks back home...." he began, and then hesitated, his cheeks flushing a little.

"That is not a monk's name," Leontes said, his tone suddenly a little cooler, letting Marcus glimpse the sort of man his uncle might be outside the warmth and loyalty commanded by the ties of blood and kinship that bound the two of them, "nor did I think you harboured any yearnings in that direction."

"No!" Marcus shook his head sharply, rushing to explain himself. "What I meant to say was, one of the monks…they had a book someone had brought to the monastery, years before—it was starting to crumble, and one of the monks was charged with copying it out afresh—it was a history, of sorts, and there was a man.…"

"I know who Maxentius was," Leontes said. "You choose an Emperor's name?"

"He did great deeds," Marcus said. "I know I am no Emperor, least of all a warrior Emperor, but Maxentius caused great buildings to be raised, and he had chronicles written of the years of his reign to which he himself contributed—the book which the monks had was only a copy, itself, but it had some of his own words in it, so the copyist told me, and he actually let me read.…"

Leontes was actually laughing, making fending-off motions with his hand. "All right, all right, my young scholar! I understand! I'm not sure that you aren't going to have just as much trouble with that name as Euphaedra had with hers—albeit for vastly different reasons—but if you can cope with that I have no problems with your choice. I shall have it entered into the Register when the offices of the Logothet's scribes open up the office tomorrow morning. If they are speedy about their work, you will have your new papers by the end of the week."

Marcus twisted the Count's ring around his finger with his other hand. "Will you want…?"

"No," Leontes said, suddenly serious again. "Keep that. It is a pledge of all that is still to come between us…my son."

CHAPTER THREE

It had been a long, cold winter.

The charcoal stove in the stone room below the marble seat tiers of the Hippodrome barely kept the room warm. Cold seeped in through the high window that seemed to admit frigid air but not nearly enough light. The air sank down to the stone flags of the floor, then sucked warmth from the flesh and bones of the humans who walked on it.

Twice during the winter, after Apphia developed a cough that wouldn't go away and the baby couldn't seem to put on the weight it needed to thrive, Batzas suggested that they find lodgings outside the stone fastness—his family, at least, because he himself was always on call, as bear keeper, and needed to be available at a moment's notice in an emergency. But Apphia just added an extra piece of charcoal to the brazier, hoarded carefully against such moments, or a scrounged quilt as an extra layer on the bed, and said that her place was with her husband, wherever that was.

Until the day that there was no more charcoal to add, and the cold northern wind that blew endlessly through the empty streets of Visant in the winter found its deadly way into the stone room, and the baby could find no more strength to fight it. While the family slept one winter night, with Batzas and Apphia in their bed and Simonis and Danelis in theirs all curled up against each other for warmth, the baby, Batzas's cherished son, simply gave up. Batzas and Apphia had slept with the baby cradled between them on the cold nights, but even that didn't help, in the end—on this morning, when they all woke, it was to find the cold and lifeless little body on their pallet.

It was bad for a while after that. Batzas and Apphia did not talk much. It was the threshold of spring; Batzas threw himself into the work with the animals which he would soon be required to display up in the Hippodrome arena, and Apphia, grown white and quiet, made her life revolve around her two remaining children—to the extent that Simonis found herself running from her home and her mother's stifling presence whenever she could snatch a chance.

Back in Cyrenais she had been known to frequent her father's animal pens by the time she was barely able to toddle. The small menagerie in Cyrenais, consisting of a couple of small brown bears, a trio of flea-bitten wolves and two mangy middle-aged lions, seemed not to mind the presence of the small human cub, who would stand outside their cages and sing to them in some weird childish nonsense language that only she and they seemed to understand. One time she had watched, increasingly upset, as one of the lions limped up and down its cage, whimpering, favouring one obviously painful paw. Simonis had slipped through the bars of the cage—just barely wide enough to allow a small child to pass—and had stepped inside the cage with the wounded lion. There wasn't a witness, after, who could swear as to what exactly had happened next—because by the time the alarm was raised what everyone saw was nothing short of extraordinary. The small girl sat beside the lion, scolding it as though it was one of her wax dolls, while the lion lay docile with a paw in the child's lap as she picked at something caught between the pads.

She removed the offending splinter, getting blood all over the front of her dress in the process. Apphia, who had been told only that Simonis was in the lion's den and had come running when she heard, fainted dead away when Simonis, wearing her blood-stained shift, had finally been enticed out of the lion's' cage and presented to her mother. It took some time to convince Apphia that her toddler was, in fact, both completely unhurt and utterly mystified as to why everyone was making such a fuss.

The law had been laid down, after that, and Simonis was expressly forbidden to go near the animals—but child and beasts knew better, and she had had to be hauled away from her friends in their cages time and again in the months and years that followed.

"She has the gift for it," people told Batzas, "it is a shame she isn't a son."

Because only a son, of course, could inherit the animal-keeper's position, once Batzas's own tenure was ended.

But then a son *was* born, and Batzas had allowed himself to hope that the boy might grow up with Simonis's gifts and propensities; and then they had left the island, and come to Visant.

And now there was no son any more.

But they had all forgotten about Simonis and her affinity for the beasts. She had been told, repeatedly, that the animals of the Visant Hippodrome's menagerie were not like the quiet, gentle, half-tame beasts she had left behind in Cyrenais—and then, because they thought they had repeated the warning often enough or because life's circumstances intervened and they forgot about continuing to warn her, they had stopped. And the baby boy had died, and her parents were distracted and distant, and Simonis remembered the animals.

She found her way down into the animal pens beneath the Hippodrome, and found a way, also, of staying invisible, unnoticed. The animal pens were stone, too, but the beasts penned here had often been taken from warmer climes and did not like the cold—so the cages were heated by a constant stream of hot water running in pipes underneath the floors, kept hot by a system of furnaces whose attendants worked shifts and never allowed the fires to go out. It was warm down here, much warmer than her own stone cavern of a room, and Simonis had found a corner in the White Jewel section of the menagerie— for this place was large enough that each faction kept its own animals—and had simply curled up on a warm spot and observed.

She watched her father working with his bears, for bears were all he was responsible for in Visant—every animal kind had its own attendant in this menagerie. He was clad only in a loincloth and sandals, his hair tied back with a leather thong and chest slick with sweat, and he worked with a younger man by the name of Locinus who had been hired to the position that Batzas himself had come here to occupy, that of bear-keeper's assistant. In other cages, lion-keepers and leopard-keepers and elephant-keepers tended to their own charges. It was a busy, hot place, smelling of animal musk and human sweat, and often of something else, something nebulous, a sense of animal unease, a feeling of incipient panic that the keepers had come to recognise and fear because it often presaged a concentrated outbreak of frenzied fury amongst the animals, set off by the smallest thing.

It was set off, one time Simonis was there, by something rather more significant—and it had started with Batzas's bears.

The trouble started when a cub born to one of the White Jewel faction's she-bears was sold—and the buyer's agents had come to collect it. The mother had first growled menacingly, hovering protectively in front of her baby, and when that didn't seem to get the message across to the determined humans who were going after the cub she began to roar, shaking her great shaggy head from side to side, shifting from one paw to the other in a way that left no doubt that the long sharp claws would be used without hesitation if anyone attempted to come any closer.

Several men corralled the mother bear, in the end, and dragged out the rather placid cub who seemed docile and sleepy and didn't object too hard to being pulled away from its mother's side. But once they had the cub and the cage slammed shut again the mother bear allowed her fury full reign, and her angry roars echoed up and down the stone casements, which set off the lions, which set off the elephants, and before long all the animals were bellowing and howling and trumpeting and the whole place was pandemonium.

"Simonis, get out of here and go home!" Batzas said, but that was all he had time for before he and his assistant were both yanked away to deal with the potential disaster of the panic.

Simonis, however, found her attention drawn to the anguished and angry mother bear, throwing herself against the bars of her cage again and again. After watching this for a few minutes, she marched over to stand just beyond paw's-reach, planted her feet squarely on the warm stone, and began to sing to the bear in exactly the same way she had once sung to the elderly lions of Cyrenais.

For a while the bear seemed rather more intent on trying to swat this new annoyance away than on paying actual attention to it, her roaring undiminished, her great paws scrabbling against the bars of the cage. But then she suddenly ceased to bellow, cocked her head and fixed Simonis with its small, intelligent eyes, and seemed to pause and listen to the child's song.

Nobody else noticed the little pool of sudden silence that had descended on the bear's cage; all the keepers had their hands full calming their other charges, with commands or with the lash. It was only in the aftermath, with the tail of the menagerie panic barely stepped on, that Locinus, Batzas's assistant, happened to look more closely into the bear cage where all the trouble had started—and then do a double take, and clutch at Batzas's upper arm.

"Batzas," he said in a low, intense voice, "your daughter."

"She was here, earlier," Batzas said, still a little distracted by the situation. "Again. I sent her home."

"No. Batzas. Your *daughter*."

Batzas became aware that Locinus was pointing with his free hand, the other still clamped around Batzas's arm, and followed the line of the pointing finger—and suddenly gasped as though all the breath had been kicked out of his body.

Inside the bear cage, curled comfortably into the side of the mother bear who had started all the trouble, Simonis appeared to be fast asleep; the bear's own eyes were barely open, its enormous head resting on the ground next to the child.

Batzas tried to say something through bloodless lips, and failed to make a sound come out.

"How do we get her out of there?" Locinus said. "If we try it by force—right after what we just went through—what if the animal thinks it's another kind of cub?"

"I can't leave my daughter sleeping in a bear's den," Batzas said.

"You'll set it all off again," Locinus said, glancing around for help. He caught the eye of one of the lion keepers and motioned him over, and then another keeper noticed the clutch of silent staring men and came to see what the new problem was, and after a few minutes the group had grown to five or six—all staring in helpless fascination at the child and the bear.

"She's *your* daughter," one of the other trainers said, actually sounding admiring.

"She used to do this," Batzas said. "Back on the island. When she was very, very young."

"How did you get her out of there back in Cyrenais?"

"We had…a different kind of animal," Batzas said. "Simonis came out when she was ready. If the animals complained she actually scolded them—stood there and *scolded* a lion into letting her leave. But it was an old lion. This…."

"You may have to let her scold the bear," the lion-keeper said. "There's no hauling her out of there right now, not after we've just spent the two hours calming the whole place down. It will just all start again."

"But if the bear…." Batzas began, going white, clutching back at Locinus. "That's my child. My *daughter*. I couldn't face my wife, not if anything…."

"I don't think the bear has murderous intentions," the lion-keeper said. "We should watch her. When she wakes and tries to leave…that's when we might all be needed. Right now…Batzas…there's very little you can do."

The bear is more valuable than the child. The unspoken words hung in the air. Unless the bear killed a human being, the bear could not be harmed.

Simonis dozed in the bear cage for almost an hour before she suddenly woke and sat up, rubbing her eyes. The first thing she saw was Batzas, crouched in front of the cage, his eyes not leaving the child at the bear's side.

"Pappa," she said.

The bear stirred, with a soft whuffle.

Batzas spoke, keeping his voice very low. "How did you get inside the cage?"

Simonis pointed to where a slightly wider gap opened up between a cage bar and an iron wall. "I fit," she said.

"All right," Batzas said, still calm. "Now I need you to come right back out, the same way. Come to me."

Simonis stood, and the bear lifted her head, instantly alert. Batzas held his breath as the child reached out to the great shaggy animal, holding out her hand open-palmed.

"It's all right," Simonis said. "You'll be fine now. I promise."

The bear growled softly as Simonis turned and walked away to the gap, and squeezed through. When she was all but out, Batzas leapt to his feet and snatched her the rest of the way, scraping her ankle against the stone wall, raising a wail from the child and an answering grumble from the bear.

"It's all right," Simonis gasped, twisting her head around to stare back at the bear. "Pappa, you're hurting me."

But Batzas had collapsed back into a crouch, holding his daughter very tightly against him, his eyes squeezed shut. "Child," he whispered, "oh, *child*, these are not the pets you left behind...don't you understand, I could have lost you too...don't ever do this, don't *ever*...promise me...."

"I promise," Simonis said, mystified, not entirely clear on what she was promising or what the drama was. The bear had been comfortable. Friendly. A haven.

Of course she would come back.

And she did. She broke her promise again and again, slipping in between the bar and the wall all that spring and into summer. She had always been small-boned and compact; at some point she would simply cease to fit through her gap sooner or later and the bear visits would be over, but until that time there seemed to be little anybody could do to prevent her from visiting her bear, and in time the keepers got used to it and if they glimpsed the small body half-buried in the bear's shaggy side they merely raised an eyebrow—especially when it began to dawn on everybody that the menagerie was calmest when Simonis was in with the bear, that the calm quiet contentment in the bear's cage was almost as contagious as the panics that they were so keen to avoid. The bear, who was not precisely friendly to any other human, seemed to dote on the child and to enjoy the feel of the small furless body against her side.

They comforted each other, the bear-mother with the lost cub and the solitary human child who could not seem to find her place amongst her own kind.

And the summer races unfolded as they always did, and then the summer season was coming to a close, and the bite of autumn was once again in the air.

And this winter, it was Batzas himself who was not well.

His son had succumbed to Visant; his wife had barely managed to get over the cough which she had picked up the previous season; Danelis seemed to respond by acquiring a persistent and unlovely sniffle which lasted from the first touch of the winter winds to well after the races started in the spring; Simonis lurched through a series of colds and mild fevers, hardly recovering from one before she was halfway into the next—but Batzas had seemed to weather the transition to Visant in his stride, that first season. But by the time the second winter came around, Batzas himself began to suffer from a strange wheezing in his breath, and the hard muscles of his arms and abdomen seemed to wither as the last of the island's sun-warmed brown faded from his skin and left his face to alternate between a wan pallor and cheeks hectic with some inner fire. After several weeks of keeping his wife and daughters awake by being unable to control the coughing fits he succumbed to in the night, he took to sleeping on his own pallet, apart from them, muffling the sound of his laboured breathing in his bedclothes.

His mood changed, too, from an optimistic and ambitious man who was still of no great age and with potential to achieve much to a melancholy shadow of his former self much given to picking over the past rather than looking into the future.

"In Cyrenais," he told Apphia, "they used to cheer me when I took the animals out into the arena."

"They do that here," Apphia said.

"No," Batzas said, shaking his head slowly. "Here they cheer the animals— they cheer the faction—they cheer the bears of the White Jewel faction rather than the bear-keeper who cares for them and trains them. It could be anyone. They don't see me. They don't care at all about who I am, so long as the bears perform to their satisfaction."

"That isn't true," Apphia said loyally. "You do great work with the animals, and the White Jewel people know it...."

Batzas coughed into a square of cloth, glanced at it, and put it away quickly before Apphia could see it. "That's probably why Locinus has been able to keep the place running without me for three days now," he said. "They probably don't even notice that I'm gone. I should go down and check on...."

"No," Apphia said, pushing him back down onto the pallet as he tried to rise. "Not yet. Give it another day. Locinus was in here to report just this morning. Everything is fine. You can take a bit of time to get better."

Batzas didn't argue too hard. It didn't seem to matter, in one way; in another, it mattered a great deal, because what he was doing—or not doing—became a very important factor in the future of his entire family. But he could not seem to make his legs hold him upright, just at that moment. Perhaps Apphia was right—one more day…

But the days stretched into weeks, and the bitter winter continued. For some reason they all clasped their hands and spoke of spring as though it would be the answer to all their prayers. When spring comes—when the season starts again—when the wind stops—it would all be well, then, everything would be well.

But the day before the racing season started, one day before the season of bounty and goodwill was due to begin, Apphia woke up in the cold grey half-light of just before the dawn with an icy premonition that something was very wrong. She lay still for a moment, listening—her daughters' breathing was close by, quiet, steady, the sound of sleeping children, for once unmarred by sniffles or rasping throats. But over on the far side of the arras where Batzas slept…

Apphia slipped off her pallet, and padded in bare feet across the stone floors and their radiating chill. Batzas seemed to be asleep, at first glance, although his breathing was laboured and shallow—but as she came closer she realised that his eyes were not closed, glittering and far too bright in the gloom. His breath seemed to be strangling in his throat, his mouth half open, his cheeks that same hectic flushed red that had been there far too often this winter. And yet, despite the apparent flush of heat on his face, when Apphia's groping hand met and clasped her husband's his fingers were chilled, clammy.

Her own breath caught as her free hand flew to her throat.

Batzas licked his dry, chapped lips weakly, and tried to speak; no sound came out except a long slow sigh. Apphia leaned closer, trying to understand, and became aware that he was repeating two words over and over again.

Forgive me. Forgive me.

And then even that was gone. All was gone. What strength there had been in his hand vanished suddenly, his fingers limp in her grasp. His tortured breathing caught on a last harsh gasp of air, and was still.

Forgive me.

Apphia hunched her shoulders, bringing Batzas's dead hand to her lips, trying to smother her sudden racking sobs lest she wake her daughters—but one of them, at least, was already awake. When Apphia looked up again, blinking several times to clear her vision of tears, she saw Simonis standing rigid with shock, one hand clamped on the arras, staring at her parents with wide eyes.

Apphia suddenly straightened. If they were to survive, if this small family was to survive, it was up to her now. "I hope *you* can forgive *me* for what I am about to do…" she whispered letting her eyes drop one more time to Batzas's face. Then she laid the dead hand back very gently back on his chest, and stood up.

"Stay here, Simonis," she said. "Please, this once, just obey me and stay here. There are things I need to take care of, right now, before anyone knows… before anyone *knows*. Stay here, and watch your sister. Can you do that?"

Simonis simply nodded, mute.

Apphia dressed hurriedly, thrust her feet into sandals, drew a fold of her wrap over her head.

"Stay," she said one more time, pausing at the door to look back on her older daughter. "I will be back as soon as I can."

It was to be a long and bitter day.

Danelis woke and first whimpered and then screamed when she toddled over to what she thought was her sleeping father, who was cold and would not respond to her touch. She would not be comforted. Apphia returned some two hours after she had left the girls, her hair straggling and untidy and her cheeks as flushed as her husband's had been in the moments before he had died.

"I came to check on you," she said, "but I have to go out again—Simonis, there is bread in the box, and you can heat up yesterday's cabbage—can you make sure you and your sister eat something? I have to report.…" She glanced back at Batzas, almost unwillingly, as though it pained her to look. "Ah, child, I wish there was some way to spare you from being here when they come…I have to go and see the Master now, do you remember him?…we went to see him on the day we came—I have to talk to him—but they drew the red silk curtain at the Imperial Box yesterday, the races are about to start, as though he'll have time to listen, to care…Simonis, Locinus will be in to check on you too, be respectful to him, he will be your new father.…"

She seemed rattled, nervous, talking too quickly and not saying enough. Simonis's eyes simply grew bigger and darker, and she said nothing.

Apphia left again; Locinus came an hour or so later and tried to speak gently to the girls, but Danelis was white and silent now and would not utter a word, and Simonis answered him in unwilling monosyllables that seemed ripped from her. He had sighed and left, driven by his own responsibilities and duties. And then they were alone again, the two little girls, alone with their father's body.

There seemed to be no way that it could get worse, any of it, and then it did.

Two dour-faced morgue-men came and wrapped the body of Batzas in a linen shroud, and took him up between them, carrying him away as though in a swaying hammock. A part of Simonis was screaming in anguish—*wait, wait, I haven't even said goodbye yet*…but it was all inside of her, and not a sound escaped her while she watched the men go about their work. Danelis had started crying again when they left, and cried until she exhausted herself, finally dropping off into a fitful sleep curled up against her sister, sucking on her thumb again as though she was back to being a baby.

When Apphia returned the second time she was as pale as she had been flushed before, and wrapped in an icy calm that frightened Simonis far more than anything else had done that day. She carried two wreaths woven from fading laurel and a handful of fresh flowers, and laid them aside on what had been Batzas's bed with an air of purpose.

"I will heat water," Apphia said. "You and your sister must wash. Go and get your best dresses out of the box, the white linen ones you've been saving. Go on, there's a good girl. Let me have Danelis."

It was a day that Simonis could not seem to do other than obey, her mind recording every moment and storing it away until she was sure that every etched instant of it would be permanently fixed in her memory, never to be erased— all leading up to something now, something big, even bigger than her father's death, and the blank uncertainty of the future suddenly terrified her. She did as her mother had asked, taking out the white dresses and smoothing them out, laying them out on her mother's bed.

By the time she was done, Danelis had been woken and scrubbed down until she was glowing pink. Apphia sent her over to the bed to put the dress on and turned her attention to Simonis, who stood without resistance as her own body was washed down with a cloth and barely lukewarm water and then obediently put on her own white shift.

Apphia reached out for the two garlands, and laid one on each girl's head— and then took each child's hand and led them both out of the stone room, talking to them in a quiet, intense voice.

"Do exactly as I say," she whispered. "We are going up to the arena. A race is about to start, don't be afraid, there will be plenty of flash and noise, but we will wait until it is over. And when I give you the signal, I want you to walk over to the box where the White Jewel people are sitting, where Amantius is sitting, you remember him, don't you? Don't say anything, just go up to the box and then kneel before it, both of you, and lift your arms up to it. Do you understand what I am telling you?"

"But…why…." Simonis had finally found her voice, her curiosity, as though the thing that was recording the events of this day in her mind suddenly required some sort of an explanation for it all.

"I promised Locinus when I married him this morning that I would make sure he inherited the bear keeper job," Apphia whispered, her grip painful on Simonis's fingers, her words falling like stones into Simonis's mind. "But Amantius…I think he has already been bribed, that the job has already been bought, if they turn us out Locinus might not keep us, and we will starve on the streets. You two children, you are supplicants. He may listen to you, he may hear *you*, the way he didn't listen to me this morning. It is for you that I did this, that you do this now. Promise me, Simonis. Promise me…."

But she didn't seem to know precisely what the promise was supposed to be, and anyway it was already too late for more. They were out in the main gate, and the race had already started—they were just in time to see the chariots rounding the curve, the horses at full gallop, spraying sand into the gate as they turned. The lead chariot blue, with a golden crown painted on its side; the second chariot, following closely was all black. This seemed to trouble Apphia—she sucked in her breath as the charioteers whipped past, lashing their horses mercilessly.

"We're losing," she whispered hopelessly, watching the third and fourth chariot—one green with a white jewel motif stencilled all around it and the other painted a vivid scarlet—drove side by side around the curve, fighting for the inner track. Even as they watched, disaster struck as the wheels of the two chariots briefly touched. The White Jewel chariot tilted dangerously, all its weight on one wheel, and for a moment it was uncertain whether it would survive—but the experienced charioteer threw his weight to the side of the chariot that was off the ground, and managed to establish control of his greys. The scarlet chariot, the one that looked as though it might gain the edge, was not so lucky, or perhaps its driver was less experienced in the Hippodrome arena. It veered out of control, scraped its inside wheel on the inner kerb of the monument-laden spine that lay mid-arena, and overturned with a sudden, frightening noise, splintering as it crashed. The charioteer had had the presence of mind to cut the reins at the last possible moment, and was flung clear of the wreckage to lie still and bloodied on the churned white sands. The four magnificent matched bays who had pulled the chariot raced ahead on their own, no longer encumbered by the drag of any weight behind them.

The crowd roared as the chariots raced into the straight, even as attendants ran into the arena to pull the unconscious driver out of harm's way while others gathered up what debris they could, followed by another pair who scattered fresh white sand over the blood on the track.

"We've lost this one," Apphia said, staring at the remaining three chariots already far down the straight. "I would have wished…Amantius might have been more inclined…." She chewed on her lip, visibly upset.

Another roar from the far end of the Hippodrome signified that the race had ended. Behind them, the gates to the underground menagerie levels had opened, and several of the handlers emerged with a number of the beasts. None of them looked at Apphia, studiously keeping their eyes straight ahead or on their animal charges. From behind them a troupe of acrobats ran out and sprinted down the straight, waving ribbon banners and raising a cheer from the winning side of the Hippodrome where the Golden Crown and the Obsidian Knife faction supporters were seated, and a sullen rumble of discontent from the side that housed the White Jewel faction and its junior branch, the Scarlet Banner, the one whose charioteer had met with the accident earlier. Someone had managed to grab and calm down the loose bays from the scarlet chariot; the other three chariots, pulled by lathered horses with heaving flanks, came round to be directed out of the main gate towards the stables and a handler followed leading the bays, whose eyes were still rolling with barely controlled panic after their accident. The acrobats had started tumbling over one another further down on the straight.

Apphia tightened her grip briefly on her girls' hands, and then let go, giving them both a little push forward.

"Now," she said quietly. "Do it now. Go to the box. Don't look back. Remember what I told you."

Danelis stood as though transfixed, and Simonis reached out for the hand that Apphia had dropped and stepped forward, pulling her sister behind her. Danelis stumbled a little, but then followed, pliant, like a doll without a will of her own.

The tiers of the Hippodrome rose above them as they stepped into the arena, its stone walls gathering and amplifying the roar and murmur of the crowds. But the two girls quickly moved into a pool of silence; Simonis did not look anywhere but straight ahead, straight into the box, and her cheeks were suddenly burning with the shame of this moment—they were literally here to beg for their lives, for survival. Their mother had already promised herself to another man, before the body of Batzas has been cold—she had had to do it, because a woman alone, a woman with two small children, had no chance. But if the White Jewel faction and its Master did not grant the bear-keeper position to Locinus…it was all in vain, everything was in vain, all the humiliations were for nothing.

Danelis did not understand the moment. Simonis did, completely. When they came to within a couple of paces of the White Jewel box Simonis fell to her knees on the sand, pulling her sister down beside her, and then dropped Danelis's hand and looked straight up at the box, lifting both her own arms, her hands palms up. Danelis, lost and confused, looked over at her sister and slowly did the same.

"What is it?" A voice from the box drifted down to them.

Simonis saw a man look down at them, saw recognition on his face, saw him lean over and whisper something into the ear of another man who sat in the middle of the box, a white jewel on a golden chain resting on his chest. The man called Amantius. Simonis remembered his face. She watched that face, saw the lips curl into the faintest of sneers, and then a subtle hand signal to a third man, the faction orator, who rose and lifted an arm out to the crowd behind the box who had started to call out questions.

"The children are the daughters of Batzas, the White Jewel bear-keeper," the orator said in a trained, carrying voice. "The bear-keeper died this morning. His wife apparently couldn't wait until he was buried to marry his assistant— and now wishes the bear-keeper's job to pass to her new husband. That is what the children are asking. What say you, White Jewel?"

The short silence that followed his words was broken, suddenly, by a boo from somewhere high to the left—and that, the first response heard by the crowd, was fatal. Others followed. Some were standing, with the traditional thumbs-down gesture of denial.

"Let the wench go to her new husband, then! If she couldn't wait to bury the old one!"

"It is none of our business!"

"Let the children be taken from here! Take the children away!"

Simonis burned. *My mother loved my father*, she thought, her thoughts incandescent with fury and helpless despair. *You know nothing of this! Nothing!*

A soldier on security detail came hurrying over, and Danelis, seeing him approaching, whimpered again.

"No," said Simonis fiercely, "do not let them see you cry. No tears."

She rose unsteadily to her feet, pulling Danelis up, looking around for the first time…and became aware that another carrying voice was speaking, from across the curve, in the box of the Master of the Golden Crown faction from which someone was beckoning Simonis to come over.

Faction loyalty was something carried deeply, but Simonis felt her humiliation at the hands of the White Jewel people still hot on her cheeks. Apphia was making frantic motions at her from the portico, but Simonis lifted her chin and tugged at Danelis's hand again.

"Come. Quiet, now. Come."

She crossed over to the other box, walking slowly, with the grace of something wounded and proud that refused to acknowledge the pain. By the time she reached the same position in front of this box as the one she had left behind at the feet of the White Jewel dignitaries, she halted, looking up, but did not kneel again.

"Child," the orator said, "do we understand right? Your father has just died, and your faction is throwing you and your family out into the street?"

There was a rumble at Simonis's back as the White Jewel stands became aware of what was going on, but she ignored it.

"Yes, sir," she said, and somehow her thin childish voice managed to carry just as well as the orator's own.

"It is as we have always known, then," the Master of the Golden Crown spoke, standing up. "White Jewel has no honour, and no compassion. They have lost today's race and they are taking the loss out on a helpless family in tragic circumstances. What say you, Golden Crown?"

A roar greeted his words, and at first Simonis could not tell what it signified— but then the Master turned back to her again, and he was smiling. "It is decided, then," he said. "Golden Crown needs a bear-keeper, too. Go, child, and gather your family. Quarters shall be made ready for you in our compound, and your new father may start his work tomorrow morning."

The words *thank you* trembled on Simonis's lips, but she did not say them out loud. She simply stood for a moment, her great dark eyes locked with the Master's, and then she bowed her head briefly, a royal acknowledgment, and turned away.

She was aware of several things. The jeers of the White Jewel people across the arena; the cheers of the Golden Crown crowd to her right; the vision of her mother in the portico, who had fallen to her knees with both hands stuffed into her mouth and was crying openly; a sense that she had somehow crossed a boundary of sorts, and would never quite be a child again or claim innocence.

She was not yet seven years old.

CHAPTER FOUR

The City of Gold did not allow for long childhoods, and Marcus's metamorphosis from country boy to city youth seemed to happen almost overnight.

The young man who now went by the name of Maxentius quickly, if guiltily, abandoned his early vows to write home every day. His days were full and busy and he often found himself running on the thin fuel of only a few hours of sleep a night and food snatched in passing.

Most of his afternoons and often late into the night Maxentius applied himself to his beloved books in the halls of the University, learning the rudiments of two new languages, polishing his reading skills and practising his writing hand. But his uncle, Leontes, had made good on the promise that Maxentius would be trained as a soldier—and the youth spent most of his mornings in the practice yard, being drilled with the javelin and the sword.

"Let's see what you know," the weapons-master said on his first day, handing him a much-battered rattan practice blade. He looked around at the rest of his class, thought for a moment, and picked out a scrawny youngster a head shorter than Maxentius and by the looks of things at least two years younger. "Here," the weapons-master said, "you two square off. I want to see what I'm up against."

Maxentius felt his cheeks burning—that he should be thought so incompetent to be given that *child* as an opponent!—but the child in question gave him a broad confident grin, somehow shifted on his feet without Maxentius noticing, and delivered a wallop to Maxentius's upper arm that made him stagger and nearly drop his weapon.

The weapons-master sighed deeply.

The other boy swung again, and this time Maxentius parried, wildly, and somehow managed to meet the other blade coming down more by accident than design. He grunted, and tried for an attack of his own—and was fought off effortlessly, even gracefully, as his opponent danced out of his reach.

They went at it for a few moments, with Maxentius flailing the practice sword with little success and less finesse, ending the bout with sweat dripping into his eyes and his hair sticking to his temples in damp tendrils. His opponent smirked as they saluted one another with the swords at the end of the match.

He retired to bed sore, and got up with stiff muscles and a collection of spectacular bruises to which he only added over the next couple of days as the weapons-master matched him against various opponents of varying degrees of skill. Against one he lasted barely two minutes before he found himself measuring his full length on the sandy practice ground, with his ears ringing and the world alarmingly unsteady as he tried to struggle upright.

His first week in the practice yards of the Palace militia came to an inglorious, humiliating end as the weapons-master took the rattan sword from him at the close of the final session.

"It's a damned good thing that you had not been anywhere near an actual honed blade," the weapons-master said. "You handle a sword like a barbarian waving a cudgel…or a peasant wielding a shovel. Look at you—you're black and blue. All week you've allowed yourself to be smashed and walloped by any comer—I'll give you credit for still being on your feet."

There was laughter as Maxentius took his leave, his fists clenched and his head bowed, his jaw tight. Burning with shame at this public humiliation, he took it upon himself to spend "spare" hours he didn't have practising by himself in the privacy of his uncle's yard, taking the hard-won results of those sessions back into the practice yards. He hid in the cloisters and watched the soldiers proper as they went through their training and practice bouts, and then copied what he had seen there on his own, trying to reproduce the footwork and the arc of the swinging sword, coming to a clumsy approximation of a series of actual fighting forms that he honed until his arms shook with the strain and wasn't sure he could even hold the weapon any more.

He practised stubbornly, alone, in silence. At the end of the first month, matched against a new opponent whom he had not fought before, Maxentius held his own—more, he managed to land a couple of blows of his own, something that he carefully did not allow to astonish or to delight him until the bout was over and the two antagonists, having saluted one another in a signal that the encounter was over, were sizing one another up, panting a little.

"Well," the weapons-master said. He was standing a little to the side, his arms crossed, his feet planted wide, having paid close attention to this particular session for almost its entire duration. His face was expressionless; he would give nothing, not a flicker of a smile, not a glint of approval in his eye. But the words, however grudging they seemed, were balm to Maxentius's wounded spirit and battered body. "Well. We might make a soldier out of you yet, boy."

Maxentius himself had no ambitions for a career in that field, and thereafter contented himself with simply keeping his skills at a level that did not draw any further scathing commentary from his instructors. As for anything that came from his peer group—and there had been a few pointed remarks aimed at him from that quarter by the more ambitious and more skilled contemporaries—he discovered that a sharp tongue could be as useful as a blade, and that he was more than adept enough in the use of *that* weapon.

It had begun with juvenile things—childish retaliations, in response to childish taunts.

"You'd better marry up," one of his tormentors had jeered once, after a particularly humiliating failure in the practice yard. "Your name might be written in the Patrician Register but you're no more than a peasant after all...."

"You'd better marry up, too," Maxentius had responded through clenched teeth. "You wouldn't want to marry another ass like yourself."

He had paid for that one with more bruises. But as they honed their own skills with physical weapons, so he honed his own skill with cutting words, and after a while his own ability with a sword improved too. He got fewer physical bruises and he healed fast—but his tormentors quickly learned that the kind of verbal jabs that he could deliver often hurt far more, and healed far slower, than anything they could do to him. He could give as good as he got, and eventually they let him be.

Marcus made few friends, but that was all right—he had no time for frivolity, anyway. And those with whom he did make a connection met with unqualified approval from his uncle, who was keeping a close eye on his foster son. It appeared that young Maxentius had a fine instinct for picking good men, people both capable and trustworthy. He might have been written into the

Register of Patricians but young Maxentius picked his friends with a peasant's skill, people who might not have had all the outer polish of nobility but who could be trusted with a task and expected to perform it with diligence and honesty. Before long it was Maxentius—despite his youth—who was in charge of the servants, military complement, and secretaries who served Leontes's household.

He was still an innocent in a lot of ways, with the simplicity and the often still raw manners of his country origins—a boy who struggled to understand the layers upon layers of complexity and intricacy on which the society of the City of Gold was built. That innocence could not last, though.

It was no accident, perhaps, that the aristocracy was partial to pearls as personal adornment. Visant was a vibrant, pulsing, almost living creature. Boys like Maxentius were grit irritating the city's innards; they would either be coated and transformed into something smooth and polished and ready to take up a place in society…or they would be digested and destroyed.

"You were up late last night," Leontes said by way of greeting one morning, nearly a year and a half after Maxentius had first come to live in his uncle's house.

Maxentius ran a hand through his untidy hair. "I was up *all* night," he said. "One of your secretaries came in with a couple of things that needed immediate attention, and I thought…." He paused, grimacing at his uncle. "Did I disturb you?"

"I was awake," Leontes said, "and your aunt would sleep through an earthquake. You didn't disturb us. This is your home. It will always be that. But I've been thinking—you need your own space. You're a young man, and you have taken on a lot of work that needs a proper office space. I think I may have a solution."

"What's that, uncle?"

"All in good time. But first, there is one other matter." Leontes reached out and rested a heavy hand on Maxentius's shoulder. "I didn't want to rush it, or you, but I think it's been long enough. You are turning seventeen not too long from now. Before that happens…how do you feel about finally making it official, filing the paperwork?"

"For what?"

"We talked about this," Leontes said gravely. "I want to formally adopt you, as my own son, my heir. The papers have been ready since the day you accepted my invitation to come to the city."

Maxentius dropped his eyes for a moment, biting his lip, and then lifted his head and met his uncle's eyes with his own steady grey gaze.

"You are renouncing your right to inherit a farm," Leontes said, answering the unspoken words that hung between the two of them.

"You have been more than a father to me, but I am still renouncing the man who truly sired me," Maxentius said. "I knew this day was coming, and I expected it, and I have accepted it—but I still feel a little…I still feel…." He broke off, suddenly awkward.

"You will be my son according to the law," Leontes said. "Calling me father, addressing your aunt as 'mother', that is not required inside these walls. You were not a baby when you left your home, you have your memories, and I cannot expect to uproot them from your mind any more than I can pour the blood from my own veins into yours and claim that you were born of my own loins."

"I love you as a father," Maxentius said, swallowing.

"I know. And I am proud of my son and what he has accomplished."

"Let it be done," Maxentius said. "Yes, let it be done."

"It shall be arranged," Leontes said.

In a handful of days, it was. In the end the whole thing was absurdly simple—an Imperial secretary paid Leontes and his family a visit, unfolded a papyrus scroll, asked Maxentius if he consented to be the lawful son of Leontes and then asked Leontes if he consented to accept Maxentius as his son and the heir of all his possessions. A seal was affixed to the document attesting to their consent to these things, the Imperial secretary promised that a copy of the document would be made and sent around for the Count's own papers, congratulated the new family, and left.

Maxentius found his hands shaking after the man had gathered up his scrolls, seals and inkwells and departed.

"I don't feel any different," he said carefully.

"I should hope not," Leontes said. "I've laid down some of the good vintage for this day. I think it's time for it to be cracked open. Let us celebrate this day!"

Euphaedra, smiling tremulously, joined them in a toast and then, embracing her new son, left the two men alone.

"Let us go for a ride," Leontes said suddenly. "It is good luck to give out alms to the poor when good fortune comes to you, and we will do this, you and I—let it be our first act together, as father and son. But there is also something that I wish to show you."

He called for a servant to saddle two horses and retired to his rooms to change into full formal finery, to mark the occasion of his first outing in public as a father with his son. Mystified but increasingly curious, certain that although Leontes was correct about the custom of distributing alms on an auspicious occasion this time it was at least partly an excuse for something quite different, Maxentius dutifully followed suit. They rode out from the Palace gate, a splendid pair, into the streets of Visant, the sun glinting off gilt dress boots and golden insignia. Leontes did not stint his coin, and their path was strewn with the blessings called out by the recipients of golden solidi that he threw out. But although he rode out a little way along the wide main avenue, he turned off at the first open forum into the side streets and then appeared to double back along convoluted back ways towards the wall of the Palace and the great golden cliffs of the Hippodrome rearing above everything with its four great banners on top.

"Where are we going?" Maxentius asked at last, because it was obvious that Leontes had a destination.

"I said I had something to show you," Leontes said. "And here it is, there, to the side. See that gate?"

Maxentius twisted in his saddle to peer at the man-height wall Leontes had indicated, with a gate set in it. The gate was open, and appeared to be rather ill-attached to one side; the wall itself was moss-grown, and largely in bad repair but mostly intact.

"What's behind it?" Maxentius asked.

"Let's go see," Leontes said, turning his horse and urging it towards the gate.

The garden beyond the gate was unkempt and overgrown, but it bore traces of once having been pleasant and cared for. Untidy cypresses marched along the far side, towards the Hippodrome, and the effect was not unpleasing. The line led the eye along high grasses which had been left to go to seed and a tangle of untended flowers, up along the darker green of the cypress trees, and on to the golden stone of the Hippodrome wall.

The path they were riding on was wide, straight, paved with stone, and in surprisingly good shape. It curved slightly as it came to another low wall with an arched gate, followed through beyond it, and once through the second gate the first glimpse of the house which this garden sheltered could be had, still chequered, hidden behind trees and shrubs, but the red tiles of its roof were visible, and a corner of a second-storey balcony.

"What is this place?" Maxentius asked, curious.

"It is called the House of Peacocks," Leontes said. "I am told that a visiting Prince built this place many years ago—someone with great influence at the Court, I would surmise, because this is a house whose grounds run all the way down to the sea, with its own little wooden wharf below. It is unusable right now, of course, being mostly rotted away—but still, it is there."

"But who owns it? Who would have left it to fall apart like this?"

"As to that, land taxes are expensive if you are forced to pay a lot of them at once," Leontes said mysteriously. "Would you like to see inside?"

Maxentius turned with a raised eyebrow. "*You* have access?"

"Indeed," Leontes said, swinging down from his horse and looping its reins loosely, soldier-style, around a nearby low branch. "Come."

Maxentius leapt off his own mount and followed his new father up a set of shallow stone stairs and across an open flagged terrace. The door opened to Leontes's touch; he stepped inside, and Maxentius followed warily.

The entrance hall was open and airy, and quite empty. It had a once-exquisite mosaic floor which showed a peacock in full plumage, but it was showing signs of damage in places as though a horse had been allowed to prance upon it.

"The House of Peacocks? That?" Maxentius said, nodding at the mosaic as he paused to scrutinise it.

"Apparently there were live ones around, too, in their time. Not, I think, now," Leontes said.

A great staircase led up to the second storey from the middle of the entrance hallway, and it beckoned—but now Maxentius's curiosity was wholly aroused and he took the time to examine the rooms which opened off the main hall—one of them, a small feasting chamber, furnished with faded banqueting couches, according to the ancient custom, which were now lined up tidily against one wall. There was a serviceable kitchen area off beyond that, boasting an open roasting hearth wide enough to take an entire medium-sized pig and bread baking slits built in.

"Come upstairs," Leontes said.

Maxentius dutifully climbed the stair to the second floor, and discovered four sleeping chambers, several of which opened up to a wide balcony with a carved stone balustrade and yet more mosaic on the floor—abstract, this time, with no peacock images although the artist appeared to be rather fond of tesserae of a particular shade of deep peacock blue. Beyond, the view opened up to a sloping garden full of more cypresses and a grove of dark gnarled olive trees. The slope led the eye all the way out to where the treetops stopped and the sun glinted on open sea.

"This is magnificent," Maxentius said. "It's been let go, badly, but this is a wonderful house. Whose is it?"

"Yours," Leontes said serenely. "If you want it."

Maxentius turned sharply to stare at Leontes. *"Mine?"*

"Today is your birthday, of sorts," Leontes said. "You can think of it as a birthday present, if you like."

"But how can you…where did…this place belongs to *you*? To give away?"

Leontes leaned heavily on the balustrade with both hands, staring out at sea. "This place has a history," he said. "In all honesty, I may not be giving you much more than a headache. But yes, it is mine to give away. I won it."

"Won it?"

Leontes sighed. "If you must know," he said, "as I have said, this place was built by some visiting princeling who got leave to do so from the Imperial Palace—which is just over there, by the way, beyond that much higher wall on the far side. What the precise circumstances of that were, and just how long they lasted, I confess I do not know. The house has passed through several hands since then, the latest of those being a certain discontented Senator whom I caught deeply embroiled in an arguably silly but nonetheless treasonous plot against the Emperor. He was very, very contrite about it at the time—or at the very least, he was extremely sorry that he had got caught at it—and he swore he would not only pull out of the conspiracy immediately but would give me some of the other names—if only I agreed not to say anything about his involvement to the Emperor. I agreed, after some thought, but he felt…obliged…to give me further payment for silence. Nothing open, of course, or questions would be asked. So we played a game of dice, and he lost. The prize was the House of Peacocks. I'm not sure I got that much of a bargain, frankly, but I *am* in a position to write off the taxes on it, particularly since I had another favour coming.…"

"Who was this Senator?"

"Nobody you need worry about," Leontes said, in a tone of voice that made the hair lift on the nape of Maxentius's neck.

"What happened to him? You didn't go to the Emperor…?"

"Well, no," Leontes said. "I promised not to speak of this to the *Emperor*. I may have, however, let slip a mention of it to Sarrus.…"

I had another favour coming. Maxentius nodded. "And the Grand Chamberlain Sarrus waived the land taxes on this place for you," he said.

Leontes happened to look up and caught the look on Maxentius's face—a mix of bitter understanding, a little disgust, and a remnant of that shock that still held him in its grip. The Count straightened, brushing invisible lint off his formal finery.

"Son," he said, "one of the reasons that I wanted you here was to remind me that a straight road is still possible. Live long enough in Visant, and you get used to the fact that there is always a curve or a corner and you have to count on there being someone hidden just out of sight and not necessarily friendly. You have to live one jump ahead of everyone else. Sometimes that means...." His lips thinned for a moment, and twisted into a grimace that was equal parts smile and sneer. *There are no straight roads in Visant,*" he said, with quiet emphasis. "You'd better learn that fast, if you are to survive here."

"You want me to remind you that there's a straight road but you want me to learn that there aren't any?" Maxentius said. "That's a hard task, my father."

"I know. I'm sorry. But that's just the way things are."

"But there *is* a straight road in Visant," Maxentius said. "The main avenue from the Palace gate...."

"...Leads straight out of the city," Leontes said, and this time it was a smile, even though it had more wryness than mirth in it. "And you are always free to take it, anyone is, so long as you wish to leave Visant. But if you would stay here and live in this place, you play by its rules. And Maxentius...you are able. I have watched you these last few months, and you've taken everything that was thrown at you and you've held your own. You have great potential to succeed here. This place...." He waved a hand, indicating the lovely, decaying house and its wild gardens. "This place, it's just a beginning. I have a post for you in the Imperial offices; you will be stepping in at a high level, with several people under you, as a supervisor. It's a good income, enough to fix this place up, and you'll need it, you'll need the room to live and work without tripping over your elders at every turn. You're a man today. A man with a position in the Empire. And this...this could be home."

"I want to see the rest of the garden," Maxentius said quietly, after a long pause.

"Lead the way," Leontes said, with a sweeping bow.

The main hallway turned out to have another set of doors in the far wall, leading onto yet another paved terrace with a low balustrade and then to steps leading down into the green wilderness beyond. There was a trickle of a stream running crosswise through the property, and they paused on a tiny wooden bridge to glance down at the clear water running over rocks and sand. Then on, down, the slope steeper now with the path turning into a stairway, all the way down to a narrow wooden wharf sticking on posts covered with barnacles and slimy damp seaweed. Leontes had mentioned that it might be unusable, but to

Maxentius's untrained eye the wharf looked serviceable enough if one didn't attempt to tie to it a fully-laden grain ship from across the Middle Sea.

He stood staring for a moment, holding the wrist of his right hand in his left on the small of his back, listening to the lap of small waves on a tiny crescent of shingled beach, breathing in the scent of wet weed and salty sea. Leontes stood to the side and a little behind, saying nothing, his own expression a little bleak, as though he was conscious of his first act as a father being something that his son found disappointing and even distasteful. But after a few long moments Maxentius drew in a deep breath and released his hands, bringing one up to rub his jaw thoughtfully.

"All right," he said faintly. "All right. Let's go back up."

They were halfway up the slope that led back to the house when a shrill cry suddenly rent the still air, and Maxentius flinched, looking about wildly, his hand going back towards his sword. He turned his head slowly as he became aware that Leontes was laughing softly.

"Relax," he said. "Look, up there, on the balcony."

The clean lines of the stone balustrade were broken by something that Maxentius could not quite parse at first, but then, as he blinked and stared, finally resolved into the shape of a bird with a small head and bulbous body, with a magnificent and improbable tail hanging down over the edge of the balustrade.

"I thought they were all gone," Leontes said, "but apparently one or two still remain. Behold, a peacock in the House of Peacocks. Looks like quite a large, healthy specimen, too. I wonder if he's got a harem of hens somewhere about."

"I might have to look into that," Maxentius said.

Leontes turned his head sharply. "You'll take the place?"

"I am here," Maxentius said. "The road, straight or not, brought me here. I will stay, for a while at least. Time will tell whether I was right."

"I will get the scribes to seal the transfer today," Leontes said. "And I'll get someone to come and fix those gates. Now that the place is occupied again by a lawful owner, it will not do to have any kind of riffraff just wandering in. I'll have a few of my men sweep the grounds, too—it isn't inconceivable that some street urchin has made a burrow for himself in here. And maybe even one or two pots of peacock soup. You will want to have a security detail here, too—some of the Palace guard layabouts can probably be better used here than lounging about at dice in their rooming houses. I will see to all that; you can make plans to move in whenever you are ready. There is no hurry to leave my house; you are my son, and that, too, belongs to you."

There is no straight road in Visant.

The words echoed in Maxentius's mind; there was a roaring in his ears, and his heart was beating very fast as he looked around at the land that would soon be written into the Imperial registers as his own. Under his own name. He, Maxentius, not yet seventeen years old. He would own a small palace, in Visant, in the City of Gold. He tried to retrace the steps of how he had got here, and found that he could not, that his trail tangled in his memory and faded from his mind's eye and his tracks were lost in a shimmering, confusing mist that surrounded him on all sides until the only part of the road he could see at all was the space required to take the next step forward, one more step, that was all. Behind and beyond, all was mystery, all was unknown.

For all Maxentius's ties to the city, for all the anchors that Leontes had provided when he had brought him here, Maxentius had never felt as though he belonged to Visant—he was always on the fringes somehow, always visiting, it was never 'home,' not in the way he thought of his true-father's farm as 'home.'

But now, suddenly, with the turn of the dice, with vows not quite broken but somehow skirted, with favours being exchanged and politics being played— in spite of all of that, so foreign to what he had once been, once, when he had first set foot in the city—in spite of it all, standing on the stone flags of the terrace of the House of Peacocks, Maxentius was conscious of the roots that had begun to bind him to this place. Shallow they still might be, and vulnerable—there were many things he still had to learn to do, to be—this place had put the first layer of nacre on the piece of grit that had once been a boy from the back country of the Empire. Maxentius was aware of it upon himself, like a second skin. The Visant skin. The armour made by, and against, the heart of an Empire.

CHAPTER FIVE

Simonis had always had a peculiar gift of living in the *now*, dealing with the circumstances immediately surrounding her. It wasn't that she had a particularly bad memory of things past—on the contrary, it was meticulous and specific and she could still clearly and affectionately recall the sunny island town where she had been born and those whom she had left behind there, both human and animal. It wasn't that she didn't care about the future, because if nothing else her father's sudden death had proved to her how quickly and how radically a future can change, turning on things sometimes large and sometimes seemingly insignificant at the time they occurred. For a child her age she even exhibited an almost uncanny shrewdness when it came to extrapolating her past and her present into a number of possible futures opening up from any single trigger event.

It was just that sometimes the instant gratification of something that seemed to be immensely important at this or that particular time and no other, now or never again, was something that she needed above all else. The impulses and needs of *now* simply blocked any warnings or extrapolations into *will be* or *might be*, and all other voices would simply fall silent, all except the single insistent one telling Simonis that the moment she held in her hand was all there would ever be.

It was under the command of that voice that the child she had once been had returned to the old lions back in Cyrenais, despite being told over and over again not to do so. It was under the command of that voice that here, in the Hippodrome of the City of Gold, she returned to the White Jewel faction's she-bear whose cub had been torn from her and with whom Simonis had forged such an odd relationship while her father was still in charge of the White Jewel bears.

Out in the arena, when she and her sister had gone to beg for her father's living to be restored to the family, Simonis had been publicly repudiated and humiliated by the White Jewel faction. She had turned away from them with a smouldering resentment that had quickly hardened into bitterness, even an edge of hate. But the bear had not been part of that. Simonis had never thought of the animal as a White Jewel bear; the bear was simply her friend. And when her life changed again—new faction, new father, her mother's belly quickly swelling with what would be a new sibling—Simonis took refuge in the *now*, and the moment told her that she had no friends left. None, except that bear.

The first time she returned to the bear's cage, less than a month after the public faction change out in the Hippodrome arena, she was lucky—she had picked a good time, between feedings, with everything sleepy and relatively sparsely attended, and she had escaped everyone's notice completely when she slipped into the White Jewel section of the menagerie and into the bear's cage. The bear had been happy to see the child, and that same calm that the White Jewel animal pens had learned to know while Simonis was in with her friend descended on the menagerie. And she never stayed long, mindful of the fact that she was no longer sanctioned to be there.

The second time she had to slip past a suspicious slave who had been engaged in tossing parts of a bloody sheep carcass into the leopards' enclosure—but she escaped without being caught.

The third time, several months later and with her mother almost due to deliver Simonis's newest sibling, Simonis lingered too long in the bear cage. Without meaning to do so she fell into old habits and the security she had always known in this place, and fell asleep against the bear's comforting flank. The first she knew about an unfolding disaster was when she was woken up by shouting.

There seemed to be a lot of people clustered outside the bear's cage, yelling and waving their arms about; it took Simonis a moment to rub her eyes and blink herself back into coherent wakefulness, and try to make sense of what they wanted.

Which seemed to be simply that she get out of the bear's cage, immediately.

The bear was watchful, roused; Simonis could feel the tenseness of shoulder muscles underneath the shaggy fur in which she was nestled. She patted the bear on her side.

"It's all right," she murmured, "they're just making a fuss. I shouldn't have fallen asleep, it's my fault. It's all right."

But it wasn't all right. And what had started out as a mild uproar quickly degenerated into disaster, and then tragedy. The new bear keeper actually unlocked the door to the bear's cage and reached in to the child, backed by an armed assistant brandishing a trident in one hand and a long sword in the other, even as a couple of other keepers threw out urgent calls not to do so. Simonis instinctively recoiled from the grasp of the enraged man, frightened by the fury that twisted his features into a feral snarl, and the bear's instincts kicked in. Yet again the humans were trying to take her cub from her; she surged to her feet and roared. Simonis was flung free. The young and inexperienced assistant panicked and attacked the animal. The bear, now wounded, retaliated by reaching out and lashing out at her enemies with one lethal swipe of a massive paw, claws fully extended. The new White Jewel bear keeper dived out of the way, catching just a glancing blow which still managed to dislocate his left shoulder, leaving a deep slash that sliced his upper arm open to the bone; the assistant who had wielded the original weapons was not so lucky. As the bear reared to her back legs and then came down for the kill, the assistant managed to hold the sword at precisely the right angle and the bear came down full on it. But she still managed to sweep aside the trident, breaking the shaft like it was straw, and then sank her claws into his side and slashed across his abdomen, lifting him off his feet and slamming him against the far side of the bars where he lay motionless in a spreading pool of blood.

By this stage the menagerie was in an uproar, all the other animals having picked up on the intensity of what was going on in the bear enclosure and giving full voice to their unease. The keepers scattered, summoned by howls of animal panic and outrage, to deal with their own charges before more beasts or men came to grief. Somehow Simonis and the wounded bear keeper were dragged out of the cage and the door slammed in the enraged bear's face, and even after they had all retreated to a safe distance the bear continued to roar and fling herself against the bars, shaking them in their foundations, her fur matted with her own blood and her enemy's.

Everyone was too busy, at that particular moment, to notice Simonis. They dealt with the immediate emergencies. Simonis, although blood-splashed, was not hurt. Once one of the younger assistant lion keepers—who had known her during Batzas's tenure as bear keeper and knew about her relationship with the bear –gripped her firmly by the shoulder and escorted her to the exit.

"They will remember this," he said to her in a low voice. "I will do what I can. But do not come back here. Not ever. Do you understand? You belong elsewhere now. They will not be forgiving."

"I understand." Simonis gulped air, flooded with guilt and a prescient dread. "What will they do?"

"To you? I don't know. I hope nothing. I will see that they know the background to this before they…." He broke off, realising that her gaze was not on him, that her eyes were wide and staring and focused somewhere behind him. Where the bear was. He sighed. "To the bear…?" he said softly, and her eyes snapped back to his face. "She has killed now," he said, tightening his grip on Simonis's shoulder for a moment. "And she is wounded. There can't be much…." He broke off again, his lips thinning into a grim line. "Go home," he said, giving Simonis a little shake. "Don't come back here. Go."

Simonis turned and fled without looking back, the menagerie still echoing in her wake with human shouts and animal roars.

She heard what happened after, from her stepfather, two days later. The new White Jewel bear-keeper would live, but he would be out of commission for a while until his shoulder and arm healed and even then it was debatable whether he would ever have full use of them again. The assistant keeper had been dead by the time they had managed to get him out of the bear cage. There were several other casualties in the aftermath, both human and animal, in the menagerie panic that the incident had triggered. And Simonis's bear… was dead.

The young lion keeper and some of the other animal handlers in the White Jewel menagerie had apparently made sure that their own version of events had been put out as the official story. But it had been Locinus, who had been unaware of Simonis's visits back to the White Jewel faction, who had been the one reprimanded in private by both the White Jewel faction and the Golden Crown faction for permitting his stepdaughter to return to her old haunts—and he turned his resentment and his outrage into a towering fury against Simonis.

"They were *this* close to turning us all out onto the street!" Locinus shouted at her. "Did you even think about how this might have affected me…affected all of us? They took us in as an act of charity, Simonis, and I have been working day and night to make sure they never regretted that, and now you—you go and do this…." He shook his head, momentarily incoherent with rage. "I should turn you out," he said, "just turn you out and make sure that I am not tainted...."

"*Locinus*!" Apphia gasped, surging forward, one hand protectively around her swelling belly where a new child grew but all her mind and spirit suddenly focused on protecting the child already out there, the child of a man who had trained animals, had trained *bears*—the child who had always loved the beasts and had never been able to understand just why this was not appropriate for a girl-child.

"Stay out of this," Locinus said through gritted teeth, his dark eyes flashing. But then he happened to glance at Apphia, saw her weaving on her feet with the suddenness of her move and ready to collapse underneath the weight of her belly and the ankles swollen with a difficult pregnancy, and his rage suddenly evaporated. His shoulders slumped, and he turned away from a Simonis who stood trembling before him with her eyes half-closed, expecting a blow at any moment. "Don't ever," he said to Simonis without looking at her again, "let me hear of you doing the like of this again."

And then he turned and walked away, slamming the door of their quarters as hard as he could behind him.

"Simonis," Apphia said, sitting down heavily, "if he abandons us...."

"He *won't*," Simonis said. "And why is it wrong? If I wanted to go and see the bear...."

"The bear is not a pet," Apphia said. "Simonis, Simonis, we have been through this. You cannot be a keeper. They will not let you. There are things a woman may do and there are things that it is impossible...."

"I know," Simonis said bleakly. "I know all things that it is impossible for me to do."

She escaped to the streets, in the aftermath, wandering into the markets without purpose or aim, drifting in and out of crowds and trying to lose herself in a mass of people, getting yelled at for getting in the way when she was barely present—but one or two of the kinder vendors saw the white-faced shock that was still in her face and offered her a slightly bruised fruit which would have been hard to sell anyway, or a taste of new honey. Simonis accepted kindness and meanness alike without responding to either, until the sun started to go down and the shadows lengthened and she found herself alone and far from home, barefoot and wearing just a thin shift, her hair uncombed, her huge dark eyes hot and stinging with the tears which she had not shed that day, with only one bruised and sticky pomegranate in her hand.

Initially Simonis found herself almost bewildered, not entirely certain where she was. That was quickly replaced by something else—not fear, precisely, but rather a slow unease as she paused to take stock and realised that she, in turn, was the focus of other interested parties. A brace of young men who might have been off-duty soldiers lounged insolently in a nearby doorway.

"Hey," said one of the men, just loudly enough for Simonis to hear. "What have we here? Look, a toy!"

Simonis froze for a moment, but only for a moment. Then a roar suddenly began inside her mind, a roar that nobody else could hear but herself, something that filled her own being until her small frame shook with it—the roar of her bear, the bear whom she might have doomed by the very act of loving it. With a sudden surge of defiance, her fingers tightened around the pomegranate she still clutched and then her arm went back, without her conscious knowledge, and she threw the fruit at the leering youths.

The pomegranate smashed on the wall beside the men rather than on the person of any one of them; juice and seeds flew out and spattered the intended targets. They uncoiled from the doorway, no longer languid, but riled and outraged and with the leers turned into snarls. Simonis found herself no more than a child again, the bear-presence having left her as quickly as it had come, and her own bewilderment and confusion was replaced by a sudden and overpowering terror. She turned and ran, slipping into the nearest side street which offered shadows and concealment, without any regard for actual direction or destination. All she wanted at that moment was simply to be somewhere *else*.

She ran blindly, without heed to her surroundings, intent only on getting away—and when she collided with another person it was a moment of unexpected force that drove the breath from her body.

The man she had run into didn't appear to be surprised by the encounter. He scooped her out of the way and behind him with an economical motion of his left hand, and then, as he brought the arm back to his side, shrugged the short cloak he wore off his left shoulder revealing a lean and wiry body clad only in a knee-length sleeveless linen tunic cinched at the waist and across the chest with a soldier's leather belt, and with dusty soldier-issue sandals on his bare feet.

The men pursuing Simonis came to an uncertain halt as they suddenly realised that it was no longer an insolent and vulnerable child who stood before them but rather a man who stood with the easy grace and power of someone trained in the use of weapons and not afraid to apply that knowledge.

"An urchin ran into the street," one of Simonis's pursuers said. "You don't happen to have noticed where the little devil went...? It...threw a...."

"I'll take care of the child," said her rescuer evenly.

It was only then, when he spoke, that Simonis recognised him. The rough gravelly voice belonged to the man whom the Hippodrome knew as Cicatrice, the dance master and chief choreographer of the Golden Crown faction—and a man who jealously guarded the secrets of his past. Everyone knew that he had once been a soldier—but how he had come by the crippled right arm which had cut his army career short was not a question that many knew the answer to. Even his name was mystery, bestowed on him by the Hippodrome for his disability—Cicatrice, Scar. If anyone at the Hippodrome actually knew what the man's real name was, they weren't telling.

"We claim…" one of the other men began, but the edge of arrogance that had tinged his words had begun to melt away even as he had started to speak. He and his companions had initially seen only the obvious—that they firmly outnumbered the crippled man whose right arm, with its clawed hand, hung uselessly at his side. But there was something in the way that the sound left hand sat on the pommel of a short sword that suddenly gave the young thugs pause.

But then Simonis, who had frozen into the shadows where she had been pushed, finally stirred, and one of the younger men suddenly pointed.

"Behind him!" he yelped in triumph, starting forward.

He was well-muscled, taller by a head than the man standing guard over Simonis, but that abruptly became meaningless as Cicatrice shrugged his cloak fully off both shoulders, taking a step forward himself.

"I would think again if I were you," he said quietly, almost gently, his tone frighteningly at odds with his words. "I was with Bassanios on the Afaris and Thera Pass campaigns; I was Ursus in Bassanios's own Mihr Lodge; you pups think you are my match?"

Something reminded Simonis powerfully of the instant when she carried the bear's shadow—because that was what Cicatrice was doing now, exactly that, his physical body crippled and outnumbered but his presence suddenly huge and terrifying. And it worked, because the pursuers took a couple of steps back, as though they had been attacked, and then turned and slunk away. It would have taken more than a handful of youths to face down Cicatrice just then. It would have taken an army.

And Simonis suddenly realised that she was in possession of a secret, perhaps the only bit of real truth that anybody knew about Cicatrice.

He had been a soldier, everyone was already aware of that much. But he had not been a common grunt. He had apparently been a career soldier, one who had been with Bassanios, a legendary general, on campaigns whose names were themselves legend. And then there was the Mihr Lodge aspect. It was a forbidden faith, proscribed for nearly a century, but it was an open secret that the ban had merely driven it into obscurity and not oblivion. Little was known about it except that it was a soldier's faith, and that it was still widely practised, if only clandestinely, by the hard men who fought on the Empire's frontiers.

And "ursus" meant "bear".

Simonis started trembling again, and that seemed to bring her companion's attention back to her. He had shrunk back down to being just a man—of less than average height, his body lean and muscled, marred only by the way the fingers of his right hand curled dead and claw-like around the ruined palm. His hair was cropped short, a helmet of tight black curls cut close to his head—that, and a magnificent beak of a nose, gave him an air of a bust of some ancient emperor suddenly come to life. But his eyes were not the blind eyes of the statue. They were so dark to be almost black, but they caught and reflected what little light there was in the shadowed street, giving him a curious other-worldly look, a spirit or a demon who was all-seeing, all-knowing.

He reached out with his good hand to help her to her feet, shaking down his cloak to cover his shoulders again, but not before Simonis glimpsed a tattoo high on his right shoulder, an area usually covered by a sleeve—a dark half-circle with rays bursting from it.

"You're the bear girl," he said.

"You came to look for me?" Simonis gasped, disconcerted by his apparent awareness of her precise identity.

"Not particularly, although some are doing so," Cicatrice said. "It's just that I make it my business to know what is going on. The bear keeper was an idiot, and probably deserved what he got—but you yourself appear in remarkably good shape after a bear encounter. You knew to get out of the way when a keeper did not?"

"The bear was my friend," Simonis said.

"Ah," Cicatrice said, inclining his head a little. "You choose strange friends. My condolences, then. But perhaps it is time you got back behind defended walls. Come on."

"You…" Simonis began, hanging back as he started to move, causing him to pause and turn to look at her again with those strange wild dark eyes.

"Yes?" he inquired.

"Ursus," Simonis said helplessly, in the grip of a superstitious dread. "You are a bear too."

Cicatrice stood motionless for a moment and then sighed deeply.

"You never heard me say that word," he said. "Do you understand me?"

"But you—"

His fingers tightened for a moment, hard enough that Simonis winced and thought she could already feel the bruises forming there. But then he decided against whatever physical action he was contemplating and sighed again. "You would," he said, "be doing me a great favour by your silence."

The words echoed in Simonis's mind. It was as if they had nudged open a great door and there was space beyond, space for her to move and dream and grow. It was the difference between her mother's constant credo of what Simonis was *not* allowed to do or be, and a sudden sense of all the things that she *could* be if given a chance.

"I won't say anything," she said, and paused just long enough for Cicatrice's fingers to relax slightly. "If you can help me work with the animals. In the Hippodrome."

His fingers tightened again, and then, incongruously, he laughed.

"You would *bargain* with me?"

Simonis stood her ground. She was an unprepossessing sight—a slight child, her hair an uncombed mess, her feet filthy and a little bloodied from her mad dash across uneven cobbles into the shadows and this man's presence, her hands stained and still sticky from the pomegranate juice—but Cicatrice abruptly reached out and tilted her chin up with his good hand, staring into her eyes, his expression serious.

"Well, not bears," he said at length. "But mimes work with the animals. If you possess an ounce of grace or flexibility, you can be trained."

"And you can make this happen?"

He dropped her chin, straightened. "If you can keep your tongue still, I can make this happen."

A ghost of a smile appeared on Simonis's face. "Done," she said, and then spit into her hand and held it out to him.

Cicatrice threw his head back and roared with laughter. "Perhaps later," he said, after he was done guffawing, "when you're cleaned up. In the meantime my word is my bond."

Simonis nodded gravely, wiped her hands as best she could on her dirty dress, and fell into step beside him. Cicatrice didn't seem inclined to make small-talk, as sparing with words as his reputation had him, but Simonis had a head full of new ideas, and could not stop herself from asking one more question.

"You have a mark—on your arm. The tattoo. The sun. Is that from the Mihr Lodge?"

Cicatrice turned sharply with a scowl, and then his features rearranged into something else, a strange expression of sudden and pointed interest. "Just when did you manage to make that out?" he murmured.

"You hide it," Simonis said.

"Invictus!" Cicatrice said explosively, with an air of invoking a deity. "Yes, by the Unconquered Sun of Mihr, that's what the tattoo means. And yes, I hide it. By which I mean that this, too, is covered under your vow of silence. Are we clear?"

"I will say nothing," Simonis said, only partially cowed, the rest of her hopelessly curious and intrigued at the secrecy of it all. "But you didn't hide it out *there*, tonight...."

"Because it didn't matter out there tonight," Cicatrice growled. "Enough questions. Come on, it's time you got back to the Hippodrome."

Simonis's family had been divided in their reactions to her return home that night. Apphia had wept passionate tears of relief; Danelis had simply smiled and nodded, giving no further indication as to whether her sister's disappearance and then reappearance had given her any anxiety or concern; Locinus was still not speaking to Simonis at all and merely looked grim. In the days that followed things were tense in the household, not made any easier that the whole situation had put the heavily pregnant Apphia under an immense amount of stress and her body responded by going into labour. It was still some weeks before her earliest expected due date, and the pregnancy had not been an easy one for her anyway; there were concerns, and not one but two of the Hippodrome midwives were in attendance on her while her husband took up lodgings with his assistant keeper until such time as things settled down at home. Her older daughters were looked after on a perfunctory basis by the neighbouring families whenever anybody thought about it, but mostly left to fend for themselves.

There was no word from Cicatrice about his promise, but a small package of mysterious provenance did get delivered to Simonis while she waited for word on her mother and the new baby—a small leather pouch which proved to contain a single curved claw. There was no word with it, no explanation, and it was delivered by a boy who had obviously been paid to hand it over—but Simonis knew it for what it was, one of the claws from her doomed bear, and an act of kindness from someone at the White Jewel menagerie, perhaps the young lion keeper who had allowed her to escape.

For all the pious service that the people of the City of Gold and the Empire over which it reigned gave to the One God in whose name it ruled, the deep roots of pagan beliefs of centuries past, and the various small nods offered to superseded faiths which had come and gone between the times of myth and legend and the present times, were still very much a part of the fabric of the Empire. The city of Visant was not immune to them, not even at the highest levels, and in the world of the Hippodrome and its people —who were often expressly excluded from sacraments offered by the High Church on the grounds that they were a lower caste of human and therefore unworthy—the old superstitions were particularly strong, even when kept hidden from public view.

It was a common enough thing for a citizen of Visant to have an inanimate object of some sort—a stone, a shell, a piece of bone or of wood or a scrap of fabric a *stoicheon*. It was something that its owner considered as having his or her life bound into it, and if the object was stolen or harmed then the life of its owner also hung in the balance. There was no accepted systematic set of beliefs that governed the nature of one of these things, or when or how one might be obtained—it seemed to be left to the individual to choose every aspect of the *stoicheon*, from its basic identity to the time and place at which it was acquired and whether or not to display it openly as a talisman or else hide it somewhere safe where it would moulder in quiet oblivion and guard the bearer's life from harm.

When the bear claw dropped into Simonis's hand she had not a moment's doubt that her own *stoicheon* had just made its way into her possession, that this was merely the final seal on a bargain already struck out in the streets of Visant when she had first heard the bear roar inside her. The true priests did not come down to the Hippodrome, unless somebody was at death's door and needed absolution before they were permitted to slip out of their body and into the Elysian Fields, where the souls of men went to worship the One God in the afterlife—but the Hippodrome folk were not sanctified anyway, their babies hardly ever baptised into the faith, their marriages blessed by their own clergy and not the formally and ceremonially anointed priesthood that served the higher-born of the city. Many of the Hippodrome people believed in the One God anyway and prayed to him where they could as best as they knew how. Simonis had been brought up in that faith herself, although she had never particularly believed in anything greater than the Hippodrome itself. But now, with her mother's life hanging in the balance and a guilty sense that she herself and her behaviour over the previous week were to blame for some of that, she found that she needed to pray to something that was more powerful than she herself was. However, instead of the holy silences of the temples of the One God, what she heard deep in her soul was the roar of that bear that had made her throw the pomegranate at the men who had meant her harm—and now she held a physical link with that animal, the spirit that had been her protector, the bear claw that was her own *stoicheon*. And it was to that spirit that she prayed, if prayer it was. She climbed climbing to the very top of the Hippodrome at twilight—up to where she had climbed when she had first come to the Hippodrome, to the place where she had first looked out over Visant and called it hers. With the city spilling beneath her gaze and filling with shadows as the day slowly died, she clutched the claw in her hand until the point dug into her palm and drew blood.

"Anything," she promised in a whisper, closing her eyes against street and sea and sky and looking into the darkness within where all true power lay. "Anything, I will do anything you ask—I will always do your bidding, Bear Spirit. Just make it all right. Make her all right. Don't take my mother."

She had not heard anyone else approach, and when she heard a voice speak right next to her it was as though the words had come in answer to her prayer.

"Your mother is expected to live. You have a new sister."

Simonis's eyes flew open and she closed her hand even more tightly around the bear claw. Cicatrice stood only a pace or two away, his majestic nose casting sharp shadows over a slight sardonic grin that twisted his mouth. Beside him, bearing a smoking torch whose light had cast the shadows on Cicatrice's face, stood a slender, long-legged girl, her long hair twisted up in a number of coiled snakelike braids around her head. Her face still bore the last traces of childish curves but was already sharpening into angles of an adult beauty, and her body was ripening into a woman's, small pert breasts accentuated rather than concealed by her garb.

The light was already too low to make out details such as the precise colour of the girl's hair or eyes, but Simonis already knew that the hair was a deep mahogany red and the eyes a smoky violet blue—because without having been introduced to Cicatrice's companion she knew who she was.

The Hippodrome was a tight-knit, incestuous family—identities were often inferred long before a unfamiliar face was attached to a name. Occupations marked a Hippodrome resident—charioteer, animal keeper, smith, stonemason, dancer—far more readily than any name could do, because even people who did not know one another individually had a solid knowledge of who did what job in which faction.

This particular girl's reputation went before her.

Circassaë.

A solo dancer at fourteen, she was accomplished, sought after, in demand as a performer both in the Hippodrome and at private parties at the homes of Senators and Imperial officials. Even Simonis, young as she was, had heard the stories that swirled around Circassaë: that she had already had a liaison with a senior officer of the Palace guard and possibly an assistant Praetorian Prefect as well—not just dalliances for a single night, but relationships lasting at least a few months at a time. Only a few years into her career as a Golden Crown dancer, Circassaë was rumoured to have a private stash of gifts and jewellery which would see her through several fallow years, if those should ever knock on her door.

"Simonis," Cicatrice said, performing the unnecessary introductions anyway, "meet Circassaë. You will be her apprentice and, for the time being, at her beck and call until you learn the basics of that aspect of your craft. As for the rest of it…you will learn that from me."

"The rest of what?" Simonis asked, her head swivelling from one face to another, the young dancer to the old soldier, back and forth, uneasily aware that there was more going on here than she knew.

Circassaë smiled, but it was not an entirely pleasant smile, and it never quire reached her eyes.

"He means," she said softly, the faintest trace of an accent in her speech, "that from now on you're one of us. You're a spy."

Cicatrice lifted an eyebrow, and then suddenly brought his good hand up to his mouth, spat into his palm, and held out his hand to Simonis without saying another word.

Still clutching the bear claw protectively in one hand, Simonis slowly brought up the other and allowed it to slip into the old soldier's firm grip.

He squeezed her fingers once, and then dropped her hand.

"Come on," he said, his voice suddenly crisp and official, "it's time we got back. There's arrangements to be made. There is work to do."

CHAPTER SIX

It quickly became unremarkable for Maxentius to walk the inner sanctums of the Imperial Palace. The place that had once made him dizzy with the nearly impossible task of orienting himself within its labyrinthine coils, was now familiar and ordinary; now he'd turn a corner and wonder irritably when they would get around to fixing a spot in a mosaic where a couple of tesserae had cracked or fallen leaving a gap in the pattern.

It did not take him long to start carving himself a path—starting from the solid, safe position which his adoptive father had procured for him in the Imperial administration. The aptitude he showed for his work, his knack for treating Senators and base-born supplicants with equal grace without once seeming to slight the one or patronise the other, and his apparent affable incorruptibility were noticed, and then acted upon by his superiors. It may have been in part the Imperial instinct to pass off as much responsibility as possible while retaining rank and title. But Maxentius did not seem to mind having more responsibility or hard work unloaded on him. In fact, he seemed to thrive on it. He quickly leapfrogged up the promotion ladder—and found himself, a little to his astonishment, in a the position of being one of the inner-circle Imperial secretaries less than three years after he had first picked up quill in Imperial service.

Sarrus, the eunuch Imperial Grand Chamberlain who ran the Palace with an iron hand and a long memory, was the only high-level official who seemed to be acutely wary of young Maxentius. Sarrus gave an impression of remembering quite clearly some of the events that had been stepping stones to Maxentius's rapid advancement—and the part that he, Sarrus himself, had played in those events. He had not forgotten the House of Peacocks, nor how it had come to be in Maxentius's possession. Maxentius would glance up from his work sometimes to find Sarrus standing quite still in some doorway, staring at him through narrowed eyes.

The Chamberlain was, in the manner of his kind, a pale-skinned and corpulent man with a bull-like neck and thick wrists; his pate was quite hairless, his lips full and moist, his fingers pudgy, his jowls pendulous—his voice thin and almost reedy, which often caught people meeting him for the first time by surprise because that body and that voice did not fit together. But for all his bulk and apparent innocuousness the man could move with the stealth of a cat and his small, pale eyes glinted with a ferocious and dangerous intelligence—it was not an accident that he had been in supreme charge of everything surrounding the Emperor almost since Valerian Augustus had ascended the throne, now nearly twenty years ago. He knew everything, he knew everybody, he was subtle but he nonetheless managed to be closely involved with all the minutiae of the palace and anything that concerned the Emperor…and his eye had lit on Maxentius as potential trouble.

"I have done nothing to offend him or get in his way," Maxentius told Leontes over a late supper at the House of Peacocks. "I swear, if I know he is involved in something, if he has an interest in something, I take pains to look the other way or be elsewhere.…"

"Son," Leontes said shrewdly, "you yourself just defined your trouble with Sarrus. 'If I know he is involved in something,' you said. That implies that you *do* know what Sarrus is involved in at any given time. And he is often involved in things that he would rather were not all that widely known. And if he knows that you know that he is involved…well…do you begin to see the problem?"

"The alternative," Maxentius said, "is worse."

"The alternative being…?"

"Not knowing. Never looking up from my feet, never seeing anything, never paying any attention at all—walking blind and deaf through a lion's den."

Leontes shrugged. "So long as he cannot pin anything on you—and he cannot, for there I too have some say in the matter, even if you were not so upright and blameless in your character—he cannot act against you. Other than outright assassination, of course—but you are hardly important enough to warrant *that*."

Maxentius allowed himself a wince. "Thank you. I feel *much* safer now."

Leontes chuckled. "Just don't let Valerian look on you with too much favour," he said. "Any inkling that his own stature is threatened, and Sarrus might well take action to remove the threat."

"How am I to encourage or prevent an Emperor from taking a liking to me? Or otherwise?" Maxentius said, spreading his arms wide in a frustrated gesture. "How am I even to know what the Emperor is thinking?"

"This Emperor, perhaps," Leontes said. "Valerian is too old to dissemble any more. I'm told he is giving more and more thought to his succession—he is old and tired and he doesn't particularly want the weight of the Empire any more. For a man who never really wanted it in the first place, he has carried it long and well. But when the widow of his predecessor chose him and married him, he was a young man, and he had a young man's ambition—coupled with a sense of entitlement and of wanting to pass on his good fortune to his sons. But there were no sons."

"There are the nephews," Maxentius said. "They're the sons of his sister. Just like I am...he might have, just as you...."

"But he never adopted them as his own," Leontes said. "He might be regretting it now, but it's way too late for that. Besides, even he has to see that the one who would by all rights inherit—Petronus, the eldest—is not fit for the Imperial diadem, nor does he want it. Severus is a good general, and probably better in that place than on the throne. And Gennadius is a fop."

"But one of them is going to inherit," Maxentius said.

"If nothing happens in between now and Valerian's death," Leontes said. "And if *he* chooses. If he leaves it to the nephews to fight it out, I'm afraid that it would come to blows—and even though only one of them is a soldier the other two have plenty of influence and plenty of backing at Court—and that would translate into arms and men."

"Would you have to take sides?"

"Inevitably," Leontes said, "and throw my Guard in, too. And frankly I like the look of none of them at all. Has the Emperor ever said anything at all, in your hearing...?"

Maxentius gave him a thin smile. "That sort of question is precisely the reason Sarrus wants me out of his sphere," he said.

Leontes lifted an imaginary blade in a soldier's salute, acknowledging a hit. "Point," he said. "Well, try not to look as if you're listening, but don't be deaf if anything does fall into your lap. It would be good to know beforehand which way the wind will blow when Valerian Augustus is done with this world."

If Maxentius had hoped that he would have enough time to forget this conversation, it was not to be—because it was only six weeks later that he entered the aging Emperor's presence, bearing an armful of edicts that needed the Imperial seal. He knelt as he entered, as usual, bowing his head, waiting for an invitation to enter.

"Come in, come in, you're letting in a draft," Valerian said querulously. He was still being arrayed for his afternoon audience, with two body servants busy about his robes and another waiting patiently with the Imperial diadem on a cushioned platform upholstered in rich purple silk, ready to present it when the Emperor was ready to receive it.

Maxentius shifted his papers into a more secure grip and obeyed. "I am sorry to intrude, August," he said, "but these need your eye before the audience begins. Two of them pertain to matters that will be presented to you by applicants waiting even now in the audience chamber...."

The Emperor raised a hand, waving his body servants away, and they took a few respectful steps back.

"We are running late," Valerian said. "Let us get on with it, or the audience will take all day. "What is it that you need from me?"

Maxentius presented the two top parchment rolls, opening them up for the Emperor's perusal, but Valerian barely skimmed them. He looked tired and old; there were bags under his eyes, as though he hadn't slept much lately—the people in the audience chamber would probably never get close enough to notice, but Maxentius saw them from where he knelt at the Emperor's feet.

He thought he had learned to school his features by this time, but either he was less good at it than he had hoped or Valerian was far more observant than he gave an impression of being.

"Do I look that bad, young man?" he asked, his voice a little plaintive.

Maxentius was betrayed into a quick, shocked glance upwards, and met the Emperor's eyes, and looked back down again.

"You look tired, August," he said, after a pause.

Valerian sighed deeply. "I am," he said. "The Empire weighs on me. And those who stand to inherit—*God* chose me, lad. Who am I to go choosing another? Why does not God make His will known again?"

Maxentius sank his teeth into his lip, biting back the comment that God made His will known as far as Valerian was concerned by having the previous Emperor's widow pick him as her consort and the next Emperor. That

Empress Eirene's first husband had had very little to say in the matter at all. That everything turned on a throw of the dice of fate, like so many things did in Visant. But none of these things was it politic to mention to an Emperor.

"Then, August, perhaps the matter should be left in God's hands," Maxentius said, controlling his impulses and coming up with something that he thought would be as safe and innocuous as he could make it.

He asked permission to withdraw and Valerian, looking thoughtful, gave it.

Maxentius might have let his words slip from his memory but the next time he had occasion to enter Valerian's presence with more things for the Emperor to sign, Valerian himself brought the matter up—and this time Sarrus, his eyes narrowed to mere slits, was within earshot to hear it all.

"God," Valerian said conversationally, nodding in Maxentius's direction, "does not appear to want to meddle in the affairs of the Empire. I did as you said, young man, and tried to let God decide—but apparently I am not to be allowed to set this responsibility down."

"As…as I said, August?" Maxentius said, baffled, trying not to look at Sarrus.

"Indeed," Valerian said. "I asked them all to dinner at the Palace—Severus was in the city, resting from a campaign, and the other two are always available to feed at the royal table, bless them. I thought, with them all here, God could choose. So I invited them to stay the night, and had three couches prepared for their rest. And under the cushions of one of the couches, I left a parchment that spoke of my will, and God's—*Regnum*, I wrote, and whoever brought it to me in the morning, him I would anoint as my successor.…"

His voice faded away. Maxentius, trembling, knew better than to ask what happened next—but it looked very much like might never know the outcome of the Emperor's ruse.

But Sarrus could ask.

"And which one is it, August?" he said softly in his high girlish voice.

"None," Valerian said. "Severus chose a couch which did not bear the scroll. And Petronus and Gennadius…chose to share a couch that night. Not the one with the scroll. That one lay empty until the scroll was retrieved for me the next morning.…"

"Is there anything further that you require the secretary for, August?" Sarrus said silkily.

"Eh? …No. You may go, young man. We are done."

Maxentius bowed and backed away, as protocol demanded—and was not surprised to find Sarrus waiting for him in the corridor as he left the room.

"You," Sarrus said, "were never meant to hear that conversation."

The unspoken hung between them—*do I need to make arrangements to silence you?*

Maxentius looked up, his eyes steady. "I have heard the Emperor say nothing, except that he will do as God wills," he said.

"Good," Sarrus said. "But as everyone knows this about Valerian Augustus already, you do not need to repeat even that. Do I make myself clear?"

"Perfectly clear," Maxentius said.

"If I hear it noised about...."

"Hear what, Excellency? That the Emperor will do God's will when it is made clear to him? I will of course keep my silence—but it is hardly something that you will have cause to trace to me should you hear it said in the street. As you yourself just said—this is something that everyone already knows."

Sarrus's fleshy lips thinned as he frowned at Maxentius. "You know very well what I mean," he said. "Have a care, young one. You aren't inviolate."

Maxentius gave him a bow commensurate with his rank and turned away, only then allowing himself to take a deep breath, to still his heart. He knew something about the Emperor, about the Empire, about the succession, that nobody else did. And it was yet to be seen if Sarrus would take steps to make sure that nobody else ever would.

Valerian seemed to be content to let things drift over the months that followed. No further word was given on succession matters—except that Petronus, Gennadius, and Severus were subtly distanced from the throne. This might not have been wholly Valerian's doing; Maxentius could see that it also played into Sarrus's own vision of the future that the three nephews be removed from the inner circle. Sarrus was grooming his own candidate for Valerian's throne—a man who would wear the Imperial Purple at public occasions, as Sarrus could not do since he was a eunuch and traditionally barred from wearing the diadem himself, but a man who would be wholly beholden to Sarrus for his position and would be inclined to accept being the face of the Emperor that looked outwards, leaving Sarrus himself to get on with ruling the Empire.

But fate seemed intent that Maxentius be privy to succession developments, because it was on yet another occasion when it was his turn to present the Emperor with the day's scrolls and parchments requiring a signature and a seal that things took another step forward.

Valerian had remembered him—not his name, apparently, but certainly his face, and his presence on earlier occasions.

"It's the pious young man who advised me to put my legacy into God's hands," the Emperor said, receiving a scroll from a kneeling Maxentius.

Startled, Maxentius nearly dropped his end of the scroll. "August?" he said warily.

"I had a dream last night, you know," Valerian said. He was not looking at Maxentius; his head was turned towards a rich tapestry hanging on one of the walls, as though he were reading the particulars of his dream from the weave. "You were right, you know. Leave it to God. That is what I intend to do."

Three or four body servants busy about the room appeared to be doing what they were trained to do, not allowing any conversation they were accidentally privy to in the Imperial chamber to actually percolate into their consciousness—but Maxentius could see at least one of them turn his head ever so slightly at the Emperor's words. Not far enough to actually look in that direction, but a definite cocking of the ear, a gesture of listening. Not sure what to do with this information, or at least not sure yet, Maxentius filed away the servant's face and his action as possibly useful in the future. But the Emperor was speaking again.

"God spoke to me, clearly, just before I woke this morning," Valerian said. "It is God, not I, who will choose the man who will follow me. And it's simple. It is my Nameday feast three days from now—and God will reveal to me then who will be the next Emperor in Visant. I will spend my Nameday praising God's name, and on the morning that follows that day the first man who walks into my chamber will be God's anointed."

The listening servant could not help a twitch of the eyebrow, and then turned away, busying himself with something else.

"As God wills it," Maxentius murmured, receiving back his scrolls. "August, have I leave to go?"

Valerian waved him away without any further word.

Maxentius eased himself out of the Imperial presence and then leaned back against the wall in the corridor, closing his eyes. His heart was beating oddly fast, and he was taking shallow, rapid breaths, as though he were fighting for every gulp of air.

It was his adoptive father's voice that came to haunt him in that moment.

There are no straight roads in Visant.

The road he was walking with such care here in the Imperial Palace had just turned on him, doubling back on itself in a blind curve, and he found himself at once frantically thinking about the possible futures that spilled ahead of him in chaotic profusion and in the grip of a cold, calculating plan which was sifting through those shards and choosing pieces to fit into a particular vision.

The morning after the Emperor's Nameday.

The first man who walked into the room.

Maxentius had not thought he had ambition—or at least not that level of ambition. But he astonished himself with his first thought, the first instinct, which was quite simply, *What if it were I?*

But the cold logical part of him dismissed that thought immediately. He was too young. Too untried. He was a peasant boy barely promoted into patrician ranks. The people might love the idea of the peasant Emperor, particularly one chosen by God himself, but the Senators would never stand for it, and nor would the army—and all three were needed to acclaim an Emperor to the throne of Visant. Besides, the logistics of the whole thing would have been impossible. He was a secretary of the Imperial office, to be sure, but he would find it hard to rig a business so urgent as to require him to be received by the Emperor first thing in the morning…even if he could get past the fact that he had been there when Valerian had spoken of the dream, had known about it, and could not protest his innocence if discovered in the Emperor's chambers at dawn.

So. Not I.

And his own face faded from his mind, to be replaced with another.

Leontes.

The army would back him. He is one of them, a soldier's soldier, he fought in the ranks. The people would acclaim him. The Senate…well, we can cross that bridge when we come to that.

The subject of the Emperor's Nameday came up in conversation quite naturally within the next few days.

"There's a procession, of course," Leontes said. "And I'm to lead it, with my Guard. And then there's the presentation to the Emperor, afterwards—from the court, from the ambassadors—and I'll be stretched to the limit to cover that. These big court days, when everyone gets free access, they're logistical nightmares. The Guards…."

"What sort of presentation is involved?"

"Gifts. From everyone you can think of, and everything you can think of. Last year the Emperor got presented with a herd of specially bred long-haired goats, a gift from some distant Imperial outpost. It was all I could do not to let the entire damned herd into the audience chamber at once so that the gift-giver could show them all off. I had to let one in, because he insisted the Emperor had to see the goat and how special it was, and the consequences of that were…predictable."

"I wouldn't have thought goat herding was one of the requirements of your job," Maxentius said, grinning.

"I've herded worse in my time," Leontes grumbled. "Well, I've still got work to do. There are always glitches in the plan. One just came up. Got to go deal with it."

Maxentius watched Leontes depart, looking at his uncle in a whole new way. Sure, his hair was grey—but his step was full of spring and energy, his sinews were tight and his muscles firm, he had passion and a quiet sort of power. He might not seek a crown, but he would wear one well.

There was a choice to be made. Tell Leontes about the Emperor's dream and make sure he went into the Imperial chambers knowing what he might be setting into motion. Tell Leontes nothing, and make sure he walked into that room innocent of subterfuge.

There are no straight roads in Visant.

Maxentius said nothing to Leontes, in the end.

But early on the morning after the Emperor's Nameday Leontes found himself waiting in the antechamber of the Imperial chamber, arrayed in full Guard finery, a final Nameday presentation in his hand—something that should have been according to protocol presented the previous day. But Maxentius had intercepted this particular offering, delayed it just long enough for its presentation at the appropriate time to have become logistically impossible. Thus, the morning audience with the Emperor, with the last gift.

A nameday celebration was above everything else a celebration of life and living, and superstition and popular belief held it to be bad luck, particularly for someone like an Emperor of a realm, if something related to that celebration was too long delayed—as though it somehow shortened the rest of the recipient's days on earth.

Leontes was the only one waiting to see the Emperor this early, alone in the anteroom, and when he was ushered into the Imperial presence the Emperor was not yet arrayed for the morning audiences but sat alone in a throne-like chair in his chamber, wrapped in a brocaded robe.

Valerian looked up as Leontes entered and went down on one knee in obeisance just inside the door.

"Oh," Valerian said, "so it's to be you."

"August?" Leontes said, puzzled, lifting his head marginally.

"God said he would reveal to me my successor—the first man who walked into my chambers on the morning after my Nameday. It is you, Leontes, Count of the Guard. You will sit on the throne of Visant after I am dead."

Leontes actually looked up and squarely met the Emperor's eyes, his own gaze frankly astonished. "But, August, I merely came...."

"No matter. Leave what you have brought. We will talk more later."

Blindsided, yet aware of dismissal, Leontes laid his final Nameday presentation on the floor and bowed himself out of the chamber.

Maxentius had made sure he was crossing a particular courtyard just as his adoptive father came into it on his way from the Emperor. They both stopped, acknowledging the other.

"You would not believe," Leontes said, "what Valerian Augustus just said to me. I can only hope it's just an old man's dream, and that nobody else ever hears of it."

"Why?" Maxentius said. There was nothing in his expression or his voice to hint at the fact that he already knew, that he had already made sure that a small bag of gold had passed to the servant who had listened on the morning that Valerian had first made his announcement, that Valerian's dream—and, now, the identity of the man who had fulfilled that dream—was already starting to make the rounds at forums and taverns and street drinking fountains and the betting rooms at the Hippodrome.

"Let it lie," Leontes said. He sighed deeply, looking up at the sky. "It is a burden just to contemplate that of which he spoke. But happily…it is no more than a dream."

It is more than a dream. It is the curved road unfolding in front of you. Maxentius gave his adoptive father a small bow, pleading pressure of work, and Leontes, still under the influence of his experience in the Imperial chamber, nodded briefly and gave Maxentius leave to go, himself striding off across the courtyard in pursuit of his own duties and responsibilities.

When Leontes's own trusted body-servant, a man who had been with him since he had achieved his first rank in the army that was high enough to warrant a personal orderly, asked diffidently if it was true that Leontes was to be the next Emperor, Leontes had to face the fact that the dream had escaped the inner sanctum and was the stuff of street gossip, that Visant was buzzing with it.

What he did not realise was how hard it would be to put a lid on any of it. Summoned by Sarrus on the following day, he could honestly swear that he had held no secret ambition to the Imperial diadem, and that he had had no idea of what would transpire in the Emperor's chambers—thus unwittingly vindicating Maxentius's decision not to involve him in the planning of the whole affair. But Maxentius's name did come up in the discussion with Sarrus, when the Grand Chamberlain flatly said that he suspected Maxentius had had a hand in the course of events—even that he, Sarrus, had come to believe that Maxentius had taken that name purposefully when he had been written into the Patrician Register, that Maxentius had always been driven by ambition of his own.

"That is a flat lie," Leontes snapped. "The boy was always a bookworm. He chose the name because the Maxentius who had worn the diadem was a scholar in his own right, not because he sat on a golden throne. The only reason my son came to the City at all was because I dangled a University education in front of him."

"And with one of those, he will be content to be a secretary forever?" Sarrus said. "You may not know your…son as well as you think you do. I've been watching him closely."

"Then you will no doubt have evidence of any action he took—in this or any other affair," Leontes said. "We live under Imperial Law, and all of us are bound by it. Maxentius. I. You. Even the Emperor, who makes the laws, has to live by them. It has always been possible to find the loopholes and to act from beyond the law—but I have eyes and ears everywhere, Sarrus, and if Maxentius comes to harm by your word, even if it is not your hand that wields the blade or the poison, I *will* make sure that justice is done."

"I will meditate on what justice needs to be done," Sarrus said.

Leontes did not cross paths with Maxentius for the rest of that day, but the conversation with Sarrus weighed on him, etching deep frown lines at the corners of his mouth. Euphaedra noticed something bothered him, and asked—she had obviously yet to hear the bazaar rumours herself—but something kept him from telling her of the matter, something that crystallised as he stepped softly into their bedroom that night, long after she had already retired, and stood watching her for a moment as she slept.

She had never been beautiful or graceful. In her youth she had been pretty, with lustrous hair and big luminous eyes that were of a strange dark green hue which had always reminded Leontes of moss under water—but even then she had had the coarse features of a peasant girl from some Imperial backwater who had once been taken as a slave by a passing army. She had always held the promise of what she would become, of what she now was, a short and dumpy woman with thick wrists and solid ankles and a rounded barren belly that had never swelled with child.

She had played the game of Countess faithfully, wearing the kind of clothes that patricians wore, wearing rings on her short fingers, and silk dyed a deep dark green which Leontes had procured to set off those oddly beautiful eyes. But to make her the consort of an Emperor? Would that be fair to the slave girl whom he had married?

It was late when he was announced at the House of Peacocks, but the lights still burned in the chamber Maxentius had furnished as his study and Maxentius himself looked tired and bleary-eyed as he stood to receive his adoptive father.

"I have to know," Leontes said abruptly, without preamble. "Was it your doing?"

Maxentius hesitated. "I knew about the dream," he said softly, after a long pause.

"You sent me in there?"

"He could have done worse," Maxentius murmured.

"Why?" Leontes said, his eyes burning, unsure of what he felt—fury, incredulity, a dawning awe, a strange swelling exultation. But the question remained, hanging there between the two of them. "Why put me on that spot? Why did you think that I would ever want...that I was not content with...." He shook his head once, sharply, as though to rid himself of some persistent gnat-like thought. "When you first came to Visant," he said slowly, "you were so young. Now...now it feels like you are so much older than I. This city has got its claws into you—what did I do, bringing you here...?"

"Uncle," Maxentius said. "*Father.* Nothing may yet come of it all. But when the time comes, think—would you rather Gennadius on the throne, a man who will take his latest favourite's word that the sun is shining even when he can clearly see the rain from his window? Or some puppet the Senate or Sarrus would put up?"

"When Gratianus died...the Emperor before Valerian...it was Eirene who chose him then, who put him in her bed, on the throne," Leontes said through bloodless lips.

"Someone always chooses," Maxentius said gently. "What harm to let the people think that this time it really was God who gave the Emperor his word?"

You may not know your son as well as you think you do. Maxentius had not been present at the interview with Sarrus, but those words were now written on Leontes's face as clearly as if Sarrus had just spoken them in this room. Leontes, suddenly aware of Maxentius's eyes upon him, bent his head and covered his face with his palm, pressing his thumb and his fingers into both temples.

"What have you done?" Leontes whispered, very softly. It wasn't clear if he was addressing Maxentius, or himself.

Out in the shadow-filled garden, somewhere in the quiet darkness, a peacock's scream rent the night, as if an oracle had replied.

CHAPTER SEVEN

Simonis's prayers might have been answered in the most literal way—her mother survived, and the new baby, although its own health was fragile at first, quickly passed out of immediate danger—but in real terms she had already lost her family. Cicatrice had made arrangements with Locinus even before Apphia had had a chance to recover enough to be asked for her consent, and Simonis, still shy of her ninth birthday, moved to the dancers' dormitory.

Her education there, on several levels, was swift and brutal.

In the dancers' hall, her role was to fetch and carry for, and otherwise attend, Circassaë, and the older girl kept her busy.

She was not given much of a chance to ease into her new role. The day after she arrived at the dormitory hall and with barely a handful of hours to come to terms with where she was, Circassaë dumped a ripped costume into Simonis's arms and told her new-minted serving girl that she needed it fixed for her next performance. That night. Simonis began to remonstrate that she had never done sewing this fine before, but she was already talking to Circassaë's back; gritting her teeth, she did the best she could. Her reward was a sharp reprimand on her sewing abilities, and two more costumes on which to practice. She had hardly had a chance to get properly busy on those when Circassaë told her to drop everything and go to the market to purchase a new batch of henna hairdye with which the young dancer kept her hair its magnificent and unusual colour.

"It's the wrong powder," Circassaë had sniffed when Simonis had returned. "Go back and exchange it."

"But they won't take...." Simonis began, only to have Circassaë wave her hand in dismissal.

"They will take it back. Tell them who sent you. Oh, and while you're out, you might as well get me a new supply of kohl, too. Not the cheap stuff that they sell out where you got the henna. There's a better shop, just off the perfumers' forum, and you'd better not get lost finding it. Have you finished with the costumes yet?"

Simonis kept her head down and did as she was told, because there was a challenge in Circassaë's eyes that spoke eloquently of a report on Simonis's behaviour being prepared for Cicatrice, a report that might affect Simonis's entire future. For the time being, whatever was being handed to her, she would take it.

The strategy appeared to bear fruit, because she soon graduated to acting as an accessory to accentuate Circassaë's status in the Hippodrome society— trotting in the young dancer's wake, dressed as a serving girl, when Circassaë ventured forth into the streets. She quickly realised that it was a stepping stone, training for the next stage of her work, a period in which she learned how to blend into the background while keeping her eyes and ears open, a spy in plain sight. It was almost anticlimactic when Cicatrice declared Simonis to be ready for society and finally permitted her to go as Circassaë's attendant to one of the private parties at the home of an Imperial Senator.

Simonis had grown up in the Hippodrome world, and the closest she had come to a patrician house had been seeing them from the street when she had come to Visant. Now, for the first time, she had crossed a threshold and ventured inside one of these establishments, and she drank it all in like a draught of an intoxicating elixir.

The Senator's guests had dined in the classical way that night, reclining on banquet couches, with silent slaves anticipating every unspoken wish of their master's companions and circulating with platters of sumptuous victuals and goblets of fine wine presented to individuals who needed only to reach for something no more than an arm's length away. It was summer, and the banquet hall was open to the garden, with only a thin silk curtain stirring in the evening breeze to separate the one from the other; the terrace outside was all sun-warmed stone and smooth mosaic floors, made magical in the moonlight and the flickering light cast by cresset lights set on the balustrade.

Simonis, after making sure her duties to Circassaë were done—the dancer's costume immaculate, her make-up perfect—crept out onto the terrace by herself and stood half-hidden in the shadow beside the open doors, her sandals in her hand and her feet bare on the mosaic floor with her toes curled on the tesserae. Inside the musicians started up and the dancers were about to begin— outside, she heard cicadas, and glimpsed what she thought might have been moonlight on the sea far away.

There had been no women in the banquet hall, but now, unexpectedly, Simonis heard a smothered giggle and a whispered exchange in high girlish voices. She could not make out what was said, but she watched as two young women, clad in gold-trimmed dalmatics and their hair dressed in a complicated style, crept onto the terrace and tried to sneak unobtrusively into a position where they could catch a glimpse of the inside of the men's banquet chamber.

They did not notice Simonis, who shrank further into the shadows, too busy trying to stay unseen themselves—but they seemed incapable of self-control or silence. Simonis's lip curled a little as she watched their clumsy attempts to creep closer—but she knew that her own presence was not sanctioned here, even less than that of these young patrician girls, who were not under any of their society's rules permitted to be anywhere near this close to a men-only feast, with all its attendant ribaldry and licence.

They didn't get nearly close enough, however, and were suddenly stopped in their tracks by a voice that managed to be at once quiet and yet leave no doubt as to its absolute authority.

"Lia. Thais. No further."

The girls flinched at the sound of their names, turning to the woman who had spoken. She was wrapped in an embroidered silk stola and a jewelled head-dress on her carefully coiffed head, waiting with an air of firm expectation at the edge of the terrace. The younger girls seemed to lose the edge of their gaiety at the appearance of the woman, and meekly withdrew from the dangerous proximity of the banquet room's windows. The woman waited until they were abreast of her, and then shepherded them ahead with a firm yet gentle hand. She paused, lifting her head a little, and, presenting Simonis with a regal profile in silhouette. Then she turned and followed the other two away from the light and music in the banquet hall.

Society's rules might have barred her from the banquet, but her dignity and presence were those of a queen, and Simonis had found herself holding her breath as the woman walked away with a high-stepping patrician grace.

That could be me, she thought, unexpectedly, passionately, with a mixture of envy and a sense of entitlement that didn't seem to be diametrically opposed to one another in that moment. *That should be me. One day. One day that will be me.*

Queen of her household. Ruler of her realm.

Patrician.

The reality of her life rushed back with a reek of wine, rancid fat, and sweat and musk of the back rooms of the dancers' halls and the great houses' kitchens. She, Simonis, had about as much chance of ever living this life as she had of growing wings and flying with the eagles. She was to be trained as an actress, an acrobat, a mime…a courtesan. Courtesans could have liaisons with patrician men, but they were short and passionate affairs that could not endure even if both parties wished them to. Marriage outside of her class was forbidden to an actress, by the letter of Imperial law.

Cicatrice called Simonis and Circassaë in after the troupe returned to the dancers' hall from the party.

"Now tell me," he said to Simonis, "who was there?"

Simonis stared at him. "How would I know their names?"

"You will," Cicatrice said. "For now, let me worry about names. You tell me what you saw."

Circassaë crossed her arms and stared at the younger girl with a slight smile, offering nothing more than a sense of anticipation—apparently this was some sort of test that she too had had once had to pass, and she was waiting to see how the next candidate would do at the task.

Simonis took a deep breath.

"The one giving the party was fat," she said, "and he wore a laurel crown. I don't remember if you told us what he was celebrating tonight, but he looked smirky, as though he had thrown the party because he had got something that someone else wanted and was showing off."

"He got word of having been awarded a promotion, and a step up in the Imperial offices," Cicatrice said. "Very good. What else?"

"An older, thin man. He looked a little sick, uncomfortable, as though he didn't really want to be there. I think he retired early."

"Your host's father in law," Cicatrice said, nodding. "He didn't want to see this promotion go to his son-in-law. But I think also that he truly is sick of some physical malady, too. I know that he had the physician summoned to his house twice last month, and none of the rest of his household is ailing—and his slaves have been buying medicinal herbs in the markets. What else?"

"Three men who didn't look like they were really guests."

"What does that mean?"

"They were on the couches, but they were not paying attention to the dancers or the food. They were watching the rest of them. Two of the other guests went off with dancers, after, and one with a boy. One wanted Circassaë to go with him but she refused him, and he was not happy."

"I thought I had been more discreet than that," Circassaë said, uncrossing her arms and straightening. "If he thinks I slighted him in public...."

"He was unhappy, not resentful or vengeful," Simonis said. "Just resigned. And I saw...the girls."

"The girls? What girls?"

"There were two young women, out on the terrace, trying to get a look inside at the banquet. One of them at least looked marriageable; they were wearing gold-edged robes, and then there was the woman who came after them. Lia...and...and Thais—I think those were their names."

"What did she look like?"

"Like a queen," Simonis said dreamily. "She wore a crown and she had dark hair and a long thin face...."

"Pasiphaë," Cicatrice said. "She is connected to the Emperor's own family. Agorus's second wife. The girls aren't her children, she is their stepmother and she has managed no children of her own. Agorus keeps her because she gives him status at Court—but now, with this promotion, he gets a step closer himself. That's partly why his father-in-law looked so sickened tonight. If Agorus lets his new state go to his head he might yet put Pasiphaë aside and get himself another wife, a younger and prettier woman who might give him the son he so desperately wants. And her family...they have the lineage but not the money, not any more. If he divorces her, they could be in real trouble—they are deep in debt, and it is only she who keeps them out of trouble with the Prefecture.... All right, you two. You can go now. Simonis, you did well tonight."

They were dismissed; Circassaë reached out and touched Simonis on the elbow and they withdrew, closing the door softly behind them, and padded along a deserted corridor back towards their own quarters.

"He promised me that he'd get me work with the animals," Simonis murmured, her voice barely above a breath. But Circassaë heard, and turned her head slightly.

"Aren't you?" she said. "With the most feral and dangerous animals of all...? Trust me, a lion mauling you can recover from, and at least you can wear your scars with pride. The wounds that *men* give you are deep inside, and sometimes never heal at all, and you have to hide the scars all your life. He *has* already thrown you to the wolves. It's just that you haven't had a chance to be gnawed on by the ones with the sharpest teeth. Give it time."

"What did he do to you?" Simonis asked abruptly, staring at the older girl.

Circassaë shrugged. "My mother was a slave taken on campaign. She never knew who the soldier was that left her belly filled with me—and she remained a slave until the day she died. I was four. Somebody bought me at a slave auction, and then thought better of it, and left me at the gates of the Antacia Hippodrome. They took me in, taught me to dance. At some point—I can't have been much older than you when you walked into that Arena to beg for your life—I was the fourth dancer from the left at some Hippodrome show when Cicatrice saw something in me, bought my contract, brought me back here, and made me what I am. But make no mistake—it was not out of the goodness of his heart. It's as good a life as I could have hoped for, but it does not come cheap. It was *he* who decided when it was time for me to take a lover, it was he who chose my first lover for me. As he will no doubt choose yours, when the time comes."

Simonis had known that it would come for her—for the women of the Hippodrome the only way to choose chastity was to renounce all the living, laughing world, put on a nun's veil and take a vow of silence for the rest of their days. For the rest, they could not be other than their society allowed them to be. Actresses were not permitted to marry outside of their caste—and if one had to take lovers, why not make it part of the trade? But Simonis had never thought about the physical reality of it all. Her knowledge of the carnal aspect of her new trade was extensive—she could hardly fail to realise what went on between the dancers and the patrician men for whom they performed, once the show was over—but, until now, it was all largely theoretical, and it was a life that belonged to somebody else. Other women. Other...*women*. She suddenly realised that somehow she was very close to being considered one of those women, that she was further away from her childhood, short as it had been, than she knew. Her throat went dry at Circassaë's words, and she swallowed, hard, faced with an imminence of something that was suddenly not in as distant a future as she had believed it to be.

But it didn't happen quickly—it was as though Cicatrice was patiently honing his new weapon, waiting for the right time to use it. Simonis continued to visit patricians' houses as Circassaë's attendant and brought back reports of what she had observed; in the meantime, her training as a performer in her own right accelerated, her teachers and mentors having discovered that she had two unexpected gifts.

One was that her small but perfectly formed body turned out to be capable of uncanny feats of acrobatics—her spine was infinitely flexible and she could bend over backwards until her palms were flat on the floor between her feet and the back of her head almost touched her buttocks, or fold herself into an impossible shape in order to fit (apparently comfortably) into a box which looked too small to hold a toddler-sized child.

The other—and she herself didn't consider that much of a gift, at first—was that she was able to make people laugh.

She had fought that one, at first.

"They are laughing *with* you, not *at* you," Circassaë said at last, both admiring and exasperated. "That is not something that many can do."

"I don't want people to laugh at all," Simonis said stubbornly.

"You will," Circassaë said shrewdly, "when it's the laughter that gets golden solidi thrown at you in appreciation. And you can get them. I've seen enough mimes and comic performers to know that a good one commands twice the price of someone like me—anyone can throw a party and have a dozen dancers in to perform, and for most of them it wouldn't matter if it was any *particular* dancer that was hired. But the gift of laughter…is harder to coax. I've seen others try and do that, and fail. I've seen you get it without trying. Cicatrice chose well when he picked you."

By the time she was twelve Simonis was doing solo spots of her own at the Hippodrome intermissions and at the same private parties where she had once gone as Circassaë's servant girl. She was entirely unselfconscious about her body, perhaps because it was yet to develop obvious feminine lines. But there was something about her nonetheless that started drawing the eye of the men. Cicatrice sharpened her choreography, using her in scenes that showed the myriad seductions of mortal women by the old pagan gods, and at last fulfilled his old promise of getting Simonis to work with her beloved animals. It was one of these scenes—the dalliance between the great god Xeuxes and the maiden Ladaë—that finally tipped Simonis into a kind of notoriety in the city, and into adulthood.

They had substituted a handful of geese for the swan in whose shape Xeuxes had tempted Ladaë in the myth. As the maiden, Simonis had danced around the stage dressed in several layers of filmy veil-like wraps that fluttered around her body, discarding them one by one as she let them drop into insubstantial translucent heaps on the mosaic floor. Then, finally miming a surrender to her fate and wearing no more than the short linen skirt that the city's modesty laws demanded of even semi-public performances, she lay on her back on a bench or couch, whatever was handy at the venue, and an attendant came in to sprinkle barley seeds on her bare belly and the folds of her modesty skirt and another attendant released the trained geese who came in and patiently pecked the grain off her body.

Her breasts were starting to bud; her body was growing up. The first time she performed her Ladaë act she had roused to applause at the finale, smiling and bowing to her audience, and had met at least one pair of eyes that were hot with hunger and desire…aimed, for the first time in her life, at herself. Cicatrice himself had been at that particular party, and had not failed to notice the reaction that Simonis's act had produced. It did not take him long, after that, to choose (as Circassaë had said that he would) the first man who would share her bed.

Cicatrice hand-picked him—Virgillus, well-placed in the halls of the Magister Oficii through which all kinds of information flowed but not ranked highly enough to be wary nor particularly cagey about what he might know or might inadvertently spill. He wasn't young and naïve—Cicatrice already valued Simonis, with her instinctive shrewdness and her powers of observation, far too highly to waste her on a mark that would be too easy—but he would not prove to be too tough for the inexperienced young fledgling courtesan to crack, if there was something there that could be useful for Cicatrice's valuable information archives.

When the message came with the time and place of an engagement, Simonis did not realise at first that there would be anything different involved than just another of the private parties at some Senatorial home. But there was something about it, something *different*. She had not really thought about the details of that instinctive reaction, but when she mentioned to Circassaë, in passing, that she had a performance that night, Circassaë had frowned delicately.

"I don't recall a troupe engagement tonight," she said. "What did he say, exactly?"

"Just a name, an address, and that there would be transport provided for me…."

"Only you."

"What?"

"Only for you. Transport only for you. Simonis…he's picked your first. Tonight you are going to be on a very different stage. Oh, but he does not know, does not care, does not *understand*…he might have warned you…."

Simonis grew very white. "You think that he…?"

"I know. This is the way he did it to me. Listen, little girl, for I will tell you a few things that Cicatrice can't. The first time is *always* difficult, because whatever I tell you, whatever you think you know, it all ceases to matter once you're there, once you're in the dance. You might be frightened—you must not show your fear. You might be disappointed—you must not show that you are upset. No tears. No whimpers. No weakness. Not *there*, not then. If he hurts you, bite down on it and smile; if he pleases you, never show him how much. What are you planning to wear tonight?"

"I hadn't thought about that yet."

"I will help you choose, later. You need to go into his bed a woman, and yet you don't want to try too hard, so that he cannot help but see the child underneath all the paint and the jewels...do you *have* any jewels? Something fit to wear to a night like this, I mean, not just childish trinkets?"

"I have a pair of earrings," Simonis said. "One of them has a broken clasp, though—and I don't know if it can be mended before I have to go...."

"I have some hair jewels," Circassaë said. "I will lend you those—you have magnificent hair, we can dress that with the pins—and we will keep the make up to a minimum, kohl maybe, some rouge. Come see me an hour before you are due to go."

"Thank you," Simonis said.

"I have walked this path," Circassaë said abruptly. "It is not an easy road. The least I can do is show you how to avoid the traps."

Simonis left her, then, and tried to find a place of solitude for a while, a place where she could gather her thoughts and try and control the flush that crept into her cheeks and the heart that thudded painfully against her ribs. But this was the Hippodrome at the height of the season, and places of solitude were difficult to come by. Simonis found herself missing the sanctuary of her long-gone bear protectress, but that was no longer available to her as an option. She did clutch at the bear claw talisman she wore on a thong around her neck and close her eyes for a moment in something very much like prayer. But the bear made her think of her father, and her father made her think of her mother. Although Apphia had not played a huge part in Simonis's life for some time, Simonis suddenly found herself missing her mother, and the advice a mother might be able to offer on a day like this took on an urgent importance that she could not shake. She knew that she had rarely found Apphia able to provide what she needed—but it seemed unthinkable to even consider going to her first lover without at least telling her mother about it.

So she made her way to Locinus's quarters. Apphia, whose job it was to produce at least a portion of the scents and paints that the Hippodrome dancers used in their trade, looked up from decanting a batch of rose-water into small pottery jars and straightened in surprise as Simonis walked in.

"I was not expecting you," she said by way of greeting.

"I wasn't expecting to be here," Simonis said. "Can I help you with that?"

"If you like," Apphia said, settling back down and nodding towards a second stool in the corner. Simonis fetched it and began to line up the empty jars to hold for her mother while she poured the scented water from the larger pot where it had been infused.

"I am to go to a man tonight," Simonis murmured, without looking up, her hands folded around a jar. The stream of rose water might have shivered for a moment as Apphia's hand shook, but then it steadied again.

"You are so young…."Apphia said quietly. "Tell me. Who is he?"

"His name is Virgillus. Cicatrice wants…something from him. I don't know. I am to get it, somehow." She deftly swapped jars, with Apphia barely needing to stop the flow of rosewater. "I remember…."

"What do you remember, my daughter?"

"That one time I went to one of the parties, with Circassaë and the dancers," Simonis said. "That time I saw the Domna, the lady of the house, the one who ruled that domain. I remember, I looked on her, and I wanted…I wanted to be…."

The rosewater stopped, and after a moment Simonis looked up quizzically. Her mother was sitting back, the big pot cradled in her lap, staring at her oldest daughter with a strange small smile.

"Those of us who marry at all, marry into our tribe," she said. "To bear the children to replenish our tribe. I married, and Batzas and I made *you*. But you were born into *this* world, Simonis. What you saw was a fable, an enchanted story told to children, something like those ancient legends that you now dance for the patricians—something that you can pretend to be, but which you cannot ever, ever, have. This man…this…Virgillus?—for you, he is the first— but for him, you will not be. There will be those who came before you. There are already children growing up who will be following in your footsteps. You cannot be more to him than…."

Simonis let a jar slip though her fingers, not sure whether she felt devastated or furious. She might have known that her mother would focus on the things that she could *not* be. Instead of finding a sense of calm and peace all she had done was stir a hornet's nest of unease, and frustration, and anger; it seemed to fit the shattered remains of the jar that lay at her feet.

"I know he won't *marry* me," Simonis snapped "I know I cannot be a keeper of bears; I know that I cannot be a patrician wife. I'm not sure that I can be a wife at all, now, with Cicatrice holding me in that claw of his and training me to do his bidding—"

She caught herself, aware that she had been about to spill the real nature of her relationship to Cicatrice, the true shape of this night—not just the first time that her body would be given to a man but also the first real test of her usefulness to Cicatrice, of her ability to extract useful and timely information from the bedmates who would be chosen for her.

Something that her mother would never understand. Could not, because she was not allowed to know.

Simonis fought her temper, made her passions subside, reached down to start gathering up the pieces of the jar. "I'm sorry," she said. "I'm sorry I dropped this...."

She became aware of the weight of Apphia's gaze on her, and looked up to meet her mother's eyes, filled with unexpected tears.

"There has never been anything that I could really do for you," Apphia said. "Not even now. Not even this. You were too young when things happened to us...I tried to hold a family together, and yet all I did was...."

Simonis reached over and laid a hand over Apphia's. She felt as though she ought to say something, do something, but Apphia was not an old lion with a wounded paw from which Simonis could pull a thorn and heal the hurt. There were too many things between them, too many things that could have been said and never were, or said too soon.

"I have to go," she said abruptly, getting up and pushing her stool away, careful not to knock over any more of the jars. "I have to find Circassaë, she promised to help me get ready...."

"Simonis."

Apphia's voice came a beat too late, even as Simonis was opening the door of the room, about to step outside.

"Mother," she said, hesitating, without turning around. She didn't think she could bear to see the expression on her mother's face in that moment.

"Don't lose yourself," Apphia said. "Never forget who you really are. Don't break your heart."

It was kindly meant, but Simonis heard the same thing that she had heard her mother tell her all of her life—*you cannot do this... you cannot be this.* She nodded, her movements sharp, abrupt.

"My heart is my own," she said. "I will remember."

When she ran into Cicatrice, on her way back to the dancers' hall, it was wholly unexpected; if she had planned to do so it would have been later, when she was more composed, more in charge of herself, less at the mercy of her complicated and complex emotions. Cicatrice, being who he was, did not fail to grasp the details of the situation immediately.

"You've been crying," he said.

"No," Simonis said, lifting her chin. She had not, in fact, given way to tears—but they were there, hot and prickling behind her eyes, and Cicatrice could sense them even though they had not been spilled.

"Are you afraid?" he asked, his voice oddly gentle.

"No," Simonis said again, but her hand clenched at her side and this, too, he saw.

"Remember this—I would not throw you away," he said, letting his good hand rest on her shoulder for a moment. "If I did not think you were ready, that you could do this thing, you would not be here. And there is much to gain, from this moment on."

"I will never be anything but a dalliance, a distraction," Simonis said, her lips suddenly dry.

Cicatrice allowed his eyebrow to inch upward a fraction. "Oh?" he said. "My dear girl, you have more to learn than you know. Entire Empires have been ruled from between silken sheets, my dear—you might say that ruling an Empire is sometimes as simple as ruling an Emperor, and where the cold chilled beds are provided by marriages of state, where families are united and not men and women, it is the…what did you call it? The *dalliance*…? It is the woman who is chosen rather than imposed, the woman who shares passion rather than protocol, whose hand is on the tiller. If you know how, you can have all the power you ever wanted, more than you know what you would do with. And it starts tonight."

Simonis stared at him. "You chose this man. You chose him…to teach me?"

"I think you have things to learn from each other," Cicatrice chuckled. "What you do tonight, that is between you and him. What you talk about…that is my concern. I will expect a full report."

Simonis dropped her eyes, allowing her hand to slowly unclench and relax at her side. "I'd better go. Circassaë is waiting for me."

"I know," Cicatrice said. And then, unexpectedly, added, "Don't forget to enjoy yourself tonight. A big part of this is all about *you*."

Circassaë spent an hour carefully coiling Simonis's unruly curls into a fashionable style which also threw into prominence her high cheekbones and the fine arches of her eyebrows over the dark, brilliant eyes. They did very little make-up, in the end—a touch of colour for Simonis's lips, a little rouge on her cheeks and on the underside of her breasts. It was Circassaë who drew a fine veil over her handiwork and escorted Simonis to the sedan chair that had been procured for her transportation; for a moment, leaning out of the conveyance, Simonis clung tightly to the older girl's hand, saying nothing, but the expression on her face as glimpsed through the translucent veil eloquent enough.

Circassaë squeezed her fingers, and then let go, stepping back.

"Go," she said, "and may fortune attend you."

"Will you wait up for me?"

"You will not be back," Circassaë said gently, "until morning."

The four slaves who had been brought to carry the chair lifted the poles to their shoulders with a grunt; it swayed unsteadily and Simonis fell back against the cushions inside. When she lifted the side curtain to look back, Circassaë was gone.

She was met at the front door of Virgillus's house by a woman slave—a girl not much older than herself, dressed in a plain gown cinched at the waist with a woven belt dyed a vivid blue, her hair piled simply on top of her head. Simonis took refuge in haughtiness, stepping from the chair with a high-handed grace and sweeping up the shallow steps to Virgillus' door without acknowledging the presence of anybody at all, and waited with a hint of impatience in the inner vestibule while the girl closed the door and, after a hesitation, beckoned her forward. Simonis was surprised to catch a look of frank envy in the slave's eyes as she stole one long apprising glance at Simonis's finery, a little astonished that someone out here would be envious of *her*. But the girl turned her back and padded down the hallway lit with several extravagant torches, and then into a large room with an open hearth in which a fire had been lit—mostly for atmosphere, because it was warm enough for the room to be open to the outside through a pair of wide doors which gave onto a shadowed terrace. It was not that unlike the tesseraed terrace where Simonis had first seen Pasiphaë, the lady, the patrician, the woman whom her mother had told her in no uncertain terms that she could never be.

And yet, the slave girl was jealous.

You can have all the power you ever wanted, more than you know what you would do with. And it starts tonight.

Cicatrice's voice echoed in her mind as clearly as if he had just whispered into her ear; when another, different, voice spoke, Simonis actually jumped, startled.

"Welcome," Virgillus said. "Come over here, to the fire. I have wine."

She came, slowly—part of it was hesitation, but she was not unaware of what this might look like from the outside, the slow and steady walk which belonged not to a slave who had been summoned but to a free woman who chose to come of her own will. When she stood before him at last and he reached out to take the veil from her hair, she stood with her back straight and met his eyes as he allowed his hand to drop with the fine translucent muslin still clasped between his fingers.

"He said you were beautiful," Virgillus said. "He did not tell me nearly enough."

He had offered wine, but somehow that was forgotten—he reached out to take the first jewelled clip from her hair, and Simonis, after a pang of pure frustration that she could not quite help—*it took so long to put it all up!*—became aware of quite a different sensation as one pin followed another and he finally shook her hair loose around her shoulders, burying his fingers into it and combing them out through the long wavy tresses. Little was said. Simonis—w whose colour was high but who was almost preternaturally aware of every filigreed nuance of emotion and need and totally in control of them—reached out herself to undo the brooch that held her gown together at the shoulder, and then let the material drop, pooling at her feet.

Simonis had been dancing before men's eyes for years now, shedding translucent veils, baring her body to their gaze. The linen modesty skirt required of all dancers was no more than a rather hypocritical nod to the city's by-laws—although it had been pared down to the smallest permissible scrap, which really left little enough to the imagination and often acted rather more than an inflammation to desire than a quenching of it, that flimsy bit of cloth had always been there between Simonis and her audience. The last veil.

But she wore nothing underneath her gown, and now stood for the first time in her life completely open to a man's gaze, clothed only in the glossy dark curls of her hair. It spilled over her shoulders, cascaded down her back, some of it snaking forward to fall over her breasts, giving a tantalizing glimpse of small dark nipples playing hide and seek amongst the curls. In some ways she preferred this, the honesty of this, to the fake barrier of the modesty skirt. This was who she was, in the end, this body, this form; until now she had been dangled before men as a bribe, or as bait, or as promise—they had always been allowed to look and admire the image she and her dressers and make-up artists had worked so hard to perfect, but never to touch the substance of it all.

She had been an illusion of a woman, dancing in men's fantasies, letting them find fulfilment elsewhere, quenching the thirsts she might have aroused in them by sheathing their desires in the more solid bodies of some other female body.

Until now. Until tonight. Until the last veil was gone.

Simonis watched Virgillus's face change a little as he traced the shape of the young body revealed to his gaze with a fingertip from shoulder to hip, shivering a little as the hand opened to rest on her hipbone, and then slipping back to the small of her back. She may never have lain with a man, but she was of the Hippodrome; she knew the smell of sex, and the way it made men's breath come faster, and she recognised it now, here, in this room—ready to swallow her whole, to mark her at last as the Hippodrome's own.

When he bent his head to kiss her, she let herself surrender to it, one of her arms lifting to his shoulder, his neck, her hand coming to rest on the close-cut iron-grey hair. His tongue teased her lips open, explored her small teeth, touched its tip to her own tongue's tip as though the two were wary sentient creatures in their own right greeting each other in the manner of their kind. She arched against him, bending under his hand, and a small sound escaped her, a sound that was the voice of the slow fire which was building inside of her, making her blood surge in her veins.

Her other hand, the one that was resting on his chest, spasmed in the folds of his draped toga. It gave a little, and Simonis pushed back against him, letting her other hand come to his chest, gathering the rich folds of the fabric up and pulling it away from his shoulder, unfolding it, tugging impatiently when it caught and hearing him chuckle a little as his own fingers came up to cover hers, to shape her hand, to let her release a stubborn snag. She stilled when it was done, her head tilted a little, gazing at his own naked body with fascination, and wariness, and a little bit of apprehension that she was unable to quite hide—but also with her lips parted a little, and her eyes wide with a kind of wonder.

"I did not know...." she began, and then fell silent, the wariness and the wonder battling in her mind, one hand coming down from Virgillus's chest to come to a fluttering rest on her own hipbone, fingers reaching around the curve of her leg, exploring how the geography of these two bodies might be made to fit together.

Virgillus could not help his lips curving into a small smile at that sight. But then it was gone, and he was serious again, gathering her up closer to him, moulding her body to the changed shape of his own.

"I am sorry," he whispered, his lips against hers. "It is the first time, for you. It will probably hurt."

"You can never hurt me," Simonis said, lifting her eyes to meet his own.

He took a far different meaning from her words than she had put into them, and that was all right. Cicatrice had chosen well for the first man to take possession of Simonis's body. There *was* pain—she was braced for that, expecting it—but Virgillus did not let her focus on that expectation. Instead, he took his time finding his way around the young body, its breasts still round with childhood, legs still long and coltish and hips only beginning to swell out into a womanly curve from a slender waist. He forced nothing, allowing her to respond with instinct and awakened desire, letting his hands linger on smooth skin, wander into places where no man's hands had been before, pausing to allow her own tentative exploratory touches. He was kindly, gentle, old enough to allow things to unfold at a pace that did not leave Simonis feeling rushed or pressured and yet with enough urgency to ignite a passionate response in herself. When the pain did come, as he entered her, it was fleeting, swiftly subsumed into other things, and the cry he drew from her, as one of her hands tightened on his shoulder and the other twisted the furs on which he had laid her into a tight, savage grip, was not born of the pain.

"Are you sure you are all right?" he had asked, afterwards, solicitous of her well-being in the aftermath, as she lay in the crook of his arm curled up like a kitten with the rich luxuriant waves of her hair cloaking them both in dark shadows. It was, perhaps, a moment of misgiving—because she could still give the impression of being so young, such a child.

But the eyes she turned on him were smoky, languorous, knowing—she was all woman in that moment. "Oh, yes," she said. Only that. And it was enough, for a while.

Simonis couldn't quite recall, after, whether it had been Virgillus who had started the game with the still child-like woman he held in his arms or if she herself had initiated it—but somehow they had got into a playful contest of telling each other something that the other did not know in exchange for the same in return. Simonis told of the old lions of Cyrenais and how she had once taken it upon herself to doctor a hurt paw in the lions' den, and Virgillus had laughed in delight and called her a brave and unusual soul.

"I'm afraid I have no such wonderful secrets from my past," he said, wrapping a curl of her hair around his finger and tracing the curve of her breast with its feathered end. "I had a thoroughly boring life—I was born into an upstanding family, had an unexceptional education just like everyone else I knew, and then found a place in the Imperial service when I was old enough to do so. Promoted twice, but at least once it was because somebody died in the traces and they needed to haul everyone up on the service ladder by one rung;

I supposed I was lucky that it happened between bribes to some higher official, and nobody was brought in from the outside and installed in the empty slot. I wish I had something exciting to tell you in return—but I've never even seen your islands. I have never been more than a day's ride away from Visant—it's ironic, I work in an office where daily requests from exotic ambassadors from foreign lands come through me, but the ambassadors are the closest I've ever come to seeing the Empire. It has always come to me, and has never allowed me to go out to meet it."

"Are you sorry?" Simonis asked, curious.

"Sometimes," Virgillus admitted with a sigh. "When I hear strange accents, or I see Annubian princes come in their lion skins and dyed feathers, or when the traders from the north come through with furs of bear and lynx and wolf to offer to the Emperor, or merchants from Xin or Syai come through with treasures from far away—sometimes I wish I knew more of them and the places they come from than just a whiff of a strange scent or the sound of a language that falls strangely on my ears when they converse amongst themselves in whispers before they call in the interpreters. I've been at audiences that the Emperor has granted in his Throne Room, and I've seen the foreigners impressed by the Imperial grandeur, and I have wondered sometimes what they would have to show me."

"All I've ever known," Simonis said, "is the Hippodrome."

"I suppose you have your own share of exotics come through there," Virgillus said, smiling. "The dancers from the Crescent kingdoms, or the traders from the far south who bring you the exotic beasts. Have you ever wished that you could go to these places?"

Simonis considered this with her head inclined a little. "Sometimes," she admitted. "I haven't really thought about it. But you are cheating."

"Cheating? I? How so?"

"I told you something about me, now it's your turn," Simonis said.

"But I have already said I have no secret exotic past," Virgillus said.

"Then tell me something about the future. Something that hasn't happened yet. What's the most exciting thing that is going to happen in the city next year?"

"You," he said, tracing the length of her body from shoulder to thigh with his fingertips, making her shiver at the touch. "And I mean that. They haven't begun to realise what you are yet. This city will wake up to you—tomorrow, next week, a month from now—and when that happens you won't have the time of day for me again."

"You're cheating again," Simonis murmured but she had coloured a little at the compliment, and dropped her eyes for a moment to hide her pleasure and confusion.

"All right," Virgillus said, tugging playfully at her hair, "not you, then. Let's see. Wait, I know. Have you ever actually seen one of the wild tribes—a Vannid, or a Vesigar?"

"I don't know. Should I have? How would I know? Why? What do they look like?"

"Well, the Vannid tribesmen are dark, and they tattoo their cheekbones—I am told it has something to do with the number of enemies they have slain, and the ones whose faces are blue with tattoos are dangerous men indeed, quick tempered and prone to kill first and ask questions later...."

"I've never seen one of those, I am certain I would have remembered!"

"I don't think they travel much, or have much to do with cities," Virgillus said. "I confess I have never seen one with my own eyes either, and what I tell you I have heard others tell—have you ever read the writings of Eleazar bar Yabin?"

"Who is he?"

"He travels around the world, seeking lost places and making maps of them for those who would follow him. He has written about many wild tribes that nobody else has ever seen. The Vannid tribesmen are as wild and lost as they come—but the Vesigars, now—they're almost civilised. They pray to a multitude of gods, of course, they are still barbarians, but I know that the man who is now their king has spent several years of his boyhood here in the city. He still cannot sign his name, but ever since he set foot in Visant he is supposed to have admired the Empire and tried to emulate it as best his could. And has always wished to have closer ties with it."

"Is he coming back to the city?" Simonis said, her eyes opening wide. "Will we get to see him?"

"Not he," Virgillus said. "He is sending his son here, Rathauric by name— for what reason, I don't know. As far as I can make out, this is a young man too old for the schoolroom but apparently too young to hold any kind of official responsibility at his father's court...even if he were allowed to do so."

"Allowed to? Why wouldn't he be?"

"From what I hear the lad is illegitimate, born of a concubine and not of the Queen. That may well have a bearing on whether he can inherit from King Vathalric at all, under their law. Possibly that is part of the reason that he is being sent here—to learn first-hand about how an Empire is run and to take that knowledge back to his people. Perhaps I was wrong, and there *is* an education planned after all, just not a formal one from the University halls. But him, you may well see—at the Hippodrome, if nowhere else. He's a young man and his blood will run hot—and no doubt he will have money to spend when the bets open at the races. But I am not at all sure how open this is going to be—whether his name and his rank will even be revealed, or if he is to come here under an assumed identity. Hostage, or honoured guest? Who knows…? So, there, you have your bargain with me. Watch out for a fair-haired barbarian prince in the late summer." He reached out and ruffled her hair. "Don't let him turn your head."

When they parted, Virgillus gave Simonis the first piece of real jewellery she had ever owned, a necklace with a bright garnet fitted into a hammered gold setting.

"The solidi," he said, passing on the pouch containing a sum agreed on between himself and Cicatrice before the tryst had been allowed to proceed, "you will probably have to share with others. This necklet, that's for you. It came from somewhere far away—it's a barbarian piece, look at the way it has been worked, they do not handle gems so in Visant—and I am afraid it is of no great value as these things are reckoned in the city markets. But it's a pretty thing, and it's mine to give, and it gives me pleasure to think of you wearing it, of that gold touching that soft skin at your throat." He traced the line of her collar bone with a finger as he spoke, making Simonis shiver. "Don't forget me."

Cicatrice had been very interested to learn about the arrival of the Vesigar prince, and very pleased with the results of Simonis's first liaison. Virgillus sent her a few messages in the aftermath, and they met once or twice in the months that followed—but Virgillus had proved right in his prophetic words that Simonis herself would prove to be the city's next star. She had poise, she had charm, she had the gift of laughter—and she had Cicatrice behind her, a shrewd and experienced guide who shaped and supervised her career. Simonis quickly proved to be a popular attraction at both the Hippodrome and on the party circuit in the city after dark. Her days as Circassaë's slave girl were numbered as she too acquired a busy schedule, a wardrobe of filmy costumes which needed maintenance, and a need for an errand-runner of her own.

She had also been sent by Cicatrice to some half-dozen or so new lovers. These were carefully chosen, but Virgillus had been the last gift of gentleness that Cicatrice had bestowed upon her.

Her second tryst was with a wealthy patrician, who staying behind by arrangement after a dancing engagement with the troupe at one of his lavish dinner parties. The house was not unlike the one where she had hidden, when she had still been innocent, outside the banquet hall on the terrace inlaid with rich mosaic; she could not help but remember that house as her patrician lover's thick fingers crusted with golden rings spread her thighs for him to enter her, and wonder whether he had a sad, lonely, aristocratic wife waiting for him in the women's wing of the house, knowing where he was, what he was doing and whom with, resigned that it would not end with Simonis, that there would be other dancers in his bed almost before Simonis herself had left it, knowing that the man had a taste for the kind of young and supple flesh that she, the wife, could no longer offer. She had to take a little time out from the trade after her third assignation, from which she returned bruised and even bloodied—she had brought back the information for which Cicatrice had sent her to this particular man, but her lover and source had had a taste for rough play, and had demanded absolute, and very physical, submission. Simonis had remembered Circassaë's words and had tried to hide her emotions as best she could but she had actually felt fear, and the signs of fear which she was unable to stop from escaping her seemed to drive her partner to ever greater heights of arousal.

"They will not *all* be kind," Circassaë had said, rubbing salve into raw flesh where Simonis's wrists had been bound too tightly. "You were lucky with Virgillus. Don't use him as something to compare the others to. It's the worst of them that you need to keep in your mind—because then everything that comes your way can be borne...."

Simonis had taken the advice to heart, and learned her lessons, as hard as they sometimes were. By the time that summer came and she turned thirteen years old she became one of the youngest performers in the Visant Hippodrome, and also one of the most sought after.

But Cicatrice still controlled it all—and the higher she climbed, the more sought after she became, the more valuable she grew to his enterprise and the more exacting and stringent the things he required of her. The Hippodrome spymaster knew she was capable of extracting the kind of information that he wanted access to—but all too often it came locked into the shape of men ever more highly placed, more trusted, deeper and deeper into the hierarchy...and older. They had no problem with liaisons with somebody of Simonis's tender years, but she began to chafe at being urged into the beds of men whose grown children had children not far from her own age.

She did see the Vesigar prince in the Hippodrome on a number of occasions, just as Virgillus had foretold—but she did not get anywhere near him. The women he took from the Hippodrome were not part of Cicatrice's network;

they were expendable, empty-headed, no more than a warm body for a man's bed, and if they came to grief or to bodily harm, not much would be lost by the Hippodrome as a whole. There was not much that was important to Visant that Cicatrice could learn directly from what was by all accounts a hot-headed, quarrelsome foreign would-be princeling prone to picking knife fights with the wrong people—and anything that he needed to know *about* the Vesigar prince he could learn through other channels, better informed channels, through men to whom he could send the likes of Simonis and get far more for his money than just a pleasant tumble for the girl and a bag-full of the solidi which the prince was reportedly rather free with.

Simonis, who had never taken kindly to being told what to do or what not to do, balked directly only once, refusing an assignation with an aged Imperial functionary, certain that one of two scenarios would play out. Either she would have to endure the old man's fumblings, and she could not make up her mind whether she was more afraid that he would succeed or that he would fail at possessing her, or else he would not make the attempt himself at all and would get what he wanted from her by handing her over to a younger and rougher man, perhaps more than one, while he watched. Circassaë's advice was still valid—Simonis could probably live through both if she had to—but neither situation appealed, and neither was inconceivable. She had simply recoiled, just this once, from putting herself in that position, of being wasted utterly on someone incapable of either enjoying her company or giving her enjoyment without the potential of her possibly getting mauled, possibly more seriously hurt, in the process.

But she was left in no doubt as to just how much power Cicatrice wielded over her life after she told him that no information was worth that price, as her engagements took a sudden dive for no apparent reason over one of the busiest months of the Hippodrome calendar. She had a few contacts of her own by that time and managed to tide herself over the lean patch—but she had acquired a taste for the good life by that time, and she had not had time to become as well established as she needed to be to make a go of things on her own. When Cicatrice finally sent her a message with no more than a time and a place, she went, meekly enough. It was something she stored away for the future, the smouldering resentment of being owned, of being given orders and expected to obey them. She would not make the mistake of openly defying Cicatrice again—but she had learned enough, by this time, to know how to do things subtly and quietly, and she had plans of her own.

She had taken the lesson to heart. She was still commanded and controlled by Cicatrice but she bided her time and appeared to be pliant and obedient enough over the next year. It seemed to be enough time for Cicatrice to let his eye slip off her for a moment or two as he gathered in new recruits and needed to spend more of his time, energy and attention in starting their training. Simonis used the lull to initiate a few liaisons of her own, sweetening the pot for Cicatrice by bringing in information he had not expected, something for nothing, as it were. Simonis weighed one man against another, never staying too long in any orbit, always keeping an eye out for an opportunity she could exploit, any loophole that was wide enough to let her slip through.

When a chance finally came, it was some time later. She had turned fifteen that summer and, once the season had closed at the Hippodrome, picked her own off-season lover that year. Gallienus might not have been the kind of man someone with Simonis's standing could have chosen—at least, not yet. He was well-off, that was true, but he was still far too newly arrived in the city from the Crescent kingdoms' city of Thyra to be well placed for any instant advancement—but that was only because he was still learning how the system worked. For that, Simonis was an ideal teacher. As the summer turned and the cold autumn winds began to scour the streets of Visant, Simonis and Gallienus retired to a villa near the sea and closed out the world while she showed him how to grease his paths through the complicated Imperial bureaucracy, placing himself well for any potential opportunities to fall into his lap—and when one did, Simonis was there to help him figure out how to put it to best use.

They pored over the parchments together—an offer of a Governorship, admittedly far from the Imperial capital and somewhere on the ancient Afaris coast, close to the half-mythical lands from whence came the barbarian Vannid tribesmen of the tattooed faces of whom Simonis had heard, years ago now, from Virgillus of the Imperial foreign office. But it was for sale nonetheless, and cheap at the price, and a Governor was still a Governor and in a few years Gallienus could return to Visant in triumph, wealthy, and with a title which nobody could take away from him and which could be a stepping stone for greater things.

"It's still exile," he mused, looking at a crudely drawn map lying between the two of them as they lay, Simonis's long legs twined with his own, on a nest of furs piled before the villa's large fireplace which had served them as a couch for that afternoon's dalliance. The map showed the province Gallienus was considering taking into his hand, an open stretch of sea between the Afaris coast and the City of Gold, wide and empty and a long way to go from the centre of all things.

"But it's three cities," Simonis said. It had been she who had brought up the subject now, while they were still slow-eyed with the aftermath of shared passion. "Three cities, and a huge back country. With a Governor's garrison at your command. Remember, a long way from Visant doesn't just mean exile—it also means that you are far more independent, and nobody will question your decisions. You are free to do what you want, as long as you don't betray the Empire, and anything you collect there will be yours."

"I have the money," Gallienus said, frowning. "It would be a simple thing. I would need to sign a document, and hand over a pouch...."

"And you would be Governor," Simonis said, lying back, allowing the firelight to play along her body, allowing the coverlet draped artfully on her hip her to slip just enough to get Gallienus's attention rapidly focused on something that was no longer the prospect of ruling three cities on the Afaris coast.

But as he reached out for her she stopped him, lacing her fingers into his own and unleashing upon him the full power of the beautiful dark eyes which were justly famous in the City.

"But there is more to this than just gold," Simonis murmured, holding his gaze with her own, taking the moment, playing a dangerous game and knowing that the price she herself might be called on to pay if this gambit went wrong would be far more than Gallienus even knew.

"What is it?" he asked, his cheeks flushed, his voice hoarse with his desire.

Simonis held him at bay for just another moment longer, and then allowed his hand to drop until it just brushed the shape of her breast under the coverlet. "Take me with you," she whispered. "You have to take me with you."

CHAPTER EIGHT

Valerian Augustus might have been pondering his legacy and the identity of his successor, but the God who apparently gave him such a generous vision of who that successor might be did not seem to be in a hurry to take the aging Emperor from his throne.

"I all but ran down Sarrus in the garden the other day," Leontes reported to Maxentius over a breakfast meeting. "On his way from the Emperor's chambers. It seems that Valerian Augustus was not, uh, feeling all that well that morning. Sarrus growled something about how he hoped that if he ever thought about growing old, someone should smother him in his bed."

"There wouldn't be a lack of takers," Maxentius said.

Leontes allowed himself a quick grunt that might have passed for a laugh. "Neither of them are on their deathbeds yet. And don't underestimate Sarrus."

But it was obvious to everyone that the Emperor was feeling his years. He was getting more prone to the megrims and ill-tempers of age every day. In a way that made him more and more conscious of who and what he was. He was incapable of grasping the concept of stepping aside in favour of a younger man, and taking his ease in the days of his twilight years; he was Emperor, chosen for his crown by a woman who was herself the daughter and wife of Emperors, and he had been placed on his throne by the will of God and the acclamation of his people. Emperors did not resign, or retire. They died wearing their crown. Valerian, however heavy he found that crown at times, was powerless to lay it down. When the end came, it would come—until then, he was Augustus, Emperor, even though much of the workload that an Emperor would ordinarily have shouldered now fell to underlings who performed the work and set the finished projects at the foot of the throne to be blessed with the Emperor's seal.

Sarrus already had a couple of his own people in key positions—but somehow Valerian had imprinted on the face of young Maxentius, who found himself raised by no less than Imperial decree from the ranks of secretaries and scribes to being directly responsible to the two Senators in charge of directing the Imperial Foreign Office. One of these two men was a Sarrus protégé and made Maxentius's life a little more difficult whenever he could—just because he knew Sarrus would have approved of that. But Maxentius's astonishing facility for assimilating knowledge, and particularly his knack for learning languages simply by paying attention, worked in his favour. He also quickly proved that he was close-mouthed, trustworthy, and—perhaps most importantly—impervious to bribery. That alone made him a useful man for his particular position, because despite the outward veneer that the Imperial City had laid upon him he remained at his core a country boy, grown into a man of relatively simple tastes and appetites, who considered himself more than amply endowed with everything he needed for his needs to be met.

It was, perhaps, his possession of the House of Peacocks, a discreet yet palatial residence where he lived alone, except for the presence of a handful of servants and secretaries, that brought him to mind as the potential host when King Vathalric chose to send his son Rathauric to Visant. Rathauric, born of a king and a royal mistress and with two living siblings whose mother was Vathalric's consort Queen, was not in line—at least officially—for his father's throne. But he had been raised in the king's own household, and had never been treated as anything other than royal. It didn't entirely work in his favour—he had all the arrogance and vanity of royalty without ever having had it curbed by a sense of royal responsibility. That was something that Maxentius found out quickly when the Rathauric arrived to be quartered in his house—Maxentius had had to step in and put a stop to a wild party that the young prince planned, despite the fact that he was not, in fact, supposed to advertise his identity and presence in Visant. He was there supposedly on a somewhat covert mission of being fostered at the pre-eminent court of the age, learning (at least his father apparently hoped so) the craft of statesmanship at the place where the rules of reigning over an empire had been forged – but it was not something that was meant to be common knowledge.

But that was not the way things worked out in the end.

"All I know is that it would have been impossible for him to have such a party if the guest list was not aware of who he really was," Maxentius said to his father, having dressed down his royal guest rather sharply and left him practically under house-arrest at the House of Peacocks while he sought Leontes's advice. "Few people on that list would have come to a party thrown by a barbarian from the provinces—I saw it, and it had some high-ranking names on it. They *know* who he is. And now so does the rest of the city."

"You think the guests were out to find favour where they could?" Leontes asked. "Rathauric might not be in line to be the next King, but he's close to the Vesigar throne—and if somebody has trading interests in the region, he would be a good contact to have, once he goes back home."

"Does everyone in this city only think of gain?" Maxentius asked sharply.

"In the long run," said Leontes. "If you don't look out for yourself you get under the wheels of the chariot of your neighbour, who is protecting his own interests. But Rathauric's presence here wasn't supposed to be all that widely known."

"I don't know *who* leaked it. All I can tell you is that I know none of my people did—they know better than to speak of what goes on in my house— and that leaves the office, but I can't conceive of who...."

"There are always leaks," Leontes said, a little grimly. "You cannot stop loose tongues in this city. I don't know *who*, precisely, but I have a good idea of *how*. There's a man—once a good soldier, but betrayed and disillusioned and now too crippled to be of any use as a fighting man—who found a niche in the Hippodrome, it's been there many years now. I've never been able to prove it to the satisfaction of the law and he's too canny to take out of the picture the quick and dirty way—but although he is technically one of the Golden Crown faction's top choreographers, and don't ask how a soldier comes down to being the dance-master for a troupe of acrobats, I can tell a trained hand when I see one at work and I know that he is the hub of something down there."

"He sounds...conspicuous," Maxentius said. "If he is the one gathering information...."

"Not he, himself," Leontes said. "I said he was the *hub* of something. He has a good network, he deals in information, I know that much because I bought information from that quarter myself—indirectly of course. He doesn't know I know about it."

"But if you know there's a leak and you've done nothing about it...?"

"He was a soldier, once," Leontes said curtly. "One has a responsibility."

"You're protecting the man?"

"He has his uses," Leontes said. "I think he runs a covey of young women, the dancers and mimes of the Golden Crown troupe—they are for hire, they perform at enough private parties at the houses of high-ranking Senators to have overheard more than just the identity of a stray foreign visitor—and of course there's always the potential that they pay for their information with far more than just a dance. And men will spill far more than their seed for a pretty young woman who knows how to ask the right questions."

"You said he was skirting the law," Maxentius said. "If there is a way of taking this down...."

"I find it useful," Leontes said. "It's better, after all, to know precisely where the snake is hiding in the tall grass rather than step on one by accident. So long as I know there's a spy I can deal with that—I've 'leaked' information before, things that I knew were not true but which it was useful to have others act upon while under the misapprehension that they were."

"All right, but what am I to do with Rathauric now, with his real identity known to far too many people in high places?"

Leontes shrugged. "Go with it," he said. "After all, *he* wasn't the spy—and if he were, then all the better that his name and rank be known, isn't it? It would be all the harder for him to gather and pass on any information we *don't* want the Vesigar court to know, if people know enough to be wary about him."

"He has money," Maxentius said. "He didn't come here destitute. Whatever his father has in mind for him, it isn't to starve in Visant. He behaves like a prince, not a common tribesman."

"Then let him," Leontes said. "I will make sure that there is a security detail on him, that isn't your problem. He will be followed, and he will be safe from assassins, at least. You—you just make sure that he *doesn't* get access to anything that his father might find too useful. Beyond that...you're providing him with bed and board, and that is all you are required to do."

Maxentius went home with an ill grace; he was prepared to put up with the house-guest quartered on him, but he didn't have to like it. The Vesigar princeling was more or less of an age with himself, but the two young men couldn't have been more different in interests and inclinations. If Vathalric had intended for his son's sojourn in Visant to be any kind of formal education— the kind that Maxentius, as a boy, had come rushing to the city to receive— the Vesigar king was sadly mistaken; Rathauric was less interested in the City's learning than in the city's wine, women, and revelry. The young Maxentius's knowledge of the Hippodrome, when he first came to Visant, had been limited to more or less its geographical location and its reputation. Rathauric, on the other hand, quickly learned to know the Hippodrome and its denizens rather too well. He flung money around freely, making extravagant bets on the races and not caring if he lost, which made him instantly likeable amongst the Hippodrome's racegoers—and he lost little time in running the gamut of the Hippodrome's women.

After the first few times, he knew better than to bring them home to Maxentius's spare, almost ascetic, household—Maxentius had made his disapproval and his sense of a potential for trouble clear, and Rathauric had quickly been provided with a bolthole where he could take his women. Oddly, with that particular issue removed from the equation, the relationship between the two young men began to develop into a steady friendship—they found that they complemented one another, with Maxentius (although the younger by more than a year) providing a stable, solid grounding for the fiery Rathauric who served, in turn, to kindle Maxentius's own slower-burning passions into a higher flame. Giving Maxentius a potentially powerful aristocratic ally—even if Rathauric never claimed the Vesigar throne himself—was hardly the result that those who mooted Rathauric's quartering in Maxentius's house had had in mind, but after the first few weeks of difficult adjustment, the two young men had both begun to conceive a grudging liking for one another and then, as Rathauric's visit lengthened into months, an ability to see past what they had initially perceived as unforgivable faults and beyond into mutual respect.

There was no pressing need for Rathauric's presence back at his father's court, and the Emperor didn't seem to care whether the young man stayed or went—and Rathauric was finding the city congenial. King Vathalric made sure that his son's upkeep was paid for with barbarian gold which arrived in regular shipments, and beyond that, everybody seemed to be content to let things slide. It was with some astonishment that Maxentius woke up to his house-guest's first anniversary in the city. Once again he consulted with Leontes as to what his best course of action would be—but Leontes counselled that he throw Rathauric a year-mind party, celebrating the day of his first arrival into Visant, and leave it at that.

But Visant, the City of Gold, as usual had its own plans.

Maxentius usually left the reins of his social life in the hands of Arkadios—an experienced senior servant of his own inner chambers, a eunuch once trained directly by Sarrus whom Leontes had rescued from Sarrus's wrath, perhaps literally saving his life, and who had since sworn eternal loyalty to the house of his saviour. Arkadios was a taciturn man of middle age who had gifts Maxentius valued highly—he wasted no words on unnecessary chatter, he performed the tasks he was set quickly and capably, and he never bothered his master with irrelevant matters.

Because he knew that last attribute was true, Maxentius always paid attention to Arkadios when the eunuch *did* choose to disturb him at his work—because the matters he brought to his attention would never be trivial. Arkadios kept a finger on the social pulse of the city, and knew what parties Maxentius should be seen at, and which ones he could safely afford to ignore—and it was Arkadios who saw to it that Maxentius did show his face at the correct social events, properly dressed for them, even when his young master muttered darkly about the waste of time and the frippery that he was required to wear.

It was Arkadios, naturally, who was in charge of planning Rathauric's anniversary party. But about a week before it was due to happen, he brought another invitation into Maxentius's study.

"I know, *despotes*—I know that you already have the anniversary party to go to this week—but this invitation came in late, and I don't think that it is a gathering that you should shun. There will be important people there, people whom you should know."

"I don't suppose they can make an appointment at the office in the morning," Maxentius grumbled, taking the parchment that Arkadios held dangling from his hand. "And it's late in the season. Who, what?"

"A young man who is strongly tipped to become the next Governor in one of the distant provinces," Arkadios said. "He has climbed fast and far since he came to the City, and he has made some dangerous friends, and worse enemies—and when his Governorship is over and he returns to Visant there will be scores to settle. It will be important then to know whose fancy he has taken, and whose enmity he has earned."

"He won't be back from his province for years," Maxentius said.

"And he may not go to the province at all," Arkadios returned. "This is a man to watch. You should be seen watching."

"Oh, all right," Maxentius said grudgingly. "Send an acceptance. It's always good to keep one's eyes open."

It *was* late in the season, the very end of summer, rather later than parties like this were usually thrown. The wind was already cool in the streets outside, and the doors of the banqueting chamber were closed against the night as the guests began to arrive.

For some reason Maxentius had been expecting a rather more intimate gathering than what he found when he turned up at the house of the Senator who was giving the party for the possible Governor candidate, Gallienus, late of the city of Thyra in the Crescent Kingdoms to the east of Visant. Maxentius sized him up at the introduction, saw the proud tilt of the man's head and the glint of something that was almost arrogance in his eye, and knew that Arkadios had been right in his assessment—this would be a man to like or to despise, but he would leave nobody ambivalent towards him. There was raw ambition in Gallienus, something he did not bother to hide, and Maxentius instantly had his guard up. This was a man who might be capable of anything to further his goals, once he was shown how. It would be a damned good thing, Maxentius decided as he walked away from the man of the hour and into the already crowded reception room beyond, that Gallienus would be safely away from the city for at least two years. They could deal with him when he came back—*if* he came back. Then they would have had time to size him up, to let his record as Governor speak for him, to prepare for him.

The social circuit of Visant had long since taught Maxentius how to put on a social face, feigning an interest in the most boring of dinner conversation, and he was cursed all through dinner with the company of a Senator well past his prime, whose favourite topic seemed to be himself and the many ways that his body was letting him down. It was with a sense of relief that Maxentius realised that the night's entertainments were about to begin, and that he would have a respite from his garrulous and ailing dinner companion.

The party's host had outdone himself where the entertainment arrangements had been concerned, because he had two rival troupes there that night. The evening was opened by the Golden Crown dancers—first an intricate and graceful knot of a dance by the main group of dancers, and then a solo, by a young woman with wine-dark hair and kohl-rimmed eyes, barefoot, her shoulders glistening with gold dust. Maxentius knew her—he had seen her dance before. Circassaë, the pride of the Golden Crown dancers. The party's host had obviously spared no expense.

She was a professional in so many ways—she danced for no man alone and yet gave the impression that she danced only for the one whose eye she deliberately caught and lingeringly held as she executed some exquisite step of her dance. Even Maxentius felt those dark eyes on him, her look having an almost physical weight to it, a sense of something fragile yet infinitely strong landing on his skin. She ended her dance almost entirely nude but with the full wealth of her glorious hair released and veiling her body to below her hips, and she smiled through the mahogany strands of it as she bent to pick up the handful of gold solidi that had been thrown at her feet as her dance had ended.

The program stopped there for a moment while the dancers regrouped and the next faction took the floor, and Maxentius used the lull to excuse himself and withdraw for a moment of solitude and fresh air.

The inner courtyard garden was empty, and the chill of early autumn had started to find its way into the stone walls. The fountain in the midst of the court was still, and there was an autumnal scent to the evening air, a memory of blossom, a promise of the damp cool Visant autumn to come. It was refreshing after the close, stuffy air of the banqueting chamber, and Maxentius stood with his feet apart, his hands linked on the small of his back, his head thrown back, taking deep breaths of it.

He was always very aware of his surroundings. The sound that he heard was almost inaudible, the merest whisper of a light footfall. He whipped his head around in that direction instantly, narrowing his eyes into the shadows.

"Who is there?"

The shadows did not yield a face—but he could discern a shape there, a shape that was too graceful and slender to be a man, a shape veiled in long dark hair shifting in the breeze.

"Ask for me," the shadow said. "Cicatrice is the man to speak to in the Hippodrome. Arkadios will know. Ask for me, and before your anniversary party."

"Circassaë?" Maxentius said, dropping his own voice in response to hers.

But the shadows were empty of wine-dark hair and whispered words and the soft light step of the dancer.

Maxentius might have led a largely solitary life, but he was no monk— and he had had his share of the more cultured Hippodrome courtesans. Not Circassaë, though—their paths had never crossed. And now he found himself intrigued by this stealthy approach in the night, still flushed from her dance, with a sense of urgency to her words that had nothing to do with a physical urge—she would never have done this, not she, not the experienced courtesan of her level, it was clients who asked for *her* and not the other way around. But she had taken the chance that someone else might see her out here, might hear what she had said.

The anniversary party. Rathauric's anniversary party. That was supposed to be a surprise, known to a bare handful of people—the servants in charge of organising the event, and forty or so invited guests to whom the invitations had gone out less than two weeks before.

She could not have known about the party.

She had known about it.

Maxentius's jaw tightened. He prided himself on running a tight ship with his own household, with carefully picked people who would not run out and tattle on their master's affairs. One of the guests? But whom he had told? And why?

He thrust the matter of Gallienus and his potential to the back of his mind, and he forced himself to endure the rest of the evening, excusing himself at the earliest hour that etiquette would permit. At the House of Peacocks, being divested of his party finery by Arkadios, Maxentius was already giving instructions to his servant to have Circassaë sent to his house the very next night.

He sent a sedan for her, carried by slaves which belonged to Leontes; it arrived without lights, without insignia, and was admitted quietly at the gate. The woman within emerged shrouded in a dark cloak and was ushered upstairs to Maxentius's chamber by Arkadios himself. When the eunuch bowed and withdrew, closing the doors to the chamber behind him, Circassaë finally threw back the cloak from her magnificent hair; the light from the candles burning in the room and the fire that had been lit in the hearth glinted on jewels in her hair, in her ears, at her throat.

Maxentius's eyebrow rose a little.

"Extravagant costume," he commented dryly.

"I had to make it look good," Circassaë said, smiling a little.

"Well, then, let me see," Maxentius said.

She let the cloak slip to the ground and stood revealed in a sleeveless white silk dress, both slim wrists encased in golden bracelets of barbarian make, her feet barely showing beneath the hem wrapped in thonged sandals glinting with jewels.

"I am suitably honoured," Maxentius said after a moment, "that I was thought to be worth all this. I have wine. Will you have a cup?"

She stepped closer. "I will be glad of it. It was a cool night to be out."

Their hands touched briefly as he handed her the wine goblet and their eyes slid apart for a moment—but then Maxentius had himself under control again. He gestured for her to sit and she did, gracefully, folding her body in a way that made him briefly catch his breath—and then, when they were both settled, he raised his goblet to her by way of salute.

"As I said, I am honoured to be worth all this," he said. "That includes your invitation in the garden."

"I do not do that often," she said, and her voice was low and smoky again. "I go where I am sent, I go where the treasure is...."

"The man to whom you are responsible," he said slowly, tilting his head a little at his companion. "This...Cicatrice. He is scarred, or crippled, to earn that name. I know of him, and of what he does. But it would be to him that you would take your...treasure. I would be the one you take it from. That is the way this works, does it not?"

She held his gaze with her own, a completely frank and open look. "Yes, I run information," she said. "I am what he has made me. And I have taken many Palace secrets into the warrens of the Hippodrome, for him to bury, or to sell. But what I have learned now—I have no way of knowing whether he will bury or sell this one, and I will not knowingly be party to murder."

Maxentius sat up. "Murder?"

"I come about the young prince," she said. "Lord Rathauric. I know he is under your protection, at this house. I know that he has been here a year. I know that there is a party planned to mark this."

"Who...." Maxentius began, and then put down his goblet, leaning a little closer. "Well, we'll get to that. What do you know about this party which was supposed to be a secret?"

"There is...a plan," Circassaë said. "For late that night. After all the dancing is done and everyone is expected to be well in their cups. There are...tensions between the old eastern half of the Empire and the Vesigar kingdom—it would go well for some people if Lord Rathauric were to inherit the throne instead of Amalric, the King's true son. There are others, for whom it would go ill indeed if Lord Rathauric were to step any closer to the Vesigar throne than he already is—and they know that the King is often displeased with his true-son, who is a known drunk and carouser, despite being so young...."

"Not unlike Rathauric himself," Maxentius muttered. "You are exceedingly well informed on Vesigar politics."

"I am well informed on politics in general," Circassaë said. "There are good sources for what I tell you. I come to bring a warning—there is a plan to kill Lord Rathauric at his party. I am not certain what the final frame story will be—but the people behind the plot include a high-ranking Vesigar noble who is here in the city right now, keeping himself out of sight...and at least one official from the Palace, from a faction which would like nothing better than to stir up trouble right now, trouble that would need an army sent out to quell. Preferably led by the Emperor's nephew, the general. There are already other plans, about the other two nephews...."

"This is information already bought and paid for by the man you call Cicatrice," Maxentius said. "Are you not betraying your master to me right now?"

"I thought that you also should know…if the safety of the prince means anything to you, or is your responsibility in any way. As I said, I don't know where the frame story will be set.…"

Maxentius nodded to himself, thinking fast. He wondered if he had missed noticing that the Emperor was feeling more poorly than usual, if Sarrus was scenting an endgame, if Sarrus hadn't suddenly brought to mind the Emperor's dream and the man who apparently fulfilled it and now saw Leontes and Maxentius as ranged against him in a power play. If Rathauric were dead, the Emperor's nephews scattered, and suspicion of murder cast on Maxentius and perhaps Leontes himself—the way to the throne would lie a little easier for Sarrus and the man he had in mind to wear the Imperial tiara.

"I will take care of it," he said at last, after a long pause, and stood. Circassaë unfolded her legs and got to her feet also, laying aside her goblet. Standing beside one another they were almost of a height, with her only a handspan shorter; they could meet and hold one another's eyes. "There is still the matter of the source who told you about an event which was not supposed to be known outside a select circle."

Circassaë's lips curved into a small, secretive smile. "If I worked for you, would you expect me to give up my sources so easily to someone else?"

"You already work for me," he said, reaching out to lace his fingers into hers. "We just need to hammer out the terms."

"Backwards," she murmured. "I am here on a pretext you cannot turn into working for you. Any money that changes hands goes to the man who sent me here in the first place…and who will expect me to bring back treasure from *this* night, too."

"That can be arranged," Maxentius said, and kissed her,

When he lifted his head from hers again she gave a small sigh, laying the palm of her hand flat against his chest. He covered it with his own free hand.

"Can you do this? Truly?" he questioned softly. "I confess I find the prospect appealing—you can give me access to a wealth of information I would not otherwise easily get. But you are already beholden—and I would not wish you to risk your life on this."

"I already have," Circassaë said, "from the moment I chose to speak to you in the garden. If Cicatrice knew this meeting was not your doing but mine, he would…be very angry."

"He would not harm you?"

"Not permanently. Not obviously. He does not need to—I am not a slave, he doesn't own me, but he can control my existence… in other ways."

"And what does he expect you to bring him from this room?"

"He takes what I can glean," Circassaë said. "And…he already knows about the party.…"

Maxentius nodded. "Then I can give you a few extra details to sweeten the pot. They may not be entirely correct, but then that's a chance he has to take when his information comes in this manner."

She clung to his hand for a moment. "And you can stop it? The killing?"

"I have no doubt that there will be no murder done at Rathauric's party. Thanks to you. Now…let me show you how much I appreciate your coming to me with this. Consider it the first instalment on the new contract."

Circassaë was surprisingly light when he bent down to slide his right arm under her knees and sweep her up off the floor. She let her head drop on his shoulder with a sigh, closing her eyes, and he carried her over to the bed that had been made ready for them.

CHAPTER NINE

Rathauric drank and caroused on the night of his party, oblivious to what was taking place behind the scenes. Maxentius's people had set a watch on the supply of the sweet honey wine that only Rathauric, the barbarian prince from the north, had a taste for—had allowed it to be tainted with poison, and then calmly plucked the poisoner out of there after he was done. The tainted keg was disposed of; fresh wine was procured; Rathauric accepted his next goblet of it with not the faintest idea of what had been going on in the kitchens.

The man who poisoned the wine vat was a throwaway scapegoat—he had been supposed to blend in with the servants, do his work, and then quietly clear out of the house where the party had been held. He had been cheaply bought, and the original plan had been for him, too, to have quietly vanished after he had left the party—something that came to light after the man who had hired him to do the dirty work had also been picked up by the authorities. It was fairly obvious why he had needed to hire somebody else to do the dirty work. He could no more have blended in with the servants in the kitchens than he could have pretended to be Rathauric himself—he was a dark, wiry little bandy-legged horse trader from the northern steppes who had found the city to be a much more congenial environment than his distant home, with a face full of scars, and teeth black and rotten from a life-long habit of chewing betel nut and an addiction to sweet halwah. It was less easy to make the next connection—that the horse trader, who had long been known to the Prefecture in the City, had himself been bought by the middle son of a high-ranking Senatorial family with strong trading interests in the Middle Sea.

It was only when the scandal finally broke at least within the Palace circles that Rathauric realised how close he had come to death.

It was a changed and much sobered young man who sought out Maxentius on the balcony of the House of Peacocks where Maxentius, wrapped in a warm cloak, stood watching a storm rolling in from the north.

"I owe you my life," Rathauric said in a low voice, stepping up to the balustrade beside his host.

Maxentius turned his head a fraction. "This wind might put paid to that," he said pragmatically, taking in Rathauric standing there in a short sleeveless tunic that ended at his knees and his feet bare in thonged sandals.

Rathauric laughed. "You southerners are soft. I've walked barefoot across snow when I needed to. A little wind will do me no harm. But you…you stood between me and poison. That would have been rather a different matter. I was careless."

"So was I," Maxentius said, straightening. "That will not happen again."

"But you are not responsible for me," Rathauric said. "In both our worlds, I am a man, and I ought to have taken a care for my own safety. Instead, I've allowed you to protect me, like a child. I ought to have taken thought myself of what I was doing, of what I was and where I was. My father would have been very disappointed if I had allowed myself to be killed."

Maxentius's eyebrow lifted in puzzlement. "You would have been dead," he said.

"Yes, but my memory would have been reviled," Rathauric said. "I have you to thank for my legacy now, whatever that is supposed to be. But for the present…I have sent a message back home, to the court. It is time I returned."

Maxentius pondered for a moment, the rising wind stirring his fair hair. "And what," he inquired, with genuine interest, "are you going to do there once you do go back?"

Rathauric shrugged. "It is to be hoped I learned *something* while I was out here," he said, "if only that it is necessary to take responsibility for watching my own back. I am older than my half-brother, you know—by a mere three months or so, to be sure, but I am the elder nonetheless, and if that had been the only criterion it would have been I who was first in line for my father's throne. But he was the Queen's son, and my mother....." His lips tightened for a moment, and then he shook his head, resigned. "Well, but I have come to terms with that. I will not be King. Amalric will be that. But my father has made me noble—and I will be a leader of men, a landowner with many slaves, a part of the council of lords whether my brother wants me there or not. That, I am going back to. It is time I learned how to shoulder those responsibilities. It's odd....."

His voice petered out and he stood gripping the stone balustrade tightly, his eyes on the black clouds piling on the northern horizon.

"What is odd?" Maxentius asked after the silence stretched out for too long.

Rathauric turned his head a little to catch Maxentius's eye. "That I had to come this close to dying before I could understand that my father had really sent me here to learn how to live," he said. "I will miss this city, you know. And this house."

"Come inside," Maxentius said, suddenly strangely moved by his own reaction to those words. "It's starting to rain."

Rathauric stole a last look over the vista of the garden and the storm clouds and allowed himself to be led away from the balustrade. But even as he stepped into the house and ran his hands through his windblown hair, waiting for Maxentius to secure the doors behind him, his head suddenly came up like a hunting dog's.

"Come with me," he said abruptly.

Maxentius turned, startled. "What?"

"Come with me," Rathauric repeated. "Come home to Ravin with me. To my father's house."

"I have work here," Maxentius said reflexively divesting himself of his cloak. "I can't just...I don't have...why? If you need witnesses to tell your royal father of the events that have just transpired, I can send a man with all the details—including the possible identity of the Vesigar noble who was involved in the plot...yes, there was one," he said, nodding, realising as Rathauric's face changed that this was something he had not known about. "There was someone from your own people who came here to make sure you never returned."

"Then it is more important than ever that I go back, and as soon as possible," Rathauric said. He had gone rather white. "If there are people working against me—people with my father's ear—I have to...you could tell him. You could come—as an ambassador, maybe. An emissary."

"I'm not ranked high enough for those," Maxentius said. "Nor for a hostage."

Rathauric's eyes flashed. "You know that would not be the case."

"It is what some thought you might have been, when you first came here," Maxentius said. "It is what your father was, once, a long time ago. That is the way the game is played."

"They will send you if we ask for you," Rathauric said. "And now...especially now...now that you've told me that my own people can't be trusted...help me get home, Maxentius. Help me get home alive."

"You will find it hard to get a ship now," Maxentius said practically. "It's getting into storm season. If you did find a ship it would be a dangerous and sorry crossing—I've never been on a ship being tossed about on a stormy ocean but I am told it is not a pleasant experience."

"Then I will spend the winter," Rathauric said. "And I will be a burden to the city, to you, for another few months. But the first ship that puts out in the spring—before the Hippodrome opens—I have to be on it. I have to be gone. I have to be home."

"Before the Hippodrome opens?" Maxentius said, unable to stop a grin. "You'll miss the races most of all."

Rathauric returned the grin. "Yes. Well. I will need to find something else to occupy me when I get home to Ravin. And I won't think of the horses and the chariots and the beautiful women, out here in the gentle south where the lemon blossom scents the air. I'll be the warrior my father needs me to be, and leave the pastimes of youth to younger men."

"You sound like you have one foot in the grave," Maxentius said.

It had been meant as a joke, but it cut unexpectedly close to the bone and instead served to quickly sober both of them.

"Come with me," Rathauric said, and this time it was almost a plea. "I will... need a friend there. For at least a little while."

"I do not have leave," Maxentius said, but was conscious of a strange pang of regret as he spoke. It must have shown in his face because Rathauric got a strange glint in his eye.

"That," he said, "I think you can leave to me. I still have *some* influence."

Maxentius smiled and shook his head, an ambivalent gesture—it might have meant a final denial of Rathauric's request, or perhaps an indication of his scepticism of Rathauric's claim of influence. Even he wasn't sure, in that moment. But Rathauric took it as encouragement. Much to Maxentius' complete astonishment he was called in to his office about a month later and informed that he was to be seconded to an embassy accompanying Rathauric back to the Vesigar court at Ravin that spring.

"You will not lose your position," Sarrus, who had delivered the news, told him. The expression on the Chancellor's face made it plain that this situation was not one of his doing and that he would have much preferred Maxentius to be permanently out of the department. "You have a leave of absence. You will be required to report back to the office on what you learn at King Vathalric's court. Anything at all. You will let us be the judge of its importance. You will be instructed before you leave in the method and the expected frequency of your dispatches. We have been instructed to be ready to sail at first opportunity— you have a short while to set your affairs in order before you go. And I might have known."

"You might have known what, Excellency?" Maxentius retained enough presence of mind to ask that much, especially given the rapid development of this particular situation.

"When they decided to quarter Rathauric at the House of Peacocks I warned them that you'd find a way to ingratiate yourself with a foreign power," Sarrus said. "Make sure you do what the Empire asks of you, precisely and completely. Hold anything back….well…you're one misstep away from stepping into a hole not even Leontes of the Guard will be able to dig you out of."

Maxentius's lip curled a little. "I have no intention of betraying my father, my heritage, or my Empire," he said, a little curtly.

Sarrus smiled, but it was not a pleasant smile. "Yes," he said. "Of course."

Maxentius took this conversation to Leontes, who frowned as he turned it over in his mind.

"I will keep an eye on him," he said at last. "Just in case he sees fit to manufacture a tidy little package of treason himself. Did you ever find out how high into the Palace the Rathauric plot went?"

Maxentius shot him a startled look. "You think *Sarrus*…?"

"I wouldn't put it past him. I haven't figured out the angle, yet, although I can think of several ways it might have played for him. But if it was his doing, then he does get what he wanted, which is Rathauric out of the city, one way or another. And you—you are a bonus. He never expected to get rid of you."

"But he didn't seem to like it that I was going on such friendly terms," Maxentius said.

"No, of course not. You will be at the Vesigar court and beyond his influence. Watch the others in your party. At least one of them will be a Sarrus man. Make sure you take a handful of your own people along. At the very least you will need someone you trust to take dispatches back and forth for while you are there."

"I'll keep that in mind," said Maxentius dryly.

"I'll keep an eye on things back here," Leontes said.

Maxentius had no reason to suppose that Leontes would fail at that task, but he had learned the value of redundancy in the flow of information. He sent for Circassaë one more time before he left for Ravin with Rathauric.

She came to the House of Peacocks, once more resplendent, glittering with jewels, swathed in silk.

"We have to keep up appearances," she said coyly, watching him through her eyelashes as he kissed her hand upon her arrival.

"I have no problem with keeping up…appearances," he said, dropping his voice a little at the double entendre. "But there is business to discuss, too. You might have already learned that I am to leave Visant for a sojourn at the Vesigar court—for a short time, anyway. I am leaving Arkadios here, in charge of the household and as a contact for what's going on in the Palace. My father, too, will keep me informed. But as for the pulse of the city itself—I will look to you. Arkadios will have means of reaching me. You can trust him with anything."

Circassaë tilted her head a little. "So will you bring me back some barbarian gold when you return?"

Maxentius threw his head back and laughed. "Keep up your end of the bargain and I'll bring you back coffers of it," he said. "Enough that you will be embarrassed to wear it all in a single lifetime."

They left on an early spring morning, just as the first fingers of the morning sun began to touch the sea, sailing away into the glitter on the water. Maxentius had circled the inner harbour on a small yacht several times since he had come to Visant, but he had never been on a long sea voyage; he was braced for seasickness, the symptoms of which had been gleefully described to him by a far too amused Rathauric as he had boarded the ship. He was not disappointed, even though the seas were calm and winds favourable for the entire journey. By the time he was beginning to find his sea legs and actually enjoy the trip, they had already passed through the channel from the Middle Sea into the Long Sea, and were mere days away from docking at the walled harbour from which they would take horse to Ravin, the Vesigar capital.

The fort was grey stone, leavened only by a handful of colourful banners flying from the two towers at the entrance of the harbour. Rathauric, leaning against the ship's railing up front towards the prow, saw Maxentius's face as they approached and smiled a little grimly.

"You will find no Visant out here," he said. "Things are much more dour up here in the north. Here, at the coast, you can still sometimes smell the lemon-blossom—it's the sea air. But once we start inland, we'll be into bare hills. It's all stone and slate after that, and if there's trees they will be dark ones and they won't shiver and whisper in the breeze—they'll loom over you and growl dark prophecies into your ear as you sleep."

"And you wanted to come back here?" Maxentius said, startled at the sudden cynicism.

"It's home," Rathauric said. "I understand it. And to be honest I was starting to miss the flaxen-haired, white-bosomed wenches of my past. Don't get me wrong, Visant has its share of beautiful women. But here…well, you will see."

"Tell me about your family," Maxentius said.

"My mother lives in a little house apart from the palace," Rathauric said. "The King visits her there…when he pleases. I have my own quarters in the Palace proper, but suitably far away from those of Amalric, who is the heir, and my sister Rothaide and her second husband. I see the Queen seldom, on court occasions. I am not exactly a welcome guest at their own family table when intimate dinners are served. I think my father does love me, as much as he can love me under the circumstances. I have been given…opportunities, and free rein when I wanted it. In his own way, he has indulged me. But I am not the heir."

They were met at the gates of Ravin by a small delegation—small, and, as far as Maxentius's court-trained eye could discern, of second-ranked nobles. King Vathalric was making a gesture of welcoming his son home, but he could not be seen to make more than a token gesture.

"Prince," said the leader of the group sent out to greet them, making a small bow to Rathauric. He spoke in the Vesigar language, but Maxentius knew that word—*prince*—Rathauric had started teaching him a little bit of the language on the sea voyage, and one of the first things to learn had been the correct way to address the royal family. The title "prince" had been used for Amalric, not Rathauric—but it had been a title that Rathauric himself was greeted with upon his return. It might have been an empty honorific, quite possibly used deliberately in front of a visiting foreigner—but it had been used, nonetheless. Maxentius filed that away as potentially useful information. The man said more, but Maxentius's command of the language was still rarefied and he could understand none of the rest of it. It was Rathauric who finally turned to him with a quick translated summary. "My father wishes me to attend him as soon as can be contrived . Your quarters have been made ready; one of these men will take you there. We have time to change into something appropriate in which to meet a King—I will collect you in half an hour, and take you in to present you to him."

"Are you sure that it would be the right time to...." Maxentius began, but Rathauric merely twisted the corner of his mouth into a small grimace.

"If the Queen is present, there will never be a 'right time,'" he said. "Just be ready."

Vathalric Maelgin's reputation, first as a fierce warrior and then as a wise king, preceded him. He had not been a lucky man in his personal life, however. Maxentius had made sure to research him thoroughly before he came here, and knew far more than a casual visitor might. He knew that the king was in his sixties, that he had spent several years as a hostage in Visant when he was a small boy and had returned, a barely bearded youth of twenty or so summers, to claim his throne against the wishes of several powerful nobles. His first queen, pregnant with her first child, had been taken by his enemies, who had ripped the baby from her womb and sent the unborn child, a boy, back to her husband in an unequivocal declaration of war. He had destroyed those enemies with a single-minded passion that had established his right to rule— and none had challenged him since, at least not openly. He had married again and had begotten a son and heir, Amalric, and a daughter who was the apple of his eye—but the princess Rothaide seemed to have inherited her father's ill luck with her family life. She had been barely fifteen when she had first wed a man of her father's choosing—she had fallen pregnant almost immediately, but before her son had had a chance to be born her husband had contracted a virulent fever of some sort and had died raving in his bed. Rothaide had picked her second husband, Valaric, herself—the tales were legion of how she had stood up to her father in open court and told him that she had done her duty, had married according to his will and had produced an heir in line for the throne of that marriage, and that now she was going to follow her own heart. In the end, he had accepted it. Rathauric had mentioned that Rothaide's older son, the child of her first marriage, was now almost three—and that she was pregnant again, expecting Valaric's child early that summer.

Maxentius had known about all the members of the royal side of Rathauric's family, but he had not expected them all to be present when he and Rathauric stepped into the small audience chamber obviously reserved for more intimate gatherings. The Queen sat stiffly on her throne, her features set in a glacial smile. Her daughter, Rothaide, swathed in robes which concealed her pregnancy, was seated in a smaller gilt chair to one side. A man whom Maxentius supposed to be her husband stood beside her. To the side of the Queen's throne stood

Amalric, the heir, who was less than happy to see his half-brother return, and who showed those feelings openly in the frown that sat heavily on his features and on the tense set of his shoulders. His left hand rested in an almost proprietorial manner on the armrest of the throne on his other side, on which sat a man whose iron-grey hair fell long on his back, two narrow braids of it framing his face beneath a crown which was a splendour of barbarian gold. But Maxentius was given little time to observe any more before King Vathalric rose to his feet, and he and Rathauric both dropped to one knee before the throne.

"Welcome home," the king said, in the language of Visant—accented, but correct. He spoke in a voice of command—the words were gentle enough but they were almost an order. "And to your friend and Visant's envoy, welcome to Ravin. I look forward to hearing more about the heart of the Empire."

At some point during their journey to Ravin, Rathauric had described his home to Maxentius as a simpler, more direct place than complicated, subtle Visant—but Maxentius found the Vesigar court just as complicated as the inner circles of the Imperial Palace. Some things might have been expressed more openly—Amalric made no secret that he resented Rathauric and did not trust his foreign friend, the Queen was less than happy to see her husband's bastard back in the orbit of her court and was being pragmatically cultivated by some of the nobles, who were making sure that their own positions were secure whatever the current state of the power play at court—but there were undercurrents at work, and the finely honed instincts for observation and a native peasant shrewdness that he had never quite shed made Maxentius almost preternaturally ideal for the position of being the foreign envoy whose task it was to pass on all carefully gleaned information to the people to whom it might be useful back home.

The character of the old king, Vathalric, particularly intrigued Maxentius—because the King was such an unorthodox mixture of barbarian ruthlessness and polished, civilised manners and mind-set. He had turned with a white-hot fury on the faction who had challenged his standing and murdered his first wife and wreaked bloody revenge for the wrongs done to him—holding his own gory sword high over the lifeless bodies of his enemies. And yet this was a man who had, as a boy, received a certain amount of education while he was hostage in Visant—he could read in two languages, he had appointed court scribes to record his laws and edicts and the lore and tales of his tribe, and he had insisted that his children all receive a similar kind of education.

He was keenly interested in the workings of Visant, and in the Empire's young emissary. He made a point of summoning Maxentius to be present at councils open to public scrutiny, together with a personal interpreter to make sure the proceedings were fully comprehensible to him, and then wished to hear Maxentius's opinion on matters in the aftermath. King Vathalric did not let it end with formal council sessions, either—he would carry on fairly high-powered political discourse with his young guest at formal court dinners, where Maxentius would be seated close to the King at the high table. Maxentius was spending far more time in the company of the King than with Rathauric, who had been the reason he had come to Ravin in the first place.

The feasts were a bit of a shock to Maxentius, used to the all-male gatherings in Visant where the high-born wives and daughters never made an appearance in the banquet halls, and where the only female presence permitted were the hired dancers brought in for the entertainment of the men. In Ravin, the women held high state, just as the men did—and the Queen presided at the state dinners at her husband's side, with Rothaide and other noble ladies, both married and of marriageable age, present. In fact, Rothaide was a particular headache to Maxentius—an obedient daughter bound by tradition who was also highly educated, literate, and who had stood her own ground and chosen her own mate despite being royal. Maxentius found it difficult to reconcile the Rothaide who was so educated and enlightened and emancipated with the Rothaide who had actually chosen for her husband a man like Valaric, a handsome man in his prime to be sure, but by all accounts a traditional brute who held that force trumped learning and that one could not be called a man if one was ever caught with an actual book in one's hands.

They had even discussed the subject of marriage and what it meant, Maxentius and the barbarian princess, at one of King Vathalric's feasts—something that he could not ever conceive of attempting to do with a well-born Visant wife, especially not if the husband who was the subject of the conversation was sitting right there beside his lady and unable to understand one word of what she was saying to the King's guest.

"Valaric is the head of the household," Rothaide said, folding her long fingers, weighted down with gold, together and resting her chin on them, holding Maxentius's eyes with her own in a bold and direct glance that would have scandalised her peers in Visant and earned her a smouldering, resentful glare from her husband. "But I am the ranking partner of this marriage outside our home, and he does not get access to my father or to his councils except through me."

"But he is noble-born himself," Maxentius said, trying to understand. "Is he not? I understood that his house...."

"Indeed, but he is hardly the equal of the Maelgin line," Rothaide said with a fine arrogance that she appeared to be completely oblivious of showing. "Not every member of every noble house gets to sit in Council. And I knew when I chose him that he was not of the highest ranks. But he was a man, and my first husband, to whom my father gave me, had been inbred for too many generations—his own parents were first cousins to one another, and their parents were, too, and probably their parents before that. He might have had the right lineage to wed a king's daughter but he was weak, and had no spine. Valaric…doesn't let me do whatever I please."

"And that pleases you?" Maxentius said, frowning a little.

"Sometimes times, yes," she said, smiling at his puzzlement and earnest attempts to understand. "Life without an obstacle now and then is one without spice. But even when he roars and blusters I usually win, of course. Women have known how to do this throughout history. It makes it fun, though, when the man thinks he has a chance."

Maxentius shook his head with a chagrined little smile. "I am trying to picture you at the Imperial Court in Visant," he said. "You would cause a scandal…and you would rule the place within hours of your arrival. Your royal father is the iron fist of the north—but you, Princess, you are no less of an iron hand for all that you are concealed in a velvet glove."

Rothaide smiled at him almost flirtatiously, through lowered lashes. She was a true daughter of the north, her skin very white and her hair wheat-gold, and her lashes were pale and very unlike those that Maxentius was used to in the women of his own city—but he found her compelling, even though she was far from being any kind of woman that he had ever been familiar with.

Her pregnancy had ensured that she was not permitted to ride out any more, as had apparently been her habit before. But she would not stay cooped inside stone walls. At every opportunity, when the weather permitted, she walked in the Palace gardens, accompanied by a bevy of her women and frequently by Maxentius, whose company she seemed to find congenial. She questioned him at length, with avid interest, about the ways and the doings of Visant.

"I will probably never see it," she said, "and thus it is you who must tell me everything. Tell me how the streets look, and tell me of the sea of which Rathauric speaks, and tell me of this Hippodrome."

"Women of good birth do not attend the Hippodrome, Princess," he said. "Even if you were to visit the city you would not be permitted to show yourself there for the races."

She made an impatient little gesture. "I could probably win the races."

"No, lady, you may have many gifts, but driving a chariot and holding four half-wild horses to a course is probably beyond your strength," Maxentius said. "Even the charioteers of the Hippodrome have been known to fail."

"What happens when they do?"

"Accidents are...bloody...and nearly always fatal," Maxentius said.

And then she wanted to know about the details of the Hippodrome accidents, once again delighting in seeing him discomfited by this, for it was the barbarian princess who asked, from behind the mask of the silk-clad court lady who paced sedately at his side on swept garden paths.

It took him a while to get used to the Ravin court and the Vesigar ways of doing things, or at least King Vathalric's way of doing things. Maxentius sent his dispatches back to Visant dutifully, via his own trusted couriers, just as Leontes had advised—they were irregular, and he had few replies other than the occasional letter bearing family and Palace news from Leontes and rare but packed reports from Circassaë about the state of the city and the Hippodrome, and he was lulled into losing track of time. He somehow did not really register the changing of the seasons, and when one day he woke up to a world that was white and quiet he was startled to realise that he had been in Ravin for nearly as long as Rathauric had lived at the House of Peacocks in Visant. Shivering and pulling coverlets that included wolf fur closer around him, Maxentius suddenly found himself missing his house, and his gardens, and the scent and sound of Visant's spring.

"Perhaps it's time I thought of going home," he muttered to himself, eyeing the fire that had died down to embers in the hearth in his bedroom and wondering when a servant would be in to build it up again. But he rose before any such servants arrived, dressed in the cold, and made his way down into the main hall where a cheerful blaze *was* already roaring in the huge fireplace, which was big enough to hold logs that took two grown men to carry.

"Bread, and cheese," he said to a servant he collared by the hearth. "And bring some of that dried meat from the stores, also. And something warm to drink."

"Yes, Lord," the servant said, scurrying out of the hall to obey.

Maxentius found a seat close to the fire and stretched his legs out towards it with a sigh. When the servant returned with his breakfast, however, he was accompanied by another man, a dark-haired curly youth who looked just as jaundiced at the sudden chill as himself—one of his own, from home.

He sat up, searching his memory.

"Orontes," he said, recalling the name. "I had not looked for you."

The young man shifted from foot to foot. "I bring an urgent message, *despotes*."

"Bring more food, for my man," Maxentius said to the servant who had been about to withdraw. "Sit, warm yourself. You came by sea? In this season…?" His eyes narrowed a little. "What's wrong?"

Orontes pulled out a much-folded piece of parchment, sealed carefully with wax, and handed it over to his master. "Perhaps this will tell you, *despotes*."

Maxentius pushed his own breakfast towards Orontes and hunched over the parchment, opening it carefully, concealing its contents from any eyes but his own.

It was surprisingly brief, only a few lines, written in Circassaë's flowing hand.

The Emperor is rarely seen. He has given only three audiences in the last month, and none for almost three weeks now. The city is restless. You had better come home.

Maxentius stared at the message for a long moment, his jaw tight.

"How long did it take you to get this to me?" he asked Orontes brusquely.

"I have been on the road almost three weeks, *despotes*," the courier said, his mouth full of cheese and fresh-baked bread.

Three weeks. *Three weeks* had passed.

The Emperor could already be dead.

"Go back to the ship you arrived in," he said to Orontes, getting abruptly to his feet. "I will make arrangements to return to Visant immediately."

CHAPTER TEN

Afaris was not what Simonis had expected.

In truth, she was not sure what precisely she had expected at all. In the beginning, the adventure had been exciting, dangerous—she was an actress beholden to a Hippodrome faction; there was no provision for retirement or abandonment, there was in fact a law on the books (however rarely enforced) that stipulated an actual fine, and not a light one, for anyone caught trying to spirit an actress away from the Hippodrome without her faction's sanction. Presumably that was originally intended to reimburse the people for whom that actress was a source of income. Fifty gold solidi, the amount of the fine, would not have been too onerous on a man of Gallienus's obvious means—he had, after all, barely blinked at the much heftier price of purchasing his governorship. Simonis did not intend, however, to get caught—or, worse, to allow Gallienus to lull himself into a position of having 'bought' her. She had sneaked onto the ship that was to bear him away from Visant disguised as a simple slave girl; it was hard for her to keep her demeanour suitably humble and her eyes demurely down, but she only had to do it until she was safely below decks and the ship had been pushed off the wharf. She had come out of Gallienus's cabin, then, when the sea had widened between her and Visant's sea walls, and had stood watching the city recede from her much as she had once watched it approach back when she was a small child and she had first seen it from a ship's prow.

She was not the only female aboard the ship, but her status was definitely different from the other women's. However, the status that the slaves and the servants saw as higher than themselves was also a danger, because the other men on board did not see a high status at all—they saw her as the performer that she was and had been until very recently. Many of them had seen her half-naked body already in the dances she had performed at patricians' houses, and they naturally assumed that Simonis was here in a similar capacity. But Simonis was done with that. She had come with Gallienus, she had come as Gallienus's woman, she had in part come to leave behind the idea of belonging to whoever paid for her purchase price, of being something to be bartered for by the faction to which she was beholden for her food and a roof over her head—to take the first steps towards the ideal of that woman she had once seen on the moonlit balcony, the proud, if tragic, Pasiphaë. The journey to that destination might be expensive, Simonis knew that, but she had no intention of earning her passage by being a common whore. She had never been that. Even when Cicatrice had sent her out to a different man every night for weeks, she had never been that. And she would not become one now.

It took more than a month, with Gallienus stopping at various ports along the way in a sort of triumphal procession, in order to show off his new status to as many as he could, to cross the Middle Sea from Visant to the port city of Gallienus's new fiefdom. Simonis was not taken as Gallienus's companion to the banquets which were thrown for him in these ports of call, or allowed to show herself if he invited dignitaries on board his ship—she was expected to keep herself out of sight on those occasions, and allow Gallienus his stage. But for now, that was enough—that, and the fact that he was still enamoured enough to return to her on the ship after his carouses, expecting her to be waiting for him in his cabin, rather than taking advantage of the women who were no doubt offered by his hosts on-shore. Gallienus was never the most considerate of lovers, taking his own pleasure quickly without paying much heed of his partner's, but he was enthusiastic and passionate, and Simonis could console herself that later, in time, once they got off the confined spaces of the ship and had the leisure and the breathing room for more, he was good clay, and he could be moulded in the proper fashion.

Their destination was a city whose name might have been part of the trigger for Simonis's decision to take this opportunity to try and escape the Hippodrome word—the place was called Cyrene, a name very close to

Cyrenais, the town where she had been born. But if she had expected a return to the happier and less complicated days of her childhood she was quickly cured of any trace of nostalgia when she caught her first glimpse of the place. It was nothing like the island town with its olive groves and vineyards and smiling women walking barefoot on roads paved with smooth, warm stone. This Cyrene was barely more than a village, its surroundings a uniform yellow-brown barrenness reaching down to the sea, with a ramshackle sea-wall and a small lighthouse built a little way out from the shore to enclose a tiny harbour. A delegation awaited them on arrival, half of them hawk-nosed and darkly scowling local men dressed in loose pale robes and turbans with their mouths lost in an unkempt greasy bush of coarse wiry beard, and the other half plump, complacent sycophants who had been exiled from Visant for reasons only they still knew about and whose only chance of surviving in the new regime with their positions and possessions intact was to ingratiate themselves with the new Governor as quickly as they could manage to do it, and preferably before their neighbour did.

Simonis despised the latter on sight, and was a little frightened by the brooding hostile silence of the former—but in any event she was not introduced to any of them. She was wrapped in a concealing cloak and whisked off the ship by two of Gallienus's men while he himself walked regally down the gangplank, resplendent in gilt and white silk, to be greeted by his future subjects who waited for him on the shore. Simonis, turning her head as she struggled in the firm grip of her two handlers, saw one of the sycophant party sweep out a wilted-looking laurel wreath and place it on Gallienus's head, saw the arrogance that crept into his stance as he straightened with the laurel crown on his dark curls.

"Wait," she said impatiently to the two men who held her elbows, struggling to see more, "wait, I want to...."

"The Governor said to take you directly to the place where we lodge tonight," one of the men said. "We are to stay in Cyrene for a few days, meeting with the local authorities, and then we're for Bakka, the interior city, the capital. But there have been express orders from Gallienus himself for you not to be allowed to loiter out by yourself." He smiled, a little spitefully. "It might not be *safe*."

Simonis shook him off with a sudden sharp movement, stiffening her spine and reaching for her full height—which still, unfortunately, left her at the level of her handler's chest. But she had always been good at giving an impression of authority, of speaking to someone from a great height, and the gift had not left her—the man did not attempt to take hold of her arm again.

"We'll see," she said. "Very well, take me to wherever it is that I need to be."

Gallienus and his party were apparently to be lodged in a private home which had been vacated by its occupant for the Governor's convenience. Simonis was admitted—not at the front door, but via a small postern entrance in the back of an unprepossessing stone house—by a close-mouthed, silent woman wrapped in what looked like a black shroud, and beckoned inside. The entrance hall was close and tunnel-like; apparently she was to enter the place alone, since the two men who had brought her there did not follow her. Suddenly aware of a pang of fear, Simonis turned her head, reaching out to prevent the black-clad woman from shutting the door behind her.

"My luggage," she said, her voice still commendably peremptory, addressing the men who loitered outside.

"It will be brought with the rest," one of the men said. "The Governor will call if he has need of you."

There was no time for more. The woman had shaken the door loose from Simonis's fingers and pushed it to; for a moment complete darkness seemed to descend, but Simonis's eyes quickly adjusted, and she laid an open-palmed hand on the cool stone arch beside her, feeling the roughness beneath her fingers.

The woman made a motion for her to follow. Left with no other choice, Simonis did. The archway quickly opened into a wider corridor with a higher ceiling, one side of it open in a peristyle manner into an inner courtyard. It was not a lush garden—Simonis supposed there was little water to waste on the luxury of decorative plants—but there was a bank of huge yellow flowers in a patch of sunlight where it reached into the court, and in the middle of it an ancient-looking gnarled tree with glossy dark green leaves. It had a large cage hanging from one of its branches—no, several, Simonis noticed as she followed her guide down the open corridor along the side of the garden. Most were empty.

The woman in black stopped abruptly, and indicated a doorway through which she apparently wished Simonis to enter. Simonis suddenly realised that there were very few doors opening out on the peristyle—and quickly discovered why, as she ducked into the room into which she was being ushered. The room only had the one door which opened out, into the corridor. It had other openings but these led only into other rooms, with tiny windows set high into walls to prevent sun from finding its way into the cool stone chambers, rooms with no other exits. And Simonis was led deeper into this warren, room opening from room, with no way of getting outside again except the way she had come. There was no expectation of privacy if her lodging was to be in any of these rooms which linked with one another, and with no other outside passage, no other way of getting from one to another except through a third, rooms like a long and endless internal corridor separated from one another by a cotton arras over the entrance arch or sometimes nothing at all.

"Whose house is this?" Simonis whispered out loud, more to hear her own voice than anything else. The woman turned her head a little but her eyes were blank, uncomprehending. For perhaps the first time Simonis paused to reflect on the possible realities of what she had done. *What if nobody here speaks my language? Nobody who will speak to me, anyway?*

She was finally brought to one last room, a little more luxuriously appointed than the rest, with silken hangings on the wall. It looked like it had had a female occupant, or occupants, before—at least one half-open chest in which Simonis could glimpse silky garments bore mute witness to that. There was a low divan bed against one wall, draped in silk and covered with bright cushions; beside it, on a carved wooden table, food had been laid out—black unleavened bread, a platter of evil-smelling cheese, a pretty but obviously old glazed ceramic cup full of a cool sherbet. The woman waved Simonis to the table, miming eating with her free hand.

"All right," Simonis said warily. She dropped gracefully to her knees onto one of the cushions laid beside the low table apparently for this purpose and reached for the bread, breaking it in half between her hands. It tasted better than it looked, or perhaps she was just hungrier than she thought; even the cheese, which she had not thought she would be able to swallow, went down easily enough. Her silent companion waited patiently while Simonis ate, and gathered up the plates and cup when she was done.

"My luggage," Simonis said, miming the carrying of a package. Another blank look greeted her as the woman hesitated, platters in hand. Simonis clicked her tongue in frustration. "Luggage," she repeated. "My things." She crossed over to the coffer with clothes in it and lifted a corner of translucent veil that had been allowed to hang from a corner of the half-closed chest. "My things. My clothes."

The woman nodded vigorously and said something in a guttural language Simonis did not understand. She motioned again, to the chest, to herself, and the other woman. A certain confused understanding appeared to bloom in the servant's expression because she tilted her head a little, frowning delicately, and then nodded slowly. Simonis shook her head. Whatever did she mean? That the luggage would be brought? That…she sneaked another look at the chest beside her, the escaping corner of veil, back to the woman's face…that she was supposed to wear the clothes that were in the chest…?

She had entertained an idea of having a personal serving maid for herself when she came to the Governor's mansion in Bakka, and now found herself revisiting the idea with a jaundiced eye. The whole thing might prove to be more problematic than she had thought, unless the local women were exceedingly quick at learning the language in which Simonis was able to issue commands.

The silence stretched between the two women, until Simonis finally gave a brief unhappy nod and the other woman took it as a signal to withdraw. There was still light in the room, coming from the two barred windows high in the outside wall, through which Simonis was barely able to glimpse a pitiless burning sky of a washed-out blue and the corner of some other building's flat roof, adorned by a frond of what might have been a palm tree just outside of her range of vision. But the hours grew long, and the sky Simonis watched through her windows began to darken, and then flushed briefly a disconcerting shade of cinnamon and apricot before the short sunset was over and night fell. She heard cicadas outside, but no voices, no human presence at all; at some point a servant scurried in to bring more food—sweet figs, this time, and some other fruit that Simonis was not familiar with—and to light a couple of small lamps in the room. They cast a dim and flickering light, leaving the place awash in mysterious shadows, and soon with the sound of fluttering moth wings as some found their way into the room.

There was no sign of anyone with whom Simonis could be expected to communicate, least of all Gallienus himself, who seemed to have forgotten all about her. Simonis ate her figs, amused herself for a while by trying to figure out the workings of a small musical instrument not unlike a lyre which she had found leaning against the wall but failing to tease anything other than a discordant strum of tinny wires from it, and finally curled up on her side on the divan and fell asleep.

She woke to the weight of a man on top of her, and in the first instant froze, frightened, before trying to straighten her legs to give her leverage and to struggle free. But then the man laughed, and she recognised Gallienus; the breath that his laugh released into her face reeked of strong liquor, and she turned her head away, disgusted.

"You stink," she said.

"What was I supposed to do, refuse their hospitality?" Gallienus said, laughing again, sending another alcoholic breath washing over Simonis's face.

"They are a hostip…hops…they know how to keep a Governor happy, that's for sure. I came to say thank you.…"

He was pushing her knees apart with his leg as he spoke, one of his hands heavy on her shoulder and pressing her down into the cushions and the other reaching down to roughly close his fingers on her breast until it actually hurt. His eyes too bright and glittering in the guttering light of the oil lamps.

"No," she gasped, pushing ineffectually at his chest with one hand, trying to angle her hips out from underneath him, "you're *drunk*, you don't know what you.…"

"I know what I want," he said. "I want to say thank you. You made this happen. You did. Without you I may never have taken the chance. You. *You.…*"

He strained against her, grinding his hips against hers, his breath coming out in an explosive sigh even as Simonis herself gasped with pain and surprise; she was dry, completely cold to him, but he was oblivious to anything except his own needs, his one hand fumbling between her legs only long enough to guide himself before he pushed himself into her with a violent urgency. His full weight was on her, her head twisted sideways and her mouth full of the silky tassels of a cushion fringe, struggling to catch her breath as he thrust himself deeper and deeper until finally she felt his release and then he suddenly went limp, his hands loosening their relentless pressure on her shoulders and his head coming down to rest heavily on her breast, his mouth opening in a soft snore.

Simonis could not move under his dead weight. She was numb at first, and then came a sudden wash of emotions—fury, horror, fear. Back in Visant, Cicatrice would never have permitted her to be used like this, not just used and discarded like any woman off the street, no more than a female body into which Gallienus could spill his seed in his moment of triumph. *Cicatrice would have made sure you paid for it*, she thought, still fighting for every breath—she thought, at first, because he had driven the air from her lungs but then realising that it was not that, that it was because her throat was tight with tears and she could not breathe, could not gasp for air, without the anger and the grief reaching out and choking her, closing her airways. *Is this the way it's going to be? What have I done?*

She managed to squirm free at last after what seemed an eternity of sleepless hours pinned underneath Gallienus's inert body. In one corner of the room there was a terracotta ewer, which she had discovered in her investigations of what she was starting to think of as her cell and found to contain rose-scented water; now, careful not to make any noise, she extracted some filmy piece of cloth from that clothes chest that had been a the object of such confusion between her and the serving woman and dampened it with the water, sluicing away the sticky mess on her belly and her thighs. For a few minutes, slumped against the wall next to the ewer, she permitted herself the luxury of letting her tears escape—but she knew that she must never do so in Gallienus's presence. Her only defenses lay in the haughtiness she had brought here from Visant, her own sense of self-worth, the focused vision of a future for which she had done this thing and for which she had to be willing to endure whatever came. If Gallienus ever saw her weak, saw her weeping, she would have nothing at all, not even his continued interest.

He woke bad-tempered and hung over and had few words for Simonis before he left her in her room—but she did manage to make him promise to at least have her luggage delivered to her there. The first thing she did when her bundles and chests arrived was to rummage through her own personal little bag, left behind inadvertently on the ship when she had been hustled away—the bag that contained the bitter herbs that Circassaë had once shown her how to use, the herbs that cleansed her system and prevented conception. She should have had her dose before Gallienus had taken her but there was no help for that now—she took twice the amount she usually did, and hoped for the best. The clothes she had been wearing, soiled by travel and the aftermath of Gallienus's visitation, she flung into a corner and tried to forget about; but the woman who came in with her breakfast saw them there and took them away with her. Simonis noticed and said nothing. If they were taken to be cleaned, that was not up to her; if they had been merely taken, she would have been just as happy never to see them again. She choked down some breakfast despite not feeling very hungry, and then, when the woman returned to clear away, somehow and in complete desperation managed to convey her need to get out of this room and at least into the courtyard garden. The woman looked dubious, but led her to the inner court; Simonis paced it like a trapped animal, first investigating the cages hanging in the tree and their solitary, silent occupant—some sort of large gawky bird with dark plumage, with little pretension to beauty or any other apparent reason to be considered decorative enough to be kept in a cage—and had to restrain herself from plucking the petals off all the yellow flowers turning their faces to what little sun penetrated this shadowed sanctuary.

It was thus, caught and hobbled, that she was found by one of the younger men from the Governor's ship. He at least had always been pleasant to her without being obnoxious about pushing his attentions on her. She found herself dredging up a smile for him.

"You don't look well," he said courteously, eyeing the dark circles under Simonis's eyes, which a dab of concealing powder had done little to hide. "Did you not sleep well? I myself found it too hot in these airless rooms. It is to be hoped that the Governor's mansion in Bakka is better ventilated than this."

"Will you take me out and show me the city?" Simonis said, trying to steady her restless hands, giving him one of her rare and treasured smiles.

He glanced around, frowning. "But I thought the Governor said that you were to stay here until we leave for…."

"There's a ruin on the hill," Simonis said. "Out on the coast. Some ancient temple, it looked like. I would very much like to see it before we leave for Bakka."

"You'd have to wear the veil, as their women do," said her companion. "I don't think it's permitted for their women to go abroad without. Or with strange men, for that matter."

"I shared a ship with you for a month, you are hardly strange to me," Simonis said. "Please…?"

"Let me see what I can do," he said, giving her a small bow.

She waited in the courtyard, alone again, astonished at how much this trip— thought up on a whim—suddenly meant to her. If he returned with a polite expression of regret and refused to take her, she thought she would actually scream out loud—there was a trembling within her, beside her, as though the shadows were gathering up once more, as they had done before, into something greater than her, a fury shaped like a bear and just as ready to kill. But when her saviour returned it was with a full-length veil draped over his arm and word of transport arrangements being made, and Simonis felt the bear go from her, the tension in her body dissipate, even smiled as she put on the hot, uncomfortable veil.

They would, it transpired, be riding on camels, a beast that Simonis had never before had the opportunity to see close up. She watched in fascination as they stood complaining in a series of grunts and whistles, constantly chewing on something, or folded their legs at impossible angles to come down onto the ground and allow their handlers to tighten the riding gear. Once this was done to everyone's satisfaction, Simonis was motioned forward and helped into a sort of high-sided saddle box—to the edges of which she clung convulsively as the animal lurched to its feet underneath her.

"Just hold," the handler said, in her own language—obviously someone who had worked for the Governors here before. Simonis allowed herself a quick pang of relief—perhaps there *would* be somebody here who was capable of understanding her. She watched the way he folded his hands, miming holding onto the saddle, and copied him. "Just hold," he said, several times, and then, observing her doing it, nodded vigorously in approval, splitting his face into a wide gap-toothed grin. "Yes, yes, yes, Hold. Like that."

She had thought she might be afraid, but instead she was fascinated by the rhythm of the camel's walk, by the way the three camels in their little convoy paced with calm dignity one behind the other, practically stepping into the previous animal's tracks in what, almost as soon as they had left the last house behind them, turned into shifting sand dunes with only a scrap of vegetation hanging on here and there with obstinate desperation. There seemed to be no path or road, but the camels and their handler knew where they were going; presently the sand began to get a little firmer, turning rockier, and the land began to rise into a shallow slope. Not too far up the hill it became apparent that they *were* in fact following an ancient road, one almost completely covered with sand and dust but still visible underneath the drifts and winding steadily upwards.

It was with a sense of surprise, almost shock, that they crested a small rise, turned around an outcropping of bare rock, and found themselves on a flat hilltop overlooking the sea. Against the back wall of the rock stood the ruin that Simonis had observed as they sailed alongside the coast just before they turned into the harbour—incongruous, beautiful even in the sad wreckage of broken columns and once probably fabulous carved reliefs which had long since been worn away to nubs by blowing winds and scouring sand, obliterating the stories they had once told. The stone, even after all these years, was white and hard—it did not belong here, and had obviously been brought here from a great distance to show respect and worship to whatever god once lived here. But whatever god that had been, it had long since passed out of the world. The ruined temple was empty except for the unexpected whisper of wind caught between the columns, bearing the salt smell of the sea.

The drover stayed with the camels, a little way back; Simonis's other companion leaned back against one of the broken pillars and watched her as she stood staring out across the sea, the veil that had allowed her to come here in a crumpled heap at her feet and her hair blowing free. It was only when she squared her shoulders and sighed, dropping her eyes, that he spoke.

"Do you regret it?"

Simonis turned her head a fraction. "Regret it?"

"Gallienus. Tying your fate to his. Coming to this hole. Leaving Visant. You were quite a star back there—what will you do out in Bakka?"

"Perhaps I'll dance," Simonis said, with a hollow chuckle.

"They wouldn't appreciate you, even if he would let you," he said.

"I know." She lifted her eyes to the sea again, her head coming up to catch the scent of the sea breeze.

"What do you see out there?" he asked, curious.

"The past," she said, and sighed. "Thank you for bringing me out here. I suppose we had better get back. I hope you won't get into trouble for it—I'll do what I can to draw his anger if he takes you to task for it."

"He left for a local elder's house this morning, and they looked like they were keeping him for lunch. It's possible he won't even know we were gone."

"Then we'd better try and beat him back to the house," Simonis said, and smiled.

"We leave for Bakka tomorrow," her companion said. "I don't suppose there's many places like this out there."

"Or that I might be let loose to explore them," Simonis said. "Thank you, for this. Who do you supposed was worshipped here…?"

But to that neither of them had an answer. She pulled the veil back on, and climbed into her camel-back nest; they returned to a house still empty of the new Governor. Somehow suddenly wary of being seen together a moment longer, Simonis and Gallienus's man didn't speak again aside from exchanging nods and smiles, and Simonis dragged her unwilling feet back to her silken prison.

Gallienus arrived back in the mid-afternoon, sated with food and drink and adulation, but did not come to Simonis to celebrate this time. He slept elsewhere that night. But everyone was up not long after midnight, with the caravan being loaded up in preparation for the journey to Bakka, the Governor's capital.

Simonis climbed into a camel-back high saddle very similar to the one she had travelled in the day before with a degree of easy familiarity that might have set off all kinds of alarms if she had been closely observed—and it took her only a moment to realise that she ought to have never seen such a saddle before, and to make certain to fumble just a little to show how strange it was to her.

The sun's first rays stealing across the desert sands caught them almost an hour on the road; it got steadily hotter as the sun rose, and they stopped well before mid-day when they reached a small village clustered around a muddy waterhole, complete with a handful of scraggly palm trees and stunted dusty-leaved bushes, which were being cheerfully decimated even further by skinny, lethargic goats that wondered from bush to bush and nipped at the foliage. Servants pitched black tents for a noon break, and everyone took their ease for a couple of hours while the sun was hottest, blazing down from a cloudless sky bleached into a pale and lifeless memory of blue. Simonis asked no questions, cowering in her own black tent with a young girl whose sole task seemed to be to operate a plaited palm frond fan—it seemed to do no more than stir up the hot, close air. Simonis could feel rivulets of sweat running down between her shoulder blades and thought with a fierce longing of the cool marble baths in Visant. When the sun began to slide lower in the sky and the worst of the heat had broken, the caravan bustled itself together once again and continued on its way.

They reached the outskirts of Bakka close to sunset. They were expected—the inhabitants were out in the streets to await them, standing in silent knots under torches stuck into sconces on houses along the main street into the city. The caravan meandered slowly through these eerie, silent crowds until they reached a large white-washed house fronting onto a paved square. Large double gates in a wall leading away from the house were opened and the caravan wound into the outer courtyard of the Governor's mansion, with stables and camel enclosures leading off to one side and a large ornate door set into the side of the house itself between two huge blazing torches set one to either side.

With the heat of the day having sapped her energy, Simonis climbed wearily down from her camel and stood beside it, leaning on the edge of her saddle for support, awaiting instructions. She heard a voice, heavily accented but speaking her own language, welcoming the Governor to Bakka, and then she was being shepherded through that door and down a long narrow corridor and into a quiet room with cheerful yellow hangings on the walls. She was too tired to notice much, but they had passed through another of those inner courtyards to get to her room, and it had smelled pleasant, almost citrussy, and there was a freshness to it as though there was water present—but for now she was more than content to just crawl into her divan bed and fall asleep almost instantly.

When she woke the next morning, she could tell by the quality of the light that it was still very early. She listened for a moment, but there seemed to be no sign of life stirring anywhere in the house yet; feeling deliciously clandestine, she wrapped a shawl around her to hide her features just in case she ran into someone who would be offended that she was not wearing her regulation veils and padded outside into the corridor in her bare feet, after carefully checking both ways to see that she was alone.

This was a larger house than the one they had left in Cyrene, and laid out differently—the individual rooms led off actual corridors and not directly one from the other, as though there had been an influence of civilisation here that had tempered the early rustic design of the traditional homes. Simonis got as far as a trellised gate set into an archway, but that seemed to be latched or locked somehow and she couldn't get it to open—not without making more noise and commotion than she wanted to at that moment. So she peered through the slats of the lattice, and she could catch a glimpse, by craning her neck, of the courtyard through which they had walked on their way to their rooms the previous night. It was green, with myrtle and some aromatic herbs growing in beds laid out between cobbles of golden stone—and there seemed to be a second storey, with an open balcony that looked down into the courtyard from above. Simonis felt a small smile begin to tug the corner of her mouth upwards. This was better. This was much better. She could learn to like it here.

Her joy lasted only until breakfast, for which Gallienus joined her—only to announce that they would be moving on the next day. To another residence. About an hour away into the back country. A residence far more like the one in Cyrene than the Governor's mansion in Bakka

"But...*why?*" Simonis asked, appalled.

"I was told that the Governor from Visant is not a very popular figure out here," Gallienus said. "My people back in Cyrene told me, in fact, that the previous Governor was attacked at least twice...in this house. And that it is very difficult to defend. Far too open, all those balconies and stairs. You'd need more men than you could afford to keep alert out here. It's a simple matter of security."

"But they wouldn't bother with me—couldn't I stay...."

Gallienus gave her a stern look. "I can't be coming an hour into town every time I wanted a woman in my bed," he said bluntly. "If you don't come with me...well...you won't be staying in this house, either."

He was Governor. His word was law. Simonis bit her lip and didn't bother unpacking her bags. But she knew she was going to miss this house, even before she had had a chance to fully explore it. And she had an awful feeling that the one she would be taken to would be the same sort of stone warren that she had thought she had been lucky to escape from back in Cyrene.

She was not wrong.

Her quarters were sumptuous, and even crudely elegant. A personal maid had even been procured for her—one who spoke more than a few words of the Empire's vernacular, even, and if she wasn't a great conversationalist she could be trusted to understand and obey simple instructions. But the life of a lady did not consist solely of a luxurious chamber, servants, and a high-ranking man in her bed. In Visant the well-born wives had the company of other women like themselves—they would go to the baths together, and visit with one another at their homes, and gossip, and chatter, and go out in groups to buy herbs or cosmetics or silks or perfumes at the forums and the bazaars. Out here, there was nothing. Gallienus kept Simonis in the kind of state that she would once have sworn that she wanted to be kept in—and she found herself mind-numbingly, crashingly bored.

She was barely allowed out of the house and even then with a heavy escort; she was not allowed to be alone in the house, either, with some woman always in the room or within earshot; needlework quickly palled as a pastime when nothing else was really available, and there was nothing to read and even if there had been, there was nobody to discuss it with.

But all that paled into insignificance when she discovered that she had bigger problems to think about.

That double dose of bitter herbs on the first night on the Afaris coast had apparently been too little, too late—or else she had missed another crucial dose somewhere along the way. It was less than three months into her stay in Bakka that Simonis found herself pregnant.

CHAPTER ELEVEN

The journey home was miserable. The winds were against Maxentius's ship all the way, until finally they drove the battered vessel into the shelter of the nearest harbour without any guarantee as to when she would be able to sail again. Maxentius actually took this setback rather well—he was thoroughly sick of the sea and the manner in which it prevented him from keeping down anything more than water and dry ship's biscuit, and he finally called it quits, stood on the wharfside in the small harbour in the sluicing rain shaking his fist at the sea and declaring that it had won, and ordered horses for the rest of the trip to be made overland.

He took a day to recuperate from the sea voyage, sending a handful of his men ahead to arrange for relays of fresh horses to be left at strategic points on the road back to Visant, and set off on the second morning after they had made landfall. In some ways it was even more miserable than it had been while at sea, where at least they had been able to shelter in their cramped cabins from the incessant rain—but all Maxentius had to do was call to mind the smell of those cabins after a few days of the seasickness that had felled practically everyone aboard, and he was almost grateful for the gifts of driving rain and cold wind. He didn't spare the horses, his men, or himself—and he arrived at the Iron Gate in Visant's massive outer walls almost three days earlier than he would have done had he stayed on board ship. He and his escort rode over the bridge across the wide outer moat, through the gaping Iron Gate under a salute from the garrison of men guarding it, across the bridge of the deeper and narrower inner moat, and through the Red Gate into the city. The broad avenue which led straight to the Palace opened up before him, its wet paving stones glistening in the rain, and Maxentius actually pulled up, drawing his tired horse to a halt, his gaze drinking in the city, the streets, the occasional citizen hunched over with a hood over his eyes and scurrying to get out of the rain. The air smelled of rain, a whiff of sea, a hint—this close to the outer walls— of slaughterhouse. Maxentius was startled for a moment that his first thought had been *I am back*—because a part of him still remembered vividly his first arrival into the city, through this very gate, when everything that he now found familiar and recognizable was strange and new and frightening, and 'back' and 'home' were words he had associated with a very different place.

The men who had ridden ahead had already arrived in the city, and had alerted the household that the master was coming home. The gate of the House of Peacocks stood open for Maxentius, and inside Arkadios had mulled wine, a hot meal, and a change of clothes waiting. Dry, fed, his feet shod in warm slippers, Maxentius waved everyone else away and beckoned Arkadios forward to sit by him.

"I had a message to return," he said. "I came as fast as I could. Now tell me."

"It is the Emperor," Arkadios said, nodding. "I don't know how recent your news is, but he has been seen only twice in the past month—by anyone other than Sarrus and the silentiaries of his chambers. The Empire is waiting— everything has ground to a halt. There have been crowds in the Hippodrome for days now, waiting for news—despite the rain, even though it is not remotely the season for any games there. Everyone knows. It's a matter of time, now. It is just as well that you have come back."

"I need to see my father," Maxentius said.

"He knows you are here," Arkadios said. "I sent word to the Count as soon as I had word of your passing the Red Gate, and I am sure he will have had word already from the guards there."

"I should go to him," Maxentius murmured, and then let his head fall back against the backrest of his chair. "But I am so *grateful* to be off a horse's back for more than a couple of hours of snatched sleep...."

Perhaps it was his mention of the word that invoked it, because without realising that he had done so he slipped into a fitful doze. He drifted in and out of sleep for a while, but when he finally woke to full consciousness it was with a start, jerking himself upright, only to realise that Leontes was lounging comfortably on another seat before the fire, watching him with a smile.

"How long have you been here?' Maxentius said, sitting up and knuckling his eyes.

"You look exhausted. I didn't have the heart to wake you. Not too long," Leontes said. "I sent a dispatch to Ravin just over a week ago; either it flew there by magic and so did you on your way back here, or your sources in the city are pretty remarkable and you were on your way long before I thought to summon you."

"I had word," Maxentius said. "No details though."

"Not many to share. All I can tell you is that I do think that this is finally the end for Valerian Augustus, after so many false alarms. The Senate and the Church dignitaries have been gathered in the Senate House for some time now. I hear that there are four leading candidates for the succession—Celerian and Vitalles, both to some extent Sarrus's men, and then Aurelius, one of the strongest Army generals after Severus and Valentian, and…thanks to you and that wretched dream episode you cooked up with Valerian's connivance…myself."

Maxentius smiled, a wolfish grin, and ran a hand through his tousled hair. "Well, we know who the Army will favour," he said. "You've been a soldier, but you haven't been part of the field forces for many years now, not like Aurelius has. What about the City's people? I hear the Hippodrome is full every day."

"For someone who's been back in the city for only a handful of hours after an extended absence, and asleep for a couple of those, you're remarkably well informed," Leontes said. "The Hippodrome is…the Hippodrome. They have brought forward several names of their own, some of them highly unsuitable. There are factions which are demanding the return of one or the other or all three of Valerian's nephews—all of whom are conveniently far away right now, and it is hard to say whether it's by their own design or someone else's. There is a handful that—apparently seriously—is nominating last season's victor in the chariot races for the Imperial Diadem."

"And I thought the succession in the Vesigar court was a mess," Maxentius muttered.

"Oh? You should tell me more about that, when time permits. I have been reading your dispatches from Ravin with interest, but I am sure you have more to tell than what you wrote to me or even to the Imperial Office."

"Rathauric nearly died out here," Maxentius said, "but it seems to me that he is hardly in any less danger back in his own home court, what with his half-brother itching for his convenient demise. Still, he told me that at least in Ravin he would die by sword and not by poison. It seems to me that it would hardly matter, in the end—dead is dead—but it appears to hold some importance for him. But all that is neither here nor there. Tell me more of what has been going on here."

"You came back in time for things to start getting interesting," Leontes said. "We all get to go before the Senate next week—Celerian, Vitalles, Aurelius and I. Sarrus is leaning towards Celerian—this week, at least…."

"How do you know that?"

"Because he has approached at least Aurelius and myself with money," Leontes said dryly. "Off the record and off the books, of course."

"Money? What for?"

"The idea is for me, or Aurelius, or both of us, to go into the Senate chamber with full pockets," Leontes said. "And pass out solidi to any Senator who will listen, with a whisper to vote for Celerian when it comes to that. It serves to line the Senators' pockets in advance, and it also serves for the Senators to be made aware that other candidates may not be worth voting for. He seems to have homed in on those of us who might be ambivalent about this whole thing—I know that Aurelius would take the crown if chosen for it. But for him it would be duty, as he was put forward by the Army, Aurelius would prefer to be strategising battles out in the field. And I, well, ever since that dream business he must have seen that I hardly leapt to seize the opportunity at the time. He actually sounded me out on it; he knows how little I wanted to seek this particular honour. And the money…I got the distinct feeling that he would wink at it if some of the money found its way into my own pocket, my price for endorsing another candidate, taking myself out of the election. After all, why waste a vote on Leontes if he is seen to be endorsing, however underhandedly, someone else entirely? What is it?" he added, his tone suddenly changing, as he realised that Maxentius had sat forward intently, his chin cupped in his hands.

"What did you tell Sarrus?" Maxentius asked.

"I have not told him anything," Leontes said. "In this case, a silence is also a reply…."

But Maxentius was shaking his head. "No. Send word to him. Take the money. Tell him you will give the money to the Senators, just as he wishes."

Leontes frowned. "You want me to bribe…?"

"I did not say for you to tell him that you will also endorse his candidate," Maxentius said. "He is arrogant enough to assume that if you say you will take the money you are also accepting his command to endorse Celerian. But you will not mention anything about that when you accept his money. You will take the money—*only* the money—and you will use it in exactly the manner that he wishes it to be used. It will most assuredly find its way into the Senators' pockets. But you will make no promise to give it in Celerian's name. When you give out the money, if you mention any name at all, it will not be Celerian's. They will associate that money…with you."

Leontes stared at him. "But that is…" he began, and then stopped himself. "But even if the Senate so chooses, what of the Army? What of the populace?"

"The Army can be brought to heel. Not a few amongst them might resent that one general has been elevated above all the rest—or can be made to feel that way," Maxentius said. "As for the Hippodrome and the common vote… leave that to me. All that needs to happen is that they remember the dream of Valerian Augustus. But it is for the Senate to choose, and for the people to endorse the choice…." He lifted an eyebrow, cocking his head at Leontes. "You *do* want to be Emperor?"

"I am not so certain," Leontes said.

"Trust me," Maxentius said, leaning forward earnestly, "of the choices that the Empire is being given, you are the prize. *You*, my father."

"But I will have reached the throne by silence, and superstition, and bribery," Leontes said. And then laughed dryly. "But then, when was it ever different?"

"The taint of all of those you can lay on me, if you want. But what you bring to the Empire is quite different. Strength. Character. Pride. An upstanding sense of ethics."

"Why do I suddenly call to mind the day I gave you the House of Peacocks?" Leontes said with a strange smile. "You were not entirely certain of my ethics… back then."

Maxentius reached out to lay a hand on Leontes's shoulder and give it a squeeze. "That seems…a long time ago. I may have learned a few things since then. But for now—trust me. If there was a twisted way to get here, then it was I who chose it. For you…it has been a straight road. A straight road in Visant. Which you once swore to me didn't exist."

"I might live to regret having said that to you," Leontes said. "I am not sure I want this."

"But you are what the Empire needs," said Maxentius. "Send word to Sarrus tonight."

Sarrus agreed to a meeting, not entirely convinced about Leontes's apparent change of heart. Maxentius would have dearly liked to be present, to be able to read Sarrus's demeanor and be able to plan for whatever traps the Chancellor was plotting—but Leontes, by himself, with his quite genuine ambivalence about the matter at hand, was the only thing that would convince Sarrus to make a deal.

Maxentius's own access to the Senate House was limited—because the moment that word came of the Emperor's death, and that was expected at any moment, the senior members of the Senate would closet themselves away in council to debate the succession, and junior patricians like Maxentius would only be expected to support the decision which the elders had reached. He made the most of his opportunity. The Senate had summoned Leontes and the other leading candidates for accession in an informal manner and questioned them—closely, but apparently randomly—about their views on various political and ideological issues current at the time. While Leontes was on the spot, being commendably calm and relaxed about the whole procedure, Maxentius was in the ranks, listening, tallying, putting in a whisper into one ear or a good word into another, leaving a bit of Sarrus's money where it would do most good if the opportunity arose. He watched the interviews with the other candidates, too, and arrived at his own conclusions about the three men—and was not leery of sharing those with the Senators who would listen.

Aurelius, the general, was a stern man of middle age, his hair still dark and only lightly streaked with iron grey strands. He was strong, but he also gave the impression of being stubborn and quick to jump to conclusions which he would never, afterward, modify, whatever other evidence might come to light concerning any given issue. He had a good strategic mind, but his entire outlook on life had been battle, and he didn't seem comfortable in the political arena or appear to show much patience for it. This was something Maxentius made certain that some key Senators were aware of.

"If once he makes up his mind he will never change it," he said to one man, during a particularly uncompromising reply by Aurelius to some question posed from the Senate floor. "And what if he were wrong? Even men chosen by God himself can be wrong now and then. It is what makes us human...."

Vitalles had been a tax collector at one time, and was still involved with the financial aspects of the Empire. He was less beholden to Sarrus than Celerian was, but he had done some favours for the Chancellor which, granted, were more or less public knowledge—but the details of them, Maxentius implied to those who would listen, would probably never be known—and what if they weren't *all* that Vitalles had done for Sarrus, or on Sarrus's behalf? And Vitalles's reputation as a tax collector had not been that of an upright servant of the Empire—Maxentius didn't even need to bring up the point that the ex-tax collector had built himself a fat estate in the country thanks to some creative bookkeeping. And Vitalles had a large family, all of whom would have to be provided for.

"What if we found ourselves overrun by the sons and cousins and nephews and in-laws of Vitalles if he became Emperor?" one elderly Senator had grumbled in Maxentius's hearing, scowling in the direction of another man who was married to one Vitalles's nieces and could count on a nice lucrative position in the Imperial government should Vitalles ascend to the throne.

"It would take a generation to cleanse," Maxentius had agreed politely. "Those of us already in the system would probably be all right—your older son, and myself, perhaps. But it would probably be your grandsons who would have a fresh chance at an imperial posting...."

But it was Celerian in whom Maxentius saw true danger.

He was everything that was the worst in human nature. He was known to be close to Sarrus, to whom he owed his current position of Count of Private Estates, responsible for the Emperor's personal properties and revenues—promoted into that high place over one of the Emperor's own nephews who was known to have coveted the job. He had his arms up to the elbows in all kinds of deals and machinations, and did not seem to mind just how dirty his hands got in the process; he knew exactly how much the Emperor himself was worth and where the treasure was stored. He was a consummate politician with a silver tongue and a ready but false smile for all, and the only reason he was not susceptible to bribes was because Sarrus kept him well supplied with money from his own not inconsiderable coffers. He was also, of the four candidates put forward for succession, the only one who had been patrician-born, which counted for far too much (as far as Maxentius was concerned) with some of the older Senators. Celerian knew how to say what people wanted to hear, but he was no weak reed that bent in the wind for all that; Maxentius was not at all sure if Sarrus wasn't overplaying his hand by backing him—it was possible that Celerian would be the kind of Emperor that Sarrus wanted, one amenable to Sarrus's nudges and suggestions as to how the Empire should be run, but it was far more likely that Celerian would say what *Sarrus* wanted to hear, but only long enough for him to get installed on the throne of Visant, and after that he would be something else, something new, something unknown, and something that Maxentius instinctively feared.

Celerian knew him for an enemy. Maxentius was more aware than ever of the murky depths of the other man's personality, when their eyes occasionally met and locked across the Senate floor. Neither of them allowed any betraying emotion to cross their features, if they happened to focus on one another—it would be a stiff formal nod in either direction, and then they would sweep away from one another in pursuit of their own business. But Maxentius caught a glint of complacency in the other man's smouldering gaze. As though the election was already done. As though Celerian already felt the weight of the diadem on his brow.

One way or another, when this was all over, one of them would be dead. Maxentius sensed this in his bones.

But another man had to die first, and the Emperor kept them waiting for nearly three more weeks.

When the silentiaries, the Emperor's own body servants, sent word that Valerian Augustus had finally breathed his last, the Senate house shut down with uncanny speed, admitting only the senior Senators and the servants to tend to their needs. The four candidates were locked out; so were younger patricians like Maxentius, who would have no real vote in what the Senate elders decided.

But his work in the Senate house was already done. He had accomplished what he could there. With its doors closed against him, with the Senators debating in one chamber and the Church dignitaries in another, Maxentius switched his attentions to the Hippodrome.

Now that the news of the death of the Emperor was made public, the kathisma at the Hippodrome draped in black silk until a new Emperor was announced and would step into the royal box to be acclaimed, there was vigorous debate in the ranks of the gathered populace at the Hippodrome. Now and then a sufficient number of them would gather to give loud enough voice to one candidate or another and would congregate in vocal crowds demanding that the Imperial insignia be handed over so that their own candidate could be adorned. But the soldiers standing guard below the kathisma and at the locked and barred doors which led from it directly to the Palace, real soldiers from the City's own defence legion and not Leontes's Palace Guard, remained silent and immovable, deaf to pleas and denunciations and acclamation alike.

Maxentius already had people seeded in the crowds, in all the four factions. Their orders were simply to find something wrong with every single candidate they heard discussed in the Hippodrome—to plant suspicion of weakness or malice or greed or any other flaw or weakness they could find at the door of every man whose name was brought up as a potential future Emperor…save one. And if Leontes's name was mentioned by others in some similar wise they were not to argue or to defend, but simply to bring up the Emperor's Dream, and to remind the superstitions populace that God had already chosen, that all they had to do was add their voice to the acclaim.

The Senate deliberations were far from locked down, and nor was the Senate isolated from the Hippodrome sentiment—news leaked in both directions, and there seemed to be two distinct sets of candidates for the throne, one discussed in the Senate House, the other in the Hippodrome stands, and they did not appear to intersect with one another.

Except for one man.

Leontes.

The Empire's loyal soldier for decades. Trusted confidant to the Emperor-who-was, now lying dead in state on a purple-draped bier, who could not be laid to rest until his successor ascended the vacant throne. The man the old Emperor himself had chosen to succeed him. Yet common-born, like the folk in the Hippodrome—a man whom they could understand, whom they could see understanding them.

The Senate tried to compromise, and sent out the name of Vitalles—but the Army did not approve, and the Hippodrome populace booed. The Senate already knew that Aurelius would never have been accepted by the people. Choosing Celerian would have pleased many in the Senate, but after several days of discussion, it was becoming painfully obvious to everyone concerned that there was only one man who would keep the City united.

Maxentius himself was down in the Hippodrome when the two guards in the kathisma, apparently in response to an unheard command from within, reached out and began to strip down the black banners from the kathisma walls and railings, revealing purple underneath. Down in the stands and the arena the voices swelled into a roar as a phalanx of Palace Guards in full regalia came out on the kathisma and stood shoulder to shoulder, facing the crowds, their faces impassive, their bodies concealing what was happening in the kathisma behind them. Maxentius found his heart beating painfully as he watched, rapt, for the drama to play itself out. When the Guards parted to reveal their erstwhile commander, standing alone in the kathisma draped in the purple of royalty and with a crown of golden laurels on his head, the Hippodrome crowd cried out as one, a shout ripped from thousands of throats.

"Leontes Augustus! Long life and long reign, Emperor!"

Maxentius suddenly sat down on a marble bench, his knees weak, and buried his face in hands that trembled.

There are no straight roads in Visant. But the one that had led him here—to this place, to this moment—with his uncle, his adoptive father, standing in the royal box in the Hippodrome in the City of Gold with the golden laurels of the Emperor on his brow—Maxentius found it hard to trace his path from the farm in the green hills of the Empire's quiet distant provinces to the crowds roaring Leontes's name. He knew that he ought to make his way back to the Senate House, to the Palace—there was work to be done, more work than ever, now—but somehow he could not move; the weight of the crowd's jubilation heavy on him; he was almost ready to unman himself and shed tears right here in full public view where he could then never show his face again.

But after a few moments the rush of feelings subsided into something bearable, and he drew his hands across his face, looking up again. It seemed to him that quite a long time had passed, really, but Leontes was still there—throwing, as was tradition, largesse into the crowds, the last coins that would be minted with the name of his predecessor imprinted on them. The next time the royal mint roared into production it would be with a new set of coins—coins marking the beginning of the reign of Leontes Augustus. Leaving the crowds to scramble for the coins, Maxentius shouldered his way through the throng and down to the arena level, making his way across to the gate that would take him onto the road leading back to the Palace.

It was almost inconceivable that any message meant for him would find him in the chaos that was the Hippodrome that day, but somehow the boy that he found tugging at the sleeve of his tunic knew who he was, and furthermore had been entrusted with a message for him—an assignation, to be more precise, at a particular perfumer's shop in the forum right outside the Bronze Gates to the Imperial Palace.

The woman who waited for him inside the shop was unmistakable for all that she had laid down her usual glitter and was wearing a plain linen gown and a light concealing cloak over it. But Circassaë didn't need jewels to sparkle. When she turned to face Maxentius, her eyes were more brilliant than any gems.

"I owe you," Maxentius said without preamble, stepping up to her and taking one of her hands to his lips.

"Then it all worked out as you wanted?"

"It would have gone ill if I had waited to return until my father bethought himself to send for me," Maxentius said. "It was almost too late when *you* called. But I was in time, I was here when I needed to be here. I owe you."

"When do I get my gold?" she said, her lips curving up into a smile.

He chuckled quietly. "I haven't forgotten," he said. "You will have your gold."

"Then here is something else you should know, so that I may properly earn it," Circassaë said, lowering her voice. "It is second hand, heard from a sister in the service, not my own sworn word—but it is something you ought to keep in mind. Celerian…had plans for this contingency. And your father is not yet completely Emperor, not until he is crowned in the Cathedral. Tell him to be careful. That, or…."

She didn't finish. She didn't need to. Maxentius's jaw clenched as the smile faded.

"I had known from the beginning. It was to be Celerian's life or mine."

"Sarrus will…."

"There are things," Maxentius said bleakly, "that will have to be done now. Once again—for this, for all that came before—I owe you. I will not forget."

She withdrew her hand from his after a moment, and gave him a nod.

"Then go. Do what you have to do. If you need me—for anything—let me know."

He said no more, giving her a long look and then a small respectful bow before he turned and swept out of the shop and out into the empty forum, turning resolutely towards the Bronze Gate and the Palace.

Where his father waited.

Where his father…the Emperor…waited.

CHAPTER TWELVE

Simonis hated her pregnancy.

There were a lot of reasons she might have given for that—her frustration and fury at herself for having slipped up badly enough to let this happen by accident and the utterly unfortunate timing of it, the discomfort of being heavy and uncomfortable in the sweltering heat of Bakka, the morning sickness that afflicted her with pitiless regularity for the first three months of it and then left her feeling merely sick in the morning and sick and miserable for the rest of the day, the way her swelling belly distorted the slim athletic body she had always been so proud of, and the effect she could see on Gallienus.

Perhaps not least amongst these reasons was also an unreasoning terror at the prospect of having to give birth—and to do it here, alone, away from everything she knew, every support system she could have counted on back in Visant if this disaster had happened to her there. In her more rational moments she knew that women gave birth here, too, just as they did anywhere else, and most of them and their children managed to live through it. But she was finding it difficult enough to communicate with the locals about far more mundane things, and she found herself more and more tearful and frightened as the days passed and the birth-date began to loom.

Weak. The pregnancy had made her weak. And she hated it, and herself, and Gallienus, and the unborn son she had yet to deliver.

For of course it would be a son. That was an article of faith—nobody doubted the truth of it for a moment, not Simonis, not Gallienus, not even the swarthy and silent midwife who had been procured for Simonis's confinement and who managed, despite a dearth of shared vocabulary, to intimate that she believed Simonis was carrying a boy. And a son was a prize worth the effort—something that Simonis had to fight to remember when her pains came upon her at the appointed time, and she screamed and writhed on her childbed for endless sweat-soaked hours, far too long, watching her strength ebb as the day faded around her and the baby not yet come.

Simonis was all but unconscious when her child finally squirmed forth into the world. The midwife brought her something she had to struggle to see, her vision blurred with exhaustion and pain; she heard the midwife speaking, but did not understand a word of it. She tried to reach out to touch the lustily screaming infant still smeared with blood and the fluids of birth, but could not seem to lift her arm to reach far enough—and then she passed out, her vision fading into black, her arm dropping lifelessly down beside her.

When she woke to consciousness again, weak but finally able to take stock of her surroundings, she found the midwife was still there in the room. The baby, cleaned up now, its skin startlingly pale and its mouth a tiny pink rosebud, was sleeping, swaddled in cotton wrappings in a woven basket beside the bed.

Simonis lifted herself up on one elbow, with some difficulty, to lean over the basket and stare at this thing that she had brought into the world.

The midwife noticed the movement and came bustling over, clucking at her, but Simonis could not understand whether the sounds were meant to be a sign of pleasure or of annoyance. She did bring over a cup of some cool liquid, and Simonis drank gratefully.

"Gallienus?" she asked, surprised at how hoarse her own voice sounded to her ears.

The midwife shook her head. No, Gallienus hadn't come to see her, or the child.

Simonis wondered how long it had been…if he had stayed away because he had been told she was sleeping. But surely he would have come to see his son…?

She glanced back at the midwife, then back at the child, made a gesture of wanting to reach for the baby, but the midwife shook her head slightly.

"Sleep," she said, one of the few words she did know in a shared language. "You sleep, need rest. She sleep, too."

Simonis lay back with a sigh, closing her eyes…and then opened them again, wide.

"She?"

The midwife must have got it wrong. Made a mistake with the pronoun.

She glanced at the child. Her child. Her son.

Her eyes closed once more. She did not believe she could sleep again, not so soon, but somehow she did, slipping right back into dreamless slumber; when she next woke, she was far more focused and alert. She wondered how long she had slept—when last she had opened her eyes it had been daytime but now it was night, with a single oil lamp lit and guttering on a low table across the room from her.

The midwife was gone, and Simonis was alone. Alone, that is, except for the baby—who was also awake, lying on its back in the basket, turning its head this way and that and uttering small whimpering noises.

Simonis sat up, and reached for the child; its head lolled a little as she lifted the small swaddled form and Simonis instinctively braced the neck with one hand, bringing the tiny thing to lie against her side, cradled in the crook of her arm. She traced the outline of its face with her finger—its button nose, the rosebud mouth, a fine fuzz of hair on its head.

"What shall we call you?" she murmured to the baby, smiling a little, completely taken aback at the rush of feelings that flooded her—she had forgotten that she had ever hated being pregnant, hated the thought of having this child, feared the moment of childbirth. "What will you grow up to be…? Let me see you.…"

She unwrapped the swaddling a little way, freeing the child's arms, smiling as its tiny fingers closed around her own thumb. The baby turned its face jerkily against the support of Simonis's arm and looked at its mother with great blue eyes, its mouth opening like a baby bird's.

Simonis's breasts grew suddenly heavy, swollen.

"Are you hungry?" she whispered. "We don't know how to do this, do we, either of us. But we'll figure it out. Let me see.…"

She settled back more securely, passing the child across her body, turning it into her bosom, opening herself up to questing fingers, a whimpering mouth which could not seem to make the connection between the nipple being offered to it and the idea of food.

"This way. Here," Simonis cooed as she guided the baby's mouth against her breast. "There. Like that." She gasped a little as the child wrapped its rosebud mouth around the nipple, tugging, its hand coming to rest on the curve of Simonis's breast, its fingers opening and closing reflexively as it suckled vigorously.

She was lost in the moment, falling in love with this child born of her body, watching as it started to drowse on her breast. When she finally separated from it, she laid the baby down on the bed to re-wrap its swaddling…and stared in shock as she unwrapped the pale, perfect body of a girl.

Simonis actually looked around in consternation—there must have been another woman who had given birth here. There must have been another baby. Where was hers? Where was her son…?

The boy who was supposed to have been born. The son who would *be* Gallienus, would be a trader, a soldier, a governor, a senator. Not another girl who would grow up to be beholden to another Gallienus in the days to come. Another woman who would dance and smile and seduce for the Hippodrome…

"You aren't mine," she whispered. "You can't be mine…."

But she was hers, this tiny girl-child. She knew it in her bones, in her blood, in the deepest corners of her heart into which the tiny thing had already stolen and made a home there. The child born from her body, her flesh and blood and now her mother's milk inside it.

She knew now why Gallienus had not come. If she had borne a son, he would have come. He might have married her, even, in time. For the girl…

Simonis wanted nothing more than to lay the child aside and turn her head away, pretend that all this had never happened, that the past months of misery and pain and frustration had been a bad dream. But it was already too late for that—she had looked into her daughter's eyes, unknowing, and she was caught, snared, trapped. There was already something stirring in her that swore a silent vow that this child *would* have it, have everything that Simonis herself had wanted. Would have it, if her mother had to die for her to get it.

She allowed herself to cry. But she cried silently, while holding her daughter in her arms.

Gallienus showed very little interest in the baby, except inasmuch as she impinged on his own access to Simonis. He was not even consulted on the child's name—Simonis named her Chryseis, a name that would be fit for the lady that the baby would grow up to be some day. Gallienus's only early edict had been to forbid Simonis to breastfeed her child, so that her breasts might dry out and return to being a part of Simonis's body to which he, and not his daughter, had first claim. Simonis allowed him to procure a woman to be wet-nurse for the child, but thereafter she and the wet-nurse came to a silent understanding, and Gallienus was largely ignored on the matter—and if he complained about the tenderness of Simonis's breasts, or that they were still milky, she turned eyes of innocence on him and said she did not know why she still had milk; and he did not know enough, or care enough, to pursue the subject.

Things settled down to an uneasy truce after a while. It had been Simonis's choice to range herself with Gallienus—the two of them against the world, and perhaps one day she would be a Governor's lady. It surprised her how little she wanted that any more—but she stayed in the room where he had lodged her, and nurtured her child, because now it was different—it was Simonis and Chryseis against the world, and Gallienus was not even in the picture when she told her daughter whispered fairy tales about how it would all be some day. And the baby thrived, and smiled, and grew; and at some point her mother's sixteenth birthday came and went, unnoticed.

Chryseis was almost six months old when Simonis heard a sound in the doorway to her room and turned to see one of Gallienus's men waiting there. She straightened from where she had been bending over the baby's cradle, a little puzzled. It was late, the oil lamps already lit, well past the hour for social calls or a time when she could have expected to be disturbed.

"Can I help you?" she asked, quietly, so as not to wake the baby.

"Gallienus sent me," the man said, still standing in the doorway.

"Yes…?" Simonis said, still not understanding. And then she did, suddenly, and the colour flooded into her cheeks. "Gallienus. Gallienus sent you…to me."

The man stepped into the room, beginning to smile. "Indeed," he said. "He told me there were…things you were particularly good at."

"Gallienus," Simonis said, and her voice was ice, "does not own me."

The man halted, mid-step. "What was that?"

"I came here a free woman. I am no slave to be handed around the garrison room when he gets tired of me. We have an arrangement, he and I—it's been a while since *he* has paid for what he finds in his bed."

Confused, the man frowned at her. "I can pay…."

Simonis suddenly changed, softened, glancing at her visitor with seductive eyes from behind lowered eyelashes—the look that had conquered Senators, generals, high-ranking Imperial officials with vastly more experience than this lieutenant of a provincial Governor. "Come inside," she said, her voice smoky, husky. "Please, do come in."

He did, looking hypnotised.

Simonis ran an apprising eye over his body as he drew his tunic off. He was a good specimen of manhood, this was not going to be difficult or unpleasant; at least Gallienus hadn't sent her one of the dour local hawk-nosed greybeards with whom she could barely have communicated. That had been a tactical mistake on his part, though—because Simonis could communicate all too well with this particular partner. She very quickly had it out of him as to exactly who he was and what capacity he served Gallienus in—a second son of a prominent Visant merchant family, sent out to the Afaris provinces to try and make his own way in the world. He had come here as representative of his family's interests, and intent on pursuing his own; his weak spots were the lack of financial standing with which he had arrived in this outpost, and all the hopes he had pinned on improving his fortunes in Gallienus's employ.

"But he is planning on increasing taxes on free trade," Simonis said as she lay with her lover, tracing the muscles of his chest with her finger. "You will have to pay almost twice as much to load a caravan, as early as next year."

"No," he said, "there will be tax exemptions…he said.…."

"The things he says and the things he does are all too often not the same," Simonis said. "If there is an exemption it will last for only a short time. And it will be offered to the senior traders. Not to you. If I were you, I would ship out any wares you may have—before year's end, certainly, in the next few weeks if you can. Slowly, of course. It would not do to suddenly empty your warehouse for no particular reason. But I would store your merchandise…elsewhere…a day's ride or so outside the furthest reaches of Gallienus's writ. Before the writ becomes law."

There was a moment of silence, and then Simonis saw a sudden clenching of the jaw as the man whom the Governor had sent to her bed turned his head away.

"I will do that," he said, his voice flat. "Thank you."

It did not occur to him—at least not right then—that she had just betrayed the man who owned them both; but she did refuse his offer of money, after, as he tried to stammer his way into payment for the night she had spent with him.

"I may be able to use a favour from you at some time to come," she said, giving him yet another of her long-lashed smoky glances. "Let us leave it at that."

He looked a little bit queasy, as though aware that he was stepping on quicksand, but did not argue the point.

Simonis sent word to Gallienus the next morning, phrased demurely enough, but nonetheless consisting of a summons to see her. The Governor kept her waiting for a full day—but she was ready for him when he came to her rooms the next evening. She greeted him wearing her finest clothes, her wrists and throat and ears and hair glittering with jewels; she could see his eyes kindle as he came in through the door, his face change, his nostrils flare with a sudden lust. But as he smiled and strode into the room she made a sudden imperious gesture, her hand a flat-palmed signal that told him to come no further.

"What is this?" he said.

"I am not your whore," she said, her voice low and steady. "Yes, I asked you to take me with you to Afaris—and you did that. But the bargain was not that I should be shared out amongst your men. I came with *you*. And you broke your end of that covenant last night. I am not yours to bestow—*you do not own me.*"

His smile widened a little, but did not reach his small eyes which glittered with smugness, even malice. "He still owes me for last night."

"No," Simonis said. "He owed *me*. And he has settled that debt. But you and I...."

"Of course I *own* you," Gallienus said, gesturing around the room "All of this, I have provided for you. Your food, your shelter, even a woman to care for that wretched brat—I could have taken the child away from you, you know, and given it to some childless family here in Bakka. I would have been within my rights."

"Chryseis is not your child, she is mine," Simonis said. But her heart had missed a beat at that threat, and Gallienus did not fail to notice. His smile broadened a notch.

"I can still do that," he said, taking a step towards the baby.

Simonis felt the bear shadow gather within her, around her. She stepped into his path and there was that something in her face that made Galllienus's smile disappear.

"Touch her and I will kill you myself," she spat out through clenched teeth.

"Then take the brat, and go," he snarled. "Go, I am tired of you. Your attitude, your sharp tongue, your condescending ways."

She had expected this; it did not surprise her.

"I can be packed and out of here in the morning," she said. "You owe us passage...."

He laughed, and it was not pleasant. "*Now*," he said. "Get out. Right now. Take the child, and get out. I owe you nothing. *Nothing*. Packed? You have nothing to pack. You own nothing, except that child. Take it, and go."

"I own what I stand up in," she said. She had hoped for better, but she had anticipated this, too. Ordinarily she relied on her own bright eyes and lustrous hair to be her decoration—she would have disdained to go out in public as gaudy with jewels as she was that night. But if she was to be turned out in the street, she needed all the wealth she could take out of here. And this was something that Gallienus could not, in honour, refuse.

But he could pretend that he could. It was threat and bluster, but he made a good show of it, spitting out of the side of his mouth onto the floor at his feet. "Go, before I send you out barefoot and naked."

She held his eyes for a long moment, and then sighed, shaking her head slightly, her eyes falling away. "I had such hopes for you," she said softly. "What a disappointment you have turned out to be."

He growled, low in his throat. Simonis did not allow it to unnerve her. She gathered up Chryseis from her basket, wrapping her up in a woven blanket on which she had been laid, and reached out for her own cloak, draped across the bench next to the baby's bed.

"What you stand in," Gallienus said, his voice cutting into her, mid-motion. "You are standing. I am letting you take the child, Nothing else. Go."

Simonis straightened, leaving the cloak where it lay. She shifted Chryseis into a more secure grip in her arms and walked slowly out of the room, without looking back.

The woman engaged as wet-nurse for Chryseis took them in for the night. The next evening, wrapped in a borrowed cloak, Simonis went to see the man whom Gallienus had sent into her bed.

She knew better than to go to his office, where Gallienus might have been told of her presence there. She waited for him when he was locking up for the day, stepping out of the shadows, calling him by name; he actually flinched at the sound, as though he were hearing the voice of destiny.

"I said I would ask you for a favour some day. That day has come, a little sooner than I might have wished, but under the circumstances it is not unexpected."

"What are you doing here?" he said, looking around carefully to see if anyone was watching. "Gallienus...."

"He has cast me out, me and the child, both," Simonis said. "Last night. I spent the day sheltering with a friend here in Bakka, but I can't stay here. I need passage. Home, back to Visant."

"As far as I know there are no ships due to sail for Visant for another month, at least—maybe longer," he said carefully. "As for those that might be in harbour, bound for elsewhere...he cast you out? He will have already sent word to Cyrene, the harbour will know. You will find no ship's captain willing to take on a passenger proscribed by the Governor."

"I can pay," Simonis said, opening her hand to reveal a jewelled hair pin, closing it again to conceal it against prying eyes.

"It isn't a matter of money. Any man who does this would incur the Governor's anger. Harbour privileges…are already expensive."

"I have to get out of Bakka. He hasn't thought about this yet, but I know far too much about him now, about the way he works, what he thinks, his plans for the year to come. Once he remembers all that…he will come after me. After me, and after Chryseis. I need to go home. If not by ship…how?"

He hesitated. "I have taken your advice," he said, his voice dropping even lower. "I have a caravan departing for Hyria in two days, it's a small city about four days' journey to the east, the closest place that I can easily reach that is outside the Governor's direct jurisdiction. I have purchased a storehouse there, to store surplus stock in. But that's as far as the caravan will go, before turning back. I can get you as far as Hyria—but after that, you're on your own. It isn't a seaport, it's an inland town, but then there are no real seaports to speak of between Cyrene and the city of Rhakotis."

"Then I shall find my way to Rhakotis," Simonis said. "He cannot touch me there."

"It lies…another week or so further east, if you find an honest caravan that sets a decent speed. And I cannot guarantee that you will find a caravan that leaves immediately…."

"I'll take my chances."

He squared his jaw. "Come to my house tonight," he said. "I will make sure you are safely in the caravan when it leaves Bakka. Make very sure that nobody sees you coming to me—especially after this, after having approached me out here in the open…."

Simonis smiled at him from the shadows cast on her face by the folds of her cloak, her head carefully bowed and out of any stray light that might have crept in to reveal her features. "Toss me a copper coin and tell me to stop bothering you," she said.

Flushing, he did as directed, pulling a coin out of a pouch at his waist and waving the 'beggar' away.

Chryseis's wet-nurse parted from the child tearfully when the hour came for Simonis and her daughter to leave; she would not take anything in exchange for sheltering the two of them while they were waiting for the caravan to gather, but Simonis closed her hand around a small jewelled hair pin anyway.

She did not have much luggage. Her jewels she had secreted in several small pouches on her person, hidden underneath her simple robe; she wore a length of cotton cloth diagonally across her body, and into it, like a hammock, she had tucked her child. The over-garment she wore over this was a home-made *djellaba,* a kind of cloak worn by the locals, and her dark hair she had hidden under a drab undyed turban. Her heart was beating rather fast as the caravan started out—at any moment she expected the camels to come to a halt, and some officious guardsman sniffing around in case he could claim a reward by returning escaping property to his Governor. But the caravan shook off the dust of Bakka without incident and passed into the back-country; with every sunset they were getting further and further away from Gallienus and his reach. But Simonis only allowed herself to draw a first deep breath of relief when the mud-and-wattle houses of Hyria began to rise around them, and the caravan came to a halt outside the warehouse which had been its destination.

Simonis asked the caravan leader if he knew of any other caravans leaving Hyria and going further east; he shrugged, and pointed her to a low, dung-coloured building which apparently served as some sort of dispatch office. But things took a turn for the worse here, because there didn't seem to be a common language in which Simonis could make her wishes understood—not even when she attempted her few words of the local language, the things she had been taught by servants while still living in Bakka or had picked up by herself with her quick ear and natural wit. But either there were no caravans ready to leave, or the man sitting cross-legged on a platform surrounded by tally sticks and untidy piles of papyrus had neither the ability nor the interest to answer Simonis's questions.

She repeated the name of the eastern city several times, as if repetition could force comprehension—but the man's entire response to her increasingly desperate "Rhakotis! *Rhakotis!*" was to shake his head with an impassive expression and go back to his work.

Tired and defeated, with the baby awake and getting fractious and hungry, Simonis finally sighed and gave up. She would find a place to stay tonight, and after that she would simply haunt the office until such time as a caravan captain came by—and try and communicate directly with someone who could offer her a berth in their caravan. She had been told it lay only another week's journey further east—it was something that she might have contemplated doing on her own, if she had not been taught a sharp lesson about the harshness of travelling through the desert country since she had landed in Afaris. The desert was unforgiving—it gave no quarter, there were no landmarks to cue a sense of direction, and there was no knowing where water was to be found. If she got lost, she would be dead very quickly.

The only place which seemed to offer lodging was a flea-bitten hostelry whose proprietors seemed not a little dubious about renting a room to a lone woman with a child. But in the first stroke of somewhat better fortune since she had left Bakka, at least one of the men gathered before the building apparently spoke enough of the *coiné*, the trade language of Visant, to gain a rudimentary understanding of Simonis's predicament—and it was he that, first, procured her a safe room for that night (not at the lodgings where she had first gone, but in an entirely different and completely anonymous house nearby where she would have never even thought of applying) and also gave her welcome word of a Rhakotis caravan which had come to Hyria only a few days before and which was now about ready to turn around and head home. He was not part of that caravan, but he apparently knew the second-in-command to the caravan's leader, and actually told Simonis that he would leave word with the man in the morning.

"You are very kind," she told this stranger, warily, wondering if she ought to squander an entire piece of jewellery to pay for his assistance—she had not had the chance to change any of her hoard for actual money yet, and certainly he might have saved her life and the life of her child, but she wasn't sure if offering him an entire gold bangle in return would be appropriate recompense.

But he reached out with one gnarled brown finger, dirt encrusted under the dark fingernail, to gently trace the outline of Chryseis's small, bad-tempered face.

"I have," he said, nodding at the child. "My baby die, not long before. Pretty child."

"Thank you," Simonis said, sudden tears sparkling in her eyes.

He sniffed once, hard, and turned away. "I go speak caravan. Word at office, tomorrow."

Chryseis was still too young to care much about anything other than her own comfort. She suckled at her mother's breast; sated, she regained her good humour and babbled happily at Simonis for a while before drifting off to sleep. Simonis herself didn't sleep much. She was awake when the sun rose, and by the time it had fully cleared the horizon she was waiting at the dispatch office door.

The official from the day before had apparently miraculously found his tongue overnight, because he was able—however appalling his grammar and mangled pronunciation of *coiné* might have been—to let her know that the

Rhakotis caravan would be departing a few hours before sunset. He quoted her a price of passage—horrendously inflated, but by this stage she was too much invested in this to care—but refused her offer of a piece of jewellery as payment, probably because it would have proved a little too difficult to take his portion of the bribe money from that when he passed the rest over to the caravan master and he was too busy, or too lazy, to take it to the bazaar to sell it himself. He pointed Simonis there instead; after a few false starts she did find somebody willing to buy a couple of her bracelets for a brace of small goathide pouches of silver coin. She spent some of it on a tiny pointed dagger she could conceal within arm's reach if she felt in need of protection, and on a small waterskin, filling that at the well in the middle of the village and leaving a single silver coin in payment for that. Then she returned to the office to pay the dispatcher. He accepted her pouch, and told her brusquely to present herself back at the office by noon.

When she returned to the caravan office at the appointed time, it was to see the bustle of an assembling caravan already evident, although no animals were yet in sight. The official bent the rules so far as to allow her to wait inside, out of the sun, because of the baby; but he did it will an ill grace, and frowned mightily every time Chryseis made any small noise. Eventually a wiry, long-faced man with eyes that glittered as though they had been oiled came into the office and said something in a guttural voice. The official barely looked up, indicating Simonis with an almost imperceptible nod of his head. The bright-eyed man turned to her.

"I am Ommar," he said. "Caravan Master. We are about to set out. You are our passenger?"

"Yes."

"Where is your luggage?"

"I have only these," Simonis said, indicating her child and her water skin.

Ommar's eyebrows went up a little at that. "Then come. A camel is made ready. We will ride, and then make break for a few hours—and then we will ride again until sunrise. Then we rest until the heat of the day is over again. We have to make good speed."

"I won't slow you down," Simonis said.

She had assumed that this would be no more than a trading caravan, assembled to deliver goods from one town to another, lean and spare, but she was surprised at what it actually turned out to be—more of a nomadic clutch of families who wandered the desert and ferried trade goods to earn a bit of money on the side. It had not been that obvious when they had started out, but when they stopped to make first camp, the place was suddenly over-run by scurrying female forms, instinctively drawing veils across their features as they noticed a stranger in their midst, and small children getting underfoot. Simonis was not really able to get a good sense of the whole thing, because Ommar had dropped by with a very clear invitation for her to stay close to her own tent and not mingle much with the families. A silent woman with huge, curious, dark eyes brought Simonis some food, and refilled her water skin; apart from her, only one or two of the bolder children skirted close to her campsite to peer slack-jawed at her, and then scurried away if she made eye contact or smiled.

She was left to herself that night. But the next camp they made, she was surprised to see Ommar himself striding over to where she sat by the small fire she had had lit for her own use outside the tent she had been allotted. He crouched by the fire, his bright eyes reflecting the flames as though he had been a demon, showing nothing for her to read.

"Everything all right?" he asked. His accent had got stronger, somehow, out here in the desert—as though any veneer of civilization he might have had sloughed away from him like a shed snakeskin.

"Yes," Simonis said carefully. "Thank you."

He reached out a long-fingered hand and curled it around her knee, his smile widening a little. "Good," he said.

There had been no more to it than that one gesture–but Simonis suddenly started reckoning a little desperately as to how much longer she would need to spend in this caravan. The woman who brought her the food that night was older than the girl who had done so the night before, and her eyes were heavy-lidded and resentful. But she might well be a wife, certainly someone who shared a man's bed, who might be less than happy at this unattached and attractive female who had intruded into the family circle. She said nothing, even when Simonis offered her a few words of conversation in *coiné*, but Simonis got the distinct impression that it was because of disdain and not ignorance.

Ommar came to her campsite the next night, also. This time, he wore a more serious face.

"We may have to detour, a little. Trouble. We might take a few more days to reach Rhakotis."

"How many days? What is the trouble?" Simonis asked.

"That is not for you to know," he said. "But we will be on our way longer. You need to pay me more money."

Simonis stared at him for a long moment. "How much more?"

His mouth lifted a little at the corners, showing a glint of white teeth. "Perhaps…not money."

His hand had found its way to her knee again.

Conscious that she might be walking into danger, Simonis reached out and gently removed it, laying it down on the sand beside her.

"No," she said quietly. "That was not part of the bargain. How much more?"

The thing that might have been the beginning of a smile had vanished, his features gathered into a scowl. "You refuse me?"

"It was not part of the bargain. How much more?"

"Perhaps more than you can afford to give," he said. He got to his feet in a single angry motion and strode away, leaving Simonis trembling in the night.

The woman who brought her food, the same one as before, treated her to the same moody silence. But that was broken the following morning, as the camp was stirring. Simonis, who was assisted at every camp-stop to put up her tent, but was now expected to stow it away by herself when camp was being broken in preparation for departure, was battling a recalcitrant tangled line when a low female voice addressed her from behind, in *coiné*, soft but virulent.

"You spurned him? Do you know what you have done? He came to his second wife last night, and nothing she did was good enough for him. He broke her arm…."

Simonis straightened and turned, but there was already nobody there.

"Not my responsibility," she whispered, gathering up her daughter, who let out a protesting squawk at being held so tightly. "Not. My. Responsibility…."

Ommar didn't come near her again, but that day the caravan veered a little more to the north, to the point where Simonis, when they made camp, was almost certain that she could catch the distant scent of salt and sea. She risked confrontation by stepping outside her little exclusion zone, out towards the edge of the camp, peering away into the darkness, wondering if she could perhaps catch sight of moonlight on water—and it was perhaps this that enabled her to catch sight of Ommar talking in a quiet, furtive manner to another, younger man.

She had paused at the sight, too far away to hear what they were talking about even if she could have understood their language, and then realised that the longer she stood staring the more chance there was of her being noticed—and she emphatically didn't want to attract any more notice than she had to. Adjusting Chryseis in her hammock across the front of her body—she never left the child alone and out of her sight, especially not after Ommar's advances—she literally jumped a foot back as she realised that the woman who had brought her food was standing right behind her, having come up noiselessly on bare feet.

"He is sending his nephew ahead," the woman said in her low smoky alto, her *coiné* almost fluent. "There's a man in Rhakotis who will be waiting to buy you when we arrive in the city. We're only a few days out, now."

"*Buy* me?" Simonis said, staring at the woman.

"I am Chaman, his wife," the woman said, smiling in a way that made the hair on Simonis's nape rise in sudden apprehension. "I gave him the idea."

"To sell me? I paid him for passage, he had the money in advance...."

"He wanted you."

"That was not part of our deal."

"He wanted you. When he doesn't get what he wants he is upset and angry and we all pay the price."

"I thought he broke your arm...."

"His *second* wife. Gulbat. He did. But when I suggested he should sell you, his mood changed." Her smile widened a little. "He made me very happy last night. I made him forget all about you once he had made up his mind to get a good price for you in Rhakotis...."

Simonis, through a haze of fear, began to feel the slow hot burn of anger. "What right does he have to sell me and my child?"

"Your child...? Oh, no. You. Just you. The man to whom you are to go will have no use for a mewling brat yet unweaned."

Simonis instinctively gathered her daughter closer. "Do you not have children of your own?"

"Not yet. Nor will, while he lusts for other women. Maybe I will take the child myself." Chaman reached out for Chryseis. "You could always run," she said silkily. "We are but a couple of days out of Rhakotis. You could take a skin of water and go. Yes, you should go. If you kept to the seashore you would hardly have to worry about being lost in the desert. The sea lies that way." She flung out an arm, pointing. "Not too far away. You can reach it quickly. Then you need to hide somewhere while he searches for you, but I can make sure he doesn't search too hard...."

Before Simonis had a chance to respond to this, Chaman was gone, suddenly, as though she had melted away into the shadows like a demon.

Simonis found herself trembling in the wake of that encounter. The rational part of her knew that going off on her own—even now, this close to Rhakotis—would probably mean death for her and her baby. But the alternative—the alternative was worse. She had realised that she had taken a bad fall when she had left Gallienus's house, but she had not realised that she had yet to hit bottom, or that the bottom would be this far down.

She thought she would sleep on it, give it one more day—but she slept with the baby-hammock wrapped around her and the child securely in it, and her little dagger in her hand. Dozed, rather, because the sleep was shallow and fitful and she kept starting awake as she thought she heard footsteps approaching. Finally she could take no more of it. The idea of being torn from her daughter tortured her. Better death than that—if that was what the One God had written in her destiny. She checked her water skin—it had been filled; she could survive on that for a day or two, until she reached Rhakotis, surely.

She slipped away well before dawn—going, instinctively, in the opposite direction from that which Chaman had indicated. She was proved right—if she had followed Chaman's directions she would have gone straight into deep desert, and her bones would have been bleaching in the sun in less than two days. But instead she quickly came to a place where the sand swept down to the shore, the sea inky dark in the night. She dared not go down to the water—if they did look for her, they would see her tracks on the wetter sand, quite easily. But there didn't seem to be anywhere to hide—until, a little desperately, she saw a rocky outcrop a little to her right and headed towards it across the softer dunes which spilled over her trail and erased it from sight. There was a crack between two large rocks, no more than that, hardly enough to conceal a grown human being, and far more likely than not to have already been picked as a resting place by some poisonous creature like an asp or a scorpion—but there was no time to think about that now, and Simonis trusted to God. She stepped into the damp cool place and curled up against the stone, cradling Chryseis against her with one hand and her precious water skin in the other.

"It is all right. It will be all right."

She did not realise that she had gone to sleep—or that she had even been capable of it—but she woke to full sunlight creeping into her shelter, throwing blinding glittering sparkles from the sea straight into her eyes. She was hungry, but she had not thought to bring food; she nursed Chryseis, there in the shadows, before taking a careful look around and emerging into the light and heat. The weight of the sun smote her like an anvil, and for the first time she felt a pang of misgiving—was it worth this? Did Chaman send her to her death after all? But she squared her shoulders and turned to the east, towards Rhakotis, and began walking, keeping the bright sea to her left.

She walked until she was numb, empty, her mind as washed-out clean as the pale sky that hung above her; once she came across another rocky outcropping and crouched in its pitiful shadow for as long as the shadow remained, but the hospitality was short-lived. All of her was focused on protecting Chryseis who, either sensing the increasing desperation that was building in her mother or herself sapped by the oppressive weight of the heat and light, barely let out a whimper; the backs of Simonis's own hands and her feet reddened with sunburn. She doled out the precious water sparingly, wondering once, briefly, if Chaman had lied about this too, if Rhakotis was not a week or more away, if she and Chryseis would die here on the shore and never be missed by any other living being. When night came, she could find no sheltering place to hold her, but simply collapsed in a fold of the sand, curled protectively around her child.

She thought she might have dreamed the rest. Bony hands on her shoulders, urging her to get up; the glimpse of a creature that beckoned to her from a few paces away—something that might have been a wraith of the desert or an angel, a wizened face crumpled into skin burned by years of harsh sun into a weathered prune, long stringy hair hanging over neck and shoulders with only two bright, living, compassionate eyes to show that Simonis wasn't following a corpse; the weightless feel of those hands as they came to rest on her again helping her move, when it became apparent that she was not about to do so under her own power; the stumble across night-cool desert sands under her feet; the feel of water trickled onto her cracked lips, in some dark and quiet sheltered place, lying on smooth stone. The helplessness of sensing a whimpering Chryseis taken from her side while she moaned and fought weakly and scrabbled to keep hold of the child—and then the baby's cries tapering off into a blessed quiet, and Simonis herself hovering between sleep and wakefulness, sensing Chryseis being returned to her embrace at some point, and then a voice, low, fluttery, almost other-worldly, whispering in her ear in what Simonis could have sworn was *coiné*—"*Go back. Go back to the city.*"

She woke hungry, still dazed. The creature she had followed into this lair—she took a closer look, recognised that it had long empty dugs drooping inside its rags, that this had once been a woman—crouched at the entrance of a shallow cave that held Simonis and Chryseis further in the back; Simonis must have made a noise as she stirred, because those bright eyes turned back to her, and the woman rose to her feet, beckoning again. It seemed to be dusk outside.

There was little choice to be had. It was follow, or stay here and die.

Her unlikely guide led out into the night desert, and they walked in silence, the wraith, the woman from Visant, and the cradled baby, for some time. They walked away from the sea, and Simonis was vaguely aware that she should have protested at that, that the sea was her one reliable signpost in the trackless wastes—but her guide seemed to know what she was doing.

All the more so when she suddenly halted on the crest of a large dune and glanced back at Simonis, pointing downslope.

Simonis allowed her eyes to follow the pointing finger, and saw that they had circled around to the sea again—the sea, glittering distant in the light of a tall lighthouse built well out on the water. And on the shore…dark shadows of walls in the moonlight.

Rhakotis.

"Thank.…" Simonis began, turning back to the wraith-guide, but she was already alone again. "Thank you," she whispered anyway, to the night air, to the One God who had sent her the angel.

There were walls and towers—a city—civilisation. Simonis's breath caught on a sob. She could rebuild—she could start again. She had done it before.

There were walls, and gates, but there was little that could threaten Rhakotis from the desert, and the city was not at war—Simonis slipped in without being stopped by perfunctory border guards. But somewhere along the way, and she could not remember how or where, she had lost her worldly wealth. The last pouch of her silver coins, the remaining pouches of the jewel hoard she had taken from Bakka—it was all gone, aside from the bearclaw *stoicheon*, which was never far from her, and a simple little necklace of tiny blue jewels and little value, which she had continued to wear because their colour had reminded her of Chryseis's eyes the first time she had looked into them. She was penniless; she had not eaten and had barely slept for nearly three days. The streets of Rhakotis, paved with a smooth dark stone, dazed and confused her—confused *her*, Simonis, once of Visant. She followed one winding street down to the docks, found nothing there to sustain her, followed another street back into the main city and found herself in a main square flanked on two sides by two temples. One, its age obviously measured in centuries, had been simply taken over by a new religion from an older one, the carvings and symbols of the ancient gods of the place existing quite companionably with the insignia of the place's new celestial masters. The other was new, built of that same bright hard white stone that Simonis had last seen in the ruins on the Cyrene headland, on the day she had first landed on the Afaris coast.

For some reason, that memory suddenly drew her now—the last time she had asked for something, and it had been granted to her.

She started to climb the wide shallow steps leading up to the columned front of the temple, church, cathedral, whatever the place was. She made it to the second step, and collapsed, lying with one arm still protectively wrapped around Chryseis. That was the last thing she heard before she passed out—the wailing, frightened cry of her child.

CHAPTER THIRTEEN

Simonis woke in a bed.

For the longest moment she lay there with her eyes closed, restless fingertips exploring bedclothes which were so thoroughly unexpected—simple, to be sure, and of relatively coarse weave, nothing that spoke of opulence, or even small luxury, but after her ordeal in the desert even the coarsest sheets on the hardest bed were sheer delight.

And then she remembered something, something *missing*, and her eyes flew open in panic.

Chryseis. Where is Chryseis?

The room she found herself in was improbable—a small cell with a low ceiling and a single small barred window, the bed pushed against one wall and a small pedestal beside it on which an unlit candle stood in an iron holder. The door was closed, and looked solid; for a moment Simonis wondered feverishly if she had transgressed some law she was not aware of when she had entered Rhakotis, and had been incarcerated for it. But there was no sense of imprisonment here. The cell was small, to be sure, and bare except for the basics—the bed, the pedestal, the candle, a small piece of rag-woven rug on the stone floor, the wooden Wheel hung on the wall….

The wooden Wheel on the wall. It was a monastic cell, not a prison.

Where was Chryseis? Simonis felt as though her heart had been removed from her body and was beating somewhere else, apart from her—even if it hadn't been for the heaviness in her breasts, which literally ached for Chryseis.

She turned back the covers on the bed with a shaking hand and discovered that she was clean, and naked underneath a linen shift in which she had been dressed when laid into this bed. There had to have been a certain process associated with all of these things, and it troubled her a little that she could not recall any of it—but Chryseis's name burned like fire in her mind, and she swung her feet out of the bed. They seemed to have been wrapped in something, though, like thin bootees, and she stumbled as she stood up on the rag rug. Her head spun, and the light coming in through the little window suddenly seemed a little too bright; she closed her eyes, covering them with one hand.

"You're up?"

The voice was female, soft, and came from the direction of the doorway.

Simonis turned to look, too fast, and sat down rather abruptly on the bed. The door had been opened a little way and an ascetic, long-nosed face wrapped in a black wimple and veil was peering around it. The expression on it was friendly, but Simonis got the distinct feeling that this woman didn't often smile to strangers.

But she had spoken in *coiné*, the language that Simonis understood; at least one horror fell from her at that, the fear that she would spend endless fruitless hours trying to communicate with uncomprehending and uncaring people while she tried to find her child.

That was the first thing that came out of her mouth. "Chryseis?"

"If you mean your baby, she is being taken care of," the nun said, opening the door a little further and stepping into the room. "We thought it best that you were given a chance to rest. Now that you are up and awake, we will bring the child to you. She is quite safe, you need have no fear, and she seems to have taken remarkably little harm from any of what seems to have befallen the two of you. When the Bishop found you on the steps of the cathedral you were in a swoon, parched, and you looked like you hadn't eaten for a while. And your hands...."

Simonis glanced down at her hands as the nun spoke. Her fingers had been left free and she could see, now that her attention had been drawn to them, that they had been badly sunburned—and indeed glistened with some sort of salve. The rest of her hands, from the base of her fingers to her wrist, were wrapped in a thin linen bandage, with something suppurating from underneath.

"It all blistered," the nun said. "We put ointment on the burns when they brought you here, but it was all badly blistered. We did what we could. The tops of your feet, too. You probably won't be wearing shoes until the swelling and the redness dies down."

"Chryseis," Simonis said again. "Please, can I see her?"

"I will go and let them know to bring her," the nun said. "In the meantime, please, do stay in bed. At least for today. You won't be walking far on those feet, anyway—and I will bring you your daughter, and some food, and water. And someone will be by to change the ointment on your hands."

"Thank you," Simonis said faintly.

"As the Wheel wills it," the nun said, tucking her hands into the sleeves of her habit. "I will be back."

Simonis had grown up in the shadow of the Hippodrome. The One God, to one like her, had always shown his stern and unforgiving face—Hippodrome folk were not precisely barred from attending mass in the great cathedrals, but neither were they encouraged to come and pray there. They were served by a second-layer, almost lay, clergy who ministered to the Hippodrome sick and dying, to their weddings and their funerals, at the Hippodrome chapels and often in people's homes.

Simonis had been brought up in a world where the One God ruled the heavens and the lives and fates of the men and women who lived beneath it—but she had never had any particular reason to trust the One God as the guardian of her own destiny, or his gospel as being the supreme holy truth above all other. She did not quite believe the nun's words until she did return, bearing a freshly swaddled squirming bundle in her arms, and Chryseis was physically handed to her once again.

The nun was accompanied by another sister, a younger one with a shy smile on her lips and wearing the lighter veil of the novitiate, which allowed dark curls to escape the restraining bands of the veil that framed her face. The second sister had brought a plain wooden tray on which rested two bowls and a brimming cup.

"You have to eat," the older nun told Simonis. "A little at a time. And you have to keep drinking. A lot. You were parched when you came here. Your little girl was a lot better off than you were when you were both brought to us."

"I remember…the white church," Simonis murmured, taking spoonfuls of the gruel in one of the bowls. She kept Chryseis tucked into the crook of her arm as though she were afraid that if she handed the child to anyone she would be spirited away again. "And after that…nothing."

"The Bishop had been out that day. He and his entourage practically tripped over you on the stair when they returned to the cathedral. He was about to order that you be taken away and be given a decent burial when one of the priests of his company heard something—your baby," the nun said. "You might say she saved your life. When they found a living child they took another look at the mother. And so you came to this place."

"Who brought me here?"

"His name is Father Honorius. He has asked about you. Perhaps when you are feeling better you can come to one of the services when he is celebrant."

Simonis, Hippodrome-bred, recoiled a little at that. Did these nuns even know who Simonis was, what she was? Would this gentle invitation into the church vanish like censer smoke when they found out? Would Father Honorius regret his act of charity...?

"That's enough for now," the older nun said, removing the tray from Simonis's hands. "Rest now. Perhaps tomorrow you can tell us more about how you came to lie as one dead on the steps of the cathedral. Do you want me to take the child?"

Simonis tightened her grasp on Chryseis. "*Chryseis*. Her name is Chryseis. Please don't take her."

"We will set up a basket for Chryseis right here by your own bed," the nun said. "What a lovely name that is. Please, be easy. The child is safe from harm here."

When Simonis was finally allowed to go outside for the first time, she was astonished and delighted to explore the inner cloisters of the convent with their neat herb gardens filled with medicinal plants for salves and poultices. Nothing was huge or out of scale, just enough of everything was present to maintain a fine balance. This was the nuns' own preserve, behind a closed and securely locked iron grille and gate. The garden extended a little bit beyond the gate, a ring of thick-skinned, sappy, low-growing desert-resistant plants which nevertheless managed a semblance of beauty and grace planted around several carved statues.

One of the nuns caught Simonis peering at the statues through the grille, and, smiling, fetched a key and led her out amongst the stone people.

"Who are they?" Simonis asked.

"Some of them are here to help us remember people whose souls the One God has long since gathered to himself," the nun said. "That one, the large one at the end, that was the man who first preached the word of the One God in Rhakotis, long ago. Our cathedral, the one you chose to seek sanctuary in, is named for him. Others were put here to commemorate other holy people. There are those among us to whom God speaks more closely, more loudly—to us they may even appear to be mad—but they have an air of sanctity to them. They are revered. Some have gone off into the desert and lived there for years, for decades, all alone—existing on what the One God sees fit to lay before them. People have been known to go off on pilgrimages to these holy hermits and leave their prayers with them—for speaking to them is only a step removed from speaking to God.…"

"I think I may have met one of them," Simonis murmured, staring up at one of the statues. It looked nothing like her desert wraith, the woman who had led her to Rhakotis out of the wilderness, but suddenly the voice was clear in her mind, as clear as though the words were being spoken into her ear right at that moment: *Go back to the city.*

The nun was looking at Simonis, her face alight with interest. "You never spoke of what happened to you before you came to us. Of how you survived the desert with nothing but a near-empty water skin and a small child in the folds of your garment. Are you telling me that one of our holy people helped you?"

"It was a woman. I think it was a woman. She had long straggly hair, and leathery skin, and if she still had teeth there can't have been many. She looked as though she had been there forever—for a thousand years—but she spoke *coiné*—or maybe she just said something and that was what I heard.…"

"She *spoke* to you?"

Simonis turned to stare at the nun, frowning lightly. "I—yes, I think—you know who this is?"

"There is only one of the holy ones that we know of who is a woman—and only one who would, if she spoke at all, use that language. But Matthea has taken a vow of silence—she has not spoken for years. For decades, even. People sometimes encounter her, and she signals them, and maybe sometimes blesses them, but she has not spoken to anyone for as long as anyone can remember. We don't know much about her, other than her name, and that she did, once, long ago, come to Rhakotis from the heartland of the Empire. She *spoke* to you? Then you are blessed indeed. What did she tell you?"

"I think…I think to go home," Simonis murmured.

But she didn't relish the prospect. She had hoped to return to Visant in some kind of glory, not like a beggar asking for charity from her city, her people, perhaps from Cicatrice, if he would forgive her and accept her back in her previous capacity. She did have a little gold stashed away in Visant, she had been prudent enough to leave herself some reserves, but it was bitter to go back to claim them when she had expected never to need them again. There was also the small but vital fact that as far as the city bureaucracy was concerned, she was still *in* the city, never having officially left it, and that might make her re-entry difficult—she had no paperwork to satisfy the guards, at wharf or land gate.

Something about the statue garden, or something that the nun had said, suddenly made Simonis more curious about the faith of the One God than she had ever been before. It was also something to concentrate on, to keep thinking about, an excuse to put the possible unpalatable logistics of her journey back to Visant out of her mind for the time being.

Simonis and Father Honorius, the priest who had brought her to the abbey infirmary, were introduced to one another by one of the nuns who had been nursing her, and Simonis, on impulse, had gone down on one knee before the priest and lifted up the hem of his cassock to her lips.

"My dear child," he had said, reaching down to lift her, "I am not God that you should thank me thus. It was God who delivered you to our church; I merely lent the arms to carry you to a place where you could be cared for."

"Still," Simonis said. "I owe you my life."

"If that is so, then use it to find joy," Father Honorius said. "You are, I think, very young…and yet I see the weight of worlds in your eyes. If ever you need to lay that weight aside, I am here to listen should you need an ear. What you tell me will go no further, if you forbid that—and it may ease your soul. But be that as it may—you are always, under any circumstances, welcome in my church."

She took him up on that invitation, and sat in the back of the church for many a service where Father Honorius had been the celebrant, and found herself fascinated by what he had to say on the fundamentals of the faith which had shaped her own life. Sometimes the things he spoke of were strange, even unbelievable. In her own experience, she had often found the faith that she at least paid lip service to be less than successful in practising the mercy and justice that it preached in the pulpit when it came to the harsh lives of those whom the establishment considered to have fallen beyond possibility of redemption, forced by circumstances to fall short of a suitably dutiful and pious life.

But at least some of what she heard preached so openly here in Rhakotis, by high-ranking priests and even the princes of the church like the Bishop himself, would be considered rank heresy in Visant…and yet it was heresy that made far more sense to Simonis than the orthodox dogma had ever done.

She had no way of knowing if Father Honorius had noticed her, there in the back, but he put that to rest, when she all but ran him down one morning as he came out of a side door to the church and walked briskly across the upper landing to the stair leading down to the square.

The same stair, as it happened, where they had first 'met' one another, where he had heard Chryseis's cry and stooped to take another look at the woman whom all had taken for dead.

Simonis stopped, a little flustered, her lips already shaping an apology. But Father Honorius had merely smiled.

"It is good to see you here at the church again," he said. "I have noticed you have been spending quite a bit of time here."

"It is…you preach very differently than they do in Visant," Simonis said awkwardly.

Father Honorius smiled a small, secret smile. "They have lost no opportunity in reminding us of it," he said. "Does it vex you?"

She looked at him with an expression that was a mixture of guilt and rebellion. "I was never much of a believer," she said.

"And yet you spend hours of your time here, away from your child, listening to us speak of faith in the cathedral," Father Honorius said. "Well, if you have any questions, I would be glad to be of service in trying to give you some answers—even if you don't consider yourself to be a person of deep faith. In fact—if you are not expected elsewhere—you might walk with me. I have an errand to run, and I could use the company—and perhaps even the assistance."

Simonis hesitated only for the briefest instant before nodding and falling into step beside him. "Have you ever *been* to Visant?" she asked him.

"I? No. Not in person. The Bishop has, Bishop Timoteo, the man you heard preaching today. Why?"

"This," Simonis said, lifting her arms in an expansive gesture, indicating the Rhakotis street on which they walked side by side, the priest and the woman in the plain gown with her hair braided away from her face—the way that passers-by nodded at Father Honorius, sometimes at Simonis, but nobody showed any sign of astonishment or disapproval to see the two of them walking together. "This would never happen in Visant. The priests in the City, priests of your own rank here in Rhakotis, do not walk the streets with women, particularly women who…." She caught herself, hesitated. Nobody appeared to be aware of her past here, and she had no wish to be the one to broach the subject. But then she carried on, "And a priest would never ask a woman if she wanted answers to questions of faith. In Visant, a woman's lot is not to question—women are expected to confine themselves to being prayerful and pious, to attend services regularly, perhaps devote themselves to charitable works if they are wealthy enough. Visant women are taken to have no business in meddling in the affairs of the church, and that includes discussing anything to do with it with any of the clergy."

"Yes," Father Honorius said, "it is different here in Rhakotis. Here, women can become as holy as any man—I am told you may have met one of our holy women yourself out in the desert, Matthea."

"That would not happen in Visant."

"What, a woman who is called holy?"

"Father," Simonis said, "in Visant a woman is the property of her husband, or of her father, the man who is in a position to choose her husband. If she has any rank at all, that is. The other women in the city, they are just property, that is all—they belong to whoever can claim them. Some of them are cloistered in the nunneries, to be sure, and I suppose they are the property of the One God—but in Visant many women view the cloister as an escape rather than a vocation."

"God does not own property," Father Honorius said, "and a human being certainly ought not to be such. But I do begin to see what you mean about your own faith. It may not be based in a refusal to believe—but rather in a lack of insight into what the Church actually thinks and feels and preaches. If I can be of any assistance in clarifying any of our teachings, it would be my duty and my privilege to provide that for you…. but ah, here we are. Might we defer our discussion until we start for home?"

Simonis glanced up and suddenly felt the blood drain from her face—the banners that hung from the walls they were approaching were familiar to her. The factions of Visant—White Jewel, Golden Crown, Obsidian Knife, Scarlet Banner.

This was the Hippodrome. The Hippodrome of Rhakotis.

Of course there was one. Simonis knew that—this was the third-largest city of the Empire, it stood to reason that it would have its own arena. But she had made a point of trying to forget about its existence, of avoiding its shadow, the taint of its association—not while she was in the holy places, being treated well, with her child safe from beggary and the street…and the Hippodrome itself.

He knows, was the first panicked thought that came into her head as Father Honorius stepped up to a door in a plain house a little down the street from the back gate of the Hippodrome. When it was opened to his knock, he began to step inside and then turned with a quizzical look as Simonis hesitated out in the street.

"When I said you might be of assistance," he said quietly, "it is now. You are free to wait for me out here, of course—but it would be greatly appreciated if you could help me."

"What can I do?" Simonis said, through bloodless lips.

"Comfort," Father Honorius said simply. "Come with me. Please."

Because it was he who asked, because she owed him, Simonis came—unwillingly and slowly, her hands clenched into fists at her sides, concealed in her skirts. Right until the moment she stepped across the threshold, she entertained thoughts of breaking and running, of going straight back to the infirmary, collecting her baby, and running for her life...before they all turned on her, and made her go. As they could. As they *would*, as they were sure to do, when they found out what she was. But she didn't run, and the door closed behind her, and she and Father Honorius were beckoned deeper inside by a young woman who had invited them in. Her eyes were red and swollen with weeping.

The house was fiercely plain, its walls whitewashed and devoid of all decoration except for a White Jewel banner hung on the one wall where the light struck in the room, its furnishings simple and battered as though they had seen a good deal of use in several lifetimes preceding their arrival in this house. In a tiny cell-like room in the back, an old woman lay in a low pallet bed, her eyes closed, breathing shallowly. One of her hands had slipped from where her hands had obviously been arranged on her breast, and dangled off the edge of her bed; Simonis, after hesitating at the door, realised that she and Father Honorius were alone with the old woman, and reached out instinctively to lift the hand and restore it to its place—but the thin bony fingers closed weakly around hers, and she froze, half-crouched by the bed, glancing up at the priest.

Father Honorius had taken out a scarf embroidered with the symbol of the Wheel and kissed it, draping it around his neck. He nodded at Simonis, half-kneeling by the bed.

"You're doing fine," he whispered. "Hold her hand, she needs the comfort of the human touch."

He took the woman's free hand in both of his own and bowed his head over the bed, beginning a soft chant. Simonis crouched with her own head bowed, holding on to the aged hand that had been entrusted to her—it was as though it was faith itself that was being offered to her in this moment, a belief in something bigger and stronger than herself, a sense of a faint light filling the dark room. But she could not hold on to it—not even as Father Honorius concluded his benediction and beckoned to Simonis to follow him out of the room, leaving the old woman breathing a little easier, as though she were now merely asleep and not fighting for each gasp of breath. But Simonis's own fear had surged back as she stepped into the corridor once more—fear, and confusion—*He knows! He knows everything! And yet he came, he came himself to ease a dying woman's last hours—a dying woman who belongs to the Hippodrome…*

She had bitten down on it, hard. Father Honorius had said nothing—and she would not start this, she *would* not…but the words were in her throat already, in her mouth. They walked away together from the house in silence, she and the priest, but it was Simonis, after all, who broke that silence with the things that had to be said.

"She is…of the Hippodrome," Simonis said, carefully, hesitating over every word.

"Yes?" said Father Honorius, both answering her question and asking one of his own.

Simonis swallowed, truth bubbling out of her. "In Visant…this would never have happened. When my father died they sent the grave diggers for his body. No priest would have come to him." She had kept her eyes down, staring at the paving stones at her feet, from the moment they had left the house where the dying woman was; now she lifted them at last, full of tears, to search for Father Honorius's face. "That's where I grew up. In Visant's gutters. In the deep dark places where the priests of the One God would not go."

"That's where you left the faith that you should have carried, that should have carried you," Father Honorius said softly. "In the hands of the priests who did not wish to get those hands dirty."

Simonis wiped her nose on the back of her hand, like a child. "Yes, well, that is exactly it. The things you preach in the church. About the Messiah being the living God. Not a human child fathered on a human woman by a divine spirit."

"How does that matter, or change things?"

"I was…I suppose I *am*…a dancer in the Hippodrome in Visant," Simonis said. "I danced all the seduction legends of the pagan ages—Xeuxes, the seducer of mortal women whose half-divine children peopled half the living world, and all the other Gods who ruled men in their own image—how were the deeds of the old Gods at all different from what the scriptures say happened when the One God swept them all aside? The way I have always heard it preached, the One God reached down to us by sending his Messiah, a prophet of his word, a son of his spirit. But how was that ever different from having a son of Xeuxes—one of the many—ruling over us?"

"Your old gods required constant and unending sacrifice if they were to be expected to continue to show favour on the devout in their temples," Father Honorius said.

Simonis shrugged unhappily. "But…the Wheel. That could be called a sacrifice, too."

"It was—and it wasn't," Father Honorius said. "Or, in a way, it was an inadvertent sacrifice by man. If there was a sacrifice, the One God made it on behalf of mankind, providing his own sacrificial offering. You might say that the ancient Eastern Empire, the one that rose and fell before our own time, tried to stop a new faith which it could not control—it grew afraid, and took the Messiah, and bound him to the wheel of death and left him out there in the desert to die of it—and then, when they came to get the body, there was nothing there…." He paused. "*And the One God had reached down and gathered him into heaven, so that he might sit at His right hand and speak for the common man in whose company he had walked on earth for a time,*" he added after a moment, quoting from the scriptures.

"But the scriptures never said that he *was* a man,' Simonis said. "Or at least the parts that I know did not."

"The scriptures, like so many things, can depend on who interprets them," Father Honorius said.

"Yes, and in Visant they say that the Messiah was the son of the One God, literally, fathered by him upon a mortal woman and raised as a mortal child—half-human, like the children of the ancient Gods like Xeuxes were. They say that this is the only reason why he speaks for us—because he was, at least half of him was, for at least a little while, one of us."

"Yes," Father Honorius said. "And here in Rhakotis, we see the Messiah as being, in Himself, God—that he may have taken on human form as a disguise, something that would allow him to walk amongst us unremarked, to get to know us, to understand us. And thus the central mystery, such as you have heard it preached in Visant, disappears—they found no body on the Wheel when they came for it because there had never *been* a real body, a human body, that could die there. It had always been an illusion, created by a divine power. No more than that."

"Then there was nothing human in the Messiah at all."

"Not as we see it. There can be no ambiguity in the nature of God—and the Messiah cannot have been human and divine, both, because then he would be fully neither." He paused. "You are finding the Rhakotis interpretation of the scriptures to be less…derivative…of the ways practised by the gods of old?"

"It makes *sense* to me," Simonis said in a low voice. "I have known far too many men—far too many men's bodies—I know their faults and their frailty and their flaws, and it would only weaken the divine half to have it watered down by that." She turned her head fractionally, but they had already rounded a corner, gone down a different street, and the banners hanging off the Hippodrome walls were out of sight.

Father Honorius caught the small movement. "Is there something else?"

"You won't tell them…?"

"Tell what? To whom? The sisters at the infirmary that your past involves the Hippodrome?"

Simonis turned back to look at him, her eyes still unaccountably full of tears. "Chryseis," she said. "She is safe there. And I had hoped that for her, the Hippodrome world…."

"Child," he said, "in some ways Rhakotis and your Visant are not that different after all. For some the cloister is a vocation, for some a refuge—those who went there because they were good women and because they want to be doing the work of the One God would not judge you…and those who ended up there because they themselves were fleeing worlds like the Hippodrome *could* not judge you because they would be sitting in judgment on themselves in doing so. And they all know that only God can be their judge, in the end—theirs, and yours. They won't turn you out, until you are ready to go, until you have a plan."

"I have no idea what to do next," Simonis said.

"God will make it clear," Father Honorius said. "What you choose to do next, that remains up to you—but at the very least you stopped to look at a signpost today which you had never considered to be important before. We can leave it at that, for now."

One unexpected consequence of the sudden return to the Hippodrome sphere was that Simonis—for all that she was grateful that her child had the security of the cloister, where the nuns doted on Chryseis and seemed to be happy that she was among them—looked at her baby and no longer saw only the child. There was more to her, suddenly, than just her dark curls and laughing eyes and small grasping hands. There was the memory of her father. Much of that was less than pleasant, but too much of it was—and then those memories led to others, and Simonis's body woke again to longings she had thought the desert had burned out of her. She felt irrationally guilty, harbouring such impure thoughts in the quiet sanctified corridors of the cloister—of stealing glances at the young men in the street through her eyelashes and being unable to prevent a small smile from coming to her lips as she allowed her imagination to briefly toy with them in her mind. She did not want to go back to the Hippodrome life—she did not want to belong to whoever had the asking price—she did not want to return to being a courtesan spy for Cicatrice in Visant, or to any kind of life where she trafficked with herself as her major, and perhaps only, asset. But she did miss the heat and the passion of being with a man, that was the One God's own truth—and in a way that was the road onto which the sainted Matthea's words had been guiding her all along.

Go back to the city.

But she did not have a good enough reason to leave Rhakotis for Visant. Not then. Not yet. Not until the baby was a little older....

Not until word came from across the Middle Sea that things had changed in Visant. That the old Emperor had finally closed his eyes for the last time, and that a new Emperor wore the purple.

The old Emperor had been sympathetic to Rhakotis and its schismatics. The new Emperor's first edicts strongly suggested that this would no longer be the case. The new Emperor was of the orthodox faith, and would act to ensure that the orthodox dogma was followed in his city...and in his Empire, where he could enforce his will.

Rhakotis would suffer for this. So would its clergy—the Bishop, Father Honorius, the other priests who had been kind to Simonis.

Go back, the desert saint had told her. *Go back to the city.*

She had meant Visant, after all. And now there was a reason.

Simonis would leave Rhakotis, and return to Visant under whatever circumstances the situation demanded; she would lie and cheat to get back into the Queen City if she had to. She had to leave one of the cities that she loved in order to return to another—so that she could be a voice for the luminous and visionary Rhakotis in the bastion of orthodox faith that was Visant—speaking for the City of Light in the City of Gold.

CHAPTER FOURTEEN

It was almost two weeks before the whirlwind subsided long enough for the city to take a deep breath.

Valerian, the old Emperor, had to be properly laid to rest in his sarcophagus, with the Emperor-elect and his closest entourage in constant attendance, before the Palace officials and the Patriatch could turn their hands to planning the solemn procession to the great cathedral of Holy Wisdom, and the long and lavish Coronation Service. Leontes, who had seen at least one of these events from the outside, seemed resigned to being the centerpiece of one this time; Maxentius, who was one of the people involved on the Palace side of things, was astonished at how fast the hours of his day disappeared and how few hours his nights seemed to have over the crucial few days.

They prayed for a respite from the cold and the rain of the season—and the One God seemed to smile on the new Emperor by blessing the city with a day of unseasonable warmth and brightness. Leontes walked to his Coronation, bareheaded in the sunshine; he was clad in a costly but very simple garment, a robe without trim or embellishment but very finely woven, a running thread of gold in the fabric catching the sun, with a fur-lined cloak thrown around his shoulders to keep out the chill. He emerged from the Bronze Gate of the Imperial Palace and stepped out on the broad public avenue, extensively repaired and levelled so that the Emperor would not stumble on any uneven cobble or pothole in his path, and sprinkled with rose-scented sawdust, all the way between the Palace gate and the great double doors of the cathedral. The route had been decorated with sweet-smelling wreaths, all the more extravagant, seeing as to what season it was, and weaving garlands of flowers was a costly, if not downright impossible, affair at that time.

The streets were lined by the cheering populace, with a couple of staged encounters where those who had planned the procession had seeded their own people with pre-scripted acclamations—but few of those were even necessary, especially given that the fountains along the route to the church had been drained of water and filled with wine. Leontes himself was preceded by standard-bearers who carried banners with the insignia of the Empire and of Leontes himself; he was followed, in strict protocol-ruled order, by the serried ranks of state dignitaries and Senators in ceremonial robes. Around the Emperor's own person marched an honour guard of the Palace Guards whose commander he had but lately been, men who knew Leontes well, who held their heads high and wore expressions of fierce pride that their Count had been raised to this high estate.

Few Imperial consorts had been crowned as Empress-regnant, Augusta, a full equal to the man who sat on the Imperial throne—for some, the honour had never come, and for others it came only after years as the Emperor's wife, often after she had produced an Imperial heir. Euphaedra would not have wanted the title, would not have sought it, and Leontes had decided not to crown her as Augusta—she would share his life, and his throne, as she had always done, but without the weight of the Empire on her own head. Euphaedra waited for his arrival at the cathedral with the rest of the court ladies who had gathered around her when she stepped into her new rank, seated on a throne-like chair of her own, but hidden behind the carved screen that partitioned off the women's gallery. She watched from her protected place as Leontes walked into the cathedral, and down the aisle left for him in the crowded church interior, and then bowed before the Patriatch of Visant who glittered in his most lavish regalia. Leontes heard the service from the body of the church, below the dais, from the front row of the dignitaries and aristocracy of Visant—and then, at the Patriarch's signal, he climbed the last few steps to where a golden throne waited for him. He stood while an attendant wrapped the purple-and-gold *loros* around him like a toga and then sat down carefully on the throne. The Patriarch motioned forward a young attendant who bore the Imperial Diadem on a purple silk cushion.

Maxentius had seen this before, in Valerian's chambers, and he held his breath as the Patriarch took up the crown, held it high as if he were offering it to the One God first or calling down a blessing upon it, and then placed it slowly on Leontes's grizzled head.

There was a lavish breakfast, after, in the Patriarch's quarters adjoining the cathedral; the new-crowned Emperor and the Patriarch and the inner circle of the court shared freshly baked bread and quince paste and new cheese. When that was over, the Emperor and his consort received a final blessing from the Patriarch, and the court procession returned to the Palace.

And then the pomp and the glory was over, and the real hard work had to begin.

Leontes's household had been moved to the Emperor's quarters in the inner maze of the Palace at some time during these whirlwind few days, with Leontes himself not quite sure when or precisely how—he just found himself ensconced in the proper place when the time came, with most things put away neatly by the silentiaries of the Inner Chambers who were now his own intimate body servants, before he had to deal with any of it. A few things remained, left out to his hand and awaiting his dispensation—but it was a remarkably tidy and quiet room that met Maxentius's eyes when he came in answer to his uncle's summons on the afternoon of the coronation.

"Augustus," Maxentius said with a slight smile, entering the room and making a bow as he did so.

"She cried," Leontes said without preamble. "Euphaedra. She would not really tell me, but I could see it in her face, and one of her ladies kept a crushed handkerchief out of sight very badly."

"Would she have preferred it if you had crowned her Augusta?" Maxentius asked.

"No, it wasn't that. It was just…we had a certain life, she and I. A certain understanding. I knew what she was and what she was capable of, what she could stretch to. I think she is holding it against me that I accepted the throne. Just the tiniest bit, but she is. It's as though I betrayed that early covenant. But between you and me, I have a feeling that she will keep a great deal of state from here on, whether or not she is expected to, whether or not she wears an Augusta's crown. She has always been nothing if not conscious of her responsibilities."

"I will go and pay my respects tomorrow," Maxentius said.

"She would like that," Leontes smiled. "Now come in, sit, before the whole circus begins again. I have little bit of a gap—and there are things, there are people, that we need to talk about."

"I saw one of those people at your coronation," Maxentius said, taking the offered chair. "If looks could have killed, you would have fallen down dead from your throne before the Patriarch ever put the diadem on your head. And I, it seems, would have followed immediately after."

Leontes nodded. "We need to deal with Sarrus, one way or another," he said softly. "He cannot, of course remain in the positions which he held under Valerian. I cannot have a Grand Chancellor who does not trust me, does not like me, and would be constantly working to undermine me at every turn. And yet...I cannot retire him and send him out to pasture—he is not a man who will take kindly to that, or even accept it. I might remove him from court, but he would continue to work against me from wherever I sent him—and unless I purge the *entire* senior staff of the Palace and replace everyone on the Council, I cannot be certain who still owes any sort of allegiance or affection to him, and who might resent me for whatever sins Sarrus sees fit to pin upon me. And I cannot imprison him, for he has done nothing that warrants a cell."

"He tried to buy an election for a minion," Maxentius said.

"He *tried*. We *did*. And with his money," Leontes said tersely.

"Given the candidates who were presented," Maxentius said, "it was a well-haggled bargain. Aurelius would have been an iron tyrant. Vitalles would have bent over backwards to spread out the tentacles of his own friends and family into every conceivable niche. Celerian...." His lips tightened. "We are still going to have to deal with Celerian."

Leontes turned sharply to stare at Maxentius. "What are you saying?"

"Let's just say that I had...warning...that Celerian might not go down without a fight. But leave Celerian to me. You were speaking of Sarrus, and the first step to pulling Celerian's fangs is to take away his strongest prop."

"But as I was saying—" Leontes spread his hands in a gesture that was almost one of helplessness. "I cannot retire him, and I cannot keep him in his present post—what do I do with the man?"

"All he wanted," Maxentius said thoughtfully, stroking his chin with his fingers, "is the chance to have a hand in the ruling of the Empire—to have things done in the ways that he deems proper and fit. That's why he sponsored a candidate—a candidate who was supposed to be his public face to the world while he pulled all the strings in the background...well...give him that. Exactly that."

"As *Chancellor*?"

"Hardly. As you say, that's a shade too much power. But he has been here for so long, he has been in the center of things for so many years, that he definitely does have a huge and eclectic store of knowledge and insight. Use that. *Not* as Chancellor—I think that he would be the first to be very suspicious if you were to offer him the possibility of retaining that title. But bring him in—make an occasion of it, full court day, give him his hour in the sun—call him in and offer him a seat on the Council. A permanent Advisor Emeritus post. Tell him how valuable his experience and the wisdom born of so many years of faithful service are, and remain, to the Empire—even with Valerian dead and gone. A lifetime seat at the Council—make it a full decree, give him a document with an Imperial seal on it. If he comes up with ideas that are too preposterous for words, it's those who sit around the Council table with him who will tell him so. You won't have to. He will never be your friend, but he might at the very least be an honourable enemy, and one on whom you can keep a close eye if he is a part of your own government."

"What did you mean," Leontes said, serious again, his sudden brilliant smile vanishing as quickly as it had arrived, "let you take care of Celerian?"

"He's being watched," Maxentius said curtly. "I've put men on him the first opportunity I got, straight after you appeared in? at? the Hippodrome. He hasn't made a move since that I haven't known about. I know whom he has talked to, and what they said. If he talked in his sleep I would know what he dreams about."

"Do you have a plan?"

"I won't start anything, but if he does, I will be ready," Maxentius said. "And I'm very much afraid that he is going to find it…difficult…to get travelling papers out of Visant for the foreseeable future. I want him where I can lay my hands on him if I need to, not plotting secretly from some distant estate where he is beyond my reach. I am watching him. And I will be more than interested to see which way he jumps when you get Sarrus to join the orthodoxy rather than the opposition…."

"Assuming I can get Sarrus to do it," Leontes said. "Don't underestimate the old fox, he might balk—and then we're back to square one."

"He won't balk," Maxentius said.

Sarrus didn't balk. Leontes offered him the Emeritus Councilor seat in full court audience, as Maxentius had suggested—it was deliberately set up as a solemn occasion, and phrased by Leontes as a request which Sarrus could graciously grant the Emperor rather than just an offer of a court position as a bribe for silence or complicity. Sarrus did take a long moment to think about it; his expression, as always, was difficult to read, and his eyes did flicker to Maxentius and stayed on him long enough for Maxentius to piece together the basic thought process: Sarrus was no fool and could no doubt see clearly how the scenario he was being asked to consider could be used to effectively hobble him—but it also carried a permanent exalted status in the highest of Imperial circles, and he could not think of a downside to that, especially presented in the way that it had been. He accepted the offer.

Leontes had the props ready—the Imperial Letter of Appointment on heavy parchment, sealed with scarlet ribbons and in gold; a heavy belt of office, substantial enough to encircle even Sarrus's considerable girth; a pouch full of golden solidi as a down payment on the salary he would be drawing in his new position. Maxentius himself had counted up those coins; he was rather wishing he could be present when Sarrus counted them in the privacy of his own chambers and discovered the sum contained in the pouch precisely equalled the sum he had handed to Leontes when he had first thought of buying the Imperial Diadem for Celerian.

As for Celerian himself, it did not take him long after the Sarrus audience to make his move. Suddenly cut off from access to Imperial funds and high levels of information, and finding himself thwarted by what appeared, on the face of it, to be simple bureaucratic incompetence when he attempted to leave Visant, he was trapped, frustrated, and furious.

And he knew very well where the source of his troubles lay.

Still, when he made his move, it was an audacious one—and although Maxentius had been speaking nothing less than the truth when he told Leontes that he was having Celerian watched, the man was still good enough to manage to give his watchers the slip, several times. They were mostly able to pick him up again before too much time had passed, but less than a week after Sarrus's induction into the Imperial Council, Maxentius's men reported that Celerian had gone missing again—and this time his absence had stretched for more than twenty-four hours. Maxentius did not like Celerian out of his sight, but he was far from worried—the man would find it very difficult if not impossible to escape the city, and as long as he was boxed in within Visant itself, anything he attempted to do there would come to light sooner rather than later.

But Celerian appeared to have reserves that Maxentius had not quite taken into account.

It was with a sense of shock that he recognised Celerian's voice behind him on his own balcony, inside the secure House of Peacocks, as he stood watching clouds scudding across an angry gray sky—it seemed to have become a habit over time, his tracking the clouds from the vantage point of his balcony. It helped him think, in some strange way—clearing his head of anything irrelevant or too obtrusive, leaving his mind empty of everything but billowing clouds and sky and leaving himself a fresh and uncluttered space to think and plan in while never forgetting the idea that a storm was on the way.

He had been aware that this storm was coming. He had not realised that it was already upon him.

"You haven't won," Celerian said, in a voice that was low and dripping with venom. "Whatever you think you can do to me, you haven't won. The game of thrones is never over."

Maxentius turned, slowly, to face the intruder.

"How did you get in here?"

Celerian laughed. "I could tell you I paid a great deal for a magic potion which turned me into a bird, and I flew in here on wings of bone and feather. The truth, as always, is uglier—one of your men betrayed you, and another is dead. I paid well for a man—not giving my own name, please, you pick your guards better than *that*—to gain entry into the garden. It was harder to slip into the house, alas—there's the man who had to die. And once inside the house, well, you don't have a guard at every door. It was easy enough to find out where you were. And here I am."

"And the reason you are here is…?"

The oily storm-light suddenly glinted on a naked dagger blade clutched tightly in Celerian's hand. "Now you, too, die," Celerian said. "And once you are dead…I will find my way back to where I was, before. Your father is an old man, too—he can only reign so long. And if his reign is a little shorter than anybody anticipated—well, that too would be the will of the One God, wouldn't it?"

It was a direct threat against the man now Emperor . It was enough to bring Celerian instant death, or a short and brutal life in a lightless dungeon, never seeing the sky, the sun, or another human face again. But Maxentius had been the only witness to it—and Celerian intended Maxentius to die.

Maxentius had been shocked, astonished, angry at the lapse in his own security—but now, for the first time, he knew a touch of fear. If he did fall here, Leontes would never be safe again.

His heart was beating fast, but he managed to keep his voice calm and even when he spoke. "You do realise that the man you murdered at the door to my house is not the only armed guard within earshot?"

"If you wanted to call for help, if you were able, you would have done it already," Celerian said.

"And if you wanted to kill me, if you were able, you would have done it already," Maxentius said. "That truth which you called ugly only a few moments ago—you will have to get out of this place the same way you got in. The guard at the gate will have been changed. There are too many who know your face. The *truth* is if you succeed in killing me here and leaving my dead body in your wake, you know very well that you would never make it out of here alive—and any botched attempt on your part would leave you even worse off. I might not die at all…and you might live to regret what you did."

"Are you so tired of your life, that you would bandy words with me in a moment like this?"

Maxentius shrugged. "What would you have me do?"

"Be afraid," Celerian spat.

Maxentius actually managed a sharp bark of a laugh. "If you had thought this through," he said, "it would have been just as easy to send someone else in to do the dirty work. Or even better, do it somewhere else, other than here, my own house, where such an assassin would almost inevitably be caught and identified and traced back to you. You're a dead man, doing this, either way. It was foolish. I had expected…more of you."

Celerian shifted his grip on the dagger. "But if I had sent someone else," he said, "I could not have watched you die."

He had signalled his move, and Maxentius was ready for it.

It seemed such a very long time ago now that Maxentius had stopped another assassin—not aimed at himself, but at Rathauric, house-guest at the House of Peacocks and bastard-born prince of the Vesigar people. Once the attempt had been safely thwarted and in the past, while Rathauric and Maxentius were on their way to Rathauric's own home at the Vesigar court in Ravin, Rathauric had spoken with some bitterness about the method that had been chosen for his demise.

"Poison," he had said, "the coward's way. The easy way. The assassin never puts himself in danger. Where I come from, if there was a quarrel over supper one night, there will have been half a dozen challenges with knife or sword before breakfast the next morning—if someone wants you dead the least they can do is actually kill you themselves."

"Are you saying everyone in Ravin had better know how to wield a knife, or else?" Maxentius had asked.

"At the very least, defend yourself against one," Rathauric had said.

"Perhaps you had better teach me, then," Maxentius had said, darkly amused.

He had meant it half in jest, but Rathauric had taken him seriously. It was hard to learn the proper moves aboard a swaying ship, but by the time they had crossed the sea from Visant to the port which was the gateway to Ravin, Maxentius had had the basics down, and Rathauric had made sure that the lessons had been reinforced once they had both stepped on terra firma.

In the days before he had known Rathauric, Maxentius might not have been as able to defend himself, unarmed, against an attack by a sharp blade—and perhaps that was precisely what Celerian was counting on. But the memory of Rathauric's lessons kicked in, and Maxentius moved with a precision and a grace that the Vesigar prince would have been proud to see in his pupil. By the time Celerian had lunged forward with the thrusting dagger, Maxentius was already not in the place where he had been a moment before. He ducked to the side, grabbed hold of Celerian's other wrist, and danced under Celerian's arm and behind him, twisting his arm painfully high up on his back. Off balance, Celerian tried to reverse his grip on his dagger and stab backwards to where Maxentius was, but Maxentius was ready for that too—his own hand sliding down the other's arm and twisting the awkwardly held dagger out of Celerian's fingers. Before he quite knew how he had got himself into this, Celerian found himself face first into the wall of the house, his left arm twisted up like a pretzel and his shoulder bent back hard enough to be on the verge of dislocation, with his own knife held sharp edge first lodged between the stone wall and his side.

The winter storm which Maxentius had been watching as it approached the city chose this moment to break over them. Cold rain sluiced down from a low, iron-grey sky; the two men were instantly soaked, their wet hair plastered down across their faces.

He should have been cold and wet and shivering, but Maxentius barely noticed the storm, a fever building inside him.

He had practised endlessly with weapons of war. He knew how to acquit himself in a swordfight, how to defend himself in a knife brawl—but all of it, all of that knowledge, had been theoretical until now, until this moment out on the terrace of the House of Peacocks in the rain.

He had never killed a man before.

Celerian's face was turned sideways, pressed against the stone wall; Maxentius saw the other man's teeth beginning to chatter, and the clenching of his jaw as he tried to make it stop.

"I knew in the Senate room, when I first saw you, that this day would come." Maxentius said in a low voice, into Celerian's ear. "A knife, a poisoned cup—whatever it took—you would have come after me with your teeth if that was necessary. Your life or mine. That's why I could not let you leave the city—because if you were once out of my sight I could never sleep in safety again. I would not kill you in cold blood, but I needed to flush you out, to make you come after me...so that when I made an end of it I would know that it was truly ended, and I would have done nothing more than defend myself."

"Kill me then," Celerian gasped. "You say you would not kill me in cold blood, but your blood is very cold—or you would not be standing here talking to me about the circumstances of my death...."

"*You* did," Maxentius said.

His wrist barely moved, but the knife suddenly turned, sank into flesh. Celerian drew a deep ragged breath, his eyes going wide, as the blade found his heart; Maxentius let him fall, a sudden dead weight, and slide down the wall leaving a bloody smear.

It was both fortunate and unfortunate that it was not the faithful and taciturn Arkadios who came running in answer to Maxentius's summons—Arkadios would have ensured that everything that needed to be done now would be done efficiently and discreetly, but Arkadios would have been too close, as he always was, and he might have tried to stand in Celerian's way when he had first found his way into the house, and would have probably paid for that with his life. But Arkadios was not there; he was out on an errand for Maxentius. It was his second in command who came in his stead, and stood staring with wide, shocked eyes at the dead body on the terrace and Maxentius himself soaked to the skin and sprayed with blood.

"We had an intruder," Maxentius said. "Remove the guard on duty at the front gate and lock him up somewhere until I decide what is to be done with him—he turned a blind eye when that man gained entry into the garden. There is also, apparently, a dead body somewhere near the house, another of the guards on duty tonight. Take care of that. Have the men sweep the grounds, just to make sure there are no further surprises."

"Yes, Excellency," the white-faced eunuch stammered. "And I'll send someone...to take...the body...."

Maxentius stepped inside from the terrace, and stood dripping and shivering a pace or two into the room. He suddenly became aware that his fingers were trembling uncontrollably, that the smell of blood that was still in his nose came not from the corpse outside but from his own clothes and hands. He felt the bile rise in his throat—Rathauric had showed him how to fight, but not how to kill a man—he had had to find that out the hard way, by himself.

"Have them draw me a bath," Maxentius said abruptly to the eunuch, dropping his arms to his sides and clenching his shaking hands into fists. "And burn these clothes when I take them off. I do not wish to smell the blood on them again."

He did not think he could sleep, after, but he retired to bed anyway and sleep did find him...of a sort. A sleep haunted by Celerian's face against the stone, both washed in the cold winter rain of Visant; by the glitter of a dagger blade in stormlight. By a vision of Sarrus's expression as he counted the gold solidi in the privacy of his own quarters, musing that every man who stepped up to the public podium in the Empire's Queen City had his price.

When he woke, he instinctively tried to reach for innocence. But although there was a picture in his mind's eye of the day on which he had first received his Uncle's invitation to the city—of his opening a letter under his mother's gaze, not knowing yet how it would change his life forever—a boy and his mother poring over a piece of parchment with a Visant seal—he could no longer remember what they said to one another, although they must have spoken; he could no longer call to mind the innocent eagerness that had been in his heart.

Maxentius belonged to Visant now. That bond was sealed with blood—the blood that had mixed with the rain on the tesserae of the balcony of the House of Peacocks in winter.

CHAPTER FIFTEEN

Returning to Visant remained a tantalizing vision for Simonis as she struggled to come to terms with the reality of her decision. It was the wrong time of year for a direct sailing between Rhakotis and Visant—but even had there been a dozen ships waiting in harbour, Simonis still had to face the simple fact that she had no money. She could not pay for passage, and nothing with which even theoretically to smooth her entry into the City of Gold—oh, how apt the name suddenly seemed to her!—once the ship docked there.

She remembered all too clearly her first arrival in Visant, when she was a five-year-old child—and the importance of having the correct paperwork. There was no getting past that; Visant was not Rhakotis, and its gates were not automatically open to her.

She had no money, and no papers.

She had both, inside the city. She had had the foresight to secrete away a certain amount of treasure when she had left Visant—and she could access that easily once she got into the city—but she could not bribe somebody to take her there or let her in with money she could not prove that she had. Until she could solve that problem, she fretted, and haunted the docks, staring at empty seas or at ships she could not board.

In the meantime, she tried to pay back some of her debt to the nuns who had helped nurse her back to health by taking up any small chores that they felt they could safely or ethically entrust to her.

There was not all that much that she could do, but she had grown up inside the Hippodrome where the human body could be hurt or damaged in any number of ways—from the broken bones of the accidents in the arena to a difficult childbirth, or chronic illness, or the twisted pain of old age. There were healers or midwives to be had for the most complicated—but a lot of the time the Hippodrome folk doctored themselves, and Simonis was no stranger to the stillroom or the sickbed. It had been Simonis who was on hand to receive a heavily pregnant woman who was not yet at term—but she had been beaten by her husband and she had managed to make her way to the infirmary barely in time for her tiny and barely viable child to be born. It had been Simonis who had stepped up to the woman screaming in pain and anguish, who had kept up a gentle, soothing stream of words washing past the patient, who had received the baby into her own hands and had tried to do everything possible to make sure it lived. She had failed; the baby, after struggling to breathe with a nose and lungs not quite ready for the outside world, died less than an hour after it had been born. It was she who went to tell the mother of this, and who held the woman in her arms and rocked her gently while she screamed and wept and squeezed Simonis's arms with a fierce passionate strength of which she had not even been aware and which had left hand-shaped bruises on Simonis's skin afterwards.

The sisters had said very little—but little had needed to be said, after all. They had simply bowed their heads in mute thanks, as was their way, and they let Simonis express her gratitude to the sisters for her own care and the care they had taken of Chryseis in the eminently practical way of allowing her to supervise patient care in the infirmary, when the sisters were needed elsewhere, or when they required time to attend a special prayer meeting or service. For Simonis, it was a duty she felt capable of fulfilling—and it gave her a quiet place she could begin to learn patience and practice calm, where she could both indulge in unfettered fretting in solitude and plot out her next move in great and often highly impractical detail at the same time.

It was a place of sick people, and she never took Chryseis with her when her duties took her there—but she always carried the child in her heart. Simonis would rise early and look in on Chryseis as she slept—and then make her way to her post, bringing the image of her daughter's face with her. She would sift through the memories in her mind's eye as she sat by a patient's bedside, smiling to herself, her hands busy with the spindle the nuns had given her and taught her how to use, often humming the lullaby melodies that she had used to lull Chryseis to sleep when she was much younger, reflecting on the inescapable fact that Chryseis was no longer the tiny baby with whom she had fled Gallienus's house.

It was during one of these early mornings, when all the nuns were at worship in their small church, that Simonis found herself patient-sitting a man who had been brought into the infirmary only a day or so before, unconscious, shaking with fever. The nuns had been doing what they could with herbs and cold poultices, but he had remained feverish, moaning occasionally as he twisted on his pallet bed, his forehead beaded with sweat and his thin hair and white beard matted with it. They had dosed him with his herbs before dawn, and there was little for Simonis to do except occasionally lay a cloth wetted with cool water on his brow and wrap his wrists in soaked rags, cooling his pulse points and trying to make him more comfortable.

She had been lost in one of her reveries, humming one of Chryseis's favourite lullabies and watching her daughter grow up all over again in her mind's eye, until she was wrenched back into reality by a weak, quiet voice from the pallet bed.

She turned her head sharply, and met dark eyes in the wan face of the convalescent—open, and lucid. There was even a thin wraith of a smile on his wasted features, and his hands, with their long, bony fingers, curled in a conscious gesture to tug at his damp bedclothes.

"Did you speak?" Simonis said, in *coiné*, certain she had heard him say something—but he had either spoken too softly for her to understand, or else he had uttered words in a language she did not know.

But he responded in kind, his own *coiné* flawless but accented with the inflexion of the Crescent Kingdoms.

"I apologise," he said. "I don't remember this room—I recall the beginning of a bad headache in a wayside serai maybe a day's ride from Rhakotis.... Was I ill? When my fever comes upon me I tend to fall back on the language of my childhood, which often means I address strangers in a tongue they cannot possibly understand. Is there water...?"

Simonis filled a cup from a pottery jar and brought it over to him, supporting his head as he drank. After several long swallows he lifted a hand in a weak gesture, and Simonis took the cup from his lips. His head fell back on the pillow; apparently even this small effort exhausted him. But his eyes were bright and curious and far from tired, and watched her with interest.

"I was listening," he said, "to the tune which you were humming. It seems to me as though I should almost know it, but I cannot bring it to mind. Perhaps it is the fever. What is it?"

"It's what I sing to my daughter when she goes to sleep," Simonis said.

"Ah. A lullaby. They are the same throughout the world, no matter the place where they began—melodies of love and protection. Does yours have words to it?"

Simonis smiled. "In two languages," she said. "My mother sang it to me, in her own native tongue—her own mother came from somewhere near Virytos, on the Crescent Kingdom coast. And then, later, I heard that or something very like it sung to another child, my half sister, in Visant—and it had different words, then, in a different language."

"I know Virytos," the old man said. "It is a beautiful place. Was that where you were born, too?"

"No. I was born in Cyrenais, a little town on the island of Kypra."

"I know that place, too," he said. His thin fingers tugged at his blanket. "Is it cold in here…?"

"I will get you a fresh blanket, now that your fever has broken," Simonis said.

She left to fetch the blanket, and when she returned she thought that the old man had fallen asleep again, his head lying back and his mouth open as though he was snoring. But his eyelids lifted again as she came into the room, and he watched her approach.

"You are no nun," he said quietly.

"I am just helping out," Simonis said. "I was a patient here, just like you."

"You suffer from the shiver fever too?"

"No, I…it is a long story," Simonis said. "Let me have that other blanket."

She slipped the sweat-soaked clammy bed covering off him, revealing a shift, much like the one she had found herself dressed in when she first woke in this place, clinging damply to a pair of thin, stick-like legs and rucked up over bony hips. Simonis pursed her lips.

"I really should change that shift," she said. "Your fever has broken, but you don't want to lie there in the damp, it can't be good for you. Let me see what I can find. Here, hang on to the old blanket for a bit until I can clean you up."

Simonis rummaged around in the chests where the nuns kept their clean linens until she found a clean shift that looked like it might be the right size. She also gathered up a basin and a washcloth, and returned to the sickroom armed with clean water and fresh clothing. The old man managed a dry laugh.

"For certain you are no nun if you intend to wash me and change me," he said.

Simonis gave him a wry grin. "You're a little older than I'm used to," she said, "but I've seen a man's body before. I'm probably doing a good deed twice over—this, you need, and if I don't do it now it *will* be some nun who will come in to finish the job. Now can you sit up a little and help me get this thing off you?"

He chuckled as he tried to hoist himself on his elbows and assist her as much as he could; he was very weak, and it took a little struggle, but in the end they accomplished the task between them, leaving him dressed in a fresh nightshirt under a clean blanket, and even his hair and beard had been given a perfunctory rinse and smoothed down into some kind of order.

"Thank you," he said at length, when it was all accomplished. "I think...I think I can sleep now, and rest, for a change, without the fever stalking my dreams. Will you return?"

"If the sisters need me to help," Simonis said.

"I would very much like you to," the old man said faintly. "Are you literate? I would very much like to have...the words to that lullaby of yours...transcribed for me...."

And then his eyes closed, and he was asleep, just like that, as though someone had cut a puppet's strings.

It wasn't really duty that took Simonis back to the old man's sickroom—she found herself curious about him, about his educated manner of speaking and his comments about knowing the various places associated with her own life and history, so much at odds with his apparently finding himself thrown to the mercy of the abbey infirmary in Rhakotis, an indigent left to the charity of the church. When she returned to see him, he was much improved, a more natural colour back in his cheeks. His lanky frame, and the high cheekbones and hooked nose that lent an almost emaciated air to his face, seemed to be more part of his natural constitution than due to his disease. The deep-set dark eyes sparkled in recognition as Simonis knocked on the door and peered into the room.

"It's my angel of lullabies," he said warmly. "I was hoping you would return. I think I was still a little...out of it on the occasion of our last meeting—I seem to remember asking you to come back and see me, but I wasn't certain if I had done so, or merely thought about doing it and never quite spoke my thoughts out loud."

"You did ask. I'm glad to see you are feeling a little better," Simonis said.

"Ah, the fever. It comes and goes. I contracted it a long time ago, on my travels, and it seems I will carry it with me until I die. It isn't deadly, merely debilitating; and sometimes I find myself convalescing in very strange places. But it also means I have met a great many strangers who have become my friends, and even colleagues."

"Colleagues? What is it that you do?"

"My dear, do forgive me. We have already been more intimately acquainted than I have been used to, but I do not believe that we have actually been introduced. I am a traveller, and a mapmaker, and a chronicler of people and of places. My name is Eleazar bar Yabin."

Simonis suddenly heard an echo of a long-vanished voice in her mind, the voice of Virgillus, her first lover. *Have you read Eleazar bar Yabin…?*

"The Vannid tribesmen," she said.

Eleazar blinked at her. "I have been acquainted with some, yes," he said.

"I have heard about you. Years ago. When I was young."

"My dear," Eleazar said gently, "from the looks of you now, anything that qualifies as *years* ago would have made you not merely young, but a child."

"It was in Visant," Simonis said.

"Ah," Eleazar said, and his eyes were filled with understanding. He said nothing, though, merely waited for her to continue—and she took another step into the room.

"I am Simonis," she said. "Daughter of Batzas, the bear-keeper."

"I am pleased to make your acquaintance, Simonis bet Batzas, as you would be known in my own tongue. They tell me that I am not going anywhere for at least another five or six days, and it would be pleasant to spend some of that time speaking with you about the places you have known, and of how you came to know of my travels with the Vannid tribesmen. Tell me, do you happen to know if any luggage came here with me? My bags of parchments and pens…?"

"They are not in the room," Simonis said. "I should think the nuns would have brought your belongings here to you had you arrived with any. But I can find out."

"And perhaps procure some new writing materials, if my bag cannot be found?" Eleazar asked diffidently. "If that is not too much trouble. If the bag has been lost, then my notes from my last trip are gone also and I had better write down what I remember before the fever takes the last of it from my mind."

He tried to sit up but could not seem to make his body obey him, his arms refusing his weight as he tried to prop himself up on them. Simonis came closer and helped him sit up in his bed, shaking her head over him.

"You are probably in no shape to sit up for very long and write out all your thoughts right now," she said. "I'll see what I can do about the materials—and perhaps if you don't mind another's hand, I could help you. If you tell me what to set down, I can write the notes for you."

Eleazar chuckled. "If so, then it will be the first time I will have to translate my own notes back into my own language, instead of translating from that into *coiné* and then into the classical form for the academics at the universities to deign to look at. I will be more than happy to take you up on that offer, Simonis of Visant—and perhaps as I tell you my story, you might tell me some of yours...?"

Simonis did not know what she expected from the strange collaboration which sprang up between Eleazar bar Yabin and herself—world traveller and his amanuensis—but she found herself astonished at the precision of his memory when it came to relating facts, incidents, or descriptions of people he had met. That didn't mean that she could not see the gaping holes which he ignored, the things he did not find interesting or relevant; at first she kept her head down and her mouth shut and simply wrote down what he dictated—but she was who she was, in the end, and keeping silent over something she felt should be talked about had never been one of her virtues.

Eleazar had been talking, on their third day together, about a southern tribe he had sojourned amongst for a while—he described them as tall, lanky, blacker than ebony, and given to running everywhere.

Simonis put her pen down as he came to that point, and regarded him quizzically.

"Why?" she said.

"Why what?" Eleazar said, a little irritably, jerked out of memory mode and dictation mindset.

"Why do they run?"

"To get to where they are going, of course."

"Yes, but why run? You said yourself the climate was hot, and the air dry, and water scarce. I would think running would make those people tired faster, probably more thirsty, and just how much quicker can they get from place to place if they race there? I mean, the caravans in the desert at the back of Rhakotis—they often make camp over the heat of the day and only move in late afternoons or early mornings, or sometimes at night, if the leader is confident—but that makes sense for them, because of the desert, because of the sun. So why do these southern black men run?"

"Because they…because…." Eleazar pressed his lips together in a thin line, making his mouth almost disappear into his beard. "I don't believe I asked them."

Simonis ducked her head, picking up a quill again. "Where were we?" she said apologetically.

Eleazar shook himself and continued with his dictation, but it was plain that he was unhappy. The next morning he made a sharp gesture when Simonis arrived with her writing paraphernalia, dismissing the job at hand.

"I was turning over in my mind some of the things I was saying yesterday," he said. "I found that I could pick more holes in my memory than I know what to do with. What took you so long to call me on it?"

"I know of you. You're a great man," Simonis said. "It isn't for the likes of me to say what you should…."

"But it is," he interrupted. "It *is*. I know that some day I shall have to go back now, retrace my steps and start again. I cannot write about those regions, not now, not when I am so uncertain about everything that I do not remember and should have asked about."

"It might have been the fever," Simonis said.

"Or I'm just getting old," Eleazar said. "I probably wouldn't notice the simplest things that I know so very well, if I went back tomorrow to the village where I was born. I need to retrain my memory, obviously, learn to trust it again. Pah!" He turned his head away briefly, in a gesture of pure frustration. "I don't feel like doing any more work today. Tell me more about *your* travels."

"So you can tell me which questions *I* failed to ask?" Simonis said with a smile.

"So that I can listen, and perhaps learn from fresh eyes," Eleazar said. "Start at the beginning, on Kypra, and then go on from there. Tell me about you."

Simonis would have scoffed if anyone had suggested to her that she could trust someone well enough, at this short acquaintance, to tell him the things she began to tell him—but somehow Eleazar was somebody she trusted, even though some part of her was certain that elements from her own story would find their way into his own traveller's tales somewhere.

She skated over some it—but she did tell Eleazar how and where she had first heard of him, and then how she had left Visant…and how she now wanted, *needed*, to go back.

"I have thought about it," she said, her hands folded in her lap, fingers laced tightly together. "I cannot take ship there and walk in—so it must be done differently. I can think of three ways I could do it—I suppose I could smuggle myself across the Narrows in a boat somehow, pay somebody to put me down on some private wharf or jetty which might not be that well guarded, and then try and scramble back into the city, dodging the guards on that private estate. Or I could put on a nun's habit and go beg at some landward gate to be allowed inside to visit some shrine or another—and then vanish into the secret places that I know, if they start looking for that nun, later, when there is no record of her leaving the city . They give out these temporary passes, sometimes, to pilgrims at the city gates—but as far as I've heard tell it's arbitrary, and often done on a guard's whim, and I could not count on it. And either of those ways would probably need money anyway, money to pay for passage or for bribes, and I don't have that kind of money in hand. And it all depends on luck anyway, and the way my luck has been running lately...."

"You said three ways. That's two," Eleazar said.

Simonis looked up. "The Hippodrome," she said. "The factions will often exchange or import dancers or other performers from other Hippodromes, elsewhere, across the length and breadth of the Empire. If I can slip in as one of a group of dancers—well—the guards would pay little mind other than to take notes as to which of us to seek out at the Hippodrome later. Faction business is faction business, and the guards know better than to mess with the Golden Crown or the White Jewel—they'd glance at the papers and make sure the number on the page tallied with the number of people in front of them, and meddle no more than that, probably. But...."

"But it would mean going back to the Hippodrome and begging once again," Eleazar said.

Simonis turned her head away sharply. "I don't want to do that," she said. "I will do it if I have to, but I don't want to go that way. It would probably be done, it could be done, but the price...could be high. I would have to tell them far too much. Everything I was...everything I have done...it might all get back to Visant with me, and I would never shed it again, and it might blight everything anyway, and if I go this route and I can't work when I get back into the city.... And then there's Chryseis. I hate leading Chryseis back into that world."

"Would they even let you take the child?" Eleazar asked gently. "If you were going in as a dancer, as a performer, would they let you carry in a toddler, and ask no questions...?"

Simonis was chagrinned to find tears filling her eyes. "Yes, there is that. And that's partly why I am still here," she said. "If it had been just me...but there's her to think of now, and every one of the roads I have spoken of is risky or downright impossible if Chryseis is with me. She is safe here in Rhakotis, and happy....

"Visant is home for you, not for her," Eleazar said, nodding.

"I can fake it when it comes to papers for me—but she...she never existed in Visant." Simonis sighed, wiping a tear brimming at the corner of her eye with the back of her hand. "It is *I* who want to go home. It isn't fair...and yet it breaks my heart, to think of leaving her behind, even if I tell myself that I can come for her later, or send for her to come to me...."

"You said there were three ways."

Simonis nodded, swallowing hard, not looking at him.

"What if I suggested a fourth?"

After a moment of silence Simonis looked up again, her brow furrowed, to look up at him. "What?" she asked. "In the end, it's always the same trouble—getting inside. I left without sanction, so I don't have permission to return—I cannot have papers to enter a place I have never left...."

"You cannot, perhaps," Eleazar said gently. "But I can. I do. I can get you into the city."

She stared at him, her mouth falling open. "You?" she said. "How?"

"I have a pass. The University made sure of that. I am welcome in Visant when I need to go there. I could go back this time...with a companion."

Simonis sniffed. "They might not let you take in a woman as easily as you think."

"There are many ways around that," Eleazar said. "We can dress you as a boy. We can even be married. Oh, don't worry I would not hold you to such a vow—I am too old a man for a child like yourself, and you are not of my faith, after all—but that is not something that the guards need to know, if they should even ask."

"Why?" Simonis asked. "Why would you do this? I told you, I have no money...."

"You were kind to me. You were a good nurse when it mattered, and then you were an even better secretary. I suspect I could use a bit of both. But if I asked for something in return it would not be in terms of money. You see...you woke something in me, twice over. First you pulled me up on my shortcomings, no longer being what I once was, a pair of eyes which fed a memory and an insatiable curiosity—now I miss things, don't ask the right questions, question if I even notice the important details, let alone remember them. I want you to help me recapture that gift that I once had of seeing, of *knowing*...."

"You want me to go back south with you?"

"No. Oh, no, that would be another trip entirely, and one for me to make. No, it's something else, it's you—your going home, your memory of home, the way you carry it all in you like a jewel. I want to go home, too, Simonis." He paused. "And I want you to come with me."

"I don't understand," she whispered.

"I can take you to the gates of Visant itself," Eleazar said. "And through them. But first…you come with me to my home. To the Crescent Kingdom's back roads, perhaps through Virytos where your mother was born, retracing the steps of my youth—I've written on so many strange places of this world but I don't think I have ever really chronicled the land that is my own home country…and I want to borrow your eyes to see it again, new, fresh, as though I have never seen it before. No, it will still not be a trip to take your Chryseis on—because I have no idea where I will go, yet, or how long it will take me to get there. But if you come to my home with me, Simonis, I will take you to the threshold of yours, and hand you safely in. No, don't answer yet," he added, as she drew breath to speak. "This is something that you might want to think about, and I can certainly appreciate that. Take all the time that you need—but in the meantime…I think we might have some more work to do, if you are willing."

Simonis shut her mouth with an effort and reached for parchment and stylus. She kept her head down and her expression hidden from Eleazar, transcribing his words onto the page. This was an unexpected solution to all of her problems—she would have company, she would have protection, she would even have something to occupy her hours and days—but she turned it all in her mind like a glittering gem, over and over again, and wondered if the price of her return was not even higher than she had ever thought she would pay. She had used her body as a bargaining chip before—she was used to that, knew the currency, knew her value on the market. But Eleazar bar Yabin did not want her body. He wanted her mind, her eyes, her spirit, her passion…and he wanted her to leave her heart behind here, in Rhakotis, where her daughter would remain.

She knew she would do it, of course. She had known it almost as soon as the words had left his lips. But she still had to convince her breaking heart.

CHAPTER SIXTEEN

The Crescent Kingdoms had been semi-mythical, legendary places in the cradle stories that Apphia had told Simonis and Danelis when they were very young. Simonis found the reality of it all a little overwhelming, even with a guide as familiar with, and knowledgeable about, the place as Eleazar bar Yabin.

Leaving Rhakotis had been hard, more difficult than Simonis had imagined it would be. Chryseis was left in trust with a family the nuns vouched for, with children her own age. Simonis swore, in tears, that she would send for the child within a year, two at the most, or even return to fetch Chryseis herself as soon as she was able—but there were words spoken of not letting Chryseis forget who she was, who her real mother was, and that spoke of things left unsaid, of the possibility that Chryseis would grow to be old enough to ask questions about her past before Simonis would come and claim her. Simonis broke her necklace, the one that she had kept beca`use it reminded her of her daughter's eyes, and left it with Chryseis, as a token, taking only three of the stones away with her—one, at least, as a keepsake and the others maybe for proof, to send with whoever she would send to get Chryseis when the time came. She left a letter, also, with Father Honorius, her entire story. She asked him to watch over her daughter, to ensure Chryseis's wellbeing, and to only open the letter should somebody come asking to take Chryseis away—because it would contain knowledge only she, Simonis, had, and if the messenger was not able to accurately answer Father Honorius's questions, then the child should not be given up to him.

She went back twice, to hug her daughter, to promise in whispers that she would return. The second time she all but broke, deciding to either stay here with Chryseis or to take the child with her.

But she could not do those things. Eleazar bar Yabin was her road to Visant, where she had to go, and the road was closed to Chryseis for now. Simonis did not turn to watch the walls of Rhakotis fall behind them as the east-bound caravan they had joined wound its way out of its gate—knowing that she would not see the walls for her tears.

She could not stop crying for hours, as the caravan—some eighty camels, and maybe fifty human souls including herself and Eleazar—followed its well-worn path, eventually coming to and then skirting the great river delta that emptied into the Middle Sea, angling south until they entered a region of lush riverside, tilled fields, and villages full of barefoot squealing brown children who ran beside the caravan, their faces alight with curiosity. The green of the fields through which the caravan road wound had her constantly craning her neck to peer at their edges, often lost in heat shimmer, seeking the presence of the sand desert which she knew had to be there, just around the corner and out of sight. But she could only glimpse that, sometimes, out of the corner of her eye, like a wraith of doom waiting at the door of this hard-working and seemingly content community.

"They build and rebuild every year," Eleazar told her as they rode along, seeing her fascination, more than happy to make sure her thoughts turned from her lost child. "These fields, this is a gift of that river. The flood wipes everything out every year, but it leaves a fresh layer of fertile river dirt behind when it recedes—and they plant again, and hope to harvest before the next flood comes."

"They don't seem surprised to see us," Simonis said.

Eleazar chuckled. "Oh, they make a nice living easing the passage of caravans. It's just that they don't feel an urge to follow a caravan once it passes the boundary of their own village and is no longer their business, or a source of income for them. We are mayflies to them, ephemera, ghosts—things that come, and pass, and go, and are forgotten. They don't remember faces well—when a stranger is here they will know him for as long as he is with them, but they will greet him as a stranger again if he returns, even if it's only a span of a few weeks between the two visits. He is not one of them, therefore he is not really worth remembering."

The caravan—man and beast—was fed in the riverside villages, and then ferried across the broad river on flat, floating platforms while the villagers waved the visitors off as they departed with as much enthusiasm as had been expended in welcoming them. Not long after the crossing, as they left the far bank's narrow edge of green fields and began to encounter desert again, Eleazar and Simonis and their two pack beasts bade farewell to the rest of their caravan, which swung further south, and struck off by themselves in a more north-easterly direction.

The terrain gradually lost the sand dunes and began to turn into something that was no less desert for that it was a harder, rockier place, a dun-coloured land with scrubby bushes fighting for survival in cracks and crevices. Away to the south there were hints of what might have been the beginnings of mountains, and Eleazar nodded at the horizon lost in the haze, his expression one of deep reverence.

"We won't be going near it, not this time, but when my own people heard God speak to us from on high it was on a mountain that lies over yonder," he said.

"Your kindred speak directly to your God?" Simonis said.

"There is word in our faith, a promise, that one day we too might have a Messiah, just like you in the faith of the One God preach has already happened," Eleazar said. "It would seem, however, that our criteria are a little different from the ones your faith has applied."

He did not explain the criteria, but a corner of Simonis's mouth quirked a little at the unspoken words that lay between them.

"Higher?" she said, softly. "Higher than being the God who chose to walk for a while among men?"

"That is an interesting question—but I am a traveller and a maker of maps and not a teacher of faith. Perhaps when we get to a city I can introduce you to someone more versed in these matters than I."

And so they left the holy mountain of Eleazar's faith at their backs and continued to the north and east, picking their way along the ancient road that linked the Crescent Kingdoms to the southern deserts. It was a road that caravans had plied for centuries, and the occasional villagers they passed on their way barely looked up at their passing, busy with their own often harsh daily lives, trying to claw life and sustenance out of inhospitable stone. They were not unwelcoming, and when night caught the two travellers on the road they knew that they could count on a place to lay their heads, in a village or even some isolated goat herder's hut—the locals didn't have that much, but they shared what they had, sparingly but freely enough. It was yet another way of life that Simonis found foreign and not a little incomprehensible.

She did not understand the local language, but Eleazar often interpreted, quietly, the gist of what was going on, when he was not directly involved in some communication himself.

He explained to her once why two of the local women turned away from a stone well without filling their skins.

"They have a daily quota for that well," Eleazar said. "If they take more on any given day than they know they can, the well can sometimes run dry."

"What do they do if that happens?" Simonis asked. And then, her eyes following the two women who had come for water too late, "And what happens to them now?"

"The others will share," Eleazar said. "As for the well—sometimes they come back, after a while, and start giving water again—the well just needs time to replenish. Some wells, when they run dry, they run dry for good. And then there's nothing for it but to move, to look for water elsewhere."

Simonis glanced around at the two mules she and Eleazar rode, at the donkey that was their pack animal. "And they will give us water? And the animals?"

"They are constrained to, under their faith," Eleazar said. "Denying sustenance to a stranger is an ill deed in the sight of God. It might be God himself come to test them."

Simonis shook her head slightly. "I'm not sure that the folk in the City of Gold would do well worshipping this God," she said. "There are public wells where you can go and drink—but you wouldn't knock on a patrician's house and ask for a draught and be given it without question. People know their place in Visant."

"People know their place here," Eleazar said.

"But here it seems that any place is interchangeable," Simonis said. "You could be the villager one day, the passing stranger the next...."

"Precisely," Eleazar said. "Which is why they do it. If one day they are the ones on the road, they know that they could expect to survive there, by reason of this act of mercy and compassion which they are now in a position to offer some other traveller. There is a certain amount of comfort and security in believing that every stranger might be God come calling."

"But you said your people's Messiah would have to be a higher kind of being, not just a temptation that comes by a man's house wearing the cloak of a passing stranger," Simonis said.

"Not...*quite* what I implied," Eleazar said, smiling. "But we are not yet come to the lands where my people dwell. These that we are amongst, they are older than my kind, they were here when we came, they will like be here when we vanish. They are born of the dust of this land, and they have never strayed from it—and my people were ever wanderers. You will see, when you meet them. In some ways they are more alike to Visant than these can ever be. Perhaps it is just the veneer of civilization that gives that layer of ownership, of possession, of believing that something—a piece of land, a gourd of water, a golden coin—belongs to you and to you alone and that you are not required to share it with others who are also God's creation. As I said, that is for a teacher to ponder, not for the likes of me. But you will see."

He did not give her a map of where they were going, or even an indication of where they were headed by dropping the name of a place that she might recognise. Every now and then, especially as they came closer to the heartlands of the Crescent Kingdoms, he would pause on a rise on the road and point to a place in a valley below and give it a name that Simonis knew—but even so she was utterly taken by surprise when Eleazar did one of his sudden pauses and pointed to something that was considerably larger than the villages of wattle-and-daub or raw unworked stone which they had been passing through until that moment. A city—a real city, surrounded by high stone walls, with glimpses of many rooftops within. Unexpected after their travels in the sparsely populated hinterlands, and oddly precious, like a mirage in the desert.

There was only one such city in the Kingdoms, and with his very next words Eleazar confirmed its identity.

"Challim," he said. "The City of the Rock. It's still today and the better part of tomorrow, I think, before we get there—but that is one of the holiest cities in the world, for your faith as well as my own. Your One God's Messiah is said to have died out in the desert that stretches beyond it, the place where they once used to pitch the Wheels."

"Will we pass by that place?" Simonis asked, suddenly filled with a superstitious awe.

"It is a site of pilgrimage," he said. "Has been one for a long time. I intend that we should stay in the city for a little while, so if you like you may certainly visit the Place of the Wheel. I think you might find it interesting. I am told that people of particularly deep faith—yours, that is, not my own—have been known to have visions there, and the Church treats them as genuine miracles."

"It is unlikely to happen to me," Simonis said. "But I should like to see it, now I am here."

"And who knows?" Eleazar said, smiling at her. "After all, you told me of the mute saint in the desert who speaks to nobody yet spoke to you when she helped you across the burning sands. You won't find a Matthea here—there are plenty of places for a man or woman of faith to go in the city, but there are few wild religious hermits out here.... But the more important thing, Simonis bet Batzas, is that this is *my* city down there, just as Visant is your own." His voice cracked a little, and Simonis tore her eyes from distant Challim to Eleazar's face. His eyes were suspiciously bright as he gazed on the distant rooftops, his hands resting lightly but tensely on the reins of his mule. "This is my own homecoming," he whispered. "Look on the city, Simonis. Tell me what you see."

Simonis talked to Eleazar in a low voice while they rode closer to Challim, until her voice grew hoarse—as though she had a blind man's hand in her own and he depended on her for survival. She described to him things she knew he could see, things she knew he knew far better than she did—but this was what he wanted for her, the loan of her eyes, of her observation, of her imperfect understanding but fresh vision.

She described, as they approached the city, the paved roads leading to the gates in its massive walls—roads worn down by generations of feet belonging to pilgrims, to merchants, to holy men and to invading armies. She described the dusty crumbling walls themselves, a memory now of what they once were, and the desultory guards set at the open gates which looked like they would be loath to close again in an emergency and if they did would not stand up to much more than a loud shout before they shivered into oblivion. She described the crowds that milled in the road leading into the city from the main gate, with its souks and market squares opening to the sides, and street vendors shouting their wares in the hot and busy street—so like and yet so completely unlike the great dignified avenue which led from the outer wall to the Bronze Gate of the Imperial Palace in Visant. She described the women veiled in black, only their dark eyes flashing from shrouded faces, and hawk-faced men cloaked in the white robes of the princes of the desert, striding along with jewelled daggers stuck prominently into sheaths at their waist. She described the barefoot boys darting in and out of these crowds, expertly driving (and keeping together) a handful of bleating goats before them, and girls balancing cages with live squawking chickens on their heads with a degree of grace and elegance which the cargo did not seem to merit.

Eleazar did not interrupt, but listened with a rapt expression on his face, his own eyes focused not on the things Simonis talked about but somewhere else entirely, only barely paying enough attention to guide his mule through the crowds.

When he drew to a halt, outside a non-descript house on a terrace where the crowds had thinned out and the street had slowly started turning into a shallow stairway? or a single stair?, he finally lifted a hand in a signal for her to stop, and she fell silent at last, grateful for the reprieve.

"I owe you a greater debt than you know," Eleazar said. "We are home, for now, this is the house of my uncle where we can find lodgings while we stay in the city. I think I shall retire for a while, and write down all the marvellous things that I had forgotten about my city in the years that I have been away from it, the things that you have just opened my eyes to all over again. I suggest you rest—but tomorrow, if you like, I will get my uncle to find someone to take you up to where the Wheel was, the place where your One God sent his Messiah to die. You said you might want to see it, and I will find plenty to keep me occupied while you do that."

He gestured to her dismount from her mule and knock on the door, and now, in response, a grille opened up in the scarred wood and a wary eye looked out and then fumbling hands seemed to begin working on the inner lock to let them in.

"How long do you intend to stay in the city?" Simonis managed to ask as the door to their lodgings was laboriously opened for them.

"Challim makes its own time," Eleazar said. "I would say, not long. But I do not know what that means to Challim today, or what it will mean tomorrow. I know you want to go home. I will not forget that."

They had no time for more; the gate had opened and a bearded man in striped robes had taken Eleazar, who had also dismounted from his mule, into an exuberant embrace. Eleazar half turned to gesture Simonis in, too, and thus they were welcomed into the house of Amnon bar Ahiram.

It was Amnon's wife, Yehudith, who came to Simonis the next morning with an invitation.

"My husband's nephew tells us that you would like to see the place of the Wheel," Yehudith said. "I would be happy to accompany you, if you wish to go today—Amnon and Eleazar are not like to show their faces in public today, they have too much to catch up on, Eleazar has not been to this house for almost ten years."

"Thank you," Simonis said haltingly, in Yehudith's own language. She had not gained anything like fluency, and was still far more adept at listening quietly to others speak (and understanding far more than anyone gave her credit for), but she was a quick study, and in Eleazar's company and under his teachings she had managed to gather up a small, useful vocabulary of his mother tongue.

Yehudith, who had spoken in accented but fluent *coiné*, smiled in genuine delight at Simonis's attempt to wrap her mouth around the unfamiliar syllables.

"If you stay for a little while," she said, "I will teach you more of our language, if you like. It is the language that he whom your faith has called your Messiah spoke while he lived amongst humans—it was as one of our own people that he walked this earth, you know. But we should get going—I'm afraid we are going to have to walk most of the way, and we shouldn't waste the cool of the morning—you should tell me if it all becomes too much for you, you are not of our skies and the heat is like to get oppressive. But there will be water, on the way. Many pilgrims walk this path."

The two women, with modestly draped veils covering their hair and shielding their eyes from the sun, walked down the narrow stepped street that led from Amnon's front door, and down into a main thoroughfare. They plunged into what appeared to be a chaotic mass of people, all bent on pursuing their own business, walking in every direction, slipping past one another in the crowds or shoving those who got in their way aside so that they could hurry past. Yehudith kept a hand on Simonis's elbow, deftly threading a path for the two of them through the crowds, until they passed out of the busiest part of the town and fell in with a group of people who seemed to be, by and large, all going in the same direction. The heat built quickly, and Simonis was grateful for the occasional pipes from which water, tepid but still welcome, trickled into stone troughs, where people stopped to cup a hand under the flow and take a few swallows, or wet a kerchief and mop at sweaty brows. It all seemed to take far longer than it must have done in reality. They walked out of what Simonis thought was a remnant of a gate in some wall, if not the city's original outer enclosure than some other, smaller, citadel; and then down a rutted road lined with a few thin trees which, thankfully, gave a little bit of pale shade; then even those were gone, and they walked along a dusty road under a pitiless sun, and just as Simonis was starting to question whether her faith was in fact strong enough to endure this, Yehudith paused and pointed.

"Almost there," she said. "Look, there, on the hill."

Simonis lifted her head. The road they were on wound up the slope of a small hill; at its crown, something that appeared to be a lightning-blasted tree rose starkly into the hot pale sky. She could see little else from her vantage point, except a line of other people like herself and Yehudith plodding patiently, faithfully, up the hill towards the top, small black shapes in the heat shimmer between her and the hillside.

She had been almost ready to give up and turn back—but now, seeing the place itself, a stubborn curiosity woke, and she heaved a deep parched sigh and took another step forward.

Simonis climbed the holy hill, doggedly, with a certain kind of obstinate resolve. It was, in a sense, for Father Honorius's sake that she did this as much as her own—for the sake of the creed of Rhakotis, because she had to see the place where it had all begun, even though the Wheel was long gone and there was nothing left except a memory of sanctity, of holiness, something divine that left a trace on the human world. Something in Simonis wanted, *needed*, to be there to touch that whisper of memory. Even if nothing was left but a ghost of faith, it would be, in some sense, proof of what she had been gathering into herself over the months she had spent listening to the preachers in Rhakotis. There was no real evidence at the top of Challim's hill, but standing on it would, in some way, be the proof of Simonis's own faith.

She was out of breath and her lips were dry and cracked when the two of them finally crested the hill. It was not quite flat at the top—there was a ledge, and then a small flat plateau which held the blasted tree, and was supposed also to have been the place where the Wheels had been raised, although it didn't seem to be big enough for more than one or two at the most. Beyond that lay a gentle valley, like a hollowed-out bowl, ending up at another ridge beyond which the hill began its far downward slope.

Down in the hollow, an open pavilion had been raised—a simple striped awning held up by several sturdy poles, stirring in the gentle breeze that swept this hilltop. The poles were covered with fluttering ribbons which had writing on them, writing which Simonis could not read. A couple of men wearing dark robes and head-cloths draped over their close-cropped hair appeared to be doing a brisk trade underneath the pavilion itself, sitting cross-legged on a mat on the ground behind a low rough-hewn table and accepting coins from pilgrims in return for…Simonis craned her neck, trying to see.

"What are they doing?" she asked.

"Prayer pebbles," Yehudith said. "Look, up there, under the tree."

Pilgrims who had purchased what did, indeed, appear to be a pebble climbed the short slope between the pavilion and the dead tree. A number of them knelt there already, heads bowed in prayer, and then laid their pebble reverently on top of one of three small cairns which had been built up there from the pebbles of those that had gone before them.

"They bring their prayers here," Yehudith said. "And they leave them there, in physical form, as the stone they take to the cairn. Some bring their own stones, finding a symbol of their prayer long before they bring it here to leave it for God to read. And it is more enduring than candles or paper or even mere words. These are prayers cast in stone, left here for God to consider in time, they remain as long the stones remain. Or such is the belief of the faithful, anyway. Would you like to leave one of your own?"

Simonis hesitated. Her faith was a strange thing, strong but silent, and she had hardly ever 'prayed' in the sense that she had knelt down and talked to God directly, asking for help or a blessing on herself or another, or anything at all. But there were things now that she could ask, the One God already knew there were.

Reclaiming her daughter.

Returning to Visant.

Rebuilding a life.

But leaving the wishes of her heart on that cairn of faith in the shape of a dumb stone? Did she have enough faith to believe that anything given to God in this wise would ever be heard, or accepted, or granted?

Yehudith was looking at her with a question still in her eyes, and Simonis had to make a decision.

"All right," she said at last. "Perhaps I will."

If God was listening, who was to say how he heard a prayer? Perhaps unspoken words wrapped in those dumb stones were stronger than chanted prayers of the service in the Rhakotis cathedral—who was Simonis to judge that?

Yehudith, of a different faith and mindful of the rules of her own presence in this place, hung back as Simonis descended into the pavilion and passed over a small coin that Yehudith had slipped her in exchange for a tiny gray pebble, irregular in shape, its texture and colour utterly foreign to this place—and that was somehow oddly apt, the fact that this stone must have been brought here from some distance away, just as Simonis herself was a stranger here. The man who selected the pebble for her and handed it over smiled at her, showing a gap where a tooth was missing, and waved her up the slope towards the cairns.

She climbed slowly, the gray pebble clutched in her hand, shuffling through her priorities—she had one pebble, one prayer, she could not ask for everything. Her mind was quite empty when she came to the cairn and knelt at the base of it, her hands folded in her lap with the pebble cradled between her fingers. On some level she was conscious that she had made a decision not to make a decision, to leave it up to the One God which one of her wishes he would promise to grant, which of them she should ask for and be sure of having it given to her—but what came into her mind was none of the specifics that had been swarming in her thoughts only a few short moments before. It was something quiet and huge, like a shadow of wings being raised above her.

Give me the life I am meant to live, she thought. Just that.

The words hung in the emptiness of a starlit void; somewhere, a long way away, she thought she could the roar of her father's bears, or perhaps of a jubilant Hippodrome crowd in a moment of victory as a chariot rounded the final curve—or the cry of a small child, or the sound of voices singing prayers in an echoing space of a huge cathedral. And then it all spun into silence, and she laid the pebble, very gently, on the cairn beside her.

It had seemed to fit into a particular little hollow—but even as she watched, it teetered on an edge she had not noticed, fell over another small stone just below it and triggered its own slide, and before she knew it the entire cairn was moving, slipping, tumbling, as the lower edge gave way and the entire thing spilled down into the hollow with the pavilion in it in a small avalanche of rushing stones.

Simonis had scrambled to her feet, aghast, her hands flying to her throat—but the people in the pavilion didn't seem to be upset about what had happened, and even the other pilgrims were looking up, smiling, nodding in what seemed to be approval. One woman, closer to her than the rest, called out something that Simonis didn't understand; she shook her head and gave a small shrug of her shoulders, signalling her ignorance. The woman switched to bad *coiné*, the trade language of the Empire.

"No look so scared. Is *good* thing. Means it come true, you and all other stones. You pray true and God tell that it come true."

Simonis managed a small smile, her hands falling to her side, and scrambled back down into the hollow and then to where Yehudith waited for her.

"I don't understand," she said to the other woman as she came up to her, glancing back the way she had come, toward the hollow where a couple of small boys were now gleefully darting about, gathering up the stones and piling them all back behind the two pebble-sellers in the pavilion, apparently to be sold again.

"Yours was the prayer that God heard," Yehudith said. "That is the way they tell it. The cairns do not last—they are not stable, they are not meant to be. Sooner or later somebody puts down a final stone and they fall—and it is believed that that last stone, the stone before the fall, is the prayer that God hears, and that means that all the prayers that had been in that cairn have now been heard, and will come true. You have been blessed, for your stone to have done this today."

Simonis shook her head a little. It seemed like superstition—but then, there was a fine line between superstition and true faith, and there always had been. And the faithful had always had their own little superstitions tricks to keep the deity they worshipped happy. It had been so in ancient times—Simonis knew that much, she had danced enough legends that told of such superstitious acts—and it was still so to this day.

Perhaps God *did* hear her prayer.

Perhaps God would answer her prayer. Perhaps all of her choices had not been so ill after all. Perhaps she was living the life she was supposed to live, that all that she had been and done had brought her to this place, that she was already—she had always been—on a road which was taking her into a future she could not yet see, a future that would mean something, a life still to be lived where her existence would matter, a world that would be changed by the fact that she had existed in it.

Her hand crept to the *stoicheon* at her throat, the bear's claw that she always wore, and as her fingers touched it she thought she could hear the bear's roar somewhere deep inside her, in answer to the rapid beat of her heart—she could not tell whether she felt terror or exhilaration.

She only knew that she *believed*.

CHAPTER SEVENTEEN

Eleazar bar Yabin had been born a rolling stone. He had been genuinely happy to come home to the city of Challim, to the circle of his family—but that did not last long. Simonis could see it bubbling from underneath the veneer of his sense of peace, of homecoming—the urge to go further, deeper, into places where no foreigner had seen, to write about people and places which his world had not known before Eleazar walked there and wrote of it.

It started with excursions that got longer and longer. Eleazar gathered up Simonis, his 'eyes', and they would go out from the city on wanderings that were at first only day trips. Quickly the trips turned into journeys where night caught them on the road, and they were obliged to seek shelter with goat herders or in villages too poor and insignificant to be marked on maps. They returned to Challim the following day so that Eleazar could write it all up in his journals. Then the one night away turned into two. And then three. And then, one day, Eleazar decided that the time had come to go on rather than return to the city—and they simply turned their backs on the dusty road that led back to the walls of Challim and continued on their journey through the Crescent Kingdoms.

Simonis's job was to be the eyes of the expedition, to watch, to see, to tell Eleazar what she could observe. She had always been good at this; she had long had the gift to assimilate her surroundings and assess them; it was that which had made her so valuable to Cicatrice to begin with—but now the ability was trained and honed, and she could walk into a village and one glance around the dusty houses would tell her who lived there, how they lived, what they grew or herded for their sustenance and how successful they were at it, what Gods they worshipped (and there were a surprising number of those along the road), and even hazard a shrewd guess as to whether the village would be there within a year's time for other travellers to pass through, or if the sands of time and the desert would cover its remains in far less time than that.

Eleazar took her to Virytos, as he had promised, and Simonis breathed in the air scented by sea and cedars and tried to imagine her mother as a little girl in these streets. But they didn't stay there long; Eleazar had a fire in him now, and he needed to keep moving. He had needed Simonis to awaken his passions once again, to open his eyes to things he had got used to taking for granted—but this trip through the lands of his own childhood had accomplished that, and he was already yearning for other journeys, dreaming of writing about other places that men of his own Empire had not seen. Simonis watched him at the end of each day of their travels, tracing the elegant convoluted characters of his own language, which she could not read, in a leather journal he had with him, squinting at pages by fire-light at camp and then by lantern-light late into the night, gathering up all of his visions into what might become another book—one no less treasured for being about things that its readers might find a little more familiar than Eleazar's usually far more exotic trips.

By the time they drew close to the Eastern Gate of Antacia—the third-biggest city in the Empire, and by all accounts the one most devoted to the pursuit of pleasure—the fire in Eleazar was well and truly lit, and Simonis wondered how long they would even stay in the city before he got the itch to leave, to go on, to fulfill the promise he had made to her of delivering her back to Visant and be free to pursue his own goals. They found lodgings near the Angels Gate, at the far end of the colonnaded main avenue that led down from the Eastern Gate, with the mountain and the steeply climbing houses that covered its foothills on their left. It had been a long day, and Simonis retired immediately, leaving Eleazar sitting up with a blanket over his shoulders and squinting into his journal for his daily ritual of entering that day's travels.

When she woke, some hours later, his candle was guttering but still alight—and when she peered around the arras that divided her own sleeping quarters from his part of the room, she saw Eleazar himself asleep at the writing table, his head pillowed on his arm, snoring softly. She rose from her own pallet and gently shook him into only a semblance of wakefulness, long enough to guide him on unsteady feet to where his own sleeping pallet was laid out, and help him stretch out on it, laying the blanket over him. Just before she blew out the candle she glanced at his work—the writing on the last page was showing his tiredness, all cramped and uneven, and the last lines he had smeared as he had fallen asleep upon his page. Indeed, he was still wearing the ink on his cheek and on his sleeve as he slept. Simonis disturbed nothing, leaving the journal just as he had left it, for him to pick up the threads of his work where he had left off, and then returned to her own bed, falling quickly back to sleep.

When she woke again it was morning, and Eleazar was already back at work at the table—she could hear from where she lay the scratch of his pen on the parchment.

He looked up as she peered around the arras.

"I thought you would still be asleep," she said.

"I had a few good hours," said Eleazar. "Thank you for helping me to bed. Sometimes time runs away from me. Have you ever been to Antacia?"

"All I have known of the world was the little town I was born and Visant—and then, after, the journey of which you already know," Simonis said. "No, I have never been here."

"You've seen Visant, and you've seen Rhakotis," Eleazar said. "Why don't you go and explore this morning? I shall expect a full report on all you saw, of course, later—but I still have work to do here, my dear, and I'd rather I caught up with all of this today before all kinds of new things come in and need to be set into their place. Go and see the river; the bridges of Antacia are renowned for their grace, and the island where the Palace and the Hippodrome are is very beautiful. We shall meet back here for evening meal, and then we can plan the rest of the voyage."

"All right," Simonis said. "Remember to eat something before the evening meal."

Eleazar smiled at her. "I shall, indeed. And you do likewise. Take some money; you will find things in Antacia's markets that you haven't seen for a while. You will be tempted."

Simonis fastened her worn pair of walking sandals onto her ankles and wrapped her shawl around her head, and ventured forth into the city as she had been bid. The colonnaded street leading back towards the Eastern Gate suddenly reminded her forcefully of Visant, and she was conscious of a vivid pang of homesickness, all the stronger now that she was getting ever closer to the City of Gold. Eleazar had been right, and she purchased several pieces of ripe fruit in one of the markets, the fruit that usually grew in climates milder than the ones which she had lived in over the last few years of her life, and bit into them, closing her eyes and letting the juices run down her chin, letting herself sink into the pure sweet pleasure of a child given a favourite treat. It was after, straightening from the water pipe where she had paused to rinse her sticky hands and the juices from her lips and chin, that she caught a glimpse of a woman who was startlingly familiar—a woman whose own wrap, of golden gauze, had slipped well down her carefully dressed hair...hair the colour of wine...hair that Simonis remembered well.

"*Circassaë?*"

The name was barely breathed out loud, no more than a whisper, but the woman with the wine-coloured hair turned at it, and met her eyes. Her own face changed, from inquiry to shock to sudden and unfeigned delight—and then she was almost running towards Simonis, an attendant struggling to keep up, and the two women embraced in the street, laughing.

"Simonis? *Simonis?* Is it really you? When you...just...vanished.... Cicatrice thought you were dead. I didn't believe it, but he said.... Where have you been? What are you doing here?"

"I thought *you* were back in Visant!" Simonis said. "How come Cicatrice let you get this far away from him?"

"Oh, but that's a long story, and I want to hear yours first. Let me look at you." She held Simonis at an arm's length, her hands, glittering with jewelled rings, on Simonis's shoulders, and finally clicked her tongue against the roof of her mouth. "You haven't been taking care of your skin," she said reproachfully. "Your face was fine as alabaster, now your complexion is darkened into ivory, and they prize that less in Visant—if that is where you are headed...?"

"Oh yes," Simonis breathed. "I'm going back."

"What are your plans, then? Oh, come, we shall sit down and share a cup of sherbet and you must tell me everything—*everything*—and then—oh—look at my hands, they're shaking!" Circassaë laughed unsteadily. "Seeing you...it's as though the last few years have never been, and you and I are still sharing supper in the back rooms and awaiting word of the next engagement...."

"It's...complicated..." Simonis said. "You still haven't said, why are you here?"

"My mother...came here somehow, or was from here. When Maxentius wanted to know the circumstances of this city—oh, but you don't know, the heretic creed is gathering strength here in the east of the Empire, and the Bishops have gone so far as to threaten excommunication for the worst, and Maxentius thought that Antacia was listening a little too closely to the deviant preachers and the unwashed saints of the desert. That's why I am here, to see what is believed out here, and who believes it. It happened to mesh well with my own desires, as it happened—I wanted to come back here, and find out...."

The 'heretic creed' could only be the teachings of Rhakotis, but something else caught Simonis's ear first. "Maxentius?"

Circassaë smiled coyly. "Cicatrice is hardly my only master," she said. "Or I could say that he is not my master at all any more. It is true that when this whole thing began I worked for them both, sending them word of whatever was necessary for them to know. But it's been a while now since I left the Hippodrome—I'm effectively retired, my dear, except as a hostess of glittering parties in Visant, in my own household…and Maxentius's eyes and ears when he needs them."

"But who, exactly, is...."

"You've seen him around the city. He was the son of the Count of the Palace Guards, Leontes." Circassaë watched Simonis's face with a small smile, waiting for the connection.

And Simonis made it, sat up. "Leontes? The *Emperor*? The new Emperor? You work for the Emperor now?"

"Not quite. For Maxentius. I have never met Leontes Augustus."

"But Maxentius is...."

"The prince of the city now, yes. And he made it that way—he shaped this election, he had the entire city shouting Leontes's name. And I helped, a little. That's why he trusts me."

Simonis subsided back into her seat, tilted her head a little. "Are you his lover, then?"

"When it suits us both, yes, we lie together," Circassaë said, dismissing the matter. "Sometimes, especially in the beginning, it was necessary—and the easiest way to hide the true nature of our relationship was to hide it in plain sight—after all, this is precisely what people would expect to see, a young aristocrat and a Hippodrome dancer of some small fame. But don't make it into a romance, Simonis; you of all people should know better than that. He has a shrewd mind and a good body, Maxentius, and he is both pleasant and exciting to be with—I would even, if I were pressed, call him my friend. But that's all we will ever be. But you've sidetracked me. You're the one who disappeared. Tell me everything!"

So Simonis did, haltingly, constantly starting at some point where something else needed to be explained first, going back and forth over the story of the ambitious dreams she had harboured when she had fled with Gallienus and the price she had paid for them. She told of Chryseis, of Ommar, of the desert, of holy Matthea and her command to return to the city. And then she told of Rhakotis, of the very reason that Circassaë had been sent out to Antacia in the first place, and her eyes kindled with both passion and challenge as she spoke even as her voice dropped while she recounted what might Circassaë herself and certainly those who sent her might consider heresy, right there in the open forum while other men and women passed by. And she finally circled to Eleazar bar Yabin, and how she had come to Antacia.

And then she fell silent, spent, staring at Circassaë's face.

"You have lived two lifetimes in the space of a span of a handful of years," Circassaë said at last, after a moment of silence. "Somehow I am hardly surprised at that, at least—you always had it in you to live your impulses rather than stop to consider what comes after. Only rarely have I known what it means to do that—life…has always been something that has happened to me, something that I accept and deal with as it occurs, but you, you make your own path.…" She shook her head slightly. "You have learned so much, on your road here," she said. "All the things that Maxentius sent me out here to find out… you already know. Perhaps I should send *you* back to the city to him, rather than a dry report."

Simonis managed a small laugh. "Send *me*? The daughter of a Hippodrome bear-keeper? To a prince of the city? Haven't I done enough damage, with a mere Governor?"

"Maxentius is himself a peasant's son," Circassaë said. "He might live in a palace these days, and consort with kings, but he still can be a friend to such as me…or maybe you. What *were* you thinking of doing when you got back to Visant? I don't know if it is prudent to go back to Cicatrice; he came to the Hippodrome because somebody somewhere betrayed him; he has never forgotten that and he doesn't take betrayal well—and believe me when I tell you, I have had enough years with him to know, he will not forgive this thing that you have done. He made you what you are; you used his teachings to escape him. He will never trust you again."

Simonis hesitated. "I don't know if I have thought that far ahead," she said softly. "Until now all that mattered was…simply to get back there."

"And you think your Eleazar can do that for you?"

Simonis hesitated again, suddenly far from certain, remembering Eleazar's distracted demeanour, as though he were…waiting for something to happen, something exciting, something different, something that would give him far more than simply escorting an errant Golden Crown dancer back beyond Visant's unwelcoming walls. A coldly prescient vision washed over her, making her shiver—herself, at the gates of Visant, alone.

"He promised that he would," Simonis said softly.

"Well, then," Circassaë said after a moment. "And how long did you expect to stay in Antacia? I have pleasant rooms here, and there is so much more to tell—would you join me for dinner tonight? Eleazar bar Yabin is welcome, too, of course…if he wishes to come."

The small pause was heavy with meaning, but Simonis understood the things left unspoken, and smiled. "We have stayed with people who would have destroyed a Visant man's reputation if he were to be but seen in their vicinity," she said. "I have slept safe in dens of thieves. You wrong him if you assume that he would flinch at being seen with a woman of the Hippodrome, or a courtesan, or worse. He would find you fascinating; and I suspect that you would return the favour. No, the bigger question with Eleazar would be if I could tear him away from his journal long enough. And I have to go back to our lodgings, anyway, because I said I would meet him there later for evening meal. I will try and entice him to come, but if not…and he has made no firm plans that need the both of us…then I shall certainly be there."

Circassaë gave her directions to her house and then they parted, with another embrace. Simonis wandered the city in a daze for a while, still astonished at the improbability of this meeting; her mind was roiling with all the new things that she had learned, mixed up with the old things that had brought her here in the first place.

Maxentius, who was born the son of a peasant…and was now the son of an Emperor. Eleazar bar Yabin, who burned to learn all the world had to teach him. Holy Matthea, and her whispered words—*Go back, back to the city*. Chryseis, the child left behind in Rhakotis to await her mother's summons so that they could once more be together. Circassaë, once elegant courtesan and legendary dancer, now a lady and an Imperial spy—the spy who said, *Everything that Maxentius sent me here to learn you already know*.

The words that sprang from her own heart, when she had laid down a pebble on the prayer cairn on the Hill of the Wheel in Challim. *Give me the life I am meant to live*.

That was what was foremost in her mind as she returned to the lodgings that Eleazar had procured for them, to find him waiting for her—and something in his expression made her stop in her tracks and stare at him.

"Something has happened," she said, before he had a chance to speak.

Eleazar actually looked surprised. "Am I that easy to read?"

"I have come to know you," Simonis said. "Something has happened to me this day, too. But you first. What is it?"

"I have spent most of the afternoon in the bazaars," Eleazar said. "I met…a man. A trader."

Simonis clasped her hands before her. "Where is he bound?"

"North, first, all the way into Karachay, along the inner sea whose northern shores I have never seen—and then east, further east than I have ever ventured, across mountains and over vast grassy plains where wild horses still roam and the tribes who ride them are even wilder than their mounts. And further, along the edge of a great desert, and then more mountains, and then the forests and valleys of Xin, and then far Syai, where the silk comes from."

"Eleazar bar Yabin, this is your road," Simonis said softly.

"But Visant lies to the west of here, through Tollin along the coast of the Middle Sea, all the way to the Narrows, and across," Eleazar said. "And it is there that I have promised to…."

Simonis stepped up to him and laid her hands on his shoulders, with affection, with tenderness. "You brought me safe this far," she said. "This is your road, and you should take it, or you will regret it all the days of your life—and I would not be the cause for such bitter regret, especially not for you, whom I have grown to care for. And the thing that has happened to me today…I have met a friend here in Antacia, unloooked for, a friend who can help me return to Visant. Your God or mine might have arranged it, but all happens as it must. Your road is east, to the ends of the known world. I will stay here, and when my friend is ready…I will go back to Visant."

"A friend?" Eleazar asked warily. "Someone you can trust?"

"I have known her since my first dance steps," Simonis said. "She has always looked out for me. I trust her with my life. I will be safe."

Eleazar's eyes filled with tears. "You are the daughter I have never had, child of my heart," he said, his voice trembling with emotion. "An old man's blessing upon you—and upon her too, this friend who comes to your aid when you least expect it. I have already told the man, with regret, that I cannot join him—but my heart stayed beating in his hands as he walked away from me, and he carried it into the east with him…."

"He has already gone?"

"No, but he leaves in the morning," Eleazar said.

"Then this is good bye…?"

Eleazar drew her in to him and kissed her on the forehead. "If I am to leave with the caravan, I should join them tonight, there are arrangements to be made. This place is paid for, you can stay here for at least another three days...."

"Don't worry about me," Simonis said. "And when you return...come and find me, in Visant, if I am there. When I get Chryseis back to the city...come tell her all the tales you brought back from the magical lands of the edge of the world."

"It may be pleasant to have a hearth to come back to," Eleazar said. "My dear, are you certain...?" Because when I give my word...."

"I release you from your promise," Simonis said. "My destination is within my reach, with Circassaë's help. Yours lies far from here."

"You have taught me how to see again," Eleazar said. "That is a gift beyond price."

"And you have brought me safely across unknown lands, and leave me in the care of a friend," Simonis said. "I could not have done it alone, not without you. Go well, Eleazar. May the new places you discover be everything that you dream of."

"And may homecoming be blessed for you," he said. "I will see you again. I know it."

"Then we will leave that, too in God's hands—your God's, or mine," Simonis said.

Little remained to be said, and they parted with great affection—he was still busy sorting his parchments when Simonis, who did not have much to pack, slipped out of their quarters and back down the colonnaded avenue and across one of the arched bridges into the Hippodrome sector where Circassaë's house was. Circassaë herself opened the door to her, took a long look at Simonis standing there with a small bundle of possessions at her feet, and simply drew her inside without asking any questions.

Simonis stayed with Circassaë for nearly two weeks, learning about Antacia and its people and the way they thought. The city definitely had a split in it, the numbers almost evenly divided between the orthodox (more often than not the wealthier citizens, with homes in the better neighbourhoods and owning vineyards and orchards outside the city walls) and the schismatics, those who followed more closely the creed as preached by Rhakotis, which did number a handful of the wealthy in its adherents but was by and large the faith embraced by the lower tiers of Antacia's population. The Bishop of Antacia appeared to be ambivalent about the matter. He preached orthodoxy from his pulpit, but never used his sermons to thunder against the schismatic Eastern creed or threatened excommunication. In fact, he tacitly accepted the divergent faith by the simple act of not denouncing it. There was nothing in his actions that Visant could reproach him with—he was scrupulous in his duties, and carried out his obligations to his city and his Patriarch and the Ecumenical Council which had appointed him into his high place. Simonis heard him talking to a group of young priests in the streets, once, on her way back to Circassaë's house from the baths—"They are all the One God's children," she heard the Bishop say, "and it serves no purpose for man to condemn them."

She had related that to Circassaë when she returned to the house, and Circassaë pursed her lips thoughtfully.

"His Excellency the Bishop is going to get into trouble with Visant," she said, "sooner or later."

"Sooner if you send in your report?"

"I do not judge either, I just relay the things that I find," Circassaë said. "And as for you—Simonis—you will find Visant less tolerant of the things that you now say you believe in, even less than Antacia is, and never for a moment should you forget that you are no longer in Rhakotis. Believe what you need to, but for the love of the One God, in whichever incarnation your faith is willing to accept him, do not speak of this in public in Visant's forums. They will come for you. Leontes Augustus is a convert to the faith, himself—he was born in the lands where half-barbarian pagan gods still have a foothold, remember, although he left there so very long ago. And then he was a soldier, and they still secretly worship Mihr in underground temples today, let alone when Leontes himself was young. Now—now he has to show himself as the defender of the faith, and he cannot let this slide. Be careful what you say in the streets."

"I cannot believe the city would be so closed to a new idea," Simonis said stubbornly.

"Believe it," Circassaë said, "whatever else you believe, believe that. Things might change, in time—but for now, Visant believes what the Emperor believes, what the Patriarch believes, what the Bishops tell the people to believe."

Simonis had her own plans for when she returned to the city, but Circassaë was in earnest, and her advice was after all rooted in far more recent experience than Simonis's own, when it came to Visant and its doing. Simonis held her tongue.

Her time in Antacia came to an end one morning as she and Circassaë broke their fast, reclining in old-fashioned style on couches around a low table. Circassaë sipped delicately at her cup of fragrant tea, and then put it down on the table before her, very carefully, keeping her eyes on the vessel.

"There is a small caravan leaving for Visant in two days," she said quietly. "Only some dozen people or so, a quiet, discreet group of traders. I have negotiated passage for you with them—I have dispatches you can carry to the city for me, and I will give you a personal letter of introduction for Maxentius. I believe he needs to hear all that you know, as well as the things I have learned here."

"Will the things I know about Rhakotis be used to persecute them…?" Simonis asked.

"That is not in your hands, or mine," Circassaë said. "What there is to know, they will find out eventually anyway—and isn't it better that they hear about the state of affairs from a voice sympathetic to their position, rather than some spy eager to curry favour by saying what he thinks his master wants to hear?"

"But you told me not to speak of the things I learned in Rhakotis."

"In the *streets*, yes, but I have never suggested that Maxentius doesn't need to know it," Circassaë said. "And besides.…" She smiled mysteriously, veiling her eyes with her lashes.

Simonis raised an eyebrow in inquiry, and waited. Circassaë glanced up coyly, and then laughed out loud at the expression on Simonis's face.

"I think you might interest him," she said, "and I honestly do think that you would like him. In an odd way, you complement one another—he is fair to your dark, he is cool pragmatic north to your hot passionate south, but for all your differences, you are still the bear-keeper's daughter and he the peasant's son, and you probably have far more in common than either of you realises. And besides—you will need a friend in Visant. And it helps if that friend is as highly placed as this, especially if you have to survive the wrath of Cicatrice out on the street."

"You're giving up the prince of the city to me?" Simonis said, laughing in her turn.

"Let's say I am willing to lend him, if he is willing to be lent," Circassaë said. "Go, say your farewells to whatever you might want to say farewell to in Antacia. I am staying for a little while longer, to find out the things that I came here to find for myself—but as for the things Maxentius needs, back in Visant, I'll have everything ready for you by tonight."

Simonis joined the caravan to Visant quietly and without fanfare, travelling in seclusion in the back of a spartan but comfortable cart which allowed her to watch out of the back, as the walls of Antacia grew smaller and smaller, until they disappeared altogether when the road plunged into the hills and the caravan turned out of sight. She carried with her a green silk bag, Circassaë's gift, which contained a bottle of expensive scent, a pot of rouge from Antacia's markets, one of Circassaë's own silk handkerchiefs, a handful of silver talents, doctored papers to allow her entry into Visant as one of Golden Crown's emissaries, and a couple of letters with Circassaë's seal. It was far more than she had arrived with when she had first seen the city, enough to begin life anew.

She had been asleep when they had reached the Narrows, and had not, as she had wanted, been able to watch as the great walls of Visant grew visibly larger as they approached. But she was awake when they loaded the caravan onto the ferry that would take it across the Narrows and into the inner harbour of the city, and although the vessel was not as large nor as fast as the one that had brought her own small self and her family to Visant so many years ago, she was still coming into the harbour, by sea, and she was seeing the City of Gold once more from the water just as she had done when she was five years old and had yet to know what it would mean to her. She saw the golden walls of the Hippodrome, and the curve of the city's sea walls as they turned into the harbour, and she had to keep a hand pressing hard on her breast, because her heart was beating so fast that she was certain it would leave her body if she didn't hold it down. Her lips were parted as the ferry rounded the harbour walls, and her cheeks bore a hectic flush that owed nothing to the pot of Antacia's finest rouge.

She held her breath as the harbour guards inspected her papers, but after a close scrutiny the papers appeared to pass muster. They returned the papers to her, and waved her past. She stepped once again onto the cobbles of the streets that twisted around the outer edges of the harbour, where the poor people lived and where the astrologers and soothsayers plied their trade. She spotted a booth only a few paces away and almost succumbed to the temptation to have her stars read for her, to have an auspicious chart cast in honour of her return— but then the words of Matthea from the deserts of Rhakotis came back to her, a haunting whisper. She already had her fortune, and she had fulfilled it.

Simonis was back. Back in the city.

There was still work to do. She allowed herself a couple of hours of sheer freedom, wandering the streets, walking up and down the great avenue that led from the palace gates, buying sugared treats and sweetmeats only the Queen City could offer from vendors plying their trade out in the Forums, losing herself in the crowds and listening to her heart sing. She stayed away from the Hippodrome; there would be time enough for that, if it became necessary. When she had had her fill of the city and its throngs, she made her way to a secluded and undistinguished house in a narrow twisted street. She knocked on an unremarkable door. A figure who wore a shrouding shawl over its head, and who might have glanced up and down the street a little too carefully, admitted her. When Simonis left, less than an hour later, she carried at least a part of the small hoard of treasure she left behind in Visant when she fled.

It was enough to negotiate the lease of a small house in a respectable neighbourhood, and the purchase of a wardrobe of well-made but not ostentatious clothes, as well as a simple spindle and a load of raw wool to be delivered to her new address later. The furnishings in her new home were simple—a bed, a warm coverlet, a plain wooden table, a couple of chairs. Once everything was arranged to her satisfaction, she called in a messenger from a trusted courier service and paid him handsomely to deliver three letters to Maxentius at the House of Peacocks—Circassaë's report, the personal letter she had written to Maxentius introducing Simonis, and a short note from Simonis herself giving her current location and indicating that, should he wish to see her, she would await his word.

She did not know what, in fact, she expected by way of return to all these messages—whether, she ought to expect an acknowledgment at all. If anything, she had probably thought she would see some sort of terse summons inviting her to attend Maxentius at his convenience at some point—but she wasn't precisely waiting at her window for a courier to deliver even that. She had learned patience on her travels, and now she put it to use, occupying her time spinning wool into fine thread, which she wound into balls of yarn to be taken back to the merchant to be sold in the open market.

She was deftly finishing off her third ball of yarn one evening, two days after she had sent her messages to the House of Peacocks, sitting out on the steps of her house with a basket of wool at her feet, when she became aware that she was being watched. She looked up slowly, without fear or even surprise, and met a pair of grey eyes beneath a shock of flaxen hair. Her fingers stopped winding her thread, and she laid her hands in her lap, tilting her head a little, waiting, her dark hair only loosely tied back on the nape of her neck, a ruby-red shawl wrapped around her shoulders.

The fair-haired man stepped forward.

"You are the one of whom Circassaë writes," he said, and his voice was pleasant, deep, masculine.

Simonis freed one hand and offered it to him, without standing up; he took another step closer and closed his fingers around her own. Her eyes were steady on his.

"I got your letters," he said. "I am Maxentius."

TWO

The Two Queens

CHAPTER EIGHTEEN

The woman wearing a saffron-dyed silk wrap over a pale green gown hesitated, as the guard at the gate leading to the inner sanctum of the Imperial Palace in Visant lifted his spear and nodded at her to pass. Everything about her was brand new: her gown, her sandals, the style of her hair dressed around the jewelled gleam of a small diadem, the gold at her throat and wrist, even her name—the name that had been her password here, the name newly written into Visant's Patrician Register. She who had once been Simonis of the Hippodrome was now Callidora.

'Gift of Beauty', it meant.

Maxentius had chosen it for her less than a week before, when she dithered over choosing her own, once he had started the process of implementing her new rank.

"I have never thought of myself as anything other than Simonis," she had said. "I have never been anyone other than myself. I'm not sure I *want* to be."

"This does not mean giving up who you already are. You are adding a layer, not erasing your personality," Maxentius had said. "I remember well when my uncle and adopted father, Leontes, asked me to choose my own new name. I could barely think. And then I knew what I wanted to aspire to, what I wanted to be, and I chose the name of a scholar and a wise man...."

"And an Emperor," Simonis had said, raising an eyebrow.

"That meant nothing to me at the time, although it did give Leontes pause," Maxentius said. "But we cannot use your own name in the Register, particularly not yours, which you have made known out there in your time. You need another layer, too, more than I ever did when I was a boy."

Simonis shook her head in a gesture that was not quite denial, but rather a wry and possibly hurt acknowledgment of an inescapable truth. "There was always the chance that it would come to this," she said softly.

"To what?" Maxentius asked, taken aback.

"That being with me would bring shame on you. That you picked...."

"If that were in question you would never have set foot in this house at all, or if you had, you would have been long gone by now. Instead, we are speaking about making you into a patrician of Visant. How could you possibly think that of me?" He suddenly grinned at her, struck by an inspired idea. "Think of it as a stage name," he said. "If that helps." And then, when she still hesitated, added, "And if you honestly can't think of one...will you trust me to choose for you?"

She eventually agreed to that...and she was astonished and moved by what he eventually chose. Callidora, he had named her, Gift of Beauty—but it was he who was giving this gift, raising a girl from the gutters of the Hippodrome to the ranks of patricians and aristocracy simply because he could, because it was within his power, and because he wanted to introduce her to Leontes, and getting a patrician into the Emperor's presence for a private meeting was so much easier than smuggling in a woman who had once earned a living as an actress on the Hippodrome stage.

Maxentius waited for her a few steps beyond the gate, halting to turn and look at her as she paused at the threshold of the Palace, looking around with enormous eyes. The corner of his mouth lifted in a strange, small smile.

"It gets worse from here," he promised earnestly. "When I first stepped into the Palace, many years ago, I thought I would never get out again—it's a maze, a labyrinth, countless Emperors added whatever they wanted wherever the whim took them and there is no rhyme or reason to the place—but it is quite beautiful."

Callidora smiled and took the hand he was holding out to her, stepping across the threshold of the gate without any further hesitation. Maxentius held on to her hand as they walked along the path into the inner garden, telling her about the things she was seeing, pointing out the worn statuary that was once part of the spoils from some long-ago barbarian war or conquest, pausing to let her look at a mosaic on a fountain, finally guiding her to a building faced with sea-green marble and with two more guards waiting on either side of the massive iron-framed door.

The guards did not challenge them. They passed through the door and into a great hall from which several corridors opened up in several directions; Maxentius led her down the widest one, past arched windows looking into secret gardens, then deeper into the maw of the palace, along a twisting corridor which changed into marble stairs several times leading them ever higher until their journey ended at a set of lacquer-coated doors. These opened into a lavish anteroom, furnished with upholstered benches set against walls inlaid in abstract mosaic patterns and lit with a number of bright oil lamps set into shallow niches. Another set of doors waited at the far end of the room, solid dark wood, polished and oiled until it gleamed, bound with bands of iron. Callidora might have hesitated again, faced with the door into the private quarters of the Emperor, but Maxentius did not, and he still held her hand. She stepped into the room beside him, and then sank into an obeisance as a resplendent figure, seated in a comfortable chair by the window with a foot propped up on a footstool, turned his head.

She had had little more than a glimpse before she had lowered her eyes, but then Maxentius strengthened his grip on her fingers and she rose to her feet again, lifting her head, squaring her chin, and meeting the eyes of Leontes Augustus.

"So," the Emperor said, looking at her with undisguised interest. "You are Maxentius's Callidora."

Callidora could still clearly remember the first night that she and Maxentius had met. She had still been Simonis and had greeted him on the doorstep of her own small house with new-spun wool at her feet. She invited him in, and they started an easy conversation on the only topic that they, so far, had in common—Circassaë.

It had yielded unexpected insights for both of them—Simonis had been surprised at the depth of his respect for Circassaë, and Maxentius had been equally taken aback at Simonis's obvious affection for her. It was sufficiently intriguing to pique an interest in one another and in the circumstances under which Circassaë had touched both their lives—but it was clear that any discourse on matters more sensitive could not really take place in Simonis's house, under the inquisitive curiosity of her neighbours and their inevitable recognition of

Maxentius, as this would place Simonis's own continued quiet existence in this place in jeopardy. So he had not stayed long, that night—only long enough for them to take stock of one another, body and mind and spirit, and to realise that at one point they had already felt comfortable enough with one another to spend the space of several minutes in a long, shared, companionable silence. The courtesan and the courtier both knew the value of such a quiet refuge, and it was on both their minds when he finally left her house, leaving word that he would send for her the next day.

And he did, sending a litter with white silk hangings borne by a quartet of strong and silent ebony-coloured slaves who wore gold bands on their muscled arms—there was no insignia on the litter's accoutrements, but it was obviously sent by someone of exalted status and high rank. Maxentius himself might have chosen not to return to Simonis's house, but he had definitely marked her, singled her out in the neighbourhood, and even if the silk hangings hid the street from her as she was carried away from her door, she could feel the weight of her neighbours' eyes on the litter as it departed, and felt almost surprised that the four muscled slaves did not stagger under the extra burden of that concentrated curiosity.

The litter was admitted at the gate of the House of Peacocks, and the man who waited for her at the front door of the house introduced himself as Arkadios, the head of Maxentius's household. Arkadios conducted Simonis up the wide stair sweeping up from the main hall, and into a study where a fire burned in the hearth. There was another door that stood ajar, giving a glimpse onto a wide terrace, and Arkadios indicated that with a sweep of his arm.

"The *despotes* is waiting for you," he said.

Simonis thanked him and he bowed lightly, withdrawing and closing the inner door behind him. She crossed the room and slipped out onto the balcony, pausing to smile in delight at the view that opened up before her.

And then Maxentius turned from where he had been leaning on the stone balustrade, gazing out over the same view, and met her eyes.

"Welcome to the House of Peacocks," Maxentius said.

He was wearing a very simple robe with sleeves that fell to his elbows, belted with a knotted woven sash; his feet were bare in leather sandals, and two broad golden wristlets locked around each forearm, accentuating brown skin and the muscle underneath. Part of Simonis looked at him in cool appraisal, measuring the manner of the man in his own environment, something that she had been trained to do in her years with Cicatrice; another part of her astonished her by a sudden rush of unexpected heat in her loins, sending colour into her cheeks.

But she controlled it, inclined her head in response to his welcome; he gestured with one arm and she realised that a table with two chairs had been set against the wall, with an awning raised above them, stirring in the breeze.

"Will you join me? I've had Arkadios prepare us a simple meal...."

The food that had been laid out on the table had touches of luxury, with victuals that let Simonis know without a doubt that she was dining in a patrician household—but they all seemed to be for her own pleasure, while Maxentius himself preferred simpler fare. They broke bread together for the first time, and it felt like it had never been different, as though neither of them had ever eaten without the other's company before. When they were done, and the trenchers on which they had supped had been pushed away from them, Maxentius finally turned to look at her again—and Simonis, veteran of many an encounter, had to lace her fingers together in her lap lest he see her hand suddenly tremble at a sudden premonition, a fleeting memory of her prayer at the Hill of the Wheel. *Give me the life I am meant to live*, she had asked her God, and it seemed to her that this moment here on the balcony of the House of Peacocks in the City of Gold was an answer to that prayer.

"So," Maxentius said softly. "I have heard your name noised about before, in the city—you had some fame in the Golden Crown circles, although I don't think I ever had an opportunity to see you perform. Then you vanish from sight, but there is no record of your ever having officially left Visant. Then you turn up in Antacia, years later, with information that makes someone like Circassaë send you straight to me."

"I have been much further than Antacia," Simonis said in a low voice, bracing herself.

"I have Circassaë's reports," Maxentius said. "You are not here to be interrogated. What you choose to tell me is up to you—and how you gained whatever knowledge you have to share, I do not need to know if you don't wish to tell me."

She looked up. "You already seem to know quite a bit."

"I make it my business to know," he said. "And I already know enough about women like Circassaë not to take anyone from her circle lightly. The One God knows that I have things in my own past of which I may not want to boast—our lives are what they are and all we can do is live them. But it seems to me that it is given to some of us to lead a far more exciting existence than others do."

"You helped elect an Emperor," Simonis said.

"Who told you that?"

"Circassaë. In Antacia. I was in Rhakotis when it happened, and I only heard that a new Emperor was on the throne. She…told me some of the story behind it. When it comes to exciting, that is a far greater accomplishment than I have managed in my life. My highest achievement was to help a man to a governorship of a distant backwards province in Afaris."

"And run there with him?"

"And then run from him," she said.

"To Rhakotis? What was in Rhakotis?"

"The road home…or so I thought…it turned out to be a rather long road, in the end."

Maxentius leaned back in his chair and stretched out his legs in front of him, crossing them at the ankles. "A relatively recent governorship," he said. "That could only have been Bakka. So, Visant to Bakka, and then to Rhakotis, then to Antacia…you've seen so much more of the world than I, Simonis. Tell me about it."

She started haltingly, not sure of what he wanted to hear, not certain of how much she wanted to tell. Circassaë had said that he was interested in the Crescent Kingdoms in terms of politics and its religious affiliations, so she started there, telling him about the places she had seen with Eleazar bar Yabin—and when she mentioned his name Maxentius had sat up, startled, and questioned her more closely about Eleazar. Then rose and went into his study and returned with a precious hand-copied transcribed volume describing one of the journeys that Eleazar bar Yabin had made many years before. Simonis told him of the man Eleazar had become, and they pored over the book together, and then talked some more of Challim and the Hill of the Wheel. She found herself telling him about the prayer cairns, and of climbing up the slope to the cairn with a prayer of her own in her hand, and then of the fall of the pebbles and what it was supposed to have meant. She had made it into an entertaining tale, in the end, and told of her consternation as she watched the cairn tumble before she was aware that it had been a sign from God.

"And what did you pray for?" Maxentius asked, and suddenly it was serious again, without warning, and she realised that they had been sitting very close, their heads bent over Eleazar's book, and that she could feel his breath on her cheek as he spoke.

"Give me the life I am meant to live," she whispered. And lifted her head, just a little.

"It was a good prayer," he said softly, and kissed her.

When he lifted his mouth from hers, a few minutes later, his fingers caressed for a moment the back of her head where they had been buried in her hair, and then he took the hand away and ran it unsteadily through his own hair, shaking his head a little. His gray eyes searched hers briefly, and then he pushed his chair away and stood, taking a few long strides that took him to the balustrade on which he leaned heavily with both hands, his head bowed, his back to her.

Simonis sat very still for an instant, waiting to be certain that her legs would support her if she stood up—and then did stand, carefully, leaning on the table. Some part of her registered with some surprise that the sun was close to setting, that they had been talking for hours, and that she had not sensed the time go past.

The small noise of her moving seemed to startle him, and he turned, first his head, then his whole body, reaching out for her.

"I am sorry," he said. "I did not mean to do that."

"Perhaps it would be best if I...."

He shook his head. "No. No, you don't understand. I have few people with whom I can...and even fewer women who make me forget that I.... By the One God, Circassaë said I would not find you commonplace—and she was right." He stopped, drew in his breath in a deep sigh. "Before this night, Simonis, before you came I had not realised...that I was lonely."

"You have an entire court at your command," she said.

"And few friends within it. Your prayer...*the life I am meant to live*.... I had thought I was doing that, just that, living the life I had chosen for myself in the instant I left my home and came here to Visant to find a new family, a new home, a new world. I learned how to live in it, but there was a part of me that was always on the outside looking in and yearning for things I could not have, or even understand." He hesitated. "Will you stay?"

It was not a command, not even a request—it was almost a plea.

But something in Simonis was holding back, suddenly terrified. "No," she whispered, and was astonished at how much it hurt to watch something in his eyes die at the word. "Not tonight."

"And if I send for you tomorrow, will you come back?"

"If you command me...."

He shook his head, and this time it was a sharp, violent motion. "I do not command you. All I can do is tell you that I would like to see you here again. I will send the litter, tomorrow. And hope."

He crossed back to her and took her hands in his, briefly, bringing them to his lips; and then dropped them, stepping back, suddenly oddly formal. "I will have Arkadios make the arrangements to take you back to your home," he said.

On impulse, she stepped up to him and stood on tiptoe to reach up and kiss him on the cheek, smiling as his eyes softened again at the gesture. "Thank you for today," she said. "Circassaë was right about you, too."

She wasn't certain that she had made the right choice, and she slept badly that night, alone in her narrow bed, tossing and turning wide-eyed in the dark, second-guessing herself and wondering if he would even send for her again at all—and all her fears seemed to be justified on the next day, because the litter he had promised to send for her never came. She had not realised that she was waiting for it until she caught herself tensing for what she recognised must have been the third or fourth time at a noise out in the street, waiting for a knock at the door, her shoulders stiff, and then drooping in resignation when the knock, yet again, did not come.

By nightfall she was pacing, her emotions a roil of regret, disappointment, anger that alternated between being focused on herself and her cowardly retreat from the House of Peacocks and on Maxentius for being a man like other men, a man who promised something and then never came through. When it became too dark to see, she lit a candle and, if she had had parchment and pen ready, would have written a long and bitter letter to Circassaë telling her about the magical afternoon and the wasted chance with Maxentius. But she had none of the required writing implements on hand, and so instead she began saying it all out loud, talking to her absent friend as though Circassaë was sitting in the room with her, still pacing her floor with quick, nervous steps.

"I don't know why I left," Simonis muttered to herself. "I *don't know*! I never expected him to kiss me…well, I did, of course, but not then, not like that, not like he meant it…but if I had stayed right then it would have been just another body in his bed and he would have sent me away the next morning and would have never thought about me again, but maybe I should have stayed anyway… it's been so *long*, and he was a man, and he was pleasant, and he seemed to care, and what if it *had* ended the next morning? It would not have been the first time. Oh, I should have stayed, and done whatever he wanted…but he *lied*, he lied to me, he said he would send for me, and he didn't even send word, not a word, nothing, it's as though none of it ever happened…."

But it had happened. Simonis's memories of the House of Peacocks were vivid—the voice of Arkadios telling her that the *despotes* was waiting, the repast on the terrace (she could barely remember what she ate, now, but her tongue tingled at the memory anyway as though she had eaten at a table from Heaven itself), the view from the mosaic-floored balcony across lush gardens and a glimpse of Hippodrome walls and then the sea beyond, the feel of Maxentius's fingers in her hair and his mouth on hers, the deep honeyed light of a sun near to setting, the scent of cypress and some sharp herby green smell she could not quite identify drifting up from the gardens. It had all happened. And he had asked her to stay so that it all might happen again.

And she had fled.

Give me the life I am meant to live. Had she been offered the answer to her prayer on the Hill of the Wheel, and had thrown it away?

By the end of the second near-sleepless night she was almost spent, hollowed out by so much emotional turmoil that she could barely find it in her to get up that morning. The ghost of Circassaë still seemed to be there with her, because she continued her monologue where she had left off, except that her voice was lower, darker, flatter.

"I know why I left," she whispered to herself, finally, listlessly gathering up the spilled wax from last night's candle. "I'm afraid. If I had let it happen then, and lost it, I would have felt worse than I feel right now. This will pass. This will pass. I have survived even Gallienus, I can survive a pleasant afternoon and its tempting trail of might-have-beens. I will live through it all. I've done it before. I'll do it again." She buried her face in her hands. "But if it had worked out...." she whispered into her palms. "If the promise had been true—and what it if did last—I could bring Chryseis home, right now—my baby girl...."

She hated crying. Hated being weak. Hated being brought here to this low place by what was in effect so little—wishes and prayers and a few kind words and a single kiss, although that kiss might have meant the world if anything had come of it.

"Don't be ridiculous," she said to the invisible Circassaë. "You yourself said it—don't make it into a romance, not the likes of him, and the likes of me. It would have been no more than a bedding. That is why he never sent for me again—if I balked then I was too difficult, and why bother when there are plenty more willing, who would have given their eyes for a chance like I had? People like us don't fall in love. I don't fall in love, not like this, not without thinking—not so fast, not so soon...and even if I were so rash as to do it, why would he ever fall in love with me? He barely knows anything about me and what he does know is all lurid Hippodrome gossip...and your letter, yes, your letter, I wonder what you said to him in that letter...."

She dragged herself through the business of the day, pulling out her spindle and the rest of the wool that needed spinning up—but she was careless, and distracted, and the thread was weak and uneven and kept splitting and unravelling underneath her impatient and shaking fingers. And when she put the task aside things were no better—she paced, like a caged beast, trying to batter her emotions into submission and hating herself for having succumbed to them so violently.

When the knock on her door came, as the day was starting to grey into twilight, she almost missed it at first, so wrapped up was she in her own misery; it was only at the second knock, once it penetrated her fogged mind, that she sighed and crossed the room to open the door.

"Forgive me," Maxentius said.

That was all. He did not stand there offering excuses or elaborate explanations. His reasons for not sending for her were as irrational, perhaps, as her own self-doubts—he, too had berated himself for being gullible, for being weak, for succumbing so fast to the charms of a woman who had literally walked into his house from the Visant streets. If he had sent for her the next day, he had told himself, he would be telling her that she had power in her hand. But it had been a long time since he had been that relaxed and comfortable in the company of a woman—a woman he had not even really been conscious of wanting until he kissed her, and the unexpected heart-stopping joy of that kiss had taken him completely by surprise. He had let it take him, that feeling, and he had let her leave only by telling himself, and her, that he would send for her again the next day. But in the cold light of that day he had been appalled at having even contemplated that much of a surrender to his emotions. He had read Circassaë's letter again, several times, searching for whatever it was she had written ? that must have triggered his actions—and found nothing that would have justified his actions, not directly. There was only Simonis herself, and the hours that had vanished while the two of them had been together. But while he waited and vacillated the day had fled, and then night had fallen, and he knew that he had already broken his promise to her. That consumed most of the second day—that guilt, on top of everything else that he had been thinking and feeling. He prowled his house like a caged tiger until he could not stand it any longer and, afraid that she would reject a litter if he sent it now and it came alone and without any word of explanation, he had ordered a horse saddled and had come himself—to make sure, because he needed her to tell him that she understood.

After a moment of silence Simonis reached up to lay a hand on his unshaven cheek, very gently, her eyes not leaving his.

No words were spoken. None were necessary. He covered her hand with his own, briefly, and then linked his fingers through hers, and the two hands fell between them without letting go of one another as he stepped back and she followed him, across the threshold of her house and into the street. Maxentius released her long enough to turn and vault into his saddle and then turned to her again, silently stretching out his arms to her—and she came, leaving the front door open behind her, and reached out for his hands, and let herself be hoisted up onto the saddle before him cradled in the circle of one arm while he urged the horse forward with one sure hand on the reins and the pressure of his knees.

They rode back through the streets of the city where the shadows were starting to gather. His arm was snaked around her waist, with his hand wide to hold her, his thumb—almost without him knowing it—brushing the underside of her breast in small rhythmic motions; she leaned into him, her inside leg hard against his belly and his thigh and very aware of his response to her body's proximity to his own, turned sideways so that her arms were locked around his waist and her breasts against the solid muscle of his chest, her ear resting on the very place where she could hear the steady beating of his heart.

She did not know if anyone saw them pass. She did not care. Her eyes were closed, and she was content just to let the moment claim her and own her, certain where this was leading, and allowing herself to be lost in the quiet joy of that knowledge.

Simonis opened her eyes briefly as they passed through the gates of the House of Peacocks, and it felt oddly...like coming home. She knew with a preternatural clarity that she would never again return to the little house on the narrow street where she had thought she would begin to rebuild her life in the City of Gold. But the shadows were deeper here, on the path which led from the gate to the house itself, and she let her eyes close again, knowing this ride was almost over, not wanting it to stop, never wanting to have Maxentius take his hand from where it rested on the swell of her breast, never wanting to release him from the circle of her own arms.

She was almost bereft when she felt the horse come to a stop. For a moment they both sat very still, without moving, and then he brushed his lips over the edge of her ear and reached out behind him with his free hand to unlace her fingers from behind him. Simonis allowed him to assist her to slip down from the saddle, turning to seek him even as her feet touched the ground—and he was already there, beside her, having paused only to loop the horse's reins over a convenient branch, leaving the animal at the front of the house where someone would retrieve it and care for it, and then he slipped one arm around Simonis's shoulders and bent to slide the other under her knees, sweeping her up into his arms and carrying her into the house and up the stairs to the bedchamber on the upper storey.

Arkadios, as always, had lit the lamps and the candles in Maxentius's study, but none in the bedchamber—it was customary for Maxentius to carry such light as he needed with him from the study when he retired at night, usually very late. But tonight the lamps stayed guttering in the study. In the bedchamber, the heavy draperies that usually covered the windows had been pushed aside to allow the cold white light of a near-full moon to flood into the room.

They were incapable of letting go of one another; as Maxentius set Simonis down on her feet, her arms lifted to fold around his neck and his tightened around her shoulders, stroked down the arch of her back to the curve of her buttocks, claiming her mouth in a deep kiss that drew her soul from her body—a kiss that they had never shared before, that had already lasted a thousand years, and would last a thousand more. When they drew apart to draw breath, they searched one another's eyes, dark and mysterious in the moonlight, and then her mouth curved into a small smile and she let her hands slide over his shoulders, down his chest.

"Let me," she murmured, her lips so close to his that he felt the words against his mouth rather than heard them.

The acceptance of that simple request was almost passed and understood directly, mind to mind. He said nothing out loud, but she took a small step back, the first time she had taken her body from his since he had taken her hand on the doorstep of her house, and began very slowly and methodically to remove his clothing, starting with dropping down onto one knee and unlacing his sandals and throwing them one after the other into a darkened corner as he stepped out of them and stood in his bare feet. She curled her hands around his calves, slipped them upwards, touched him gently at the back of his knees, allowed her fingers to slide a little further up, and then took them away just as she reached the middle of his thigh, teasing, letting her fingers alight again on his arms as they swept up to his shoulders and then back over his chest again, reaching down to unfasten the belt of his tunic, her hands alighting briefly and tantalizingly on his hips as she spread her fingers wide over hipbone and the small of his back before she caught the fabric of the tunic between individual fingers and drew the flat of her hands, tunic and all, up over his toso and over his head.

When finally he stood before her, naked and ready and reaching for her, she shook her head very slightly, her hands flat on his chest and her palms over his nipples, pushing him back gently towards the bed.

"No. Let me."

He submitted to her touch, subsided on the bed, and lifted his head to watch with close, concentrated attention as she stood before him in the moonlight, her two slender arms raised to take down her hair and then slowly remove her own robe and sandals, he finally reaching for her as she shook her hair down over her shoulders and stepped into his embrace, burying his face between her breasts.

She had done that much—that slow undressing, that had been the courtesan's way, the way of coming into an encounter, of easing into the body of a stranger, of coming to terms with what was to come after. But even that had felt different this night than it had ever felt to her before—because this time she had not done it for any of the old reasons. She had done it because she had wanted the moment to last forever, not because she had wanted to titillate, or tease, or delay the coupling for as long as she could until she had to submit to the embraces of yet another man whom she did not love—and for whom she might have to pretend, and to lie. She did not want to lie to this man, in this place. This seemed like the first honest moment of her life, the first time she had come to a bed willingly and eagerly and openly, without secrets, without ulterior motives, without a price on it all. This…this was free, freely given, or else it cost too much to put a price on it at all.

She folded her arms about his neck and head, holding him to her breasts, standing with her legs slightly apart and her knees straddling his own, and then allowing him to draw her down against him, letting her thighs slide around his waist, arching her neck to allow his mouth to find its way from her breasts back to her lips pausing to drink in the hollow at the base of her throat where a small pulse beat wildly. She let out a small cry as she felt him inside her, a cry equal parts wonder and triumph, and his arms tightened around her at the sound as he allowed himself to fall back against the bed, pulling her down on top of him as he did so, without relinquishing his hold on her. Their lips found one another's again, and each drank the other in, touching, tasting.

Simonis laughed softly as he finally lifted his mouth from hers for a moment, and he tilted his head a little, drawing his face back so he could look at her, one eyebrow quizzically lifted.

"What?" he questioned, his voice low and husky.

"You. This. It feels like the first time."

"It is," he said. "It will always be."

"But I've been here forever," Simonis protested against his chest, as he drew her back against him, reaching down to pull her thigh higher over his hipbone, opening her up to him.

"That, too," he said.

And after that, they did not talk for a while. Little remained to be said out loud that their bodies could not convey to one another, skin to skin.

Simonis and Maxentius explored each other in the dark and by moonlight. His skin had long since lost the bronze glow that had been his when he had been the son of a peasant, working in the sun; his life in Visant had been very different, and the only parts of him where the colour lingered were his forearms, often bared to the elements where the rest of him had been shrouded by armour, or cloak, or formal tunic. He had no battle scars, his skin smooth under Simonis's fingers, his skin pale and soft and vulnerable where his collarbones met to make the hollow of his throat and where she had buried her face, nuzzling at his neck with gentle lips. But he was no soft slug, for all that, and the hands that traced the shape of her own body were strong, capable, his palm gentle against her breast and his fingers, long and supple, cupped around it, his thumb teasing the small brown nipple until it was hard under his touch. She shivered and arched against him as those hands moved further down, his thumb brushing the valley between her belly and the fold of her thigh where it lay against him, curving down against the smoothness of her hip and buttock until it slipped back to the thigh again from a different angle, underneath, finding all the places of her body where so many men had trespassed over the years, where no man had really touched her before.

She let him take her…and then she took him right back, straddling his hips as he lay back against the bed, straining her hips against his with both hands. They opened up to each other, allowed no place—mind or body—to remain unexplored, thought themselves spent over and and over again only to find the passion flaring once more after a pause spent wrapped in one another's limbs, and never knowing which of them reached out first, to touch, to hold, to gather back up what had been allowed to fall away, making one of the two of them over and and over again until neither was sure any more where one body ended and the other began.

The hours of another sleepless night for them both quickly added up like beads on a string and the moon finally set and then the sky began to lighten before they finally fell asleep, tangled up in the bedclothes and one another.

When Simonis started awake, it was to find Maxentius lying beside her, propped up on one elbow, his grey eyes resting on her face. She blinked, turning her head on the pillow to look at him more directly; he smiled and with his free hand reached out to smooth an errant curl of dark hair from her cheek.

"Before this day begins," he said gently, without preamble, "there is something of which we must speak."

Simonis clenched her hand into a fist inder the bedclothes, where he couldn't see. "What is it?"

"Don't look so hunted," he said. "It's just that I…that you are…how old *are* you, anyway? Watching you sleep just now, I might have been watching a child…."

"I'm not a child," she said.

"But there is the inescapable fact that I am considerably older than you."

She propped herself up on her own elbow, facing him, heedless of the sheet falling away from her breast, ignoring a sudden appreciative smile on his face.

"What are you trying to tell me?"

"I want you to stay," he said. "I want you to stay with me more than I remember wanting anything in my life. But there are ten years between us, maybe more…."

"Maxentius," she interrupted, "if you have found out anything about me you have to know this—I have been in the beds of men twice your years, and not because I wished to be there. You are not an old man, and ten years means nothing if…."

"It might," he interrupted back, raising a hand, "hear me out. I know you are young, and I know…of your past. What I need from you here, now, is just—if you find me pleasing as a companion, if you are content to have me in your bed, then I have to know that there will be no other men…."

"I will take no other lover as long as I am with you," Simonis said, reaching out to place her fingers on his lips and silence him. "There, it is said, and I will stand by it. But will you, Maxentius, prince of the city who can have any woman he desires, make me the same promise that I make you?"

Maxentius kissed her fingers and then drew her down into the circle of his arms, laughing unsteadily. "How can I not," he said, "when right now I cannot conceive of the very existence of a woman who does not wear your face?"

They fit together, somehow, just as Circassaë had foreseen—light to dark, passion to pragmatism, north to south, two points to the same compass, and the days slipped by quickly, almost too fast for Simonis to count them. The idyll lasted for more than a month, and then she realised that she had missed her courses in that month and that her body was beginning to change in an all too familiar way.

She hesitated in telling Maxentius, suddenly terrified of his reaction—but circumstances overtook her even as she hung back and waited for the perfect moment. They had sat down together for an early supper before he had to go to a late meeting with Leontes at the Palace, and it was almost in the same instant that Simonis suddenly bent over with a sudden sharp intake of breath and Maxentius sat bolt upright, staring at a spreading scarlet stain on her gown. Then all was pandemonium for a while, a rush of confusion and of agony, Simonis doubled over on the bed and moaning in pain as the doctor and the midwife whom Maxentius had summoned busied themselves around her.

In the end, when she finally came back to a level of consciousness without pain that allowed her to think clearly for the first time, Simonis opened dark eyes that swam with tears as a teardrop rolled down her cheek until it found the corner of her mouth and she tasted the salt and the bitterness of it.

Maxentius was sitting beside the bed on which she lay, his head thrown back against the back of his chair, his legs stretched out in front of him and one hand laid lightly over her own where it rested on the coverlet. Her small motion made him instantly sit up, alert, and his hand closed around hers.

"Why didn't you tell me?"

"I wasn't sure, and then there wasn't a right time...." Her breath caught in a sob. "I'm sorry...."

"For what, dear heart?" He leaned forward to brush her forehead with his lips. "For a momentary weakness of your body? You could not help this, and I would have taken joy in it if the One God...had decreed that it be otherwise than what it was. But you are young, still. There will be other...."

"There *is* another," Simonis said, clutching at his hand.

If she had mentioned Chryseis to him it had been oblique, in passing, trying to gauge how he would respond to the child's existence. He had not said anything about it, and she had been waiting to broach the subject properly, for much the same reasons that she had held back about the child the two of them had made together, who would never be born. But now the whole story came tumbling out as she lay there, vulnerable and alone, and suddenly missing her daughter with every fiber of her being—remembering the feel of the small mouth on her breast, the quiet baby she had carried across the burning sands to Rhakotis, the child who had spent more than a year apart from her mother and probably called another woman Mama by now.

It was not the most auspicious timing, and some part of Simonis was appalled at her weakness, at the laying bare of some of the most sordid episodes of her life—because she told Maxentius all of it now, told him about Gallienus, and her life with him, and why she had left him, and Ommar's hot eyes in the desert, and the desperate flight to Rhakotis. It came pouring out of her, and she could not seem to stop, even while aware that she might well be crushing this fledgling relationship into dust and ashes as he finally knew it all. Her voice finally fell into a whisper, ending on a name.

"*Chryseis…Chryseis….*"

"Hush," Maxentius said at last, when she was spent, lying back against the pillow with her eyes closed and her lips parted as they formed her daughter's name. "We will send for your child as soon as that can be arranged. I will see to it. Rest, now."

Her eyes flew open at that, and her fingers closed convulsively over his. "You would do that for me?"

"I would move the world, if I knew how," he said simply. "One small child will be a far simpler matter to manage. Sleep; you are safe. I will be here when you wake."

That was the moment in which Simonis finally relaxed into the relationship, began to believe it—right at the instant in which it might have all shattered, it suddenly shone with a glint of steel. And she sighed, and closed her eyes again, and did sleep, at last.

It was only in the days following the miscarriage that Maxentius finally spoke of Simonis to Leontes, and to Euphaedra.

He fought to find the words, in the beginning—words in which he could express to himself, let alone someone else, just what kind of a need Simonis had filled in his life. Leontes had listened in silence, a small and ambiguous smile hovering on his mouth—but Euphaedra's reaction, although he thought, after, that he should have been able to predict it, left Maxentius astonished and considerably taken aback at the time.

"Are you out of your mind?" Euphaedra had rounded on her adopted son. "Do you realise who you have become, what your future is? Are you really going to throw it all away on a circus dancer?"

"Euphaedra…" Leontes said, reaching out a restraining hand.

"You have never met her," Maxentius said. "You don't know how much she…."

"She was a courtesan, Maxentius, and that is putting it charitably. You cannot possibly contemplate taking this woman out in public anywhere where some man who has already had her would snicker and point and describe the things she had once done for *him* in *his* bed. If she were a peach on a market stall you would not buy her, she would be too bruised from too much handling. Do you realise that you are one step away from a throne? You cannot marry her, of course, that is out of the question—but with her bewitching you as she has obviously done, you are hardly likely to look at a marriage prospect that does make sense for you. I wanted to…."

"*Euphaedra*," Leontes said again, with emphasis.

"No," she said, rounding on her husband, "I know, I should know, who better, what the wrong kind of woman can mean for a man. You…you, when you married me…."

"He is Emperor," Maxentius said. "And you were his wife when he was crowned."

"He was already married to me," Euphaedra said quietly. "It could not be changed. Don't think I don't know that I—the things that I was before he made me respectable—was a factor when the Senate talked of him behind closed doors—whether I would ever embarrass the Imperial Diadem in some way. And I was a slave, once, who had no say, no choice—and that too was held against me, was held against Leontes, he should have been Count years before they raised him to that rank, and it was I…."

"Euphaedra, it had very little to do with you and everything to do with politics," Leontes said.

"I would like you to meet her," Maxentius said.

Euphaedra looked up, her eyes flashing defiance. "I will not receive a woman like that in my house," she said. She rose from her chair with as much dignity as she could muster and walked out of the room with her head held high.

Maxentius followed her with his eyes, and then turned back to look helplessly at Leontes. "I did not mean to cause a rift in the family," he said.

"She is who she is," Leontes said. "But she has taken being the Basilissa, the Queen, very seriously. Any scandal—any damage—she will trace it all back to her own background somehow. It seems that all evil began with her—that if I had not, so long ago, had the foolish idea of marrying her then I would have at the very least been Emperor sooner, that somehow she had been the weight around my neck that has been holding me back all these years."

"I think she would like Simonis," Maxentius said.

"I don't know," Leontes said shrewdly, "there might have been a bit too much friction there to make it an easy meeting. Are you really that serious about this woman?"

Maxentius frowned a little as he nodded. "I know one thing," he said. "I need her."

"Then *I* would like to meet her," Leontes said, sitting back. His foot was raised on a footstool, with an old war wound giving him trouble, and he scowled as he reached to rub at his leg in frustration. "But I am not going anywhere in a hurry. You will have to bring her here."

"Smuggle her in?" Maxentius said with a smile.

"There is always a way. I can give you a seal again, or a signet ring, as I did once with you—before you were written into the Patrician Register and were free to move about in your own right."

It had been that which had given Maxentius the idea. He had broached it with Simonis only after he had had all the papers drawn up already—all except the matter of the name that would be written into the register. And she had balked at that, at giving up her own identity, until he asked if she was willing to let him choose her new name for her. When he had come back with the completed paperwork, she had cried when she had seen the name he had chosen, the name by which the patricians, the aristocracy of Visant would know her by—'Gift of Beauty', the very name his own gift to her, and also binding her to him.

The name had not been hers for long, and she was still getting used to being called Callidora. It had remained strange and somehow apart from her right until the moment she had walked into Leontes Augustus's presence and he had addressed her by it, and she suddenly claimed it, owned it.

"So," the Emperor said. "You are Maxentius's Callidora."

"Yes," she said quietly, without taking her eyes off the Emperor's face, without turning to look at the man who stood by her side. "I am."

CHAPTER NINETEEN

The first time that Maxentius brought up the question of marriage, Callidora had laughed.

"There is a *law*," she said. "You might have done a magic trick and changed my name—but you haven't changed my past. Just because I am no longer on the stage does not mean, as far as the Imperial law books are concerned, that I am any less of an actress, and your kind does not marry my kind. Not in Visant. It's all right, Maxentius. I never expected that from you. I am content with things as they are."

Euphaedra had been far more violently opposed to the whole idea. "Not while I live and breathe," she had declared.

Leontes, who liked the mixture of earthiness and sharp intelligence that Callidora embodied, was certainly not as adamant as Euphaedra, but regretfully sided with Callidora on the matter. There was, whatever way Maxentius wanted to slice it, the law—and the law expressly forbade an actress from marrying a man who was not of that caste. Women from their social stratum could aspire to be mistresses of wealthy men, at best—and quite a few were, for long enough to retire comfortably on the proceeds of their careers when their wealthy lovers took up with younger and prettier women in their turn; those who could not manage to reach even that pinnacle of social status were still only objects of passing passions, well-paid and working in cultured circles if they were lucky, no better than they should be and at the lowest ladders of the social ladders if they were not.

Catching the attention of a man like Gallienus for long enough to form a liaison of any duration had been a high achievement for someone like the young Simonis, particularly at her age; landing the love and protection of a man of Maxentius's rank would have been beyond her wildest dreams only a few short years back. She had gained enough worldly experience during those years to be acutely aware of the value of what she already had—after she had moved into the House of Peacocks she might as well have been married to Maxentius for all the attention he paid to any other woman. But Callidora, even after he re-named her and elevated her to a high rank of her own, had never really believed in raising the bar any higher than she had already done. She was here, she was with a man who—against all odds—loved and respected her, who had given her first her own quarters and then an entire suite of rooms in his house, and her own servants to tend to her apartments and to her person. She had not really looked beyond that, other than keeping a tiny part of her mind shuttered away against the possibility that it all might end some day, quite suddenly, if someone else caught his eye.

She had never thought of the remotest possibility of marriage. Even if there had not been a law.

But Maxentius was obstinate. He kept on circling around to the subject, a number of times, after Callidora had thought she had put it to rest over and over again.

"It is the law," she kept on telling him. "I don't need this. I don't want it. I am happy with the simple fact that you are content to share your life with me—it is enough. It is the law—you might be an Emperor's son but even you cannot change the law."

"No," he had finally said in response to that particular riposte, and his smile was thoughtful. "But Leontes can."

But Euphaedra was adamant, and Callidora knew of her objections, and kept on telling Maxentius to stop wishing for the moon when he had the stars in his hand already.

And he did not want to cause Euphaedra any unnecessary grief, or Leontes any strife—and so he pulled back, biding his time, perfectly certain that the day would come when what he wanted could be made to happen, and content to wait for that day.

Euphaedra remained resolute in her objections. She could not demand that her husband never receive Callidora, but it visibly upset her that he frequently did, and that he enjoyed her company—all Euphaedra could do was make her feelings plain and retreat into her dignity and behind the walls of the Empress's quarters where Callidora was forbidden to enter.

But Euphaedra, although she might have looked sturdy and healthy enough on the outside, had already started to nurse the affliction that would end her life. By the time that the flesh began to melt from her bones and her skin turned a pallid pasty white, dark circles under her eyes, it was far too late for anything other than a waiting game. She died quietly in her sleep one night, alone, less than a year after Callidora had taken up residence in Maxentius's house. Leontes had not been with her, and he bitterly reproached himself for that.

"I could have eased the last hours, at least," he told Maxentius dully, after they had returned from Euphaedra's funeral, sitting in the Emperor's private sitting room. "I never had time. There was always something, something that needed me more. Perhaps she knew what she was about when she said that she never really wanted this for us—perhaps she would have lived a little longer, been a little happier, if I had never accepted the diadem."

"That's like her saying that you would have been Emperor sooner had you not had her for a wife," Maxentius said quietly. "I might have been more of a son to her, too, if we are to sit here talking about might have beens. I know, I have seen first-hand, what the two of you have had—and I don't believe many people are gifted with that kind of companionship. She loved you—she would have given anything for you."

"She gave up the life she really wanted," Leontes said. "She accepted that I had ambitions, but she would have been more than content to have lived out our shared days in that same soldier's tent in which we began them. She never asked for more, but I kept piling more on anyway."

"Not because you didn't love her," Maxentius said.

"I miss her," Leontes said, staring out of his window with his eyes focused somewhere on infinity and on memories of days long past. "I miss her practical little ways. I miss her down-to-earth instincts. I miss that faithful soul who was devoted enough to me to take the patrician rank when I thrust it upon her, and who thought that Euphaedra would be a nice aristocratic name to go with it."

"Nobody ever laughed at it," Maxentius said.

Leontes managed a small smile, glancing at his adopted son. "I did, you know, sometimes," he said. "I teased her about it. I should never have...."

"But nobody *else* ever laughed at it," Maxentius said. "When you did, she knew it came from love. She knew that it was yours to smile at, and anyone else who dared to do likewise would feel your wrath descend on them. She knew you loved her. She always knew that."

After a period of mourning that was proper for a wife and mother, some eight months later, Maxentius returned to Leontes to discuss the idea of the marriage law.

The first Callidora heard about this was when he invited her out into the moonlight onto their favourite balcony, and stood there together in the fresh breeze blowing in from the sea and plucking at Callidora's hair.

"There is something I want to ask you, and I am very serious," Maxentius said, reaching out to tuck a wayward strand of wind-teased hair behind her ear.

"Yes?" she said, turning her head to look at him, and then sighed as she read his face and realised what was coming." That? Again? But I told you—"

"Yes, the law. I know. You said you can't. But what if you could? What if that road was open?"

"But it is not," she said, staring at him.

"As of tomorrow morning," he said, "it will be."

"What in the world are you talking about?"

"The law is dead. Tomorrow morning, there will be a new law on the Imperial books. It was passed today, in Council, sealed with the Imperial seal, lodged in the copiers' pigeonholes. I already have a copy—if you don't want to take my word for it, it is in the study, on the writing table. Go, read it. I will wait."

"What new law?" she said, her hand clutching the edge of the ballustrade in a white-knuckled grip.

"A woman who had been an actress or worked on the stage, if properly repentant and shriven by her priest, may marry outside her stratum, if an appeal is made to the Emperor," Maxentius said. "Not even that, if she had been raised to a higher rank in between her past employment and her intent to marry." He took up both her hands in his own, having to practically tear the one hand off the stone ballustrade in order to do so. "You are free," he said quietly. "You are now free to choose for yourself."

"So I can lay down my sins, and be forgiven," Callidora said. "What about my daughter?"

Maxentius had kept his word about Chryseis. He had said very little to Callidora as she lay recovering from her miscarriage of their own child, but he had quietly set things in motion. Callidora had not been aware that she was waiting…until Maxentius came into her room one day, leaving the door ajar behind him, smiling.

"I have brought someone to see you," he said.

Callidora had tried to rise from the chair where she had been reclining, but found that she could not move, that her cheeks had taken on a hectic flush and that her heart was beating very fast. She had nodded, reluctant to trust her voice to speak, and Maxentius called out to someone waiting in the corridor.

Chryseis was no longer a baby. She was a wide-eyed toddler who was obviously a little frightened by her sudden change in surroundings, but was doing her valiant best to hide it; she was carried in the arms of a small dark woman whose face Callidora recognised as the foster mother to whose care she had entrusted Chryseis when she left Rhakotis. Chryseis, with the alabaster skin she had inherited from her mother, was a pale, luminous thing against the nut-brown face and arms of the woman who held her; but she clung to that woman, with both small white arms around her neck, as though she was the child's only anchor against a shifting world.

Callidora had been completely unprepared for the sudden stab of pain which this sight gave her. She had lifted up a hand, offered it to the child.

"Chryseis…? It's Mama. Do you remember me?"

Chryseis regarded her with a small quizzical tilt to her head, and then shook it in mute denial. Callidora finally found the strength to stand, to reach out for her daughter, but Chryseis let out a small whimper and turned to bury her face in the curve of her foster-mother's neck. The woman made small hushing noises, but the expression on her face was bordering on panic.

Callidora knew better than to snatch at the frightened toddler. Instead, she found herself humming a tune, the same lullaby she had sung to Chryseis when they had both been refugees who had found a safe haven with the nuns of Rhakotis. After a moment Chryseis lifted her head, just a little, her face still turned away, but showing signs that she was listening—and then, as the melody unwound, the head kept on turning, a little at a time, until she was looking back at Callidora, her expression a puzzled frown…until something woke in her eyes, a distant and almost lost memory of her early babyhood, a recognition, a slow re-awakening of a love she had all but forgotten had ever existed.

She had no word for her mother. She had been too young to speak when Callidora had left, and if she knew a word for 'mother' it had been given to the woman who had nursed her and raised her in Callidora's absence. But she knew, finally, who Callidora was—the memory of the lullaby brought that into her mind and her heart and her memory. Her upper body had begun to turn in the direction her head had been facing, and all of a sudden the child was twisted in the desert woman's arms, her arm reaching out towards Callidora.

Chryseis's foster-mother held on for just a moment before, with a sigh, she relinquished her hold and released the child into her mother's embrace as Callidora sank back into her chair. Chryseis wound her arms around Callidora's neck as her weight was transferred from one woman's hip to another's; Callidora's arms folded around her, one supporting the child's weight, the other coming to rest gently, ever so gently, on the back of her head where it rested on Callidora's shoulder.

The tears were falling freely from the foster mother's eyes as she watched this transformation; Callidora glanced away from her face, quickly, asked a question of Maxentius with her own eyes, received a reply from his own, and turned back to the woman who had loved Callidora's child as her own.

"Thank you," she said. "There is a place for you in this house, for as long as you want it. Thank you...for loving her."

The woman gave her a graceful bow. "I will stay...for a little while."

Having her daughter back at her side had allowed Callidora to finally let down her guard a little, to relax into the possibility that things might work out for the two of them after all—but Chryseis, although she had been snatched from the Hippodrome's physical clutches, was still tainted by her association with it, with her mother's association with it—Chryseis was, would always be, the daughter born to a Hippodrome dancer, and her future had always been something of a concern for Callidora.

Maxentius knew this. He was not above using that knowledge to get Callidora to finally change her mind on the matter of her own future.

"You are free to choose," he said now, "choose for you...and for your daughter. This affects her own future—she too is covered by the amnesty. Chryseis stands to make a good marriage in her turn. Her past is erased, just as yours is. Under the law, she becomes a patrician's daughter, the child of a woman married to a man of good standing, in good faith. There is now neither natural nor legal law that you can throw down as an obstacle if you wish to take this road. And Euphaedra, may the One God rest her soul, is no longer here to stand in your way. So I will ask you, once again—you are the second half of me, Callidora, my Gift, and now there is nothing to stand in your way. Marry me. Be my wife in the eyes of society and the law, and not just shrouded away in this house and ruling the bedchamber."

"But I love this house," Callidora whispered, tears in her eyes. "Maxentius, you don't realise...."

"We've said it all," he interrupted gently. "I know it all. I know of the risks. I know of the pitfalls, I know it *all*, damn it, Callidora. Why won't you accept that I know what I am doing?"

"Because I am terrified that if I say one wrong word this whole thing will collapse around me like a house of mirrors, and I will be left with nothing but a lifetime of regrets," she said. "I *never* want to start telling you what Euphaedra said to Leontes—that you could have done so much more, been so much more, if you had not saddled yourself with a woman like me for a wife...."

"Callidora," Maxentius said, interrupting again, "why don't you break the habit of a lifetime and finally do something you *want* to do?" He gathered her up against him, smiling at her in the moonlight. "You do *want* to marry me... don't you?"

Her hands dropped to his chest, her curling fingers crumpling the soft fabric of his robe between her fists, and then she sighed deeply, laid her palms flat against his chest and then her forehead on her fingers, the top of her head tucked underneath his chin.

"Of course I do," she whispered.

It would not be a state wedding, but Maxentius would not have it be a hole-in-the-corner affair, either. There may not have been cause for lavish pomp, but he meant to make sure that Callidora had her day. He had merchants from the silk quarter come into the House of Peacocks with samples of fine fabric for her wedding finery, and Callidora presided over a riot of colour and texture in her sitting room, fingering silks and linens and sheer veils, trying to imagine herself in garments made from all this and having to stop every so often to catch her breath and make her head stop spinning. It was Arkadios who ushered everyone in and out, kept track of who came and who brought what—but in the end even the faithful Arkadios allowed something to slip, and it was Callidora who caught it.

One of these presentations was just drawing to a close, and she had instructed Arkadios in the purchase of a certain length of white silk. He had his head down with the merchant as the transaction was being recorded, his attention focused on that task, while the merchant's assistant was busy collecting up the samples strewn around the room, assisted by a couple of household servants from Arkadios's cohorts. They were speaking to each other quietly as they worked, and Callidora might have ignored them completely if one of them hadn't giggled in a funny, excited way that made her suddenly pay attention.

They were speaking in a street argot, the kind of Hippodrome talk that Callidora had grown up around, no doubt secure in the belief that nobody in this household could possibly comprehend them.

"Ah'n just tell them a littl'bit extra's wanted over at the big house, just in case," one of them, the one who had giggled, was saying to the other. "Them's always big orders these days and if'n the bill comes in a little higher nobody really asks, ayeh? I got a fine bit o'yellow silk out o'it the other day, best thing is that none even wonders...."

Calllidora's eyes narrowed, but she did not otherwise indicate that she had either heard or understood any of what was being said—until all the samples were gathered up and the merchant and his assistant made their bows and were escorted out.

"You two," Callidora said as everyone else prepared to vacate the room, "stay."

She had used the vernacular, the educated version of the language spoken between herself and Maxentius and in which instructions were given to all the senior servants. Arkadios, however, heard a strange tone in her voice, and turned sharply, staring at the two servants being summoned, at Callidora. Then he signalled someone else, outside the room, to accompany the merchants to the gate and himself stepped back into the room, closing the door behind him with a subtle finality. The two trapped servants stood in the middle of the room, eyes darting about, suddenly uneasy.

"Ah'n might have given out a bolt of silk or three," Callidora said suddenly, using the same street argot that they had used. She saw their heads come up sharply, their eyes rolling in their heads, frantically trying to remember what it was that they had said, that she might have overheard. "But Ah'n not have the *despotes*'s own household cheatin' him on the sly because they think that Ah'n am too stupid to notice, ayeh? Ah'n know exactly how much silk was ordered, and for what. Ah'n might've let others keep track before but now Ah'n will personally oversee things from here on, ay. An' not just silk. Let me notice there's other things paid for but not delivered and Ah'n will know where to come to look for answers, ayeh? And Ah'n goin' to be payin' attention from here on. It'll be your final warning, this, ayeh? Now go."

They scuttled like mice, leaving her in possession of the battlefield.

"I will make sure that things are square below," Arkadios said, with a small smile, as he gave her a slight bow and made his own exit. "*Despoina.*"

He always called Maxentius *despotes*, 'master'. He had never called Callidora mistress before, until that moment.

Callidora suddenly remembered a little girl who had watched from the shadows as a regal woman named Pasiphaë had extended her authority over a situation once, many years ago. *You will never be that*, her mother had told her. *You will never be that lady, the Domna, the mistress of a patriarchal household. You can't be that. Don't break your heart over it.*

She remembered her own small defiant thought when first she had seen Pasiphaë on her terrace—*Some day, that will be me.*

She was not Domna, not yet. But she was *despoina*, mistress, and she stood in a house which was soon to be her own domain.

That 'some day' that a small girl had dreamed about—unexpectedly, unbelievably—had finally dawned.

Callidora had kept up a faithful correspondence with Rhakotis since she had returned to Visant, keeping an eye on the state of affairs in both cities, keeping those in Rhakotis who had been her friends apprised of what had happened to her since she had left. She wrote to Father Honorius about the impending nuptials, and he had written back to her, wishing her happiness and sending her the personal blessing of Bishop Timoteo, the schismatic head of the Rhakotis church who still held on precariously to his little enclave. But all of this was kept quiet and out of sight of the Visant clergy, with whom Callidora had to deal on a day-to-day basis in the city, and she had no doubt that the Patriarch in Visant, the head of the church, would have been outraged at this secret correspondence.

It was something that was particularly on her mind as Maxentius took her to the Cathedral of Holy Wisdom a week before the day set for their wedding, to have her presented to the Patriarch. She had gone in alone, and had knelt with a veil of embroidered translucent silk covering her bare head and her eyes modestly lowered, to receive the Patriarch's blessing; when she laid her hands in his for him to hear her confession, the cleansing of her soul before she was given in marriage, she gave the One God a sincere apology; but to the Patriarch himself she recited a carefully edited version of affairs, just enough to satisfy him into giving her absolution for her penitence of all confessed past sins. She left the Patriarch's palace purified and walking in righteousness, back into the final week of frenzied preparations for a wedding.

Maxentius knew of her connection to Rhakotis, if not the full extent of the ties that she had preserved with the schismatic city. Their divergent faiths were the one bone of contention between them; he was willing to let her pursue her own way as long as she did not flaunt it in public—but in the privacy of their bedchamber he had asked half jokingly if she thought that she was the single person alive who had received the blessings of both the Visant Patriarch and the Bishop of Rhakotis and did not disintegrate under the strain.

Her wedding to Maxentius might have been small, but the guest list more than made up for it. Leontes was present, of course, as Maxentius's father, but also as the Emperor, dressed in full Imperial regalia. Maxentius was attended by the new Count of the Palace Guard, the position Leontes had once held. And the Patriarch himself was present to perform the ceremony.

Callidora, clad in a flowing gown of pure white silk, with gold on her wrists and heavy pearls in her earlobes, her head covered in a fine translucent veil, was escorted by Arkadios to the small but exquisite chapel deep inside the Imperial Palace, where generations of Imperial heirs had been baptised at the smooth marble font before being presented at the Cathedral—an intimate place heavy with Imperial history. The eunuch handed her through the chapel doors and then closed them behind her, taking up his own position outside. Callidora walked the rest of the way alone, to where Maxentius waited at the altar with the Patriarch. He managed to give her a small secret smile before he turned, and they both knelt before the Patriarch, who lifted both hands above them in blessing and began to sing the wedding service.

She would remember this day oddly, in the years to come. Some parts of it would blur and vanish from her memory; other things she would recall in vivid detail, like the moment a golden cup was passed to Maxentius, who sipped from it, and then to her, and she had to lift her veil with one hand and balance the heavy cup with the other so that she could take her own sip of the sweet sanctified wine within—or the instant in which Maxentius slipped the marriage ring onto her finger. And then it was over, and she was married. Then came a moment even more unreal than the rest: she found herself being embraced by the Emperor as his new daughter. A part of her was fiercely grateful that she had not had to endure this in full panoply, with a wedding feast afterward, at which a hundred people could gaze on her and see the dazed look in her eyes—instead, Leontes took the newlyweds off to his own quarters for a wedding breakfast, and then released them to begin their new lives.

But the wonders of the day were not yet over, because when they returned to the House of Peacocks Maxentius drew his new wife into his study.

"There is something that I want to give you," he said. "It is traditional, after all, for a husband to give a marriage-gift to his bride on their wedding day. I waited to give you this, I wanted it to be here, out on that balcony where we first kissed. Come."

She followed him out to the terrace, watching him detour briefly to his writing table to gather up a scroll lying on top of all the other documents strewn about. He handed her the scroll as they stood at the ballustrade, still in their wedding finery, and nodded at it.

"Open it," he said. "It's your wedding present."

"You have already given me…." she began, but he shook his head.

"Just open it."

She did, and for a long time she stood staring at the contents of the scroll, her lips parted in a silent O of astonishment. When she finally looked up, all she could do was look at him with an expression so stunned that he finally had to laugh.

"You…" she began at last, in the wake of his chuckle. "You gave me…."

Maxentius glanced around, encompassing within that look the terrace they stood on, the house at their back, the gardens sweeping down to the sea.

"You said once that you always did the things you needed to do…to survive, to go on, to know you had a roof over your head somewhere. Never again, my Gift. Ever since you walked out onto this balcony and I first set eyes on your face, this house has belonged to you—all that's changed is that I have made that legal. The House of Peacocks is yours."

CHAPTER TWENTY

In the aftermath of Euphaedra's death, Leontes seemed content to drift, only occasionally taking command. Without quite knowing how things had come to pass, Maxentius found himself shouldering more and more of the administrative portion of Leontes Augustus's work—Leontes would preside over councils and receptions, but much of the material being presented at those occasions had been hammered out, drawn up, and put together by Maxentius.

Callidora saw less and less of Maxentius in the months that followed their marriage. Sometimes he came home too late and too tired to do much more than order Arkadios to find him something to eat and collapse into bed—and even when he was back in time to share the evening meal with Callidora, the topic of discussion was more often than not Court business and Empire worries. It wasn't that she didn't enjoy talking to him about those matters—she took to politics as if she had never done anything else a day in her life, and quickly established herself in a position where Maxentius deeply valued any insight or suggestion that she might make after hearing him out on a sticky problem and often relied on her for the solutions.

It wasn't always the huge problems that needed solutions, it was the little things—not the thorn barriers but the pebbles that would lodge in a hoof and make a horse lame for leagues before anyone could figure out what had done it.

The Empire's courier system, for instance, was always a fraught issue—it was necessary; it was a lifeline for the more far-flung outposts of the Empire. But it was expensive to run and often unreliable for anything but the military and tactical dispatches which absolutely had to get through, and even those were often sent by other channels to avoid the mail backlogs on the country roads.

"The trouble is the supplies," Maxentius had told Callidora. "If one outpost gets them and another gets wind of it, then the second outpost comes running to the city whining, cap in hand, to demand the like. If one outpost runs out of hay or oats for the relay horses kept in the stables, no other outpost will help out. They all hoard their own supplies as though their very existence depended on it."

"It does," Callidora said. "Look, why don't you make it the business of the villages surrounding the outpost to maintain the thing? It works for everyone— you could make it a law that a tithe of their taxes simply goes directly to the mail stables on their territory, and in lieu of money, they can pay in feed or tackle or labour to keep the stables in good repair and the courier huts roofed and winterproofed. They can't come running back to you then if anything goes wrong—it would have been their own responsibility to set it right."

"They can come whining about their neighbours' post and how *they* aren't pulling their weight," Maxentius grumbled.

"Yes but that's a grievance, and it can go to a court and not to the Imperial exchequer," Callidora said. "You can try the system out in one mail segment and see how it works out—and if it functions, then implement it everywhere."

They had tried Callidora's idea out on one mail route. It shook down remarkably well, and very quickly the system was being implemented everywhere.

Callidora weighed in on far more important issues than this, when Maxentius presented her with a problem—and revelled in being allowed, even encouraged, to use her head, thrilled that her ideas and thoughts were considered important, that she herself had a role, however peripheral, in the running of an Empire. But there were times when she found herself unexpectedly understanding Euphaedra, feeling a twinge or resentment when the business of Empire tore Maxentius away again and again, yearning every so often for the simpler days, when all they had to worry about was how to spend their day together.

She got him to herself for a rare evening one night—she waited for him in their bed when he came home, her eyes smoky and inviting and her hair loose and tumbled about her shoulders—and he did not needed more invitation than that, his body responding to hers even as he walked into his bedroom and his eyes lighted on her. They did not have very long, but that didn't make much of a difference—even if they had been presented with an entire uninterrupted day together, they would have thought it too short a time to share all that they had to give one another. But Callidora had been quick to learn that it was the moments that mattered—a lingering intimate touch in passing here, an extra hour spent in bed there, whenever she could snatch it from the jaws of his many responsibilities—and she knew how to make the best of the times they had together. After, their bodies still langourous with the memories of the other's touch, they sat down to a shared dinner in Maxentius's sitting room; he was barelegged, wearing only a linen tunic, and she was clad in a simple wrap gown which showed an expanse of white thigh when she sat down. It was rare, these days, to have an opportunity like this, and Callidora revelled in it—and was equally pleased that Maxentius had begun to relax, the lines etched into his forehead smoothing out as he laughed at something she said—when Arkadios knocked on the door diffidently and, when commanded to enter, slipped in with an expression on his face that made Callidora sit up and scowl furiously. This was business—this was business again—when for once she had thought she had managed to tear Maxentius's mind away from it all…

But Arkadios had news of a different sort than Callidora had expected.

"*Despotes*," the eunuch said, "forgive me for disturbing you, but there is a visitor waiting downstairs whom I think you will wish to receive immediately. He has travelled a long way to see you."

"Oh, Arkadios—can you not give him lodgings for the night and have him state his business tomorrow…" Callidora began, but Maxentius was staring at Arkadios's face.

"Wait," he said. "Arkadios, who is it?"

"Rathauric, *despotes*," Arkadios said. "The Vesigar prince."

Callidora sat back, closing her mouth. This was not something in which she could meddle.

"Bring him to me," Maxentius said. And then, when Arkadios bowed and slipped out of the room again to do his master's bidding, Maxentius turned to Callidora, reaching for her hand, bringing her fingers to his lips. "It's a long way for him to come," he said, almost apologetically. "If it wasn't important…."

"I understand," she said. "Do you wish me to leave you?"

"No, stay, at least until he gets here," Maxentius said, lacing his fingers into hers. "I would like you to meet him. After—well, it depends on what he has come here to discuss."

"As you wish," she said, smiling at him. He did not seem to remember how she was dressed—or meant for her to make an impression on Rathauric.

In a way, she was pleased that he had asked. She was curious—Rathauric had been one of the first secrets she had carried to Cicatrice, the first thing she had won from the first man who had been her lover. Callidora hadn't thought of Virgillus for years—now she suddenly remembered him, vividly, and wondered if he was still around somewhere, a cog in the Imperial machine. It was peculiar that the imminent presence of a barbarian prince should remind Callidora of a competent, kind, but undistinguished Imperial official, but there it was—and she was quickly out of time for pondering the idea, because Arkadios returned swiftly, bringing Maxentius's guest with him.

Callidora did not hide her interest, giving the visitor a long apprising stare as he was ushered into the room. She could see what had given Arkadios the incentive to interrupt his master's dinner with Rathauric's arrival—he certainly looked far different than the glittering prince whom she had caught glimpses of when she had been a young girl in the Hippodrome. He looked as if he had aged more than decade in that time, as though every year that had passed had counted for two for him. He had lost weight and his face was thinner, more drawn; his eyes were ringed with dark circles as though he had not slept much of late; his attire, dusty and stained, was not something in which a prince would have expected or even wished to be presented to a host of even a casual friendly visit—and there was a darkness in his face, in his eyes, that quickly told Callidora that this visit was far from a casual one.

"Maxentius, I apologise…" Rathauric began almost before he was fully in the room, and then caught sight of Callidora, and abruptly halted, his eyes darting from her face to Maxentius's and then back again. And then he collected himself, and gathered up what dignity he could, and gave Callidora a small bow. "I apologise twice over," he said, courtly manners deemed appropriate and dragged out to be put into service, despite the urgency that Callidora could still sense was driving him.

"Rathauric," Maxentius said, making a small but equally courtly gesture in Callidora's direction with his free hand, "may I present my wife. Callidora, this is my friend, Rathauric, son of Vathalric Maelgin, King of the Vesigar tribe."

The expression on Rathauric's face changed to astonishment, for just an instant, before he schooled his features again—but Callidora had seen it, and felt laughter bubble up inside her, something wholly inappropriate for the circumstances. So she contented herself with answering his bow with a courtly inclination of her head, and then turned to Maxentius.

"It would seem that the two of you have a few things to catch up on," she said. "I will retire. Prince Rathauric, I am honoured to meet you at last, having heard so much of you in the past. I hope we have a chance to speak again."

She rose, squeezing Maxentius's fingers once before letting go of his hand and gathering up her gown with a casual motion which still managed to allow one last glimpse of white thigh before she swept it out of sight with a swathe of fabric, and walked towards the door.

Rathauric, still astonished but enough in control of himself to mind his manners, bowed to her again as he held the door open for her. But when it closed behind her, he finally drew a ragged breath and pushed back the fair hair falling into his face with one unsteady hand.

"By all the Old Gods," he said, "you turn your back for an instant and when you look back everyone is married. I suppose congratulations are in order. I am sorry to barge in like this, uninvited, but I had no idea that your house has a mistress now—and I need your help."

"We have wine," Maxentius said. "You look as though you might need something stronger. Shall I have Arkadios...?"

Rathauric shook his head. "No. I need to talk to you. Leave Arkadios out of it."

"Sit," Maxentius said. "You look like death. What happened?"

"I killed the favoured heir. I killed Amalric," Rathauric said without preamble, subsiding heavily on the seat Maxentius had indicated. Maxentius, halfway through the gesture of pouring a goblet of red wine, stopped in mid-motion, his head snapping to face his guest.

"You *what*?"

"That was never my intention," Rathauric said. "But when you are defending yourself against six attackers at once you don't stop to look at their faces."

"Six...." Maxentius finished pouring the wine, poured another full goblet for himself, and crossed the room, handing one vessel to his guest. "You had better start from the beginning."

Rathauric took another swallow, nearly draining his goblet. "Amalric never liked me," he said. "He hated it that I came back at all from Visant—I could not prove it, but it would not have surprised me in the least if I learned that he was ultimately responsible for that little plot which would have made certain that I never returned to Ravin at all. But I did come back, and my father made no secret of the fact that this pleased him, and Amalric and the Queen made no secret of the fact that it did not please them."

"I know all this," Maxentius said. "I was there to see your return. I would have been blind not to see the way you were received by Amalric and his mother.

But you had your father, the King, in your corner—enough to make him stop his Queen or his heir, if they showed signs of going too far. What changed?"

"I'm not entirely sure," Rathauric said. "It could have been any of a number of things. Vathalric Maelgin is no longer the young man that he once was, and perhaps he is slower to see, or to act; my sister had her second child, a girl, which meant that the succession was more than ever on Amalric, and after him Rothaide's young son…and then, after that, possibly me, even with my parentage, because my father favoured me. It might have been those things. It might simply have been the fact that Amalric decided that he had had enough of his father's bastard at the court, and decided to act upon it. I have no way of knowing."

"Perhaps you'd better tell me exactly what happened," Maxentius said.

"It had been a more than usually excruciating feast," Rathauric said morosely, "as I recall. I drank far more than I should have. When one too many subtle things were insinuated about my mother—or at the very least the things that my mead-soaked brain told me were so insinuated—I lost my temper, called one or two of the worst offenders whoresons in public, and left in a fury. Turned out that the whoresons included one of my father's own knights—but also certainly at least one of Amalric's own posse, who had probably started the whole thing anyway. The royal knight took umbrage at being called a whoreson by the King's bastard, and—I heard about all this later, from Rothaide— demanded that the King curb my tongue. The King apparently told him that his own tongue had brought the insult upon him. But Amalric was ready to jump on this, and kept the knight I had insulted at a slow boil of resentment and outrage. Then, one night, maybe a week or so after the whole incident, they decided that they had waited long enough for the King to take action, and they would take matters into their own hands instead.…"

"Who did? The knight you insulted?"

"Him, and they got him drunk beforehand, so much that he could hardly stand when they confronted me—him, and Amalric's own hand-picked men. I took the measure of the knight early enough—he was little trouble, one swipe with the flat of my sword and he was down. I turned to the other five, and they all came at me at once—I had sword and dagger, both, but one of them got my left arm and I dropped the dagger, and by that time I no longer had the luxury of fighting until I *won*, I was in a fight for my life, and I knew it. So I picked out the leader, or the man I believed was the leader…and as it turned out I was bitterly right."

"Amalric came himself?"

"My guess is that he wanted to be certain that the job was done this time," Rathauric said, his voice harsh. "But I did not know who it was—they had taken the precaution of wearing masks, just in case anyone did see them, and they all wore chain armour cowls so I couldn't see their hair, and the whole battle was fought in a back alley by guttering torchlight anyway. By all the Gods, I swear I did not know who it was when my sword bit into his neck and his lifeblood spurted out to soak me where I stood. The rest of them fled, after this one fell; I did not know why, then. I was not too drunk to fight but I had drunk enough to take their flight as a compliment to my own prowess. I left the bodies there—the one I had killed, and the other, the knight, who was merely stunned—and I walked away. The next day...."

Maxentius refilled Rathauric's empty goblet. "The next day...?" he said softly.

"The next day I was shaken awake in my own quarters, by Rothaide, no less," Rathauric said. "Her eyes were swollen with weeping, and she told me everything. The knight had come to in the alley, eventually, and had realised that there was a dead body beside him. He was holding no blade in his own hand, and was unhurt—but his memory of the night before was hazy, so when he saw the dead man had a mask on he reached out to remove it...."

"And found Amalric?"

Rathauric nodded. "The knight went straight back to my father with the story. I don't know which story, precisely. They were still closeted, when Rothaide came for me—all she knew was that Amalric was dead, his body had been brought back and had been laid out in state in the hall amid much weeping—and the rumour was that I had been the murderer. Actually there were many rumours—at least one of them was true, that I had slain the Prince in self-defense, but most of them were lurid exaggerations of what had really happened, fed, probably, by Amalric's friends who had left him there, who had to draw attention away from themselves. And who better a scapegoat...?"

"But it was self-defense," Maxentius said. "Surely if you went to your father...."

"I did," Rathauric said, "but by the time I got there the Queen had already said her piece. It was a blood debt now, and there was little he could do. He did not want to see me dead—but he could not allow me to stay. He himself made some of the arrangements that let me escape—but it's exile, Maxentius. I cannot go back to Ravin. At the very least, not while the Queen lives. And now it's all on Rothaide and that prancing fool she married—she's Maelgwn, the last princess of the blood, and it's her son who will be the next Maelgin king.

Vathalric Maelgin will not live forever—and whether Rothaide likes it or not it is Valaric who will have the charge of bringing up the next king of the Vesigar people, or even of being regent until the child is of age to rule in his own right. And he knows that, more's the pity." Rathauric drew his free hand over his face, as though to chase away a nightmare. "She will need a friend, in times to come, Maxentius," he said. "Be her friend. I cannot protect her—not any longer—not against anything."

"No less can I," Maxentius pointed out. "Not all the way from Visant, not against her own husband and her father and her people."

"I told her a lot about you," Rathauric said. "She might well turn to you if she needs you. Be there for her in my place."

The hand that held the goblet trembled a little, and Maxentius rescued the vessel before Rathauric dropped it.

"How long were you on the road? Did you come here by sea or by land?"

"By land. I could not risk a ship. I did not want anyone to know where I was headed."

"They know you were in Visant. They know you have friends here. They might have assumed...."

Rathauric gave him a tired smile. "That is why I cannot stay," he said. "I have no wish to tangle you up in unpleasantness with Ravin. But I needed, at the very least, to have one man look me in the eye and not draw a blade to end me—and I wanted to tell you about Rothaide, and ask you to look out for her—and I also wanted to ask if I may tell my mother to send any message she might have for me here, to you. I don't know where I am headed next, but I will find a way to let you know where I land, or possibly make my own way back here from time to time, even if I have to wait outside the walls to get the news from home...."

"How *did* you get into the city?" Maxentius said. "The guards at the gate...."

"I sent in a message from the gate, to the House of Peacocks," Rathauric said. "With my signet. Arkadios must have received it, and recognised my seal, and taken it upon himself to send back a message saying that I was expected, I did not realise that it had not been you until he met me at the gate, and I realised you had no idea yet that I had come. If he overstepped his authority, be kind to him. He knows that you are my friend."

"If the message had reached me, I would have sent back the same response," Maxentius said."You're married," Rathauric said, with a slow smile. "You still have to tell me about that."

"Unless you plan to fade with the dawn, then there will be time enough for that tomorrow," Maxentius said. "You're exhausted; I will have a guest chamber prepared—in fact, it would astonish me if Arkadios has not got one ready by now—and at the very least you will get one good night's sleep here. And tomorrow, we will talk again of what must be done. Perhaps I can talk to the King for you...."

Rathauric had stood up, and he was weaving on his feet. But he did manage to shake his head at Maxentius's suggestion, a very small movement, as though anything more physically hurt.

"That is done," he said, slurring a little. "He is Maelgin, I killed his son and his heir, he cannot take me back now in honour. I must carve a new life out for myself somewhere."

Maxentius stepped up to his side, grabbing one of Rathauric's arms and draping it over his own shoulders, wedging himself against Rathauric's body for support and staggering a little as Rathauric sagged against him.

"Bed," he said. "You can barely stand. We will talk tomorrow."

Callidora had her own suite of rooms, including a bedchamber. She seldom made much use of it, preferring to share Maxentius's own bed—but that night she had retired to her own quarters, leaving Maxentius free to deal with Rathauric's unexpected arrival on his own, without the need to worry about whether he would find her underfoot at the worst possible moment. He looked in on her the next morning when he rose, but she was still asleep, burrowed into the pillows of her bed. He stood over her for a moment, smiling, reaching out to sweep a tangle of hair gently from her cheek so that he could see her face. She stirred, but did not wake, and he left her undisturbed.

He might have supposed Rathauric to be still asleep, too, after the rigors of his journey to Visant and the events that had led up to it—but Rathauric was already up and dressed by the time Maxentius knocked on the guest room door.

"Arkadios is a treasure beyond price," Rathauric said conversationally as Maxentius entered the room. "I didn't really think I needed a hangover cure until he came up with one this morning. My bones might ache, but my head doesn't hurt any more."

"Are you hungry? There is breakfast...."

"No. I should go. If you can do two things for me—no, three—"

"Of course your mother can send messages here. You can do likewise, if you wish. I will make sure that a courier gets your messages to her."

"I was thinking of asking Arkadios to pack up some travel rations for me, actually, on a more urgent practical matter," Rathauric said, grinning wryly.

"That, and I would beg the means to leave the city without having to deal with bureaucratic tangles. And please—look out for Rothaide, I mean that. She is not really in a good place right now...."

"That's four things," Maxentius said, laughing. "I can't promise to meddle in the affairs of Ravin, but I will keep an ear on the ground." He shook his head. "Amalric," he said. "What ill spirit guided your sword?"

"If it had not been him, it would have been me, sooner or later," Rathauric said grimly.

His life or mine. It was a disturbing echo of his own choice, with Celerian, on a terrace only a few paces away. "You saved my life, you know," he said to Rathauric.

"Oh?" Rathauric said, cocking an eyebrow at him.

"A candidate for Emperor who got passed over at the Senate vote...came after me with a blade. Right here, in this house. If you had not drilled me in self-defense back when I was in Ravin with you, you might not have had this safe house to come back to."

"And you are all right...?" Rathauric said sharply, narrowing his eyes, his shoulders tensing. When Maxentius nodded, Rathauric shrugged, relaxing again. "Well, that actually makes me feel a little better about all this, dropping in on you from nowhere to lay more trouble at your door. Make my apologies to your lady, would you? I'd prefer to leave as soon as that can be arranged. I will try and stay in touch, as best I can. You...." Rathauric glanced around at the well-appointed guest chamber, but it was obviously not all that he meant by his next words. "Congratulations, on everything—on all this. You are closer to a much more powerful throne right now than I have ever been to Vathalric Maelgin's, and you have a beautiful woman in your bed besides—it seems to me you have done well for yourself over the last few years."

"The world has treated me well, and the One God wills it so," Maxentius said, shrugging, a small smile dancing on the corner of his mouth.

"You have helped shape Visant,' Rathauric said. "Now take it, and hold it."

They clasped each other's arm briefly, a farewell between brothers of the sword, and then Rathauric released his grip with a sigh and looked away.

"If I had not done a stupid thing..." he said. "That should teach me, I have an evil temper when I drink too much. I've already done the worst I could do, but from here on...it might help me if I remembered that, before I get too deep into my cups. Thank you for helping me. I realise this isn't your fight, and that Visant might not want to get too deeply involved—but thank you, for the little things."

"Arkadios will have your travel rations ready," Maxentius said.

In less than an hour, he was gone. Callidora rose almost an hour after that and came knocking on Maxentius's study door, remarkably well put together for that hour in the morning.

"Arkadios tells me he is gone already, your friend," she said, sounding just a little disappointed. "It certainly was a fleeting visit. What brings him here?"

"He had to…leave home under disastrous circumstances," Maxentius said. "He calls me friend, so he came to me."

"For help?"

"Of sorts. It seems he leaves a trail of catastrophe in his wake, back in Ravin. I need to tell Leontes and the council about the new situation. The succession in the Vesigar court might have just got…complicated."

"But is it something that Visant needs to be involved in?"

"Visant—I don't know. We'll have to watch the situation; I might send an envoy out there on some pretext to see what the lay of the land is. I certainly don't want to have to get tangled up in some local scrap—but if the Maelgin dynasty is at stake, then we have to know who the players are. As it stands, only Rothaide and her son stand between the end of the true Maelgin line."

"Rothaide?"

"Rathauric's half-sister. King Vathalric Maelgin's daughter. Beautiful, headstrong, intelligent, she should have been a warrior but she was born in a woman's body. But the Vesigar tribesmen will not be ruled by a woman's hand. That's one of the things Rathauric came here to ask of me."

"What did he ask?" Callidora said, conscious of the faintest flutter of unease at the tone of admiration in her husband's tone when he spoke of this northern princess who was his friend's sister.

"To be there for her, if need be. As Visant…as myself." Maxentius sighed, and reached out for her hand, rubbing the soft inside of her wrist with his thumb. "But there's nothing that I can do about that right now, except keep watch. I'll let Leontes know about the situation after breakfast—which I shall stay and have here with you, seeing as our dinner was interrupted last night. I wish that the circumstances in which Rathauric came here had been different. I would have liked to introduce the two of you properly. I think you would have found much in each other to like."

Callidora smiled, accepting his caress, letting him snake his other arm around her waist, held her peace—and felt the first tiny stirrings of the shadow bear that was her protector, the spirit of her *stoicheon*. It was not a roar, not yet—but the beast was awake, and watching. And it had a name now, to worry on.

The princess of the north. Rothaide, the last of the Maelgin line.

CHAPTER TWENTY ONE

They tell me he either sleeps too soundly and will not wake, or spends the nights sleepless," Arkadios said quietly, apparently as a complete non sequitur, waiting at Callidora's elbow while she pored over some household accounts.

But she understood him; it was only days before that she had asked him to find out what he could, through his own channels, about Leontes Augustus—Callidora herself had seen the Emperor look tired and pale, his skin almost waxen, the last few times she had seen him, but Leontes? had told her that everything was all right. He had told Maxentius the same thing—if he admitted to anything, it was only that it was the old war wound that pained him more and more often these days. The war wound had been blamed for a lot, increasingly so, over the past year—but Callidora had been increasingly certain that he was not telling her, or even Maxentius, the whole truth.

Callidora laid down the accounts, looked up at Arkadios. "Has he been seen by anybody?"

"He refuses attention, I am told," Arkadios murmured. "But there are rumours that he takes a powder at night—and that how he sleeps that night it depends on how much of it he takes."

"Maxentius said he won't talk about it," Callidora said.

"Weakness is the fear of Leontes Augustus," Arkadios said. "I was in his household long before he appointed me to the House of Peacocks when Maxentius came here. I remember that war wound. He was sometimes troubled by it, yes—and he kept that to himself, letting nobody know, except some who were necessary to bind it or brace it until the pangs passed, and he was in control of it again, and of himself. But *despoina* Euphaedra is gone now, and there is nobody for him to lean on...."

"If he would let me...."

Arkadios shook his head once, regretfully. "You are his son's wife, *despoina*, not his own. But some time soon he will have to speak to his son about this. I am not saying that Leontes Augustus is as death's door, not yet, but I think he well remembers the succession mess that his predecessor left behind—and if he wishes to make sure of his legacy, he will have to do something about the future very soon."

Callidora gathered up her accounts, squaring the pile into a neat stack, and sighed. "Leontes might reign, but Maxentius already rules," she said softly.

"Precisely," Arkadios said. "And my sources tell me that Leontes Augustus plans to address that very thing, soon, by decree."

Less than a month later, in Winter Court, the decree came. In the splendour of his throne room, before the assembled dignitaries from both Visant itself and from the furthest reaches of the Empire, his pallor camouflaged by careful make-up, Leontes called on Maxentius to attend him. When Maxentius came down on one knee before the Emperor in answer to the summons, Leontes presented him with a scroll naming him *nobilissimus*, the highest rank in the Empire...and more than that, naming Maxentius directly not only as Leontes Augustus's chosen successor but as fully his equal, a co-Emperor with all the rights and privileges of that rank, ensuring a seamless sideways step to succession when the time came for Leontes himself to step aside.

Leontes had warned Maxentius that he meant to raise him to *nobilissimus* rank, and Maxentius was waiting for it. The other took him utterly by surprise, and not just him—the court was abuzz with it, after the Emperor's announcement, and it was as well that it was the last order of business because nothing else of any importance could have been done in the aftermath.

After court was over, Maxentius and Callidora both retired with Leontes to the anteroom behind the throne chamber, so that the Emperor might get divested of his regalia before returning to his own quarters.

"You both know it," Leontes said, submitting to silentiaries' practised ministrations. "You've been worrying about my health for months. If I look the way I feel, I am sure you had good cause to worry about it. This needed to be done, Maxentius. You were there the last time. I know that with you I leave the Empire in good hands. I would not want a repeat of the last succession run, when the wolves were snapping at Valerian Augustus's heels even before he was dead and then stood ready to rend his Empire apart after he was gone."

"Well, he did have his dream," Maxentius said, smiling a little wryly.

"I've had no prophetic dreams. I don't appear to be on such intimate terms with the One God as he was at the end," Leontes said. "But if I had to stake my life and my legacy on one prophecy that I could make then, it would be that you should follow behind me, as you are already beside me, as you have been beside me for months, perhaps even since the very beginning of it all, in every sense but the one that I have formally added today. You haven't suddenly become Emperor today, my son. You've been one for a while—it's the empty title that I add today, just to make the rest of the Empire aware of it." He paused. "And there is the fact that I would like to see you crowned before I die," he said.

"Most Emperors don't get that luxury," Maxentius said gently, finding himself oddly moved by Leontes's words.

"Not because they are forbidden to, or unable," Leontes said. "In the early days of the Empire it was customary, in fact, to crown a Junior Emperor who would shoulder some of the responsibilities of the Empire, right along the Senior Emperor who would reign over it. It made sense—the Junior Emperor, younger and more hale by definition, would be the war commander, should the Empire need one, and lead the army into battles—without leaving the Empire headless and in the potentially devastating situation of being leaderless at the worst of times."

"Are you planning a war, Leontes Augustus?" Callidora asked.

Leontes smiled at her, reaching out with a reassuring hand. "Not in the foreseeable future. I have no plans to turn Maxentius into a general. But it was time he was called by his proper title. He has earned it."

But despite Leontes's words and the proclamation, the coronation that Leontes said he wished to see did not eventuate at the Winter court, and it was early spring before the matter was brought up again—because Leontes's health took a turn for the worse as the days warmed, and he realised that he had far less time than even he had believed. The complicated protocols for Maxentius's coronation ceremony was suddenly stepped up to a much higher priority. Leontes gave his panicked functionaries less than a month to set it all up because he wanted it to coincide with Holy Week, culminating with the day on which the body of the One God's Messiah had been taken up into Heaven.

Maxentius was abruptly busier than ever, the demands of the running of an Empire now added to the preparations for the coming ceremonial. But he had taken the time to sit down with Leontes and Callidora, and set out his own plans for the coronation ceremony.

"If you think I've been working beside you all this time," he said to Leontes, "then you have to know that it is also true that Callidora has been working beside me. She has been more than my wife, whom I love—she has been my partner and my ally and my counsel. You did not crown Euphaedra as Augusta, my father, and you had your reasons, and they remain good and valid for you and for her—but I have my Empress right here, and I intend that she should be crowned Augusta at my side."

Callidora turned to stare at him with wide eyes. Leontes hesitated, but then tilted his head slightly, a gesture of resignation, of acceptance.

"Perhaps I should have seen this coming," he murmured. "My dear," he said, turning to Callidora, "in the two hundred years since Emperors have been crowned here in Visant, twenty six men have worn the Imperial Diadem in their turn. Only nine women have ever been so honoured before you. I hope you realise what is being laid at your feet here."

"Maxentius," Callidora said, breathless, "I don't know that I...."

He reached for her hand. "Truly," he said, "it is no different in this instance than what the Emperor has already done for me. You have already worn the robes of this title, for as long as you have stood by my side. All I am doing is making sure the world knows what I know about you."

Her eyes filled with unexpected tears, and she came down on one knee before the chair on which he sat, bending her head over his hands. "But what if I fail," she said, "what if they hate me? Maxentius, you might have changed my name and dressed my body in silk and gold—but they will never forget who I was, and the Hippodrome. The city will never forgive me that, the hubris of a dancer who clawed her way up to the very pinnacle of the Empire and claimed the throne itself. It might hurt *you*—your own standing...."

"They've already had quite long enough to get used to the fact that where I go, you are at my side," Maxentius said, getting to his feet and raising her up from her obeisance, too. "I am resolved on this, for my part, Callidora—*you* are what makes it possible for me to endure the weight of this crown."

"Only nine," Leontes said softly. "Maxentius—Euphaedra was who she was, and it was an easy decision for me not to name her Empress in her own right. There are good reasons why only nine women have worn this crown. It is a double-edged sword, this gift that you give your consort. It is yours to give, of course—and yours to accept, Callidora, if you so choose. The choices are with you both. But think on it, before you fully resolve on the matter. Make sure you understand…all that it entails. Euphaedra's life remained her own, in the end, even living here in the safety and privilege of the Palace, these walls—this crown, my own—protected her from the world when the world was hungry for her. You give that up—that peace andprotection —if you once allow the diadem to be set on your own head, Callidora."

"When have I ever sought peace and protection?" Callidora asked. "If there was something going on I was always in the center of it anyway. I know how to protect myself."

"You may have the resources to pile barricades between yourself and what is out there, waiting—but when you are Augusta, when the storm breaks, it breaks on *you*, not on those walls."

"On us both," Maxentius said. "I will never let you stand alone."

She searched his eyes, found only love, trust, absolute resolve; turned to look at Leontes, and found something that was an incongruous cross between affection and sympathy. But then the bear shadow in her stretched and rose, and pride lifted her head and squared her jaw, and she straightened, feeling the weight of Empire come to rest on her slim shoulders.She was strong enough for this. She knew that.

But still. It was Maxentius's word that had brought this to her. *His* faith.

"I will do it, then," she said. "If you will it."

Leontes sighed, and sat back. "So be it, then," he said, and he was Augustus in that moment, Emperor, his voice a command.

Court protocol separated Maxentius and Callidora for the handful of days preceding the coronation itself.

Maxentius had not taken a break from his duties at the Palace, and found himself working almost every minute of every day—be it a resolution of disputes in council, dealing with the day-to-day running and petty concerns of the Palace which overflowed from Leontes's plate to his own, or frantic preparations for a ceremony that would change his life profoundly and for which, now that it was imminent, far too little time seemed to have been allotted. He found himself dictating letters while being fitted for his coronation garb, or eating a meal in the middle of the night and wondering whether it was supposed to be breakfast or dinner.

On the last night before his coronation he knelt in a prayer vigil in the Patriarch's own chapel in the Cathedral of Holy Wisdom, dressed in the simple coarse robe of a monk, with shifts of drowsy priests accompanying himself and the Patriarch as they sought the blessing of the One God upon the day that was to come—Maxentius noticed that at least one of his vigil companions was frankly asleep in the corner of the Patriarch's chapel before the night was done.

But Maxentius himself was awake—more awake than he had ever been in his life, despite feeling as though he had been set adrift in a strange and wholly unreal dream He caught himself wondering with a degree of earnest but somehow disembodied interest as to what he would have been doing right then, at that precise moment, if he had never received Leontes's letter or accepted his offer to come to Visant and become his son. That road had been walked long ago, its route set and solid, and he knew that playing the what-if game was useless—he was who he was, he was what Visant had made him—Visant, and a man called Leontes, and a woman called Callidora. He fully realised that nothing would graphically change in the wake of the coronation—he would still be Maxentius, and Leontes would still be Leontes Augustus, and they would do the same things on the day after the coronation as they had done in the days that led up to it. But he would have a new title after his name—he himself would be Augustus, and it would make everything different.

Callidora, her own days a flurry of activity, had had her own fittings for garments that promised to be richer than she could have ever imagined an article of clothing could possibly be. She held her own vigil on the night before the coronation, in the Imperial Chapel in which she had been married, and only she knew that one of the assorted clergy who shared that night with her was a monk who had been sent all the way from Rhakotis with Bishop Timoteo's blessing on her new estate. But she might have been alone, for all the notice she took of any of the holy people who kept the vigil with her, praying in soft voices until they filled the frescoed and marble-columned chapel with a whisper of entreaties to Heaven to bless the woman who knelt on the step before the altar itself. Callidora's back was straight, her eyes wide and all but unseeing for all that they rested on the shadow of the representation of the Wheel that hung before her—because although her physical body was here, her mind was far away, remembering the road that she had travelled to reach this quiet holy place, this trembling night.

She remembered with vivid clarity the musky scent of the old lion in Kypra, whose paw she had healed when she had been too young to understand the meaning of fear; the texture of the white sand in the Hippodrome arena when she had walked out with her sister to beg for her family's survival; the men who had come to take Batzas's body from the stone room in which he had died; the feel of a hundred men's hands as they reached for her body, with gentleness or with passion or with rough carelessness; the weight of a dying old woman's hand in her own while a priest intoned the last blessing; the laughter of the small girl-child who had been born of her body and whom she had carried safely between the hammer of the sun and the anvil of the empty desert outside Rhakotis—the daughter whom Maxentius had extracted from Rhakotis for Callidora, and who even now slept quietly in her own room back in the House of Peacocks; the quality of light in the twilights of the Crescent Kingdoms; the glint of sunlight on the walls of Antacia...or on the golden stone of Visant's own Hippodrome, where it had all begun, a place not too far away physically from where she knelt in prayer that night but which might as well have belonged in another world. Her hands trembled with all of it—the pride, fear, regret, passion, determination and love that she carried in her, the light and the darkness of her soul.

If Maxentius managed to snatch a brief moment of sleep in between his own vigil and the procession that would take him to the Cathedral, Callidora did not. She rose from her knees in the Imperial chapel as one of the nuns touched her shoulder to let her known that dawn had come, and walked straight back to her rooms where her dressers waited. She did not say a word to anyone, allowing them to dress her and style her hair and lay the veil upon her head that she would wear in the streets, and then letting herself be escorted to fill her appointed place in the coronation procession.

Maxentius led the way in the procession—himself, this time, walking within the protective phalanx of the Palace Guards whom Leontes had once commanded, just as Leontes himself had done on his own coronation day. His head was bare in the cool spring sunshine, the wind tangling his hair, and the acclamations from the street were loud, for he had always been a popular personage in the city. Behind him, some distance away, another phalanx of guards surrounded a smaller figure, veiled in white and wrapped in a simple dark cloak that shrouded her form. The street throngs were not as well versed in Visant's history—for the most part, the things that had happened to anyone more than a generation removed from them held no real significance at all, and they neither knew nor cared, in that moment, that Callidora was only the tenth woman recorded in the Imperial rolls of Visant as being crowned

Augusta in her own right. But they sensed that they were in the presence of something unusual, perhaps even unique—the roar of acclamation that marked Maxentius's passage had quietened down into an expectant silence by the time that Callidora passed, and for her part she could not but wonder what the silence meant. Were they in awe of what she represented on that day? Or did they resent that an upstart like her had such a prominent place in the procession that wound its way to the doors of the great Cathedral?

Maxentius remembered Leontes's coronation, remembered the feelings that carried him through the ceremony that day, but it was as though he had imagined all of that, because the reality of his own coronation was quite different. He knelt at his father the Emperor's feet. Leontes, wearing a crown of golden laurel leaves, stood on the dais before the Cathedral's great altar, first laid the purple cloak of royalty, the Imperial *chlamys*, over Maxentius's shoulders, letting it flow down his back and fall around the younger man and cover him from shoulder to the soles of his shoes. Then Leontes turned to solemnly accept the Imperial Diadem from the Patriarch—and himself placed the crown on the head of his adopted son and chosen successor, making a gesture of blessing over the new-crowned young Emperor. Then he stepped back and was helped by one of his silentiaries into a throne-like chair that had been placed to one side.

If there had been a quiet susurrus in the Cathedral before, it suddenly vanished altogether, as all those present took a deep breath and then held it. In the profound silence, Maxentius rose to his feet, the Imperial Diadem glittering in the candlelight as he turned his head, and held out a hand to the main body of the Cathedral.

Callidora shed her cloak, and stood—and the candlelight caught and flamed in the jewels that adorned her gown. Her head and face were still covered by the fine white veil in which she had walked from the Palace to the Cathedral. She ascended the three shallow steps to the altar dais and sank down on both knees before Maxentius, lifting her head to look at him, her hands raised in a gesture of prayer. He reached out and removed the veil, letting it fall to the side; she gazed at him steadily, dark eyes holding his grey gaze.

Are you sure of this?

I know what I am doing.

The exchange remained unsaid, but it might as well have been spoken out loud; they both heard and understood the other. She kept her gaze on him as he turned to accept a second blessed crown from the Patriarch's hand, and only closed her eyes as they filled with that crown, with his hands, as they came closer and closer until she eventually felt the weight of the diadem bite into her forehead. The great pendant pearls cascaded down her temples and onto her shoulders, settling down with an inexorable pressure that made her suddenly terrified that she would fail beneath the crown, crumple right there by the altar, show everyone what a weak vessel she really was. But she did not fall, and her shoulders remained straight, as Maxentius threw her own cloak of purple around them. Her chin was high, her head held with a high pride, and she rose to her feet with a feline grace at the slight pressure of Maxentius's hand on her own, her eyes opening as she turned at his side to face the serried ranks of people in the Cathedral. Her people. The people whose Empress she had just been crowned by the hand of love and God's blessing.

Give me the life I am meant to live, she had asked of the One God. And God had placed the crown of Visant on her head.

At the breakfast provided in the Patriarch's quarters, later, Leontes brought in some unexpected guests.

Maxentius had never gone back to his home, to the farm in the rolling hills where his blood-family lived. He had sent dutiful letters, frequently at first and then more rarely as the years and the responsibilities piled on, and he had always made sure that he sent a tithe of his own revenues to bolster the fortunes of the family farm. But he had never, himself, returned—nor had any of his family ever shown the slightest desire to come to Visant in their turn and see him. He was gone from the farm, he was Leontes's son in the letter of the law, and his own family had stepped back and allowed him to live the life he had chosen in the city.

But Leontes had thought it only right that his sister should see her son crowned an Emperor—and he had sent for the family, without telling Maxentius. Only Dunia had come, Maxentius's mother, with two of her younger sons—her husband, Maxentius's true father, had died only a few months before, during a hard winter, and the rest of her brood was back home working the farm, with all the demands that spring placed upon it. Maxentius's brothers barely remembered him, knew of him as an almost fairy-tale figure who had left the land to become a prince, and now they hung back, owl-eyed, staring at the crown on his head that had really made him royal. Dunia herself had hesitated, unsure of protocol now, until Maxentius himself embraced her. Then she clung to him, unable to keep herself from weeping.

"I'm not sure if my memory fails me, but I seem to remember that I was heartsick when you decided to go, to leave the farm and to seek your own fortune. Had I known then what was in store for you, that *this* lay in your future, I would have taken more joy in it," Dunia said.

Maxentius brought Callidora forward to introduce her, and there was something in Dunia's eyes that made Callidora think that Dunia would have been rather more in agreement with Euphaedra on the subject of her son's choice of bride than Maxentius might like to think. But that was long done, and now Callidora was Empress, and Dunia first sank down in a deep obeisance to her son's wife before Maxentius laughed and said that they were family, and they were allowed to embrace.

Callidora's own family, of course, could not be here. Not the Hippodrome folk. Not the bear keeper's widow, and her new husband, and Callidora's own siblings. She might have been raised to the rank of patrician, but they had not. Neither had Dunia and her sons, of course, but they were honest free-born farmers, not tainted by the Hippodrome. Callidora understood this, and she of all people knew how completely her mother would have failed to fit into the gathered company—but that didn't stop her from feeling just one pang of regret, perhaps even resentment, before she admitted to herself that realistically it had been impossible.

Dunia and the family had been whisked off to their own guest quarters in the Palace proper, afterwards—but for Maxentius and Callidora there was at least one more stop to make.

Callidora supposed she should have expected the strength of her own emotions in this moment—but she was still taken aback at the way her whole body shook with the beat of her heart as she walked at Maxentius's side, stepping from the Palace out into the Kathisma, the royal box in the Hippodrome, where the populace waited to receive them. She shook off his hand when he tried to take hers, and glanced sideways at him in an oblique apology—*I love you, but here I stand alone.* He respected that, but she could feel the weight of his eyes on her as the Kathisma doors opened and they stepped out onto the balcony.

There was a private area to the side, latticed with elaborate carvings, where an Empress might have sat in quiet seclusion should she, as a woman of good standing who was not normally supposed to set foot in the underworld of the Hippodrome, choose to visit the Kathisma to watch a race or two—Empresses had, after all, been known to have favoured certain factions, and had had more than a passing interest in what went on in the arena. But this day was not a day for seclusion—this was a day when they walked out into the Kathisma side by side, Emperor and Empress, crowned by God by the hand of the Patriarch, and now come to accept the acclamations of their people.

And they came, the shouts, the words that Maxentius remembered hearing when he himself had been down amongst the crowd and it had been Leontes up here in the royal box—except that this time they were calling *his* name. Maxentius Augustus.

And hers. There were shouts for Callidora Augusta. They all knew who she was, who she had been, and they could not help feeling ambivalent about it—but some had made a decision, and were shouting out her name, in joy, in praise. And Callidora stood as though carved of some beautiful alabaster stone, only her eyes moving underneath the jewels of her diadem.

Her roving gaze was finally met and held by a pair of familiar eyes, whose slow fire froze her where she stood glittering in the Kathisma. Against all odds, in that mass of shouting and pushing humanity in the arena and covering the stands, one man locked eyes with the new Empress; when he realised that he had her attention, he smiled, a slow, wolfish smile that she knew well, and brought his fist to his heart in a soldier's salute.

Cicatrice.

The shadow-bear that was always within Callidora responded to the multitude below, to the proprietary and almost possessive smile of the man who had once owned her days and her nights—rose and roared until she could hear nothing more than that roar, drowning out every human sound and every human emotion until all she was was that roar of raw power, which was equal parts triumph, challenge, a baring of claws that told someone like Cicatrice, *You cannot hurt me now*—it was then, at last, that she reached unsteadily for Maxentius, for the hand of the man who loved her, grateful that he was beside her and that his fingers were warm and strong as they closed about her own, because she knew that if she had been alone in that moment, she would never have been completely human again.

Until Maxentius guided her back into the corridor to the Palace, and she reached up to with her free hand to catch a tear rolling down her cheek, Callidora did not know that she was crying.

CHAPTER TWENTY TWO

I t was only four months after the coronation, on a hot night in late summer with the air heavy and humid and dry thunder rumbling in the distance, that Leontes Augustus died.

He had spent the final few weeks in bed, miserable with the heat and the oppressive, moody, brooding weather which always seemed on the point of breaking but never quite broke, and it had seemed to soothe him to have Callidora sit with him—and so she did that, for several hours every day, plying her embroidery needle in a craft that she had never had either the patience nor much aptitude for in the past, but which helped pass the hours and kept her hands busy, while she talked to Leontes or listened quietly while he spoke of his own life.

She learned much about Euphaedra in these hours she shared with Leontes, which gave her a whole new respect for the woman who had once been no better than a slave, before she had caught the eye of the young soldier, who Leontes had once been, and captured his heart—and his respect. It had been Euphaedra who had nursed him when he had first been felled with that war wound that now came back to haunt him. It had been Euphaedra who had kept his spirits up during the low times, and shared uninhibitedly in his joy when things had been good—Euphaedra who had loved him enough to stand by him even when he chose to take the crown of Visant, knowing that she herself could never reach that high, never be adequate for that role, content to fade into the background so that the man whom she loved could take the world into his hand. She had believed in him, and he had loved her. He spoke of her often during his last days, almost looking forward to his own death so that he could be with her again.

He often drifted, speaking of disjointed or disconnected things, going as far back as his boyhood in the green hills of the back country where he and Maxentius had both come from, or as close as the day before, lucidly inquiring of Callidora as to whether she thought his leg was turning worse, because he was starting to lose all feeling in his foot. There were times he began to tell her something and would then be overtaken, often mid-sentence, by suddenly falling asleep—and then, disconcertingly, picking up where he had left off when the quick snatch of slumber passed and he started awake again.

She had become used to these pauses, and on the night of dry thunder she had thought, at first, that it had been one of these that had claimed him again. But when it went on for a shade too long, she laid down her needle and her embroidery and leaned over to look in on him—and realised that he was lying with a small smile on his face, as though he had just glimpsed something he loved, and his eyes wide open but not seeing any longer anything that was of this world.

Callidora wept for Leontes the way she had never wept for her own father. Maxentius had been the one who had found her, and raised her up, and stood beside her—but without Leontes none of it would have ever happened. He had accepted her, taken her in as his own, and had never once treated her as anything other than a favourite daughter—even, sometimes, flying in the face of his beloved Euphaedra's objections.

When Callidora closed his eyes for the last time, she laid over him the almost-completed thing that she had been embroidering—a coverlet where the last thing her needle had created was his not-quite-finished name. But what was there was enough—*LEONTES AVGVST*, it said, in golden thread, and N days later they laid that offering into his marble sarcophagus with him, when the Patriarch sang him to his rest in the tombs of the Kings.

The transition in the aftermath was seamless enough, as Leontes had hoped it might be. Callidora and Maxentius left the House of Peacocks and moved into the Imperial Palace—he into the quarters lately occupied by Leontes, she into the purple porphyry chambers that were the Empress's apartments. She walked down the long twisting corridor alone, the first time she set foot into those rooms, the walls red marble and the arched roof above her head set in mosaics made of semi-precious stones and gold. There were concealed cubbyholes for guards at every turn, so that the Empress might sleep safe and that none whom she had not invited might take an unsanctioned step into her domain. Carved marble arches spanned windows and doors, doors that opened into secret gardens where porphyry fountains spilled from marble basin to marble basin and cooled the air. The receiving rooms—for an Empress often kept her own resplendent court, rival to that of the Emperor—were large and well-appointed, with rich carpets covering the floor and walls adorned with marble inlay and mosaic. There was even a frescoed chapel for private devotions. Callidora was also informed, somewhat diffidently, that there were other places close by under her own personal control—underground stone chambers to house the Empress's own treasury, and even a set of cells where those who displeased an Empress might be set to languish until they saw the error of their ways.

The children born from an Imperial bed had always been referred to as having been 'born in the purple', and for the first time Callidora knew that those had not been merely metaphor, a play on words and on the state of being born royal – the richness of the Empress's bedchamber lay in the magnificent porphyry columns that rose to support the domed roof, the huge bed with its cloth-of-gold canopy resting on a dais of purple marble in the middle of the large square room. Callidora had never quickened with child again after that early miscarriage, and it had been years now since that day – she glanced around the room with a sudden deep regret, her hand going instinctively to her still flat belly.

The rhythm of Maxentius's days, and her own, changed when they stepped up to full Imperial duties.

Imperial protocol now divided them, and they were expected to keep their own households and courts—but they had seldom spent a night apart since they had met, and they still, one way or another, contrived to share a bed. The Emperor usually began his day with servants bringing him water in a silver basin, and a few small things to break his fast—figs, dates, barley cakes. But Maxentius's silentiaries quickly learned that sometimes this particular Emperor would arrive back in his own quarters straight from his Empress's bed, and keep the morning rituals waiting on his pleasure—or else they had to deal with the realities of finding the drowsy Empress also in the Imperial bed when they came to rouse their master, the bedclothes fallen back to reveal a white shoulder or an expanse of alabaster back.

But that was the end of indulgence. After he ate, Maxentius was assisted to dress in his Imperial finery for his morning duties—the purple *chlamys* he had received at his coronation, the Imperial Diadem itself with its heavy pendant pearls—all while being kept advised of early morning news or developments on pending issues, often being interrupted by secretaries offering documents for his signature and seal. From there he made his way to the great audience hall, to take up his place on the golden throne behind a concealing curtain which, when he was ready, the Grand Chamberlain would pull aside to reveal him to those waiting in the hall. At some time around noon the Grand Chamberlain would declare the morning audience closed, and usher out the crowds who still remained, telling them to return that afternoon (if another open audience was on the schedule) or the next day; Maxentius would have maybe an hour and a half to snatch a mid-day meal, which he more often than not managed to share with Callidora, and by early afternoon it was back into the audience hall, or into the Council Chamber with his ministers, or into the smaller receiving chamber to receive foreign dignitaries and ambassadors.

Callidora, who had the luxury of flexibility, ordered her own days with a little more leisure built in. She usually rose at mid-morning, from her own bed or her husband's, and made her way to the private baths in the Imperial gardens, with attendants trotting behind bearing ointments, perfumes, and soft drying cloths. She would take her ease at the baths for an hour or so, and then usually spend some time with her daughter in the nursery wing. If time permitted, she might allow a single audience or two before she joined Maxentius for lunch. She did her own real work in the afternoons, and then she and Maxentius would come together again at twilight, to touch, to lie in one another's arms and talk about their day, to discuss the state of the Empire and the Imperial courts, reminisce about the past, or plan the weeks ahead.

Maxentius came to Callidora's chambers for their nightly repast one evening, not long after Leontes's death. She met him at the door of her bedchamber, wrapped in a length of lemon-coloured silk which set off to perfection her dark eyes and the tumbled dark curls which spilled over her breast and shoulders; he had come in carrying something in his hand, but at the sight of her his eyes lit up in appreciation, and he cast that which he carried away from him, reaching instead to lift her up into his arms and carry her over to the waiting bed, laying her down on her back so that her rich hair spilled across the bedclothes. Callidora allowed one of her legs to slip from his hand and begin to slide up, locking over his hips as she opened herself to receive him, already aroused and ready as he brought his body down on hers, smiling at her as he felt one of her hands slip between them to guide him into her, and then throwing her head back, biting her lip, as their hips strained together.

Maxentius unwrapped the yellow silk, slowly, exploring every inch of revealed skin as he did so, making Callidora, seasoned courtesan that she had once been, giggle helplessly with the sheer joy of it, like a bride. But they knew one another well by this time, and the codes of touch and response. Hhis fingers would linger, and her hip would fall open and then close again over his leg, trapping his arm between his thigh and hers and his fingers inside her. It was a gentle intermission, by mutual consent, before the passion flared again and they came together once more, the sweat of their passion making their bodies slide against one another and making Callidora's curls cling wetly to her temple and neck.

They lay against the pillows on the Empress's enormous bed, after, Callidora's head tucked under Maxentius's chin as she balanced a precarious half-full goblet of wine on his drawn-up knee.

"I have a present for you," he said, gathering up his own wine goblet to take a sip.

She shifted her head a little so that she could look up at him.

"What is it?"

"An old friend of yours," he said laconically. "He's back in the city, fat with his revenues, and wishes an audience with the Emperor. I'll see him—eventually. But in the meantime...."

He balanced his goblet precariously on a small inlaid table by the side of the bed, and reached for a rolled-up parchment scroll on the floor beside the bed, almost completely concealed by tumbled bedclothes—the thing that he had brought into the bedchamber with him, and had tossed away..

"Here," he said. "I thought you might want to know."

Callidora's heart had lurched painfully—she had unrolled the scroll even as he spoke, and the name leapt out at her—*Gallienus*—returning to Visant for the first time, apparently, since he had left it for Bakka, asking for permission to pay his respects to the new Emperor, apparently intending to return to his lair in Bakka after that and continue to preside over the province for as long as he could hold on to the position, raking in the taxes and revenues as he went along.

She looked up, her eyes hard. "I may have a debt to pay here," she said.

"I thought you might," Maxentius said. "As I said...I'll see him. Eventually. When I do, I will abide by what you want done with him. Just send me whatever you want signed—I give him to you."

"It's time I settled more than one debt," Callidora murmured thoughtfully.

She had summoned her secretary the next day and had several messages prepared, summoning three men into her presence.

Gallienus had been the first. His invitation to attend an audience had been carefully couched so as not to say directly that it would be an audience with the *Emperor*, and he had simply assumed that it would be. He had been schooled carefully about the "new protocol" in approaching the Imperial person—he was to prostrate himself before the throne, and kiss the hem of the Emperor's garment; this was startling and unexpected, he had been expecting to be received on a much higher level as befitted a Governor of an Imperial province. He was vain enough to resent this, and it had preoccupied him rather to the detriment of his noticing, at first, where he was being conducted. It was more or less at the door of Callidora's audience hall that he suddenly realised that this couldn't possibly be the Emperor's own quarters, but by that stage he was being ushered inside, and nudged to perform the prostration, which he did…and only woke up that something was indeed not right when he realised that the delicate foot being offered to him in its jewelled shoe, the hem of a costly garment grazing the instep, was not a man's foot at all. Suitably startled by this, he instinctively glanced up, the hem of the Imperial garment already in his hand…and then dropped it as though it burned him as his eyes met the glittering ones of the girl he had once known as Simonis.

"As we are old acquaintances, I asked my husband if we might meet privately before his busy schedule finds room for you," Callidora said, her voice pleasant and low. She was smiling, but the smile was not something calculated to set a visitor at ease.

Gallienus scrambled back, still on his knees, staring. "But you are…" he began, "You can't be….How…?"

"The One God gives what gifts he chooses," Callidora said primly, sitting back more comfortably in her chair. "I give you leave to sit, if you like," she added, glancing to one side and giving a small nod, at which signal a muscular young man stepped out from the shadow of the wall and brought out a rough three-legged stool which he placed beside Gallienus, sweeping him with a long apprising look that was almost insolent. In any other circumstances, Gallienus might have demanded that the slave be disciplined, but he had been quite robbed of speech. He saw the carefully built edifice of his future crumbling to dust around him, realising that he could not possibly hope for mercy from the woman whom he had once cast aside, who now sat in judgment upon him.

He took the stool, perching on it with his knees up under his chin, feeling ridiculous and knowing that this had been precisely what she had intended.

"So," she said, "what brings you back to Visant?"

"You are all right!" Gallienus said at last, finding some portion of his aplomb. "I had feared you dead—you and the child, both....."

"The child is doing well," Callidora said affably, as though she were discussing her daughter with a well-meaning stranger. "She is growing up, and I think she will grow up beautiful, not favouring her father much."

Gallienus latched onto what he thought was the most valuable asset in this conversation—he and the woman on that throne shared a child, after all, and it was an undeniable connection; if he could convince her of his earnest and sincere interest, perhaps something could be salvaged out of the mess after all.

"Daughters should be as beautiful as their mothers, that is only right," he said. He had to think for a moment, trying to remember what his daughter had been called, but then he had it, and smiled a little wider. "Chryseis, wasn't it... Might it be possible for me to see...?"

But he had miscalculated, and Callidora sat up, straighter, her eyes flashing fury. "You have no right to even utter that name," she said to him, her voice suddenly an edged blade. "You abandoned your own flesh and blood to whatever shame or death chose to claim her; if you could have left her strangled when she was born you would have done it. I am willing to stake this throne and all the joy in my life that you have not thought of her, not once, since the day you cast us both out into the street in Bakka—where you stayed, to gather up all that it had to offer you. Well *I* gave you Bakka, and now I can take it away, Gallienus." She sat back again, tilting her head a little, the smile creeping back onto her lips. "On second thought...perhaps not," she murmured. "You enjoy Bakka so much, why not return it to you...?"

Gallienus opened his eyes wide, suddenly hopeful. "You are generous," he began, "and I...."

She raised a hand to stop him, made another gesture which brought in a scribe with a small table, a blank parchment, an inkwell and a pen. Callidora favoured Gallienus with another long measured stare, and then reached for the pen, dipped it into the ink, and wrote steadily for a few moments, and then signed what she had written with a flourish. Then she laid down the pen, and the scribe blotted the parchment with sand, waited until all was safely dry, rolled the parchment up into a tight roll, tied it with a scarlet ribbon, and sealed it with a blob of wax melted over a small flame. Callidora herself pressed her seal—

the Empress's seal—into the wax and gathered up the scroll into both hands, holding it lightly in her left and tapping her right palm gently with it.

"You will abide by whatever I have written here," she said, "and you will take it directly to my husband's court and present it to him yourself, within three days. If it has been tampered with in that time he will know it. You will not see me again."

"Simonis…" Gallienus began, starting to get up.

She whipped the scroll around, pointing it at him, and he fell to one knee at the gesture, as though the parchment roll had been a sword. "I have not given you leave to speak further," she said. "Now take this, and go."

He crawled out like a worm. When he managed apparently to leapfrog a number of applicants in the next morning's audition with the Emperor, he actually entertained some hope that things might yet turn out well, that she had had him at her feet, the girl whom he had once had at his pleasure in his bed, and that she had been content with that. But when the scroll with the Empress's seal was handed to the Emperor himself, Gallienus's stomach suddenly turned with a premonition of an imminent doom.

"So be it," Maxentius had said, lifting his head after having broken the seal and perused Callidora's scroll. "What my Empress has decreed, shall be done. You return to Bakka with the next available ship, Gallienus, and you return as an exile—you are never permitted to return to the city of Visant again, or leave Bakka without express permission as given to you from an Imperial hand. Oh, and yes—you return as private citizen. Another Governor shall be appointed at our earliest convenience and dispatched to take over the reins of that province."

Gallienus turned a sickly greenish pale as said the Emperor spoke, but Callidora was not done with him yet. Maxentius glanced back down at the scroll, and then at the hapless ex-Governor again. "Your tenure as Governor shall be subject to an Imperial inquiry," Maxentius added, almost as an afterthought. "Any revenue found to have been acquired through dubious channels shall immediately be recovered as a fine and paid straight into the Imperial treasury. We are done with this matter."

He added his own seal to that of the Empress on the scarlet ribbon binding the scroll, and a couple of guards stepped up to escort the sweating, waxen-faced Gallienus from the room. They took him straight down to the harbour, and he was kept there under guard until the first suitable ship presented itself. He watched the walls of Visant recede as the ship put out to sea—and did not know that Callidora had come to the wharf to watch him go, her face bare of makeup and her hair blowing free, looking like any girl growing up in Visant's streets, only her glittering eyes giving away the fact that she had been the driving force behind the exile of the man whom she could see staring hollow-eyed back at the city he had once thought he would conquer, the city which she had once, when she had been young and had believed many impossible things, thought that she would return one day to conquer at his side, as mistress of a small moderately wealthy household belonging to a retired Governor grown rich from his labours.

But there were two more messages that had been sent out, two more men she had summoned to her throne—and now that she got the bitter bile out of her system, the second would be even more of a pleasure.

The man ushered into her room was older than she remembered him, but other than a few lines on his face being deeper and a few more gray hairs, he did not look that much different than when they had first met.

He had not been as oblivious as Gallienus, and he knew full well who it was that had summoned him—he could not know why, and the expression on his face was wary, although guardedly pleased, as he lifted it to hers once he had performed his obeisance to the Empress.

"Virgillus," Callidora said gently, and this time her smile had genuine warmth in it. "Do you recall telling me once, a long time ago, not to forget you?"

"I hardly had these circumstances in mind, Augusta. I had merely hoped that you might have kept a soft spot for somebody like me, as you lived the days of your life...."

"I still have the necklace you gave me," Callidora said. "Some day I may pass it on to my daughter, perhaps, as a good luck charm—she might never know exactly how I came by it, but she will know that it had been a gift from an honourable man."

Virgillus bowed his head, visibly moved. "It is you who honour me, Augusta," he said. "Is there some way that I can be of service to you?"

"Are you content?" Callidora asked unexpectedly. "Did you ever manage to leave Visant and travel, or are you still reading the books of Eleazar bar Yabin and learning of your world though them?"

"I have travelled nowhere," Virgillus said. "I have done my work here in the city, and I have been content with my life. But yes, every so often I return to bar Yabin's journeys, as he set them down in the copy of his book in the University library. And it's always been a window out into the world for me."

"I travelled with him for a while," Callidora said, and Virgillus could not help a startled look at her face. Callidora actually giggled at that, at having caught him by surprise—she felt thirteen again, a child, full of delight that she had managed to surprise her elders by something that had been a delicious secret. "I told him about you, actually. So now you both know of one another. I've been all along the coast of Afaris, Virgillus, and to Rhakotis, and then across the Crescent Kingdoms and into Antacia—most of it with Eleazar, helping him take the notes for his next work...."

"Yours has been a charmed life, it would seem" Virgillus said.

"I nearly died, more than once," said Callidora, suddenly serious again.

"And I was safe, here, within the walls of Visant," Virgillus said quietly. "And yet even now, hearing you speak the names of those fabled cities out loud in this room, even if you tell me you faced death in order to see them, there is a part of me that envies you."

"I can make that happen," she said. "Virgillus...I am told I have estates now. Many of them, scattered across all sorts of small corners of the Empire. I need a man I can trust who can gather it all up and keep the records of those revenues for me, an administrator if you like, someone who will know all there is to know about the Empress's revenues and where they come from and how they are gathered up for the treasury. It would mean quite a bit of travel—I don't know if anything I own is actually all the way out in the Crescent Kingdoms, but if you wish to see them, too, then I dare say something can be purchased so that you can travel there to oversee it. What do you think?"

"You might need a younger man for such a job," Virgillus said, but his eyes had kindled.

"I said someone I could trust," Callidora said. "A younger man can be flighty and untried; I value your experience, and your fundamental decency, and your kindness. I have not, Virgillus, in all these years, forgotten you—or any of those things which you represent." She nodded at her assistant to the side, and a young secretary came out and went down on one knee before her, proffering a sealed scroll. Callidora took it, and the secretary withdrew; she turned back to Virgillus and held out the scroll to him. "Take it," she said. "If you wish it, this is yours."

He hesitated for one more instant, and then he knelt before her, taking the scroll in his right hand.

"You are gracious," he said. "I will do as you ask."

"That scroll is your letter of appointment, and you will find your salary generous," Callidora said. "I will find you an office near my rooms somewhere, to begin your work as soon as you are able to take it up—and the details of all my holdings will be there waiting for you. There will be an Imperial pass made ready for you by morning, so that you may travel at your leisure and come and go from Visant as you will."

"Forgive me one indiscretion," Virgillus said, his eyes suspiciously bright. "And it is only this—I asked a young girl not to forget me one night, but it is I who have never forgotten her. I am greatly moved that the girl once known as Simonis remembers my name, or the things we talked about on the one night of our lives that we shared. And Callidora Augusta gives me…more honour than I have ever believed I would have deserved. I will give you faithful service, Empress, and my thanks—not just for this, and for what it means—" He hefted the scroll in his hand, and then bowed his head again. "I thank you," he said, "for keeping that memory of me in your heart."

He bowed over her hand, and retired; Callidora found herself smiling after him, her eyes full of tears.

The third man she met in the House of Peacocks, with no Imperial panoply at all and only a few armed guards waiting in the shadows in case they were needed.

Cicatrice came alone, and was taken up to Callidora's sitting room on the second floor; she was not sitting on a royal throne, or wearing her gem-crusted diadem, but she might as well have been—she sat with her back straight and her head held high, and Cicatrice, who may or may not have planned to offer her an obeisance as he came into her presence, instinctively gave her a small bow.

"You have come a long way," he said, speaking first, breaking all protocol—but they had history, these two, and there was no protocol that could have come between them. Even Callidora knew that; this was why she had chosen to meet him outside the Imperial circle. "I have, it seems, wrought well—perhaps too well. Circassaë, and you, both. You were my best, you know, in all the days that I have done what I do. You, and her. And you both abandoned me." He chuckled. "And for the same man, too," he added, almost conversationally.

"We were water," Callidora said quietly. "Water in your hand. And the tighter you held us the more we slipped through your fingers. Circassaë, and me. And I would have us both safe from you, now, and from your interference. So I have come to a decision."

"I had not realised that you would have had the spirit to run," Cicatrice mused. "At first I honestly thought that something might actually have happened to you, that you might have been hurt, or worse.…"

He stepped towards a chair, as if he was planning to avail himself of it, but froze as her voice sliced through the air between them, ice and steel.

"I have not given you leave to sit."

He turned, looking genuinely astonished. "What was that?"

"I cannot stop you doing what you do," Callidora said. "You're too good at it. I have things I can be grateful to you for—but I know things about you now that I did not know before. I know you were Ursus in a Mihr lodge, and for all I know are still one—but I have learned much more, far more than you might wish me to know. Leontes Augustus knew you, or at least of you, and he told me everything that he knew before he died. So—I cannot stop you, nor would I want to, for the same reasons that were those of Leontes himself. But I *can* take you from this city."

"Take me from this city…?" Cicatrice repeated blankly.

"You may sit, now, if you will," Callidora said regally, allowing a smile to touch her lips for the first time. He did, subsiding onto the edge of the chair at his back, his eyes never leaving her face. "You will," she said softly, after a pause, "travel to Antacia—there is a ship that will take you to a port that is close to the city, and there are arrangements in place to take you the rest of the way. I have the papers drawn up, your passage all set. What you do over there…I don't care to know. But Visant is mine now, and you do not have the power any more to control me, or scare me, or fight me for it."

"It was quite a show you put on in the Kathisma on the day you were crowned," Cicatrice said. "But if there was one person in that arena that the crown and the purple could not fool, it was me, Simonis. You were Golden Crown; you are still Hippodrome. You may not think that you…."

"Do not presume," she said, her voice ice again. "I am no longer Golden Crown, or White Jewel, or any of the faction colours. I am no longer Simonis, young and alone, willing to trade all that I had or all that I was for the sake of safety and protection. I don't know what you saw that day when I stood in the Kathisma, but you forget that you saw it *as I stood in the Kathisma*. I am no longer Golden, or White, or Scarlet, or Obsidian—I am purple, I am the Empress, and I have the weight of Empire behind me now."

"And if I do not go?"

She bared her teeth. "Then I destroy you," she said.

Cicatrice was nothing if not a pragmatic man. He weighed his options, took the Empress's free pass and a bag full of money to pay for his passage, and was gone from the city before the next sunset.

Virgillus knew the name of Simonis, of course, and of the middens of the Hippodrome where she had begun. But he would never have uttered that name again, now that she was Callidora Augusta; with him, she was safe. The last of the Hippodrome past, the last trace of Simonis-that-was, she had driven from the city when Cicatrice left.

She knew she might not ever bear a child for the Empire in the bed that sat on the porphyry dais of the Empress's bedchamber—but in a way that felt very real to her she had been re-born there herself, as much born in that purple as any infant Imperial princess in her turn.

The past could not hurt her any more.

CHAPTER TWENTY THREE

The days turned into weeks, and then months, and Callidora, lulled by all the things that now filled her days as Empress, almost forgot about the Rothaide of the Vesigars, until Maxentius brought up the northern kingdom again, nearly a year and a half later. He had come to her garden after a particularly trying day full of courtiers and foreign dignitaries demanding concessions in trade or armed alliance—it had seemed only one more thing on top of that when he tossed Callidora a parchment roll. It was simple enough on the outside, and yet she received it with her hackles raised, as though he had handed her a burning brand.

"What is this?"

"The Ravin situation just got complicated," Maxentius said tersely. "I need to think about this before I can deal with it. I thought you should know. Take a look."

The roll proved to contain not one but several letters, and Callidora flipped through them quickly. The first, right on top of the sheaf, was written in an uneven, unpractised hand, in an idiosyncratic variant of the High Tongue of the Empire—not the trade language of *coiné*, but an earnest attempt at court dialect and vocabulary, although the spelling sometimes bore only a passing resemblance to the word it was intended to convey, a kind of letter that someone who spoke a language fairly fluently but was not completely literate in it might put together.

Callidora glanced up. "Who…?"

"Read it," Maxentius said.

She skimmed it. The letter addressed Maxentius as the "all-powerful Emperor", and it was in essence a declaration of allegiance and a plea for protection all at once. It was signed *Magnaric Maelgin.*

"*Magnaric* Maelgin? Who is Magnaric?"

"Rothaide's son," Maxentius said, resting his head on the stone wall behind the bench on which he sat and closing his eyes. "Keep reading."

The next page seemed to be a hastily-penned copy of what read like a royal decree, naming Magnaric as the heir to the Vesigar kingdom, to ascend the throne when he attained his majority at fifteen years of age, and appointing Rothaide Maelgwn, his mother and princess of the Maelgin line, as regent until such time. It was not signed, but it could only have come from Vathalric Maelgin, the old king, the one who held it all together in the north—the one whose heir his other, illegitimate, son had killed.

The third letter was a short note apparently from Rothaide herself, her hand elegant and educated, which addressed Maxentius in courtly and formal manner and seemed to have been written in order to accompany her son's missive—and said very little other than that she, Rothaide, would write again soon and explain the situation in more detail. Callidora read that one closely but there was nothing there, nothing except chill cold formality of court protocol, from one royal hand to another—and yet Callidora scoured the letter looking for more, and wondering, when she could not find it, if there had been another more personal note which Maxentius had not shown her, would never show her—the friendly letter between a young Emperor and a princess of the north who…who….

There was a piece missing, and Callidora frowned at the sheaf of paper, hesitating before she picked up the last dispatch.

"Why is *she* sole regent? Is she not married?" Callidora asked after a pause.

"Read the last one," Maxentius said with a sigh, without opening his eyes.

The last letter was a copy of a letter from Rathauric's mother, originally obviously written to her son but translated and transcribed into *coiné*, something that Rathauric himself must have forwarded to Visant. It gave a few more details about the true picture in Ravin, the details that Rothaide had promised but never delivered. The situation, apparently, was a great deal more fraught and fragile than any of the rest of the letters had given their intended recipient cause to believe.

The letter from Rathauric's mother was incomplete, starting more or less mid-sentence, and Callidora bent over it with a frown, trying to make sense of what it said.

...Valaric being a typical hothead, and riding off in hot pursuit as soon as word arrived that you had been sighted within a day's ride of Ravin, my son. He and his following, some ten or twelve men, could not be dissuaded from riding off into the teeth of a winter storm, intent on finding you and bringing you back in chains to face Vathalric Maelgin, reaping the glory of returning the murderer and the fugitive back to what they repeatedly called 'the King's justice' although I for one would not have put it past the lot of them to have enacted a swifter 'justice' on the road and returned in triumph with your corpse—they would still have been the ones whose names would be shouted out as the avengers of Amalric's blood. Rothaide herself was out in the courtyard holding onto Valaric's bridle, pleading with him to stay—he shook her off, almost calling her traitress to her face, and implying that the only reason that she did not want him to go was because she was secretly in league with you, and practically accusing her of having orchestrated the murder of her own brother. Her reasons remained unclear—and even if she had been guilty of these things, which we all know that she had not been, it had all played into Valaric's hands anyway because he was stepfather to the next Maelgin king, that much closer to the throne than he could ever have dreamed of being had Amalric lived and his sister's son never been named heir. He shook her off, there in the snow, a princess of the Maelgin, his own wife—I watched it happen, I saw it all—and he and his men rode out into the blizzard. Nobody was surprised when word came, three days later when the survivors returned, that they had all been caught out in the open during the worst of the storm, and that Valaric had been one of the first to commit a stupidity and die out there in the snow. They brought back a body, all right, only not yours. Several bodies, actually. They buried five of those men who rode out into the storm less than a week after. And now Magnaric is the only remaining prince of the old blood, and Rothaide—a woman—has been named regent, should the King die before Magnaric reaches his fifteenth year. I don't need to tell you that the nobles, both in Council and out in the hall, have not taken this news all that well. Ruled by a woman...

The letter ended there, mid-sentence as it had begun. Callidora turned it over in her hands, looking for something else, something that Rathauric might have added by way of addendum or explanation, but there was nothing. This was the extent of the news from Ravin.

"Is this all?" she asked.

"All?" Maxentius said, sitting up and opening his eyes in puzzlement. "You do not think there is enough there to go on with?"

"No, I meant…this is all you received? Did Rothaide send that second letter that she spoke of?"

"If she had, it would have been in with the rest," Maxentius said curtly.

Callidora shook her head slightly, rolling all the letters back up and handing the parchment roll back to Maxentius. "What are you going to do?"

"I may send an envoy in to take a look around," Maxentius said. "I would go myself—I know the main players, and they know me—but my going there now would send all the wrong signals, and I don't want to make things any more difficult than they already are."

"*I* could go, if you wanted me to look it over," Callidora said carefully. "If you wanted me to."

"If I send the Empress I might as well go myself," Maxentius said. "I'd love your take on the situation, I remember well the training that you and Circassaë had when you were young… but you aren't that girl any more. I don't think it's for either of us to wade into that situation right now. The inevitable interpretation would be an immediate and unequivocal backing by Visant of whatever Vathalric has chosen to do—and I don't want to blunder into anything blind. I know enough about that court to know that this won't make anyone happy; Vathalric must have had a good reason for it, though, he always does. But before I throw my weight behind him I'd rather like to know what he was thinking."

"Then send Arkadios," Callidora said after a beat of silence.

Maxentius sat up. "You brought him with you from the House of Peacocks," he said. "That tells me you have grown to depend on him managing your household. Wouldn't he leave a huge hole if I sent him? Besides, he is hardly experienced in.…"

"He's perfect," Callidora said. "Yes, he's not a polished ambassador—but he is reliable, discreet, faithful. And above all, he is a shrewd observer, and he would know exactly what details you would need to know. He doesn't speak the language of the Vesigar, however."

"Not many that I could send would. It isn't an accomplishment highly rated in the diplomatic ranks of Visant," Maxentius said. "But it so happens that I have a decent translator on staff; he has been useful before, when the northern tribes sent envoys. He might prove just as useful as Arkadios's interpreter. Send Arkadios to me in the morning, and I will speak to him about this assignment—I would like to send somebody out there as soon as that might be arranged. I have to write a reply to young Magnaric's letter, anyway, and who better to carry it?"

Arkadios and his translator, a middle-aged man by the name of Menas, were dispatched to Ravin before the week was out. But before they left Visant, Callidora called Arkadios in for a private audience.

"Maxentius has been to Ravin and he knows the people at this court. I do not. Maxentius calls this Rathauric a friend—and you too have known him, when he was here in Visant. I just got one glimpse of him on that one occasion when he breezed into the House of Peacocks as though he knew it owed him sanctuary. I need to know a lot more—about all of this. You will send me copies of all the reports that you dispatch to the *despotes*, and in addition I will expect your own personal impression of the players in this game—the King, the Princess-Regent, the young heir, and anyone else whom you might consider to be of any sort of importance. This is between you and me, Arkadios."

"Yes, *despoina*," Arkadios said. "I understand. I will do as you ask."

After Arkadios arrived at the Vesigar court and was received by Vathalric Maelgin in private audience, and before attending a full and public presentation of his credentials in open court, his first impressions of the situation was that it was simplistic, or at least far less fraught than his Imperial lord and lady seemed to fear. But he had been given a task to do, and he applied himself to it conscientiously. His reports back to Visant were frequent, meticulous, and—in the case of Callidora's packet, as requested—full of deeply personal observations.

If anything, he did his job entirely too well. His detailed descriptions of the Maelgin royals served to stir up far more in Callidora than she had believed had been there. Reading Arkadios's account of Rothaide—he called her strong-minded, courageous, possessed of great poise and physical beauty with blue-gray eyes and pale gold hair—stung Callidora in unexpected places; she was ill-tempered for days, fighting a greensick jealousy of a woman she had never met, but of whom her husband had spoken in terms of great respect and approval—and now her own trusted emissary confirmed every word of that, by independent and unbiased observation.

But even a man of Arkadios's undisputed abilities was, when it came to the subtleties of this unfamiliar court, a foreigner, an outsider looking in.

What he saw, when he first arrived at the Ravin court, had looked far more solid than it had seemed from the possibilities that had been hinted at in the Ravin letters. But things were rather more fragile than Arkadios initially suspected. What he saw as Rothaide's self-confidence and power was at least partly something that had been spread over her like a cloak by the still-strong influence of Vathalric Maelgin, the ageing king—but he himself was no longer as powerful as he had once been. Vathalric backed Rothaide's decisions concerning young Magnaric—the boy was to be given an education like his mother and her brother, an Imperial education which involved the teaching of history, and penmanship, and at least one foreign language. The nobles of the court said nothing overtly, and it was many months before Menas started to overhear the grumbles and the mutterings, the stirrings of disapproval and even anger at the way the young heir was being brought up in this "womanly" way, as though it would somehow mar his ability to one day rule as a man. Arkadios started to pay much closer attention to where all the strings of discontent eventually led.

At the point where Arkadios finally decided that he had enough to send to the Emperor, in fact more or less as he was in the process of writing the dispatch about the situation, Menas, the interpreter, knocked on the door of his room to announce a late-night unexpected visitor.

"Who is it?" Arkadios asked, laying down his pen and looking up, irritated at being interrupted.

"You will wish to see him, sir," Menas said. "It is Theodren himself."

Arkadios actually glanced back at the document he had been writing almost with disbelief—this was the name he had only barely finished tracing out with his pen. He shivered with something close to superstitious awe—if he didn't know better, if he had not been of a culture that had left its pagan beliefs behind centuries ago, he would have sworn that he had just summoned the man with magic, by the simple ritual of writing down his name.

"You had better show him in," he said.

As Menas ducked out to obey, Arkadios swiftly reviewed what he knew of the man. Theodren was a scion of a Maelgin line—the last in that particular line, as it happened, since he and his wife Gudeslind were childless. He was Maelgin, but only distantly, an echo of the ruling bloodline. However, he made certain that people he came into contact with, or had business dealings with, were always fully aware of his lineage—and while he had always been too lazy to indulge in any real behind-the-scenes conspiracy against the current occupant of the Maelgin throne, that didn't mean that he wasn't a natural center to which malcontents gravitated when they wanted a sympathetic ear.

Theodren took pains for none of this to be at all obvious; he enjoyed his status of shadow-royal, and was far too protective of his own hide to stick his neck out in any intrigue which might be traced back to him and endanger his safe and relatively plush niche in the Ravin court. It was only recently that he had slipped up just a little, enough for Arkadios to notice that he was constantly surrounded by some of the most disgruntled of the Vesigar nobles—and it was precisely this that had made him decide to alert Maxentius (and Callidora) to Theodren's potential and quickly growing role in what might be a slow-brewing situation at court.

And now the man himself was here, at Arkadios's door.

Menas ushered Theodren in before Arkadios had had a chance to ponder more on that subject, and Arkadios, who had not wasted his time at the Ravin court, managed a respectable greeting in his guest's own language. Theodren smiled in what seemed to be genuine delight at this.

"I am ashamed that I am not able to return the compliment you make to me," he responded, by way of Menas the interpreter. "I understand some of your language, but I don't have enough of a command of it to converse in it. Which…is a pity, since I come to discuss a confidential matter…."

Menas's eyebrow rose just a little as he translated that, but Arkadios, diplomat and Imperial envoy, merely made a small bow.

"Menas is unfortunately necessary," he said politely, gesturing his guest to a seat by the fire, "but I can assure you that anything you have to say to me, or to the Emperor of Visant by means of my mediation, will remain absolutely private. Menas is completely trustworthy."

Theodren took the offered seat, slipping his heavy cloak off his shoulders and draping it over the chair. "That is good, because I have information which you—or your Emperor—might find useful."

"Indeed?" Arkadios said noncommittally, taking his own seat opposite the visitor. "Please, do go on. I am listening."

"It is about young Magnaric, the Maelgin heir," Theodren said. "The nobles of the court—some as high up as the Royal Council itself—are not very happy at the manner in which the young prince is being, ah, raised."

"In what way?" Arkadios inquired politely.

"Vathalric Maelgin does not appear to wish to raise up another warrior king, a protector of his people, a wolf of the north, the very thing that he himself has rooted his reign in," Theodren said, obviously choosing his words with care. "Instead, we are getting a boy trained as a scholar, as a bard, even, someone far more at home by his fireside and a warm blanket over his knees than a true son of the north."

"I am not sure how having a scholar for a king would be ill for a kingdom," Arkadios said. "The Emperor who sits on the throne of Visant is a scholar in his own right, and values learning highly."

"Indeed," Theodren said with a quick glance at Menas, who had translated those last words with a deadpan literal flatness which had quite failed to conceal the sharpness of their hidden point. "And I am certainly not implying that this would be a bad thing—but, with all due respect, the throne of Visant does not sit backed up against the frontier, as ours does—we live out on the edge, not in the pleasant and comfortable centre of all things, and at our backs are the wild mountains and beyond them the barbarian tribes of the far north, against whose incursions into Visant we, the Vesigar tribes, are the first line of defense."

He could give as well as he got, and Arkadios had to look away for a moment to give himself time to school his features and hide the small appreciative smile that had quirked the corner of his mouth. He was not here on a holiday, he was here to do a job for his *despotes*, and he could not afford frivolity.

"Point taken," Arkadios said politely, when he finally brought his gaze back to his guest. "But I remain at a loss as to how I could be of any assistance in this matter at all."

"Perhaps," Theodren suggested delicately, "a message from the Emperor might achieve what the discontented nobles here in Ravin cannot—perhaps the Emperor could suggest to King Vathalric and Rothaide Maelgwn that Magnaric might benefit from, ah, at least marginally increased training in the arts of manhood."

"But the boy is not yet nine," Arkadios said. "Surely there is plenty of time for him to be trained in the use of weapons and the art of warfare when his young bones have had a chance to toughen a little. Surely there is no harm in a child this young not being thrown into the tilting yard?"

"Ah," Theodren said softly, "but he is not a child. He is a King, or will be one. And when he is one he needs to hold the fealty and respect of those whom he rules—particularly those close to his throne. If he does not do this, then his grip on the Maelgin throne becomes…weakened."

"And you think that because he is being educated in history and penmanship while he is still this young, he might be a weak king hereafter?" Arkadios inquired after a pause. "Perhaps you could tell me just what, precisely, you had it in mind for the Emperor to offer as a suggestion for the further education of young Magnaric. I might add that the Emperor was quite impressed at the missive he originally received from the young man. He might consider a request from the child's guardians that Magnaric be fostered at the Visant court for a year or two, perhaps, but I gather this is not the sort of thing you…or the Vesigar nobles… would look kindly on? After all, it might be construed as just more of the same as far as they are concerned, an emphasis in the arts of civilisation rather than proficiency at arms and an ability to wage war."

Theodren smiled. "Well, but it was my task to let you—and the Emperor whom you serve—know of the situation," he said coolly. "Beyond that, I will not meddle. Perhaps you might pass my concerns on to Visant, and we shall leave it at that."

"I shall certainly do this," Arkadios said, truthfully enough. "I will write up a dispatch to Maxentius Augustus this very night, and it will mostly concern you and the things you have brought to my attention."

"Please convey my own personal regards to the Emperor," Theodren said with a careful emphasis that suddenly made Arkadios's hackles rise. "If there is any small service I can ever perform for the Augustus, in whatever capacity, I stand ready to do so."

Arkadios completed his report on Theodren and his concerns and sent it off the very next day, including in his own commentary that he had himself become aware of the discontent in the ranks of the nobles, but that he had no idea as to what had made Theodren come to him of his own accord at precisely the right moment to confirm Arkadios's own impressions. He also relayed Theodren's personal regards, exactly in the words in which Theodren had conveyed them, with all the implications and the hidden subtext they had contained—there had been a definite message in his words, an assurance that, if the Emperor needed an inside man at the Vesigar court, this descendant of ancient Vesigar royalty was more than happy to step into those shoes and work towards a foreign Emperor's agenda, instead of in the interests of his own people.

This is a man you might find useful, Arkadios wrote to both Maxentius and Callidora. *But you can never trust him. He will do what is needful only if he conceives it to be useful for his own plans. But if your plans happen to coincide with the thing that he wants to do, or see done—he would be second to none at accomplishing the tasks you might assign to him.*

There should have been more than enough time for Visant to weigh the situation and respond in whatever way it thought best—but three days after Magnaric's ninth birthday, at mid-winter, Vathalric Maelgin died.

Rothaide's son was now Magnaric Maelgin in his own right, a king in waiting. According to the old king's wishes, Rothaide became a full-fledged regent, at the head of the Vesigar nation until Magnaric turned fifteen and could be crowned in his own right.

The atmosphere at court quickly thickened with intrigue and resentment. Rothaide was a capable regent, and she had had enough experience with her father's Council to handle them with aplomb and grace—she quickly instituted a procedure where the young king, Magnaric, would attend the Council meetings, and she made a point of consulting with him on important issues before the Council debated on them or acted on them. It was Magnaric's childish reedy voice that made the final pronouncements in Council or in Court. Rothaide made every effort to make it as easy as possible for the nobles to deal with the unpopular prospect of having a woman as the power behind the Vesigar throne for at least the next six years.

But the uncomfortable truth was that the situation remained unpopular, and the nobles, who had resented the old king's edict when it was no more than just a royal decree, disliked the state of affairs even more, now that it had turned into their everyday reality.

Theodren drifted through this poisoned court with an affable smile and an apparent peacemaking bent. He was inevitably civil to Arkadios himself, as well, and Menas's translations of his greetings when they happened to cross paths in the castle halls were never anything other than impeccably polite and meticulously crafted to be throroughly innocuous. But Arkadios was now aware of him and of his manner, and he knew that there was always something there that Menas could not translate, something unspoken and unsaid, those words that he left hanging in the air as he left Arkadios's room, that night that he had come calling. Arkadios walked the halls of Ravin castle perpetually wary, tense, as though he were prey which was constantly aware of being stalked by an invisible predator.

It turned out that he was partially right. It was in Rothaide's own interests to be aware of what was going on in her court, and she too had been watching Theodren. Up until then she had not seemed to pay that much attention to Arkadios—but now, because Theodren always made a point of going out of his way if necessary to greet the Visant envoy, Arkadios himself had become a person of interest. He was a little chagrined, but hardly surprised, when he received the summons to wait on the Princess Regent one night.

Rothaide received him in her private sitting room, alone.

Arkadios bowed over her hand, and then stood, waiting, for her to speak. It had been a while since he had had the opportunity to get a look at her from close quarters—in fact, not since her father had died and she had taken the kingdom onto her shoulders for her son's sake, as Vathalric Maelgin had willed. It surprised and rather saddened Arkadios to see traces of this in her face; she was thinner, more drawn, her cheekbones sharper on her narrow aristocratic face. Rothaide was only a handful of years older than Callidora Augusta, but somehow, right now, in the yellow light of torches and hearth flames, she seemed much older. Arkadios, not unaware of why Callidora had wanted detailed reports on this woman, filed this information away for a future report—it might be something that the Empress would like to know.

"You may sit," Rothaide said, waving at a carved wooden chair set opposite hers beside the large fireplace.

"Thank you," Arkadios said, accepting the chair. "How may I be of service to you, *despoina*?"

He addressed her by an honorific with which he addressed Callidora herself. Rothaide, in this room, this night, was wholly Queen—and seemed to deserve it.

"You may think it pathetic of me to ask this of you, a foreigner," Rothaide said, "but you were sent here by Maxentius, and he would not have kept you here so long if you had not proved to be useful and observant."

Arkadios gave her a respectful nod, acknowledging a hit. "I thought I had been more discreet," he murmured.

"I know, and a handful of my people know," Rothaide said. "It has served me to know and allow it, because at least I know who you are and where you are, and there is hardly likely to be a duplication of effort—so I can concentrate on playing the game of kings with the Emperor with you as the intermediary. You at least are out in the open. It would make life a lot easier for everyone if you were the trusted channel through which we could communicate in either direction, and I am happy to accept that Maxentius wishes me and my people no harm. He was Rathauric's friend, after all."

"So—what would you like me to convey to the Emperor?" Arkadios asked.

"My friendship, my respect, and my continued entreaty that he keep my son under his protection should that become necessary."

"All of that, I will be happy to relay to Visant. Your son is part of the reason I am here, after all. But surely you have not called me here tonight to let me know that you are aware of my true purposes in Ravin?"

"Theodren," Rothaide said succinctly. "I could sorely use talents like yours myself right now. I cannot command you, as you are not mine to command, so—now I simply ask you. You and Theodren have been seen to speak together on several occasions, out there in the halls. Tell me what you know of him."

"My lady," Arkadios said, "if I had anything concrete to tell you, I would. He makes it a point to talk to me because he too wishes his respects sent to

Visant—as to his private reasons, I can tell you nothing of those. But I do know that he is the center around which I have seen a lot of darkness swirling, out there in your court. People whom I know have issues with your regency, or the manner in which your son is being educated, I am constantly seeing Theodren in earnest conversation with them."

"As to motivations, he is Theodren," Rothaide said. "I've known him all my life; he has ambition but he lacks the passion to pursue it himself—if things fell into his lap, however, he would take them without a qualm. Those people of whom you speak, whose company he seeks out—would Lord Adalbert be one of them?"

Arkadios hesitated, but only briefly. "Yes, *despoina*," he said. "Lord Adalbert is one. Lord Thorismund is another. Lord Ageric is a third."

"Two out of the three you have just named sit on my father's royal council," Rothaide said softly, "and the third with ambitions to rise there. All powerful. All with their own agendas. And all courting Theodren." She glanced away into the fire, and there it was again, the sudden stretching of her skin across the bones of her face, as though she were old, as though she had already endured centuries of existence. "Very well. I thank you, Arkadios. You have done me a great service tonight."

"*Despoina*," Arkadios said, rising to his feet and giving her a courtly bow.

"Perhaps we could speak again soon," Rothaide said, offering him her hand. "After you've heard back from Maxentius Augustus."

Just as Arkadios was straightening from his bow over her hand, a side door into the room opened and a small girl ran inside, an apologetic young woman scurrying in her wake.

"Amalinda! Come back here! You know your lady mother is not to be disturbed—I'm sorry, Your Grace, she *was* in bed, but then she gave us the slip and we chased her all the way here…oh…." She stopped flustered, as she realised that Rothaide was not alone.

But the child called Amalinda ran across the sitting room and into Rothaide's arms, and Arkadios suddenly revised his estimate of Rothaide's age as the years and the burdens melted from her and she cradled her daughter in her arms.

"I didn't want to sleep," the little girl explained artlessly.

Rothaide laughed, a light, lilting, joyous laugh of careless youth. "That does not mean you can run around where you will and when you will," she said in gentle reproof. "Arkadios of Visant, may I introduce my daughter, Amalinda."

The child stared at him with open curiosity; smiling, Arkadios gave another bow. "Honoured to make your acquaintance, Princess Amalinda," he said.

"How old are you? About six? You'd be of an age with Chryseis, Empress Callidora's daughter....."

Rothaide looked up sharply. "Maxentius has a *daughter*?"

"Chryseis is the Empress's child, not the Emperor's," Arkadios said, shaking his head slightly. "She's acknowledged but not flaunted; you may not have heard of her. But the Empress dotes on her daughter."

"I know little of Maxentius's Empress," Rothaide said. She nuzzled her child's hair and then handed her back to the nurse. "Back to bed now, little one, and stay there. Don't give any more trouble. Good night."

"Good night, Mama," the golden-haired little girl said dutifully, and walked out of the room with her hand in the nurse's, turning back once or twice curiously to stare at the stranger beside her mother.

Rothaide glanced at Arkadios, and smiled. "Well, that ends the day on a less formal note than you might have anticipated," she said. "I suppose you must be used to this, with a small child at court in Visant."

"The Empress spends quite a bit of time with her daughter," Arkadios said carefully. "But this...would never happen in Visant. The child has rooms in a wing of the Empress's palace, in the grounds, but she doesn't have access to the Empress's private rooms, or her formal ones. Chryseis...is loved, but not indulged."

Rothaide stared at him for a long moment and then sighed, looking away. "You may go," she said. "You have certainly given me much to think about tonight."

Rothaide played a careful game that winter, a game worthy of Callidora herself—she moved her pieces with surprising guile, telling Lord Adalbert something that she distinctly implied she did not want Lord Thorismund to know, confiding something completely different to Lord Thorismund and implying that Lord Adalbert should be left in the dark about it, baiting Lord Ageric with a dangling promise of a Council seat...should an appropriate vacancy arise. She was waiting for one of them to crack, and one did, finally, just as Theodren left the court in early spring on business for one of his country estates.

After a particularly well-planned and frustrating Council meeting, Thorismund was elegantly trapped into a traitorous snarl not only against the Princess-Regent and her son but about Vathalric Maelgin himself, calling the old King's judgment into question. He was detained by Rothaide's Guard, but promised amnesty if he revealed who his co-conspirators were. Rothaide's men picked up Ageric long before Thorismund even began to think about succumbing to the will of a mere woman, and told him that Thorismund had given him up. The other Council Lord, Adalbert, had been present when Thorismund had been taken away, as Rothaide had ensured that he should be, and decided that it might be best to spend the rest of that spring and perhaps most of the summer somewhere far away from court, only to be intercepted by Rothaide's knights and marched back to the castle. All three men disappeared into the dungeons, and did not emerge again.

Rothaide had grabbed Theodren's strongest support, leaving him without a base in the court; Magnaric, the young king, appointed—through the agency of his mother, the regent—two new lords to the royal council, loyal to Rothaide and to the will of Vathalric Maelgin.

Rothaide had won the battle...but she had lost the war.

She faced them down, Arkadios wrote in his report to Maxentius and to Callidora, *and for a time it seemed that her strength was enough. But not long after Prince Magnaric turned ten, the nobles of the Vesigar tribe tore him from his mother's arms, almost literally, and announced that they were taking over the young king's education. She has seen little of him this summer. He is living fostered in a series of the earls' houses, being trained in swordplay, in riding, in knife-fighting. And they have already introduced him, I fear, to strong drink—I've heard stories of nights with mead, where the young King was treated not as the child that he still is but as one of the men. They are trying to make him grow up, I think—to make him grow up as fast as he can, faster than he can, maybe—they are perhaps hoping for a miracle and to see his fifteenth birthday arrive much sooner than it is due. When you sent me here, things were still under control—but I very much fear that something is going to give very soon here, and I wouldn't be surprised if the weak link doesn't turn out to be Prince Magnaric himself.*

CHAPTER TWENTY FOUR

For a while Arkadios was hard-put to keep his dispatches current, so swiftly and disconcertingly did things change at the Vesigar court. Sometimes Maxentius would receive three letters from him on three successive days, a breathless waste of resources and couriers on the face of it, but every letter contained some new and vitally important piece of information that Arkadios didn't feel he could in good faith withhold until the next regular courier left for Visant.

Maxentius received one letter directly from Rothaide that was a little more personal in nature than the formal communications they had exchanged so far. She did not ask for anything directly, but it was obvious that she was desperately trying to hold together a situation which was beyond her strength to handle, and that she was looking at all the exits.

One line in particular caught Callidora's eye as she skimmed over the letter that Maxentius showed her.

"*I may find myself in need of a refuge.*" Callidora looked up at her husband. "She means Visant?"

"Or somewhere that Visant holds sway and can protect her," Maxentius said. "But being who she is, what she is, she probably means Visant."

"Did you say yes?"

"I haven't replied yet. But she is the daughter of a King who was Visant's ally, and she is the sister of my friend to whom I made a promise. And Ravin is far more stable with her at the helm than those hot-blooded earls who are hankering for somebody to butcher. If she needs a refuge, then of course she must come here."

Callidora chewed on her lip briefly. "Would you go to war over this?"

Maxentius shot her a startled look. "It hasn't come to that," he said. "Yet."

It was no answer, and it was more answer than she wanted to hear. She fretted and paced, like one of her father's bears in its cage; she, too, received regular mail from Arkadios, and she could see the shape of the Vesigar problem very clearly—no matter what her qualifications or abilities, Rothaide alone was not who the nobles of the Vesigar court wanted at the helm of their kingdom. They wanted a King, and that was the one thing that Rothaide could not be.

And although nobody had ever even so much as mentioned the possibility in her hearing, a kernel of a completely irrational fear took root deep inside Callidora—that there was one way of solving the Vesigar problem, a very simple way, and sooner or later Maxentius would realise it. He could marry Rothaide himself. It was so blindingly obvious to Callidora that she could not understand why nobody else was seeing it—Rothaide was royal, born of an ancient line of sacred kings, and she could bring entire provinces as her dowry, to fold into Maxentius's Empire. She could marry her people to his, and settle the frontier for generations with their children sitting on the Vesigar throne.

It was perfect, except that she, Callidora, had no place in that future at all. And the silence that surrounded her on the subject was suddenly not an indication that Maxentius had no such plans—only a confirmation that just the solution she had envisioned was in fact being considered, and that nobody knew how to tell her that she would soon have to vacate the Empress's porphyry halls in the Imperial Palace when the new, the *true*, Empress arrived to take possession of them.

And do what? And go where? Back to Rhakotis? Back to the Hippodrome?

She drifted through her days like a ghost, unable to settle to anything, waiting, braced for a blow that never came. Maxentius noticed, but when he asked what was amiss, she shook her head and would say nothing—because she was afraid that if she once opened her mouth, then the silence would be broken, and even that would be no protection for her any more.

At a loss, Maxentius finally said that Callidora needed to take her mind off things, and suggested that they take a trip together—up into the north, to his own childhood country, so he could show her the other half of her Empire.

"You've seen the stark and deadly lands of the desert provinces," he said, "but the rolling hills and fir-cloaked mountains, and the plains further north, can be just as beautiful, just as mystical. Some of your own estates lie up there, too. I would very much like to show you the places where I was a boy. And they haven't had a proper visit from a Visant Emperor for far too long. We can afford to take a little bit of time off from the shadow of the throne itself. Anything urgent enough to absolutely need our attention will still be able to reach us. The mail service is reliable in those parts. But until something does we can go as slowly as we like and visit anything we choose."

It would be a lavish expedition, and it tickled Callidora's vanity; she, the girl from the Hippodrome, would go on a royal progress.

The Imperial pair left the city with a great deal of pomp on a fine spring morning, accompanied by several high-ranking church officials, the Prefect of the City, and far more Palace officials than Callidora thought strictly necessary, but all of whom, once again, served to underscore the importance of the expedition. The full entourage numbered in the hundreds, in the end, and moved slowly, sometimes stretched out along narrow country roads for miles.

Callidora was actually beginning to enjoy herself, even going so far as to stop keeping a close eye on the daily dispatches that still somehow managed to catch up to them from Visant, no matter where they ended up staying. Until, that is, one particular batch of letters brought Maxentius to her with an expression on his face that sharply brought back to Callidora the complications they had originally fled from.

They were staying near a hot springs grotto, which local rumours held to have miraculous healing powers; Callidora relaxed by the gently steaming pools, barefoot and clad only in a cotton shift and brightly coloured wrap over that, when Maxentius came up to stand behind her, just out of her range of vision. She knew it was him, recognised his step, but when he halted and stood in silence for several heartbeats longer than she had expected she turned her head with a sudden quick movement to look behind her. What she saw made her scramble to her feet and turn to fully face him.

"What has happened?" she asked sharply.

Unlike his Empress, Maxentius was no longer dressed for relaxation or taking his ease—he was wearing riding leathers, and his face was grim.

"Ravin," he said abruptly. "You'd better get ready. We're going back to Visant as fast as we can."

"Maxentius…" Callidora said, half demanding, half pleading, reaching out to him with one hand, all of the fears she had thought she had forgotten flooding back into her mind.

"Here, read Arkadios's letter yourself," he said, tossing her a rolled-up parchment he held in his right hand. "And there's some mail for you, too," he added. "It arrived only a few moments ago. You may want to read it all on the way."

Her mail would contain her own reports from Arkadios, and possibly pertinent information. When Maxentius gave her a nod and another exhortation to hurry and prepare to leave, she sent an attendant to fetch her own mail bag while she subsided back onto her comfortable seat by the hot spring pool and smoothed Arkadios's letter over her lap.

For a moment it all seemed too much to take in.

Young Magnaric was dead. The Vesigar earls who had tried so hard to make the boy grow up faster had only ensured that he would never grow up at all—Arkadios was sketchy on the details, but the one thing that seemed obvious from reading between the lines of his letter was that the boy king had died from something as simple as alcohol poisoning, with his young body simply unable to cope with what he thought he had to do in order to be accepted by his earls. He was gone.

And Rothaide—proud, royal Rothaide—had apparently changed her mind about fleeing to Visant and gathering strength there to reclaim her father's kingdom. Whether it had been her son's death that broke her or some other thing that Arkadios did not yet know, Rothaide had tried a last, desperate gambit.

She had married Theodren.

He was the only other living man who carried the Maelgin bloodline, and it was the only way that her own, far stronger, claim on the Vesigar throne could be upheld.

Callidora had enough of a conscience to feel a rush of shame that her first response to reading this particular piece of news was a joyous relief that Rothaide could no longer even consider a liason with Maxentius. But then, once she was past that, it occurred to her, belatedly, that she had seen mention somewhere in Arkadios's earlier dispatches of Theodren's 'wife'. That had not seemed to be an obstacle—if he had been married to somebody else before, apparently that union had been set aside. That was confirmed a moment later when her own mailbag, fetched by her attendant, contained a letter from Gudeslind, Theodren's repudiated wife herself.

The letter was short, passionate, and pleading.

You are a wife, Gudeslind had written. The hand did not look like a woman's, it was strong, flourished, and was probably the work of a male scribe who had translated the letter into a language which the Empress of Visant could understand. *You will understand the grief and anguish and anger that I feel right now— discarded and thrown away by a man who had been my husband for nearly fifteen years, so he can go to a higher place. But it is not only I who am betrayed—I know that Theodren was approaching your husband for a position for himself in Visant, at your court, where he would have planned to go, taking me. Now, apparently, he has turned his back on it all. I no longer know what his plans are—but you may need to tell your own husband that Theodren has betrayed before, and will betray again.*

"And would you take him back if you could have him?" Callidora murmured, tapping her slender fingers against her lower lip. And then caught herself. *Why would I want her to take him back? That would mean Rothaide's marriage to him was void, and that would mean she was back in play, for Visant....*

Callidora sat by herself and pondered for a while, and then gathered up her letters, restored them all to the leather pouch in which they came, and went in search of Maxentius.

He was giving what he thought would be final orders for their departure, and frowned a little as she approached him, still barefoot and in her summer shift, her dark hair loose over her shoulders. She looked wanton, and she knew it—but that was part of the plan that she had started to set in motion.

"I understand the urgency," she said to him, handing him back his own letter from Arkadios and allowing her hand to linger just a shade longer than necessary on his wrist. "But I've been on this tour a little too long to gather up my things at the snap of a finger and have it all ready in time—and you are already ready, my love, and wish to get back to the city. If you will allow me a few days' grace—you go, go now, get back to where you need to be, and I will follow at my own pace and speed and catch up in Visant."

"I don't particularly wish to leave you alone—" Maxentius began, but Callidora laughed softly, glancing around the busy camp around them.

"I daresay you will take a few men with you," she said. "As for the rest—I would hardly be alone out here. I have half the court to dance attendance on me."

"Are you sure?" he said, but he had already turned twice to cast anxious glances in the direction where the road back to Visant lay.

"I am certain," Callidora said. And because she spoke the absolute truth, the conviction of it came through; Maxentius took her hand in his own and kissed her fingers.

"Then I will see you back at the Palace," he said.

"Go," Callidora whispered, giving his hand a quick squeeze. "Godspeed."

He was gone within the hour—he, and thirty men with him, many of them the palace officials who had accompanied them on this trip.

Callidora, watching the dust that he and his party had raised in their wake on the unpaved country road, stood with her face calm and serene like a marble statue's—but her eyes were burning, and inside she was consumed by the fires of her passions.

Back in Visant. Alone. And I sent him there. What if I come back and it's all done already—and they turn me away at the palace gates? What have I done? What if she's already on her way there—what if they meet up, there, on the balcony of the House of Peacocks—what if she changes her mind again? What if he realises what he has to do? I have to get back.... I have to get back myself....

And then another voice spoke, a deeper voice, the voice that her bear might have spoken in, had it been able to speak—a voice which had the bear's growl embedded in it, a command, a way for her to resolve the situation one way or another, to finally put the specter of the northern princess to rest.

We are only a day's ride from the shores of the Inner Sea. Somewhere on that shore there will be a boat. The boat will take you across to a harbour from which a grey road leads to Ravin. Go. Go and see for yourself.

She hesitated, biting her lip, staring at the empty road which had swallowed Maxentius and his party. And then she came to a decision. She brought her fingers to her lips and kissed them, blowing the kiss down the road down which Maxentius had gone.

I'm sorry, my love. I have to do this. I have to do this or it will destroy me.

She retired to the main house of the hostelry around which they had pitched their encampment, and gave out the word that she was feeling unwell. Nobody except a few of her very closest intimates knew that ten minutes after the announcement of her sudden malaise Callidora herself was riding hard in the opposite direction than the one that Maxentius had taken—the road that led down to the sea, and to Ravin.

It was not the first time that Callidora had found herself in a place where she was a stranger who spoke a strange language and had no fixed plan—but the harbour where her fishing boat set her down in the early hours of the morning was hardly the wilds of Afaris, and this time she had an escort, and she had money. A local man who spoke passable *coiné* was quickly found and enlisted as a guide for Callidora and the young Guardsman she had chosen to come with her to Ravin; fresh horses were procured, and the rest of the journey to the gates of Ravin was uneventful, almost anticlimactic. Callidora knew she was doing something born of a guilty impulse, and it felt wrong not to be challenged on it—the road was almost too smooth, everything too easy.

But the expression on Arkadios's face, when Menas ushered Callidora into his room and she paused dramatically by the door to slowly push back the concealing hood of her cloak, more than made up for anything, and Callidora, the actress again, smiled a quiet little smile of self-congratulation, while Arkadios pulled himself together and handed her further into the room.

"I didn't expect to see either you or the *despotes* here," Arkadios said.

"Ah, but I am *not* here," Callidora said, lifting one slender finger and laying it on her lips in a gesture that hinted at silence. "Maxentius is in Visant, or will be shortly; I am due to join him there in as short a time as I can manage—but as far as he knows I am still languishing by a certain bewitching scenic pool. We were travelling when your last letters reached us. Maxentius was deeply disturbed at the whole Ravin situation, but he went back to Visant to deal with it. I…was close enough to Ravin…to make a detour. But I am not here, Arkadios. I never was. So far, only a handful of people know of my plans—those covering for my absence from the camp, the Guard who accompanied me here and who will never betray me, and now you and Menas. But I thought…it was about time I came out and met Rothaide for myself."

"You wish to see the Queen?"

"You can arrange it, surely? I wish to speak to Theodren's wife, too."

"Rothaide Maelgwn *is* Theodren's wife."

"I meant the real one. Gudeslind. She wrote to me, you know, asking for my help. So I came."

"*Gudeslind* wrote to you?" Arkadios, with his years of experience at the Visant patrician houses and then two Emperors, was not easily flustered—but he was now. Callidora had an edge of wildness to her that he barely recognised.

"The passage was easy, and I am well rested," Callidora said. "I am more than willing to go to anyone, or they can come here to your lodging—but you must arrange it, Arkadios. As soon as possible. I need to return to Visant with all speed. We can start with Gudeslind. Tell her the Empress read her letter, and is here."

Arkadios decided that simply doing as she asked, to the best of his ability, was the only thing he could do. He made sure Callidora was comfortable, gave her a deep bow, and hurried out to set in motion the things she wanted done.

Gudeslind was a stately, elegant woman of middle age, dressed modestly and in dark colors that might have betokened widowhood; her only jewellery was a ring that she still wore on her wedding finger. Her face was etched with lines but her eyes were the clear blue of a summer sky, and her hair was light enough to hide the presence of grey well, if any was there at all.

She sank down into a deep obeisance before Callidora, her head bowed almost to the ground.

"You honour me beyond measure," Gudeslind said. She spoke passable *coiné*, enough, at any rate, to carry on a conversation.

"Why did you write to me?" Callidora said gently, reaching out to draw her out of her obeisance and guiding her towards one of the chairs in the room. "Sit, please. Talk to me. I want to understand what has happened here."

Gudeslind subsided onto the chair, her eyes never leaving Callidora's face. "I sent your man away," she said. "Twice. When he came to get me. Because I could not believe that what he said to me was true—that you had come, that you were here."

"But what do you think I can do here?" Callidora asked. "You wish for your husband back?"

Gudeslind shook her head, slowly. "I do not know. If he were here right now and begged to return, I would hesitate. He was honest with me—ah, he was honest!—he told me to my face that he was leaving, and for whom, and why...."

"Can you tell *me*?" Callidora said.

"She came to him," Gudeslind said, folding her hands in her lap. "Rothaide Maelgwn. The Princess. His own kind, or so he liked to think. I married him because he told me that he was descended from the Maelgin kings—I was young and foolish then, and a romantic young girl, and he wooed me with that. When he asked my father for me, he had a good enough name and standing for my father to accept him as a suitor and a husband, and that was more than enough for him—my father was a merchant, he had money, but no standing at court. Theodren was his means of entry into noble company, and he was willing to pay the price, even if the price was his daughter—but for me, when we first met, Theodren he swept me off my feet, filled my head with dreams...."

"Did you think you would become a queen?" Callidora said.

"I was young," Gudeslind said, shrugging a little. "I would have believed anything. I thought that if I could marry him, I would already be a queen, because I would be married to a man of royal blood. And my children would...."

She stopped, stared at her hands, suddenly silent.

"But you never had children," Callidora said.

Gudeslind shook her head mutely.

"Did he want them? Theodren?"

"He never said," Gudeslind whispered. "If it made him unhappy, he never told me, never blamed me. Not even at the end. It wasn't because there were no children that he was walking out. It was because I, after all…was not enough of a queen. And she was."

"But you said she came to him,"

"At my house," Gudeslind said. She looked up, dry-eyed, but her eyes were blazing with pain. "She came to talk to both of us. She came to take him, the last male of the Maelgin line—she had lost her father, and her son, and it was down to her and to the young princess, Amalinda, and they could not hold against the earls. She was Vathalric Maelgin's daughter; they never forgot that—but she was a woman, and they would not suffer themselves to be ruled by a woman. She came to Theodren and she told him—she told him that she knew perfectly well who he was, *what* he was, but that his name was all that was required to make *her* reign legitimate in the eyes of the nobles."

"The price," Callidora said, "was you. Again, you."

"He turned to me when she was done speaking," Gudeslind said. "And he told me he had no wish to hurt me, but that as of that moment he was divorcing me—that he could do it, because there were no children. He had never said he wanted any, but right then, it mattered only because it gave him the excuse. If she had not come—if she had not come to him…."

"And if she had not…?"

"I know he was talking to your Empire. He met with Arkadios, the envoy. Several times. I wrote to you of that, I think. I know a little of what they talked about, I know that after Rothaide took the three lords who had been his closest allies at court, Theodren was afraid, for a while, and he was negotiating with Visant to leave here, and to go and live in your city. I think he believed that he could be treated there just like the king he thought he could never become here. But then Magnaric died, and Rothaide needed him to walk down the aisle with her, because she needed a man to throw to the earls, and then—well—here I am."

"Would *you* still come to Visant, if you could?" Callidora asked.

Gudeslind stared at her out of empty blue eyes. "I thought I might," she said after a moment, "but I am no longer so certain. I'm not sure I would belong there."

"I will talk to your husband," Callidora said.

"Rothaide's husband," Gudeslind said, a little bitterly.

"To Theodren," Callidora said firmly, putting an end to any further embellishment of that idea. "Gudeslind…do you think him a traitor? To the Vesigar? That's what you seemed to want to tell me, in your letter…."

"He finds it…easy to betray," Gudeslind said. "He makes promises he cannot keep, or never had any intention of keeping, as long as they get him something he wants. No—you asked if I wanted him back. I wasn't sure, but no, I don't, not now. And I don't envy Rothaide her marriage—because sooner or later he will betray her too." She paused, looked up, met Callidora's eyes squarely. "He might have already done it."

"Oh?"

"She hasn't been seen in public for at least a couple of weeks," Gudeslind said. "I do not attend court, so I don't know if she has withdrawn to the palace itself and simply does not venture out of it. It could be nothing. All I know is that she is…gone."

Callidora added it up in her head—approximately how long the news of Rothaide's marriage must have taken to reach Visant from Ravin, and then the time the message spent in tracking Maxentius down on his travels, as well the extra couple of days or so that she had spent travelling to Ravin herself. If Gudeslind was right, then Rothaide had disappeared from view less than a week after her marriage.

After Gudeslind left, Callidora questioned Arkadios closely. He clearly recalled seeing Rothaide in the throne room beside her new husband on the day after the marriage was announced. But there didn't seem to be many people who could swear to having seen the young Queen at all in the days following her first court as Theodren's wife.

"You wrote to us that she was married but not that she disappeared?" Callidora asked.

"I'll talk to my contacts," Arkadios said.

"Do that. And do it quickly. I have little time."

When Arkadios returned with news a few hours later, Callidora could see from his face that he brought her nothing good.

"I have found the Queen," he said. "She is not in Ravin; she is in retreat at a royal estate on a small island just off the coast, near to the place where you disembarked."

"You will take me there," Callidora said.

"*Despoina*—she might not be there of her own free will," Arkadios remonstrated. "There may be guards. There could be danger…."

"Take me there," Callidora repeated. "The guards will be far from an authority confirming their orders, and I am Visant—they will obey the Empire."

Arkadios was his usual efficient self when it came to putting together the expedition. The small party—Callidora, her attending Imperial Guard, Arkadios,

Menas, and a brace of armed men as escort, rode back to the shores of the Inner Sea and two boats were waiting for them when they got there. Callidora climbed into one with her Guard and Arkadios; the rest followed in the second. The sun had barely set, its burnished edge still showing faintly on the horizon; they were out on a flat, calm sea the colour of dull silver, the only sound the steady dip of oars into the water and an occasional splash that might have been a leaping fish. The island they approached was rocky and appeared deserted, showing no light, and they landed their small boats on the small crescent of shingle beach on which the sea broke and whispered. Arkadios clambered out first and handed Callidora out of the boat; one of the armed escort was left with the beached boats and the rowers, who settled down to wait, their backs against the boulders on the beach. Callidora led the way towards the dark fringe of aromatic cypress trees that fringed the beach as though she belonged here, as though there was nothing in the world wrong with her presence on this island. The guard who stepped out from the shadow of the trees did so almost hesitantly, uncertain as to whether to challenge or not.

"Who goes there?' he said in the end.

Callidora halted, lifting her head, and Arkadios stepped up beside her.

"I am the envoy of Maxentius Augustus, Emperor of Visant," he said. "I have messages from the Augustus, for your Queen."

"We haven't had word," the guard said. "Give me the message, I will pass it to Her Grace."

"I am the message," Callidora said, pushing aside the enveloping cloak that she wore, revealing the glitter of gold on wrists and throat and hair. "I am Callidora, the Empress of Visant, and I am here to see the Queen."

The guard was visibly taken aback, the expression on his face something that Callidora would have found amusing, in other circumstances. "But we have orders...but we can't...."

"I am guessing your orders are more concerned about who is allowed to leave this island than about who is to set foot on it," Arkadios said.

"Our orders concern the Queen, and who is to be allowed to see her," the guard said, sturdily enough. "I answer to the King...."

"And you will answer to the Emperor if you do not step aside," Callidora said.

She had counted on the probability that at least the fringe guards might not be high-born enough to stand up to an aristocrat who seemed to know what she was doing—on the simple fact that, for most such folk, previous orders issued by superiors who were not present paled in comparison to the instinctive acquiescence to crisp and authoritative orders being given by someone standing right in front of them. And she seemed to be right, so far—the guard might have dealt with an armed insurrection from the beach, by others like him, perhaps, whose obvious purpose would be to wrest the Queen from his control. But he was disarmed by Callidora's sex and the command of her presence, and after a moment he swallowed and let her pass.

It was easier, after that. They were stopped by one more guard, this one more formally attired although it was obvious that he was there as far more than just an ornamental fixture, but they had already come past one circle, which seemed to lend their presence some credibility, and a flash of Callidora's signet ring convinced him of the rest.

Eventually, climbing a shallow rocky slope, they arrived at a clearing which had a stone house in the midst of it, with red roof tile, and painted shutters framing its small windows. A pair of torches in iron sconces flickered in a sheltered entrance alcove beside a sturdy wooden door—which opened more or less just as the small party approached the house, revealing a young woman with flaxen hair in two braids on her shoulders. She froze as she saw the strangers on the path, her mouth falling open in a comical O of surprise; after a moment she drew in her breath, intending to either speak or scream. Menas hurried forward, calling out something in the Vesigar language. She hesitated, on the point of slamming the door in their faces, and then said something in response in a low voice, pointing further along the path.

"She says her lady is down on the shore by the pool," Menas said, turning his head marginally to convey the girl's words to Callidora. "She likes to watch the sunset from there."

"Thank you. I'll go on by myself from here. The rest of you, wait for me by the house."

She picked up her skirts and walked briskly down the shadowed path which the servant had indicated. It took her downhill, and then it turned into a crude but serviceable stair, with a single torch left stuck in the ground near the top of it to illuminate the first steps. Callidora negotiated the rocky steps, in-filled with shingle, with care and in as much silence as she could muster, and was rewarded by the prize for which she had come here—a glimpse of Rothaide, alone, unaware of another's presence, sitting on a large round rock beside the darkening waters, her profile perfectly presented in silhouette against a sky in which traces of sunset colours still lingered.

But a glimpse was all she got because Rothaide, like a deer, turned almost instantly towards the stair as though she had felt the weight of Callidora's eyes upon her. She rose to her feet, and Callidora took in the slender body clad in blue with a gilded belt as a girdle, the loose fair hair stirring in the evening breeze and held back only by a thin golden filet bound across her brow, a grave yet pleasant expression on the narrow aristocratic face.

The bear in Callidora's soul screamed once, as though it had been wounded, and was silent.

The two women stood looking at one another for a long moment.

Then Rothaide smiled.

"I know who you are," she said in *coiné.* "I once thought I would welcome Maxentius Augustus back to Ravin, with you perhaps at his side—but we are far from my court, are we not? And I think that chance has passed already. I have made too many ill choices along the way."

"Why did you permit him to do this?" Callidora said. The question might have seemed disjointed, illogical, not following from anything that Rothaide had said—but they both understood its meaning, that the man implied in the question was not Callidora's husband, but Rothaide's own.

"I was…*persuaded*," Rothaide said softly. "I am told you have a child. You will understand."

"He married you—and then threatened your daughter?" Callidora said.

"Not physically. At least, not precisely," Rothaide said. "He did present me with the man to whom she would be married, right there and then, unless I willingly came to this place. I don't know if I can trust his promise that Amalinda will not be chained to this animal, but I knew that if I balked he *would* have done it, and made me watch," Rothaide said.

Callidora shook her head, trying to assimilate all this. "But you are the queen," she said. "You held the power. How did he suddenly come to be able to even threaten these things, never mind accomplish them?"

"Blood debt," Rothaide said. "Before I married him, he might not have had the influence to deal with that, but once I did—well—he was King. The original arrangement was that he would wear the title lightly, like a cloak, and do the things that Kings do with their leisure, and leave me to get on with doing what my father had wanted me to do in the first place—reign. Deal with the day-to-day tasks that someone guiding the destiny and well-being of a kingdom needs to deal with in order to keep everything going—things I thought he would be too bored or too lazy to interfere with. But they came to him the day after our wedding, the families of the three lords whom I'd had killed when the first stirrings started, back when Magnaric…." She looked away for a moment. The subject was obviously painful for her. "I did not do well by my son. I didn't see another way out—those three, they had the sheer weight of numbers behind them if they chose to act, and I thought I was doing right by getting them out of the picture. But in the end that achieved nothing. It merely gave the nobles more of an excuse to take Magnaric from me. Oh, they will *love* it if Theodren manages to marry Amalinda to one of those rutting beasts...."

"Arkadios told me of what you did," Callidora said. "He said you did it to *stop* Theodren. And then...you married him. We didn't understand any of it."

"We?"

"Maxentius and I. He promised Rathauric, your half-brother, that he would...."

"Rathauric is dead," Rothaide said sharply, tossing her head.

This was more news that they had not yet heard, back in Visant. Arkadios would not have written of it. He would never have known. "I am sorry," Callidora said. "Maxentius thought highly of him."

"I would have called on him to take me from this place, and he would have come, even with a price on his head," Rothaide said. "But he is dead, gone these many months, slain in the service of a foreign prince in a war on foreign soil. All because Amalric was too jealous of him to see him for what he was—that he never coveted Amalric's throne, that he could have been an ally, a friend, a *brother*, rather than the enemy. Well, but that's done with." She reached up to push back the hair that was blowing across her face. "But I have to admit, I don't understand one thing myself. You. What are you doing here?"

"I came to see you."

"Ah," Rothaide said softly. "You came to make sure that I never found my way to Visant...."

Callidora said nothing, but the blood rushed into her cheeks; her eyes glittered in the deepening dusk, with both empathy and defiance.

Rothaide crossed the small distance that separated them, stepping delicately on the uneven shingle surface, and took Callidora's hand into her own.

"Well," she said. "Now I know. It was not your doing, none of it, I dug myself into this hole—but even if I scramble out of it, by some unlikely lucky chance, I now know there is no harbour. Not really. Maxentius would take me in, but you...would never be anything except an implacable enemy, would you?" She sighed, glanced up at the stone stair, and reached out with her free hand to gather the torch she had brought down here with her. She slid the other hand, the one she had used to take Callidora's, up her forearm to link arms with her, as two young girls, friends, might do on a pleasure outing into the country.

"Shall we go back?" she said lightly. "They must already be worried…about both of us."

Callidora wanted to pull away—this felt like the ultimate betrayal, this simple gesture of friendship, but she found she didn't have the strength to. They returned like that, arm in arm, and Callidora had the small pleasure of seeing Arkadios disconcerted yet again—he did not fluster easily, but then this clandestine visit to Ravin by his Empress was hardly something that he could have prepared for in any way. If anything, he was bearing up extremely well. But twice now she had seen it on this trip—that expression of complete bewilderment—and she knew that she would probably never see it again. Nothing she could possibly do after this would surprise Arkadios in the least.

They paused, the two queens, as they reached the level plateau before the house's front door, and Rothaide turned to face Callidora. For a moment a question fluttered in Callidora's mind, almost made it to her lips—*what if we took you back with us, right now?* But she never said it. And Rothaide knew that she never would. Leaving this island alive meant only one thing for the Vesigar queen—exile. And the road to Visant was closed.

"Give Maxentius my regards," Rothaide said, slipping her hand from Callidora's arm and letting it drop to her side. "I am glad we got this chance to talk, Callidora Augusta. Thank you…for coming."

And she sank down in obeisance—queen to empress, as rank demanded, royal to the last.

Callidora reached out to raise her and then, still holding Rothaide's hands, her own eyes full of tears, sank down in a courtesy of her own—something that rank did not demand, but that respect did. Whatever this woman's mistakes had been, she was, after all, a queen. They had been right, all of them; they had been right about Rothaide, about all that she was, or could be…and must not ever be allowed to be.

"I wish it could have been different, Rothaide Maelgwn," she said in a low voice.

"It was not meant to be," Rothaide said. "Good bye."

Callidora held her gaze for another long moment, and then turned away.

They met no guard on their way back to the beach. The boats were unmolested. Callidora climbed into hers in silence, and did not speak again until they grated on shore back on the mainland; and even then, standing beside Arkadios on the wet shingle, all she did was tell Arkadios to find her a boat or a ship to take her back across the Inner Sea. That night, if possible.

Arkadios bowed his head and turned to obey.

Callidora knew that leaving Rothaide on that island, as they had done, was tantamount to signing her death warrant—if Theodren had been able to send her there, without consequence, then it was just a matter of time. The one thing that might have been holding him back, making him keep at bay the wolves that wanted Rothaide's blood, was how Visant might react—and if news of Rothaide's confinement reached Visant while Rothaide was still alive and there was a chance of rescue, Callidora knew with bitter certainty how Visant would react. She had asked Maxentius once if he would go to war over Rothaide's fate, and he had told her it had not come to that yet. But this would be the spur to war—the rash decision of a beleaguered queen to marry the wrong man, the new husband's swift response in removing the woman who had been the path to a throne so that his own grasp upon it was made more secure—Maxentius would send the army, if he believed there was even a slim chance that he could pluck Rothaide out of the mess alive.

And if he did that.... Callidora was haunted by Gudeslind's gray face, the defeated slope of her shoulders, the sudden age that had touched her eyes and her hair. Abandoned. Cast away. For a greater prize. For a greater Kingdom.

As Callidora might be. For a greater Queen.

If Rothaide was dead...Maxentius might still come. To take his revenge.

But there was a way to do that that she, Callidora, could manage herself. Theodren had already provided the means to his own demise. If he handed over his queen to those who wanted her blood, it was because they were not prepared to have a woman ruling over them, and they were willing to follow Theodren's lead if he provided it in the traditional way of the Vesigar, a man to lead men, a Vesigar warrior, a wolf of the north. If they ever suspected him of weakness, he was done for—and he had proved that he had the seeds of that within him. He had bargained with Visant, with the soft and decadent Empire of the south, for a position there. The "wolf of the north" had been willing to trade it all for a soft bed and a jug full of southern wine. He would have sold the northern kingdom for that, if he thought he could get it.

"I have a message for Theodren," she said to Arkadios, when he returned with word of the arrangements he had made for her. "Make sure it reaches him. Tell him that Maxentius will not go to war with him...once Rothaide is dead. Tell him to believe that, no matter what the official messages from Visant might say. Tell him that, from the Empress herself. And tell him...that I know all about his dealings with Visant. And that there are some things that Visant *will* go to war over."

She looked away, her dark eyes stark, glittering with guilt, and determination, and pain. The bear was huge within her again, all was his shadow, and he was roaring defiance—Callidora told herself that she was doing nothing except giving her approval to a situation already in progress, a drama unfolding to its inevitable end. Nothing wrong—nothing except turning to defend her own life, her own love, her own existence. She could not allow Maxentius to be in a position to choose. Beneath the armour of the Empress's *chlamys*, the purple cloak, the jewelled crown, the power of a throne, Callidora was still Simonis after all—the little girl walking into a hostile arena and waiting with her heart in her mouth to hear the word that would decide her fate, her survival, whether or not she was acceptable to the faction that sat in judgment on her, with power over her life and death.

She had thought the past had no power to hurt her any more.

She was wrong.

CHAPTER TWENTY FIVE

Arkadios's next dispatch to Visant reported that Rothaide was dead.

The report was short, stark, and masterful in its ability to relay the events that Callidora had helped set in motion, without once betraying her own role in the affair. Callidora herself, who was back in Visant by then, watched Maxentius's face darken as he read Arkadios's letter.

"The bastard did it," Maxentius said. "I didn't quite believe that he would dare."

He threw the letter at her and stalked angrily away across the room to stand at a window and stare outside, his hands balled into fists.

"But according to Arkadios it wasn't Theodren who did it," Callidora said, after a long enough pause to let him think that she had skimmed the letter and did not already know, from letters of her own, what it contained. "The northern earls...."

"Theodren took her to an isolated place, and turned his back," Maxentius snapped. "If his hand did not wield the knife, he winked at the man who did it. Rothaide's blood is on his hands. But I don't understand—I never believed that this was possible. The Maelgin kings have sat on the Vesigar throne for a thousand years. How could the Vesigar earls themselves have extinguished that?"

"Theodren has Maelgin blood," Callidora murmured. "Perhaps they thought...."

"That's like saying a street cur has royal blood because his great grandsire was one of the Palace hounds," Maxentius said.

"They saw her as Empire," Callidora said. "They saw her as looking to you. They saw her educate her son, the next Maelgin King, as a weakling. You remember what Arkadios wrote when Theodren first approached him. They may have believed that they were saving the Maelgin dynasty from itself."

"And they got Theodren on the throne?" Maxentius gave a sharp, mirthless bark of a laugh. "Perhaps I should just leave them to it. They'll find out just what sort of devil's bargain they have made."

"You can destroy Theodren with a stroke," Callidora said, her face very pale, her hands twisted with each other in her lap.

Maxentius turned to her, raised an eyebrow in wordless inquiry.

"They raised their hand to Rothaide, the true Maelgin, because she was leaning to Empire," Callidora said. "Let the earls know that Theodren himself was angling for a position in Visant, and you don't have to start a war to overthrow him. The earls will do the job for you. If they could bring themselves to spill Rothaide's blood, they will hardly hesitate to make sure that Theodren gets what they think he deserves."

"And then, what?" Maxentius said. "The northern kingdom is leaderless, rudderless, and dangerous. And how do we know, when they take down the last Maelgin, who will step up to take Theodren's place? And if he won't be worse?"

"He won't be worse," Callidora said. "At least he will be an honest enemy. And he isn't the last Maelgin."

"Who is left?" Maxentius said sharply.

"Amalinda," Callidora said faintly. "Whoever takes the crown will take Rothaide's daughter. She is the last line to the legacy of the sacred kings."

Maxentius stared at her for a long time. "What would you have me do?" he said. "I have the oddest feeling that you would stop me from going to war to avenge Rothaide, or to stabilise Ravin—but you would be quite content if I went in with the legions in order to save Rothaide's daughter."

"Close the borders," Callidora said. "Cut the trade. And let them know that it would take only one more false step before you unleashed the full wrath of the Empire."

There were tears in her eyes; Rothaide's ghost was a presence in the room, pale and golden, shredding Callidora's heart not with accusation but with what was almost absolution. The memory of their encounter was etched into her mind, the quiet knowledge in Rothaide's blue eyes, the awareness of her doom—and the understanding that Callidora would do nothing to stop it.

The next news to reach Visant from Ravin was brought to Maxentius and Callidora by Arkadios himself.

"I am sorry to abandon my post without your leave, *despotes*, but I think that I have reached the end of my usefulness in Ravin. The Queen, who knew me and trusted me because of my connection with you, is gone—and Theodren, who has never really trusted me but who was willing to work with me if that suited him, is now gone also."

Callidora shot Maxentius a sharp, questioning look. He had not said that he would do what she had suggested—that he would allow Theodren's Visant aspirations to leak to his earls—but there was nothing else that could have thrown him down from his high place, not this quickly. But he was giving nothing away, his expression calm and carefully schooled, his eyes resting on Arkadios. Callidora shook her head a little to clear it, and returned her own attention back to Arkadios, who was still speaking.

"The earls would have sooner strung me up by my heels than allowed me anywhere near them," Arkadios said. "What I am…is anathema to the wolf-men of the northern court. I am an un-man to them. The only way you can get information from within Ravin now is by means of someone who has never been associated with you or with Visant. Theodren himself could not survive in Ravin now after he had been tainted by a direct association with Visant."

"Are they *seeking* war with the Empire?" Maxentius asked.

"I think they are mostly intent on turning their backs on it," Arkadios said. "But if you began the war, they would fight it. And your garrisons near the northern borders…could not hold them, at current strength. You would need to pour men and supplies into the north if you decided to pick a fight with the Vesigar King."

"What have you learned about him, before you left?"

"His name is Woldren, and he rules by right of…Amalinda," Arkadios said, and tried not to notice as Callidora winced. "I don't think that marriage has been consummated yet—she is far too young—but they were married with full pagan rites, after Theodren was driven from the palace, and then chased down like a stag and killed in the forest in the mountains above Ravin." He hesitated. "I do not know much more than that, *despotes*, I am sorry. I judged it more prudent…to leave Ravin before they remembered to turn their attention to me."

Maxentius was still scowling, his brows knitted together, but he held out a hand to Arkadios.

"You have given faithful service," he said. "Welcome home, Arkadios. Welcome home to Visant."

"I am glad you are back," Callidora said. "Your old post in my household is waiting for you, if you wish to return to it." Her eyes were huge, almost pleading, as they rested on him. "It's good to see you again, Arkadios."

Arkadios met the Empress's gaze with his own, and it was eloquent. *You never told him. You never will.*

But he was complicit himself in the plot that Callidora had hatched. When he chose not to tell the Emperor about Callidora's visit to Ravin back when she had arrived there in secret, he had chosen his side—his loyalty was to Visant, first, but after that to his *despoina*, to his lady, because he had linked his fate to hers.

He closed his eyes for an instant, and then dropped his gaze to the floor, giving Callidora a deep bow. "It would be my honour and my pleasure, *despoina*."

Whether or not she should have confessed everything, Callidora had hesitated too long, and the moment was gone. She told herself later, in self-justification, that saying anything further at this point would have served no purpose at all; she did not speak of Rothaide or of Ravin even with Arkadios in the weeks that followed, resolutely turning away from the subject of the northern kingdom, trying not to think about it any more.

But whatever Ravin had been, whatever it had meant or would still mean, was quickly rendered unimportant, almost trivial, by the vast and shadowed peril that stealthily drew near to the city—so unlooked for, so quiet and sly, that the full weight of it was upon Visant before anyone knew that the danger was real.

Callidora's first hint of trouble had come from her correspondence with the east. Rhakotis, practically on the edge of a river-delta marsh, the biggest port on the Afaris coast where everyone stopped sooner or later, the city on the frontier of a huge, lush, exotic continent, about which very little was really known outside of the writings of intrepid explorers like Eleazar bar Yabin, had always had its share of disease—and at first the mention of something that might have been a bigger problem had slipped past Callidora's notice, and into her archives. But letters speaking of sickness and death began to come in more frequently, from places closer to Visant—and even then, even with all this information and knowledge freely available to her, Callidora all but missed the signs when the sickness first set foot in Visant itself.

She was in her summer palace when she first realised something was badly wrong—a place she had had Virgillus find and purchase for her, a quiet house in pleasant grounds which lay almost directly across the Narrows from the labyrinth of the Imperial Palace in the city. The two palaces were separated by only a short boat ride, with private jetties at either end, ?but so that? Callidora could escape from the city at a moment's notice and pretend that she was far away from its troubles, even while she could be summoned at less than an hour's notice to return and deal with those troubles if they needed her attention.

Virgillus had just finished up a report on the current status of some of the more outlying of the Empress's estates, and it had all seemed good—but his expression, while gathering up his papers in preparation to leave the Empress's presence, suddenly caught Callidora's eye.

"Is there something you aren't telling me?" she asked, sitting up a bit from the couch on which she had been reclining.

Virgillus gave her a sharp glance. "I've lost two of my city staff this week," he said. "Things are a little…backed up right now."

"*Lost* them? How do you mean, lost them?"

Virgillus hesitated. "There's the sickness, Augusta," he said. "There have been deaths. More than a few, now, I gather. Quite a few in the Hippodrome, but not just there."

"No, not just there, or you would not have spoken of your own staff," Callidora said, frowning, unable to help the feeling that she would regret not having noticed this situation earlier, or an even worse feeling that something bad was coming, and that even had she seen it in time there was nothing at all she could have done about it. "Tell me about this sickness."

"It seems…bad," Virgillus said. "The reports have been hard to follow, and sometimes it seems as though people aren't all talking about the same thing— but they all die, those who get it, or most of them do anyway, and whatever the early symptoms might be, it all seems to come to the same thing in the end."

Callidora got up from her couch abruptly. "Get the boat ready," she said, "I am going back to the city. Right now."

She summoned the Palace physician when she returned to the city, sending a runner from the jetty almost before she had fully alighted from the boat herself. The message she sent left the man in no doubt about her urgency, and he did not keep her waiting long in her private audience chamber, arriving a little out of breath.

"I haven't been paying attention," Callidora said, a little grimly. "This epidemic that seems to be in the city. Tell me what is happening, and I want the truth."

"There have been four deaths connected with the Palace…and more are falling ill. I've had reports of at least five new cases since yesterday's sundown All of the four deaths so far were within the last week—two of the people worked for your own man, Virgillus; of the other two, one was a rank-and-file groundskeeper from the Palace gardens, and the other, one of the Guard. This is not something spread by human contact, Augusta. It is not contagious, by touch, by breath. But somehow it is…spreading. And now I think there are at least two more cases, right here in the Palace—one a cook in the Emperor's kitchens, the other a secretary in the tax offices. I can find no contact between them—or any of the people who died."

"What are the symptoms of this disease?" Callidora said. "And give it to me straight, without embellishment or prudery. I need to know."

"There is a mild fever, to begin with, headache, perhaps a pain in the legs or the back—nothing that seems serious, which is why the first victims never realised anything was really wrong…until too late. Everyone complains of a headache at some time, after all. But then the pain changes and deepens, a sharp, stabbing pain—in the joints of the body, in the armpits, or in the groin," the physician said. "While they're still able to complain about the pain—that's the last time they're lucid. They quickly develop a very high fever. Some slip into a restless sleep, after, from which they never wake. Others cannot sleep at all; they quickly lapse into delirium, hallucinating ghosts, and never sleep again until a convulsion takes them into death. I've heard reports of people screaming in their beds, spitting or vomiting blood—some demand to drink, but cannot swallow—there have been a few where the patient develops a sudden energy and superhuman strength and throws off the strongest men to rush out into the streets, or climbs to a rooftop and flings himself off the edge. There are other symptoms—a slurring of the speech, and then, later, a kind of death rattle deep in the throat that prevents any speech at all; bloodshot eyes; a blackening of the fingers and the toes. But all of those afflicted finally come to the same thing—in the places where they first complained that they hurt, they develop large boils and pustules which suppurate evil-smelling liquids… I've heard reports of those reaching the size of melons in some unfortunate people…and then, three or four days later…they die."

"I know of this," Callidora whispered. "I remember this. My mother told me of the tales that her own grandmother told, the last time this sickness was in the land. The black plague, they called it then. How long has it been in the city? How many are sick? Have any lived who contracted it? Why weren't we told earlier?"

"There have been survivors," the physician said. "But not many. I would say that only one in four survives—and a few of those die, after, of hunger or of some other disease, too weakened to live. As to how many are sick right now...." He shrugged his shoulders, spread his arms wide to indicate that he did not know. "I have heard talk that there have been at least a hundred cases in the Hippodrome alone so far. More, out in the city."

"Is there a panic?"

"Not yet, Augusta," the physician said carefully, but his eyes slid off hers.

Her lips tightened. "Keep me informed," she said. "I want a report every night on how the day has gone. I want to know how many are sick, and where, and how bad they are. I want to know how many live, and how many die. *Every day*, do you understand?"

"As you wish, Augusta. It shall be done."

He bowed and left her.

Callidora remained seated in her throne for a while longer, chewing on a fingernail and thinking about what she could possibly do about this, other than to demand to know how many of her people died every day. Callidora had arranged, less than year before, for her younger sister Danelis to marry well, to one of the younger Army generals. She at least was safe—or as safe as she could be—at the very least she was not still living in the crowded underbelly of the Hippodrome where a disease could rage so freely. But the rest of Callidora's family—her mother, her youngest half-sister, her stepfather—had repeatedly resisted her efforts to better their status and their living quarters. They had let Danelis go, but the rest of them remained in the Hippodrome warrens; Locinus had said that he was still bear-keeper, and must live close by his bears, and his family with him. Now, suddenly, that obstinacy might have come back to haunt him.

Maxentius was otherwise engaged, but Callidora left a message with his silentiaries that she needed to see him, and then went back to Chryseis's quarters. It was just as well that they were empty; her daughter was still at the summer palace across the Narrows, the place Callidora had named Heron House in a gentle nod to the House of Peacocks in the city, a place untramelled by court protocol, where Chryseis was allowed to run free in sleeveless summer shifts and barefoot, on the lawns of the great house….and also a place where she was gently constrained against her own wilder impulses. The girl was wilful, stubborn, unwilling and sometimes outright refusing to obey commands given by her elders—and there had been times, back at the House of Peacocks, where she could give her minders the slip and escape into the city, that Chryseis had taken advantage of security loopholes. Once it had taken Arkadios most of the day and a full contingent of house guards to find her again, and that had been bad enough. But what had galled Callidora most was that the child she had fought so hard to protect from the her own Hippodrome past seemed to find the Hippodrome more and more irresistible as she grew older—and seemed drawn to it, having to be retrieved from its precincts several times on the occasions of her escapades. Callidora had found herself speaking sharply to her little girl, but Chryseis, with her mother's flashing dark eyes and her father's temper, had not taken well to being told what she *could* or *could not* do—and Callidora had remembered, too late, what effect those words coming out of her own mother's mouth had had on her. It had only spurred her on to try and prove Apphia wrong—sometimes with disastrous consequences.

Chryseis was far too much like her sometimes. By the time she herself had been close to the age her daughter was at now, she had already been dancing for the patricians of the city for several years, and her life's lessons had been learned by living them; Chryseis was not that different. They both learned by doing, by experiencing, by being a part of life, rather than observing it from the sidelines. If she had been in the city, Chryseis would not have taken word of the plague, someone else's experience of the plague, as sufficient reason to stay safe and close behind the shelter of high palace walls. She was at an age where every truth had to be tested. She would not have believed in the solid reality of the plague. Not until she could see proof of it herself.

And be snared by it.

Callidora suddenly ached to touch the child, to inspect her armpits herself, to make sure that she was still untainted with the scourge. Chryseis had appeared to be perfectly healthy when Callidora had last seen her, but now Callidora was suddenly terrified that everything that Chryseis could see, touch, smell, or taste had the potential to kill her with this blight, the disease that took only a handful of days to ravage a grown man's body and extinguish his life. How much faster, how much worse, for a tender child? *I did not bring her out across the burning desert for her to die here like a rat*, Callidora thought furiously. It was as well that she was not in Visant itself.

Maxentius came to her very late, when candles were already half-burned; he looked tired and hollow-eyed. He paused at the entrance to her sitting room as she turned to face him, and they exchanged a long, bleak look. Then he sighed and stepped into the room, running a weary hand through his hair.

"You know," he said.

"You knew before?"

"You were at Heron House. I myself only found out less than a week ago. And the first time I was told about it…there were a few isolated cases of a bad sickness. But all too quickly…well…there have been more than three hundred deaths, so far."

For a moment Callidora seemed about to rise from her chair, but then sank back onto it without completing her motion as though her legs had refused to bear her. "Three *hundred*? You should have sent for me…."

"There was nothing you could do. There is nothing I can do. I walked to the cathedral at the last service, all the way from the Palace, asking the One God what it was that I should do, what kind of penance I should give myself, what sin I should atone for, that this should be visited on my city, on my people. But I heard nothing except the cries—people in the street who called out, *help us*. But there is no medicine that helps. Those who get it, die."

"I spoke to the physician," Callidora said through bloodless lips. "He said some live…."

"A few," Maxentius said grimly. "A very few. When you have that few living when you know that you already have three hundred dead, you know that your odds are not good."

"What can we do?" she whispered.

"Hope. Pray. Hold on." He covered the distance that separated them in two long strides and slipped one arm around her shoulders, gathering her head up against his chest with the other, holding her with dangerous, desperate strength. She reached out to wrap her own arms around his waist, burying her face into the silk covering his chest.

"I'm sorry," she whispered, her words muffled against his robe, buried in quiet sobs that shook her narrow shoulders.

"What was that?" he said, reaching to lift her head a little.

She looked at him, straight at him, straight into his eyes, and even opened her mouth to speak, to tell him everything, to tell him that it was not his sins but hers that had come home to haunt them…and found that she could not, that the words wouldn't come out, that she couldn't look into the fierce love that was in his face and confess that she had betrayed him. Instead, she found herself slipping off her chair, onto her knees, and after a brief hesitation Maxentius knelt down beside her, gathering up her hands into his own.

"I know you believe differently than I," he said. "If we both pray…perhaps one of us will be heard in the heavens."

Callidora suddenly found herself wishing fiercely for a tiny grey pebble which she could place on top of a cairn of small stones…and watch it all fall down, as faith moved it, as prayers were answered. If she had been there now, on a hillside just outside the city of Challim in the Crescent Kingdoms, it would have been easy to find exactly the prayer she needed. It would have been nothing for herself. It would have been this—only this: *Spare them. Let this plague pass.*

But that day was long gone. And it was strange—the prayer she had prayed back then, when she was still a young girl who might have lived a hard life but still retained a sort of native innocence, had been selfish, for herself and for herself alone. Now, tainted by her actions and her choices, marked with the scars of acts that had been more instinctively selfish than she had ever thought herself capable of, now she let go of the self—and prayed for her world.

The prayers seemed to do very little—the Emperor and the Empress were not the only ones on their knees, beseeching the One God for deliverance, but the One God had suddenly turned into an avenging god, and the scourge lashed the city without mercy. And it was quickly not just the city itself that they had to worry about, because things worsened to such a degree that getting reliable messages in or out of the great Gates on the outer wall soon proved to be a near-impossible task. The stricken city turned inward. There was a period during which, for all Maxentius and Callidora knew, entire provinces might have been dying out there—but the city had no way of knowing.

The numbers of the sick escalated fast, and then the bodies started mounting up; men with wheelbarrows would go around gathering them up and taking them to the cemeteries outside the city walls. When those filled, they dug long pits on their outskirts and dumped in bodies until each pit was full—and then poured lime on them to prevent further contagion, and covered them with earth. And then they started to open up the tops of the big towers, and threw bodies in there until the tower filled up, and then mortared the roof in over them.

Food supplies were interrupted—corn and grain coming in to the city slowed to a trickle, mills and bakeries ground to a halt as the people who worked them went to fill the pits and the towers where the dead were, and the plague-stricken city began to be stalked by yet another spectre: famine.

Within a month five thousand a day were dying in Visant; within two months, they had days when the body count reached twice that, sometimes three times that. Entire families were swept away, houses left standing empty with unlocked doors swinging open. People of wealth and distinction died alone, screaming, with all of their household already dead around them or fled, their final companions only the newly bold rats who had crawled out of cracks and crevices and ran down empty hallways and wide city avenues in broad daylight, no longer afraid of humans. The poorer families, with smaller quarters where more of them shared a smaller living space, sometimes all died in one pathetic heap of humanity, clinging together with their arms around one another as though they were too afraid to let go in the end.

Callidora had seen them—the solitary rich men, the huddled families. She had gone out amongst them, to do something, even she did not know what—sometimes all she did was wait beside the bedside of someone whose laboured breaths told her that death wasn't far off, and tried to pray, or at least to recapture that feeling of light and fire that she had once touched at the bedside of another dying woman, far away in Rhakotis, in what seemed to be a different lifetime.

One of the first places she had gone had been the Hippodrome—her Hippodrome, where she had begun to learn about life, where now death walked daily. The men with wheelbarrows returned to the Hippodrome often, and always left with the barrows fully loaded. When Callidora came there, hurrying through the corridors to the rooms where her family lived, the stench of death was all around her—as if the wheelbarrow men had not quite got them all, as though there were still dead bodies rotting behind closed doors, nibbled on by the Hippodrome rats.

I should have made them leave, Callidora berated herself, in guilt, in torment, in terror. *I should have taken them by force if I had to. Oh, God. Oh, God, Oh, God...*

The door to her family's room was closed, but not completely—it was barely latched, and it opened with a long squeal of unoiled hinges at the slightest touch. The stench of death was strong here, and Callidora gagged, wrapping her headscarf around her mouth and nose as she looked around.

She quickly found the source of the smell. In a bed stained with blood and pus and sweat, still breathing but barely alive, lay Apphia. Her arms were stretched out away from her body in a position that looked acutely uncomfortable, and it was easy to see why—her armpits were grotesquely swollen with suppurating black buboes, and she smelled of rotten flesh, as though she were already dead. There was a label tied to her wrist, with her name on it—that had become commonplace in the city, nobody went out without a name-tag, just in case they collapsed somewhere, died suddenly and alone—sometimes that tag was the only thing that told the men with the wheelbarrows of the identity of the corpse they threw into the back of the barrows to cart away for burial.

Someone had tied that label to Apphia's arm. Someone who counted her as being beyond human help, already among the dead.

The bile rose in the back of Callidora's throat, and a small moan escaped her even as she stuffed a fold of her headscarf into her mouth and bit on it to stop herself from screaming. At the sound Apphia's eyes flickered open, slowly, very slowly.

She murmured something that Callidora didn't understand, perhaps lapsing, in her delirium, into the language of her own childhood, the language she once spoke in the back streets of Virytos on the shores of the Crescent Kingdoms. The voice that came out of her wrecked body was barely more than a hoarse breath, but even that seemed to exhaust her, because she coughed weakly and turned her head away, wincing, as if the tiny movement of her arm sent a lancing pain into her body from the disturbed buboes.

"Mother," Callidora managed to whisper at last.

Apphia didn't respond. She didn't seem lucid, but she was alive—she was still alive—maybe there was still hope. Maybe she would be one of the ones that lived. Maybe there was a chance, if only Callidora could get her out of this room full of death…

She looked around for Locinus, but could not see him anywhere.

"You wait," she babbled, speaking quickly, her words falling over each other in her haste to get them out, tumbling from her mouth, barely making sense. "Hang on. I will get someone to take you out of here. You wait. Hang on for just a little while longer. I will be back. I will be *back*, Mother.…"

She whirled and fled, no longer Empress, just a small girl again racing to find succour and survival. There were healers in the Hippodrome. She knew there were. If she could find one, just one, get him to stay with Apphia while she went back to the Palace, or to the House of Peacocks, somewhere where she had men at her command, people she could order to come back here and carry her mother out, take her somewhere else, anywhere but here, *anywhere* but here…

She all but collided with another woman as she rounded a corner and raced back into the open area at the back of the arena, where the gates opened to the menagerie. The stench that was coming out from the animal pens nearly made her faint, and for a moment she completely failed to recognise the woman she had run into, but then the other spoke.

"We have to stop meeting by accident, Callidora Augusta...."

Callidora looked again. The hair was not the colour of wine, but ash brown shot with gray now. But the eyes were still the same—the eyes that had captivated patricians and Senators and, once, a prince of the city.

"Circassaë? Is that really you?"

"That depends on who you think I really am," Circassaë said laconically. She was carrying a pail full of water in one hand and an armful of clean rags in the other, not a trace of make-up on her face, the dull hair tied back with a simple leather thong. She looked more like a washerwoman than a once-great dancer.

Callidora clutched at Circassaë's sleeve. "I found my mother...I need to get her...."

Circassaë was shaking her head gently. "I did what I could. But when your sister died—well...Apphia didn't last much longer after that."

"When?" Callidora whispered, reeling. "When did she die?"

"The day before yesterday," Circassaë said. "The barrow-men took her yesterday. I don't think Apphia even knew."

"Where is Locinus?" Callidora asked

Circassaë pointed into the reeking animal pen area with her chin. "Probably in there, with a lot of the rest of the animal keepers, I would guess. It is an area I haven't ventured into. I am too afraid of what I will see. I heard some of the animals turn on each other, but it's been pretty quiet for a couple of days now. All the same...I don't really want to know what's down there. I don't think you want to, either."

"I didn't know," Callidora said. She knew she was babbling, crying, that she had completely lost what little control she'd had. "When I found out I came...I tried to...."

"Yours was a Hippodrome family. They would have been miserable elsewhere."

"I could have found Locinus a bear to take care of!"

"But he was working for the factions here, not for the Empire," Circassaë said gently.

"What are *you* doing down here?" Callidora said, abruptly changing the subject, wiping the tears off her cheeks with the back of her hand like a child.

"I gather up the ones still living, and we help the dying as best we can," Circassaë said. "They're my people. Whatever they and I did to hurt each other in the past, they're my people—and the city gets taken care of by others. The Hippodrome only has its own."

"Let me help," Callidora said, reaching for the rags.

Circassaë held them away from her grasp. "You can do much more out of these halls," she said gently. "This is a nightmare, Empress, but you have to stay awake—without someone with courage and heart at the head of the Empire right now, we are *all* going to perish. Let me lay cool cloths on fevered brows; you go back to your own house, and if you have gold to buy food with, send it, if you have food you can share send it, if you have physicians willing to come and tend to those who can still be saved, or priests who are willing to pray for the souls of the Hippodrome folk, send those too." She reached out and grasped Callidora's trembling hand. "Listen to me. Some of us have to live. Some of us can help others live. You can do much—go do it. I am doing the only thing I can do. You know where my house is?"

"But my mother…" Callidora whispered.

"Simonis," Circassaë said quietly, using the childhood name, the first name by which she had ever known this woman in the days when they were both so young, "it would not matter. She would not know you were there. She doesn't know anyone is there. She is past recognising you, or being aware of you. I will stay with her, for what that is worth—I will take care of your mother. Nobody else you love will die alone."

She pushed Callidora gently away, and the Empress, her face smeared with dirt and tears, stumbled out of the gate and into the silent streets. Her feet took her to the House of Peacocks out of sheer instinct and inertia, and her people there, holed up in the house and afraid, let her in and threw themselves into taking care of their lady—it gave them something to do, something with which to fill a day that wasn't a constant and nagging fear, a dread of every new moment potentially making buboes bloom on their skin.

She had not thought that she could sleep, but she cried herself into exhaustion, and slept for hours. When she woke it was dark, and she never went back to the Palace that night, turning back into the pillows and starting to weep again, great silent sobs that shook her whole body. She slept again, and woke, and cried, and slept—it was a nightmare, as Circassaë had said, and one she could not seem to wake from.

The House of Peacocks was quiet, peaceful, apart. It seemed to Callidora that she could shut its gates against the heartbreak and the tragedy of her city, take a rest here, take a breath, gather her strength for the next step; she sent word to the Palace to let Maxentius know where she was, and sent another messenger to Arkadios to command him to send a certain sum of money in gold coins down to the House of Peacocks. Arkadios, efficient as always, sent it down within the hour. But Callidora was suddenly afraid of the silence of the streets—she ventured to the gate twice, on two separate days, but then retreated to the safety of her house again and waited for...she didn't know what. For something—for a sign, for a signal, for someone to come knocking on her door to tell her that everything would be all right.

But the signal, when it came, was not what she had been expecting.

It was one of her servants telling her that another had died in the House of Peacocks that night, the buboes under her arms.

And Callidora felt the concealing curtain stripped away from her again, once more into the pitiless light, and she was appalled that she had wasted as much time as she had. She made arrangements for the woman's body to be disposed of. Then the Empress collected her bag of gold, stepped out into the streets again, and walked up to the house where Circassaë now lived.

It was quiet—in fact, it seemed to be deserted, its outside door open to the street and giving into a beautiful inner courtyard, paved with simple mosaic, with a dead fountain in the centre of it. Callidora called out, but nobody answered— she crossed the empty yard, finding the inner door similarly unlocked, and pushed into the house itself.

Everything was empty of life. It was as though nobody had ever lived in these tastefully decorated rooms at all, as though it had all been a stage set for an elaborate play which was now long over, or which had never been performed at all.

The window to one of the upstairs bedrooms was open, a pair of delicate translucent curtains shivering in the wind. Callidora glanced out of the window—the house was on a slope, and the bedroom was on an upper storey, so the window looked out over the roofs of the neighbourhood houses down-slope from it. Circassaë must have chosen this house for this particular location—because the window framed a clear view of the Hippodrome, its banners fluttering bravely on their poles. From this vantage point, it was almost easy to believe that nothing at all was wrong, that there were crowds in the Hippodrome betting on the outcome of the next race, that horses and chariots awaited at the starting gate.

But all Callidora had to do was turn her head to know that the vision was deceiving, that nothing would ever be right with the world again.

In the bed in the middle of the room with a view lay a woman, her eyes closed, her skin waxen, her fingertips blackened and bruise-coloured buboes barely visible under covers painfully drawn up as high as she could reach with her stricken arms. Her hair was loose, spilled over the pillows in stringy, sweat-soaked tangles; Callidora, in the moment before her eyes filled with tears and she could no longer see anything at all, swore she could see a glint of wine-red highlights still shimmering in the brown and gray, the memory of what once was, and now was no more.

Nobody else you love will die alone.

She had said that, she had promised it, when they had last spoken. Only a few days before.

But she had died alone, Circassaë the beautiful, her body twisted under the covers, her glory unremembered.

Callidora hesitated at Circassaë's bedside, painfully torn. If she left this house, if she left Circassaë lying there as she was, the men in the wheelbarrows might find her before Callidora could return, and she would be gone, thrown into one of the cemetery towers with a heap of other bodies, anonymous or with name-tags tied to their wrists or hanging around their necks in a pathetic effort to have someone remember who they had been. Nobody would even know where Circassaë's last resting place was. She didn't deserve that, not the friend of Callidora's childhood who still knew her milk-name, not the woman who had grown in grace until she could be friends with an Emperor's son, and yet still find it in her to wash dying men's bodies in the Hippodrome warrens and ease their last moments with a kind word. The law said that no burials—other than the Emperors in their marble sarcophagi in the catacombs of the cathedral—were allowed within the city walls. Well, these were lawless days. Callidora's lips tightened in resolve—if she had to carry Circassaë back to the House of Peacocks herself, she would do that, and then think of something to do—bury her quietly in a spot marked with a wine-red climbing rose rather than a stone marker, or give her to the sea. Anything, anything but the towers and the stench and the lime and the suffocating piled bodies of the multitudes of other plague dead...

Callidora left the room and prowled the rest of the house, looking for inspiration as to how best to accomplish her purpose. She found no other living soul, but she did find a donkey which had wandered in off the street and was cropping experimentally at some of the ornamental plants in the fountain courtyard. It still had a trailing rope halter attached, as though it had escaped from somewhere—but ownership was moot in these days, and the animal was a means to an end. She drew the donkey into the house, shutting the door behind it, just so that it wouldn't wander off again before she was ready, and went back up to the bedroom, where she struggled to wrap Circassaë into a sort of shroud made from her own silken sheets. Circassaë had been taller than Callidora, but she seemed light, as though the departure of her soul had left only her shell behind. Callidora dragged the shrouded body down to where the donkey waited patiently, and managed to drape it across the donkey's strong back. Then, leading the animal by the remnants of her halter, she walked back into the street, towards the House of Peacocks.

It seemed to take forever to get there, even with the donkey plodding in her wake without any apparent objections to following her. The guard at the gate of the House of Peacocks flinched as she walked up to the entrance with the donkey and its burden, in no doubt as to what it was carrying, and recoiling from the plague actually being blatantly brought into the gates like this. But Callidora quelled him with a look, and passed through.

Arkadios came out to meet her; he said nothing, his eyes merely going from the Empress to the beast behind her and the burden on its back.

Callidora spoke first. "It is Circassaë," she said. "I found her…in her house. She had been…tending to the sick and the dying, in the Hippodrome. She was the only one who did." She left things unspoken, things that she could not bring herself to say out loud, not without breaking down completely—*She was with my mother, in the end—she, when I could not be there, when I could do nothing….* "I could not have the barrow-men come for her. Not the anonymous grave with the nameless dead."

Arkadios reached for the donkey's halter. "Let me take care of it, *despoina*. I will find a way to make sure she is laid to rest with honour."

Callidora's hand fell away from the rope, and her shoulders sagged. "Thank you," she said dully.

"The *despotes* has been asking about you," Arkadios said.

Callidora glanced up again, at the house that Maxentius had given her, at the refuge from the storm, and sighed deeply. Circassaë had been right about that, too. She had other responsibilities now, and she could not allow herself to hide from them—not in this haven, not anywhere, not until this was over. "I had better get back to the Palace," Callidora said at last.

Callidora walked back slowly to the Bronze Gate, giving out her gold coins to those she found still living, pausing to whisper a few words over those who had already slipped away. She was recognised; people lucid enough to know that someone was with them would open rheumy eyes and see her, and breathe a single word in a hoarse whisper—*Augusta!*—and some, the living waiting with the dead, retained enough presence of mind to try and struggle to their feet, to do obeisance in thanks for the gold, in mute thanks that their Empress walked amongst them.

It was the longest walk she had taken in her life.

She went out daily, after—with more gold, and more prayers, and growing helplessness.

Perhaps she was trying to seek her own death amongst the dying, with that cold vivid conviction buried deep inside her that she herself was responsible for offending God, for bringing this down on the city—she, who had stood by and waited for a woman who had been in her way to be killed so that she, Callidora, could retain her claim to her crown and the man whom she loved. But if that was what she sought, she did not find it—the physician had told her, early on, that the disease wasn't spread by human contagion, and no matter how many dead bodies she saw and stopped to say a prayer over, the plague passed her by.

She knew that Maxentius had been doing the same thing. She knew even though he had not told her that he was, even as she had not told him of her own activities, both of them keeping it from the other, even though they knew that both of them knew, hoping that not saying it out loud would make the one who was supposedly living in ignorance less worried about the other's well-being out in the streets. But they would meet up in the Palace corridors sometimes and they would touch fingers lightly, hopelessly, in passing—or exchange an unguarded look full of anguish. It was all there for anyone who wanted to read it.

"You are all I have left," Callidora had whispered, once, as he turned to walk away from her to hurry to some other place that needed him. She did not know if he heard her. He did not stop to respond.

Callidora had not thought it could get worse—not when they had sixteen thousand bodies a day to bury somewhere, and the stench of death hung around the ill-mortared towers in which the dead mouldered away.

Not until she walked into Maxentius's room one night, and saw him sitting alone in a chair, shivering slightly, his eyes closed and skin pale and beads of sweat on his forehead. When she reached for his hand she felt the fever in him burn her fingertips even before she touched him. She snatched her hand back with an agonised gasp, and at the sound he opened his eyes—they were cloudy with pain, but still lucid.

"I have them," he whispered hoarsely, his words slurring a little. "The buboes. Help me get into bed…and then pray for me, pray for the city. But if my life is what buys their deliverance, I want you to know…I do not go to the One God with as much grace as I should, I leave far too much undone here on earth, but I will go willingly, if that is the price Visant must pay. Now help me…help me.…"

His eyes closed again, and he slumped back into his chair.

Somewhere deep inside Callidora, something huge and dark that had always given her strength before, the shadow of her bear, was huddled in a pitiful heap, soundlessly screaming.

CHAPTER TWENTY SIX

For three days Callidora kept vigil at Maxentius's bedside.

If she slept, no one saw her do it; food was brought in to her and more often than not taken away largely untouched. Her eyes grew huge and hollow in her face as she watched him fight for breath, watched the sweat of his fever plastering his fair hair to his temples. On the fourth day, with Maxentius still delirious, she stood and walked stiffly from his chamber, down into the gardens and into her own quarters where she had not set foot since Maxentius had fallen ill. Nobody approached her—one look at the terrible, burning eyes in her thin face was enough to make anyone she happened to meet scurry out of her way.

The fourth day. The fourth day brought death.

Callidora did not pause in any of her chambers. Her body rigid, her shoulders stiff, she made straight for the Empress's chapel, dark except for a handful of votive lamps that had been lit and kept perennially alight by a faithful servant. Her hair coming loose from its pins, her face drained of color, her eyes full of anguish and fear, she knelt on the step leading to the altar dais, and folded her hands together, lifting her head to the domed roof. She wasn't sure what she saw there—the light of faith, or the ghostly face of a beautiful woman with fair hair blowing across her face in the evening breeze from the sea.

"He has done nothing wrong," she whispered, her voice catching. "This is not his guilt, his debt. I was the one who schemed and plotted, I was the one who sinned, I was the one who killed or let the killing happen. If there is a price to be paid, let me…take me. Let him live, he has done nothing wrong.…"

The chapel echoed faintly with her whispers, but there was no other response—and she finally collapsed into a boneless heap on the floor before the altar, her face buried in her hands, weeping, her whole body shaking with her sobs.

At first she failed to even notice a gentle hand on her shoulder—and then, when she became aware of it, she started violently, shying away, before she realized that she knew the man who stood beside her.

Father Honorius, the Rhakotis priest who had saved her life once as she lay near to death on the steps of the Rhakotis Cathedral, had come over to Visant almost a year before at Callidora's invitation. He had come, at first, for only a short visit—and she had installed him in the rooms next to her chapel, set aside for the Empress's own priest and confessor when an Empress had someone like that in residence. Somehow his sojourn in Visant had been extended again and again, first because of his own interest in the city and its ways, then because the Bishop of Rhakotis himself had requested that Father Honorius stay a little longer, especially after he had picked up a following of his own—secret sympathisers to the Rhakotis creed in the ranks of the Visant patricians—and the Bishop thought that he could do much good placed as highly as he was, presenting and protecting his beliefs. Callidora had no objections, and had told him that he could stay for as long as he wished—she enjoyed having him near her, because he had not lost his taste for philosophical discussion and was always glad to indulge the Empress in increasingly sophisticated debate. But he was there as her friend, not her priest or her confessor. She had not told him of her Ravin adventure when she had returned to Visant.

She had spoken to nobody of what had happened in the Vesigar city; even Arkadios only knew because he had been directly involved himself. But she was beyond that, now. The devastation of the city—once teeming with more than half a million souls, now half emptied by the plague with a death toll that numbered hundreds of thousands of victims—had been a hammer that had cracked the shell of her secret. Maxentius had been the final blow, and Callidora was open now, and helpless, her soul bleeding.

"I could not help hearing what you said," Father Honorius said. "God does not make bargains like these with mortals, my child—at least not the God that you and I both believe in. You cannot offer yourself in exchange for another.

The One God does what he does for a reason—I cannot begin to tell you what his reason might be for what is happening in this city right now. But I do know that it is not your doing." He paused. "I came to you, when you were with the Emperor," he said gently. "You would not speak to me. I don't know if you were even aware that I was even there. But you are here, now—has the Emperor…?"

Callidora recoiled. "No. No. Not yet." She began to scramble to her feet. "I should get back to him. I should get back.…"

It was only Father Honorius's hand, closing around her arm and steadying her as she tried to rise too fast, that kept her from falling as her head spun with a sudden and nauseating vertigo. He guided her back down again, and she sat in a graceless heap on the step, gulping in huge breaths of air.

"Sit there quietly for a moment," Father Honorius said. "There is some wine back behind the altar."

"It's the consecrated wine, for the service," Callidora said weakly.

"Under the circumstances, I don't think the One God will mind," Father Honorius said. "I will replace what I have borrowed. Stay there."

She could not muster the strength to turn and watch him step up to the altar and bend down to rummage sacrilegiously behind the altar cloth. He returned with a plain pewter goblet half-filled with red wine, and steadied her with one hand as he offered the goblet to her with the other.

"Drink that," he said. And then, when she hesitated, "I insist. Under this roof, Empress, it is my authority that comes after the One God's will. I tell you, if nothing else damns you, drinking this wine will not do it. You have my word on that, as a priest of the One God."

Callidora held back for another moment, and then took the goblet with both hands and lifted it to her lips, closing her eyes as she drained it.

"Good," said Father Honorius. "Now, when was the last time you ate anything?"

'I don't remember," Callidora said.

"In that case I'd better get my supper. We don't want that wine going to your head on an empty stomach. It's simple fare, I'm on a fast, but it's something—and we can send for more later. Do not," he added, as he left her side and stepped away towards his own quarters that were adjacent to the chapel, "even think of going anywhere, Augusta, because you will probably not get further than a few steps before falling down. After you have eaten something, I will help you walk out of here."

He brought back some plain bread and cheese, and Callidora, who had thought that she would never want anything to pass her lips again, demolished it in a few bites, suddenly ravenous.

"Good," said Father Honorius, settling on the step next to her. "Now tell me the thing that shadows your soul. I can see that it is gnawing away at you on the inside. Tell me, because you know I can tell nobody else. Lay down that burden before God." He paused, reached out to take her hand between both of his own. "Whom, my child, have you killed?" he asked, his voice very gentle.

"A queen," Callidora whispered bleakly. "A true queen. If she had come to Visant...she would have taken my place. I was jealous, and selfish, and afraid—afraid of what would become of me, if he ever chose her, and he would have chosen her, because she was perfect, and I am...I am the bear-keeper's daughter from the Hippodrome. I was never supposed to wear a crown. All of it felt like a dream, and I was about to wake, and there was nowhere to go from here, Father, but down into the darkness. So I went to see her, because everyone told me that she was beautiful and royal and proud and she was so right for him—I had to see her, I had to see for myself. And she *was*, she was all that, and more. And she looked at me and she knew exactly what I was thinking, and that she had no hope left—and she *forgave* me, as the One God is my witness, she forgave me everything, even though she knew she was a dead woman and I would do nothing to save her, I would let it happen, I would even stand in the way of rescue, if I could without letting on that I was doing it. She knew exactly why I came...."

"Stop," Father Honorius said gently. "Tell me slowly. Tell me from the beginning."

And it finally came tumbling out, the story of the two queens, as though it had been a boil on her soul, a black plague bubo, and it had been lanced at last and the poison was coming out. She told it through her tears, she cried until her eyes were hot and dry and empty, until she could cry no more—and she told it all, how she had gone to Ravin, how she had enmeshed Arkadios, Theodren, Rothaide herself, and finally Maxentius—set up a complex chain of events that could lead to only one end.

"I might as well have taken a dagger to the island and stabbed her myself," Callidora said. "I did it all, full knowing. None of it was done in ignorance or in innocence. I wanted her dead. I wanted her out of my dream. And now...."

"And now?" Father Honorius echoed.

She lifted her tear-streaked face to stare at him. "The city," she said. "The plague. Half the city is gone; the One God knows how the rest of the Empire is doing. There has certainly been no government from Visant in the last few weeks, while we were gathering up our dead and trying to feed our living. I wanted to tell Maxentius. I just…couldn't find the words. It would have been admitting to cowardice and jealousy and complete irrationality—and I knew that I was all of those things, and I let myself be driven by them anyway. And so I kept silent. And because I more or less told Theodren that the Empire would wink at his crime if he murdered his wife, Rothaide is dead, and God is punishing the city…I *will* tell Maxentius. I'll tell him now. He may not hear me but I will tell him what I did, that it was my fault, that it was my sin.…"

"Your sin right now is hubris," Father Honorius said. "Hubris, to believe that something you did would cause God to lay the hand of divine wrath on a city full of innocent people. And you are compounding that with the sin of cowardice and despair—you've carried the burden yourself thus far and only now, at the reckoning, are you willing and even eager to share the story, to push some of the responsibility onto someone else so that you can finally stand up under the load of it before it crushes you into the ground. You have done what you have done—your penance is that Maxentius Augustus, if he lives or dies, must *never* know the full tale."

Callidora buried her face in her hands. "I need him to forgive me.…"

"He might forgive you because he loves you. But he would never forget it, or her, your Rothaide, the northern princess. She would be a ghost who stood between you from now until eternity—you will have invited her into your house yourself, and she will never leave it again." Father Honorius stopped, and allowed a pool of silence to gather around them. Callidora sat with her eyes closed, her fingers pressing into her temples, until she could finally bear the silence no longer and dropped her hands to look at the priest. "There are two things you are to take with you from the house of God tonight," he said, when she met his eyes. "The first thing is that, yes, you have sinned—and the sin is your own, and your penance is to carry it on your soul until you die. The second thing—and this is not absolution, because I cannot give you that—is that this plague out there, that is not God punishing your city for your sins. God's reasons are his own and they may become clear to us in time…or maybe they never will. But the one certain thing is that you, Augusta, did not bring the black plague into Visant."

Callidora sat in silence, her hands twisted together into her lap, and finally sighed deeply "I must go back to Maxentius," she said.

"Then I will help you get there," Father Honorius said. "And may I have your word that if I send for something to eat, you will take it? Before you, too, collapse?"

"I will eat."

"Good. Now come, let me help you. We can go by your quarters, you can change your raiment, comb your hair. You do not want the court to see you distraught like this."

She moved like an old woman, carefully, as though she might break bones if she moved too fast. One of her women was drowsing in the quiet shadowed silence of the Empress's dressing room; she leapt to her feet when she saw Callidora, her eyes widening, and Callidora shook her head a little, trying a smile, to let her know that the Emperor had not slipped away yet. The woman helped her change into a plain grey gown and wrap a red shawl around her shoulders, something that drew an inadvertent smile from Callidora, as it occurred to her that this was precisely what she had been wearing the first time Maxentius had ever seen her, spinning the wool from the market on the steps of her house in the city. She allowed her hair to be brushed and pinned up again, and then she walked down the porphyry corridor, back towards the main wing of the Imperial Palace, where the Emperor still lay suspended between life and death.

She was pale, and proud, and composed, even though she walked leaning heavily on Father Honorius's arm. He left her at the door of the Emperor's bedchamber, bowing to her, and she gave him a long look before she walked inside, alone. She heard him talking to the silentiaries waiting outside, ordering food.

The fourth day. The fourth day was drawing to a close.

She leaned over Maxentius, touching his forehead lightly with her fingers— he still burned with fever, his eyes closed, murmuring something soft and incoherent in his restless delirious sleep.

"I am here," she whispered. "I will always be here."

One of the silentiaries brought her a plate of light supper and Callidora made herself eat, even if she had to remind herself to chew and swallow. She felt better for it afterwards and even managed to fall asleep for a little while, curled up on one of the large chairs by the window. She hadn't realized that she had done so until she woke up with a start from a complicated, feverish dream and had to shake her head to orient herself and remember where she was.

The dream was evanescent, and vanished before she had time to properly think about it or pin it down. But one thing remained, the sound of one voice— Circassaë's, back at the Hippodrome—*He made you Empress. It is your Empire, as well as his. You have a responsibility...*

The Emperor had been at death's door for four days. The Empress had been lost in a fog of guilt and grief. The Empire had been drifting and leaderless.

It was *her* responsibility.

She was not unaware of the irony of the situation—she would have to do exactly the thing that Rothaide had been trying to do. She would have to grasp the thorny branch and actually become the ruling queen, and possibly face the very things that Rothaide had faced: the resentment, the jealousy, the plotting, the pain. Callidora had not been born to this, as Rothaide had been, but she had the advantage of not coming to it in a society which was never going to accept a woman's rule. There were precedents in Visant history, of widowed Empresses ruling until they could bring another Emperor to the throne by remarrying, or pass the sceptre onto another Emperor chosen by the Senate.

Maxentius seemed, if anything, worse when she bent over the bed to check on him. He was restless, and seemed to be in the grip of a bad dream or in pain.

"I will not be far," Callidora said softly. "And I will be back, every hour."

The members of the Imperial Council, who had themselves been keeping a low profile in their quarters, had arrived in the Emperor's sitting room in response to an Imperial summons, expecting to hear the worst. They found Callidora, sitting at the head of a table that had been moved into the room, waiting in silence until they had all filed in and settled into the chairs set out around the table.

"My lords," she said, when they had all arrived and turned to her expectantly, braced for bad news, "we have work to do."

"Augusta?" one of the council members said, confused.

"The Emperor…?" another said.

"The Emperor's condition is unchanged," Callidora said. "But I am here. And I need your help. The city is still out there, and the Empire. As long as there is anyone still left alive there, we have a responsibility to help them, to support them." She paused. "To reign, and to govern."

There were looks exchanged between the men at the table, some frightened, some merely confused. Sarrus, the ex-Grand Chancellor and now Emeritus Counsellor, once Maxentius's enemy, did not look at anyone else but stared at her with thoughtful eyes.

One of the other counsellors roused. "Maxentius Augusts—is he—"

"It's the fourth day," Callidora said. She clenched her hands underneath the table, driving her fingernails into her palms; she would not cry, could not, not here, not in front of these people. "We will know by morning. In the meantime, I mean to do what I can. I need to know what the epidemic is doing. I need to know how empty the granaries are, and I need to know how we can arrange for tithes from the country to start coming in—we have a city to feed, a city that is wounded and reeling and needs something solid and reliable to cling to. We need to have bread for the people. We have been burying the dead—it is time for us to look to the living. I know that none of us have been keeping too close an eye on our duties, but I will be expecting this council to meet every day for at least an hour, with up-to-date reports, and a plan of action. Organize your departments. See how much you think we have to do before we regain a grip on the city, and on the empire. If we do not start now, today, we may lose it all. I realise that this meeting was called at short notice—that none of you are prepared. By tomorrow morning...." She choked on that, despite herself, without meaning to. Tomorrow morning could bring so many things—so many things she did not wish to even begin to think about. Tomorrow morning...she might truly be Empress. The only thing left. The only person whose head bore the weight of a crown, whose shoulders bore the weight of an Empire.

If Maxentius died...

They were all thinking it, every one of them, as Callidora rose from the table, watching eleven astonished faces gaping back at her. She moved to the doors of the bedchamber, her head held high, knowing that every pair of eyes in that room was on her.

She knew that something was different the moment she closed the door of the bedchamber behind her—there was a stench in the air, as though something vile had just died in there, and Callidora stifled a cry as she gathered up her skirts and ran towards Maxentius's bed. She only realized that the court physician was already there when she all but ran him down as he straightened in her path.

"The buboes, Augusta," he said, before she asked. "They have ripened, and they're suppurating—they're draining. I have seen this in a handful of patients under my care." He paused, weighing his words carefully. "The ones who survived."

Callidora shuddered, reaching out blindly for the nearest support. "He will live?"

"It is too early to tell," the physician said, clearly unwilling to raise expectations too high too early. "But in the next few hours, we will know." He paused, looking at her with helpless compassion. "I need to clean the suppuration now. So that he is not lying in his own poisons. I will send word, the moment anything changes. In the meantime...as your physician as well as the Emperor's, I would earnestly advise that you get some rest. There is nothing you can do here, Augusta. Not any more. The rest is as God wills it. Get some sleep."

Callidora stared at him for a long moment, and then her shoulders sagged. "Do what you must," she said. "Do what you can. If he…if…."

"Augusta," the physician said gently, "you will be the first to know. Whatever happens."

She had not thought that she could sleep. The very idea of it revolted her— that she should sleep, on this fourth night—the night that might decide it all— seemed almost sacrilegious to her. But she was practical enough to realise that the physician was right, that she could do nothing right now but get in the way. But she would not go back to the Empress's porphyry bedchamber. It was too far away. She summoned a couple of the silentiaries and asked them to make her up a makeshift pallet in the next room, where she could be out of the healers' way, but close enough to wake and be summoned if she needed to come to Maxentius's side—and after tossing and turning on that narrow bed for what seemed like endless hours, finally, she slept.

It was a fitful sleep—she kept starting awake, listening for sounds, raking the shadows with her eyes to see if anyone had actually woken her—but she was always alone. Twice she actually slipped into Maxentius's chamber, both times terrified of what she might find, but he still breathed, even if his every breath sounded laboured and hard-won.

Dawn caught her awake. She sent one of the silentiaries to summon one of her women with a change of clothes and a mirror, and made herself presentable with a heavy heart, ready to face the council she had summoned back for that morning. In Maxentius's room, she found the physician again, once more sponging down the oozing buboes; she asked, with her eyes, and he shook his head. All he could tell her was that the Emperor still lived.

The council was waiting for her as she entered the sitting room. They appeared to have got over their astonishment, and now regarded her something that was a mixture of resentment and respect—and it was Sarrus, astonishingly enough, who turned out to be the spokesman.

"We are ready," he said. "You are right, the city needs us. And I am grateful that you have stepped up. I have a single piece of what might be good news— the death numbers seem to have peaked, and I am told that in the last few days there have been fewer deaths per day than have been recorded earlier. We may be over the worst of it."

"Then we have to start dealing with the aftermath," Callidora said. "Right now."

"Agreed," Sarrus said. "I haven't had much time to prepare it formally, but I do have a short report for you, of intelligence that has been accumulating in my office and which I have been remiss in not paying closer attention to before. I am in your debt, Augusta." He made a sweeping gesture with his left hand, indicating the rest of the council, who sat nodding agreement. "We all are."

The reports of the council, such as they were, did not take very long, because they all had obvious glaring gaps where things had been allowed to lapse in the general chaos of the epidemic. But Callidora listened , made suggestions where she thought she was able to make a contribution, and dismissed the council again to gather up their departments and start the bureaucratic wheels grinding once more, the machinery at the head and heart of the Empire, a government for the lost and hungry city, and the Empire beyond, who were reeling from the impact of something they were only just beginning to come to terms with.

At the end of a gruelling couple of hours of this, her head was pounding, but her eyes were eloquent with resolution—with an acceptance of that responsibility that was laid on her. Whatever else that day might bring...she was Empress. She had been truly Empress, at least for the day. If she had to be, she would continue. They had accepted her.

When she finally returned to Maxentius's room, hours later, she found him alone but for a single silentiary watcher. Callidora ignored the servant, walking hesitantly across the room, listening for Maxentius's breathing—and it was still there, still the same, still harsh and shallow and rattling in his throat.

She closed her eyes, swaying a little, and her mind was empty except for a single word.

Please, she whispered, soundlessly, hopelessly. She did not know what it was. It was not a prayer, not the way she thought of prayer. It was no more than a plea. God did not make bargains, Father Honorius had said—well, she was past making bargains. She was not asking for anything, offering anything, other than that single heartfelt word. *Please.*

And then she caught her breath as she realised that something very subtle had changed in the room. For a moment she could not put her finger on anything specific...but then, suddenly, she knew.

She had spent too many nights sleeping next to this man, in his bed. She knew what his breathing sounded like when he was asleep.

She knew what it sounded like...*when he was awake.*

With a small gasp she opened her eyes, one hand reaching down to the man lying there, the other flying to her mouth as her eyes filled with tears.

Maxentius's eyes were open, his eyelashes spiked and gummed by sleep and fever-sweat, and he squinted as though even the candle light was too bright for him. But he was definitely awake, and alert.

He tried to speak, to whisper her name, but his voice failed him, and he lay with his head back against his pillow, trying to focus on her face.

With a sob, Callidora threw herself on her knees beside his bed. "Don't talk," she said. "Don't try to talk. I am here. Do you need something? Do you want water?"

He closed his eyes, nodded weakly. The silentiary, who had bounded to his feet with a gaping mouth, had collected himself and anticipated her words, his needs; he was already beside her, a goblet of water in his hand. Callidora took it from him and gently lifted up Maxentius's head off the pillow, tilting the goblet to wet his lips, watched him take a few painful swallows and then turn away slightly indicating that he had had enough. She laid him back on the pillow and turned back to the trembling silentiary, her eyes blazing.

"Fetch the physician," she said. "Tell him…tell him it has broken." She looked down at the hand that still held the goblet, a hand that was shaking so violently that she was spilling the remaining water in the vessel on the Emperor's bed, on the floor. "Tell him the Emperor is awake. Tell him Maxentius Augustus will live."

THREE
AUGUSTA

CHAPTER TWENTY SEVEN

The Empire, and the city of Visant, had almost seven years to recover from the black plague before the summer of the comet.

It had come blazing across the night sky, a firedrake, a bright star dragging a long pale tail behind it. The church, officially, had nothing to say about it—but the soothsayers and astrologers in Visant all immediately hailed it as a sign, and began to prophesy doom and tragedy, vying with one another as to who could come up with more dire predictions. With the priests grimly silent, it wasn't hard to see whom the people would listen to.

It was at times like these that Callidora missed the company of Father Honorius, her friend from Rhakotis, whose views and opinions she valued greatly—but those same opinions, freely expressed, had finally put him in direct conflict with the Patriarch of the City. Father Honorius had left Visant under sentence of excommunication six months before, and it was only in letters now that he and Callidora could speak of things that mattered.

Callidora had started one of those letters when she arrived at Heron House, but it had progressed desultorily over the course of several long evenings, in fits and starts, rambling from this subject and that one, suffering from Father Honorius's inability to respond to her words as she spoke them. As her sixth night in Heron House began to gather around her, with the comet to come soon after, Callidora reached for the pages she had already written and shuffled through them.

Wouldn't it be a good thing if they all got it wrong, if the comet actually meant the end of seven years of bad luck? The One God knows we could use a break. Yes, I know. I have much to be grateful for, and I am still grateful for those things, every day of these last seven years. The plague was devastating, but if I had lost Maxentius to it.... I dare not even think about it. I never thought I would live to see Visant that empty, that tragic. It was bad enough, back then. You were there—you remember—it took months for the stench to abate from the towers where they had piled our dead.

She could almost hear him respond to that. "Grace," he would have told her. "Faith. Faith makes us grateful for the things we have, not covet the things we don't. And we have much to be grateful for. It was bad, but it ended."

She might have imagined him saying that when she had written those lines, too, because the next words in her letter could have been a direct response to it.

Yes, it ended—eventually, at last—and then all the other things began. First the whole clean-up after the plague—not just Visant, everywhere—and in some ways that was far worse than what had led up to it. All the things once taken for granted, now changing. There was a time that all registered households in need were issued bread in Visant—but the plague showed us how very fragile that was. The early disruption of the wheat supply—the lack of men to work the bakeries—and we had people going hungry in the city. And yes, we dealt with that, too—but at a price. The city used to be so organised, practical, smooth—the people who lived here knew how things functioned, who belonged where, what everyone's job was, and those with no business in the city were never allowed to wander in at will and make trouble. But with half our population gone—the city needed the influx of new people if it was to survive. And the new people who came...were not of Visant. We relaxed our guard.

It was different, in Rhakotis, when I walked in through your open gates so many years ago—Rhakotis never had Visant's responsibilities. After the plague...well, too many who knew how to run this city and its own peculiar needs were gone. All these raw and inexperienced people—outsiders, strangers—replaced them. And when most we needed the old guard, who understood plebeian and patrician alike and knew how to deal with both, we had new functionaries whose only priorities often seemed to be only themselves.

And at the worst possible time, too—ah, but you know all this, my friend, and I am just picking at old wounds—first the earthquake in Antancia, strong enough to bring down walls which have stood for centuries, and then the Crescent Kingdoms rising in insurrection, and the Imperial Army is suddenly stretched across thousands of miles, and we're losing border forts we've held for generations because there simply aren't enough men to hold them all, not even one of those gifted generals who would have known how best to deploy those men who are in place. No people have ever loved taxes, that is for certain. But we had to redesign the tax laws to replenish the treasury emptied by all these calamities, and from the outcry in the city you might think that everyone believes that these new laws were created to personally enrich Maxentius himself. There are those who are behaving as though they sincerely believe that every coin torn from the hands of a poor beggar at swordspoint went to buy new gems to sew on the Imperial cloak.

Callidora scowled at the page, tapping her fingers on her writing table. She, who had once asked for the life she was meant to live and been granted her wish in abundance, sounded like she was now complaining about the gift that she had received. But even she, always the strong one, always stalwart, had her moments of fragility and failure. Father Honorius, of all people, knew that well. Perhaps that was why she was so free with her complaints with him—he knew how far she had already fallen. Everything else would seem so small, in comparison.

She went back to the letter—there was not much that remained to tell.

And of course…all the people who might have made the transition easier, explained, discussed, did the job in a manner firm but kind—they were all gone, the plague took them. So now we have tax collectors who go in and bully instead. They come back to Visant with bulging saddlebags, to be sure, but also with nicknames like Cutpurse and Scissors. And of course they are resented. I would resent them myself if I were on the receiving end of their tender mercies. But I've already contributed my share—I've channelled the income from the Empress's estates into the royal treasury. Half of Antacia was rebuilt from my revenues, and not on blood money extracted from some small landowner in Tollin or the hills of Naisos.

Yes, Father Honorius, I know—I have been richly blessed. And I am not feeling sorry for myself. Not really. I try to focus on other things, too, on my daughter's marriage, which is nigh on a year old now, on the coming child that she is expecting in the spring—yes, I am to be a grandmother, I am not sure how I feel about that, right now—but everything else…it's been weighing on me lately, and sometimes I catch myself whispering that it isn't fair, that the plague took far more than ever we realised, and wonder if soothsayers in Visant don't have the right of it and the comet isn't just the final seal on our fate.

The skies had darkened as Callidora had read, and as she looked up she saw it rise, the comet she had been writing about, and spread its ghostly pale tail across the heavens. She stared at it, oddly troubled by its strange, surreal beauty. It could mean any number of things—she couldn't let it prey on her mind so. She folded the letter with a resolute motion.

"Pestilence, famine, the stirrings of war on our borders, death," Callidora murmured. "We've already had them all, the disasters, the catastrophes. What else can possibly go wrong?"

The comet flamed across the summer sky and then faded into memory. It seemed to have left in its wake nothing more than a waning wave of doomsayers who were still prophesying the end of the world—but then autumn came, and then winter, and even those voices seemed to fall silent. The things that Callidora had complained about that summer remained on-going troubles, but winter was always a quiet time, and the Empress, back in the city, began to think that she could begin to relax her guard again, to put the potential for calamity, brought by the comet, behind her.

There were disturbances in the city as the year waned to a close, and there seemed to be a disquieting angle to it all which directly involved the Hippodrome and its folk. Callidora found herself missing Circassaë more than ever, a friend who'd had vital connections to the Hippodrome and could have conveyed invaluable information which it was next to impossible for an outsider to ferret out—Callidora even thought once or twice with a pang of regret, of Cicatrice, because if anyone would have known exactly what was brewing in the warrens of the Hippodrome, it would have been that old fox. But the plague had severed what remaining direct ties Callidora herself had to the Hippodrome, and although her agents brought her reports of the details of the unrest, she was left to piece it all together herself, removed from the source, behind the Palace walls which concealed her from the world but also hid the world from her.

The two strongest factions—White Jewel and Golden Crown, both of which had shaped Callidora's own life to such a large extent—seemed to have taken their traditional rivalry to a whole new level. Callidora's main source of information on this was one Belenus, a man fairly highly placed in the hierarchy of a third faction, Obsidian Knife—traditionally strongly affiliated to the Golden Crown faction, to all practical purposes almost a junior branch of the more powerful faction. Belenus himself had approached Callidora with an offer to be her eyes and ears in the Hippodrome; he had not asked for favours and she had made no promises, but she understood his unspoken position clearly—this was a man with ambition, someone who wanted to see the Obsidian Knife faction raised to a different level, not a subsidiary, but a direct rival of their seniors in the arena, and who was willing to take a risk of approaching the throne of Visant itself if that would further his cause.

They met in the House of Peacocks when he had information for her, and as late autumn swept into the city, the frequency of Belenus's visits to

Callidora's house increased. He spoke to her of a dangerous situation where some of the Hippodrome folks were afraid of others of their kind, and some appeared to be afraid of nobody at all—and what was brewing was a dangerous mix of frustration, misery and fear on one side and arrogance and a sense of invincibility on the other.

"Some of the Golden Crown bloods have become so bold as to openly assault people on the streets; they've even broken into houses," Belenus said to Callidora. "About a week ago somebody fought back, and one of the Golden Crown boys got knifed—he died the next day, and that night they found the other man dead—the one who had dared to defend himself in the streets. The Golden Crown people went out looking for him, and they found him."

"Was there a report filed with the city Guard? With the offices of the Praetorian Prefect?" Callidora asked.

"There have been quite a few such reports filed before this one," Belenus said, a little grimly. "The Empire does not seem to assign them a high priority."

"So these deaths are not an isolated incident? Are you telling me that they aren't even anything new?"

"People have died, yes," Belenus said. "And the Empire does nothing. But this time…the Golden Crown lad who died was actually a charioteer. He was gifted, someone with great potential, but still new to the Visant arena—he would have raced his first Golden Crown chariot in the Winter Cup races this year, and much was expected from him. Those races are only a few weeks away. Now the faction is up in arms and screaming murder, because this means that their chances in the race have been substantially affected, to the point that they may race one less chariot than their competition. It means that they will almost certainly lose. And they are not happy."

"A Hippodrome charioteer has turned thug?" Callidora said, sitting back in her chair. "Things have certainly changed in the Hippodrome…."

"Winter was always a time of rest before, Augusta. As you know. But in the aftermath of the plague…it had seemed like a good idea at the time to institute a winter race, anything to take the survivors' mind off the memory of it all. And it worked. But winter races meant that the competitive spirit of summer had to be kept at fever pitch all year round. And it festered, in some. It became all about winning, all of the time, against all comers. The Golden Crown had the edge because they had always had more support amongst the higher-born—and they inherited some of their attitudes, too. So they figured that they could do what they wanted to maintain their edge. The street gangs grew out of that."

"How did I miss all this?" Callidora asked, rising abruptly from her chair and starting to pace her sitting room.

"With respect, Augusta," Belenus said, "I would venture to guess that you probably welcomed the Winter Cup when it was first proposed—and it was a good idea at the time, it was needed. If it had been allowed to proceed for only that first year, perhaps things would never have escalated. But after the *second* year, it was already thought of as tradition, and cancelling the races would have been almost impossible. If you had tried, you would have had a riot on your hands."

"And the faction gangs?"

"They've been around for a while. But it's only been getting really bad in the last month or two."

"I will speak to the Emperor," Callidora said. "Keep me informed."

She went in search of Maxentius later that night. She knew he would be awake; he was always awake these days, working late into the night, pacing the Palace corridors when he was done with the work and unable to get his racing mind to quiet down into sleep. He had been that way ever since he had come back from the brink of death during the epidemic; it was as though the price of his survival had been his peace of mind. He was sleeping only a couple of hours a night; he had lost weight, becoming more gaunt and sharp-featured, and he had become more impatient, more impulsive, as though he were shying away from difficult decisions.

Callidora had carried the weight of the Empire on her own shoulders for months, while Maxentius recuperated very slowly and painfully from the disease that had nearly taken his life. She had continued to be a part of the Imperial Council after Maxentius had returned to its head, and often it must have seemed to the council members that it was Callidora who made the final decisions. It wasn't that Maxentius was any less shrewd or perceptive than he had been before, but at some point during the debates in council he would simply step back and allow Callidora to wrap the matter up, have the final word. He had not abdicated in any way his duties and responsibilities as Emperor—if anything, he worked harder than ever, more intensely, for longer hours. It was just that these days he seemed to work best when he withdrew from other people…even from Callidora herself. When he worked alone.

Callidora found him in his study, poring over a pile of parchments under lantern-light, and walked over to lay a gentle hand on his shoulder. He turned without startling, as though he was not surprised to find her there, and gave her a slow smile.

"It's late," he said, reaching to lay his hand over her own.

"Yes, I know," she said. "It's always late for you, these days. But I need to talk to you. I've had word…about the situation in the Hippodrome."

"The faction unrest?"

"How much do you know about it?"

"I know that it's been escalating since the summer. I've been hoping it was just a phase—the post-comet madness, maybe, young bucks blowing off steam when the world failed to come to its predicted end."

"Is that why the Praetorian Prefect has been ignoring the reports that have been filed about it?"

"I was not aware that there have been that many."

It might have been her mood, but she heard his words as wilfully defensive, rationalizing his own inaction. She set her teeth a little at that. "Probably more than you know," she said, managing to rein in her irritation, but pulling her hand away from underneath his fingers and crossing her arms across her chest. "And the Hippodrome sees it as indifference, at best. At worst, you—the throne is tacitly taking sides here, and Golden Crown is assuming it has your backing for this because you—the throne, the government—haven't moved to put a stop to it. And White Jewel assumes the same thing, that you are favouring their rivals."

He reached over to tuck a stray strand of hair into place behind her ear—it was a gesture both reflexive, in that these small intimate touches had been so much second nature for them both for so long, and consciously conciliatory, from a man who knew and recognised the signs of gathering displeasure in the woman who had been his other half for so long and sought to head off the storm before it became dangerous. "The throne has always played favourites in the Hippodrome, Callidora. That is not a new thing."

"Yes, but there hasn't been killing before—killing that the Emperor, through his Prefect, does nothing about, and therefore tacitly approves…."

"As to that," Maxentius said, "if you're talking about this latest outrage, I *have* taken action on it. Seven men have been arrested, four from Golden Crown, three from White Jewel, the ringleaders of the whole affair. They're locked up in the Prefect's office, awaiting the execution of their sentence."

"Their *sentence*? They have been tried?"

"They've been up before the magistrates, and it is clear that they have all broken the laws," Maxentius said. "They gave each other up, really. Or lied about each other. Either way, they're all implicated."

"What was the sentence?"

"They will hang. All of them. It's been set for the day after tomorrow."

"I don't know if that's the wisest course of action.…" she began, but he tossed his head impatiently, drawing a hand through his tousled hair.

"You yourself just said that they saw inaction as condoning the faction killings," he said. "It's hardly biased—there are men from both the factions in the cells, and both the factions are seen to be paying the price for this. It's completely impartial. What else would you have me do? Threaten them—with what? The city's already seen far worse than I can do—disease, famine—and the only way to justice now is the straight road. I have to show them I've been watching, that the Empire doesn't sleep."

"They all know you don't sleep. They call you haunted, out in the city. There's tales of you being seen prowling the walls like a ghost at night." He pulled away from her, already beginning his restless pacing around the room. And now she reached for him once more, catching his thin wrist in both her hands. "Come to bed, love. Leave all this—it will keep until morning."

He smiled again, a gentle, tired smile, but she already knew that he would refuse.

"You go," he said. "I'll just finish up here. There's a meeting in the morning for which I need to prepare for—the new law codex.…"

There was a time she had tried to get past this—she had cajoled, wheedled, flirted, almost bullied him into the bedroom when the night's candles started burning low—but even on those nights that he had followed her to their bed and made love to her, she knew he lay beside her afterwards, restless and awake long into the night, and then, when he thought she was asleep, he would rise and walk away again, back to his study, back to his papers, back to his restlessness. Now she knew better—there were times that he finally came to bed on his own, when he was past the ragged edges of exhaustion, and that was the only time he could snatch some sleep. There were times she watched him burning up his life's energy and worried about how much longer he could last.

She sighed, squaring her shoulders, and turned to leave. But she paused at the door, and gave him one last long, troubled look.

"Is there a way you can delay this execution?" she asked quietly. "There's an ugly mood in the city, and I am afraid.…"

"I think it will send a message," Maxentius said.

"Yes," she said. "It will do that. But my instincts tell me that we don't have the whole story here. That we are perhaps punishing the scapegoats."

"Have you got something new to tell me?"

""No," Callidora said, with a sigh. "Not yet, at least. But I have a bad feeling about this."

"I can't go on feelings, Callidora. Not any more. I will follow the truth, as I know it. That's the best I can do."

Sometimes Circassaë's ghost was present very strongly for Callidora, her voice as real and vivid to her as though the woman herself were standing at her side. She heard her now, clearly, her laughter and the words she had spoken in Antacia when she had first told the girl who had been Simonis about Maxentius, the Emperor's son. *You complement one another—he is fair to your dark, he is cool pragmatic north to your hot passionate south, but you probably have far more in common than either of you realises.* They might have changed over the years, the two of them, but that still held true. Callidora worked on instinct, and heart; Maxentius, even with the occasionally rash impulsiveness that seemed to be the legacy of his resurrection from the black plague, still relied on things empirical and pragmatic, the things he saw as truth. That was just the people they both were.

He would do what he would do. She would fret about it.

It was Arkadios, who always cultivated his own sources of information, who brought Callidora the next piece of the puzzle, the morning after her conversation with Maxentius. Arkadios, who had risen through the ranks until he stepped into the position of Grand Chancellor, the same one once held by Sarrus, had a direct and guaranteed access to either Maxentius or Callidora at any time. He had come to speak to the Empress while she was being prepared for an unusual morning audience, requested by a tenant on one of her own more distant estates, someone who had travelled a long way to come and see her…probably to complain about taxes.

"There was a time that some of the folks out there would have been turned away at the gate, because they only came to Visant to make trouble," Arkadios said. "But these weren't, and now they are doing just that."

Callidora pushed aside one of her women who was combing out her hair and turned in her chair to face Arkadios, suddenly aware of a cold wash of prescience, as though all of her formless fears and anxieties were finally coming home to roost and showing their true shape.

"What do you know?" she asked sharply.

"There have been meetings," Arkadios said. "I have a couple of men who are on the fringes of the discontented—but they aren't close enough to the center to know the true agenda. All they can tell me so far is who attends—and it's those who have drifted in over the last couple of years, the dispossessed and the discontented. I've got lists—they include civil servants dismissed from posts when departments were streamlined, and minor landowners who could not cope with the heavier taxes and now find themselves ruined and humiliated—and also former dependents of wealthy men whose incomes have taken a cut and who cannot afford a retinue any more, or at least not as large a one as they used to have. And these last, they are often trained fighting men, mercenaries, and they are for hire to the highest bidder—that is what they do, that's all they know—and there have been those who are both willing and able to pay for their expertise. Money is changing hands, and people who have never carried weapons in the street before are being trained and incited to carry them now."

"The Hippodrome gangs," Callidora said suddenly, things falling into place in her mind with distressing clarity. "If they are planning anything more serious than thuggery in the streets—and from what I hear, that alone is reaching serious enough levels—they will need the sacrificial wave, the people to throw into the arena to be devoured first, a diversion…for whatever else is happening, for whatever is really being planned for those meetings. And they have it—they already have it—Maxentius has taken the Hippodrome leaders, and they are to be executed—"

Callidora was right about the mood of the city—it was ugly, and it got uglier as that day waned and the executions of the Hippodrome men drew closer. Callidora felt uneasy enough to make one last attempt to convince Maxentius to at least delay the carrying out of the sentence—but he was bent on showing that Imperial justice was swift and impartial, and she could not prove anything at all about the involvement of the non-Hippodrome participants in the charade, the men behind the whole affair, the ones in the secret meetings who plotted dissent and possible insurrection against the Empire while others took the fall for their actions.

She could not go to the execution herself—she would have been recognised, and this was a far cry from the days when she walked the streets of Visant praying over the victims of the plague. This time the victims were the seven men who waited with ropes knotted around their necks, with a large and unhappy crowd bearing witness at the edge of the execution ground. Arkadios went for her, and when he returned to her chambers later that afternoon his face told her all that she needed to know—something bad had come to pass, something that would precipitate a storm in the city. Callidora sat in her chair, gripping the armrests, and waited in silence for him to speak.

"It was like listening to distant thunder, *despoina*," Arkadios said. "There was this...rumbling...noise from the crowd. As though there were bears growling somewhere behind the front lines. I kept on hoping that there might be a desperate last-minute reprieve—but no word came, and the executioners were nervous of that crowd and therefore slipshod and careless, and then...."

"What happened?" Callidora demanded.

"Four of the men died at the end of their rope," Arkadios said. "Three... did not. One of those fell to the ground and lay there twitching for a moment or two—he was alive when he fell, but something was already wrong, perhaps he was already choking, or he broke his neck in the fall. But while everyone's attention was on him, the other two...their ropes broke. They fell, but they landed on their feet. Before anyone turned to look to them, they had fled, both of them, their hands still tied behind them—but they ran, trailing frayed rope from the nooses around their necks, and they...they both...they ran into the nearest church, *despoina*, and they holed up in there, claiming right of sanctuary."

"If the rope breaks on a hanged man he is free," Callidora said slowly. "That has always been understood."

"That's not the way the soldiers saw it," Arkadios said. "A dozen soldiers were immediately summoned to guard every exit of that church—and more of them were brought in to disperse the crowds. I stayed, in a secluded place from where I had a good view. I saw those last two men taken. The last I saw of them, they were hustled off surrounded by soldiers. I tried to find out what had become of them—I detoured to the Praetorian Prefect's offices before I came back to the Palace, but if they are back there, my contacts either don't know about it or they won't tell me."

Callidora sighed. "Who were the ones who escaped? Which faction? At least we will know from which side the worst trouble will come over this, and I can find out if the Hippodrome...." She stopped, watching Arkadios's already unhappy expression change to something else, something bleaker, something that said that he had not yet told the worst. "Is there more?" she asked, and then, thinking it through to the logical conclusion, she knew the thing he had not spoken of. "One of the men was Golden Crown, and the other was White Jewel, weren't they? Maxentius wanted to send a message with this sentence— and he sent one, he sent one that he could still live to regret...."

The Emperor's justice had certainly been impartial—he had openly laid the responsibility for the situation on both the factions, equally, without showing favour. But the balance of power in the Hippodrome had always been held in check by the rivalry of the two major players in the arena—and now Maxentius had given them reason to transcend that rivalry. A reason for both the major factions to think of the Emperor…as their common enemy.

CHAPTER TWENTY EIGHT

The botched executions had been performed on a Monday, the first day of a new week. It had not been an auspicious beginning.

The following Tuesday was the first day of the Winter Cup races in the Hippodrome. Callidora offered to accompany Maxentius to the opening ceremonies—if nothing else, then just as an advisor as to the mood of the crowd, which she was still better able to judge than Maxentius could.

"I already know that they are discontented. You don't need to be there to tell me *that*," he told her sharply. "I was the one who commanded the arrests, who gave the men over to judgment, who approved the sentence and authorized the executions. I will come to terms with them, or nobody can." His voice softened a little as he took in the worry in her eyes, and he reached over to touch her cheek. "You cannot help me in the arena," he said. "Not today."

"At least take an extra handful of the Guard. Not that they would help if the mob really turns ugly...but still...."

"That much I can do, for what it's worth" Maxentius said. "I'll take an extra dozen men. Of course, if things go as badly as you think they will, it won't matter how many extra men I have at my back unless I take the Army, and they won't fit in the Kathisma."

Maxentius appeared in the Kathisma at mid-morning, with only half a dozen more armed Palace Guard soldiers than he usually commanded as an escort—it was a gesture to Callidora, and he did not believe their presence carried any real weight in terms of an increase of his own personal safety. He did not really know what he expected of the crowd on the day. He was braced for catcalls or heckling from the stands, or even some sort of more organised protest—but the relative silence that greeted him as he stepped out into the loge of the Kathisma and laid his hands onto the stone balustrade made the hair on the back of his neck stand on end.

This was new. This was almost unprecedented.

If one faction had a grievance, it was usually openly aired on occasions like this, and the opposing factions lost no time in dismissing it or lampooning it or belittling the entire issue, until the whole thing degenerated into an exchange of highly stylised, almost poetic banter between the heralds of the two factions, and was then allowed to lapse when the real business of the day, the races, was ready to begin. The inter-faction squabbles served as a traditional prologue to the races, getting the charioteers' blood up and their competitive spirit spurred into victory, just to show the opposing faction who was right. The races were a trial-by-combat of the grievance aired in the Hippodrome that day—whichever faction won the day in the arena also carried the day in the current argument.

But there was no traditional altercation prepared for this race. There was just a silence, thrown into sharp relief by the undercurrent of low murmur that swept the stands as the Emperor appeared, and all eyes were on the Kathisma. Maxentius paused, allowing his own gaze to sweep across the packed Hippodrome, wishing that he had brought Callidora along after all, because he was at a loss as to what to make of the situation—and in that gap, in the silence that stretched taut between the Emperor and his people, two voices were raised.

Two voices, not in argument, but in unity. The heralds of the White Jewel and the Golden Crown factions, both on their feet, each in the loge box for his own faction's higher officials, both facing the Emperor in the Kathisma.

Both, giving voice to the same words in the same moment, the two trained, powerful voices filled the Hippodrome with sound.

"Clemency," they both said, in unison. "We demand clemency."

Maxentius understood that this was to be a stage-play, already scripted in advance—the only difficulty was that he, who was no doubt expected to participate in the charade, had not been given his lines.

But it would not be the first time when he had been required to land on his feet, think as fast as he spoke, finesse the moment. He signalled his own herald, the trained orator, the one who would be his voice to the Hippodrome crowd.

"Clemency? For whom?"

"Two men were delivered by the One God from the noose that a mortal judge placed around their necks," the Golden Crown herald said.

"Their judge now is their God, not a mortal man," the White Jewel herald said in response. "You, August, have no more power over them."

"They were given into your hand, and they were set free by their God, and your own."

"They sought sanctuary in a house of that God. You took them from that house."

"That was not your right."

"They were beyond mortal justice, and in God's hand."

Maxentius's own herald was at an intrinsic disadvantage here, because he could not respond on his own behalf—there was always a significant lag while the Emperor relayed what he wanted conveyed to the audience, and then the herald had to compose that message into lines of ringing rhetoric, and it all took a little time. But now he finally caught a gap in the double-pronged attack by the faction heralds, and gave Maxentius's reply. "They stood convicted as men who raped, looted, killed. You of the Hippodrome, you yourselves filed complaints about these men's deeds. You demanded that they be punished. The Emperor took the criminals that you yourselves pointed out to him, and he released you from their actions. Free and honest men—of the Hippodrome, of the city— may walk the streets unafraid once more now that these men are no longer prowling there for their next prey. You asked for the Emperor's justice—you have received it, with even hand, no faction held higher than another, all held equally responsible for the crimes that have been committed."

"They were delivered by God," the White Jewel herald said, raising his arm to point at the Kathisma. "You are but a man, like other men. You may not take upon yourself the power of judgment upon their souls."

"They were delivered by God's hand," the Golden Crown herald said, copying his counterpart's action.

Both men stood with accusing fingers pointed at the Emperor standing tall in the Kathisma, the cool breeze stirring the purple cloak that hung from his shoulders.

"Are you saying that the men whose lives you now seek back were unfairly accused?" Maxentius's herald asked, lifting his own arm to point back at the two motionless faction heralds in their boxes. "No, because they were not. Are you claiming that they were unfairly tried, or that no evidence or witnesses were brought to bear on their case? No, you cannot. You asked for Imperial justice, and a deliverance from the gangs running loose in the streets of Visant. You received it. You cannot ask for clemency for men you yourselves have accused of crimes against your own people."

"It is a pitiful justice that cannot be tempered with mercy," the Golden Crown herald said, slowly lowering his arm.

"It is not justice at all," his White Jewel counterpart said, doing likewise, "when it is done to appease an Emperor's guilt at having allowed things to get this far."

There was a moment of silence, and the two faction heralds turned their heads marginally to look at each other across the arena.

"They were murderers," Maxentius's herald said. That was his own contribution. Maxentius had offered nothing but silence to those last two remarks from the stands, and the herald could not let that silence stand. Maxentius knit his brows and frowned at the herald, who flushed and bowed his head briefly in apology.

But he had given the faction heralds the opening they had wanted.

"Would that your father had never had a son, Maxentius Augustus," the White Jewel herald said, and his words fell into the arena like stones into a deep pool, ripples of reaction starting to spread in the White Jewel stands.

"If he had remained childless, he would not have a murderer for a son," the Golden Crown herald said, completing the denunciation.

In the Kathisma, Maxentius recoiled as if physically struck.

The crowd noticed. And in that moment all was lost.

There would be no races that day. The crowd spilled from the stands, boiled over into the arena, and the cry "Murderer!" was taken up by many throats.

And one more thing was being cried out—something that hadn't been heard in the Hippodrome within living memory. The people were no longer divided by faction, kept apart and at a low boil of cheerful rivalry in the arena and the corridors of the Hippodrome. But now they were no longer calling out the name of the Golden Crown, or of the White Jewel. The cry was different. The cry was *Long live the Crown Jewel!*

One of Maxentius's people reached out to touch his shoulder, indicating the door that led from the Kathisma back down the winding stair and into the passage that connected the royal box in the Hippodrome with the heart of the Palace. It was time for retreat—now, while there was still adequate time for the door to be secured. The Emperor was not welcome in the Hippodrome that day.

Maxentius hesitated, his emotions in turmoil—he was at once furious, defensive, angry at having been put into a position where he had to be defensive, and appalled that it had come to this, after he had done what he had conceived to be his duty. But as he glanced back at the angry mob swarming and roiling on the white sands of the arena, he realised that whatever was left to be done with the situation would have to be done from somewhere else. He was no longer safe in the Kathisma.

Maxentius turned with a curt nod, and strode back through the doors, setting his foot onto the stair. He heard the door close behind him, a solid and somehow doomful sound, as though the slow scrape of wood on stone and the thud of the massive bar being dropped into place signified more than just a retreat—it signified a rout, and it was no longer a certainty that the bar would be lifted for him again. He paused at the top of the stair, scowling, and then swept his cloak aside with one hand and hurried down the stair.

Well, but they could be left to themselves for a while, until the fervour burned out. Then they would realise that they were asking for no less than a reversal of an act of Imperial justice for which they themselves had once clamoured, and they would be ready to talk sense again. Maxentius could wait.

Except that he had misjudged the situation, again. The crowd's fervor did not die down, it burned higher.

They poured out into the streets, brandishing flaming torches, shouting *Long live Crown Jewel!* as they spilled out of the Hippodrome and engulfed the city, flowing down the narrower streets in a dense, closely packed crowd, pushing and elbowing one another until they reached the wider thoroughfares closer to the collonaded avenue that led from the Bronze Gate of the Palace to the outer walls. They burst into this as a flood of water released from a dam, gathering up people as they went, and finally pooled around the massive edifice that housed the offices of the City Prefect, the chief law-enforcement official in Visant, and the holding cells where prisoners were incarcerated to await their trial, or the carrying out of their sentence.

The two heralds, at the forefront of the mob, called for the release of the two men who had escaped Maxentius's rope two days before, who had been returned to their Prefecture cells after having been extracted from the place where they had sought their sanctuary; they called out the demands, and the mob punctuated them by a raw roar of excitement and rage. They had not got what they wanted from the Emperor's hands; they were here to take matters into their own.

"To whom should I release these murderes? To the rabble?" the City Prefect replied loftily from his tower. "They have been brought here by Imperial justice. The Emperor has sent no word that they have been reprieved. Here they stay."

The mob was too far gone to take no for an answer. Their solution was simple, and drastic—they surged to the doors of the prefecture, where many of them fell as the Prefect's men defended their bastion—but they were too many, and too angry, and these doors after all had been built more to keep people in than to keep them out. The rioters broke through the defenders, leaving bodies in their wake. They poured into the prefecture hallways; they brandished the keys taken from a dead guard's belt and opened every cell door, setting all the prisoners free, not just the two whom they had asked for, and the released men enthusiastically joined their deliverers.

Whose idea it was to set the whole building on fire was quickly lost in the melee—it might well have been an act of revenge by one of the released prisoners—and by this time it was too late to do anything at all except join the mob or die at its hands. There were men wounded but still alive in the Prefecture, including the City Prefect himself, as the mob deliberately fired the Prefecture tower and then barred the doors from the outside—they heard the cries of those who burned alive as the innards of the building caught and then went up like a giant torch.

This news reached Maxentius within an hour of his retreat from the Kathisma. One of the City Prefect's men brought the message. He'd had the relatively good fortune not to have been inside the building when it was torched, but he had witnessed the entire rampage. He had escaped with nothing more than scrapes and bruises—but he had fled to the Palace, and he had brought the mob with him.

They were frustrated at the Bronze Gate; access was too limited for their numbers to make a difference, and the Palace Guard, better armed and better armoured than the rioters, were easily able to hold them at bay. The mob's one weapon, however, was fire.

One of the Guard was dispatched to the Emperor, while he was still closeted with the Prefecture refugee, with a report of the skirmish at the Bronze Gate itself.

"We threw them back, August, but they managed to get close enough for torches," the Guard reported. "There have been a few places where the fire caught—there's some damage—but the gate and the wall are mostly stone, and they will not burn easily."

Maxentius could see the signs of this if he looked out of the palace windows. First there was a smudge of distant smoke as The Bronze Gate smouldered but did not burn. But the wind suddenly changed, and it took the sparks across the great forum onto first the roof of the Senate House and then onto the great cathedral of the city, the seat of the Patriarch himself, the place where the Emperors of Visant were crowned.

If Maxentius had not known how serious the situation was, he knew it now. The red glow that lit up the streets of his city that night as the Senate House was reduced to ashes and the cathedral to burned-out rubble, were more than enough to convince him. A steady stream of people—Senators, a Bishop and his entourage—managed to flee the flames and seek refuge within the Palace walls. Maxentius left orders at the gate that all who came and asked for sanctuary were to be admitted; in the light of the blazing city, people slipped in ones and twos past the angry and apparently sleepless mob and found their way into the Imperial Palace, where Arkadios worked through the night to feed everyone and find them lodging.

The next morning a pall of black smoke still hung over the Palace, and the air was gritty with ash. Things seemed to have quietened down a little out in the city, or at least he could not hear the roar of the mob clearly any more. But then a man stumbled into the gate, one bloodied arm hanging usless by his side, his face and hands smeared with blood and black ashes, came to deliver a stark message to the Palace.

The Patriarch was trapped at the still-burning cathedral. There was no way out. The main mob seemed to have found other places to be, but there was still a large and angry crowd between the Patriarch and safety—a crowd armed with torches and knives and rocks.

The messenger from the cathedral, hollow-eyed, exhausted, prostrated himself before the Emperor. "His Holiness begs your aid, August. If you do not act, he will die with his church."

The only squad of armed men that Maxentius could send out at short notice were not Visant-born—they were part of a band of barbarian mercenaries from the north, handsome fair-haired men with steel-grey eyes and long blond hair. They were trusted men, but—in a tragic replay of what had been going on in Visant ever since the plague had swept through the city and decimated its population—they had not been in Visant very long, and they were unfamiliar with the things that were commonplace on the street.

They won through to the cathedral, and gathered up the stranded Patriarch and his entourage of tired, soot-smeared priests and acolytes, several of them staggering under the load of treasures saved from the burning church. The mercenaries surrounded these men and began their retreat to the Palace.

They were ambushed from a cross-street by a stray remnant of the previous night's mob, joined now by a handful of women, and a few monks whose sympathies were with the rioters in the aftermath of the condemned men's right of sanctuary in a church having been violated by the Imperial soldiers, monks who had no idea that their Patriarch was in the midst of the armed barbarian band.

Taken by surprise, the barbarians retaliated, giving no quarter—and now there was more blood spilled in the streets, this time by men directly under the Emperor's own orders, and the dead included women and clergy. The barbarians made it back to the Palace without any losses of their own men—but the blow to what remained of goodwill in the streets of Visant was mortal.

Thus far it had seemed to be the Hippodrome alone. But now things took a deeper turn, as new intelligence brought to Maxentius and Callidora began to reveal the true nature of the insurrection.

Several high-ranking Senators were conspicuously absent from the patrician refugees, two of them from the Imperial Council itself. One of them was Sarrus, the former Grand Chancellor. Despite his having appeared to accept Callidora's leadership in the dark days of Maxentius's illness and his long convalescence, he had never let go of the antipathy he had held from the very beginning for Maxentius himself—and now he appeared to have lent his not inconsiderable knowledge and clout to what was quickly shaping to be far more than just a riot by an out-of-control mob. It had turned political.

The next thing that landed in front of Maxentius was no longer a request for clemency for two convicted criminals. It was a demand for the immediate dismissal of three of Maxentius's most senior ministers—the Praetorian Prefect, a man by the name of Tiborus, who was responsible for the execution of Imperial law in Visant; the Quaestor, Rencellus, responsible for the formulating and drawing up the body of those laws; and Tarchus, the Master of the Imperial Treasury, who had been in charge of redrawing the tax laws and subsequently collecting the taxes the Empire called in as due.

Callidora, poring over the document that had arrived with the names of these three officials, frowned at the list.

"If it were only the street thugs, I could see the reasoning behind their wanting you to remove the people who were directly involved with the law—

they took care of the City Prefect themselves, may he rest in peace, and now the obvious next step would be to remove the men to whom he himself answered. But the poorer people…would have no reason to go after Tarchus," she said to Maxentius. "That's the Senators talking. The rich families, the ones who bled taxes under the new law when they had never bled taxes before. They resent Tarchus, and all that he has done. They must have jumped at the chance to see him fall."

"I trust those men," Maxentius said grimly. "If I did not, they would not be in their high places."

Callidora glanced out of the window next to which the two of them sat. The sky was still dark with smoke. "There's your answer to that," she said. "Whoever is really behind this is staying out of harm's way, I would think, but the disposable ones, the Hippodrome crowd, they're still out there with torches. The city is going up in flames, Maxentius."

"You think I should do this thing that they ask of me? Bow to these demands?" Maxentius demanded, drawing himself up to his full height. "Replace these men whom I trust with…with whom, exactly? Someone a charioteer in the Hippodrome might nominate to the position?"

Callidora's eyes flashed a little, at that. "Don't be surprised if you find out that some of those charioteers are far more politically knowledgeable than you think," she said. "In fact, it would not surprise me to know that not a few of them are actually on *your* side in all this. Only in an Imperial peace is there leisure for the races, and the races are their lifeblood. It's your Senators that you should fear. They might have their own candidates for the jobs of those three men. People who might hobble you for the rest of your reign."

"But if I take a stand on this, the city burns," Maxentius said, following her gaze out to the drifting smoke.

"The city is afire whatever you do," Callidora said. "All you can hope for now is to contain the flames. Any way you know how."

"I will speak to them again. At the Hippodrome."

"Yes, that worked well last time," she said, a little acidly. "What do you plan to tell them?"

"That all this has to stop, has to stop right now—we did not survive earthquakes and plagues to have our own people destroy Visant around themselves. They have to listen to reason." Callidora's face was still sceptical, and Maxentius sighed. "Surely there are still sane men in the Hippodrome?" he said. "There has to be a way to resolve this."

"Not with the Hippodrome crowd," said Callidora. "If you give them this, they will assume that *they* won it, with fire and pillage, not some political higher plan. You will be feeding the bear—the anger and the triumph—rather than calming it all down."

"Callidora, the choices are limited," Maxentius snapped. "I intend to propose a solution—I will do as they ask, I will take my chosen people from those offices, but I will replace them with other men of my own choosing. I will not be dictated to about whom I am to have in my own government."

"It's a good plan," Callidora said. "It's a pity it won't work."

"I am willing to swear amnesty for all, if this stops now," Maxentius said. "I will put them to rebuilding, rather than destruction. If I can still turn this...."

"I don't know," Callidora said faintly, unable to take her eyes off the smoke that drifted across the sky. "I don't know how you can...."

Maxentius had a proclamation nailed to the gates of the Palace, telling the rioters that he would appear in the Kathisma at sunset, to discuss the situation. How far and how fast the word would spread, he could not know—but when he stepped out into the Kathisma at the appointed hour it seemed to have worked well enough. The arena was packed with people, some still carrying torches that might have been used to light the multitudes of conflagrations in the city, wavering shadows falling everywhere.

Maxentius addressed them himself, throwing his voice out over the crowd, disdaining the use of the herald.

"I have heard your voice," he said to them, leaning heavily on the stone balustrade of the Kathisma, his knuckles white with the pressure. "I am prepared to replace the men you wish to see gone, with other men whom I deem to be capable of carrying their duties. I will issue the edicts tonight, if I have, in return, your word that you will return peaceably to your homes, and that you will help to put out the fires and to begin to rebuild what has been destroyed. For every man who does this, I swear, here and now, on the holy book of the One God...." He turned a little, gesturing, and a pale priest stepped forward holding up a huge leather-bound copy of the book Maxentius had invoked, a little singed at the edges, salvaged from the rubble of the cathedral. "I will swear, on *this*, a most holy oath that no retribution will be raised against any who committed arson or even killed in these last days. I will swear it, before you all, right now. If you will give me your word in return to do as I ask."

"Men of your choosing? Again?"

"More of the same!"

"Amnesty? Clemency? Like our friends got, after they escaped the noose?"

The catcalls came from the crowd—first one or two, but then they were picked up and echoed by others, and before long there was a growling roar coming from the mob in the arena that shook Maxentius to the core.

There had been a time when he had had a rapport with the people of Visant. There was a time that he had even been one of them—not of the Hippodrome, as Callidora had been, but Leontes had been a common soldier in his time and, in the days that Maxentius had come to Visant, a minor enough aristocrat for the rank to carry no dramatic privileges. The first of those had come when the Imperial diadem had been set on Leontes's head. Before that, before the coronation, Leontes had been a patrician amongst patricians, a citizen of Visant amongst fellow citizens, someone equally at home in a Senatorial banquet hall or talking to soldiers in the field. He had married a woman he himself had raised from a slave.

Although Leontes had enrolled Maxentius into the ranks of the patricians, he had not done anything else to spoil his adopted son or to instill any false airs of superiority within him. Maxentius had started with the novices when he had been given his first instruction in the bearing and use of arms; he had enrolled in the Visant University as a simple scholar, paying his dues, often earning his tuition by performing small services for his tutors; he had joined the ranks of Imperial bureaucracy at a step that might have been higher in the ladder than he should have, given his youth and inexperience. But once installed in his job, he had earned advance and promotion through his own efforts and hard work.

But there was no talking to the crowd any more. The talking was done. There was nothing that Maxentius had to say that the mob wished to hear—other than things Maxentius could not, and would not, say. When he turned his back to the roaring, torch-waving mass of heaving humanity in the Hippodrome arena, he knew that this game had been played, and quite possibly lost—and that the next move was up to the Senators who had taken sides with the populace whom they had urged to the use of knife and torch in the streets.

And that move, with the hand of Sarrus heavy upon it, landed on Maxentius's doorstep before that night was over.

Visant was apparently no longer calling for the removal of three problematic ministers. Now the call was for a much bigger change.

They were demanding a new Emperor.

CHAPTER TWENTY NINE

The mob around the Palace gates fluctuated in numbers—sometimes thousands strong, sometimes only a couple of hundred people—but it was never absent. They occasionally made forays into the Bronze Gate and broke on the Guard, but for the most part they seemed contented to simply camp out in the forums and surrounding streets and besiege the Palace with their mere presence.

News and the occasional refugee still managed to slip past the crowd and into the presence of Maxentius or Callidora.

Two of these messengers arrived at the Empress's quarters, both hurt and bedraggled, exhausted and frightened, their clothes singed at the edges.

One was a novice monk, barely a boy, still beardless—but with eyes that were haunted, and the memory of which would stay with Callidora for a long time to come. She knew him, by sight—he had been one of the boys in the cathedral choir, with a beautiful clear boyhood soprano, until his voice had broken spectacularly when he turned thirteen years old. By that time he had come under the influence of Callidora's sphere, and when he had stepped up to take his monastic vows, it was to a group of monks who professed the Rhakotis creed. He still looked barely old enough to wear a monastic robe—

and his wide-eyed, innocent looks had been an asset when Callidora needed messages slipped past vigilant orthodox clergy to those secretly inclined to her own version of the faith.

The young man had taken the name of Methodius in the monastery, and when he was not running Callidora's errands or those of Father Honorius, the young Brother Methodius had taken up his place in a city hospital and hospice, catering to the indigent and the poor, and particularly to the sick and battered women of the lower echelons of Visant. It was something that Callidora herself had endowed, and it was housed in the very dwelling in which she had once taken up residence herself, when she had first returned to Visant after her travels in the East—the place where she had sat spinning her wool on the steps by her front door, the place where she had first set eyes on Maxentius.

The house had been rented, back then, but after her marriage, with the revenues of the Augusta's household at her disposal and the House of Peacocks hers, Callidora had gone back and purchased the house where it had all begun—that house, and the one next to it on the street. And she had had workers knock down walls and rebuild its interiors, with monastic cells in the back and on the upper storey, wards for the sick and the needy on the ground floors. It had been a place where she had returned over and over when the plague was at its worst in Visant—the place where people who had nowhere else to go had come to die. In the aftermath of the scourge, when they had taken dozens of bodies out of that place every day, it had been scrubbed down to the bare boards and then freshly whitewashed—it was a place of faith, where death was not the end but a stepping stone to a heavenly reward, where people came to be cured if cure was possible and to be gently eased into the next life if it was not. Nobody was turned away, if there was any way at all to accommodate them—and if there was no room at all, then the young monks who worked at the place would find them alternative places to go.

"I come from your House, Augusta," Brother Methodius said to Callidora, kneeling at her feet. "At least...from the place where it used to be. I come with...terrible news...."

He was still young enough, and this was bad enough, for his control to be less than equal to the moment. He actually doubled over, pressing his forehead to his knees, sobbing hard enough to shake his whole body and retching dryly when the sobs were done, as though he were trying to rid his body of every trace of the memories that clung to him, that would not let go, that would never let go.

Callidora was white. She could smell the smoke on him, even without the telltale burns on his hands and the scorched holes in his habit. If he came as he was from her House of Healing in the city, that could mean only one thing.

"Tell me," she said, and her voice was very gentle. There was enough anguish in the youth to last him his whole lifetime; she would not add more by letting him see her own.

She signalled for water and he struggled to regain his composure, accepting gratefully a goblet of cold water and draining it in one long gulping draught.

"They did not mean it, Augusta," Brother Methodius said, turning those wide eyes up to the Empress, pleading with her to agree with him on this. "They could not have meant it. At least, I did not see anyone set it deliberately. But the city—the city is on fire, and the wind blows where it will. And even things that have not been set alight...."

Callidora's hand clenched at her side, hidden underneath the folds of her robe. "What happened, Brother Methodius?"

"I—I was upstairs," the boy monk said. "It was my quiet hour. I was in my cell, meditating...and then I heard it. The noise."

"What noise?"

"At first I thought it was something cracking, or creaking, or a howl of trapped wind somewhere. But then I heard the first screams...." He swallowed. "I couldn't even smell the smoke. Not at first. But then, when I started down the stairs...."

Callidora waited for him. There would be no hurrying this story. This was a demon that would come at its own pace, in its own time.

"By the time I was halfway down to the second level, I turned around and I could see...I could see...it was too light upstairs. And then I smelled the smoke. And the screaming was coming from both above and below. And I...I froze...there on the stairs...there were people that needed help, and they were everywhere, and I didn't know where to go...but then I thought that those below had more need, many of them were sick, and could not run, could not move, not by themselves. I had no idea who was still upstairs—they might have needed my help—but the others, those below, the sick and the hurt in the wards, they needed *me*, myself, my physical presence, my shoulder to lean on. So I turned my back on my brethren...."

He choked again, covering his face with his hands. After a moment he seemed to make his slight body stop shaking by main force of will and looked up at Callidora again.

"Downstairs..." he began, and his voice gave out, his eyes filling with tears.

Callidora's own hand was at her mouth, covering her lips, her fingers trembling on her cheek—but she said nothing, letting Brother Methodius compose himself to the best of his ability. He swallowed hard, once, twice, and then squared his shoulders and lifted his head again.

"The wards were already on fire by the time that I stepped off the stair—and then I heard the stair fall behind me as something higher up gave way. There was no going back. And in the wards—there were a couple of my brothers there, and they were trying to get some of the patients out. I saw one of them dragging a man who had come to us only a couple of days ago—he had been in a bad accident, down by the wharfs, his leg had been crushed between a docking ship and the edge of the wharf itself—he could not move, could not get out of the way, not by himself, and I could not help...seeing...he must have been too close to one of the fires, because...because his hair...his face...." He swallowed again. "Augusta, the smell...and the way his face looked...and my brother's arms were burned, too, up until his elbows, and I could see his sleeves were still smouldering at the edges...I tried to rush over to help, but there were other screams, all around me, and I turned to see...."

"The fire...?" Callidora managed, in a whisper.

"It was too late to fight that, too late already, too late by a long way. We needed to save those who were close enough to save. I had to let my brother who already had the man with the crushed foot try and get him out, by himself, as best he could. For myself—there was a girl, barely more than a child, she came to us heavily pregnant, we had no idea how close the birth she was but she looked like she might drop the baby at any moment—and she was lying on her pallet in a corner, on her back, and could not turn, and was screaming for help—and I tried to go and get her—and that was when one of the beams...."

Brother Methodius actually turned away and threw up on the Empress's woven carpet, a thin stream of greenish-white bile dribbling out of the corners of his mouth.

"I...I ran, Augusta," he said at last, wiping his lips with his sleeve. He could not meet her eyes any more. "I saw more die. One of my brethren. At least two of the patients from the ward. I heard them all calling for me, for my help... and I ran. I could hear them calling. I could smell...I could smell burned flesh. And the fire had leapt to the next house by then, too, and the street was full of ashes, and I...I ran."

"Nobody can blame you," Callidora said, her own eyes full of tears. "There was nothing you could do. Nothing. Nothing except seek your own death in there."

"But others did that, Augusta," Brother Methodius whispered. "They are with God now, all of them. And I…I live, instead. And I will never forgive myself."

"God will forgive you. You are young. Go, now, and rest—and I will make sure you are safe."

Callidora could not reach Maxentius, closeted with messengers of his own, or high-ranking officials of the state trying to find a way out of the quagmire that the riots had degenerated into.

Alone, she received word of another messenger who had got through the blockade. The second messenger was from Belenus, Callidora's Obsidian Knife contact from the Hippodrome. Belenus himself was caught up in what was going on in the arena. But a couple of his people had got through to Callidora, especially in the very early hours of the developing situation, when the noose around the Palace was not yet so tight, carrying their messages committed to memory and not on any incriminating written notes.

Belenus's information was enormously valuable. He had been able, somehow, to quickly gain the trust of at least one of the Senators whom he had found to be working with the Hippodrome factions—enough to find out more about the conspiracy than the Senator thought he had allowed to slip. It was thanks to Belenus, and the second messenger that she received on this harrowing day, that Callidora could finally breach Maxentius's defenses and go to him directly with a list of names, with Sarrus at the very top of it, of the Senators who had betrayed him.

Maxentius had stared at that list for a few long, silent moments—and although Callidora, because of all the years they had been together, could nearly always tell exactly what he was thinking, she found herself completely shut out now, his bleak fury a cold wall.

"All right," he said at last, clenching his hand so that the list of the names that she had written down for him crumpled in his fist. "All right then. Perhaps it is time to throw them all out to the wolves."

"What do you mean to do?" she asked, seized by an irrational panic.

"They came running here, for safety," Maxentius said. "What kind of safety were they seeking here, behind these walls, when that which they fight for is out there in the burning city…? They all have houses and estates out there. Let them all go to those, and barricade their own walls against the mob if they fear it. This Palace…was not built for a siege. We have, by God's grace, our own spring and our wells and our cisterns and we will not run out of water—but food is another matter, and we are not prepared to endure for too long without fresh deliveries."

He had been caught up in his own anger and frustration, but he suddenly took a closer look at Callidora's face and stopped, narrowing his eyes.

"What else has happened?"

Callidora told him, haltingly, of what she had learned from the fleeing Brother Methodius.

She might have wept over it, in his arms, if she could have found him in the immediate aftermath—but it had cooled now. It was still a vivid pain, but she had always known how to bear pain by herself. She too had been angry at first, had been appalled, had even been consumed, however briefly, by her old burden of guilt. But she had had a little time to think, and to remember Father Honorius's words to her when she had thought that the scourge of the plague had been her punishment. Hubris, he had called it. However great her guilt, she could not take the responsibility for every ill thing that came home to roost in the City of Gold.

But Maxentius had not heard this before, and his own reactions to the things she was telling him ripped open her own wounds all over again. She had thought she was numb, that she could bear it all now, that nothing further could make the burden any heavier—but she could hear the roaring of her shadow-bear in her ears, and she could not bear to look at the stark expression on Maxentius's face.

His lips had tightened into a thin line. "It might have all turned out well if the patricians hadn't started stirring the pot," he said. "The people had their own grievances. Fine. We could have settled that. We always have. But then the Senators—Sarrus—saw an opportunity in the whole mess, and threw their weight and their own agenda behind the uprising.... *They* began this. At the very least it was they who raised the stakes, and now it's a fight to the death, and there are innocents, as always, caught between the grinding stones.... They will go, all of them. All of the Senators cowering in the corners of the Palace. Within the hour."

"Not all of them have turned against you—if you turn the ones who favour you out to the wolves, Maxentius, you may be forcing their hand...."

"That is for the One God to decide. I know what I must do."

"Do you even know who is sheltering here?"

"Arkadios will have a list."

The list was long. Callidora, exhausted and uncharacteristically perfunctory, managed only a brief scan of it before Arkadios took it off to Maxentius for his approval—and there was a name somewhere on it that she knew was vitally important. But she had been hurt. She was still preoccupied, still mourning the loss of the House of Healing. The important name slipped into her mind and out again, leaving just a memory of its passing, a nagging insistence that she should have been paying closer attention.

She had sought solitude, and had walked down the length of the Imperial gardens, all the way to the private jetty and the little beach beside it that curved into the bay. The day was drawing to a close. Callidora slipped into the shadows, so perfectly suited to her mood, and wrapped them around her, and lost herself in them for a brief while. She lingered down by the water, stealing peace, knowing that there was too much light in the sky for the hour of the day that it was, knowing why that was so, the fires of Visant burning a trail of ashes on her own soul.

Eventually, tired and troubled, she drifted off into a sort of uneasy state where she was half asleep and half awake, her thoughts skating across the surface of her mind like dragonflies on a pond, alighting gently now and then, touching down and leaving ripples in their wake before launching again and disappearing into the twilight.

It was one of those ripples that finally connected the name she had seen on the list of the Senators and patricians that Maxentius meant to expel from the Palace—had already expelled from the Palace, for all Callidora knew, while she was dallying here by the sea—and the jeopardy into which Maxentius himself had thrown his reign.

The mob—backed by Sarrus and his hand-picked Senators—had called for a new Emperor. They could have picked any candidate they wanted—but that candidate had to have at least some legitimacy for the name to be acceptable to all three parts of the Visant society traditionally called upon to acclaim an Emperor: the Senate, the Army and the people themselves. Sarrus had suborned, or could suborn, the Senate; the people were running wild out in the streets, and could be gathered up into the palm of Sarrus's hand if the right name was dangled before them; the Army was still silent, but it would go with the majority, in the end, if it came to that.

The reason Callidora had not responded instantly to the name on Arkadios's list was that she was so unused to seeing it on its own—the nephews of Valerian Augustus, Emperor before Leontes who had not succeeded their uncle, almost always came as a set. But under the current strained circumstances on the eastern borders of the Empire, Severus, the general, was out on the front lines somewhere with his legions.

The eldest of the three brothers, Petronus, had not been on Arkadios' list of those taking refuge in the Palace—if he was anything at all, the man was almost preternaturally aware of any potential personal danger, and supremely adept at getting out of its way; Callidora had no difficulty imagining that he had already gone, fled Visant before the mob took to the streets, too afraid of what might happen to him if he stumbled into their path.

The youngest brother, Gennadius, was not distinguished by even that much. If someone had offered him a free banquet or a chance at a debauch, he would have gone in a heartbeat, and would have sat happily downing wine or (it was said) playing with a pretty boy, oblivious while the jaws of hell itself closed around him.

Gennadius was on Arkadios's list.

He had been amongst the first of the refugees from the city to run straight to the Palace to hide behind walls, and none of them—not Maxentius, not Callidora, not even faithful Arkadios—had thought about him as a possible potential candidate for the voices calling for a new Emperor. Instead, he had been part of the group of Senators whom Maxentius had expelled from the Palace…and he was out there now, in the city, a NOUN ripe for the plucking by the conspirators as soon as they worked out that he was in circulation.

Maxentius had just handed his enemies the man whom they could use to replace him. Gennadius was painfully perfect for Sarrus's purposes—he was no soldier, being timid and afraid of his own shadow; he had no interest in statecraft; and he was completely pliable in the right hands. With Gennadius as a figurehead emperor on the throne of Visant, the Empire would really be ruled by whichever man fought hardest for Gennadius's ear.

Callidora scrambled to her feet, breathless, aware of a sinking feeling that she had allowed her instincts to sleep, that she was far too late. She now hoisted the skirts of her robe up with both hands and raced like any hoyden up the steep garden path towards the looming walls of the Palace proper, heedless of the pins flying from her hair as she ran or of the picture she presented as she skidded to a halt at the main entrance and hurried down the endless corridors which led to Maxentius's private quarters.

He was not there, but a number of his silentiaries were; she sent at least three of them to three possible places that the Emperor might be, with an urgent message to return to his chambers.

Maxentius returned some half an hour later with the third of these, wearing an expression that was equal parts worry and exasperation.

"What is it, Callidora? He said you told him to get me at all costs—that it was urgent.…"

"I'm sorry," she said. She had had time to gather herself and she'd tidied her hair up as best she could with what pins remained, but it still half-spilled free in escaping curls down her shoulders and back; she'd got her breath back, but her cheeks were still a hectic feverish flush. "Are they gone?"

"Who?"

"The Senators whom you wanted to throw out of the Palace—are they gone?"

"Yes. They left...."

"*All* of them?"

"Yes, all—Callidora—what is the matter?"

She slumped against the chair on which she had been leaning.

"Too late," she said. "Gennadius was amongst those men, Maxentius."

He stared at her in silence.

"I saw it," she continued, knowing that she was babbling now, unable to stop. "I saw his name on the list. I saw, but I didn't look long enough or hard enough or make the connection—not until less than an hour ago—I was hoping you had delayed, that he might still be here...." She lifted her eyes to his, and they were wide, and scared. "You let loose the Emperor's nephew. They wanted a new Emperor—and now they have a candidate. He is precisely what Sarrus wants, and the stars are against us on this day—Sarrus is going to find him. One way or another, he will. I know it." She lifted her hands and pressed them against her breast. "I know it in here. I can feel it coming."

"It might still take them too long to be useful," Maxentius said, after a beat of silence.

They both knew he did not believe his own words.

A single tear spilled out of Callidora's suddenly brimming eyes, and rolled unchecked down her cheek.

"No," she said. "We're out of time."

It wasn't until just before dawn the next morning that they realised just how right she had been. Belenus had sent one more urgent message, one that was brought by sea by a single man in a rowboat, scrambling up through the gardens in the dark in search of the Empress, discovered by a pair of Palace guards who very nearly killed him before he convinced them to conduct him to Callidora.

She had not thought that she would sleep, but Arkadios, who had intercepted the messenger and knew about Belenus and his couriers, woke her from a light, restless slumber just as the sky was starting to lighten in the east.

"*Despoina*," Arkadios said grimly, "it pains me deeply to steal your sleep, but there is a man you must see...."

The messenger was thin, wiry, rat-faced, shifty-eyed—the kind of man who would not ordinarily, at first glance, command trust. But he knew the code words that Belenus and Callidora had set up, and he had shattering news.

"I was there myself, Empress. I saw it all—everything," he said, almost boastfully. "First they had gone to Petronus's house, to get him, but he was not there, but his wifewas, and she would not or could not tell them where to find him. So they threw her out of the house and set it alight. That seems to be a popular pastime out there right now." He turned his head marginally, as though he had been planning to spit, but realised in time where he was and desisted from the impulse. "Then I followed them wherever they went," he continued, "and sure enough, when they couldn't get either Petronus or Severus—too far out of reach—they found Gennadius, who had come crawling to his brother's house and found it a burned out shell, and they decided that he would do. His connections were too good, what with him being Emperor's Valerian's nephew. He was just what they needed. He did refuse them, three times, when they acclaimed him Emperor on the steps of his brother's house, some of it still in flames behind him—his sister-n-law, Petronus's wife, warned him like a sibyl— she pointed her finger at him and told him that if he accepted this it would be the death of him—but they actually kicked her down until she shut up, and the fourth time they acclaimed him Augustus he did not say no. He didn't say anything much, come to think of it, and I think he looked more terrified than exalted, but there you have it. They have their Emperor. They plan on bringing him to the Hippodrome today, this morning—they have no diadem, of course, and the doors of the Kathisma are still guarded—but they will do what they can. Before noon today, come what may, there will be two Emperors in the city of Visant."

Callidora turned to Arkadios, dark circles under eyes that burned feverishly in her thin face. "Arkadios, Maxentius...."

"I will go myself, *despoina*," Arkadios said, and was gone.

Two of the detachment of the Palace Guard who had caught Belenus's man in the gardens and brought him to the Empress were still waiting a few steps back, their attitude respectful but not deferential.

"Let him go," Callidora said. "And then—you will get your orders from Maxentius Augustus—but you should gather up your cohorts—the Kathisma...."

"Empress," one of the Guards said, interrupting politely, "we will stand, at the Kathisma—we will not allow anyone to gain entry into the Palace or the Grounds through those doors. That is our sworn duty, and we will abide by it.

But neither will we suffer anyone to issue forth upon the Kathisma from this side. Until this is settled and we know who the true Emperor is who will sit on the throne of Visant…we are the barrier between you. We are the border that may not be crossed. But we will not take up the fight, on either side." He reached out and tapped the messenger on the shoulder, none too gently. "You. Go the way you came. Nobody will stand in your way. Lady, my respects. Today will tell the full tale."

The messenger needed no further words. After a last long, apprising look at Callidora, he melted into the shadows of the morning, and was gone.

The two Guards saluted Callidora, and departed.

She was left alone, frozen where she stood, staring up at what promised to be the cloudless, deep blue sky of a perfect winter's day.

After a moment Callidora cupped her elbows with her hands, wrapping her arms around one another, realising that she was shivering. The morning air had a bite to it, to be sure, but what chilled her went far deeper than that.

Today will tell the full tale.

She was acutely aware that she might be staring at the dawn of her last day as Empress of Visant.

CHAPTER THIRTY

Maxentius called an emergency council session as soon as Arkadios brought the news of Gennadius's acclamation to him—but it still took until mid-morning for all to assemble.

The Emperor looked haggard and tired; it had been one of those nights when sleep had eluded him completely. The morning's news had not improved things, but before coming to preside over the council, Maxentius had changed into a fresh, simple robe and his fair hair, now with a few traces of grey in it, was damp and slicked back against his skull. He resembled the least, rather than the highest, of the people in the room as his councillors began to arrive, dressed in such court finery they could manage to scrape together at such short notice; the exceptions were the two generals, Valentinian and Kalos, who wore the same war-worn garb out of which they had not changed for the last few days—and Callidora herself.

She arrived last, late, and dressed in the full Imperial regalia of the Empress of Visant.

Maxentius said nothing, but his face changed, a little. She noticed and allowed herself a small pang of remorse—it had not been intended to make a point, or to show him up. It had simply been that shiver in the cold light of dawn, the sense that this might be the last day she would greet as the Augusta, and there was something in her, deep and superstitious—that shadow-bear that she always carried, perhaps—that demanded that she wear her crown on such a day.

The council had already started by the time she arrived—it took time to do justice to her regalia, and she had taken the time she needed. It had been worth it, in the end, simply for the looks on everyone's faces as she had entered—in the way that the bows offered to her were just a little deeper than usual, as though the men in the council room had been reminded just in whose presence they were. Callidora acknowledged their bows, as she walked down the length of the room, and installed herself with dignity and grace in her chair at the head of the council table, next to Maxentius.

She raked the table with her gaze. Three empty seats—Sarrus, two others. For the rest, the three men whom the mob had wanted Maxentius to replace were all present—Tiborus, the Praetorian Prefect; Rencellus, the Quaestor; Tarchus, the Master of the Imperial Treasury. Others were there, too—Masters of various administrative and legislative Imperial offices; Count Photius, the new royal physician, the successor to the healer who had presided over Maxentius's triumph over the plague and who had himself succcumbed to it in the waning days of the epidemic.

Arkadios, her friend, now Grand Chancellor, and the only man in the room save Maxentius himself whom Callidora fully trusted.

"The Palace Guards were indeed a surprise," Valentinian said after the Empress was settled in her chair, continuing the on-going topic of discussion. "And not a pleasant one. This stance of theirs—this 'neutrailty'—it's childish, this play on their deciding that neither man was Emperor until one won this tussle. I was counting on them as a last-resort back-up, here in the city—we simply cannot bring in the numbers of men it would take, quickly enough, to rely on the army itself. All told, I have maybe seven hundred men under my command here, and they include regiments that are of a mercenary nature and may or may not follow me into a pitched battle, if they are led to believe that someone else will very soon be in a position to be paying their wages. That is not a lot to hold a city with."

"That, and my five or six hundred," Kalos said grimly. "Between us, we command less than two thousand armed men. It isn't that the Palace Guard would add measurably to those numbers—but if there is a call for the army regiments outside the Palace now, I am not at all certain that I would not leave some of my men behind—men under my own command, men I trust, men who did not declare their neutrality until someone else decides who their

Emperor should be. They swore their loyalty—they swore their loyalty to *you*, Augustus, when you were crowned...."

"They swore loyalty to the crown," Maxentius said. "They don't swear to be loyal unto death to an individual—their responsibility is to defend the Palace, and to protect the man who wears the crown to which their loyalty is sworn. They have no obligation to me, personally. No, I do not blame the Guard. They are doing precisely what their oaths require them to do."

"Would you trust them with your life?"

"As long as I am Augustus and wear the diadem lawfully bestowed to me by the church and the people, yes," Maxentius said. "As long the Imperial diadem sits on my own brow, and not somebody else's."

"Well, the regalia are safe in the vaults," one of the Masters commented dryly. "At the very least they cannot crown Gennadius with that until they manage to break into the Palace itself."

A silentiary opened the door of the council chamber a crack and slipped inside.

"Begging your pardon, Your Excellencies, August—there are two men waiting, with news...."

"Bring them in!"

One of the men who stepped into the council chamber was obviously one of the Palace Guard—but he looked uncomfortable, and his uniform was incomplete, as though he had tried to divest himself of some of the more obvious marks of his occupation or identity. The other was dressed in civilian clothes, but carried himself like a soldier.

"Respects, August," the Guard said, hestitating. "I am here...on my own behalf, not as a representative of...I am not sure if I am still Guard, at all, because I deserted my post to come and bring this news to you."

"And your post was?" Maxentius said sharply.

"The Kathisma door, August. I was on duty there this morning, I and one other. I stood between the Hippodrome and the Palace this morning."

"And what did you come here to report?"

"I could not hear, not clearly, the door is thick," the Guard said. "But this much I can tell you. They have Gennadius there. In the Kathisma. Right now. And the shouts from the arena are loud enough to be heard even through the thickness of that door. He has been acclaimed, August—acclaimed in the Hippodrome, as Emperor."

"Yes," said the other man, "he speaks the truth. I have come from that arena. I saw it happen."

Kalos turned to the Emperor. "He is one of my own men, August," he said. "I sent him out as a civilian this morning—I sent a handful out—to find out what he could from the Hippodrome."

Maxentius lifted a hand for silence. "Hold," he said. And then turned back to the uncomfortable Guard. "I know what this cost," he said quietly. "I am grateful. Name what post you will, in the army or here in the Palace on my own staff, and it is yours."

He stopped short of uttering the corollary to that—*so long as I am able to give the orders here*—but they all heard it. The Guard opened his mouth to speak, but the generals exchanged glances and then Valentinian straightened, giving a formal military salute.

"I would be honoured to have you as a lieutenant," he said.

"Soldiering is all I know," the Guard said. "I accept, Excellency."

"There is an aide waiting in the anteroom," Valentinian said. "Report to him, and tell him to find you quarters and gear. I will attend to other matters personally, once this meeting is over."

The Guard bowed deeply, and retired.

Maxentius waited until the door was closed behind him, and then turned back to the other man, the witness.

"Now," he said. "Tell us."

"They used the acrobats," Kalos's man said.

"Acrobats? For what?"

"To gain entry into the Kathisma, from below, from the arena. It was quite beautiful to watch, really—a bravura performance, both the Golden Crown and the White Jewel acrobats, some of both factions' best. They made a human pyramid, from the stands—it took quite a few of them, standing on one another's shoulders, until the one at the top—I think it was a woman, actually, and a young one at that—could reach up to the edge of the balustrade and vault over into the box itself. It was beautifully done, truly, almost a dance— she gained the Kathisma, and then she helped another follow, and then they unbarred the side door to those who waited in the arena with Gennadius. And Sarrus—he was wearing a chain like a Grand Chancellor wears, much like your own, Excellency—" He nodded at Arkadios, whose lips tightened.

Valentinian and Kalos exchanged another glance.

"That is something to consider," Valentinian said softly. "The Kathisma has a direct passage to the Palace itself. And we have all seen how easy it is for trusted guards to be…not so trusted any longer. If there is an easy way to gain entry from the Hippodrome—then—"

"Easy, if you have tame acrobats," one of the administrative offices Masters said.

"And that is precisely what the Hippodrome does have, in abundance," Valentinian said. "This was a dangerous oversight."

Maxentius made a sharp gesture with his hand. "Emperors have been assassinated before, but never by acrobats from the Hippodrome," he snapped. "It hasn't been a problem for hundreds of years. If they gained entry, they would have to come one at a time down the winding stair, and then into that narrow bottleneck of a corridor below. That could be held by two men against a thousand, for as long as it took for the bodies of the dead to pile up high enough for road into the Palace to be barred to the living."

"But one betrayal," one of the Masters murmured thoughtfully. "One betrayal. *One*. Enough for those two men not to be present at the bottom of the stair. Or, as the Guard might still do, if they stood by and did nothing to stop those who swarmed down...."

Maxentius quelled him with a look. "I said I trusted the Guard to protect the Crown," he said. "I meant it." He turned back to the man who had brought in the report from the arena. "Continue," he said tightly.

"They took Gennadius up, once they had gained access to the Kathisma itself—Sarrus, and a couple of other Senators, and several bodyguards who looked well enough armed to me. They even had a couple of priests," the soldier-spy said.

"They have the Church?" Rencellus, the Quaestor, asked abruptly, sitting up in his chair. "Has the Patriarch...?"

"No, there has been nothing official," said Tiborus. "I still have ears. I would have known. It's a couple of renegade priests—it's a ploy, to make it all seem legitimate. But however they dress it up, there is one thing they cannot produce."

"The diadem," Tarchus said. Master of the Royal Treasury. There was a special office which dealt directly and only with the Imperial regalia, but they fell under his jurisdiction—and he, better than anyone, knew that the Imperial diadem and all that it meant were still safely locked away in the vaults. "They cannot crown an Emperor without a crown—and a priest off the street is hardly the Patriarch. We still have both, here, in the Palace."

"They did crown him, sort of," Kalos's man said. "One of the Senators took a gold chain from his own shoulders and draped it over Gennadius's head. There is gold on his head, and they called it a crown, and they called him an Emperor. If you ask me, he looked more petrified than anything else—there was probably a part of him that was lapping it up, who wouldn't—but there was another part of him that was ready to bolt at the first opportunity. I was close to the Kathisma, right there in the stands, I could clearly see his face."

"They demanded the true regalia. I know, because I was there when they did it," Kalos said. "I went up to the Kathisma door this morning. The Guards on duty—one of them was indeed the man who came to see the council this morning, August—spoke me fair. But they did not budge from their posts, and they made it plain that they would not hesitate to use whatever force was necessary to stop me if I tried TO WHAT?. I'm not entirely sure what changed the mind of the man who then decided to abandon his post and come here to warn you of what transpired. Be that as it may—it was while I was there that someone started thumping heavily on the door, from the Kathisma side. It was muffled, to be sure—but I am certain enough of what I thought I heard them say. They had, as they shouted, the Emperor, and now they wanted the diadem to crown him with."

"They were at the Bronze Gate with that demand, too," Valentinian said. "And at the Ivory Gate. Both were held by the Guard, and they let nobody through. That is to say, they allow anyone who wishes to do so to leave the Palace, without hindrance—but they will let nobody *enter*—not even, since you cleared the Palace, August, someone claiming refuge or sanctuary—nobody, unless there is someone there at the gate who knows the person seeking admittance and will vouch for that person. We were besieged before, but now the Guard is adding a layer to that—we could slip people in and out then, and we knew some of what was going on—but now we're all locked in here like rats in a trap. They are guarding the Palace from the city, and they are also guarding the city from the Palace."

"Then how did your man get back in, Kalos?" Maxentius demanded.

"The sea," Kalos said. "There are rowing boats, and the Palace's jetty is still open. They do not hold the harbour, or the shipping, or the sea lanes. We do know that much. The sea is the only open way."

"Are they letting anything *else* in?" one of the Masters asked abruptly. "It seems to me that we will be running short of food eventually, if nothing is allowed to come in from the outside…."

"And just from where would it come, and how would it pass through the streets without failing?" Kalos said. "We have sortied a few times—the ban on coming and going does not apply, it seems, to the troops—the One God knows the way of it, I certainly don't claim to understand what the Palace Guard are thinking—neutrality? *Now*? What kind of an ill-timed gesture of…."

"There is that," Count Photius said slowly.

Faces turned toward him, expresions quizzical. Maxentius raised an eyebrow.

"Well, the isolation, I mean," Photius said, fumbling a little under the concerted scrutiny. "That will work against us. I have a limited amount of material with which I can treat wounds or disease, and no likelihood of getting more unless it is delivered, somehow, from somewhere from the outside eventually. Once I run through the medical supplies in the Palace right now, I don't see an obvious way of getting more. Unless...."

"Unless?" Maxentius prompted.

"Well, the sea," Photius said. "They said the sea was still open. Can we use the sea to ferry in what we need?"

"The sea is still open because the men leading the insurrection haven't thought about that quite yet—they do not have sailors in their ranks, and the sea is of a secondary importance to them," said Tiborus, the Praetorian Prefect. "But they will think of it all the faster if we suddenly clog the waterways with all manner of craft and start bringing in huge amounts of supplies. No, the way to deal with this is to wait it out, lie low...."

"Wait," Tarchus said, cutting him off. "Wait a moment. The sea is open? We have a way out at our backs? I had thought us pinned down here with no escape—but now suddenly there's been one all along? August...it's been said over and over again that they cannot crown a new Emperor without the Imperial regalia, without the Patriarch. Why do we not take these things, and your own self, to safety? August—if we do not give them the regalia, they may take it into their heads to come in and take what they want, one way or another. It would be bloody and their casualties would be enormous—but they might still do it, anyway...."

"If they have their tame priests, and the Patriach is gone, what is to stop them for creating another Patriarch just the same as they created a new Emperor?" Arkadios said slowly. "It may yet come to a battle. But taking the Patriatch out of Visant right now means nothing at all—and that doesn't begin to take into account the fact that the Patriarch himself—who is, I might remind you, not present to speak for himself here—may not wish to leave at all. What do you plan to do then—kidnap the highest official in the church, stuff him in a sack, and take him out on a dinghy like a bag of turnips and against his own will?"

"But Tarchus has a point," said Rencellus. "All this—re-creating the entire society they need to make the new Emperor legitimate in the eyes of the city, of the Empire—all of this will take time. We are partly pinned here because we are so badly outnumbered. The enemy might be less disciplined than a cohort of Imperial soldiers, to be sure, and they are certainly less well armed—but when there are ten of them to one of you, I would think that your odds just went down a little, no?"

Kalos thinned his lips. "They are rabble," he said. "But they are many, and they have been kept at a fever pitch, and they are dangerous because they are drunk with their power...."

"*Now*," Rencellus said. "Of course they are. They have just seen a new 'Emperor' crowned before their eyes—this is a game of circuses with them. For the love of the One God Himself, they used Hippodrome acrobats to gain access to the Kathisma. How much more of a spectacle can this be? They're still at the height of their fury, of their excitement and their exhilaration. But let them cool down a little and think...."

One of the Masters on the other side of the table gave a short sharp laugh. "When have you ever known them to think?" he said acidly. "Let Sarrus and his henchmen keep the gold and the bread flowing long enough, they'll come running to the Hippodrome and acclaim Gennadius for as long as it takes."

"As long as it takes to do what?"

"To get the real crown on Gennadius's head," Tarchus said.

"Then the true Emperor would have to be dead," Arkadios said. "And Maxentius Augustus is not, I think, ready to lie down and die yet."

But Maxentius was staring at his councillors, his eyes lingering on face after face, reading their expressions, their thoughts, the plans and schemes hatching in their minds.

"You think I should leave the Palace? The city itself?"

"I think it would be an excellent idea, Augustus," Rencellus said, after a pause. "You will remove yourself from danger, you will have the Imperial regalia with you, and the Patriarch—if he is willing to come, that is—" He shot a quick, acid look in Arkadios's direction. "The Patriarch will be there to lend legitimacy to your own cause. And the generals would have the time to muster the army, the real army, and then we could return and make certain that Gennadius never sits on the holy throne of Visant—or at the very least does so only long enough to regret it."

"I agree, Augustus," Tarchus said. "I could have the regalia safely gathered and packed and ready to go within an hour—and the sea, the sea is still ours. And there is plenty of gold in the treasury. We will have more than enough to take with us for the army to be paid, and for all our own necessities."

"But go where?" Maxentius said. "And for how long?"

"Anywhere that the Empire reaches, Augustus," Rencellus said. "You have estates of your own to which you could pull back and regroup for the time being—or, if you wanted to stay close to the center of things, there is always a place like Antacia. It once served as a secondary capital to the Empire when it was young—it could serve as such again, until we can return and claim Visant one more time...."

The words and the voices faded around Callidora, blending into a rush of white noise...into a roar, the roar of the shadow-bear that she carried, stronger and louder and containing more raw power and fury than she had ever sensed in it before. It was as though this moment was the reason that her shadow-guardian had come to be, that all of her life, all of its trials, all of its joys, everything had served but one purpose—to bring her here, into this room, sitting at the head of this council...to be the dam holding back a deluge.

She had not even been aware that she had done it, but she found her right hand scrabbling at her throat for the bear claw *stoicheon*, the symbol of the darkness she had accepted as part of herself when she was still a child, the darkness that had risen to give her strength and to protect her so many times, and in whose name she had done unspeakable things. But she was wearing the regalia of an Empress of Visant, and the bear claw was deeply buried beneath layers of robe and cloak and jewelled collar; nonetheless she could feel it burning against her breast, searing its shape into her skin like a brand.

She noticed, in passing, that Photius, the physician, had slipped out of the room. That ought to have been important—but somehow she could not concentrate on it at that moment, as her vision narrowed until all she could see was the one man at the center of the whole controversy—Maxentius himself, on his feet now, standing before his council with his shoulders hunched a little and his brows knit together into a frown, looking tragically torn at the prospect that was being presented to him. His lips were moving—she could see it—but the blood was rushing in her veins and the roar was loud in her head, so loud that she could not believe that the roof was not coming down upon them all, shivered from its foundations by the sound. That was all she could hear. That noise. That roar. That fury.

And then it subsided enough for her to be able to comprehend words again. Maxentius appeared to have been taking a vote around the council table, and he had reached Arkadios, at the last. Callidora came back to herself in time to see the faithful Chancellor hesitate for a long moment, and then give his Emperor a small bow of deference and respect, and resignation.

"It is not ideal," Arkadios said, with difficulty, obviously carefully choosing his words. "But, *despotes*, I will do what you wish. I am, as always, at your command."

Callidora took her own census, face after face. They had all voted for flight. Every one of them.

Even Arkadios, in the end, had bowed to it.

"Are you done?" Callidora's voice had become low and throaty—level and restrained enough, but obviously concealing a barely leashed passion.

Maxentius turned, startled. "Callidora?"

The Empress of Visant rose from her chair in a single fluid motion. Callidora had always been of slight, almost fragile, build; the bulk and weight of the Imperial regalia only emphasised her slender physique. Even with the high Imperial diadem on her head, every man in that room physically towered over her. But in this moment, standing alone and a little apart, glittering with the cold fire of gems and an icy dignity in her bearing, she looked as though she was looking down on them all, her back straight, her shoulders back, her small pointed chin held high.

"I have been what I have been to this council in the past," she said, addressing the gathered men, "and when times demanded that, you have all followed me. That was in a moment of crisis, years ago—a crisis that made it forgivable, even essential, for a woman to speak out in this place. Perhaps some of you have reconsidered, since, and might consider it presumptuous of me to speak now. But it is not *you* to whom I speak—"

That last was in response to one or two of the men at the table stirring. But Callidora wasn't about to let anyone speak. They had all said more than enough already.

She turned away from the council, faced Maxentius directly. "To you, Maxentius Augustus, I say this," she said. "You may leave Visant. If you wish to save yourself, you can do it—you have the means—you have the treasure, you have the boats, and the sea awaits. But before you set one foot on that road, consider that it leads in only one direction. They tell you, your people, that you will take with you the crown, the purple, the Patriarch who set the diadem on your head—and that taking these things will somehow, magically, make every city that you set foot in become Visant. But that is not true. Visant remains here–and if you leave it, you may find it impossible to return."

"To stay in Visant might mean death, Augusta," Rencellus said, apparently unable to restrain himself from speaking out.

Callidora barely turned her head, gave him no more than a cursory glance that took the measure of the man and clearly found him wanting.

"Even if it *is* nothing less than death that awaits here, at least it is not death as a fugitive," she said levelly, in response to his words.

There could be no reply to that.

The silence in the room was profound. Maxentius searched Callidora's eyes with his own as she turned back towards him, finding there love, and pride, and, unexpectedly, pity.

Her tone had been formal, until that moment, but now suddenly something cracked and the roar sounded in her ears louder than ever. But the voice that came out of her, as though to compensate for that, was softer and more gentle than before—she had spoken as Empress, but now she spoke as woman, as wife, as mate, as someone who loved. She reached out a hand to him and Maxentius instinctively took it, his eyes wide on hers.

"You will know what you need to do," Callidora said gently. "But Maxentius… *you* gave me this. *You* placed the purple on my shoulders, the crown on my head. Do you still not have any idea what that means? You may leave, if you want to—but as for myself, I stay. If the One God chooses that I should die, then I die. But I will perish here, in this palace where you have made me queen, and I will be buried in a purple shroud."

She gently extracted her hand from his, turned her back on the gaping men gathered around the council table, and walked out of the room without looking back.

CHAPTER THIRTY ONE

Y*ou will know what you need to do.*

They were words, no more than that, but Callidora might as well have left them written on parchment with a dagger pinning them to the council table. They were a challenge, a call to action from the only woman in a room full of men—men who included two seasoned generals and an Emperor. There could be no turning away from that.

They had talked about running. Callidora had flung that back into their faces. She had not called them cowards, not exactly—but not one of them could even consider the option of flight any longer.

The alternative to that…

A full understanding of that pity in Callidora's eyes suddenly flooded through Maxentius. The alternative to sounding a retr

eat was turning to face the enemy and making a stand. And once unsheathed, a sword was always thirsty for blood.

He closed his eyes for a moment, his hands clenching into fists at his side, and then he sighed deeply, straightened his back, lifting his head. When he opened his eyes again, he gazed on his council with eyes that were glittering like cold steel.

"All right, then," he said softly. "It seems that the sea is closed to us, after all. I need a new plan."

For a long moment, nothing greeted him but silence—and then Kalos placed both hands on the table before him, bracing himself against the surface, his head bowed.

"It cannot endure," he said, the strategist, the general. "This will break, sooner or later. Right now, it's a stalemate—they have their Emperor, in the Kathisma, and we have ours, here in the Palace. But that is already stretched too thin. We have only hours, perhaps. *They* will, in some way, attack…or we have to."

Maxentius's eyes were on the door that Callidora had left through, his expression bleak.

"I know," he said. *She knew. That is why she looked at me that way. Before this day is over I will have to give orders to spill the blood of my own people—or do it myself….*

Arkadios, who knew both his master and his mistress all too well, cleared his throat to get Maxentius's attention. When the Emperor glanced over at him, Arkadios pushed back his chair and gave a small bow.

"If the Emperor will excuse me," he said, "I have duties to attend to." His eyes met Maxentius's, said the things he could not say out loud in this room—*I will go after her, despotes, I will find her.*

Maxentius nodded at him. "Very well," he said. "You may go." His eyes were more eloquent. *Go. Make sure she is all right. Make sure she doesn't take matters into her own hands….*

The silentiaries, aides, and several priests waiting in the council room antechamber looked up as the door opened and Arkadios stepped through.

There was no sign of Callidora. Even weighed down with all the trappings of Empire, she must have moved fast—which meant that she had her own plans, indeed, and Arkadios's sense of urgency climbed a notch.

His first instinct was to go to her quarters. But when he arrived there everything was quiet—and the emissary from the Imperial Treasury, guardian of the official regalia to whom the Imperial diadem and other accoutrements had to be handed over for safekeeping once the Empress was done with them, was still sitting empty-handed in the anteroom of the Empress's quarters, waiting patiently for his charge.

That meant that the Empress was still in possession of the diadem.

Arkadios made certain. "Have you seen the Augusta this morning?"

"When she left here, Chancellor, yes," the Treasury man said, rising to his feet to offer a small bow. "I am waiting for her return—I thought she was still at council…?"

The door of the outer chamber opened again, and closed.

Arkadios whirled, hoping that he had indeed pre-empted Callidora here, that it would be she who would walk into the room. Instead, he was greeted by the sight of two of Callidora's women, their arms overflowing with Imperial regalia. The women came to an abrupt halt just inside the Empress's chamber, staring at the Grand Chancellor with wide eyes.

"The Empress?" a sharp voice spoke from behind Arkadios. He recognised it—Sidonia, Callidora's senior attendant, Mistress of the Empress's Chamber. "Antonina? Cervella? What happened?"

"We...we followed her, when she left the council chamber," Antonina said. "They all stared at her as she walked through the anteroom, as though they were seeing a ghost, or an angel, someone not mortal—there was something about her, my Lord, she was transfigured, her mind made up on something. We followed her out, and she ushered us into the Emperor's own quarters, she ordered the two silentiaries who were there out, and then she made us help her take off the Imperial raiment—the diadem, the jewels, the cloak, all of it, until she stood in front of us wearing just the dark under-robe she had worn underneath it all, and her hair falling out of its braids, and she looked down at her shoes—she was wearing court shoes, the ones with jewels on the clasp—and said that it couldn't be helped...and then she made me give her the cloak that I was wearing, and wrapped that around her, and ordered Cervella and myself back here with the regalia."

"I must have walked straight past the room," Arkadios muttered. "Where is she now?"

"I...don't know, my Lord," Antonina said. "She turned us both out into the corridor, and closed the doors behind us. We...we came straight here."

"Did she say anything at all as to what she planned to do...?"

"Not to us, not directly, my Lord," Antonina said.

Cervella, the younger woman, opened her mouth as though she would have spoken, and then seemed to change her mind. But Arkadios noticed, and stepped up to her, cupping her chin in his fingers.

"You heard something," he said. "It may be important. Tell me. Now."

"She murmured something to herself, my Lord, I don't think I was meant to hear it," Cervella said, looking terrified.

"But you did hear it, and now I need to," Arkadios said.

"I only heard a few words," Cervella stammered. "*The Hippodrome only has its own.*"

Arkadios's hand dropped from Cervella's face. He looked stricken. Callidora had not spoken about Circassaë often, but she did tell Arkadios about the work that she had found the once-great dancer doing in the Hippodrome at the height of the plague epidemic. Once. Callidora had spoken about it only once—when Arkadios had come to her, discreetly, to tell her that the laws of the city had been broken for this one woman's sake and that Circassaë had been buried quietly, without ceremony and without a formal marker, in the gardens of the House of Peacocks—a secluded spot, from which it was possible to glimpse the glitter of sunlight on the sea. Callidora had thanked him, and then she had asked him if he had ever known Circassaë personally.

"We were…acquainted," Arkadios said. "I was her contact here in the House of Peacocks, if she needed to get word to Maxentius Augustus…." And then he had paused, searching Callidora's face, knowing that she had asked him quite a different question and that he had failed to answer it. "No, *despoina*," he said quietly, correcting that. "I knew far less of her than I should have. But I know that the Augustus thought very highly of her. And I know…whatever her origins or her reputation…I know that she was an artist, and a true lady."

"She was the last thing that many of them saw," Callidora said, staring into space, her gaze unfocused and her mind lost in her memories. "She was an angel of mercy, at the end, not an artist, not a lady—she wore a faded robe that might have belonged to a serving woman, and her hair had faded into drab when last I saw her. But she was an angel of mercy. *The city gets taken care of,* she said to me, *and the Hippodrome only has its own.* She was what the Hippodrome had, in the end. The only thing. The last thing. Its own."

Hippodrome.

Where the mob had just crowned a new Emperor.

The Hippodrome only has its own.

Arkadios shuddered. "Oh, dear God," he said. "I must get back at once. What hour is it?"

"The bells rang for Nones only a little while ago," Sidonia said.

Arkadios glanced up at the ceiling, but it was not that he was looking at—he was seeing the winter sky above the city, remembering the shortness of the winter days, trying to count the hours before it would be dark, to anticipate how long it would take the council to come to the same conclusion that Callidora had already done, that everything, *everything*, was centered on the Hippodrome right now. That's where the conspirators were. The new Emperor.

The people.

You will know what you need to do.

Arkadios stumbled from the Empress's chamber, and ran down the porphyry corridors.

What if Callidora had gone to the Hippodrome? What was Arkadios to tell Maxentius? What would Maxentius do? If he had come to the same conclusion as his Empress—that the Hippodrome was the one place where this could be brought to an end—would he stay his hand if he knew, if he even suspected, that he was putting the woman he loved in danger by giving the order for the generals to go in?…

Arkadios hesitated at the gate to the porphyry corridor, glancing this way and that, conflicted, and then finally made a decision. If he tried the Bronze Gate, first, he would gain immediate information. If she had not gone that way, there was still time—maybe—to send out a second boat in pursuit.

In a blind rush, he all but ran down Count Photius, the court physician, who appeared to be hurrying away from the very gate for which Arkadios himself was making. The two men staggered aside after their collision, and only then appeared to realise who the other was.

Photius blanched. "What are you still doing here?"

"What do you mean?" Arkadios asked, in a fever of urgency, but sufficiently caught by this reaction and those words to pause and listen.

"I thought the Emperor had left," Photius said. "By sea. That's what I heard—when I left the council room, they were saying…I thought that it had been decided…. That's what I said to the…." He stopped, swallowed. "Oh, may the One God be merciful to me," he whispered.

Arkadios grabbed him by the shoulders, his hands vice-like on Photius's upper arms. "What have you done?"

"There was a man," Photius said. "A messenger. At the Gate. The Guards were holding him. He said…he said he came from Gennadius…that Gennadius had sent him to the Emperor, to tell him that all those who were against him were gathered in one place right now, and that a strike against the Hippodrome…he said that Gennadius told him…I don't think they believed him…."

This was beyond neutrality. If the Guards held back this news, whether or not they had actually believed that the messenger was from Gennadius himself or merely used the name to gain entrance to the palace, this was hostile intent. Arkadios's cheeks were as flushed as Photius's were chalk-white; he shook the man. "Is the messenger still there?"

"No—he left—when I said that the Emperor was gone…."

Arkadios glanced back over his shoulder, almost expecting the mob with the torches to be coming down the corridors behind him. They were out of time, now. If the messenger Photius spoke of was indeed from Gennadius, and had gone back to the Hippodrome bearing the news that Maxentius was fled, then it was a whole new game out there—out where Callidora had gone, unknowing.

Maxentius needed to know this. The council needed to know now.

Wherever Callidora was…it was already too late.

The doorkeepers to the council chambers took one look at Arkadios's face and made no effort to stop him as he flung the doors open and burst into the council.

"*Despotes*," he said, heedless of protocol, not caring whom he interrupted, "they think that you have fled. There was a messenger at the gate, turned away by the Guard, who swore that he came from Gennadius himself—with a message that they were all there, in the Hippodrome. Right now. Right now, but perhaps not for long. If you want to save yourself, you have to act now."

"I know," Maxentius said. He was standing very straight, but he looked haunted, wounded, as though there was already a blade in his heart. He turned to the generals. "Valentinian…Kalos…gather your men. I will meet you at the Bronze Gate as soon as I am armoured."

The generals saluted, the soldiers' salute of fist on heart, and hurried out of the chamber.

"My lords," Maxentius said calmly to the rest of the gathered men, "the meeting is over. Whether we shall all see each other again…depends on what happens before this night ends. You may make your own arrangements."

They were dismissed. They glanced at one another, at the Emperor, some of them looking frightened, others confused. Everything had changed too fast, and kept changing; Maxentius had started out looking tired and weary but now he was something else again, he was steeling himself for the unthinkable, for the thing that had to be done.

You will know what you have to do.

"Arkadios," Maxentius said softly, when everyone else had filed out and he and Arkadios were the last ones left, "where is she?"

"Gone, *despotes*," Arkadios said. And then, hesitating, gave his Emperor the truth because the truth was all that he had to give. "She may be…at the Hippodrome."

Maxentius flinched as though struck.

"If we go in it will be a slaughter," he said, appalled. "I cannot watch out for one face—none of them can. Arkadios—we need just a little time, to get our forces together. That's all the time you've got. Find her. *Find her.*"

"I will, *despotes*."

Maxentius allowed himself to be escorted by his silentiaries back to his own chamber and submitted to being armoured, his sword and his dagger buckled around his waist, a helmet touched with gold and with a high crest dyed a deep dark crimson that almost shaded into purple placed on his head. There were ghosts in the room with him—Rathauric, pagan prince and friend, who had taught him to fight in close combat; Leontes, standing in the dress uniform of the Count of the Palace Guard, his face serious, mouthing the phrase, *There are no straight roads in Visant.*

No straight road had led Maxentius to this moment. But the road that led from here was as straight as they came—there was no other choice to be made, none, except to go forward and hope that there was a way out on the other side.

He found Valentinian in the first courtyard behind the Bronze Gate, with his men; Kalos, with his forces, had already gone to the smaller gate, the Ivory Gate, to implement the second half of their plan. The Bronze Gate court was a big courtyard, which housed, amongst other things, the quarters of the Palace Guard in buildings that made up fully two sides of the court. It gave Maxentius pause to realise that this space easily held all the men gathered there in their tidy army ranks.

Maxentius, his hand on the pommel of his sword, had the captain of the Bronze Gate Guard summoned into his presence. When the man came, giving him a truncated version of the obeisance due to the Emperor, Maxentius gave a prearranged signal and three soldiers stepped up to the Captain, one behind him, one to either side.

"We could do this quietly," Maxentius said. "I need all the men I have, but I will leave as many as are necessary to ensure that this gate is guarded by men whom I trust. So—you will either step aside of your own will or else I need to leave an entire troop here…to guard the Bronze Gate from intruders, and the Palace from you. I will take your word on this—I will trust your word because Leontes Augustus, who was my father, was also once your Count, and he taught me that your word as a Guard was sacred to you. So—we do not have much time. What will it be?"

The Captain stared at Maxentius for a long moment, and then sighed, bowing his head. "I will take my men into the garrison quarters," he said quietly. "We will stay there until word comes. I will give you my oath to that."

"Then go," Maxentius said.

The Captain gave him another bow, deeper this time, and called out to his detachment of Guard. Maxentius nodded to Valentinian, and the general barked a few quick, sharp orders to his own men; a number of them peeled off the outer fringe of the gathered cohort and took up the positions being vacated by the Palace Guard. The rest, with Maxentius stepping into the lead and Valentinian falling into step beside him, marched out into the street.

It was quiet out in the first Forum, as the twilight was falling. If any of the Hippodrome mob were present, they did not make their presence known—and Valentinian's men fanned out on either side of the Forum as they turned away from the main avenue and into the wider side streets that led down to the main gate of the Hippodrome, swords drawn, their footfalls soft. Now and then Maxentius thought he heard sounds out at the periphery of the formation—maybe a thud, a stifled cry, a running step quickly silenced—but it was all subdued, quiet. They walked along streets where some of the houses were burned out wrecks, some still smouldering; there were hints, in the sky, that somewhere the fires were still burning, and the air tasted of grit and ashes. Beneath Maxentius's feet things crunched and crumbled, and sometimes the pavement was slick with things he preferred not to think about.

This was what they had done to his city.

This was what he had allowed to be done.

He rounded the final corner with Valentinian, who lifted an arm in a signal for the troops to halt behind them. Between themselves and the open gates to the Hippodrome was an empty space, an open square where the street widened into a small forum. Huge torches thrust into several sconces by the gate lit the small square brightly; it was empty, and anyone stepping out onto it would be painfully visible. But there was no other way into the Hippodrome. The one advantage they still had was that those inside the arena had been too lost in their jubilant celebrations to think of posting scouts.

"Kalos should be in position at the Dead Man's Gate," Valentinian said in a low voice. "We should go."

The Dead Man's Gate. A relic of the Hippodrome's bloody past, back before gladiator fights to the death had been outlawed—the back gate of the Hippodrome used to be the postern entrance through which the losers of the gladiatorial contests had been carried out, discreetly, so as not to ruin the mood of the crowd in the arena by having to watch the removal of a dead body.

The name of the gate was all that had remained of those times. Human blood had not been deliberately shed in the Hippodrome arena for over a century.

Until now.

Maxentius nodded, and stepped forward, drawing his sword. A hiss behind him told him that the men had done likewise.

The light from the torches played along the steel of his blade, flickering hypnotically, giving it a reddish tint, as though it was already blooded. The golden stone of the Hippodrome walls also reflected the bright firelight into a reddish hue, dried blood, and Maxentius felt a roaring in his ears. He was an Emperor, annointed by the church, acclaimed, once, by the self-same crowd who now cheered Gennadius in the Hippodrome. An Emperor about to turn on his own people.

It did not matter to him in the least, right then, that they had already turned against him—that those torches, or others like them, had burned down half his city, his Patriarch's cathedral, hospitals full of the sick and the wounded. What death would come tonight…would be his to deal. And it tasted like ashes in his mouth, like the ashes that drifted in the air from the burned-out buildings in the City of Gold.

He halted as he reached the outer gate to the Hippodrome, waiting for the rest to catch up. The gate was more of a tunnel, with the outer gate that opened into the forum and then a short, wide corridor wide enough for a pair of quadrigas to be driven side by side in it, led to the inner gate, which opened into the arena itself.

Ahead of them—and they could see them now as well as hear them—was the jubilant mob. The Hippodrome crowd had forsaken the spectator tiers and isntead packed the arena, fifty thousand strong, maybe more—shoulder to shoulder, a sea of humanity, drunk on power and quite possibly wine, somehow still completely contained in themselves, enough to pay no attention whatsoever to Maxentius and his group as they lined themselves up in disciplined rows of men behind their Emperor and their General.

"Cover the width of the arena," Valentinian spoke softly to the men behind him. "When we emerge, fan out until you cover the width of the arena. Don't worry about the stands, Kalos has the first wave of his mercenaries ready to take the stands from his end. You concentrate on the arena itself—cover the width, and then move forward. And keep moving."

Maxentius stood frozen, staring at something that he had not really thought through.

To his right undulated a punch-drunk mob fifty thousand strong.

To his left…the steps up to the Kathisma, to a barred door where only a handful of bodyguards would be on duty, because no more could fit on the stair without getting in one another's way should they need to earn their pay. And beyond that…the heart of this whole thing. He could end it all, there. He could end the slaughter before it began.

The mob, or the Kathisma.

Attacking one…meant turning his back on the other.

If he miscalculated now.…

Valentinian touched his arm. "It is time. I am sure Kalos is ready."

Maxentius came to a decision. "Go," he said. "Give me four men, and go. Implement the plan as we discussed."

"August…?"

"Don't ask questions," Maxentius snapped. He turned his head, caught the eye of the four nearest soldiers at his left shoulder. "You, you, and you two. Follow me. The rest, after Valentinian. Give me just a little bit of a head start. Go. *Now!*"

He broke left, the men he had called following in tight formation behind him.

By the time the roar of the crowd changed into something different, something wilder, and he smelled the first sharp coppery tang of blood, Maxentius was already on the stair, and the attention of four burly barbarian bodybuards standing on either side of the Kathisma door was firmly on him and the escort at his back. Maxentius paused just long enough to turn his head a little, catching the eye of the nearest man.

"Take those out," he said. "I don't care how you do it. I'll take the brute on the top landing."

His men brandished their swords and raced towards their targets, taking the stairs two at a time. Maxentius himself, sword in his right hand and dagger in his left, followed by one of his soldiers, rushed his own chosen man.

The guard was long-haired, blond, obviously some barbarian mercenary procured by Sarrus; he was stocky, but none of it was fat, and his arms, circled at the wrists by boiled leather cuffs, looked like they had been torn off a small oak tree. He was not armoured, except for a leather vest over his naked chest which left those imposing arms bare and on display.

There would be no fair fight here. The gate-guard had too much to lose; Maxentius had too much to win.

Maxentius and his companion both tackled the burly barbarian at once. For a moment it seemed that even two would not be enough—he fought them off with ease, almost playing with them, baring his magnificent teeth in what might have been a feral grin. But then Valentinian's man got past the barbarian's guard and a bloody gash opened along the muscle of the blond giant's left arm.

He lost his grin then, and snarled something in a language unknown to them, and joined the fight in earnest.

It was the other man, the soldier, who took the brunt of it—Maxentius was capable, but he was not a natural warrior, he took no glory or pleasure in this. His own guard was breached at least twice—first a stab that took him in his left shoulder and then, while that was still numb, in an eerie echo of the barbarian's own first wound a long gash was opened down the length of his left upper arm which bled copiously and made the fingers of his left hand slick with his own blood and lose their grip on the dagger which tumbled harmlessly down the stone stair. Maxentius himself was a step down on the Kathisma stair from the gate guard now, and could only watch in horror as his companion tried another attack and took the barbarian's sword in the throat.

Hot blood gushed from between the soldier's fingers as he dropped his sword and brought both hands to his neck—but there was nothing he could have done. He was probably dead before he dropped, and rolled down a couple of steps before coming to rest against the gate wall, lying still.

The barbarian, gory with the blood of the man he had just killed, turned his attention to Maxentius. There was little he could do—the moment unfolded in slow motion as he watched the barbarian's massive sword lifted with both hands above its wielder's head, the expression on the wild face beneath the blowing blond hair full of triumph, and saw the man begin to bring his weapon down for the kill. Maxentius brought his useless left arm up, wrapped his fingers around the pommel of his sword and held them there with his right hand curled around them, and simply lifted his sword, thrusting upwards, in the only maneuver open to him.

It was hard to say which of them was the more surprised as the barbarian, before he had a chance to complete his killing blow, found himself impaled on the length of Maxentius's sword. He staggered, and the weight of him tore the sword from Maxentius's fragile grip. Man and weapon both tumbled down the Kathisma stair in a series of bone-jarring thumps until he fetched up sprawled in an ungainly heap at the bottom, just inside the main gate.

The other three soldiers who had come up with Maxentius had all despatched their opponents, and now came running over to the Emperor. Maxentius sent one of them down to retrieve his sword from the barbarian's body and shouted throught the door and across the open balcony of the Kathisma that jutted out onto the arena.

"It's over, Gennadius. How many more die tonight is up to you. Open this door right now."

He heard commotion in the Kathisma, raised voices, a shouted *No!* Then he heard the scrape and click as someone raised the bar. Slowly, the door swung open; Gennadius himself, the new Emperor, stood framed in it, his shoulders sloped in defeat. He reached out and dragged the gold chain from his head, letting it dangle from slack fingers of his right hand.

"You got my message?"

"I got the message that something needed to be done," Maxentius said.

A voice—Sarrus's, Maxentius thought—came from behind Gennadius.

"What do you think you're doing? They could never have...."

"*Listen*," Maxentius said, pushing Gennadius aside with his bloodied left hand and stepping past him into the Kathisma. "Every man who dies from this moment on, that blood is on *your* hands, Sarrus. Now get out of my way, and let me stop this carnage." He paused, raking the inside of the Kathisma with his eyes, taking note of the faces of the men who stood within it. "I know every one of you," he said. "You may choose to run, but you cannot hide from this. You brought this on all of us, and you will answer for it. It may go easier on you if you stay here until order is restored down there and you can be taken into full custody."

His men stepped into the Kathisma, their own swords drawn; one of them was also carrying the Emperor's sword, which he handed over hilt first with a small bow. Two of them took up positions on the inside of the door outside to the outer stair and to possible freedom, their eyes glittering, daring Sarrus and his men to attempt to escape that way. The third, on Maxentius's signal, stepped up beside Gennadius.

Maxentius himself lowered his sword point first onto the stone floor of the Kathisma, holding it loosely in his left hand; blood still dripped from it, gathering in a small pool at the apex. He stepped forward, leaned with his whole weight on his good hand clasping the ballustrade of the Kathisma balcony, and took stock for the first time of what had been happening in the arena while he had battled the barbarian on the Kathisma stair.

Valentinian's soldiers were methodical, and ruthless. They were pushing forward relentlessly, hacking their way with sword and dagger; the crowd tried to shrink from before them but there was nowhere to go—Kalos's men of whom Valentinian had spoken were doing an equally systematic job on the stands, driving those who had been up there down into the already packed arena, and people were starting to get trampled, and squeezed against monuments and the stone walls of the arena, and there were screams and shouted pleas for mercy and above all the violent stink of death and fear, the sour smell of sweat and the coppery scent of blood, and there were already bodies stretched out behind Valentinian's lines, motionless, blood pooling on the white sands of the Hippodrome arena churned up by so many feet. At least two of the bodies were women, long hair spilling on the sands beside them; another was a small boy. Maxentius saw a hand severed just above the wrist, divorced from a body, flung to one side as though it had been dropped by careless accident.

Maxentius felt the bile rise in the back of his throat and his vision faded for a moment, into white, into blindness, as though he were about to pass out from the horror of it all. But then he set his teeth, shook his head to clear it, and gripped the stone ballustrade with his good hand as though he wanted to rip it apart with his fingers.

"*Stop!*" he cried out. "In the name of the Empire, stop! It's over!"

He did not have a herald, or any means to amplify his voice—but he shouted from deep within himself, with every ounce of power, and his voice carried, miraculously, over the screaming and the dying and the clash of steel in the arena below.

It stopped in waves, as the people nearest to the Kathisma heard him, froze, stopped in mid movement, turned to stare at the royal box bathed in the flaming light of torches. They saw the defeated figure of Gennadius, their new Emperor, standing hunched and submissive beside a figure in bright armour who shone with the light of ancient gods. As the silence spread Maxentius reached up and removed his helmet, letting his face be seen, letting his hair blow free.

"It's over," he said. "Let the killing end, right now. Valentinian, tell your men to stand down. If anyone continues with violence take him into custody—the Prefecture may be burned but we have plenty of holding cells if they become necessary. The rest of you…go home. Tomorrow, we start to rebuild. Together. It's over."

He glanced at Gennadius, who glanced up, lifted both his arms, showed the golden chain that had been called a crown hanging from his hand.

"I submit myself," Gennadius said, his voice much reedier, softer, but still carrying far enough to make a difference, "to the Emperor's justice."

The Emperor's justice. The justice that had started all this.

Maxentius sent one of his men down to fetch a more substantial escort for Sarrus and his cronies, and for Gennadius—but in the end it turned out to be unnecessary because at long last, finally, the inner door of the Kathisma creaked open and a contingent of the men they had left behind in the Palace stepped through. Sarrus, the last to be escorted down the winding stair into the holding cells of the dungeons below the Palace, turned to Maxentius.

"It is *not* over," he said softly. Maxentius leaned wearily on the ballustrade, aware that there were still cries and the occaisonal sharp crack of steel on steel in the chaotic but slowly emptying arena below and that there was nothing more that he could do to stop those deaths, grateful that he had stopped far worse.

"It is not over, Maxentius Augustus. It won't be, as long as there are men like me out there to take you on."

"What did I ever do to you?" Maxentius said, staring at him.

"You stole an Empire," Sarrus said. "It could have been in my own hand." He grimaced sourly. "Twice."

"There won't be a third time," Maxentius said. "I may not have learned the first time, but I have learned now. There will never be another day like this, another night like tonight. Not so long as I sit on the throne of Visant."

A soldier nudged Sarrus, and he shook his head, folded his hands together, and stepped into the winding stair.

The man he had sent back down for reinforcements came clattering back up the stairs—accompanied by half a dozen more soldiers and Valentinian himself.

Maxentius acknowledged him with a nod, but without taking his eyes off the arena, which was currently being emptied of its spectators. He watched bodies being carried away—far too many bodies.

"How many?" Maxentius said in a low voice. "How many are dead?"

"We haven't tallied the numbers yet, August," the general said. "But there are many. There are three times the number of dead in the arena, at least, as we brought men. A number of those in the arena were armed. I think our own casualties are light enough, though. In all, I believe we lost some twenty men, at the most."

"The soldier who was with me at the stair...."

"Yes," Valentinian said. "He has been found. He will be taken care of."

"He was a brave man," Maxentius said absently.

Valentinian made a gesture towards the Emperor's left hand, still hanging uselessly at his side.

"You should have that seen to, August."

"Yes," Maxentius agreed automatically. He was aware of pain, but it was distant, as though the arm was not his own. He found it difficult to bring himself to care about his own blood right now, not when so much more of it had been spilled on the white sands of the Hippodrome. On his orders.

Valentinian bowed to the Emperor. "If you will excuse me," he said, "I think I'd better go down and supervise the aftermath of all this."

Maxentius glanced at him, nodded dismissal. Valentinian, frowning a little, took his leave.

Alone, Maxentius stood paralysed with a sudden terror, staring out into the flickering lights of the Hippodrome arena.

Was she here…? Was she…

More noise on the outer stair of the Kathisma made Maxentius turn his head sharply. He transferred his sword into his good hand and reflexively tightened his grip—but the face that showed itself from behind the half-open door was unexpected, and all the more welcome for the expression that it bore—an expression that did not foretell doom. A wild hope stirred in Maxentius's heart.

"*Despotes*," Arkadios said, his eyes very bright, "She is here. She is safe. I found her."

CHAPTER THIRTY TWO

You will know what you need to do.

Callidora knew where those words would lead Maxentius.

It had been a long journey for her. She had thought she left the Hippodrome behind—but her life's road had travelled in a circle after all, and all the choices she had made when faced with a crossroads in her path seemed to have conspired to lead her back here, back to the arena, back to the shadow of the four great banners snapping above the gate.

Maxentius would go in. He would have to. She, Callidora, had left him no other way.

And it would be the Hippodrome that would pay the price of the wrath of Empire, her people, the people who had been lured into the game of kings without being aware that the stakes, for themselves, were higher than they might have been willing to pay.

Usually the arena itself was the preserve of the men—but these were not ordinary times. Callidora knew her tribe. This would have been heady wine for the Hippodrome folk. Men would take their small sons into the Hippodrome and hoist them on their shoulders, to show them the new Emperor in the Kathisma—but this involved everyone, men and women alike, the dancers and the acrobats would be out in force and even those women who ordinarily shunned the glare of the open arena might be there that night—because these weren't the races, nor the games, these weren't amusements for their menfolk to place bets on and squabble over and cheer from the stands. This was one of those moments when the world came to the Hippodrome, when the Empire brought its glory to the arena, and the people were made aware that without them, their support, their approval, the Empire could not exist.

Maxentius's response would have to be swift, now—and brutal. When his soldiers went into the arena, they would not have time to care who was falling underneath their swords.

And Callidora had betrayed them both, the Hippodrome and Maxentius himself. It was she, glittering with the jewels of Empire, who had stood in his way when he would have turned his back on the situation—would have taken ship—would have withdrawn the swords about to be unsheathed on the people. It was she who had proposed that he turn his hand against the Hippodrome. It was she who had planted the seed for something that might have been inevitable—but that would haunt Maxentius's reign, win or lose tonight, for as long as history endured. It was her words that began it all—but it would be his actions, what he did next, that would be written into the books, would be his legacy. Callidora, the Empress, had signed the death warrants of the people who had shaped her past, and had set the seal on Maxentius's future.

You will know what you have to do.

She was ice and steel when she walked out of the council room. Two of her women, who had accompanied her there from her quarters but had been left to wait in the anteroom, scrambled to their feet and hurried to follow as she swept past them.

The Emperor's private quarters were a turn of the corridor away. Callidora flung open the doors to the antechamber, startling a silentiary on duty there; she ignored him, sweeping past him into the inner chamber, seeing him stumble to his feet, a challenge dying on his lips because she was Empress, after all, and she had a right. Two more silentiaries inside the chamber straightened from their duties as she entered, and she locked eyes first with one, then the other, and then gestured wordlessly towards the door.

They asked no questions. They bowed, and scurried out, closing the door behind them.

"Now. Quickly. Help me."

She reached out to the diadem on her head, lifting it off carefully, laying it down on the Emperor's bed; one of her women fumbled with the catch of her jewelled collar at the back, the other was unpinning the purple *chlamys* from her shoulder. Callidora began wriggling out of her rich outer gown in a fever of impatience almost before either of the women were fully done, catching her hair and tumbling it loose, finally standing before them just in a simple dark woollen gown. Shorn of her glitter, of her trappings, even of that purple that she had sworn only a few moments ago that she would be buried in, Callidora had never looked more like an Empress in her life.

A sparkle caught her eye as she stepped forward, and she glanced down, lifting one foot, and staring at the jewelled clasp on a soft court shoe that was never meant to be worn outside halls of marble and soft carpets.

"Can't be helped," she murmured. An image swam into her head—Circassaë, dull-haired, gowned in drab, who had left her own glory days behind to minister to the Hippodrome when it was in need. She, Callidora, would walk in wearing jewelled shoes, would literally set foot in there as the Empress. The irony didn't escape her, but the memory of Circassaë's words was vivid in her mind. "*The Hippodrome only has its own,*" she whispered, almost too soft for anyone else to hear—but one of the women lifted her head, turned.

Callidora had almost forgotten that they were there.

"Antonina," she said, holding out her hand, "give me your cloak. And then, both of you—" she paused as Antonina obediently undid the clasp of her own plain cloak and passed it over to the Empress. "Both of you—take the regalia, and go directly back to my chambers with them. I have work to do. Go."

Antonina hesitated, her eyes full of questions, but both women were used to obeying Callidora's word. They might have misgivings, but they had their orders; they gave her the obeisances due to the Empress, gathered up the things they had been charged with conveying back to her quarters, and left.

Alone, Callidora closed her eyes, standing very still. Once again she was back on a distant hillside, under a hot sun, and a cairn of pebbles, a tower of prayer raised up towards the One God, tumbled at her feet as she laid her own stone, her own prayer, on the rest.

Give me the life I was meant to live. She had asked for that. Only for that. But now she stood on what felt like a final crossroads, and her choice here might be what determined it all. *If I go in and warn them, I tip Maxentius's hand, and it might all be for nothing. If I do not go in, and he carries out his plan, there may be thousands dead this night. Whose blood do I take upon me...?*

It was a question without an answer—or, rather, it was a question that she had already answered. She knew she would go.

She fastened Antonina's cloak about her shoulders, pulled the cowl of her hood further forward, and slipped out into the corridor.

She made it to the Bronze Gate courtyard without being seen; she had not planned anything beyond this moment, really, and had no idea how she was going to manage this part of it. She didn't think she could slip past unnoticed, and she didn't know what the guards would do if they challenged her—let alone if they became aware of the identity of the woman they challenged.

But when she got to the gate, there seemed to be something of a commotion happening—most of the Guards' attention was on one man, babbling something in the portico, surrounded by at least three armed Guards and appearing to be earnestly trying to convince them of something.

Between them and the side of the courtyard that Callidora had hugged in order to approach the gate, there was only one remaining Guard—and his own attention was on what was going on at the far side of the portico. Behind him—between him and the wall—there was a gap. Beyond that, the portico itself provided cover—and from there it was but a step out to the open Forum, and the city.

Callidora's soft-soled court shoes made no noise as she made her decision, committed to her move, stepped out from the deepening shadows of the edge of the courtyard. The Guard did not turn towards her.

She hesitated, almost too long, when she came abreast of the man being detained in the gate itself and caught a few words—"Gennadius himself, Gennadius sent me…they are all there, and Gennadius sends to Maxentius…it won't be long before.…"

Callidora could all but hear the sands of time running out. Maxentius had hours, maybe.

She had less.

She never really knew exactly how she slipped out of the Palace, but she found herself hurrying in the city streets where the light of day was fast fading, past remnants and skeletons of houses gutted by fire leaning against their damaged or soot-smeared and singed neighbours, seeing only one or two other cloaked and huddled shapes scurrying past. Callidora spared a moment to wonder just where the mobs had all gone, the mobs that had been besieging the forum outside the Bronze Gate for days—was *everyone* at the Hippodrome? How many did the arena hold?

She had not meant to go that way, but somehow her steps took her down the street which had once held the house she had rented when she returned to Visant from her adventures in Afaris and the Crescent Kingdoms—oh, it seemed like a lifetime ago, now!—the house that had since become a hospital and a haven, the house which Brother Methodius had described to her as going up in flames and taking those it had sheltered with it.

It had been a place for people who had had nowhere else to go. Callidora's steps faltered as she approached the ruin, some parts of which were still smouldering, and she came to a complete stop as she came abreast of it, staring into the ashes and the blackened remains.

If things had been different…she might have died here. Her own ashes might have been mingled into the ones which the wind was stirring within the burned-out husk.

She could not have done anything to save the people who had died here.

But the Hippodrome…

Forgive me, she mouthed to what remained of her house, and turned away. It was not enough, not nearly enough, but it was all she had right now. She had to hoard whatever she still had left—to save the rest, to save the ones still living, to do what she could for the Hippodrome, for the children, for those who were not thinking ahead to the moment when the Empire they had poked and prodded into a corner suddenly woke and turned on them—the Empire that might have looked cowed and beaten, but which was still a wounded lion at bay.

She slipped into the Hippodrome unnoticed, as unnoticed as she had been when she had slipped out of the Palace, and paused for a moment at the edge of the crowd, craning her neck to look up at the Kathisma…where a man stood, torchlight glinting on gold in his hair, his arms lifted in acknowledgment of the mass of cheering people below.

The man whom they had called Emperor.

Not Maxentius. Not her husband. In this place, in these people's eyes, right now, she was no longer Empress.

"What am I doing…?" she whispered to herself, covering her face with her hands. "What am I doing here?" *What was I hoping to do? I cannot play both ends—I cannot send in Maxentius and then warn them he is coming—as though they would even listen to me—as though they could even hear one voice amongst the roar…*

A hand landed gently on her sleeve and she recoiled, flinching, dropping her hands and turning to face whoever had accosted her.

The woman who stood beside her was familiar, but Callidora groped for the name she knew went with that face and could not find it. She stared in silence.

"You shouldn't be here," the woman said.

"You know me?"

"I was your mother's friend, Simonis. Empress Callidora. What are you doing here? If they see you, they will give you to Gennadius like a sacrifice to the old gods."

The name came at last. "Nyssa. It's Nyssa, isn't it…?"

The other woman nodded; Callidora reached out for her arm, knotting her fingers in the fabric of the sleeve of Nyssa's robe. "Help me. You have to help me. Maxentius is coming, he is coming soon, he may be only a few steps behind me. Help me get them to safety."

"Whom, child?" Nyssa said, glancing over her shoulder at the oblivious crowd.

"The children. There are children out there. I cannot help them all, but get the women and the children out. The army won't stop for them. Help me, Nyssa. The Hippodrome only has its own—and right now, the only thing that I can give is me. Help me—enough blood is going to be spilled here tonight, even without...."

Nyssa's face had changed, her expression at war with itself.

"Come with me," Nyssa said at length, pulling at Callidora's sleeve.

They scuttled out behind the main thrust of the mob, having to push their way through some stragglers, until they found themselves pausing at the entrance that led down to the animal pens, to the faction menageries, where Callidora, when she had still been Simonis, had sought shelter and sanctuary so many times...and after she remembered that, the rest was easy for Callidora, suddenly obvious.

"Bring them here," she said intently, turning to Nyssa again, her eyes bright as though with fever. "They will be safe, down here, with the beasts. The army won't come here."

"Bring whom, Simonis?"

"Anybody you can find. Send word. Let someone go...."

"Into the *crowd?*" Nyssa said. "Even if they were disposed to listen, which they're in no mood to do, there is no way another adult human would fit in between those bodies, let alone move freely, passing the word that you want. And what would you have me do—whisper that the army is coming into the ears of women alone, tell our men—our husbands, our lovers, our fathers, our sons—nothing at all? You say the wrath of the Empire is coming—and we should warn nobody—"

Callidora lifted her hands, laid her palms flat against her temples, buried her clawed fingers in her hair. "I cannot," she said. "I cannot make it all go away. But I can do what little *does* lie in my power. There *are* women out there somewhere?"

"There are those who *could* not go," Nyssa said. "The pregnant ones who cannot move quickly, the older ones, the younger girls. The ones left behind."

"Get them down here," Callidora said. "And if a grown human can't do it… find me a few half-grown ones. Are there any boys out there who would carry the word into the crowd? Any girls, even…? I would have done this, if I had been young today, I would have gone.…"

"I know, Simonis," Nyssa said gently. "But you said Maxentius is coming—you want to get children *out* of there—and now you speak of sending them *in*—if they would not listen to grown folk, why would anyone out there heed a child tugging at their elbow spinning fairy tales about what the Empress says…?"

"Tell them to go to the ones with children," Callidora said. "Tell them to get the children out." A vision of her own Chryseis swam into her mind's eye, the loved and laughing child, the only child that her body had carried and the last that she would probably have—in her years with Maxentius, after the first miscarriage, she had never quickened again. She shut it down, before the vision showed her what it would inevitably show her next—the bloodied child, empty-eyed, the laughter fled, lying still, hacked by steel blades. Her own child was still safe; she would do what she could for these, for other people's children. The Hippodrome would take a wound this night, a deep one, and there was nothing she could do about that—nothing at all. But although her hand would not be the one wielding the swords, the guilt was hers, and the weight of it was almost enough to make her knees buckle right there on the stone flags and cry it out aloud.

But there was still this last thing that she could try. She could not stop the inexorable present…but she could try and save the future.

Her eye was caught by the glint of torchlight catching on the gems on her shoes, now grimed and torn beyond repair on the gritty, rubble-strewn streets that she had raced down. Struck by a sudden inspiration, she bent down and slipped her feet out of the jewelled shoes, gathering them up in one hand and offering them to Nyssa, as she herself remained standing barefoot on the edge where the arena sands gave way to the paving stones of the outer Hippodrome.

"Take these," she said. "Send whom you can send. Give every one of them one of those gems. That is proof. They are not making this up. The Empress says—there's proof. Get the children out. And hurry."

"Where are you going?"

"Down to the beasts," Callidora said over her shoulder, making her way down the ramp that led to the animal pens. "On this night, the beasts will be friendlier than fellow men. Send them all down here, to me. Nyssa.…" She paused, turned, her face stark under the torchlight. "Believe me. Please, believe me. And do what I ask."

Nyssa's hand closed hard on the jewelled shoes. "I believe you," she said. "I will do what I can."

Callidora padded down the ramp, her bare feet almost silent on the ancient stones. She found her heart beating very fast, the memories flooded back, the years at Maxentius's side faded as the little girl in her returned—the little girl called Simonis, who had just been called by her own name again after so long. Simonis, who had once slept nestled into the rough fur of a bear's flank, fearing nothing. Simonis, who had walked into a lion's den to pull a thorn out of a lion's paw. Simonis, who had once given her fate over to a man known as Cicatrice… because he had promised her that one day he would arrange it so that she could work with the animals.

These animals. The Hippodrome beasts, who were all, sooner or later, destined to die for the entertainment of the arena—but who symbolised only a towering sense of warmth and safety and security for a little girl who was once Simonis, child of Batzas, keeper of bears.

The animals were restless, abandoned—all the keepers had gone up to the arena, to where the crowds were, to where the new Emperor held court over the Hippodrome. Callidora was greeted by a growl from the lions as they paced their enclosure, their massive paws slapping softly down on the stones; she echoed their growl, throwing the sound back at them, and one of the lions halted, staring, its golden eyes focused directly on her. But she had already turned away, facing the single bear that stood in its cage, shaking its head back and forth, its small angry eyes leaving her in no doubt that it was displeased, angry, probably hungry, and in no mood to be trifled with.

"I was once a friend," Callidora whispered, reaching up for her bear claw, the *stoicheon* that hung at her throat. "I betrayed one of you, too—because I loved her too much, because she loved me. I know I have little right to ask— but give us sanctuary this night. Keep us safe. Let it pass over us."

The bear halted, snuffled at her, rose briefly up on its back paws—the cage had a roof of stone, too low for the bear to rear up to its full height, but even with its head ducked between its shoulders it was an imposing sight. The bear claw hung at Callidora's neck, exposed; she knew, rationally, that it could not have meant anything at all to the living bear in the cage in which her own she-bear had once been, whose spirit was present stronger than ever within Callidora and around her right now, as though her shadow-bear had come to bargain with the animals on her behalf, in their own language, on their own terms.

The first of the women whom Nyssa had shepherded down into the animal pens stumbled down the ramp not too long after—young, very young, and heavily enough pregnant that she had to hold her swinging belly with one hand as she made her careful way to where Callidora stood. Her eyes were wide, staring.

"Nyssa said…that the Empress…?"

"I am Simonis tonight," Callidora said gently. "I am the Hippodrome's own. Come, there is clean straw over there—it's a warm corner, I know, I used to curl up there and watch my father work when I was very young. Come, let's get you settled."

They came, after that—singly, in pairs, women holding infants, women holding the hands of children barely old enough to toddle, women alone, small children on their own who looked frightened and confused and whom Callidora gathered up, soothed, paired off with women who had brought children of their own. She fossicked around the keepers' duty quarters, where she had known her father to keep a food stash for the long nights that he had to work down here or for emergencies—and sure enough, nothing had changed much since Batzas had walked these halls. She took what was there, shamelessly, and distributed the keepers' secret hoards amongst the women; she sent a couple of the older children to get clean water from where it was piped down into the animal pens, gathered up the keepers' cups and passed them around, even found a skin of wine that one of the keepers had left down here, in express defiance of standing orders that no intoxicating drink was to be brought down to the animal pens, and handed that down to some of the women who looked pinched and scared enough to need some.

These were the women who had not been part of the crowd—too pregnant, too old, too many children who were too young to be left alone. But after a while some of the others began to trickle in—looking sceptical, and confused, and then increasingly astonished as the truth of the rumour they had followed here became apparent.

"The boy who got me said that the Empress…" one of the women said. "I didn't believe him, but he said that the Empress said to get out if I wanted my son to live…." She had her arm around a boy, maybe six or seven years old, who looked tearful and rebellious and ready to go tearing right back to where the excitement was the moment his mother let go of him. All too aware of that, the arm draped around the boy's shoulders was deceptively casual—she actually held him in a grip of iron, as though afraid to open her hand.

"I'm glad you finally did believe him," Callidora said. "Is it…."

"They're still there. Nothing had happened yet by the time I stepped onto the ramp."

"Are others coming?"

"Very few." That was Nyssa, coming down the ramp herself with a handful of other women. They were closely followed by a few of the boys who had been her messengers, owl-eyed as they came down the ramp and craned their necks to catch their first glimpse of the woman who had owned the gems with which they had gone into the crowds—the gems that were proof of who had sent the urgent message to retreat, to come out of the jubilant crowds. Some of Nyssa's women were her own age or older, others younger, clutching more children. "How many have you down here?"

"Not all. Not nearly enough. Maybe two or three hundred." Callidora turned to glance around the area, where women and children had found niches to settle down; women offering a breast to fretful suckling infants—women improvising makeshift games for the younger toddlers, trying to keep their minds occupied—women crouching anxiously in corners as far away from the animal cages as they could, their eyes glittering with fear—women who had taken the role of organisers, who had grasped the situation and now moved amongst the rest, soothing, helping, calming, stealing anxious glances all the while at the ramp which led back up to the arena…where their men were. Where all of the Hippodrome, and half of the city of Visant, had crowded together that night to usher in a new Imperial era.

"We still have a few scouts out there," Nyssa said. "Some of them bear the jewels from your shoes. There might still be some, a few who are coming…."

"I'm going up," Callidora said. "I am going to get a feel for it."

Nyssa appeared to want to say something, but then decided against it, and merely touched Callidora's arm. "Stay by the entrance."

There was little about Callidora, right now, to identify her as anything other than just another woman of the Hippodrome—as though she had never left the place at all—her feet bare and dirty, her hair only just held together in a loose braid which hung down her back. But her face was etched with anxiety, her eyes huge and bright, her whole body braced for what was to come. If she had been amongst the more superstitious citizens of Visant, the kind who came to high mass when celebrated by the Patriarch but secretly visited the wharfside astrologers every day, Callidora might have sworn that she could see Death stalking the Hippodrome arena that night, could feel its icy breath as it brushed past her, its cold fingers touching her shrinking flesh.

"May the One God be praised!"

The exclamation was heartfelt, if perhaps a little misplaced under the circumstances—but Callidora knew that voice, and turned to face the cowled figure of Arkadios, leaning heavily on the stone wall beside him.

"What are you doing here?" she asked.

"The *despotes* charged me to find you," Arkadios said. "To keep you—"

"Where is he?"

"On his way," Arkadios said. "Out there. Maybe a few streets away."

Callidora felt tears burning her eyes. "Oh, God have mercy on us all," she said, her voice breaking. "Will Maxentius ever forgive me for this?"

"Listen," Arkadios said sharply, turning his head a little.

She heard it, too. Or maybe she just thought she heard it, maybe it was still coming, maybe she was hearing with her heart.

A step of booted feet.

Too late.

"Come on," she said urgently, her voice barely above a whisper, reaching out to grab the edge of Arkadios's cloak. "They're here. You have to get out of here. Now."

She knew, if she waited another instant, she might meet Maxentius's own eyes across the arena...and knew that she could not bear it. What she could save, was saved, down below, with the beasts.

She let go of Arkadios's cloak, turned, ran, blinded by tears.

Nyssa stopped her at the bottom of the stair. "I think Ismeme may be about to her child, right over...." She paused, as her glance caught on Arkadios, following Callidora down the ramp.

"It's all right," Callidora said. "He is a friend. Ismeme—has she had other...?"

Nyssa shook her head. "No. Her first."

Callidora closed her eyes briefly. "I suppose it might be a sign," she whispered. "New life, tonight. Where is she?"

"Over there. On the straw."

"Arkadios. Stay here. Warn me if anybody...."

Arkadios glanced up the ramp. If anyone came down here there, was little that Arkadios could do, that any of them could do. But he merely nodded, taking up his post at the bottom of the ramp. "Yes, *despoina.*"

The sounds that drifted down into the animal quarters suddenly took on a different tone—the jubilant shouts had been replaced by faint screams, a distant ring of steel. Many of the women whimpered, cried out, began to sob—not all of them had believed, when they came here, that what the Empress had prophesied would come to pass, and was happening right now in the arena above them where men were dying. The smell of death and fear came curling down into the animal pens, disturbing the animals all over again, starting them growling, pacing, pawing at the bars of their enclosures as they caught the scent of blood.

Callidora tried to close her ears to it all, hurried over to Ismeme instead, filling her mind and heart and spirit with this, just this, an imminent birth. Ismeme, breathing hard, lifted a panicked face to stare at Callidora as she came down to crouch beside her.

"It's all right," Callidora said. "It will all be all right."

The memories of her own childbirth fears came flooding back—heavy with Chryseis, already instinctively knowing that the man who was her baby's father was not going to be of any real help or support to her, alone amongst strangers who did not speak her language, afraid of what was to come with nobody to talk to about it or to talk her through it in a way that would have made a difference, or eased her anxieties, or helped her through her pain.

"It's all right," she repeated. "You're amongst your own."

"Help me," Ismeme whispered, her eyes locked with Callidora's.

"We will all…."

Ismeme shot out a hand and locked her fingers around Callidora's wrist in a panicked, bruising grip. Callidora was her one spar right now, the one who had brought her down here, who had offered salvation, who was the reason her child would be born at all. "No, you. *You….*" Her breath caught on a gasp, and then a sob. "Oh, One God, it *hurts….*"

Callidora settled down onto her knees from her crouch, beside the pregnant girl. "All right, I am here. I won't leave you," she said, turning her head briefly to find someone who was there to carry out her orders. In that one instant, she realised that Arkadios was no longer at his post, that the ramp was empty; her heart lurched painfully, but she could not think about that. Not right now. Not with this terrified child who was about to bear a child, clinging to Callidora with superhuman strength. "Somebody, get some water. And we will need a knife."

Time vanished. There was nothing except the *now*, the rapid breathing and the moans of pain, the blood that seeped down Ismeme's legs and onto Callidora's hands and arms, spilling onto her gown, smearing onto her face as she lifted the back of a blood-streaked hand to push a loose strand of hair away from her face. She had no idea how long it all took, but it was she who received Ismeme's new-born daughter into her hands, held the child while some other hand cut the cord that tied her to her mother, saw the tiny rosebud mouth open in a face still wet with blood and birth fluids and the small, perfect hand open up like a starfish, reaching out.

"*Lady....*" A frightened, anxious voice behind Callidora brought her back to reality. "Lady...there's a man...with a sword...."

Callidora looked up, met Nyssa's eyes, wordlessly handed over the child into the other woman's arms and rose to her feet, turning, bracing herself for the sight of some stray soldier who might have heard a noise....

....And met the grey eyes of Maxentius, across an expanse of empty floor, his bloodied sword still in his right hand, the left hanging loose and useless by his side.

He in turn stared at the woman he had made his queen, his heart giving a queer lurch as he saw her standing there with her gown streaked with blood and her hands red up to her elbows, smears of blood disappearing into her hairline.

They did not speak. They could not. There was a silence between them as wide as the Middle Sea, and as deep.

And then they both took an unsteady step forward, towards each other.

"Are you hurt?" Maxentius managed to force out, a hoarse whisper.

"No," Callidora said, and reached out her arms to him. "But you are."

Arkadios, standing just behind Maxentius, took the few steps necessary to come up beside him—Maxentius released his hold on his sword as Arkadios closed his own hand on the grip, and in the same motion reached out to gather Callidora to him, his left hand hanging by his side and refusing to obey his command, but his right holding her against his chest with a strength that frightened her.

"Is it over?" she murmured, the side of her face crushed against his armour, her eyes closed.

She felt him nod, his chin moving against the top of her head. And then his right hand came around her shoulders, inched forward along the line of her jaw from behind, made her lift her head to look at him.

"Don't leave me again," he said.

Her eyes were full of tears. "Can you forgive me?"

"For what? For all that?" He jerked his head back along the ramp, back to the arena filled with death. "That was my doing, if anyone's."

"Empress...."

Callidora swallowed, turned slightly in the curve of Maxentius's arm to face the woman who had addressed her. It was Nyssa, carrying a tiny mewling bundle in the crook of her arm.

"I thought you should know," Nyssa said. "Ismeme is the wife of the Golden Crown assistant bear-keeper. This…is a bear-keeper's daughter. Ismeme asked me if I knew of a suitable name and I could only think of one." She smiled, lifted and turned the newborn a little so that Callidora could glimpse the face, still red and wrinkled but with two huge wide eyes now open and staring out into the world. "This," Nyssa said, rocking the baby gently in the cradle of her arms, "is Simonis."

EPILOGUE

ive me the life I was meant to live.

GA woman had once asked that of a God, and the God had made reply. The life that had been granted had been rich and full, filled with both good and bad in equal measure, lest the lack of one or the other should cause either complacency or resentment…and far too short.

Callidora was forty-eight years old, and she knew that she would not see another winter.

They were sitting out on the terrace where the lanterns had been lit for them, a bench set out on the mosaic floor, piled with cushions and throws for the Empress's comfort, where she could recline, nestled in the circle of Maxentius's arms around her, watching the round full moon rise in the sky, large and yellow like a golden solidus. The season was changing; yet another hot Visant summer was fading, and the first hint of coolness touched the air in the early mornings and just after sundown, the first hints of that winter which Callidora knew would come without her being there to share it with Maxentius.

Nearly thirty years had passed since they met. Almost three decades that they had been together. It didn't seem right that there would come a season they would be apart.

Callidora felt a little strange that evening, as though the moon was closer to her than it should have been. Its light felt heavier, almost like a slight but solid weight upon her skin. In that solid light, which was casting sharp-edged black shadows, she could almost see the shapes of long-gone ghosts, people who had drifted through her life and left it, leaving tracks in her memory. Circassaë, red-haired and beautiful as she had once been, danced by in her diaphanous veils, laughing. Eleazar bar Yabin, who had fulfilled his promise to return to Visant and find her, and who had been astonished, when he arrived, to find himself being received not by the girl whom he had once known as Simonis, who had been afraid that she could never gain back the City of Gold which she had so carelessly left, but by the Empress of Visant in the porphyry chambers of the Imperial Palace. Father Honorius, many years dead now, caught in Antacia when another wave of that plague that had decimated Visant had returned to sweep Antacia—and whose clutches, this time, he had not escaped.

And the living. Chryseis, now married and grown with children of her own. Arkadios, getting on in years now, but still faithfully serving his *despotes* and his *despoina* as Grand Chancellor, the long-term companion and trusted friend who knew their preferences and their secrets and did not need words to know what they were thinking, or what they needed to be done.

And something else, something that she had carried through the years, whose commands she had obeyed, whose protection she had trusted, whose presence she had never questioned. Callidora's hand strayed, as it often did, to the bear claw that she still wore around her neck, and she sighed deeply.

Maxentius stirred. "What is it?"

"I was just...remembering," she said softly. "Thinking back...to the first time...."

"The first time of what?" Maxentius said, shifting to gather her into a more comfortable embrace.

She leaned her head back against his shoulder and gave him a small smile.

"My bear," she said, her hand still at her throat. She lifted the claw a little for him to see. "This bear. The one who loved me, the one who killed for me, who died for me. She's always been with me, all the way. When my strength was not enough, she rose inside of me and roared defiance, and the strength that I had sufficed—but it was her power that carried me through. Not mine."

"You are the strongest woman I know," Maxentius said sturdily. "You needed no bear spirit to help you cope with your burdens."

She looked away, back at the moon.

"You don't know everything...."

Twenty years, and the secret was still hers—the secret of the journey to Ravin, to the island where its queen had been imprisoned…to Rothaide's understanding, and pride, and forgiveness. Father Honorius had told her that Maxentius must never know—and she had obeyed. Now, with Rothaide herself one of the ghosts drifting in the golden moonlight, it all came flooding back, sharp as the moon-shadows—the irrational fear that she would lose everything, the choice she made not to stand between Rothaide and her death…the roar of her bear in her mind, the fury, the jealousy, the pain.

She still could not tell him. It had all happened too long ago; saying anything now would open wounds long healed, and Callidora had made her peace with the fact that he would not, could never, forgive her for what she had done.

But perhaps it was all those years that had passed in between that suddenly made her start thinking about everything again—right from the beginning, when she had first allowed her shadow-bear to guide and protect her. All sorts of moments illuminated suddenly in her memory, as though the moon had crept into the dark corners of her mind and poured the eerie, heavy light over everything, until it was overflowing into every nook and cranny, leaving her no place to hide any more.

To hide from herself, least of all.

Every one of those moments, of those choices, of the things that she had done or chosen to do because she believed that she had listened to or had been guided by the great shadow of her bear-protector, whether they had been the choice to allow royal blood to be spilled while her silence gave it sanction, or the way she had stepped up to take responsibility for an Empire when Maxentius lay on the brink of death during the black plague…all they had ever had in common was Callidora herself, in the centre of it all, sometimes seeking a place to lay the responsibility when it became too heavy for herself to bear.

All the choices had been hers. All the actions.

The shadow-bear had never been a protector, or a guardian angel. It was merely the darkness of her own soul, the deepest, the most powerful, and the most raw of her own emotions.

She was the bear. Always had been.

She tilted her head a little to look up at Maxentius's profile above her; he was gazing somewhere into the distance, his head held high. Callidora tried to remember him when he had been young, when they had both been young; she had changed him, too, over the years, making her own choices, forcing his.

"What are you thinking?" she asked quietly.

He turned his head to look down on her. "Nothing," he said. "The past."

Same as her, then. She closed her eyes, a soft sigh escaping her.

But Maxentius had been thinking of a different past.

It had been the night of slaughter at the Hippodrome that had changed him, forever. He would never again be the sort of man who would consider the easy way out, a choice to avoid confrontation. He had faced that demon, and he would never shy from it again. The order to go into the Hippodrome had been only the first step in regaining control over his own Empire—in the aftermath, it had been he, the Emperor, who had had to deal with the conspirators who had started the revolt and fed it until it had so nearly taken Maxentius himself in the fires that had been allowed to rage in his city.

He had gone down to the holding cells in the dungeons beneath the Palace, after, to face Sarrus, the instigator, the driving force.

The ex-Chancellor had received the Emperor in his cell as though it had been he who had been giving an audience.

"I am owed a trial," Sarrus had said, standing with his arms crossed across his chest, his gaze as imperious as any crowned Emperor's.

Maxentius had stared at him, and had shaken his head, very slowly.

"No," he said, his voice soft but implacable. "I told you in the arena, it is over. You have had your trial; you have stood in the arena with a puppet Emperor whom you had crowned while another still lived and reigned, anointed by popular acclaim and by God himself in the person of his Bishops and the Patriarch of the church in whose authority you yourself have always claimed to believe. You have condemned yourself. I can call thousands of witnesses to that fact—thousands living, more than a thousand dead, men and women and children in the Hippodrome whose blood is on your hands. I am your judge now. You have said all you are ever going to say to anybody outside these walls. You will not have a public trial, there will not be a chance for you to play the martyr of the people, or to offer last words that would reverberate through history. You are done, Sarrus. This is the end. I come now only to tell you one thing—that I am your judge, and that I have passed sentence. You will die a traitor's death in these dungeons, alone, without an audience, tonight. And there will be no marker placed on your grave."

"What of Gennadius?" Sarrus demanded, visibly shaken. "It was *he* who accepted the crown—it was *he* who...."

"As I have been told, he refused it at least twice before you persuaded him into that acceptance. And even then...did you even know that he managed to send a messenger to me that night, to tell me that you were all there at the Hippodrome, that if I wanted to end this I could end it all, right there, right then, with all of you in the trap...? No, I didn't think so," Maxentius said, seeing Sarrus's face change. "You too were betrayed. But it does not matter, because without your influence behind it all Gennadius would never have set foot in the Kathisma at all with that gold chain upon his head. The gold chain that he accepted, that condemns him too...."

"Are you going to destroy us all?" Sarrus demanded. "With one sweep of your hand? By God—I always knew you for this. I knew your ambition, I saw it in you long before you knew it yourself. I could see the taint of it in everything you touched...."

"You were wrong about me," Maxentius said simply. "*Then*. I was an innocent then. That night at the Hippodrome...that changed it all. I can now do things I did not believe were possible. *You* taught me that." He paused, and gave Sarrus a brief inclination of the head, an acknowledgment, slight enough to be almost insulting, big enough to make his point. "You taught me how to order your death, Sarrus," he said. "Make your peace with whatever gods you do worship, because you meet them tonight."

"Wait..." Sarrus said, as Maxentius turned to leave. "Wait—I have to...."

But Maxentius was gone.

And it had all happened as he had said it would. Sarrus's body had been rotting in an unmarked grave for two decades.

Maxentius had believed that he could be satisfied with merely exiling Gennadius, to some distant province where he would be unable to do much harm—his record as Emperor, even for just a few hours, had been abject enough for him to pose no real threat, Maxentius thought. But it was Gennadius's own brother, the general Severus, who taught him otherwise.

"He is my brother, and I love him," Severus had said, having asked for and obtained a private audience with the Emperor. "But Gennadius...is a tool. He has already been used against you once. He may swear that he will never allow that to happen again...but he deludes himself when he makes that vow, and he would break it, the next time someone with a stronger will than his own comes along to whisper poison into his ear."

"So what are you suggesting that I do with him?" Maxentius had asked.

"Death, or imprisonment for life in a place from which he cannot easily escape," Severus had said. "And he is my brother. I do not give this advice lightly."

"But if he is a tool, then so are all of you, all the three brothers," Maxentius said softly. "How am I to deal with you?"

"August," Severus had said levelly, "what you do with myself or with Petronus is your decision. All I can tell you is to remind you that Petronus fled the city rather than be used by Sarrus and his friends, and that I…have never wished to sit on the throne. I am a soldier, not an Emperor. And no one could give me enough reason to change my mind on that."

Gennadius had been given a patrician's death, and he had been buried with enough honours to placate the Senators. Maxentius could afford to be magnanimous, but he could no longer afford to show mercy. His night in the Hippodrome had changed something in him—there had been little softness left, after that. He had withdrawn behind that armour that Visant had bestowed upon him, the layer of nacre that had once coated an irritant that the boy from the country, the peasant's son, had been in the shell of the City of Gold and had changed him forever into something that Visant had claimed as its own.

The city, the Hippodrome, had understood what he had done—but had found it hard to give him absolution for it. It took a long time before they stopped remembering those who had died every time they saw Maxentius's face. But the Hippodrome also remembered that the Empress had come herself to offer salvation to those who would take it, and they also remembered, at last, that it had been Maxentius who had led his soldiers into the crowd but that it had also been Maxentius who had stopped the killing. They might never have loved him, after, in the same way that they might have done before—but they respected him, and they even realised, after a while, that they had reason to be grateful.

The Empire learned to know him, in the aftermath of the rising, as brilliant, constant, just, a lawmaker and lawgiver, a strong arm and a heavy hand, a guardian of the boundaries of the Empire and of all who lived within it—but they had rarely seen him smile, and they had never again seen him vulnerable.

The only person who had still known that side of him, what softness remained, had been Callidora.

He knew that she was dying. There was no escaping that knowledge—she had been fading before his eyes, the once slender woman now almost gaunt, her cheekbones tight against skin that seemed barely able to stretch to cover them, her large eyes bigger than ever, threatening to engulf her whole face. But he had never said anything to her. He was determined to live the days that they had been given without contemplating the days that they would not be.

The days that would, perhaps, end this night, with her lying in his arms, almost weightless, her breathing shallow and barely audible.

It was she who was ill, it was she who was in almost constant pain. But looking down at her wrung his own heart with such sharp agony that he could not help a small gasp.

Callidora opened her eyes at that.

"Are you all right?"

"I was just…thinking," he said.

"Yes," she murmured, "so you said. Still about the past…?"

He smiled at her, smoothing the hair from her face.

"Maxentius," she said abruptly, her face suddenly serious, earnest, almost pleading, "forgive me."

"What do you need forgiveness for?"

"For the things I could not tell you. For being afraid that you would someday choose another in my place. For being afraid that it wouldn't last, couldn't last, that you would look away someday and find someone better suited to stand beside you…."

"I can forgive you almost anything, except the thought that you might ever have believed that of me," he said. "I chose you. I was grateful that you chose me. I am grateful right now for every day of the years that have gone by since that choosing. There is nothing to forgive, Callidora. Would you like some more wine?"

"No," she said, looking away, back at the moon. "But I think… I think I could sleep now…."

Her eyes closed again, and after a few moments her breathing slowed, quieted, and her hand slipped from the bear claw at her throat, coming to rest on her breast.

Maxentius's eyes filled with sudden tears as he watched her life ebb away, slowly, one breath at a time. He resisted the temptation to gather her to him and hold her tightly, and beg her to stay, and tell her how little meaning his life would have left in it once she was gone. But it would not have been kind.

"Good night," he said instead, his voice low, and loving, and steady, his eyes resting on her face which he could not see clearly through his tears. "Good night, Augusta."

AUTHOR'S NOTE

"The Imperial team complemented one another, even in their differences, and both were utterly loyal. Perhaps the glue of the partnership was mutual respect."—*The Empress Theodora, Partner of Justinian*, James Allan Evanx

"However it occurred…[their meeting] appears to have been a love-at-first-sight thunderbolt. It is worth remembering that among the tons of invective poured over them in subsequent years by doctrinal opponents and political enemies, not a single word accuses either of betraying the other, Their partnership was total, their love for one another complete."—*Justinian's Flea*, William Rosen

Western readers are familiar with that part of history that was Rome—the Republic, the Empire, Julius Caesar, Nero who fiddled while Rome burned—the classic tropes which are so strongly woven into the cultural fabric of our lives. They are also familiar with the European Middle Ages, the basis of so many historical novels and fantasies—the names ring with recognition, Richard the Lionheart, Charlemagne, the Crusades, Neuschwannstein Castle and its many copies, the knights and ladies of medieval England and France and Germany and Spain, King Arthur and the middle-ages-that-never-quite-were.

What many of them are not familiar with at all is what came between those two particularly fecund periods of European history, the missing step which connected the ancient Rome to the rousing and romanticised Middle Ages of Western Europe.

That missing step was Byzantium.

Perhaps because so much of its history was spent looking to the east, the Empire of Byzantium, first sibling and then heir to the Empire of Rome, simply never managed to hold the Western reader's attention. But it was a rich time, full of passion and power, and it's disappointing that the only legacy it seems to have left in the Western mind is the meaning which has accreted to the word "Byzantine" when it is used to describe something as being intricate, complicated, and perhaps too difficult to understand.

Byzantium has its own gallery of rogues and heroes, and these names are much less well known in the West. One of the best known of its Emperors, perhaps by virtue of the character and identity of the woman he made his Empress, was Justinian, whom history sometimes calls "the Great". His wife, Theodora, rose from the lowest rungs of the social ladder to the dizzying heights of Empire—a strong and outspoken woman in a world dominated by men. Much of what is known about her centers on that past, and on the things that she must have done in order to survive it. Period sources candidly name her "Theodora from the brothel", and accusations of sexual misbehaviour have never ceased to cling to her memory.

But these two, Justinian and Theodora, a somewhat scholarly man much his wife's senior and the vivid, brilliant woman who understood people and knew how to handle them, between them ruled an Empire at its most brilliant height, and their legacy includes an across-the-board betterment of women's rights, a law codex on which most of our modern law rests today, and Hagia Sophia. And the unlikely pair were blessed with the kind of enduring relationship, and a complete and utterly mutual partnership based on love, trust and a deep knowledge of one another's strengths, that not many people have had before or since they ruled Byzantium's Empire together. Their lives and times are truly the stuff of story.

Maxentius and Callidora in my story are not, precisely, the historical Justinian and Theodora. The events depicted in this novel mostly happened—but not necessarily in the order I have them in this book, or to the extent to which I chose to take them. The rising in the final section of the book, for example, has a name—Justinian and Theodora really did weather an insurrection like this, and history has recorded this time as the Nika riots—but neither of them were in the Hippodrome, as I have them in my story, to personally resolve this crisis. The Empress's speech in council, however, is real—in a period of history which has scant primary sources remaining and has been interpreted and reinterpreted any number of ways, that speech has survived, a true gem lost in a mass of glittering imitations, and although the actual words quoted by various books differ a little here and there the gist was the same—"You may go, Caesar, but I stay, and I will die wearing purple if I cannot live in it." It was Theodora, the only woman in a council full of men, in an Empire ruled by men, who saved Justinian's realm that day—at a price that it seems to be hard for modern historians to pin down. Estimates of casualties from the raid that Justinian sent to the Hippodrome range from 20 000 to 50 000 people—and yes, in my world the number was considerably smaller, because in my world my Emperor called a halt, where in the true history Justinian's general, the celebrated Belisarius, had no such word to stop him.

This is a novel of alternate history. People much like those in my book once lived and breathed and reigned, although my characters are not—*quite*—those people. Events that occur in my book may have occurred in the distant past, although not—*quite*—in the manner or the order in which they are depicted here.

I have not attempted truth, except inasmuch as I have tried to convey the emotional truth of the story that I chose to bring to a readership which might have been unfamiliar with the names of Justinian and Theodora. For those who wish to pursue independent study of the actual true events of their lives and times, there are many history books out there which will serve. The book you are holding in your hands right now is not history—not as you know it—not the compendium of times and dates which define the lives of the Imperial pair. It is, however, true *story*. If Justinian and Theodora were telling you their own story, independent of the trappings of history, legacy and empire…this is the story that they might tell.

Alma Alexander
October 2015

PS

Book club discussion questions

Interview with the author

EMPRESS

Book Club Discussion Questions

1. Is there such a thing as 'destiny' – something that is inevitable – or do you think that good things only come to those who fight for them? Do you think Simonis's prayer – "Give me the life I was meant to live" – exemplifies a fatalistic view of life, or a battle cry?

2. Do you believe in love at first sight? Do you believe that there someone out there who is 'The One' for you? Do you think that Maxentius and Simonis would have been incomplete if they had not met each other? Do you think that either life would have been diminished by the fact that the other was missing? In what way?

3. Was Cicatrice an evil villain or simply a dark angel in the young Simonis's life? Do you think he helped launch her on the path which she eventually followed? Do you think she betrayed a benefactor of sorts when she fled with Gallienus, or do you think she was escaping bondage?

4. Simonis had a "spirit animal" as a protector, her bear. What do you think about that idea? Do you have a "totem" animal spirit which you feel close to?

What other cultures had similar beliefs? How do you think a belief like this would affect Simonis's primary faith?

5. Leontes never crowned his wife as Empress. Maxentius did. Do you agree with their reasons? What do you see as the differences in status, in responsibilities? Is there a particular kind of person whom it would be cruel to ask to assume such responsibilities?

6. The Hippodrome is its own world, a microcosm of society within a great city. What happens when someone is forced to choose between the rules and laws of the Hippodrome and those of the greater world? Which would or should take precedence? Why? And what would be the consequences?

7. Discuss the meeting between Callidora and Rothaide. Their one and only face to face meeting takes place on a number of different levels with plenty of subtext. Can you tease out the layers? What is really going on in that scene?

8. During Maxentius's illness, it is Callidora, the Empress, who takes over the day-to-day governance of the Empire. Do you think this was the right decision or was she usurping authority she was never meant to hold?

9. Callidora's "payment of debts" – her meetings with Gallienus, Virgillus, and Cicatrice. What do you think of her 'payback' to all of these men?

10. Every life has turning points, moments in which a decision is taken which defines the further course of one's existence. What do you think were some of those moments for Maxentius and for Simonis?

11. EMPRESS touches on religious schism – it is a fantasy world in which Christianity as we know it does not exist, but religious differences of this sort existed in the Christian world of the REAL historical era presided over by the Byzantine Empire. In terms of the novel's context (leaving aside the dogma squabbles between the Christian princes of our own world) which view would you consider closer to your own idea of a good faith, that of Visant or that or Rhakotis?

BONUS ROUND:

Eleazar ben Yabin, the traveler, mentions an expedition to the land of Syai, "where the silk comes from" – have you read the other novels set in the geographical world of 'Empress', which take place in Syai? 'Secrets of Jin Shei' and 'Embers of Heaven' may take place in a different locale and a different time frame than 'Empress', but the author is creating a very real OTHER world, in which these historical fantasies are set, a world with a history and a world-wide geography which includes all the locales where individual novels are set. Can you begin to glimpse a time line of that alternate history throughout the historical fantasy novels of Alma Alexander?

INTERVIEW WITH THE AUTHOR

Why is storytelling so important?

There are truths that need to be spoken, internalized and understood. Many of them can be hurtful, even agonizing, if administered unadulterated. Wrap them in a layer of story, though, and they will slide down easier – and the truths they contain will be no less important for all that.

Stories awe us, entertain us, teach us, make us laugh, make us cry, make us believe in six impossible things before breakfast. Stories take us to Narnia, to the Syai Empire, and to worlds that might look a lot like the one we glimpse when we look out of the window but are somehow… somehow… different. Stories free the imagination and the mind. They make us stay up all night to finish a good book; they make our toddlers go to sleep.

Stories are quite simply the closest thing that the human race has ever come to something resembling real magic.

If you could introduce one of your characters to any character from another book, who would it be and why?

I have created a few hundred characters and they would not all relate well to the same otherwise character.

But if I should narrow this down to the intimate gathering of friends in one of my latest novels,"Midnight at Spanish Gardens", it might be Dianora from Guy Gavriel Kay's "Tigana."

She is from a much more fantastical setting, to be sure, but she would be an amazing person to talk to about the power of choice for any one of my five friends in that café at midnight at the end of the world. And I would sure love to be a fly on the wall for that conversation.

Why did you to choose to become a writer?

When someone asked Ursula Le Guin what she would be if she weren't a writer, she answered succinctly, "Dead." That's also me.

I made no conscious decision to "be a writer" – I was mugged, hauled off into a dark alley, and presented with a stark choice – write or die. I wrote my first poem at five years old; I wrote my first (unspeakably bad and thankfully deceased) novel when I was eleven, and my first reasonably GOOD and wholly original novel (which still exists, all 500-odd handwritten pages of it) at 15. I started winning writing awards at 12.

But while I always knew I was a **writer,** I realized I wanted to become an author – a writer who makes writing her sole career – when my then school brought in Lynne Reid Banks as a visiting author one rainy autumn evening.

As I watched her talk about all the furies of the writer's life – all the rejections, the writer's-block, the constant revisions, the frustration, the bad reviews, the endless waiting, I saw the light of angels in her eyes. She was telling us the unvarnished truth, but also that she could not live any other kind of life.

And the hairs on the back of my neck lifted in nearly superstitious awe, and I thought, "Yes. That. I want THAT."

That was the moment I knew what I wanted to do with the rest of my life.

Agatha Christie got her best ideas while eating green apples in the bathtub. Steven Spielberg gets his while driving. When do you get yours and why do you think this is?

I often dream mine. Sometimes I serial-dream, simply picking up a dream where I left it off the previous night.

But that is hardly the primary source of ideas.

For a writer, ideas are everywhere. Kudos to Christie and Spielberg for being able to nail down where and how they get theirs – but mine come at me from unexpected places and inconvenient times, leaving me to scribble them down on bits of paper or try to remember a single shorthand phrase which will be a trigger for the thing to unfold into a full-blown idea.

I have very little control over this. I've been known to interrupt conversations to scurry off and grab the little notebook I always carry and scribble furiously as some new thought or wonderful story idea mugs me and won't let go until it is at least recorded well enough to be recalled at a later stage when I'm actually at a keyboard and can do something about it.

What type of writer are you—one who experiences like Hemingway, or one who daydreams and fantasizes?

Well, I write mostly fantasy. If I experienced much of what I write I would be a very unique human being indeed.

Why do you choose to work in the speculative genres?

Part of the answer could be that I cut my teeth on mythology and fairy tales when it came to early reading – but that isn't really it, most children do, and for many the love affair with the fantastic does not endure past the age when poor Susan's sudden attraction for cosmetics and nylons got her kicked out of Narnia.

For me, the never-worlds held a particular kind of magic – they were worlds which had their own rules, where nothing was inevitable, where anything could happen and usually did – and it was a particular kind of joy to delve into such a world and find out the secrets it held.

Part of that was the sheer danger of going into places where the only extant maps said Here Be Dragons… partly for the pure incandescent pleasure of the possibility that there might actually be dragons to see. Once I found out that I had the sort of wings that would let me soar in these rarefied airs… why would I ever be wholly content with just walking anywhere again?

The speculative genre is not a place where the "real" and the hard and the difficult do not exist – on the contrary, it is perhaps the place where such things exist in their purest form, and as ideas can get explored, discussed, gnawed at and even possibly defanged – all while "protected" by the "fantastic" and therefore rendered invulnerable and powerful in ways that might then get translated back into our everyday reality.

Fantasy is the great power, the weapon that vanquishes anything, the knowledge that arms you against all folly and all misery. It gives of itself and of its wisdom, freely. And I am proud and humbled, all at once, to be called to call it my own.

What aspect of speculative writing do you find most challenging, and how do you address that?

A fantasy world does not need to work according to the rules of our own world – but it absolutely has to follow its own rules, whatever those rules may be in context.

One of the hardest aspects of worldbuilding is to create a world which is utterly strange and yet utterly believable and self-consistent – the flowering of the idea that everything comes at a cost, and then having to work out what the cost of things is in the world that I have created and to make sure that the trade is fair, and sustainable.

I work hard at my worlds – if I am writing a work of historical fiction, such as "Secrets of Jin Shei" or "Embers of Heaven", I will read thirty books before I write my one volume, thirty books that cover the spectrum of history, geography, memoir, biography, social customs, fashions, food, climate and related issues such as possible crops and livestock, economics, everything that makes a world tick.

90% of this won't make it into the finished book, but because I know my material it all informs the 10% that does, and there is a real sense of stability and steadiness and verisimilitude – the sense that my worlds rest on solid ground, have deep roots, and even though they may not be real, they COULD be if they so choose.

This is important to me. My fiction may be fantasy but it is also TRUE, to itself, to its story, to its genre. I dive into world creation, head first, and let it close over my head; I live in those other worlds, while creating their stories. There are times that our own reality seems dim and strange to me, when I come up for air.

What motivates you to keep writing?

The fact that I get cranky and miserable when I do not – creating stories is something that is as necessary for me, as necessary as breathing and coffee (and trust me, ask anyone who knows me, coffee is *necessary.*

Let me put it in a more graphically illustrative way. Once upon a time, two decades ago or so, I went through a truly rough emotional patch in my life – and somehow what that did was to turn off the writing spigot. The stories which coursed inside of me all of my life were simply… not there anymore. I did not have the words. I could not form them into sentences that made sense to me. I had just ground to a complete and utter linguistic HALT – there was nothing left, it was all dry, it was all just waterless dust blowing away in the wind.

The phase lasted almost a year, and by the tail end of it I was pretty nearly insane with it all. That was the moment when one of the still small voices I had been ignoring for so long finally broke through for long enough to whisper, "If you don't write… we all die."

And so I took the words that wouldn't work and hammered onto a blank page with a metaphorical hammer. Even into places where they didn't fit. Anything, anything to get the flow started again. And somehow, slowly, it did, and the stories returned.

But I *NEVER* want to go back to that place again. I know what I am, and that is what drives me – and I will always be writing, always be a writer, because that is quite simply a basic building block of what makes me… *me*.

What does your writing process look like?

Chaotic enough that I don't know if you could call it "process" – I am the ultimate so-called pantser, a writer who creates story literally by the seat of the pants, I sometimes find out what happens next in exactly the same way as a reader would – except that I am in the process of TYPING OUT AND CREATING that story that I am reading, and often freaking out about it, yelling at my characters not to be so stupid and how did they expect me to get them out of THIS mess? (They don't of course. My characters – all the best characters – have enough agency to deal with their own problems. Sometimes I feel I am just here to take dictation…)

Often I will have epiphanies while sitting in a restaurant eating breakfast with my husband – and he's learned to recognize that sudden sitting up motion I do, the change of expression on my face, as some plot bunny hops into view – and usually, if I don't whip out pen and paper myself, offers a paper napkin with a resigned little smile. Or I'll wake up in the morning and assault him with, "I got it! I figured it out!" and then he has to sit back and listen to me babble about the solution which just came to me in a dream. And then I'll pour myself a large cup of coffee, go down to my computer, and start typing.

On a good day, that's all it takes – I open up a blank page and let my fingers fall on the keyboard and that's the last conscious thing I do until I look up and see a couple of thousand words (once or twice 9,000 or 10,000 words on a given day…) staring back at me. I guess you can call it process.

When people who plan their writing, outline their novels and methodically work through things scene by scene, ask me how I write I honestly cannot tell them. All I know is that I get a story seed – and then I stuff it into a pot of good black earth and wait for something to grow, and until it does not even I know if I have a cabbage or a redwood…

Your work has been translated in many languages? What was your reaction when that started to happen?

Disbelief, actually. And after that, increasingly, more disbelief.

'The Secrets of Jin-shei' is the prime example. The languages began to pile up, and they included some which absolutely astonished me. It was almost impossible to believe that my characters would be speaking all these varied and different languages many of which I would be lucky to be able to recognize the alphabet they use.

"Secrets of Jin Shei" sold to an Italian publisher before it sold to an American house, which blew my mind. Other foreign sales followed – the Dutch, the Lithuanian, the Spanish (and the Catalan!), the Turkish… Each was an adventure. Hebrew completely threw me because to the Western-trained eye the books are UPSIDE DOWN and BACKWARDS.

BTW, 'The Secrets of Jin-shei' was a runaway bestseller in Spain and the Spanish-speaking territories, with 30,000+ copies (IN HARDCOVER) sold within the first six months of first publication.

I still get notes from readers from scattered Spanish markets – Spain itself, Mexico, Chile. For some reason the Spanish speakers loved my Chinese girls. A lot.

The most interesting translation experience was when "Embers of Heaven", written in English, was translated into my mother-tongue, Serb. The translator was in constant touch via email – in both languages, interchangeably – when she needed to pick my brain about how best to colloquially render something from one language into the other and make it all feel organic. That was just *fun*.

You state on your website that you are a Duchess by historical accident, can you expand on that?

Back in the 1100s, my family was of no real title but a reasonably wealthy landowner clan. In a very famous battle in 1389, one of my ancestors distinguished himself in battle and was rewarded by a Dukedom.

The original Dukedom is long since vanished, of course, under the weight of Balkan history – but the family is still around, and I'm a lineal descendant. Hence, Duchess.

My ancestor sustained a bad leg wound which gave him a nickname of Hromo (which literally means "gimpy") and his family took a modified form of that as a surname from that day on, my own maiden name.

At certain conventions where my family history may be familiar to some, I get people who know me greeting me with "Your Grace" in the corridors, which can be great fun if it is done while some newbie who isn't in on the "secret" happens to be wandering by. There have been some spectacularly wonderful double takes in the past.

What is the one, single food that you would never give up?

A three-way tie between coffee, cherries and chocolate.

You can learn more about me at my website and blog:
http://www.almaalexander.org/

"North, first, along the inner sea whose northern shores I have never seen – and then east, further east than I have ever ventured, across mountains and over vast grassy plains where wild horses still roam and the tribes who ride them are even wilder than their mounts. And further, along the edge of a great desert, and then more mountains, and then the forests and valleys of Xin, and then far Syai, where the silk comes from."

EMPRESS, Alma Alexander

Have *you* visited Alma Alexander's Syai yet?

"The Secrets of Jin-shei is a complete original — and a completely magical piece of writing." **Joanne Harris**, author of Chocolat and Blackberry Wine

"The Last Samurai has nothing on this complex adventure." **Belfast Telegraph**

Alma Alexander is not a writer, she is a poet. Her writing is lyrical and mesmerizing, evoking a dreamy, otherworldly feel. Her scenes are so beautifully wrought that, due the sheer musicality of her writing, – **Ginger Myrick**

"Beautifully written, with rich characterisation and captivating originality, it quickly draws you in and is a real page-turner." — **Glasgow Evening Times**

ABOUT THE AUTHOR

Alma Alexander's life so far has prepared her very well for her chosen career. She was born in a country which no longer exists on the maps, has lived and worked in seven countries on four continents (and in cyberspace!), has climbed mountains, dived in coral reefs, flown small planes, swum with dolphins, touched two-thousand-year-old tiles in a gate out of Babylon. She is a novelist, anthologist and short story writer who currently shares her life between the Pacific Northwest of the USA (where she lives with her husband and two cats) and the wonderful fantasy worlds of her own imagination. You can find out more about Alma on her website (www.AlmaAlexander.org), her Facebook page (https://www.facebook.com/pages/Alma-Alexander/67938071280) or her blog (http://anghara.livejournal.com).

ABOUT BOOK VIEW CAFÉ

Book View Café is a professional authors' cooperative offering DRM-free ebooks in multiple formats to readers around the world. With authors in a variety of genres including mystery, romance, fantasy, and science fiction, Book View Café has something for everyone.

Book View Café is good for readers because you can enjoy high-quality paper and DRM-free ebooks from your favorite authors at a reasonable price.

Book View Café is good for writers because 95% of the profit goes directly to the book's author.

Book View Café authors include Nebula, Hugo, and Philip K. Dick Award winners, Nebula, Hugo, World Fantasy, and Rita Award nominees, and *New York Times* bestsellers and notable book authors.

www.ingramcontent.com/pod-product-compliance
Lightning Source LLC
Chambersburg PA
CBHW030848030726
47495CB00005B/1434